Queen of the Sea

This book is dedicated to Kid Dylan, who loved her Island but never stopped scanning the horizon for a friend.

Copyright © 2019 by Dylan Meconis

First paperback edition 2020

Library of Congress Catalog Card Number 201896223
ISBN 978-1-5362-0498-8 (hardcover)
ISBN 978-1-5362-1517-5 (paperback)

20 21 22 23 24 25 CCP 10 9 8 7 6 5 4 3 2 1

Printed in Shenzhen, Guangdong, China

This book was typeset in Audric.
The illustrations were done in watercolor, pencil, and ink or created from hand embroidery with digital retouching.

Walker Books US
a division of
Candlewick Press
99 Dover Street
Somerville, Massachusetts 02144

www.walkerbooksus.com

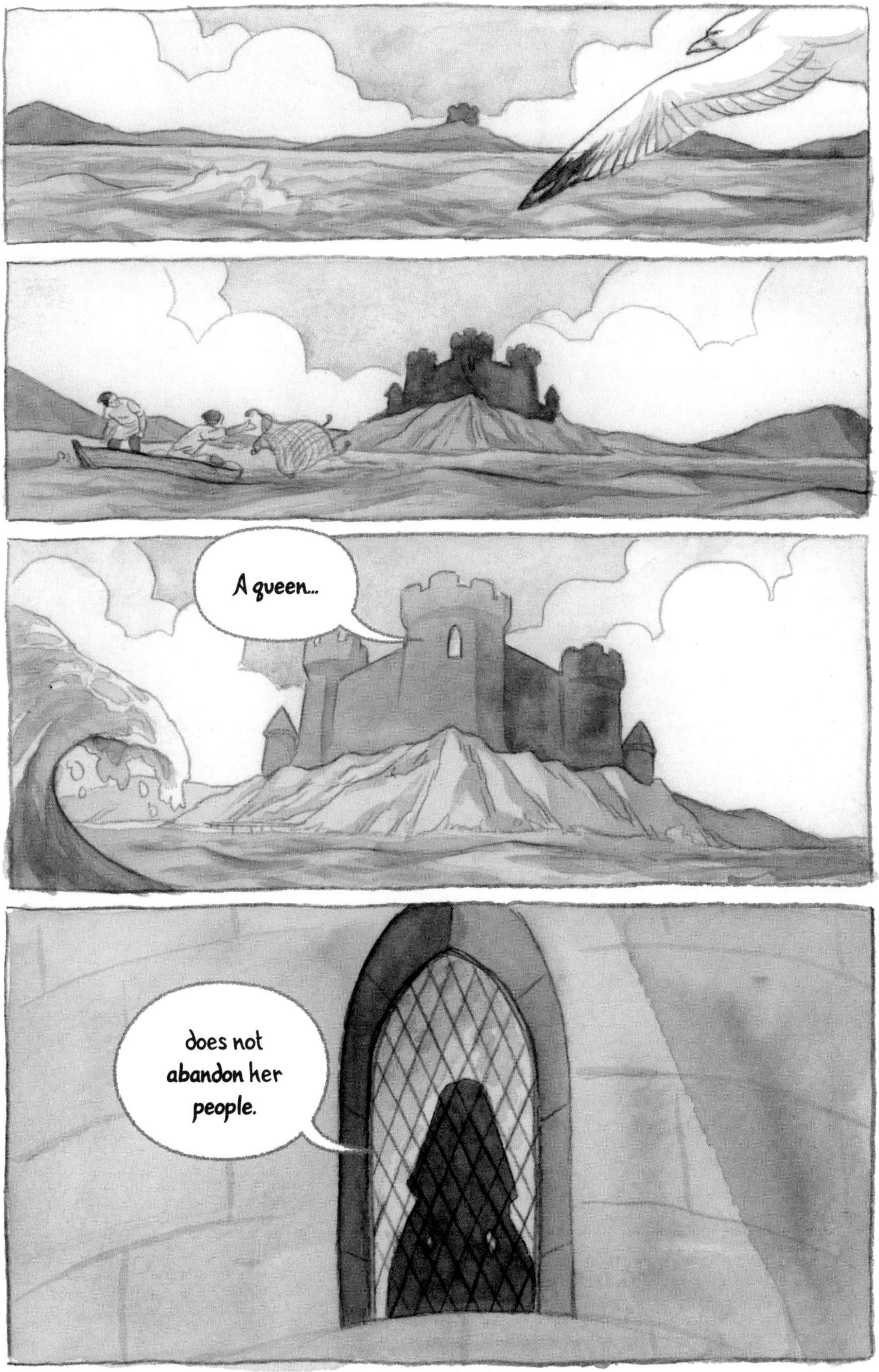
A queen...
does not abandon her people.

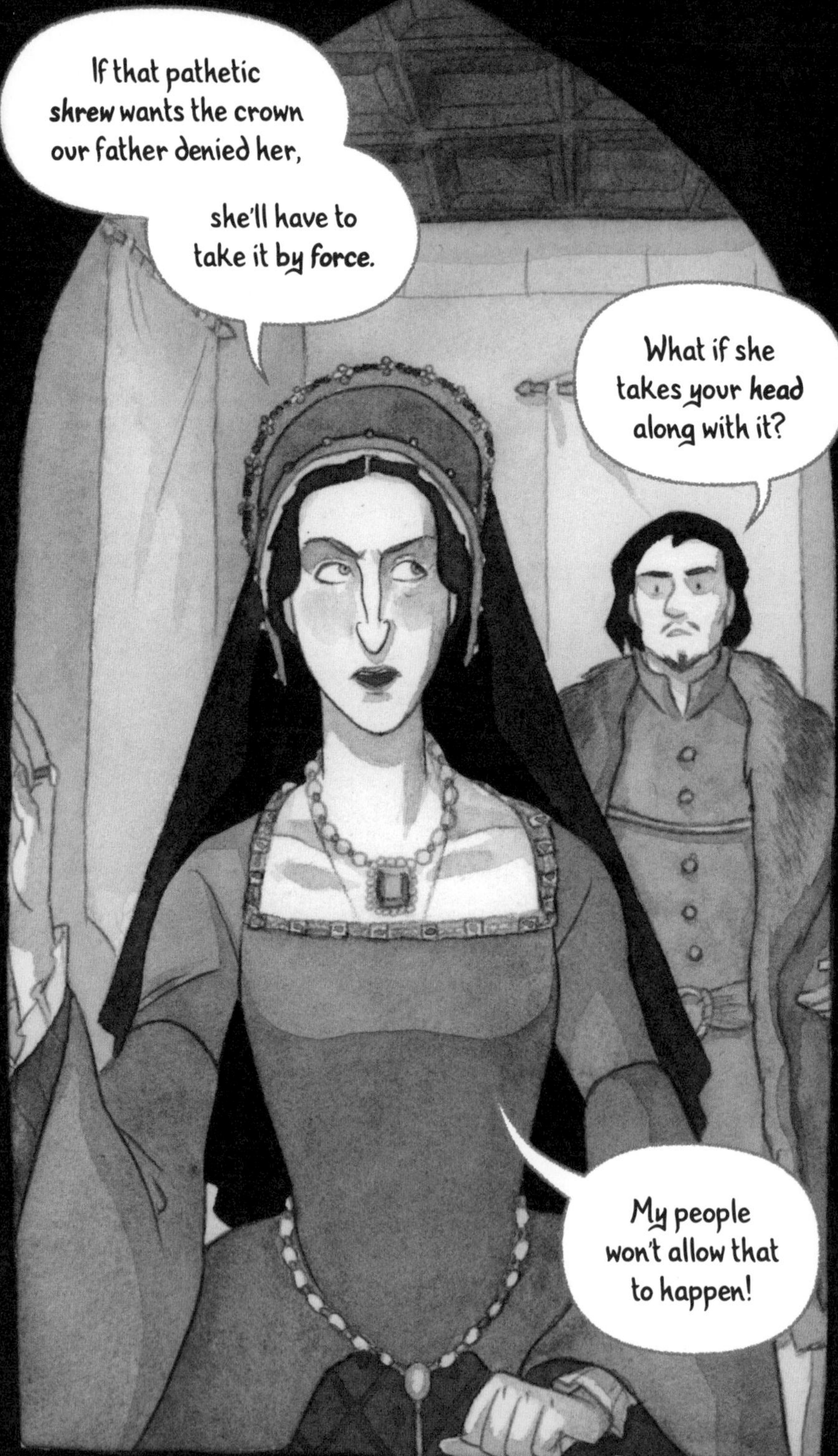
If that pathetic shrew wants the crown our father denied her,
she'll have to take it by force.
What if she takes your head along with it?
My people won't allow that to happen!

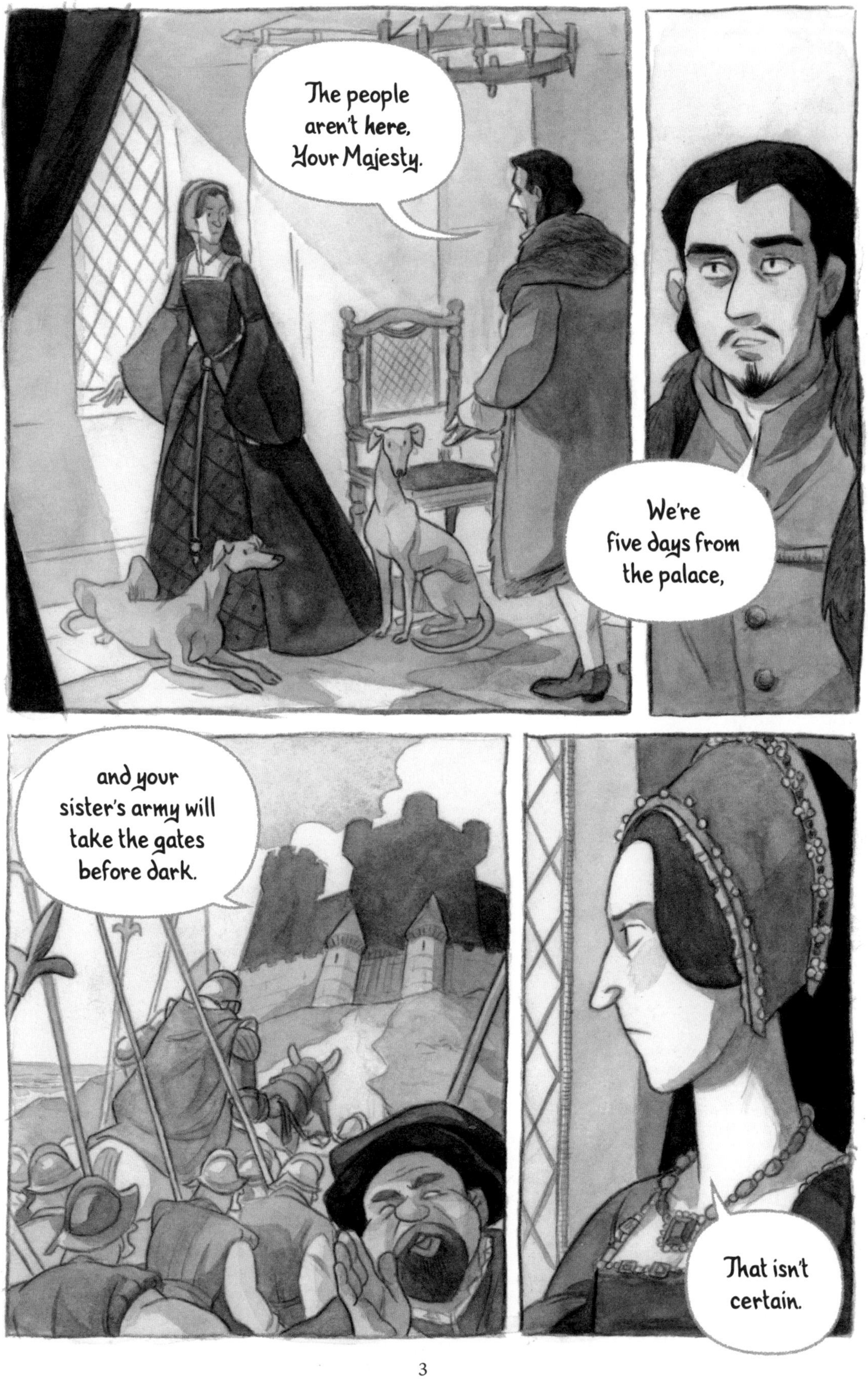
The people aren't here, Your Majesty.
We're five days from the palace,
and your sister's army will take the gates before dark.
That isn't certain.

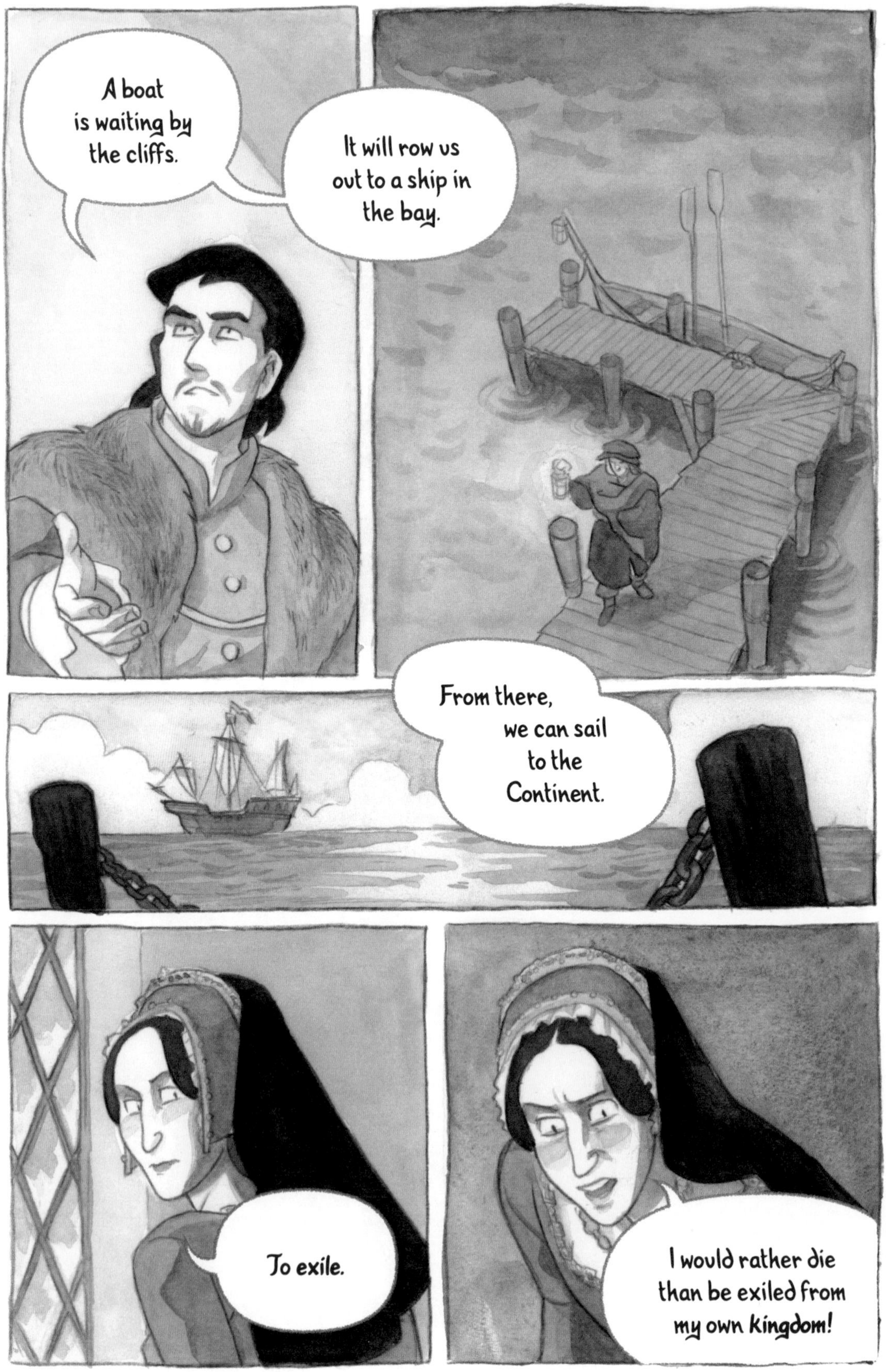
A boat is waiting by the cliffs.
It will row us out to a ship in the bay.
From there, we can sail to the Continent.
To exile.
I would rather die than be exiled from my own kingdom!

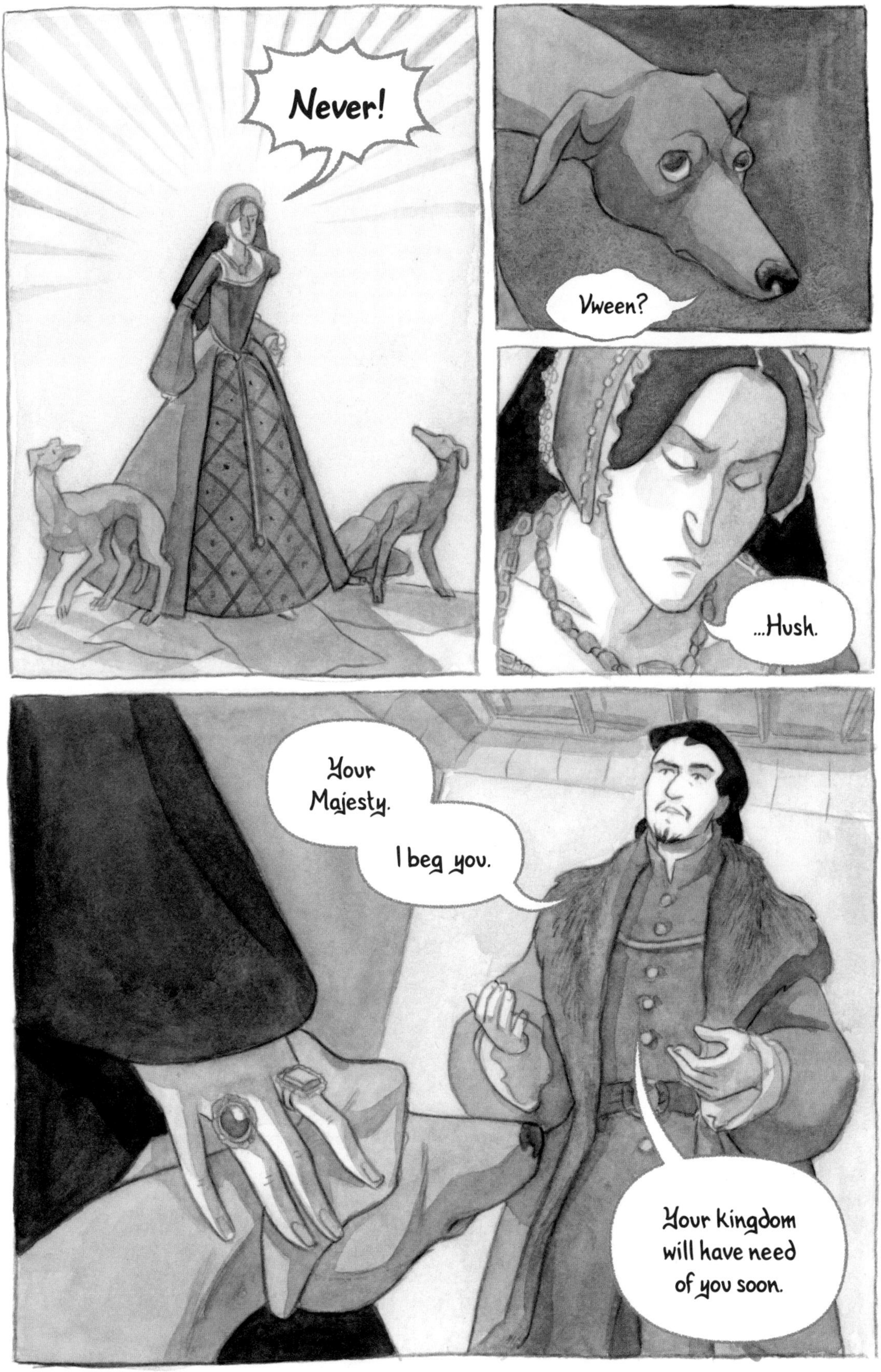

Never!
Vween?
...Hush.
Your Majesty.
I beg you.
Your kingdom will have need of you soon.

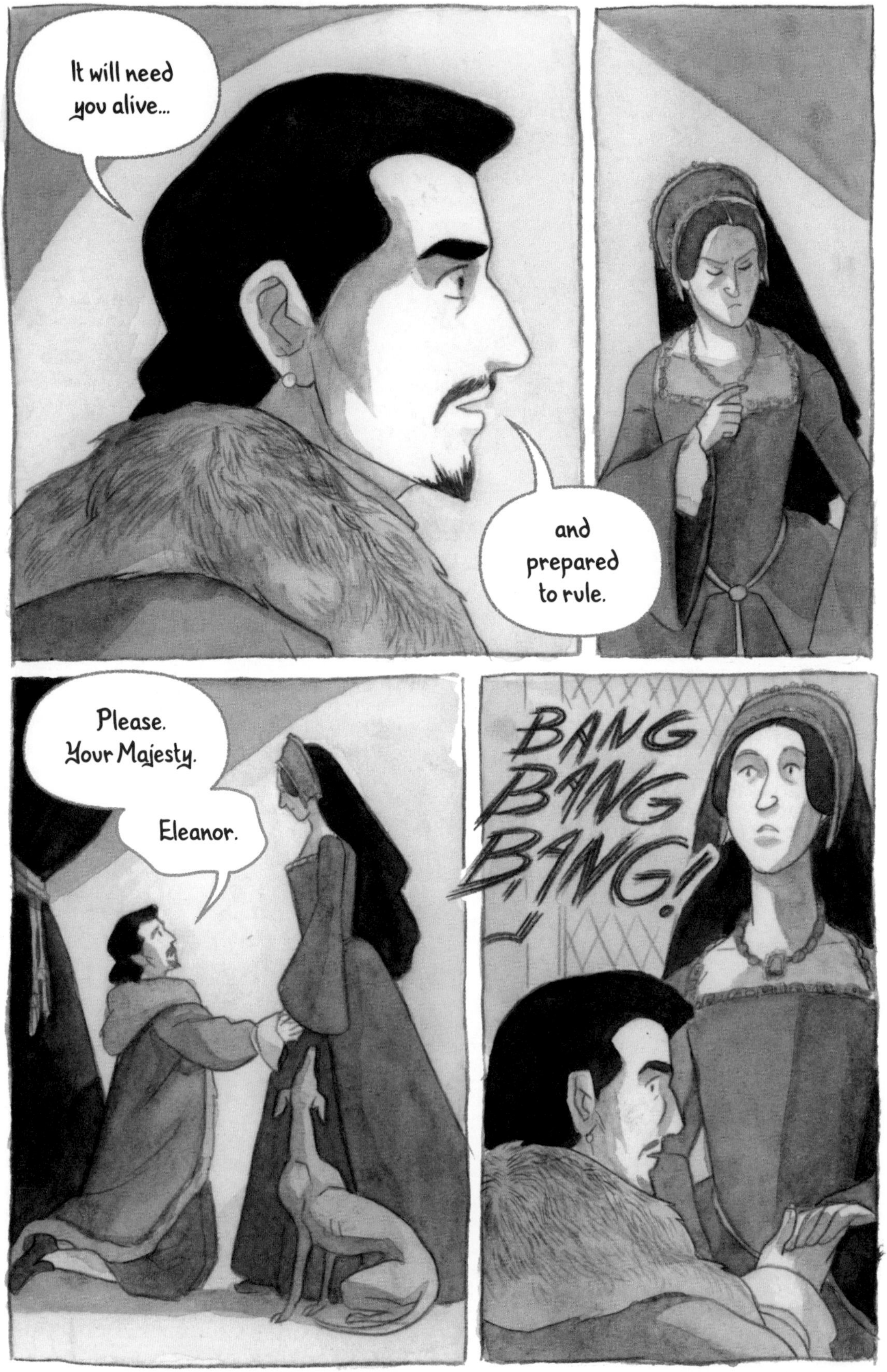
It will need you alive...
and prepared to rule.
Please. Your Majesty.
Eleanor.
BANG BANG BANG!

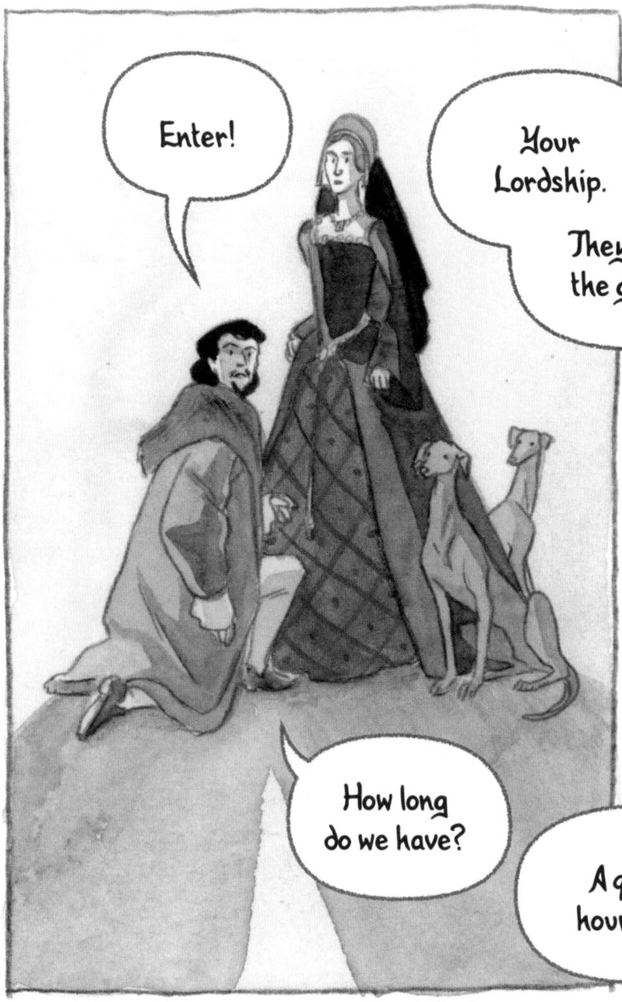
Enter!
Your Lordship.
They're at the gates.
How long do we have?
A quarter hour or less.

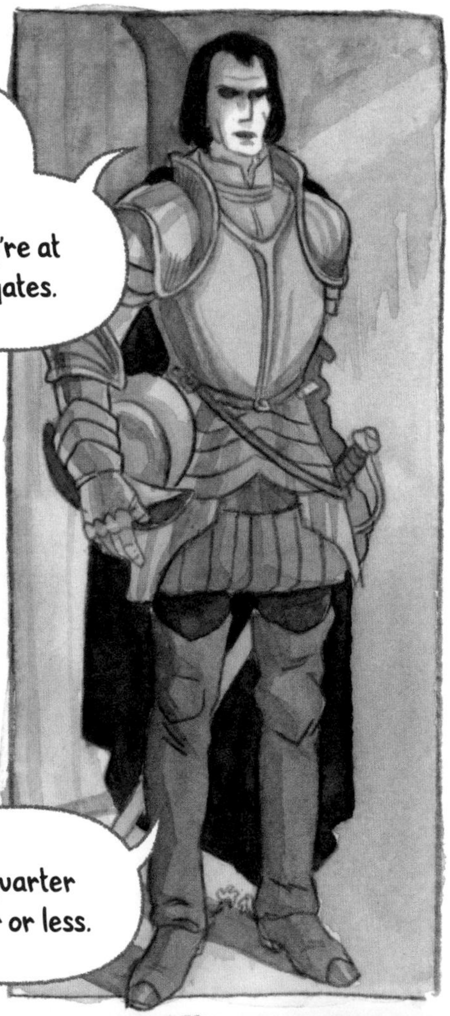

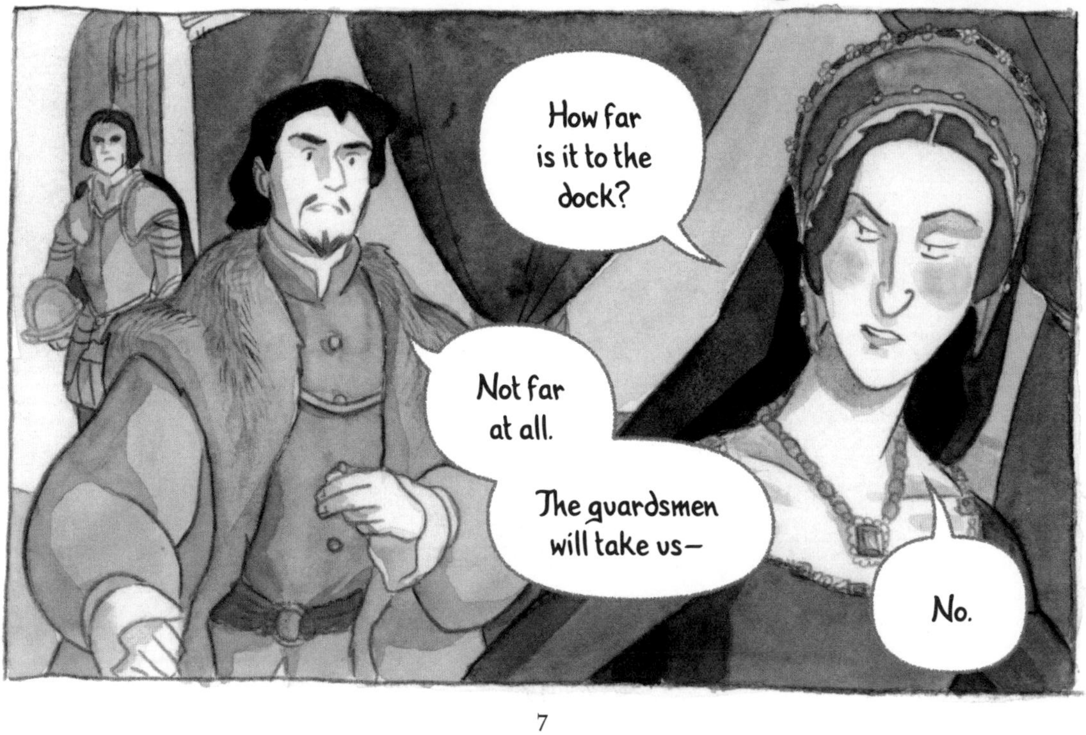
How far is it to the dock?
Not far at all.
The guardsmen will take us—
No.

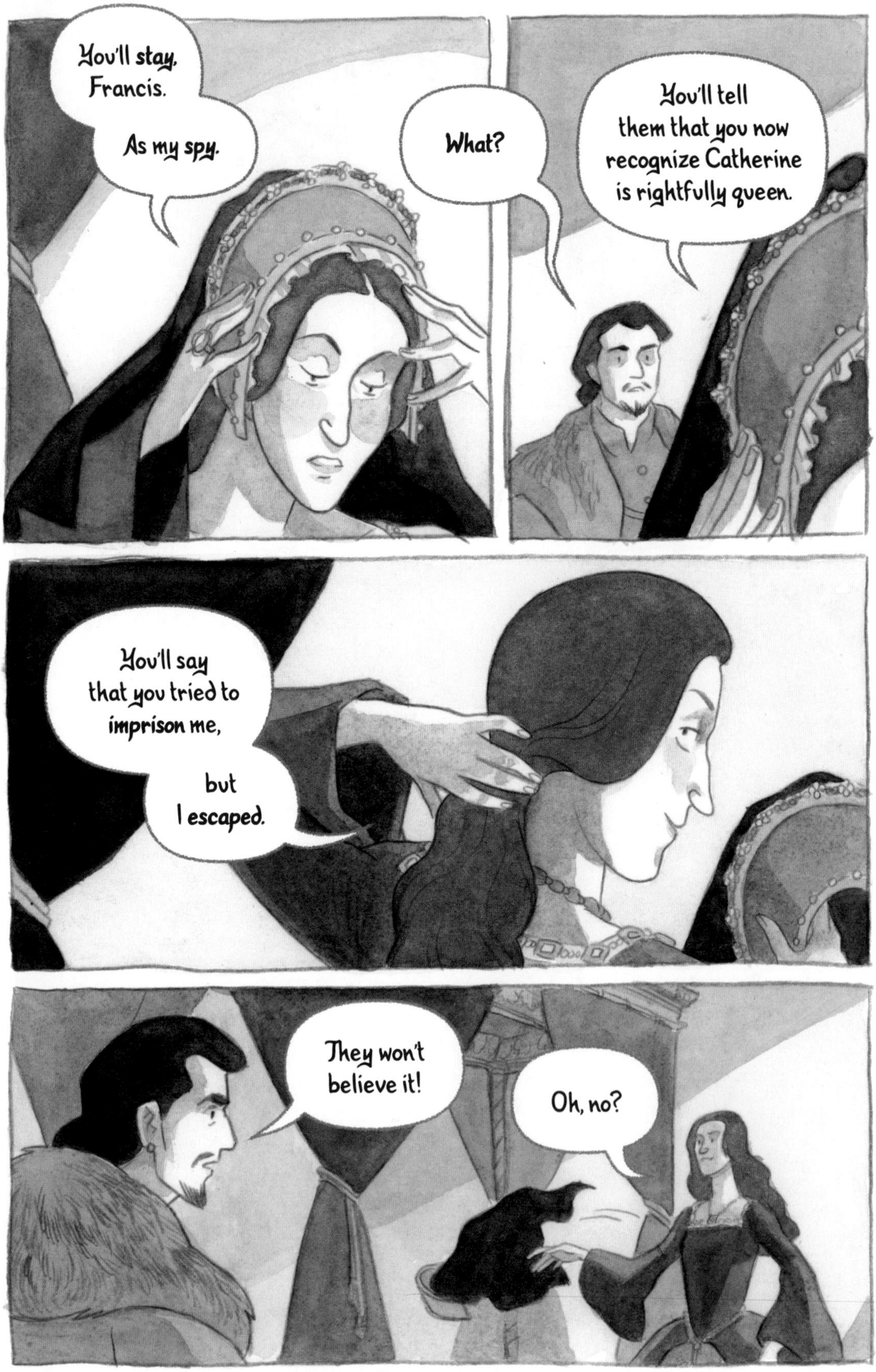
You'll stay, Francis.
As my spy.
What?
You'll tell them that you now recognize Catherine is rightfully queen.
You'll say that you tried to imprison me,
but I escaped.
They won't believe it!
Oh, no?

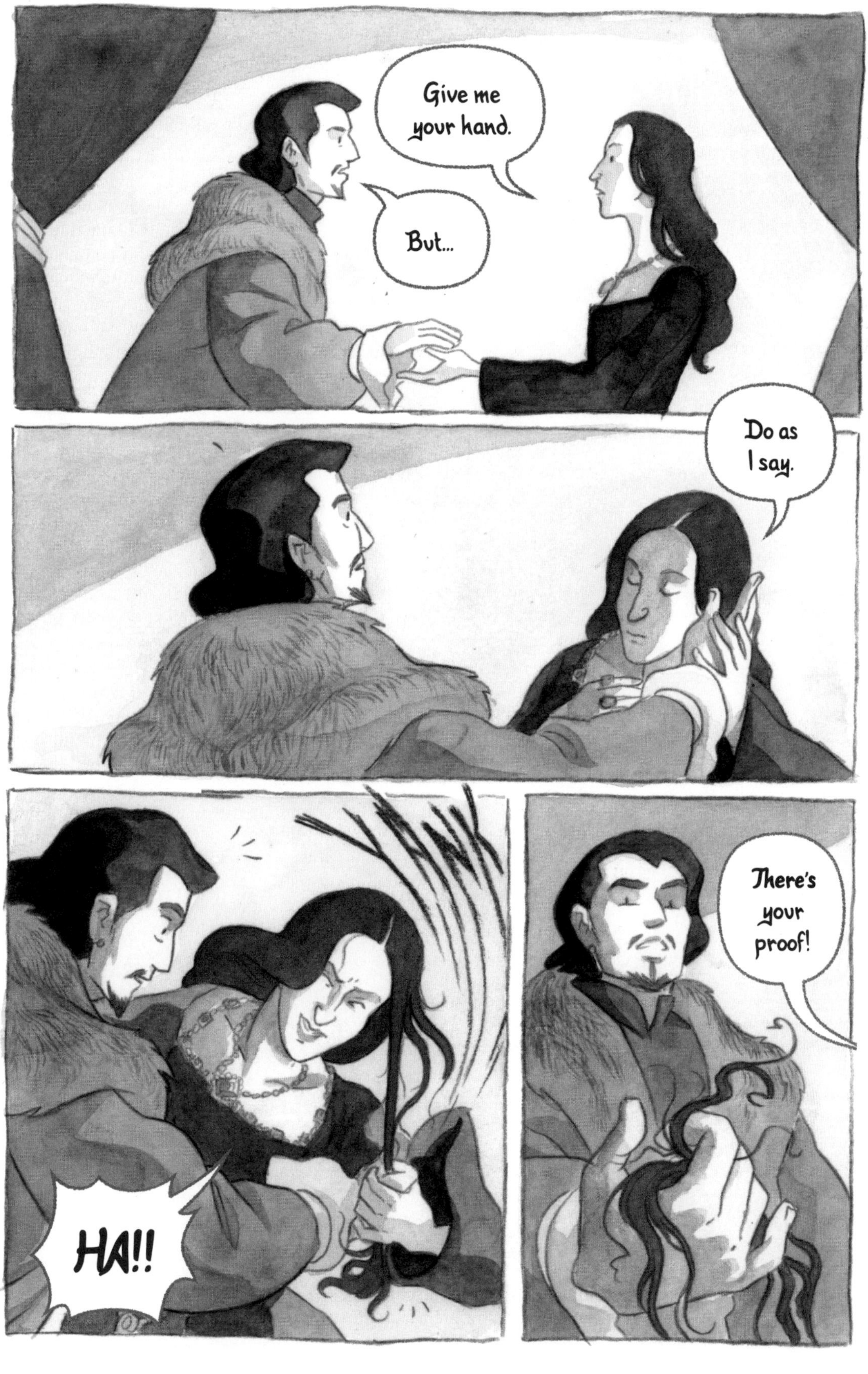
Give me your hand.
But...
Do as I say.
HA!!
There's your proof!

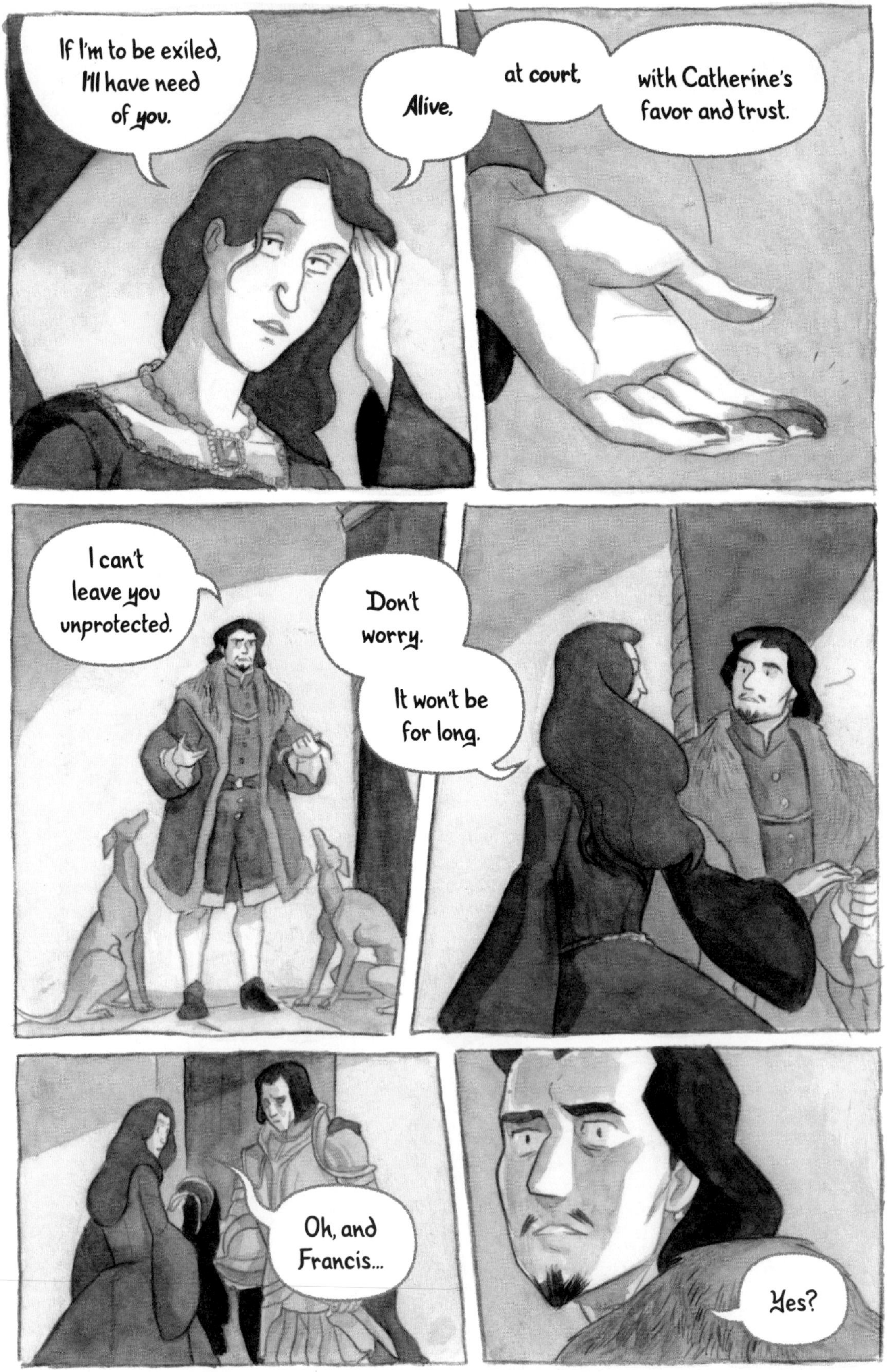
If I'm to be exiled, I'll have need of you.
Alive,
at court,
with Catherine's favor and trust.
I can't leave you unprotected.
Don't worry.
It won't be for long.
Oh, and Francis...
Yes?

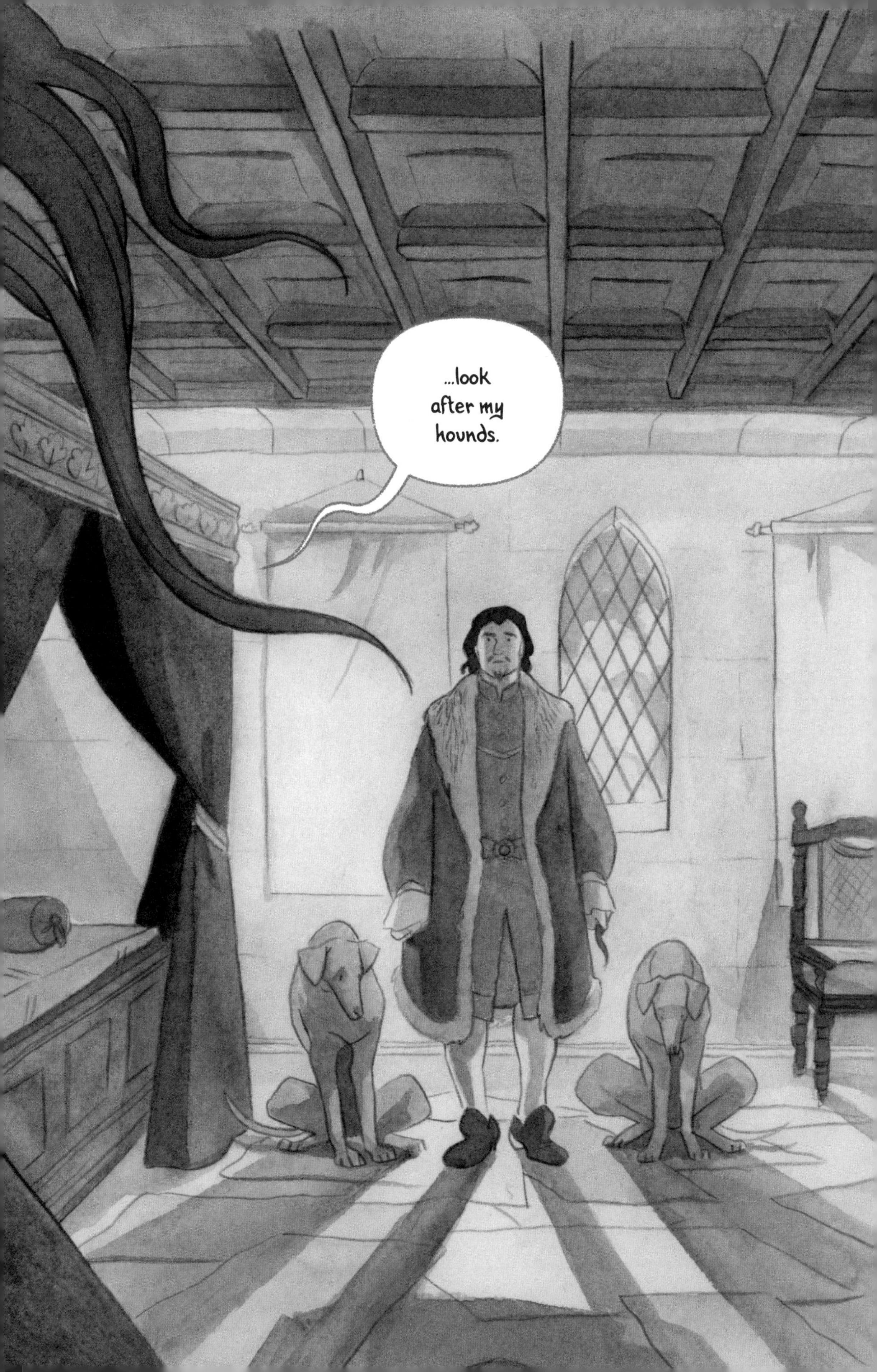
...look after my hounds.

I wasn't born on
the Island.

If you're reading this to find out what
happened to the true queen of Albion,
that's the first thing you should know.

Trust me.

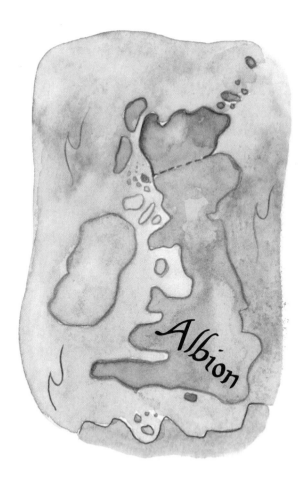

The funny thing is,

I don't know where I was born.

It might have been on a much, much bigger island, not too far away, called *Albion*.

Albion is also the name of the kingdom our little Island belongs to.

There are many other islands included in the kingdom of Albion, of all sizes and shapes.

In fact, the whole kingdom is nothing but islands. I suppose that I could have been born on any of them!

I don't even know the exact day I was born— only that it was almost twelve years ago.

We celebrate my birth on Saint Elysia's Day instead. That's the day I was brought to the Island aboard a ship called the *Regina Maris*.

I can't remember that day at all. I was only a baby.

But I do know exactly what happened, down to the last detail. How?

Well, starting on the morning of my sixth Saint Elysia's Day on the Island,

I decided to ask every single person on the Island about it.

That may sound like a lot of work for a very small girl.

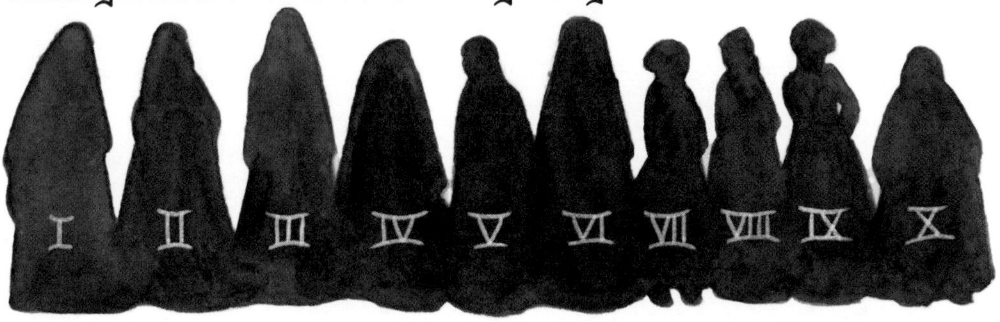
I
II
III
IV
V
VI
VII
VIII
IX
X

But since there were only ten other people on the Island, it didn't take very long at all.

And since the *Regina Maris* is the only ship that comes to the Island, and since it only visits twice a year...

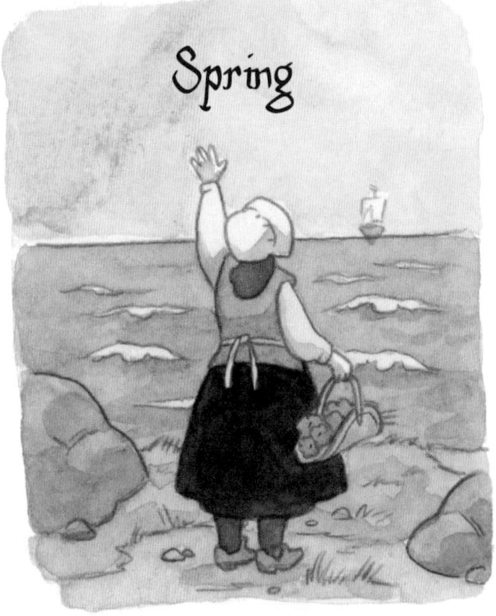
Spring

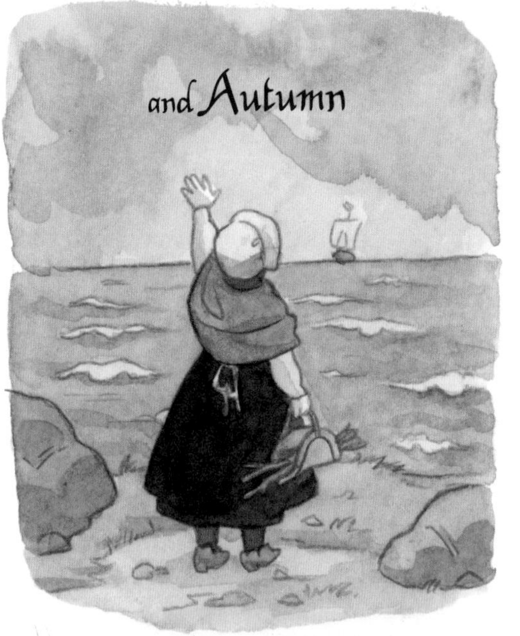
and Autumn

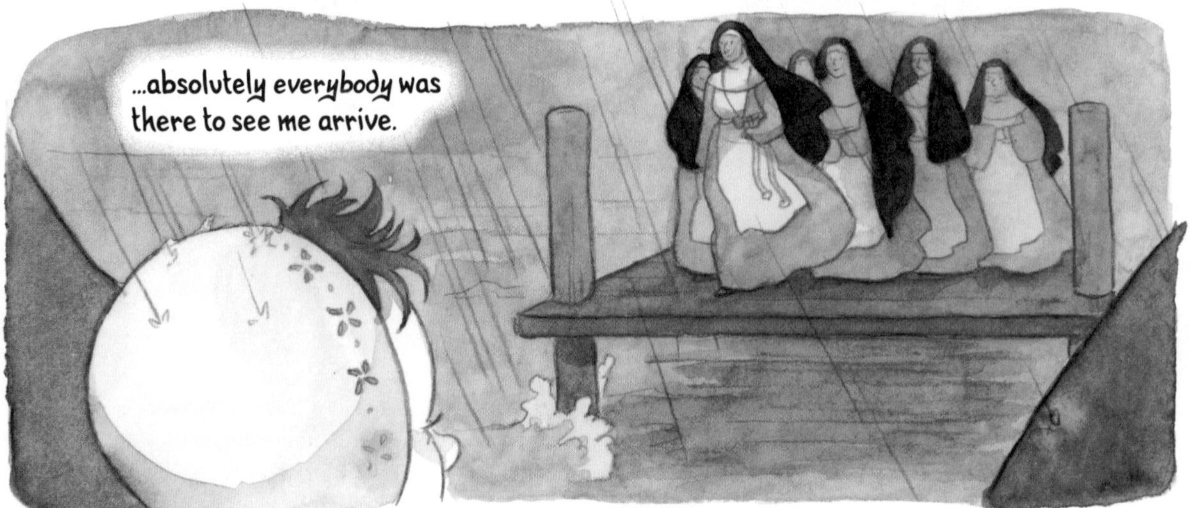
...absolutely everybody was there to see me arrive.

My name is **Margaret**, by the way.

Not "Lady Margaret of Somewhere" or "Sister Margaret" or even "Mistress Margaret So-and-So." Just Margaret.

Margaret means **pearl**, which makes it a good name for me. Pearls are hidden inside oysters, deep beneath the waves, and our Island is hidden far from the rest of Albion, deep into the Silver Sea. Our Island is so small, and so far away, that it doesn't have a proper name. It isn't even on some maps!

The only reason that anybody lives there at all is the **convent**. A convent is a place where women go to lead very religious lives together without ordinary people around to distract them.

A woman who makes a promise to live forever in a convent becomes a nun and calls herself a sister. After you become a nun you aren't allowed to get married or have any children.

Being a nun is not very easy, but there are plenty of reasons to become one, especially if you like to help people. Different orders help different people.

Some Kinds of Nuns (But There Are Others!)

Clarites
Nurse
the sick

Wandering Sisters
Shelter travelers

Lamentines
Pray for
prisoners

Elysians
That's us!

The convent on the Island belongs to the **Elysian order**.

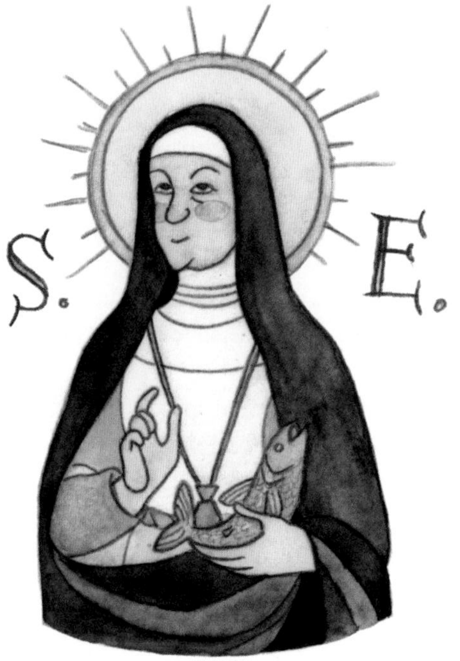
S. E.

Elysian nuns live by the sea and honor **Saint Elysia** by taking care of sailors and their families.

Our part of the Silver Sea is full of storms and tricky currents.

The convent was built here so that Elysian sisters could pray for the safety of all the ships that go by and take care of anybody who washes up on the Island after a shipwreck.

Those are important jobs, but nowadays the sisters don't have to do them very often. Not many ships sail by anymore.

In the past, every time Albion declared war on its enemy kingdom, **Gallia**...

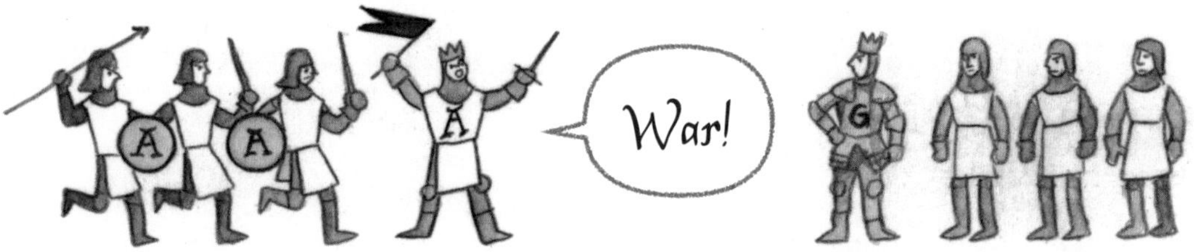
War!

or Gallia declared war on Albion,

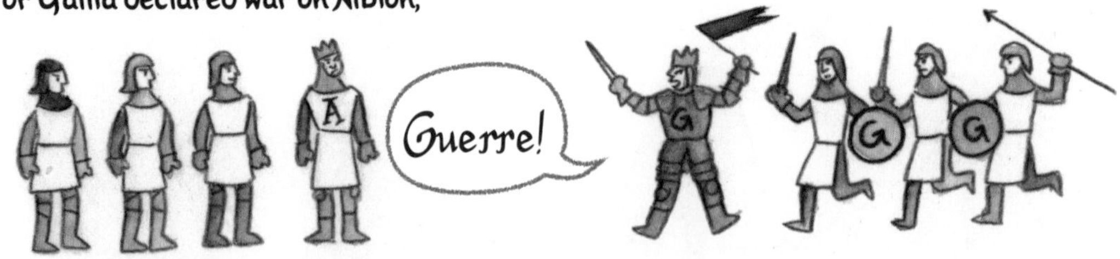
Guerre!

or **everybody** just decided it was time for another war,

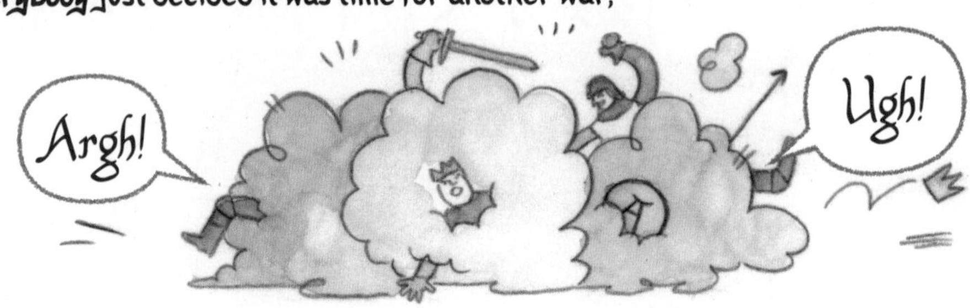
Argh!
Ugh!

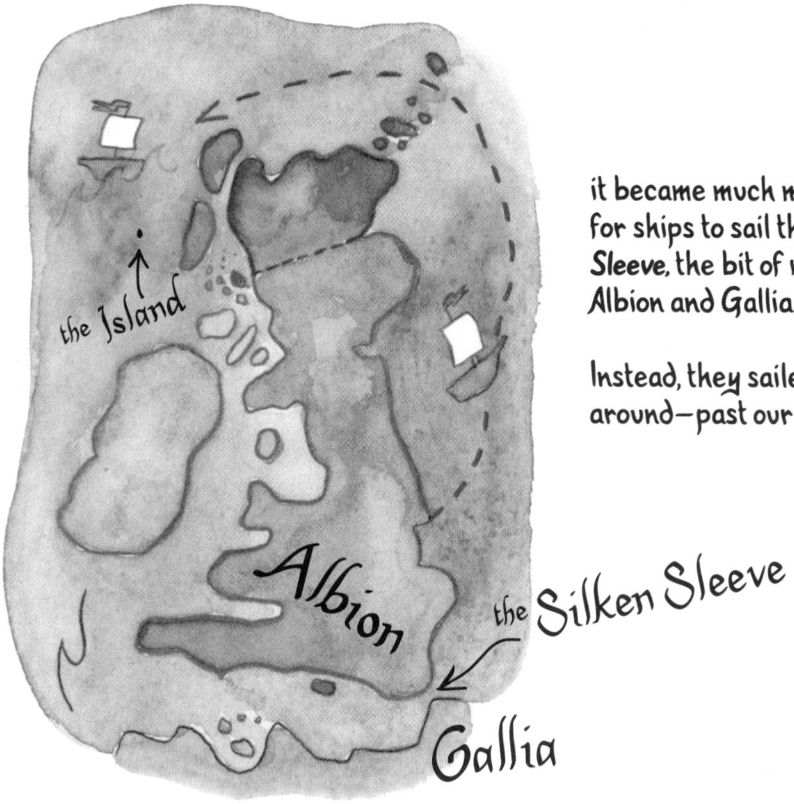
the Island
Albion
the Silken Sleeve
Gallia

it became much more dangerous for ships to sail through the ***Silken Sleeve***, the bit of water between Albion and Gallia.

Instead, they sailed the long way around—past our Island.

Then our king, **Edmund**, ended the wars for good. He defeated Gallia so badly that they declared a truce. So now nobody needs to take the long, dangerous route past us.

The only sailors who the sisters of the Island have to pray for these days are the ones who belong to the *Regina Maris*. And the only person who washed up on the Island needing their care and attention...was me.

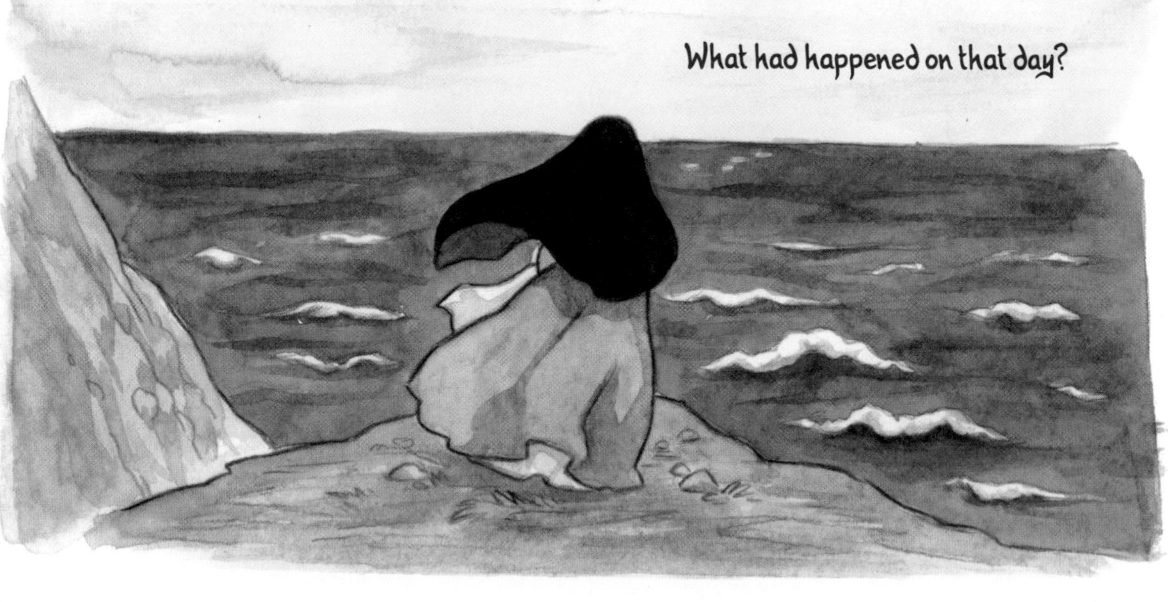
What had happened on that day?

First I asked...

All of the

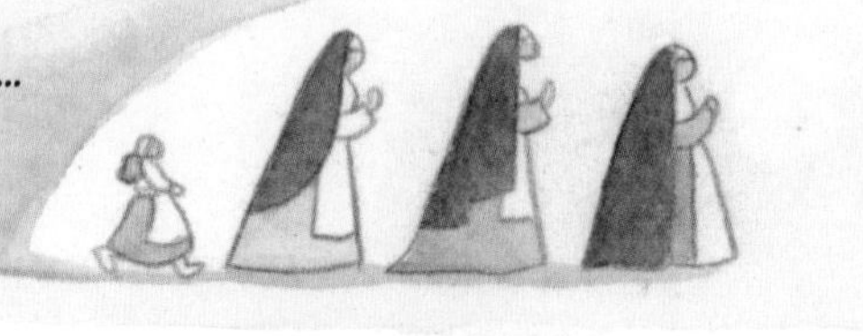

Sister Agnes

...is the ***Prioress,*** which means she's the head of the convent. She writes letters and makes decisions.

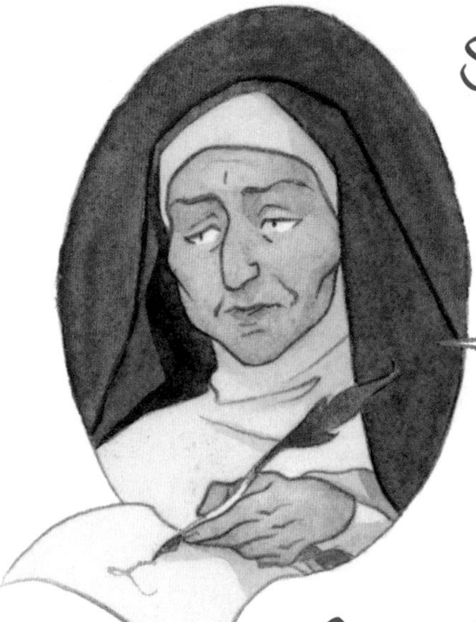
It was raining,
so I tucked you beneath my habit.

Sister Sybil

...is the ***Librarian.*** She keeps all the records and the calendar, too.

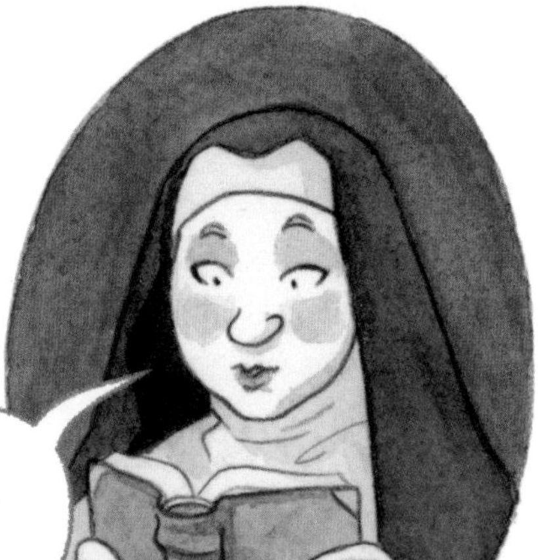
It was a Friday!

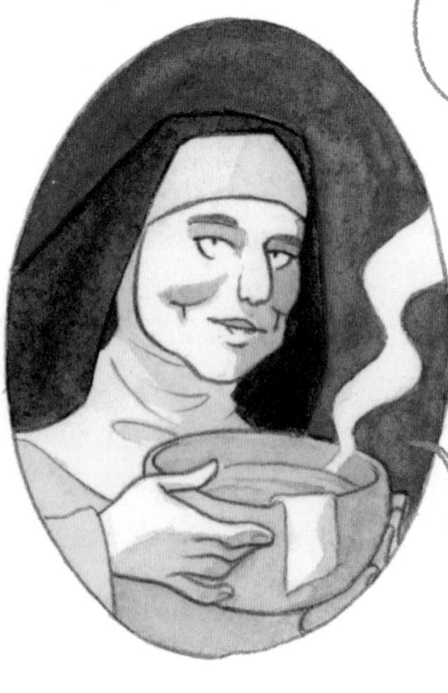

Sister Edith

...is the ***Infirmarian.*** She makes all the medicines and takes care of anybody sick or injured in the infirmary.

You had a slight fever.

Sisters

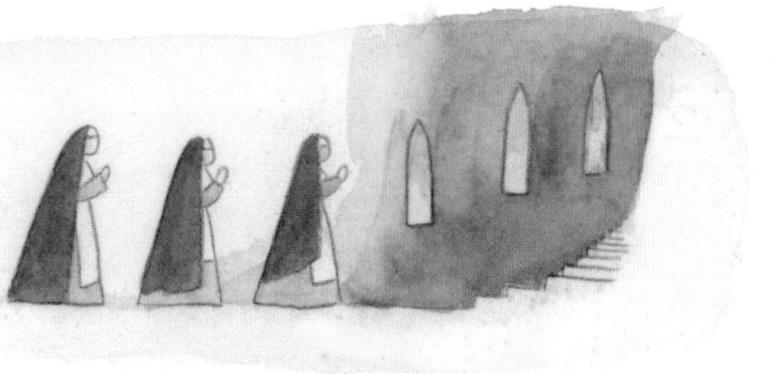

Sister Barbara...is the **Sacrist.**
She makes sure we have enough candles and incense, and cleans and decorates the church.

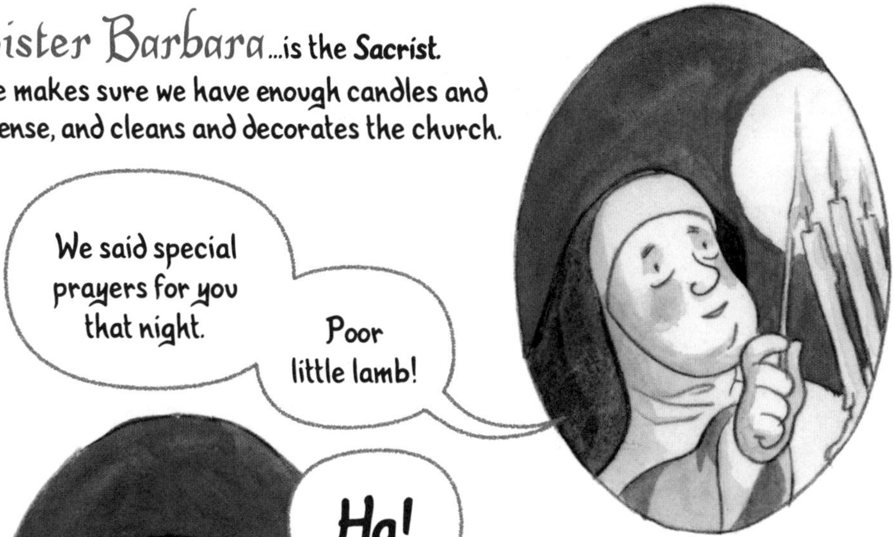

We said special prayers for you that night.
Poor little lamb!

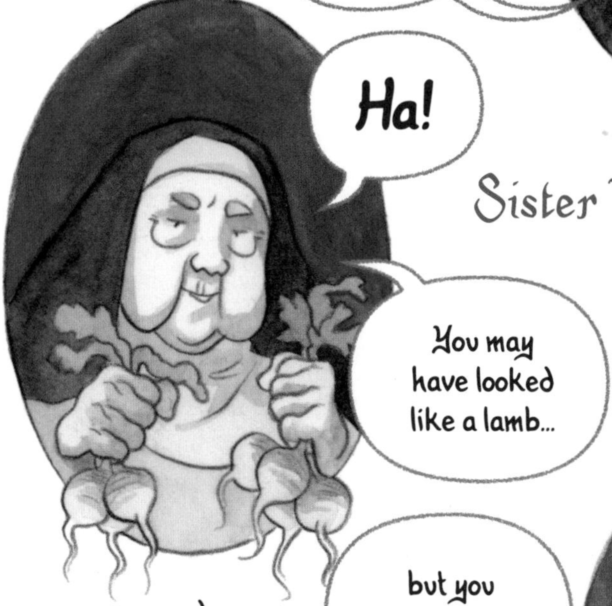

Ha!
You may have looked like a lamb...

Sister Wynefreed

...is the **Cellarer.**
It's her job to see that we have enough food in the gardens and cellar.

and...

Sister Philippa

...takes care of all the animals in our farmyard.

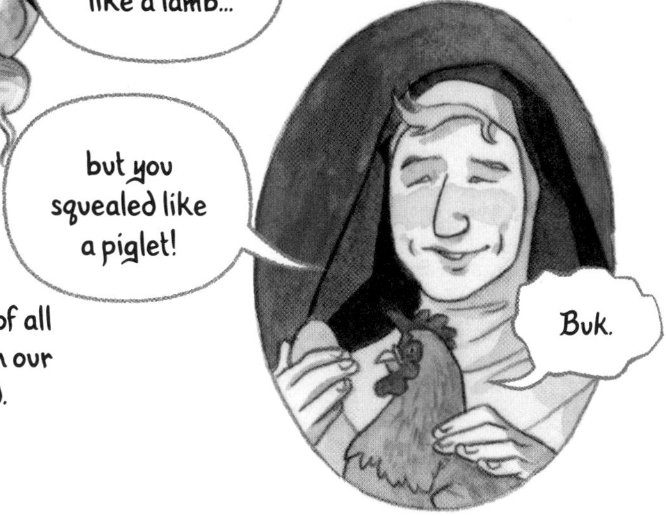

but you squealed like a piglet!
Buk.

Next, I asked... the Servants

Maud is the **Kitchener**, which means she's in charge of...yes, the kitchen.

Her husband was a ship's captain. Elysian nuns saved his life once.

After he died, Maud took their daughters and came to work on the Island.

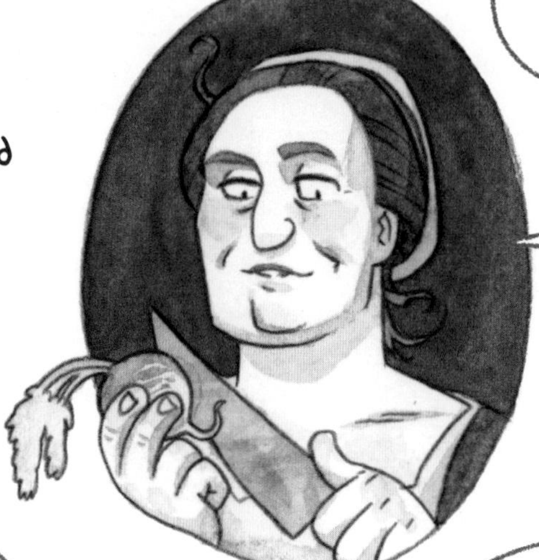
I fed you sweet milk porridge,
though you looked too small even to be weaned.

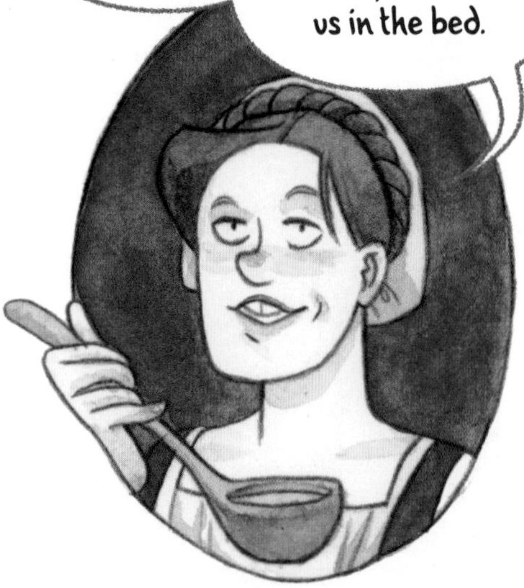
You wouldn't stop crying...
until I put you to sleep between us in the bed.

Bess is Maud's older daughter. She mostly helps with cooking.

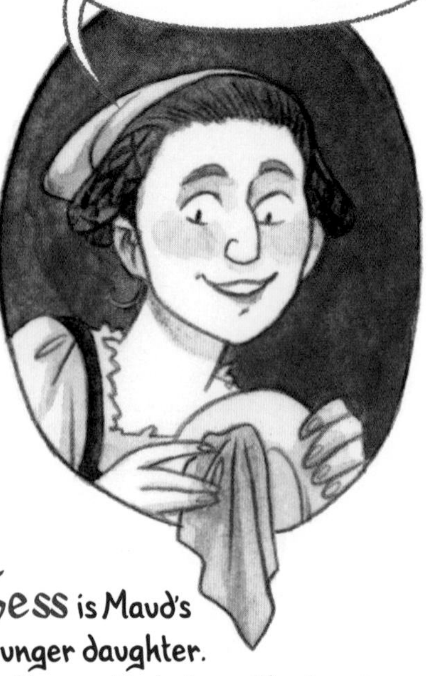
I put an iron horseshoe over the door,
so the fairies wouldn't steal you and replace you with an imp.

Tess is Maud's younger daughter. She mostly helps with cleaning.

Last of all, I tried to ask...

Father Ambrose

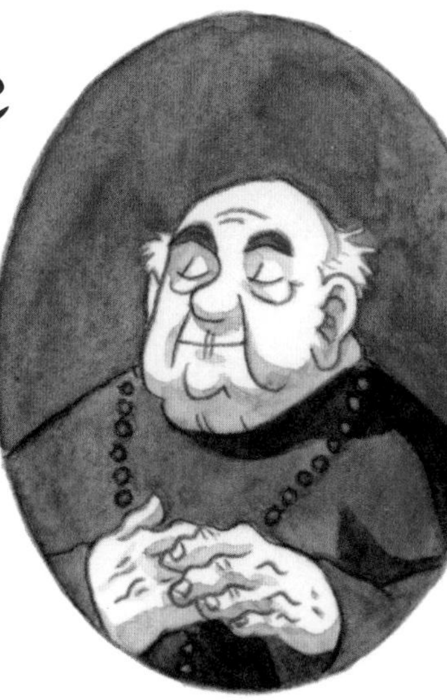

Nuns are generally very holy people. But there are some important things that only a priest can do, and only men are allowed to become priests.

In a normal convent, a priest would visit once in a while to take care of all those things and then travel on to other convents and leave the sisters in peace. But since we're so far away from other convents, Father Ambrose just stays put.

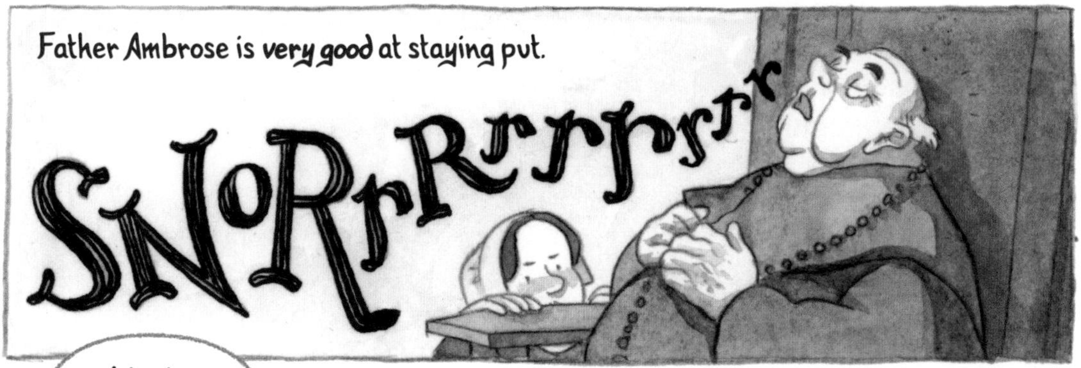
Father Ambrose is *very good* at staying put.
SNORrRrrrrrr

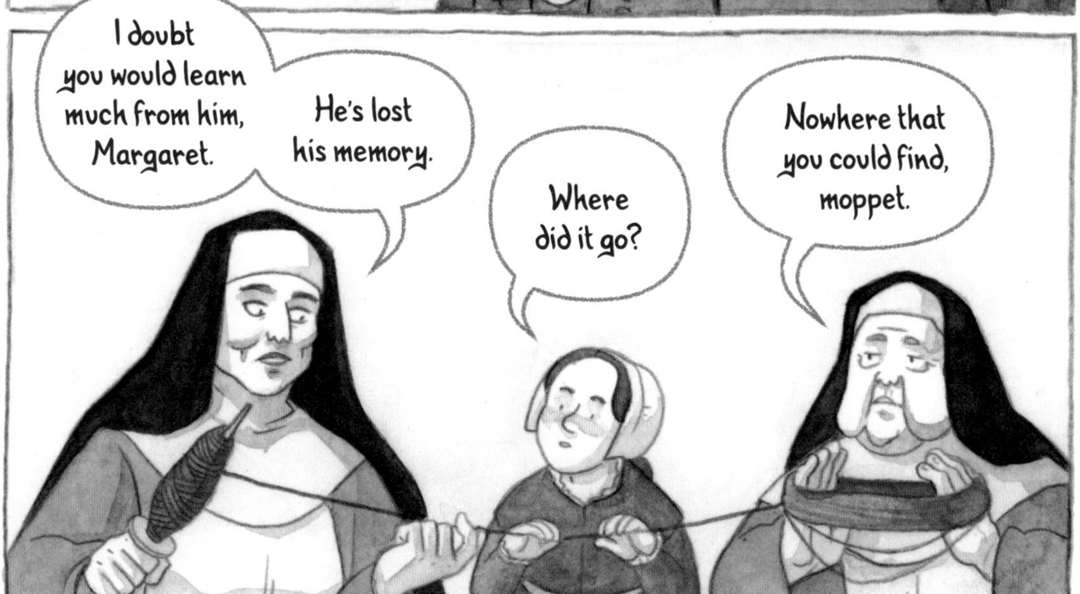
I doubt you would learn much from him, Margaret.
He's lost his memory.
Where did it go?
Nowhere that you could find, moppet.

I didn't learn much from the other residents of the Island, either.

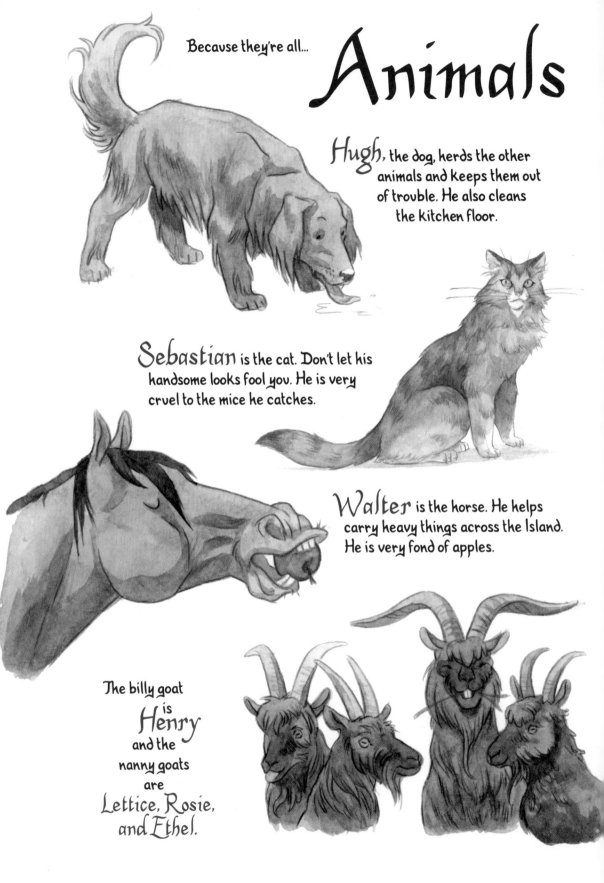

Because they're all...

Animals

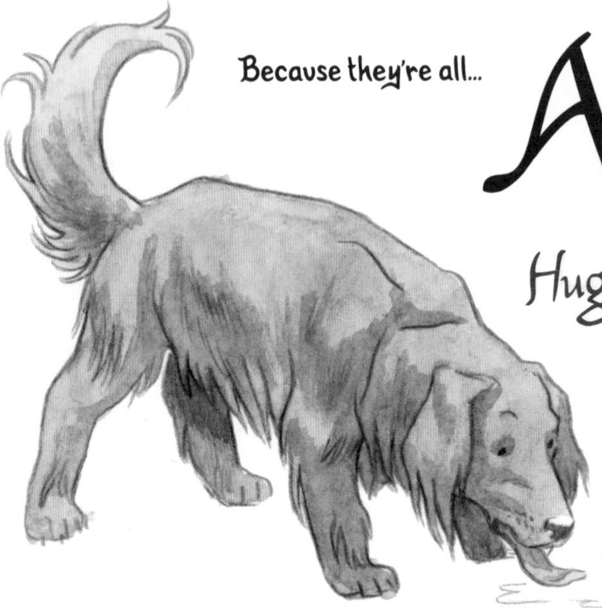

Hugh, the dog, herds the other animals and keeps them out of trouble. He also cleans the kitchen floor.

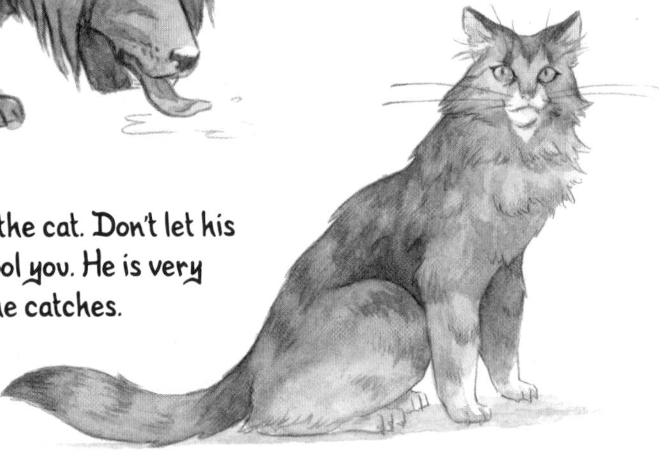

Sebastian is the cat. Don't let his handsome looks fool you. He is very cruel to the mice he catches.

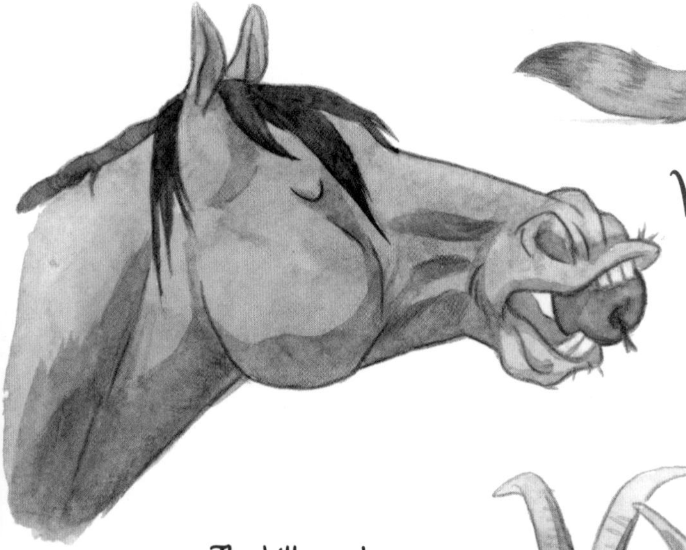

Walter is the horse. He helps carry heavy things across the Island. He is very fond of apples.

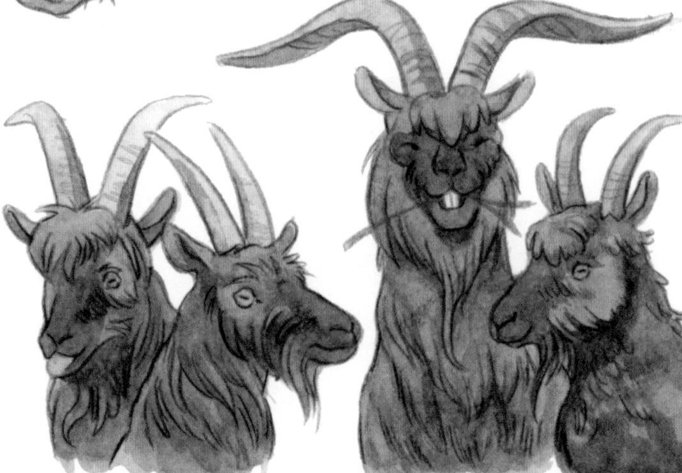

The billy goat is Henry and the nanny goats are Lettice, Rosie, and Ethel.

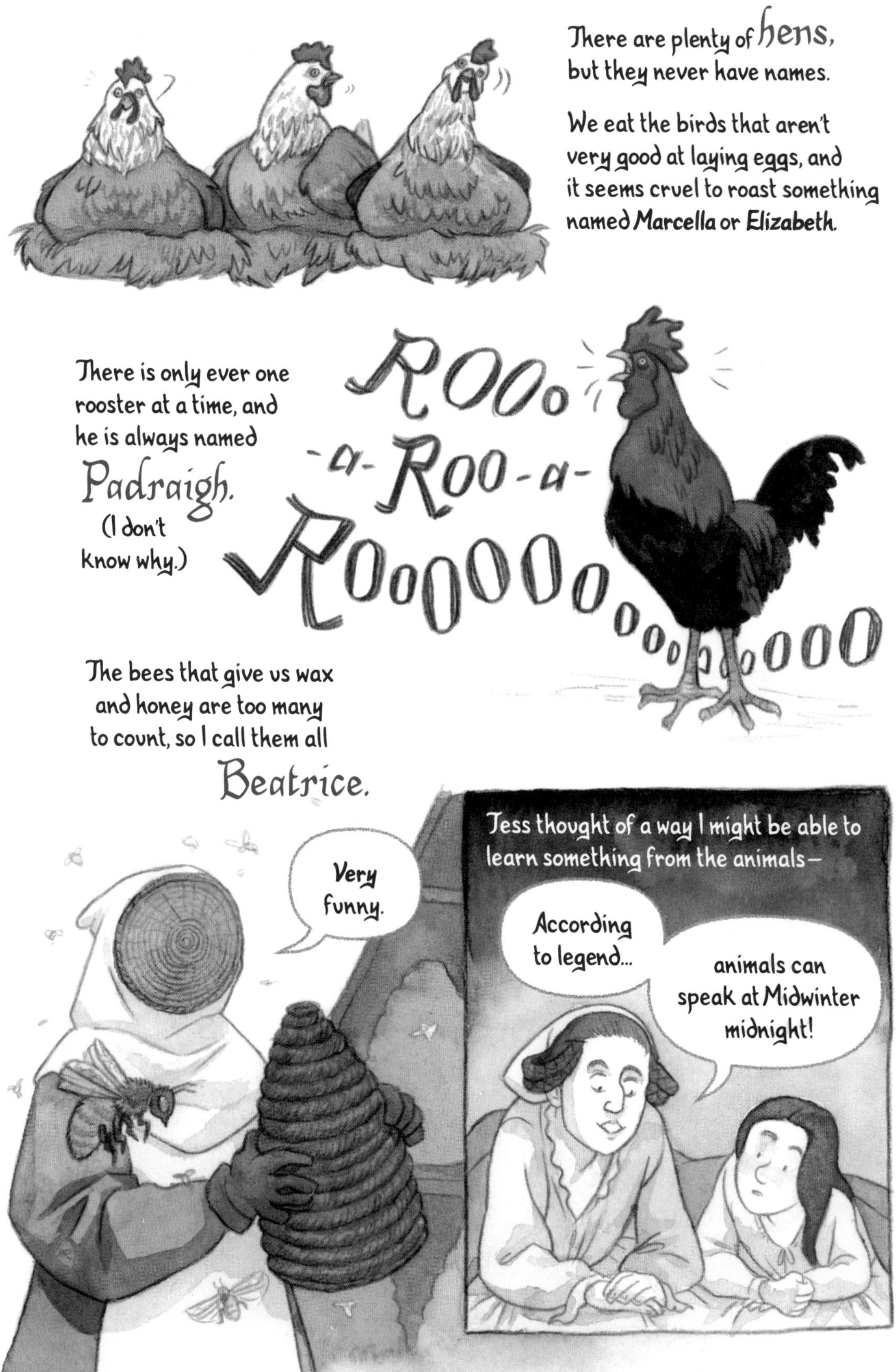
There are plenty of hens, but they never have names.
We eat the birds that aren't very good at laying eggs, and it seems cruel to roast something named Marcella or Elizabeth.
There is only ever one rooster at a time, and he is always named Padraigh.
(I don't know why.)
ROOo-a-ROO-a-ROOOOOOoooooOOO
The bees that give us wax and honey are too many to count, so I call them all Beatrice.
Very funny.
Tess thought of a way I might be able to learn something from the animals—
According to legend...
animals can speak at Midwinter midnight!

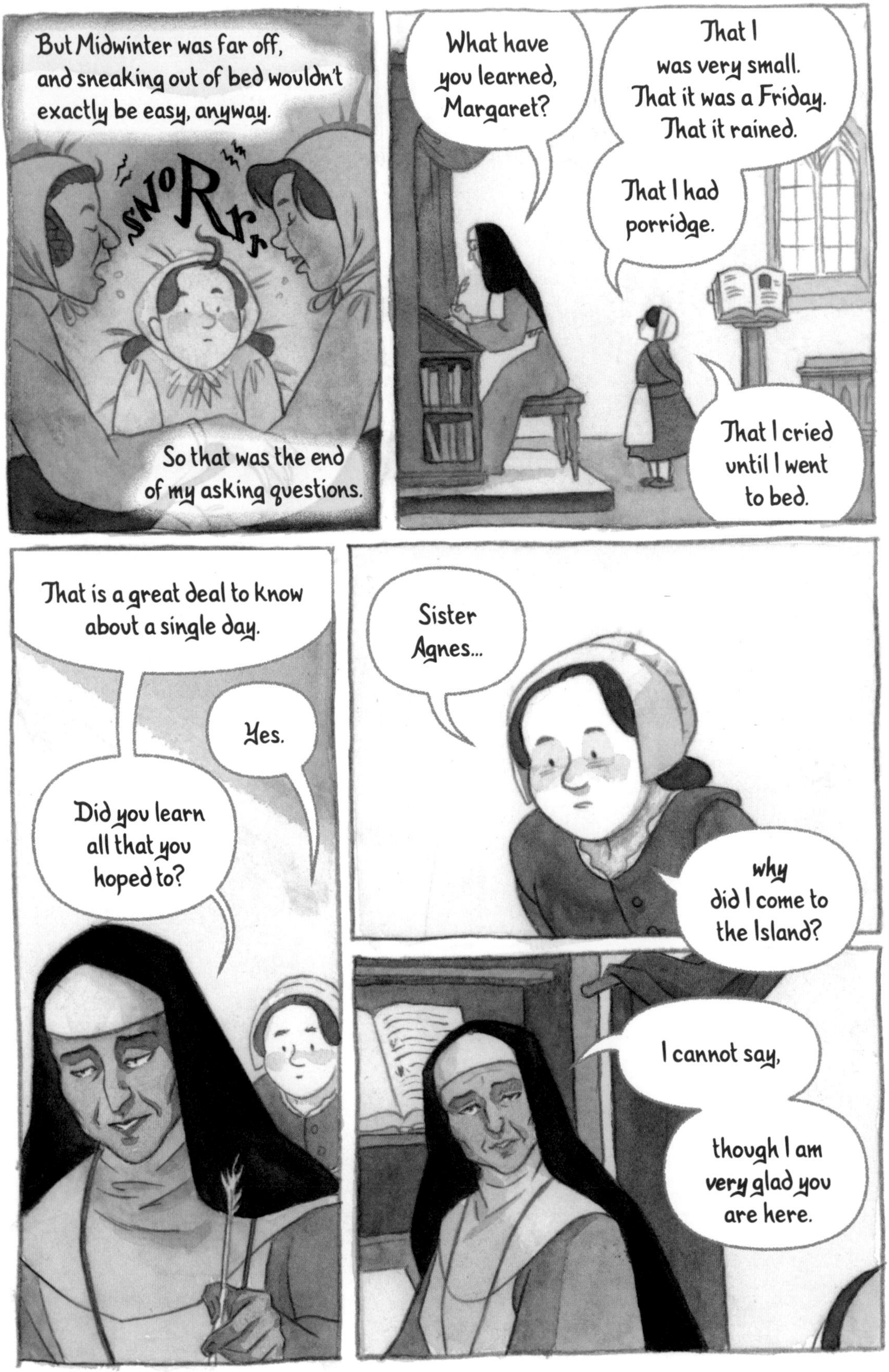
But Midwinter was far off, and sneaking out of bed wouldn't exactly be easy, anyway.
SNORRrr
So that was the end of my asking questions.
What have you learned, Margaret?
That I was very small. That it was a Friday. That it rained.
That I had porridge.
That I cried until I went to bed.
That is a great deal to know about a single day.
Yes.
Did you learn all that you hoped to?
Sister Agnes...
why did I come to the Island?
I cannot say,
though I am very glad you are here.

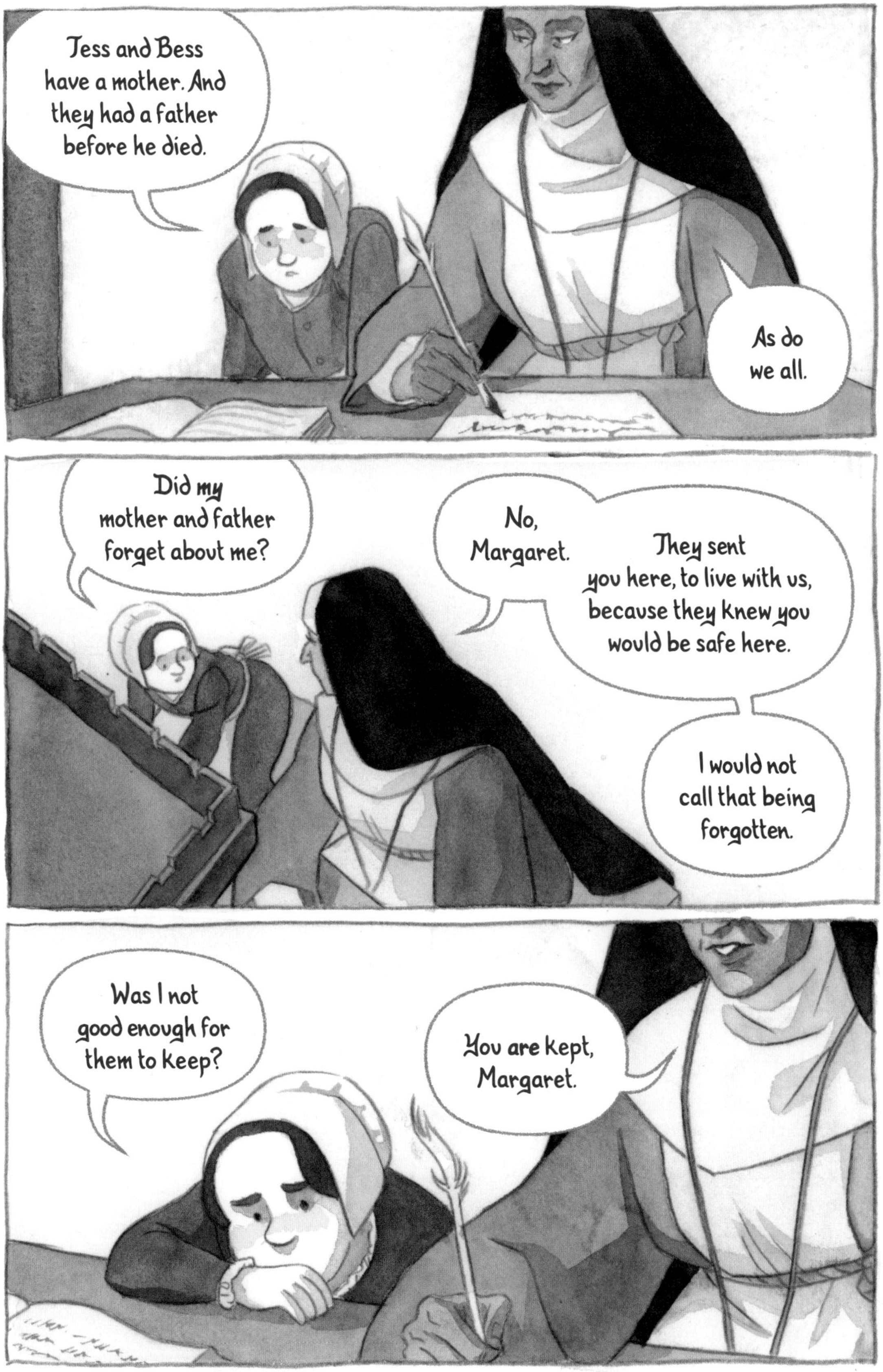
Jess and Bess have a mother. And they had a father before he died.
As do we all.
Did my mother and father forget about me?
No, Margaret.
They sent you here, to live with us, because they knew you would be safe here.
I would not call that being forgotten.
Was I not good enough for them to keep?
You are kept, Margaret.

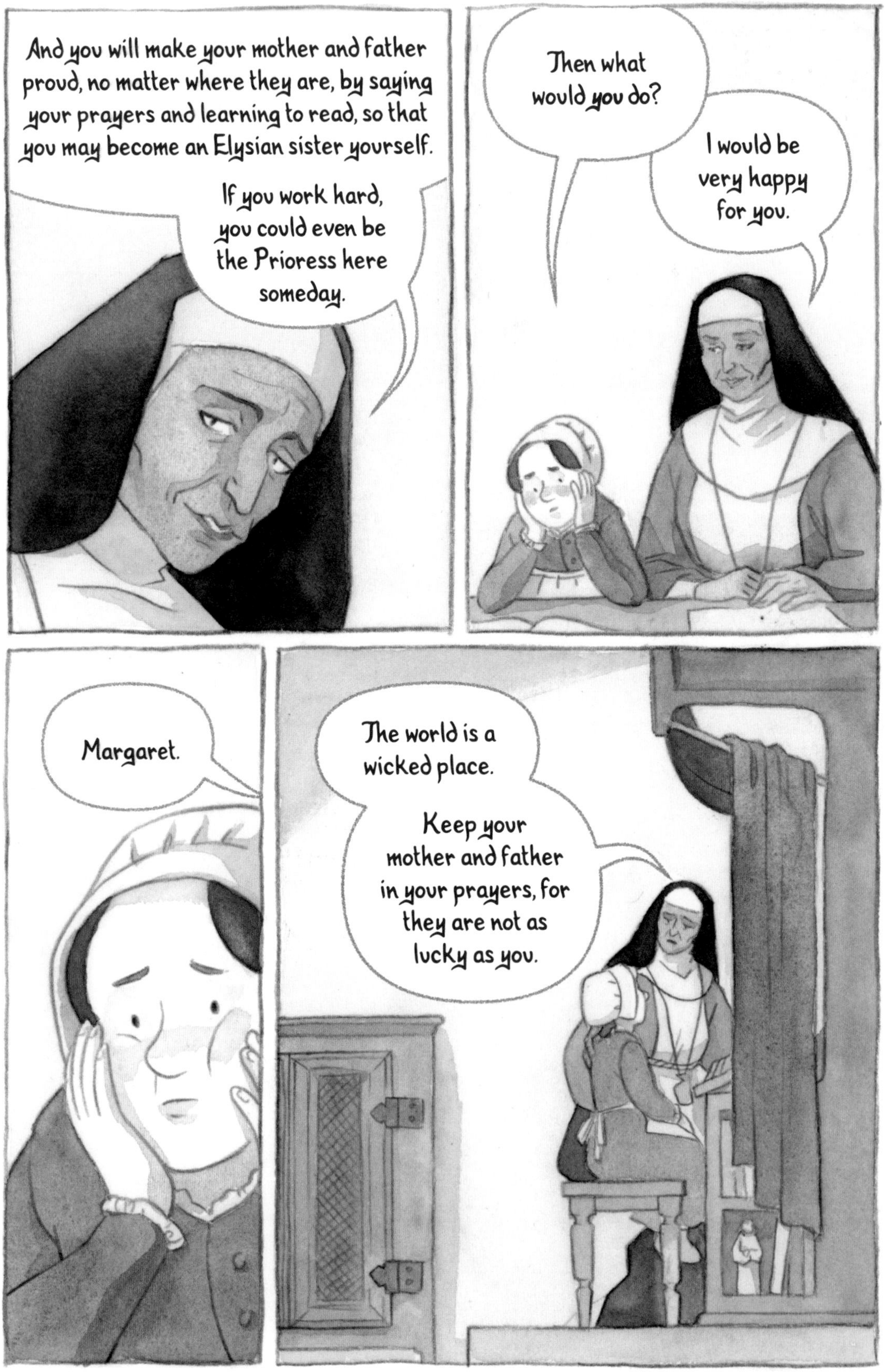
And you will make your mother and father proud, no matter where they are, by saying your prayers and learning to read, so that you may become an Elysian sister yourself.
If you work hard, you could even be the Prioress here someday.
Then what would you do?
I would be very happy for you.
Margaret.
The world is a wicked place.
Keep your mother and father in your prayers, for they are not as lucky as you.

The other "child" on the Island was in a painting hung in the **Chapter House**, which is the big room where everybody gathers for important meetings or special announcements.

It was a picture of

King Edmund,

the ruler of Albion, with his daughter Eleanor.

At first, because of her red hair, I thought that the little girl in the picture might be **me**.

(Although her ball was much fancier than my wooden one.)

No, dear. That's the **crown princess**.

What does that mean, Sister Sybil?

It means she is the king's daughter and that she will rule the kingdom after him. Unless he has a son.

I found out later that she wasn't even holding a ball to play with but an important thing called a **globus cruciger** that represents the whole world and means you are a person who rules over part of it. (With God's permission, of course.)

So I wasn't jealous of her useless ball anymore. But she did have a father who let her sit on his lap. I thought that he must be very proud of her and love her very much.

Sometimes I would visit the painting of the princess
and her father the king and imagine for a little while
that it really was me sitting on his lap, and that he told
me stories of the wicked world and all the ways a good
and kind ruler could make it better.

Or I would visit the statue of the Mournful Mother
and pretend that I had once been a baby made of
wood on her lap, and that She had brought me to life
and given me to the sisters of the Island so that one
of her children wouldn't grow up to be so sad.

No one could be sad living on the Island, I thought. But since my living there
meant that I couldn't have my real mother and father with me, I decided that
it was reasonable to ask God for something in return.

The one thing
I **really** wanted...

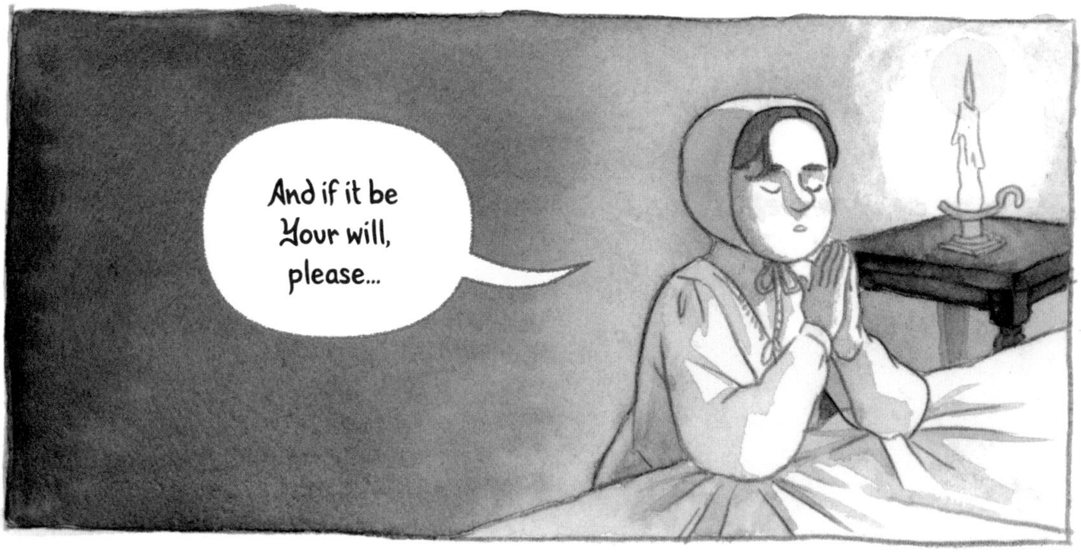
And if it be Your will, please...

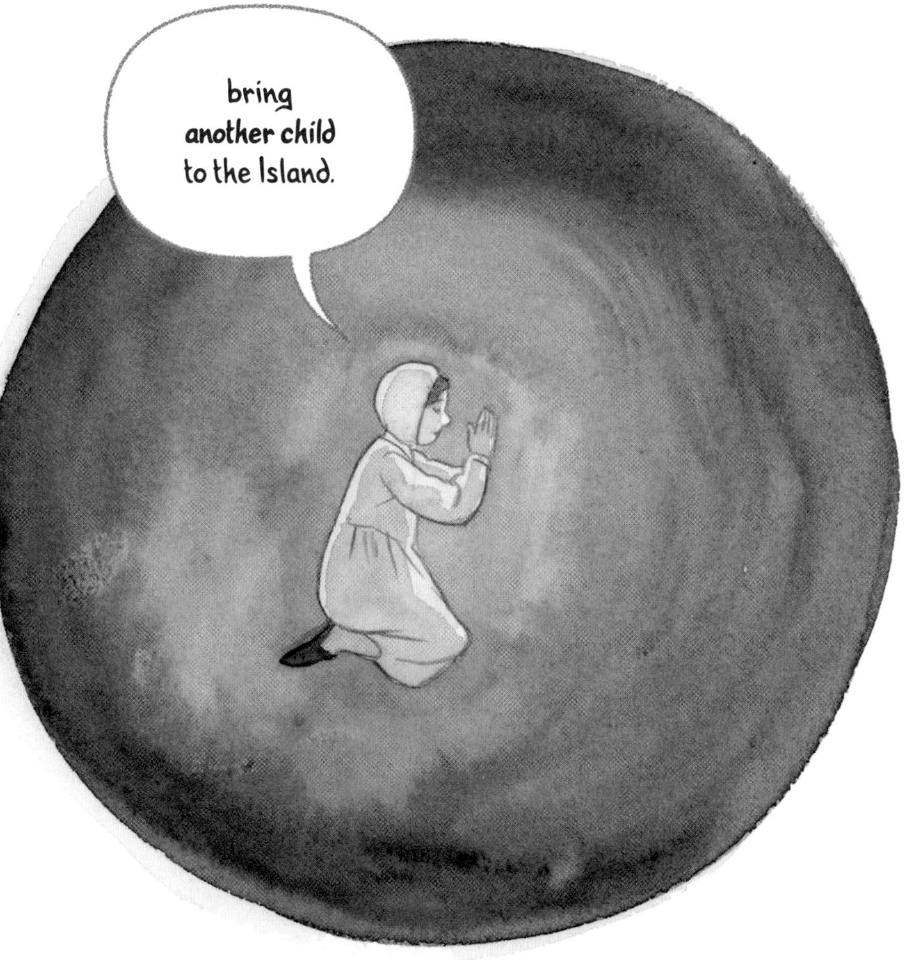
bring another child to the Island.

That is how I met William.

In the first six years I had lived on the Island,

nobody new had come to stay. (Well, other than chickens.)

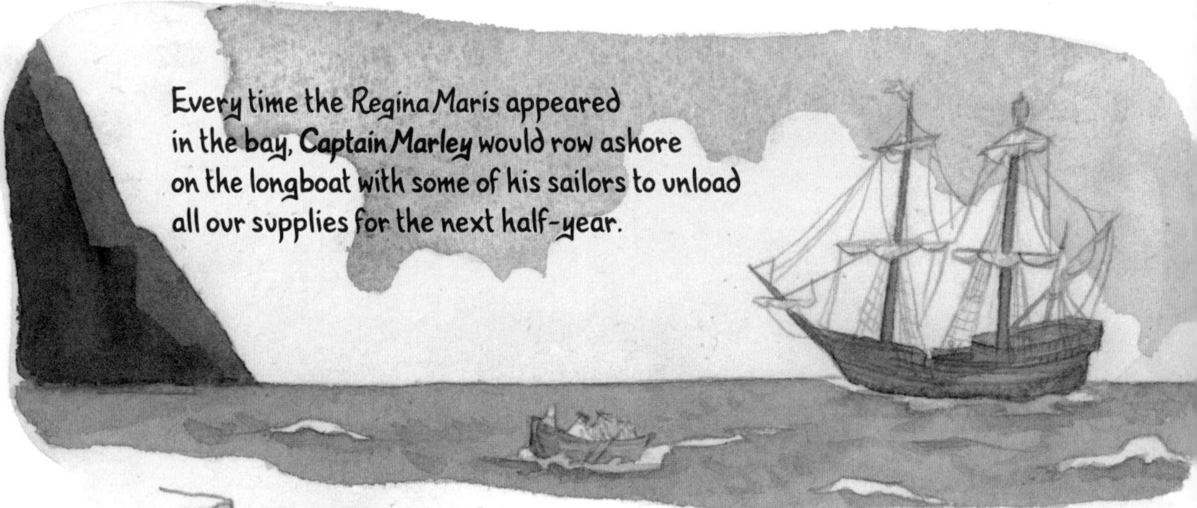

Every time the *Regina Maris* appeared in the bay, Captain Marley would row ashore on the longboat with some of his sailors to unload all our supplies for the next half-year.

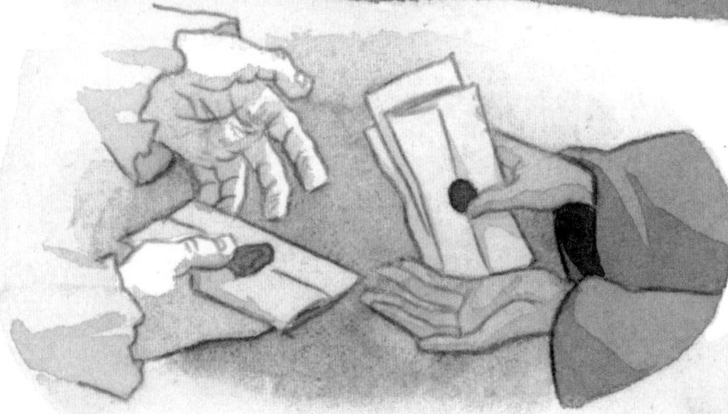

Next, Captain Marley would share a meal with Sister Agnes, tell her all the news from Albion, and exchange all the letters and packages they had to send or to deliver.

Then all the sailors would row back to the ship before dark,

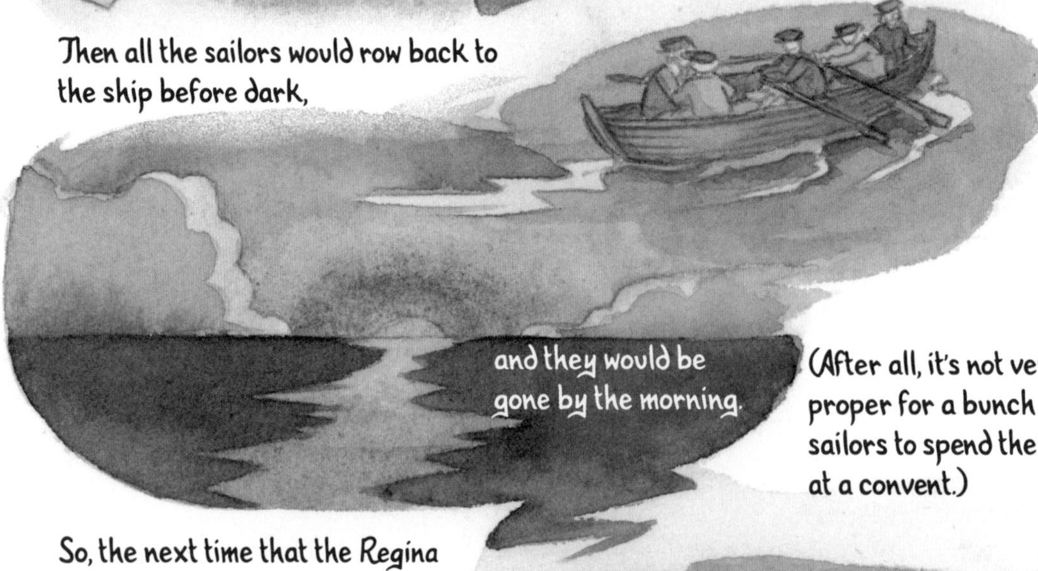

and they would be gone by the morning.

(After all, it's not very proper for a bunch of sailors to spend the night at a convent.)

So, the next time that the *Regina Maris* arrived in the bay, I could tell right away that something was different.

For one thing,

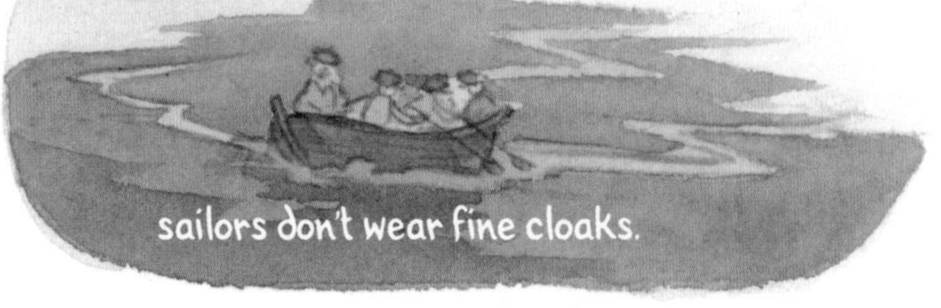

sailors don't wear fine cloaks.

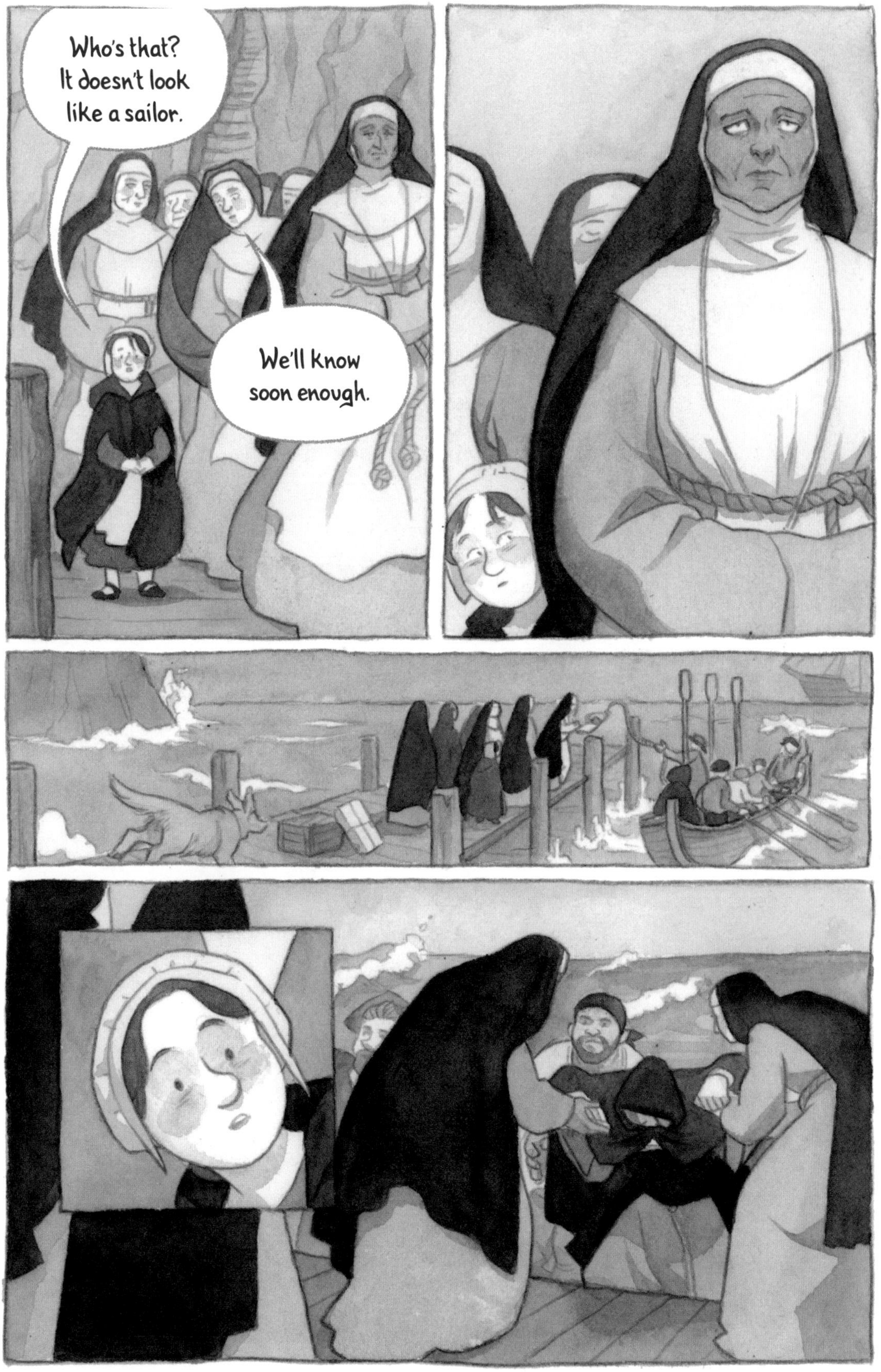
Who's that? It doesn't look like a sailor.
We'll know soon enough.

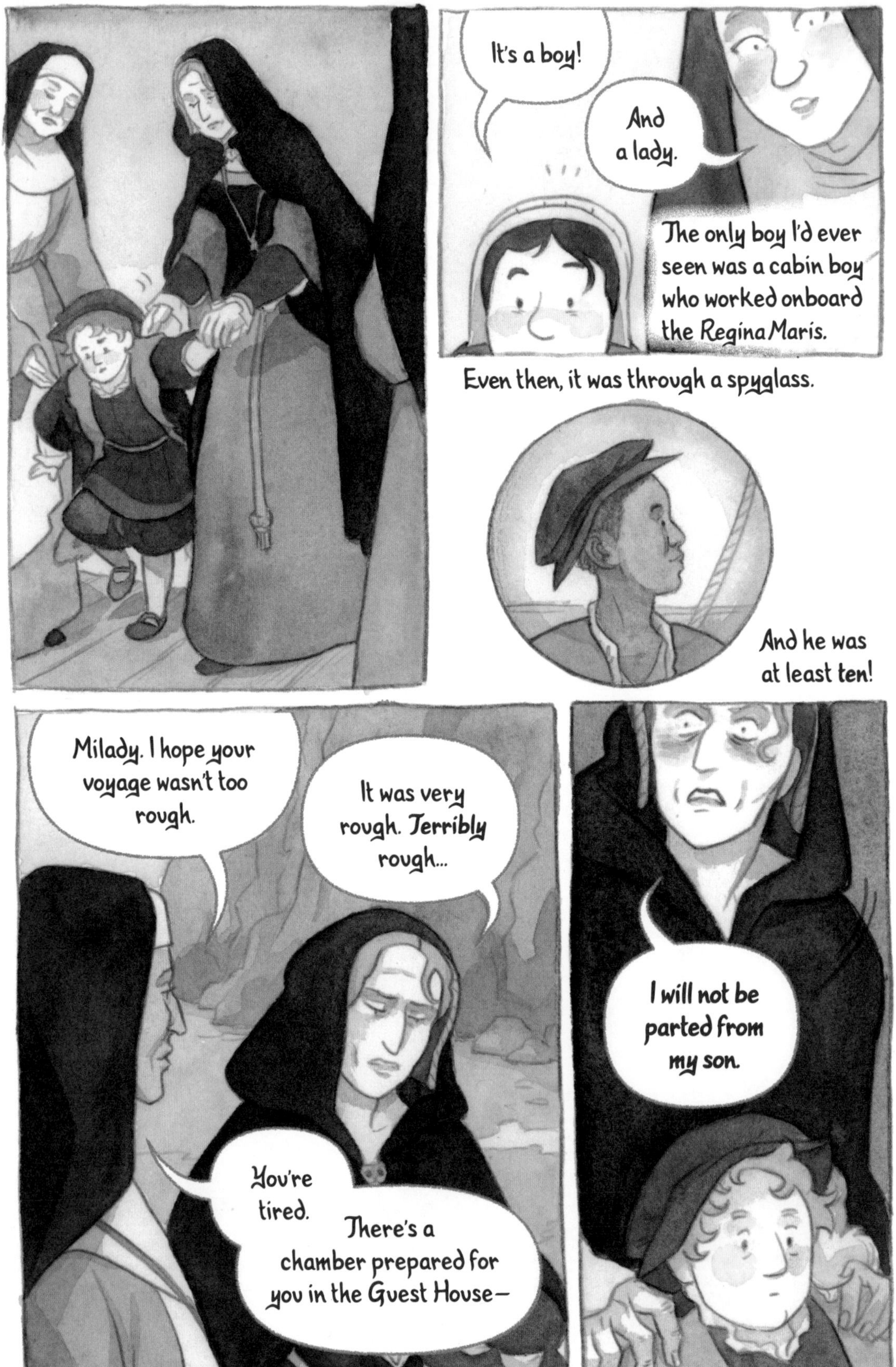
It's a boy!
And a lady.
The only boy I'd ever seen was a cabin boy who worked onboard the *Regina Maris*.
Even then, it was through a spyglass.
And he was at least ten!
Milady. I hope your voyage wasn't too rough.
It was very rough. Terribly rough...
You're tired.
There's a chamber prepared for you in the Guest House–
I will not be parted from my son.

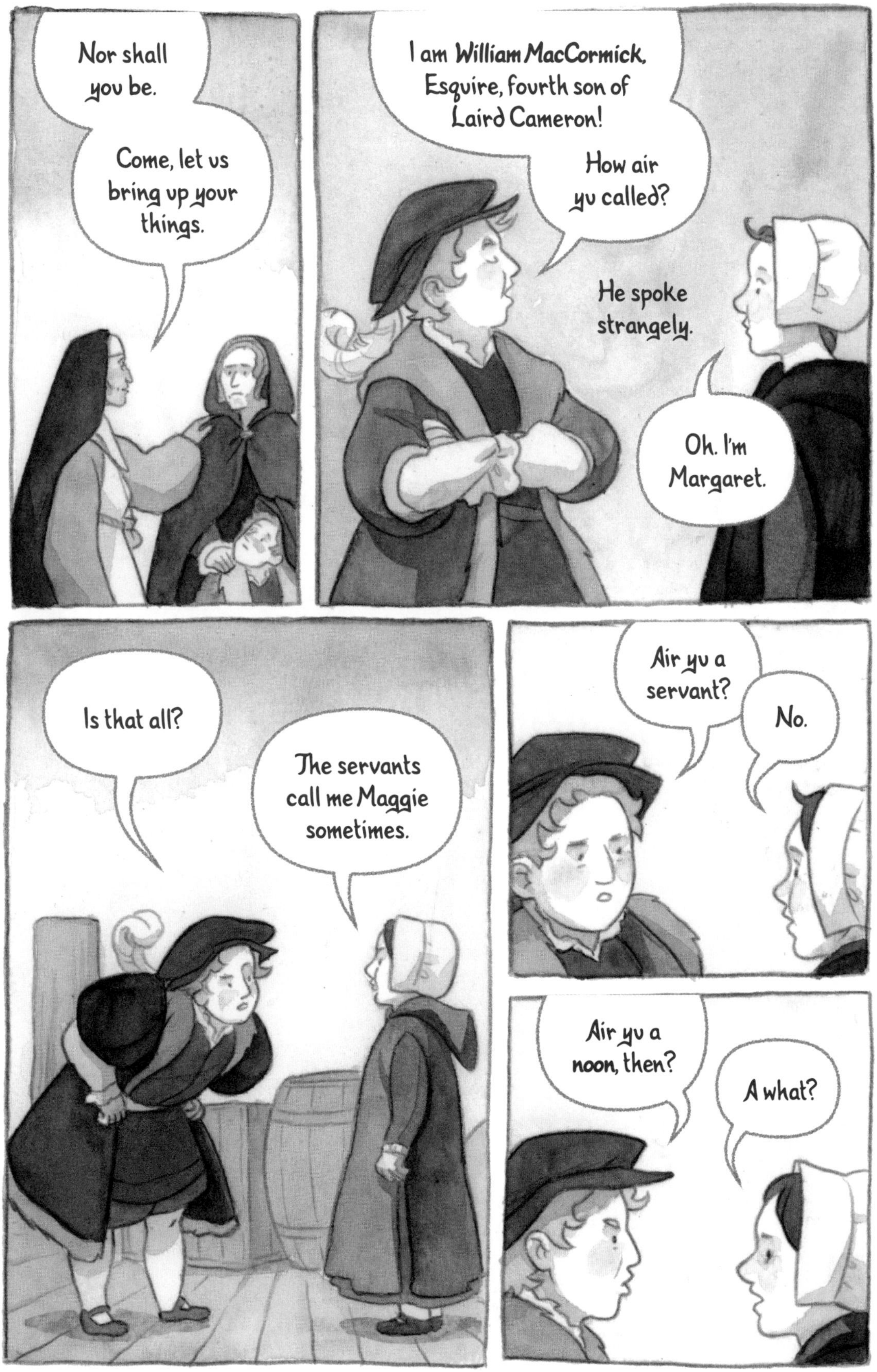
Nor shall you be.
Come, let us bring up your things.
I am William MacCormick, Esquire, fourth son of Laird Cameron!
How air yu called?
He spoke strangely.
Oh. I'm Margaret.
Is that all?
The servants call me Maggie sometimes.
Air yu a servant?
No.
Air yu a noon, then?
A what?

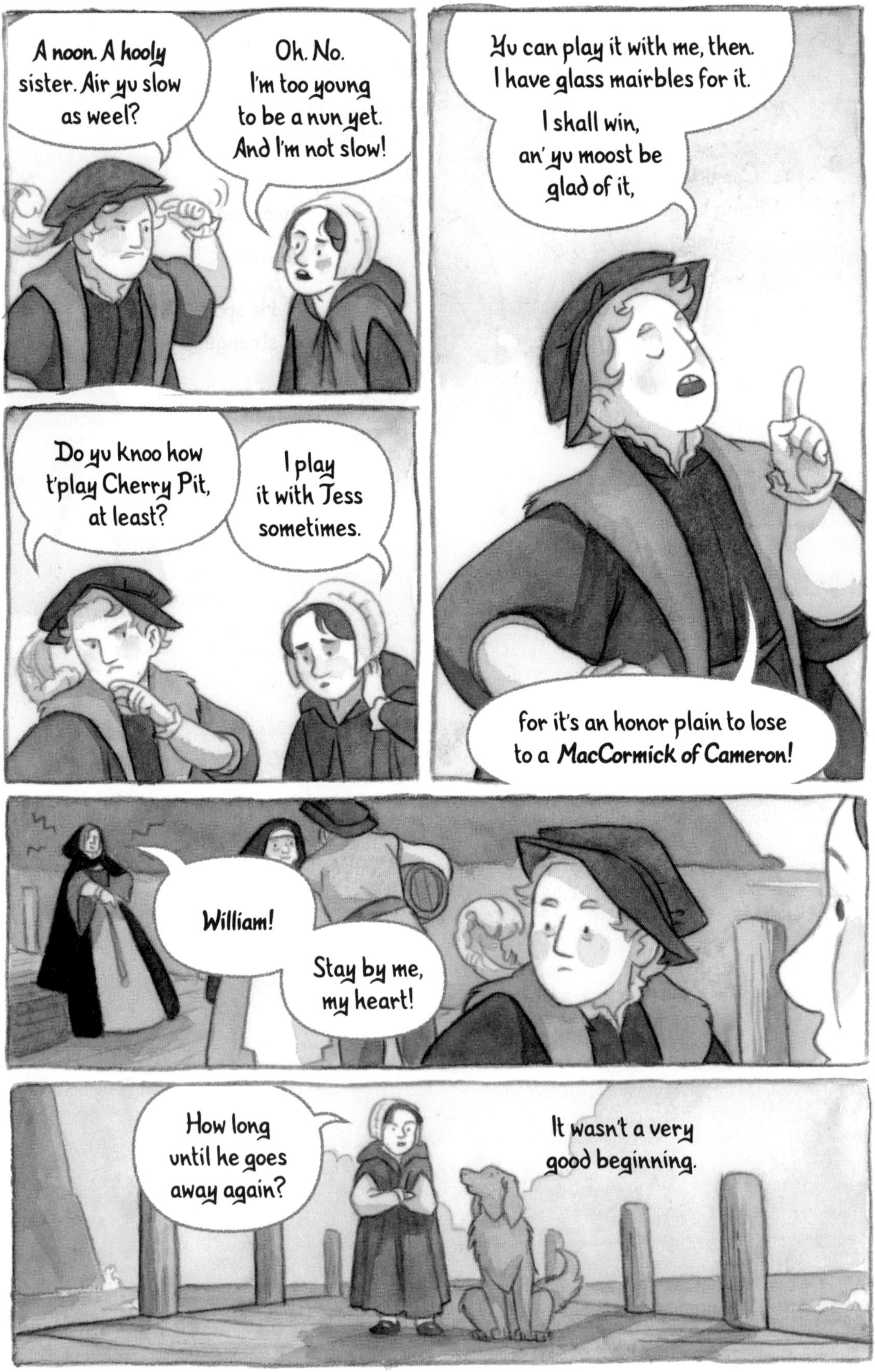
A noon. A hooly sister. Air yu slow as weel?
Oh. No. I'm too young to be a nun yet. And I'm not slow!
Yu can play it with me, then. I have glass mairbles for it.
I shall win, an' yu moost be glad of it,
Do yu knoo how t'play Cherry Pit, at least?
I play it with Jess sometimes.
for it's an honor plain to lose to a MacCormick of Cameron!
William!
Stay by me, my heart!
How long until he goes away again?
It wasn't a very good beginning.

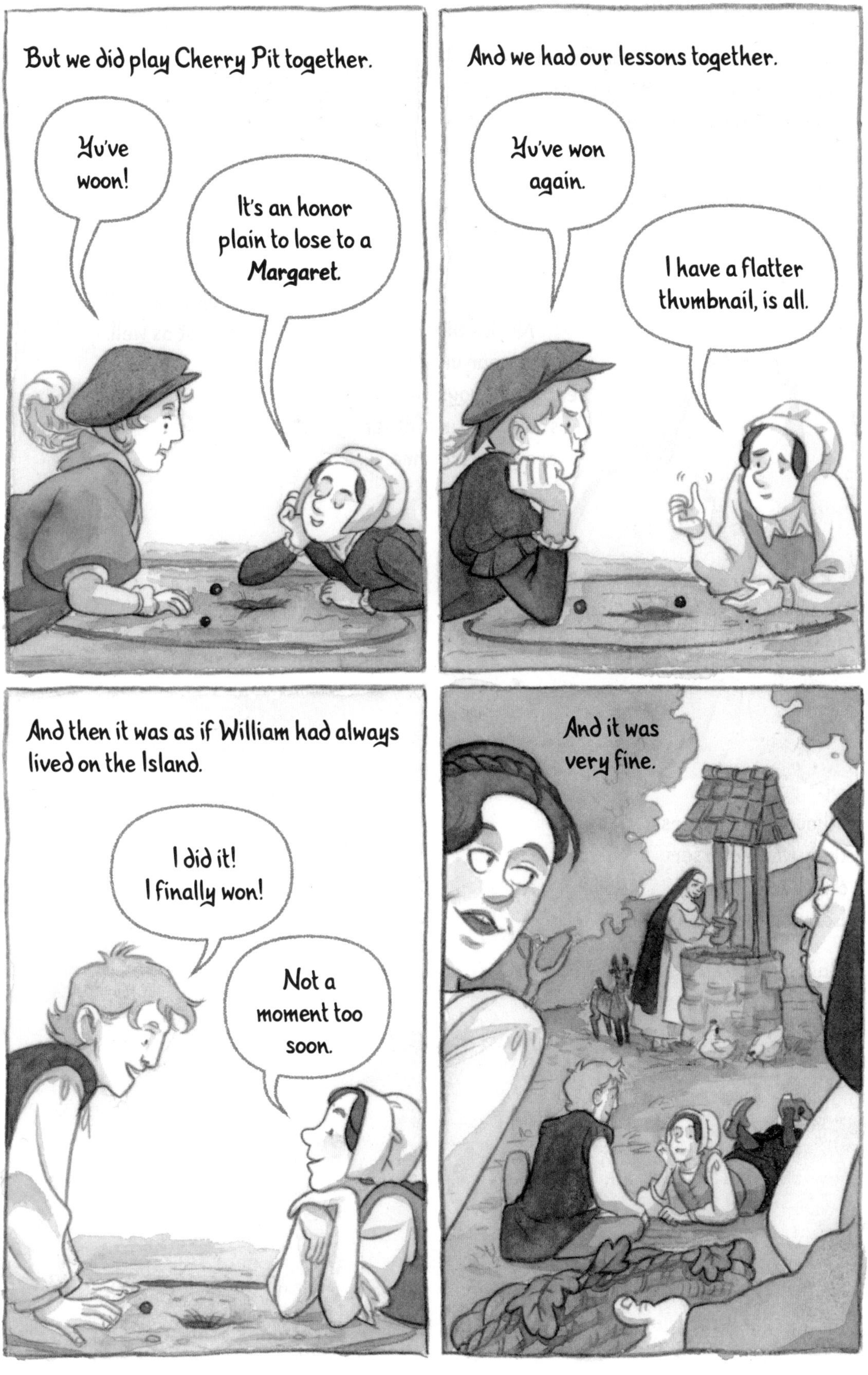

But we did play Cherry Pit together.
Yu've woon!
It's an honor plain to lose to a Margaret.
And we had our lessons together.
Yu've won again.
I have a flatter thumbnail, is all.
And then it was as if William had always lived on the Island.
I did it! I finally won!
Not a moment too soon.
And it was very fine.

But William's mother, Lady Cameron, didn't fit in so well, not even after three years. Some days she never left her bed. She hardly ever helped the sisters with their embroidery, which paid for all the food we could not grow ourselves. I thought she was very selfish.

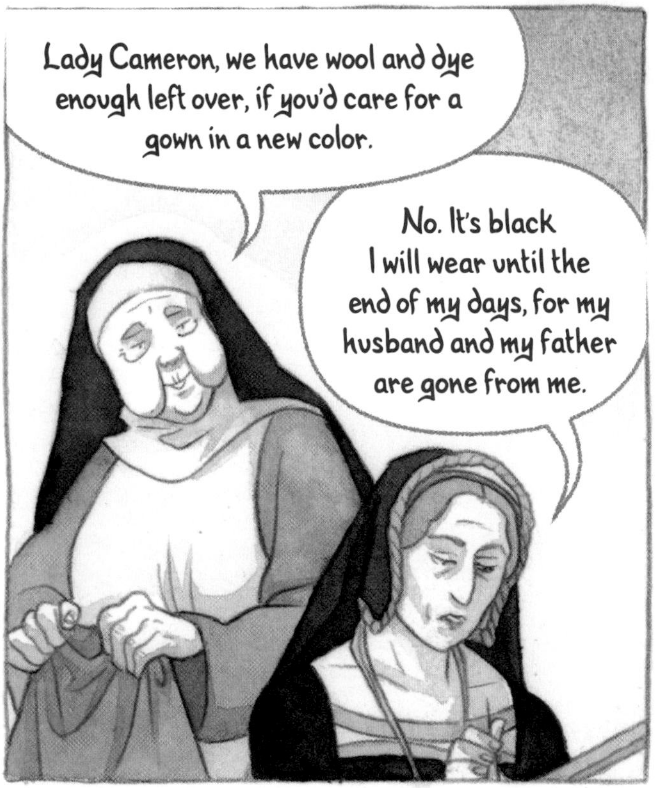
Lady Cameron, we have wool and dye enough left over, if you'd care for a gown in a new color.
No. It's black I will wear until the end of my days, for my husband and my father are gone from me.

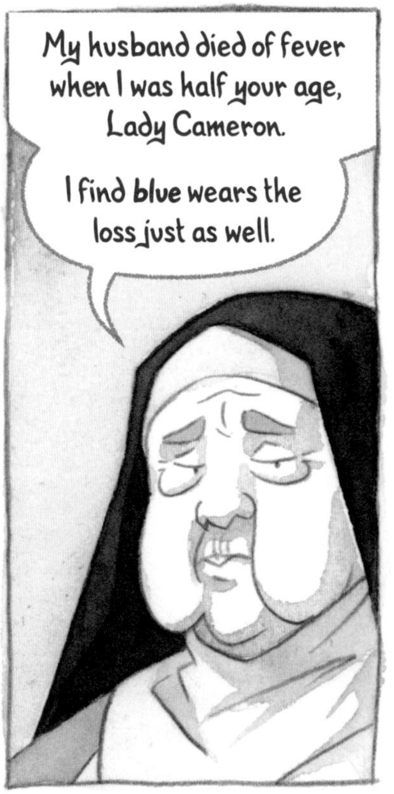
My husband died of fever when I was half your age, Lady Cameron.
I find **blue** wears the loss just as well.

I thought the sisters had all grown up as foundlings, like me, or had taken vows because they wanted to serve Saint Elysia instead of being married. Sister Wynefreed had not only had a husband, but lost him! Yet she had found peace in the sisterhood. So why did Lady Cameron not take her vows and find peace, too?

Maybe it had something to do with how her husband had died.

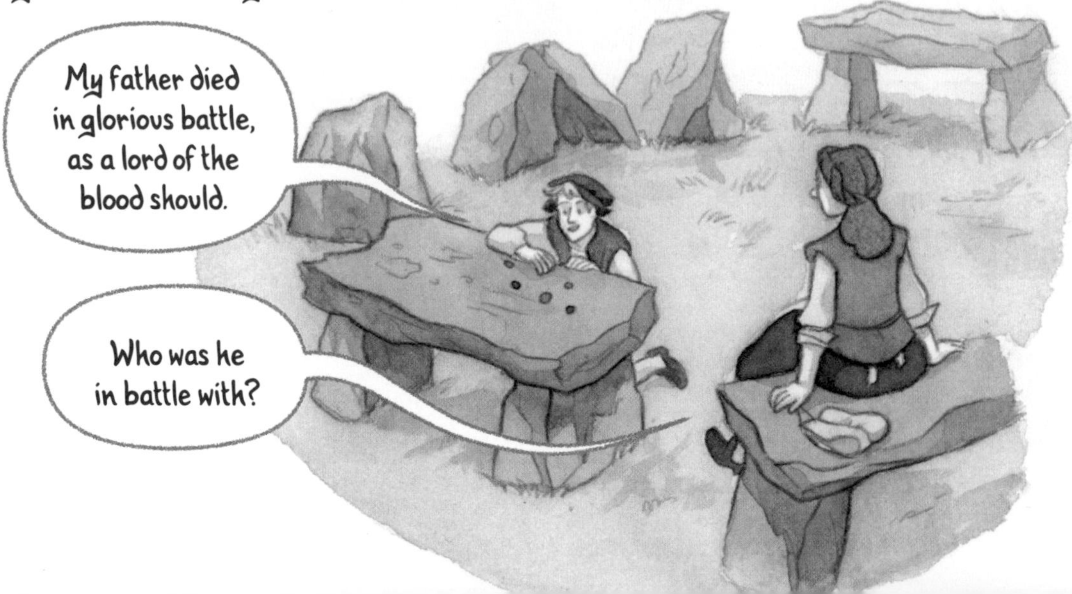
My father died in glorious battle, as a lord of the blood should.
Who was he in battle with?

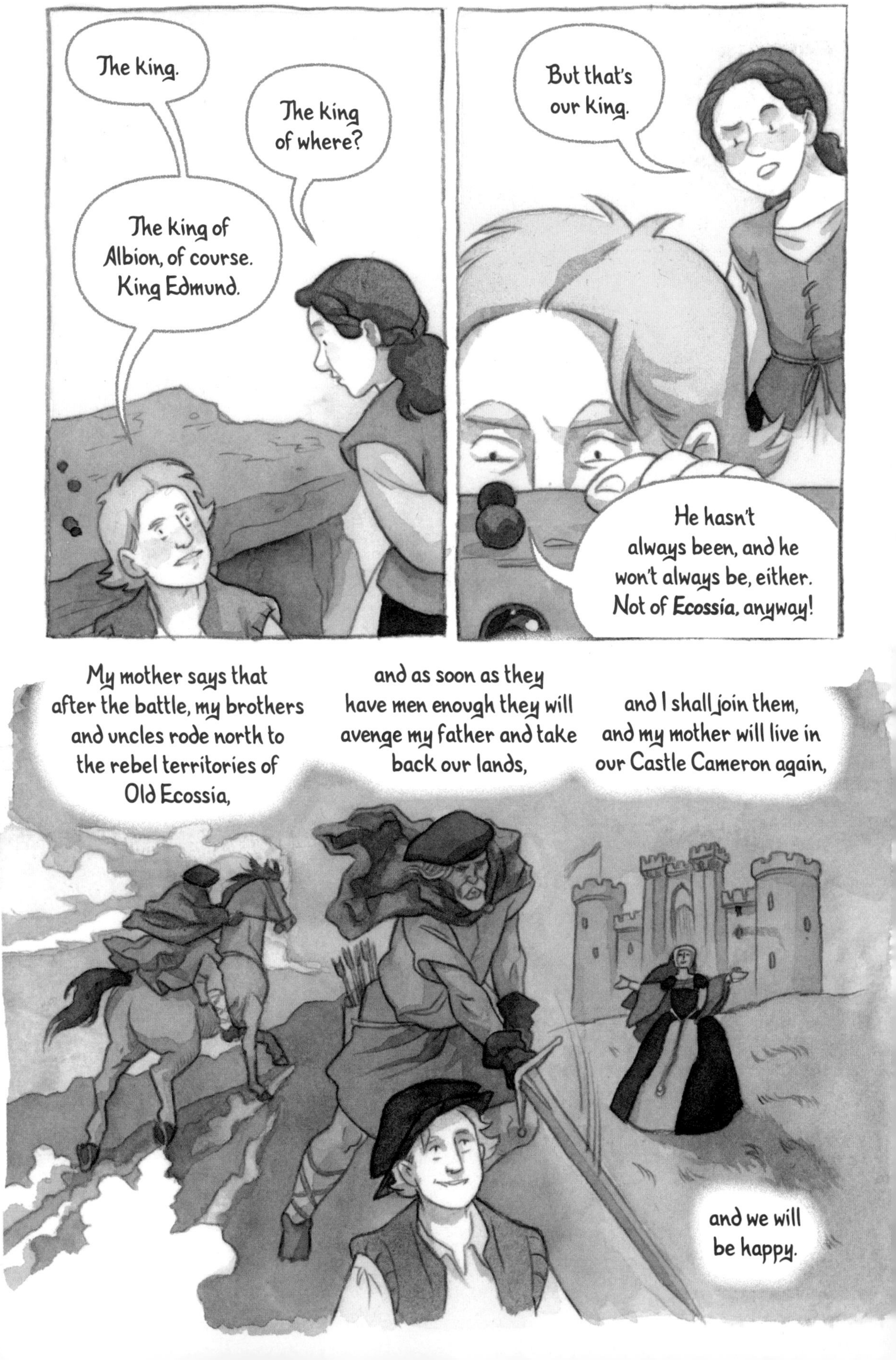
The king.
The king of where?
The king of Albion, of course. King Edmund.
But that's our king.
He hasn't always been, and he won't always be, either. Not of Ecossia, anyway!
My mother says that after the battle, my brothers and uncles rode north to the rebel territories of Old Ecossia,
and as soon as they have men enough they will avenge my father and take back our lands,
and I shall join them, and my mother will live in our Castle Cameron again,
and we will be happy.

I was confused because a good king wouldn't take anybody's home away, and King Edmund was a good king. And because I thought that William was already happy. Who needed anything more than what was on the Island? We explored every inch of it together.

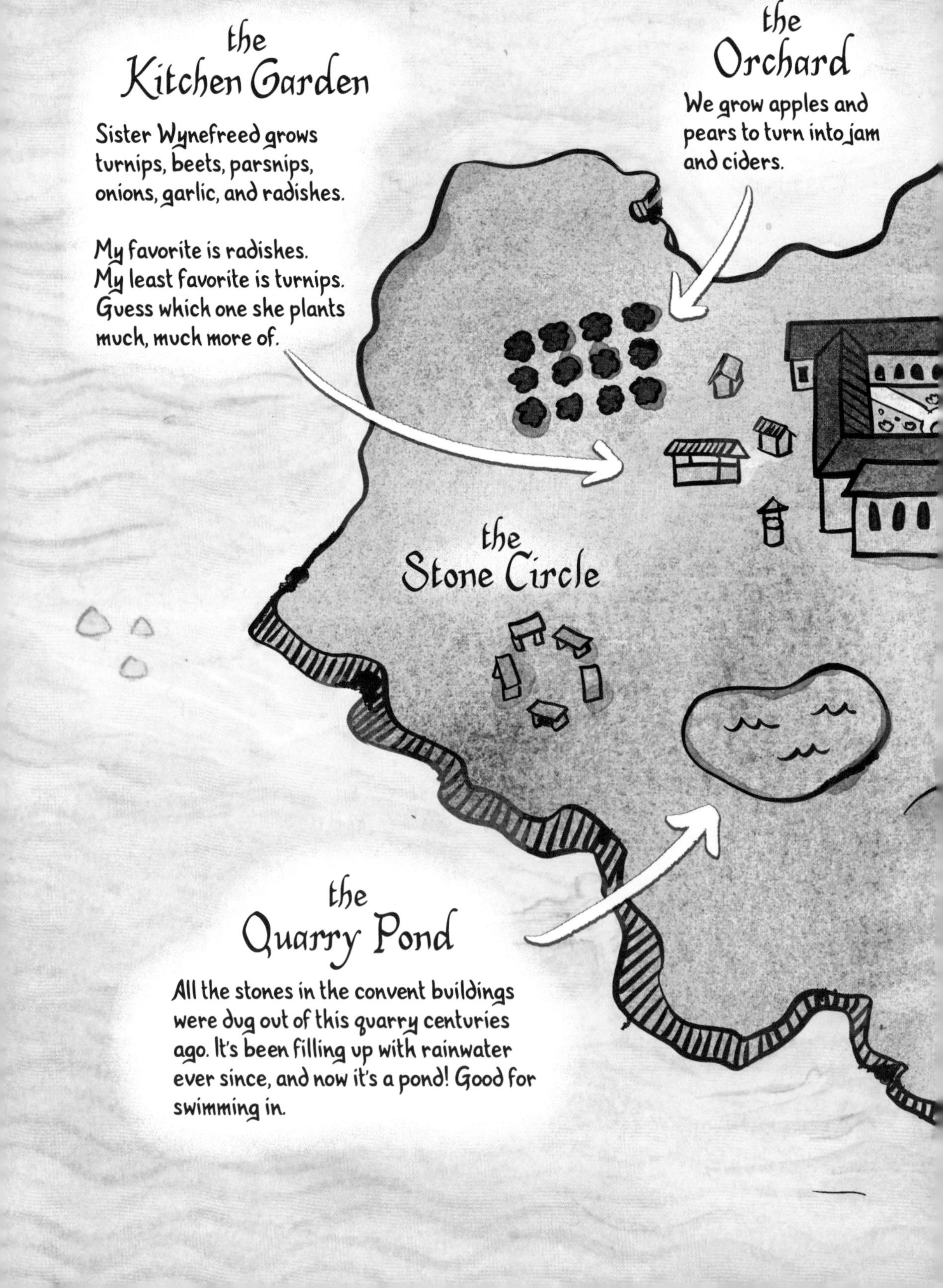
the Kitchen Garden
Sister Wynefreed grows turnips, beets, parsnips, onions, garlic, and radishes.
My favorite is radishes. My least favorite is turnips. Guess which one she plants much, much more of.
the Orchard
We grow apples and pears to turn into jam and ciders.
the Stone Circle
the Quarry Pond
All the stones in the convent buildings were dug out of this quarry centuries ago. It's been filling up with rainwater ever since, and now it's a pond! Good for swimming in.

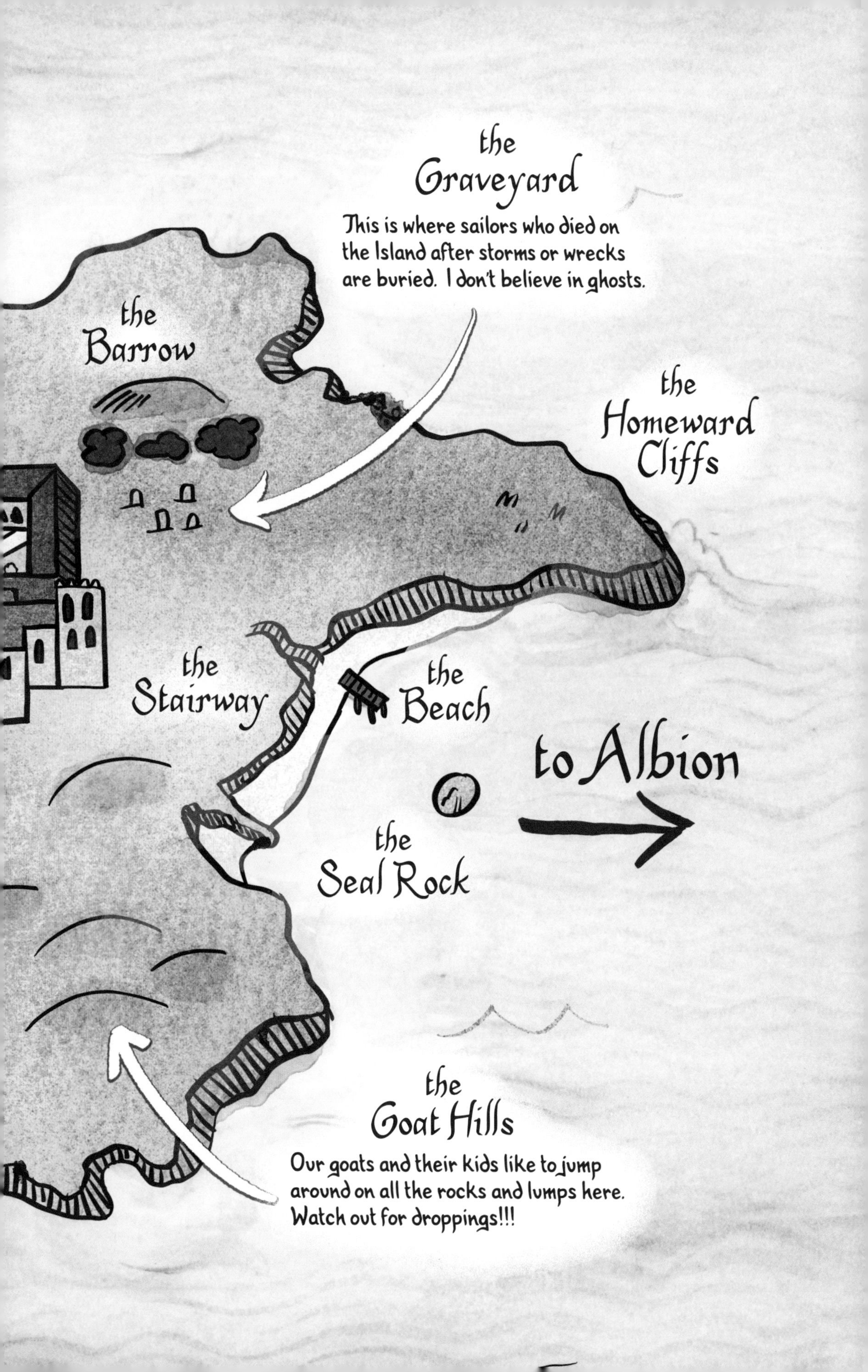
the Graveyard
This is where sailors who died on the Island after storms or wrecks are buried. I don't believe in ghosts.
the Barrow
the Homeward Cliffs
the Stairway
the Beach
to Albion
the Seal Rock
the Goat Hills
Our goats and their kids like to jump around on all the rocks and lumps here. Watch out for droppings!!!

Some parts of the Island were more unusual or interesting than others. For example, in the east part of the Island are...

the Homeward Cliffs.

The Island has cliffs all around it, but these are the highest by far. The wind on this part of the Island is so strong that hardly anything can grow. It faces Albion, but the only thing you'll see here is the sea, the sea, the sea.

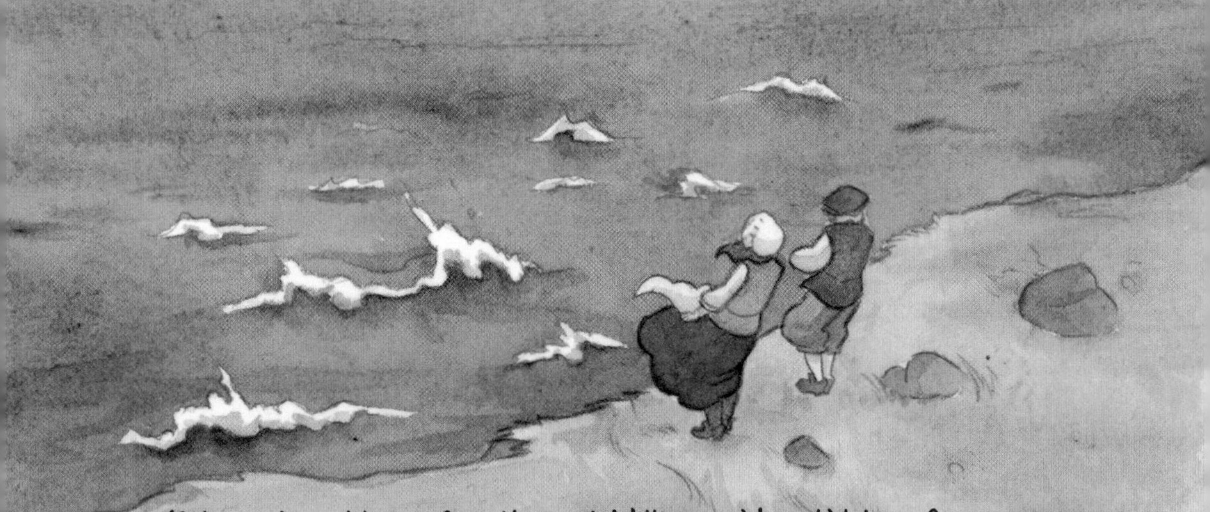

If the wind was blowing from the west, William and I would let go of leaves or feathers to see whose was carried away farther or fastest.

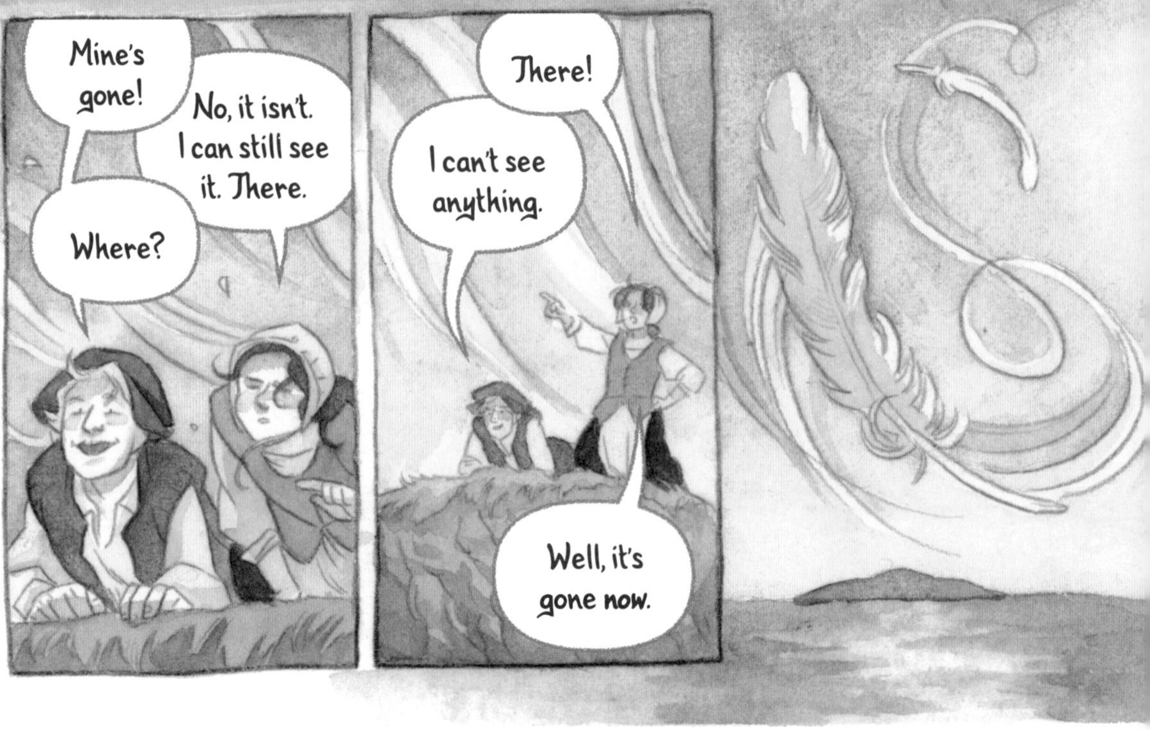
Mine's gone!
No, it isn't. I can still see it. There.
Where?
There!
I can't see anything.
Well, it's gone now.

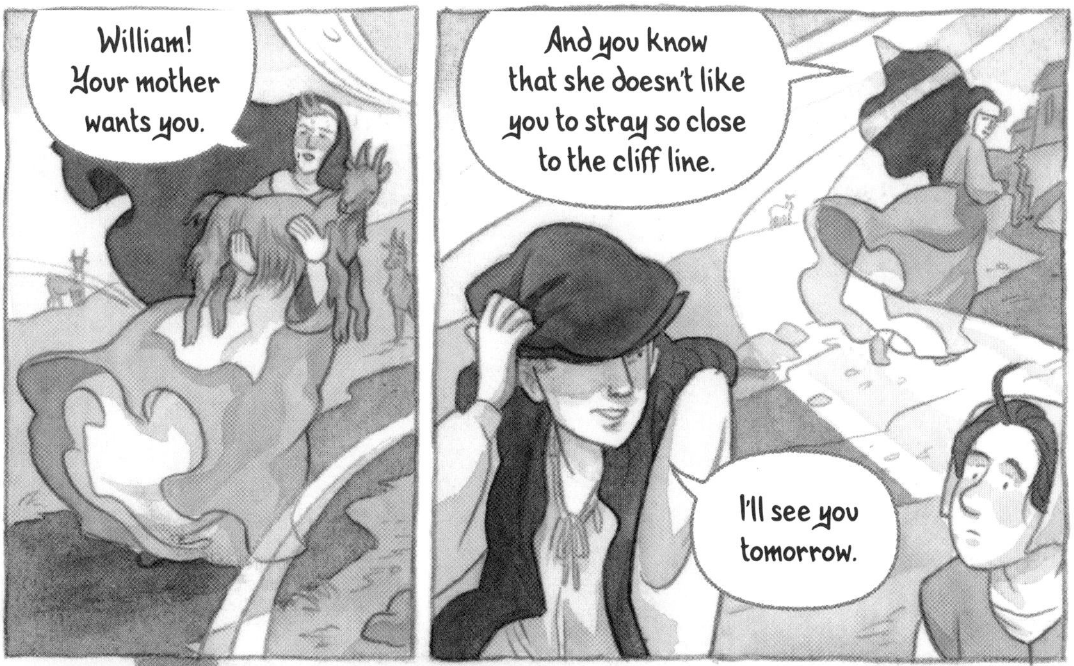
William! Your mother wants you.
And you know that she doesn't like you to stray so close to the cliff line.
I'll see you tomorrow.

On the north side of the church is a strangely shaped hill called... the Barrow.

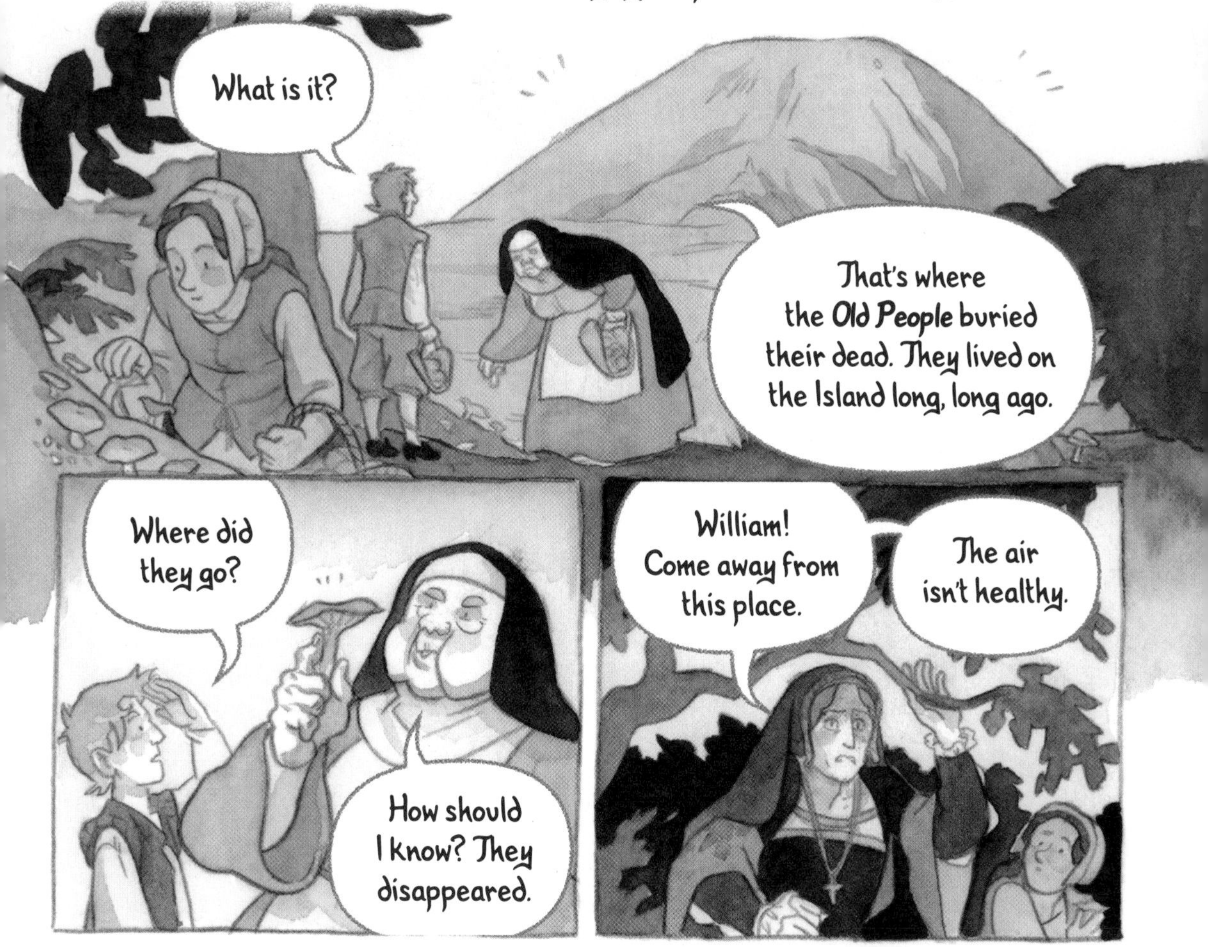
What is it?
That's where the *Old People* buried their dead. They lived on the Island long, long ago.
Where did they go?
How should I know? They disappeared.
William! Come away from this place.
The air isn't healthy.

The Barrow isn't the only sign that the Old People left behind. In the middle of the Island is a ring of carefully balanced rocks called...

the Stone Circle

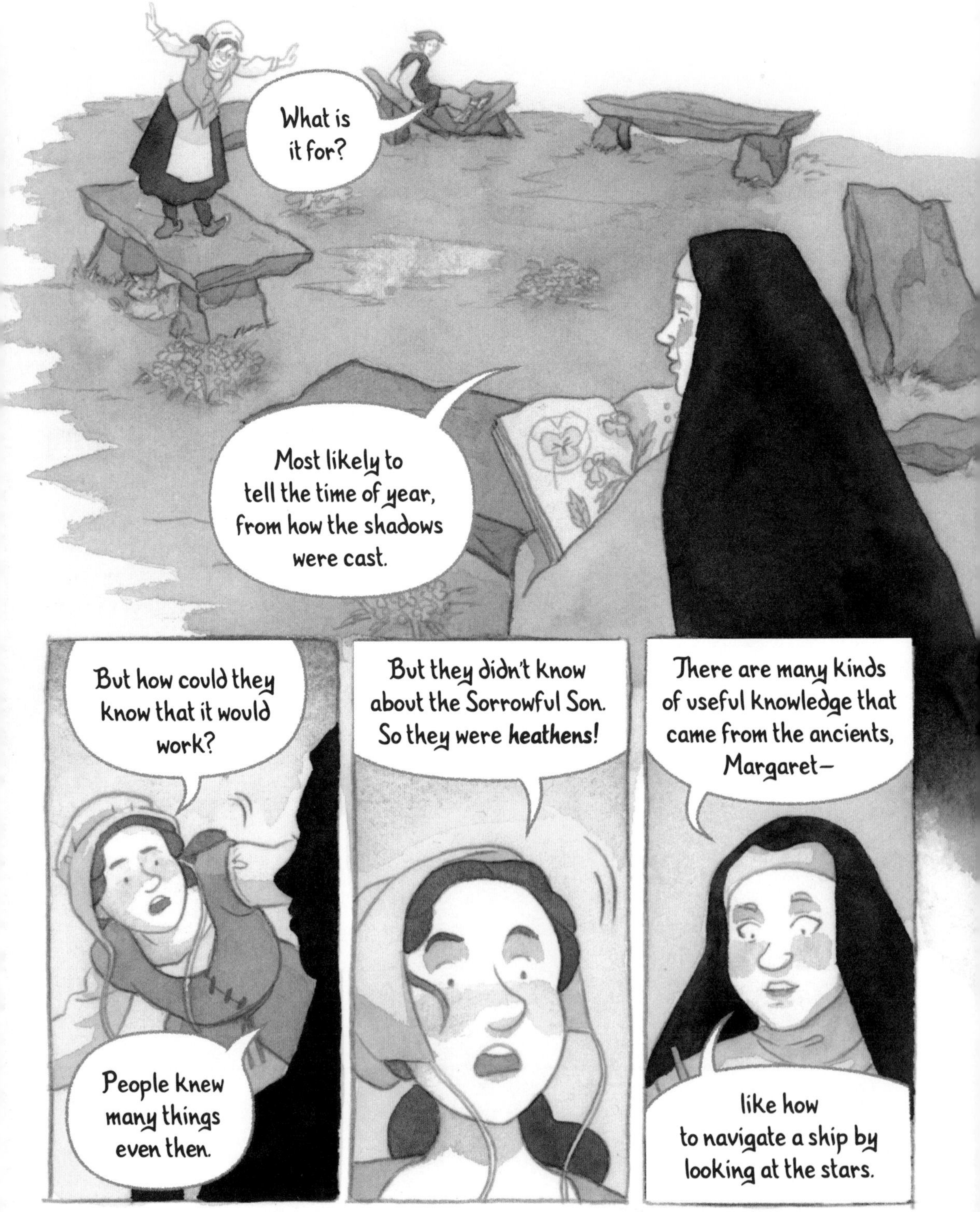
What is it for?
Most likely to tell the time of year, from how the shadows were cast.
But how could they know that it would work?
People knew many things even then.
But they didn't know about the Sorrowful Son. So they were *heathens!*
There are many kinds of useful knowledge that came from the ancients, Margaret—
like how to navigate a ship by looking at the stars.

There's only one place on the Island where you can get down to the sea (well, without jumping).

The Stairway is a path that goes down through the cliffside that leads to the beach.

Sister Sybil taught us that the Stairway probably began when an ancient stream carved a groove into the cliffside.

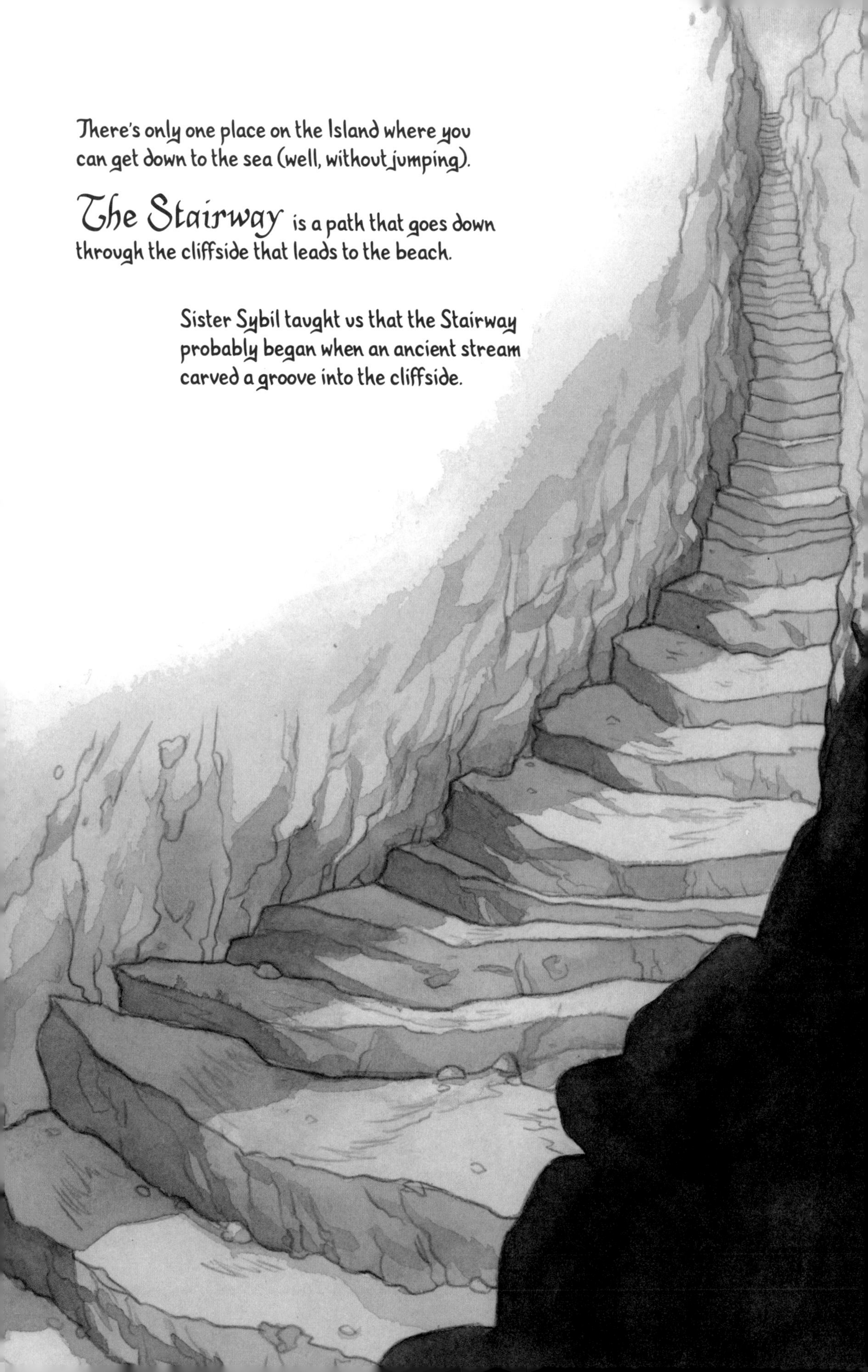

Eventually the stream went dry, and the Old People used its old bed as a pathway to climb up and down between the top of the Island and the Beach.

Then, hundreds of years later, the same people who built the convent carved the rock into an actual staircase to make it even easier to bring things up from the beach. It's still steep, but not so bad unless you're carrying something heavy.

(Unfortunately, the driftwood that we bring up from the beach to dry out and burn as fuel is very heavy!)

So many feet have gone up and down the stairs that the middle part of every step is worn down. Someday the Stairway may turn *back* into a streambed!

The noise of the waves is very strange in the Stairway. It sounds small and far away, but loud at the same time, like the sound of Sister Philippa's beehives.

Sometimes when the wind blows straight into the Stairway, it feels like it's trying to suck away your breath.

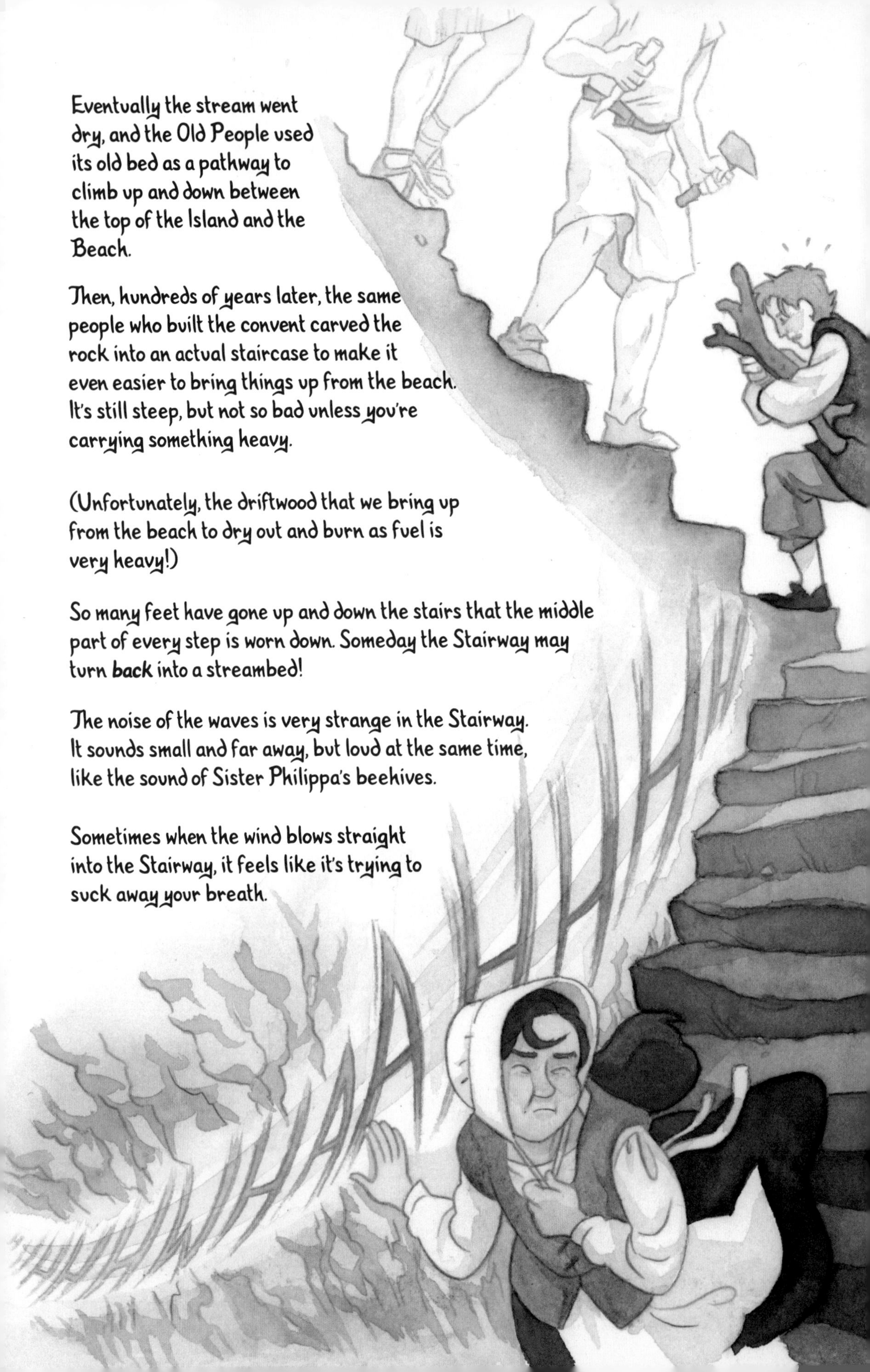

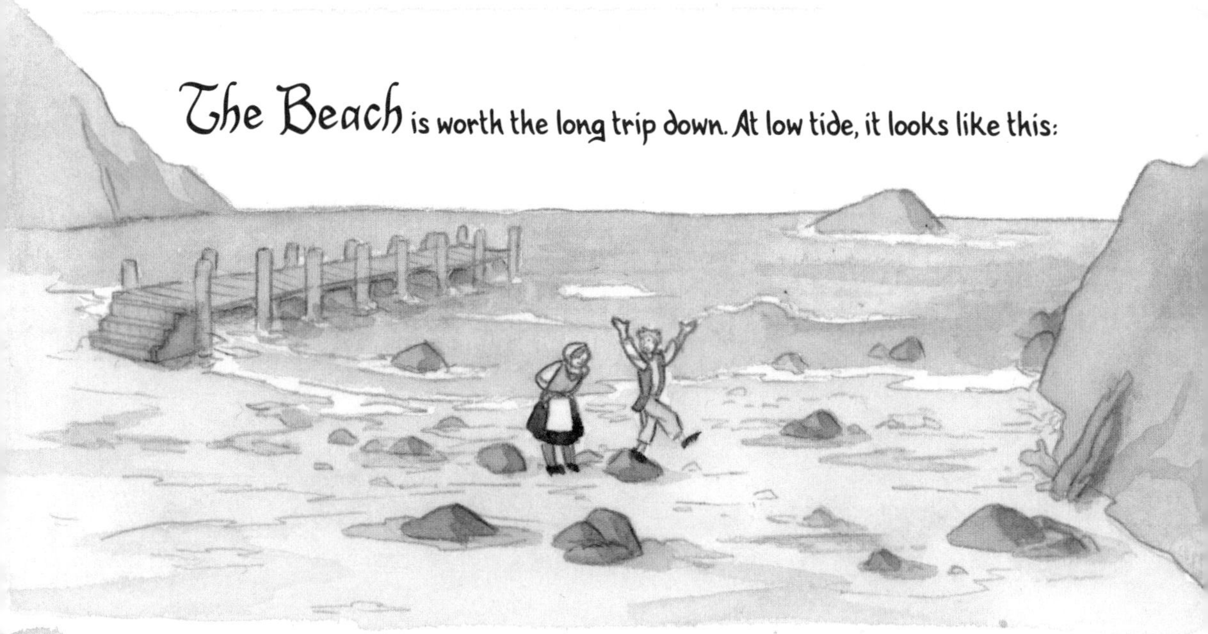
The Beach is worth the long trip down. At low tide, it looks like this:

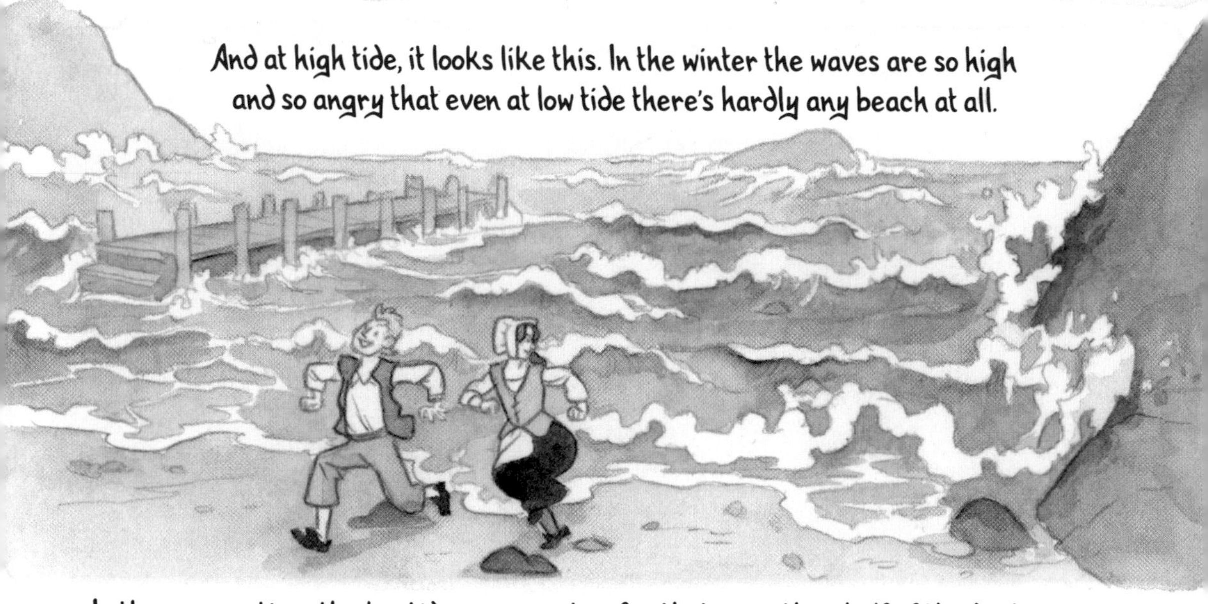
And at high tide, it looks like this. In the winter the waves are so high and so angry that even at low tide there's hardly any beach at all.

In the summertime, the low tide can go out so far that more than half of the dock is on dry land, and all the creatures who live near the tide line go thirsty for a few hours.

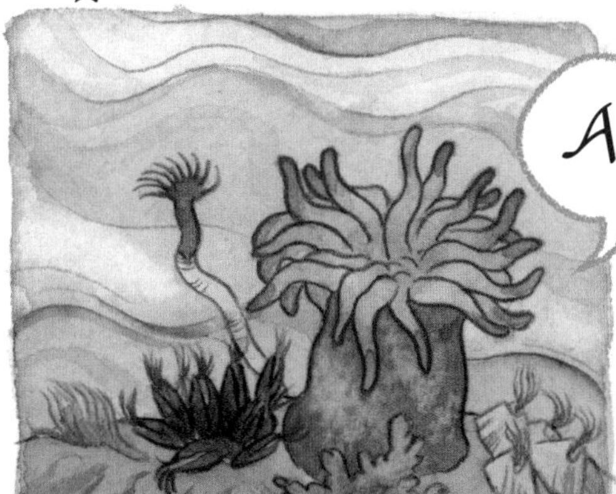
Ahhh...

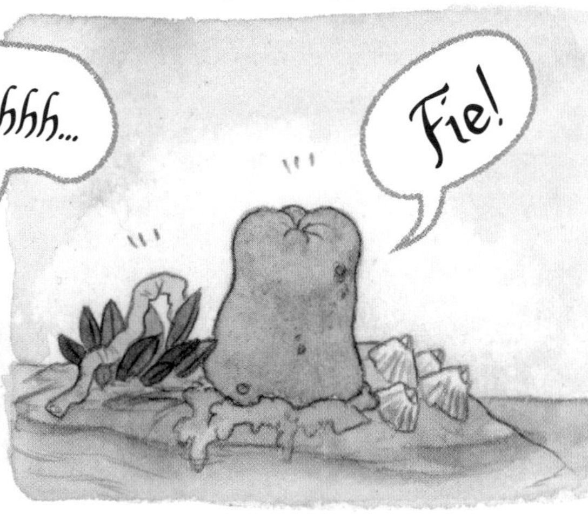
Fie!

The convent has a little fishing boat that you can launch from the dock. It's a coracle, which is a sort of basket boat woven out of strips of wood and grass.

You couldn't sail anywhere with it, but it's easy to row out into the bay, where the tastiest fish live.

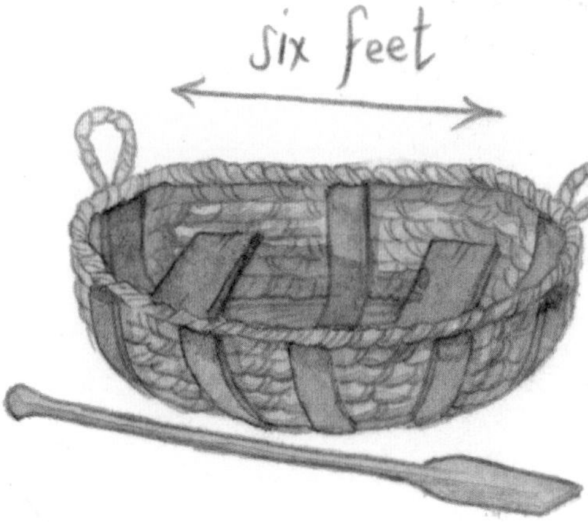
six feet

Fishing does get a little dull. You cast your nets or put out your lines and then there isn't much else to do.

The water is usually too cold to swim in—although that doesn't mean it hasn't happened!

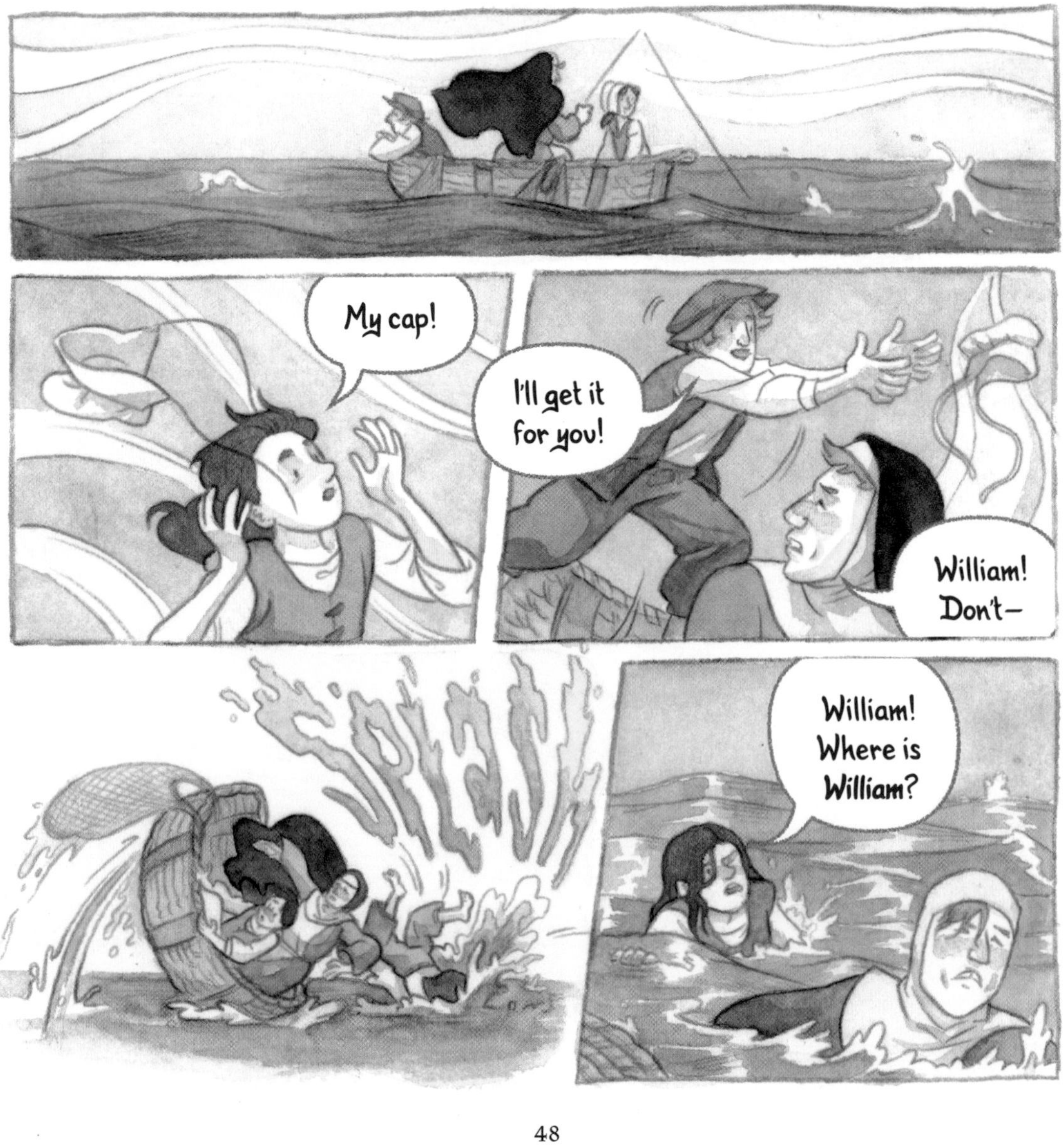
My cap!
I'll get it for you!
William! Don't—
Splash
William! Where is William?

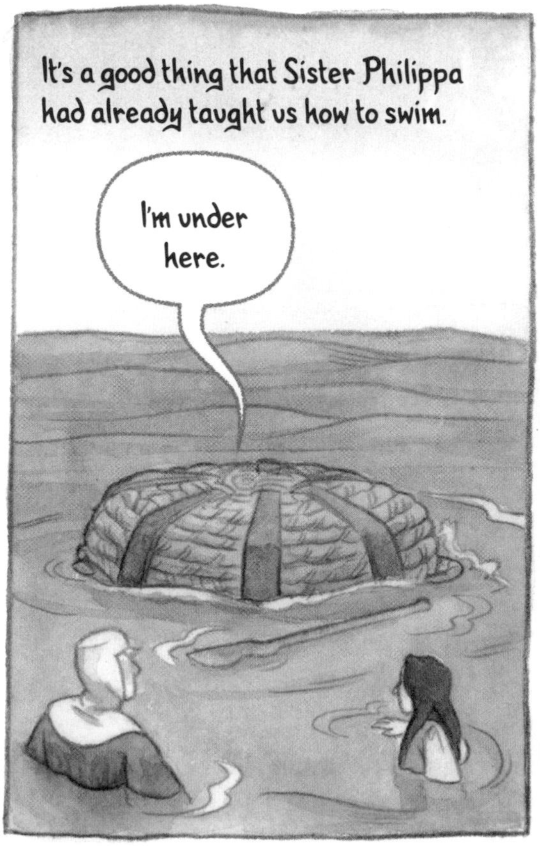
It's a good thing that Sister Philippa had already taught us how to swim.
I'm under here.

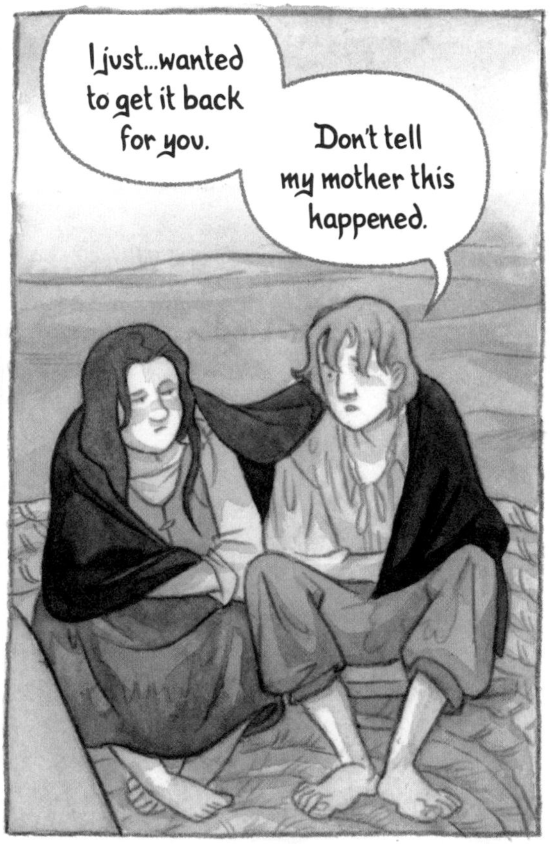
I just...wanted to get it back for you.
Don't tell my mother this happened.

But Lady Cameron did find out about it, from Sister Philippa. Nuns aren't allowed to lie. Lady Cameron told Sister Agnes that William couldn't go out in the coracle anymore, and that he and I weren't allowed to see each other for—

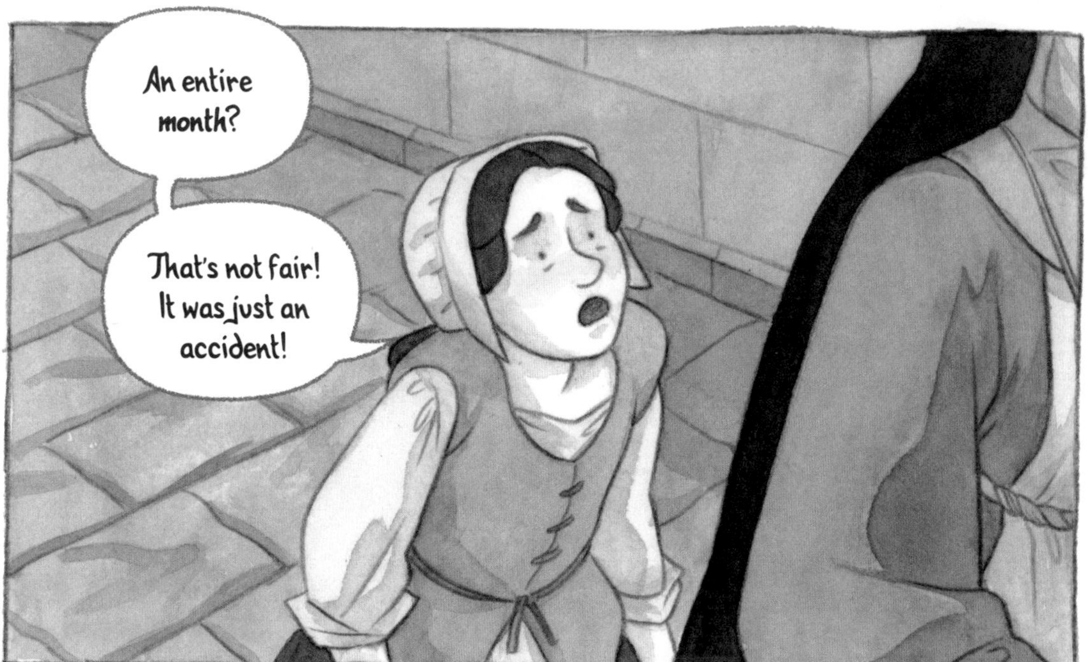
An entire month?
That's not fair! It was just an accident!

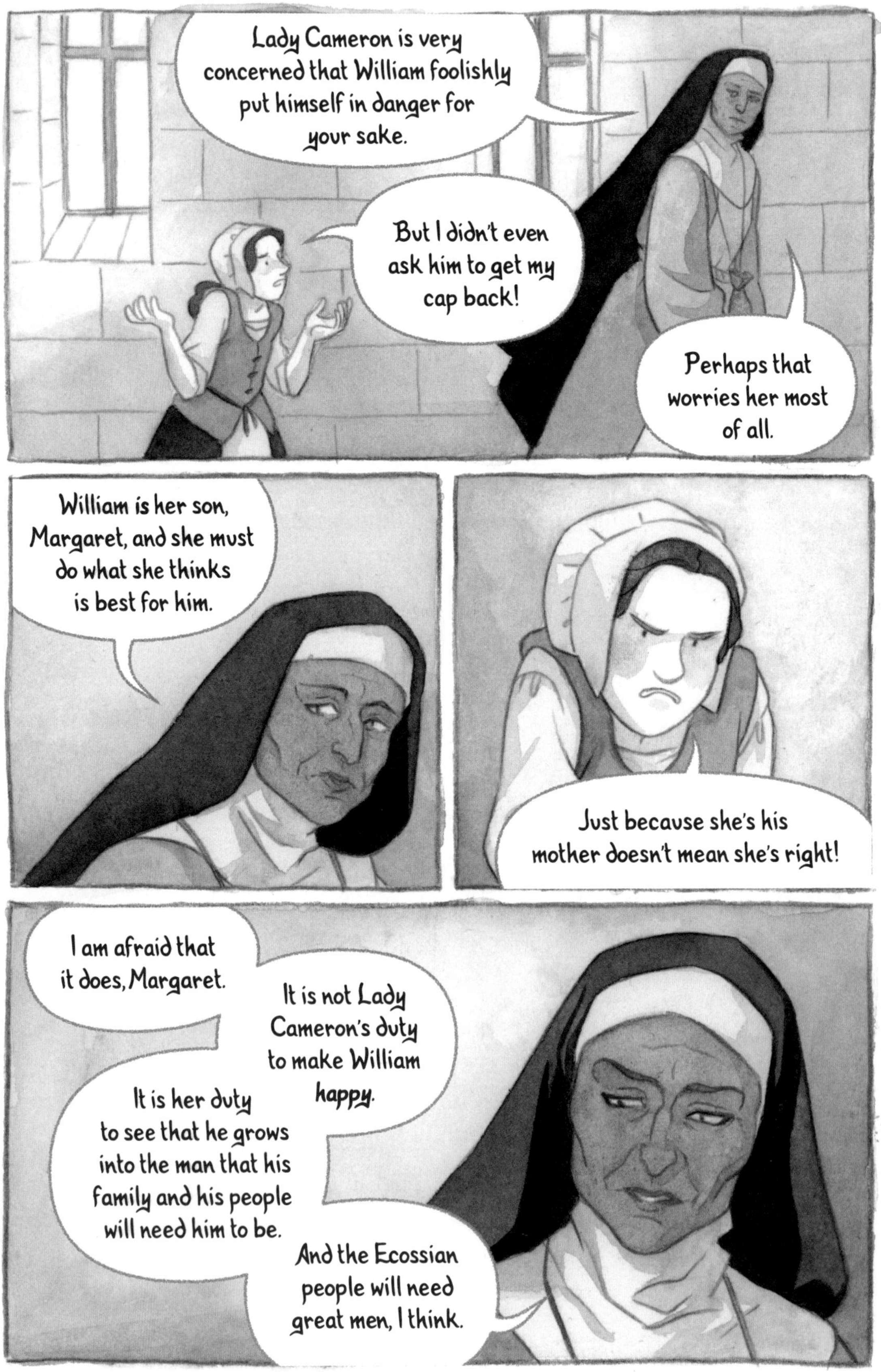
Lady Cameron is very concerned that William foolishly put himself in danger for your sake.
But I didn't even ask him to get my cap back!
Perhaps that worries her most of all.
William is her son, Margaret, and she must do what she thinks is best for him.
Just because she's his mother doesn't mean she's right!
I am afraid that it does, Margaret.
It is not Lady Cameron's duty to make William *happy*.
It is her duty to see that he grows into the man that his family and his people will need him to be.
And the Ecossian people will need great men, I think.

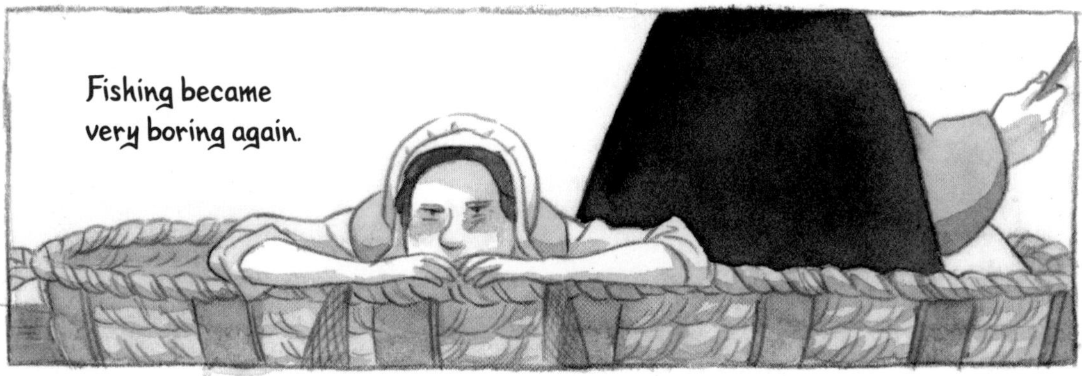
Fishing became
very boring again.

Thankfully, Sister Philippa became too busy with the farm, so Jess took me instead. As the fish moved into the cooler water of the bay, we drifted close enough for me to spy on the inhabitants of—

the Seal Rock

All the seals in the nearby sea gather there to sun themselves, sleep with their pups, or gossip between fish hunts.

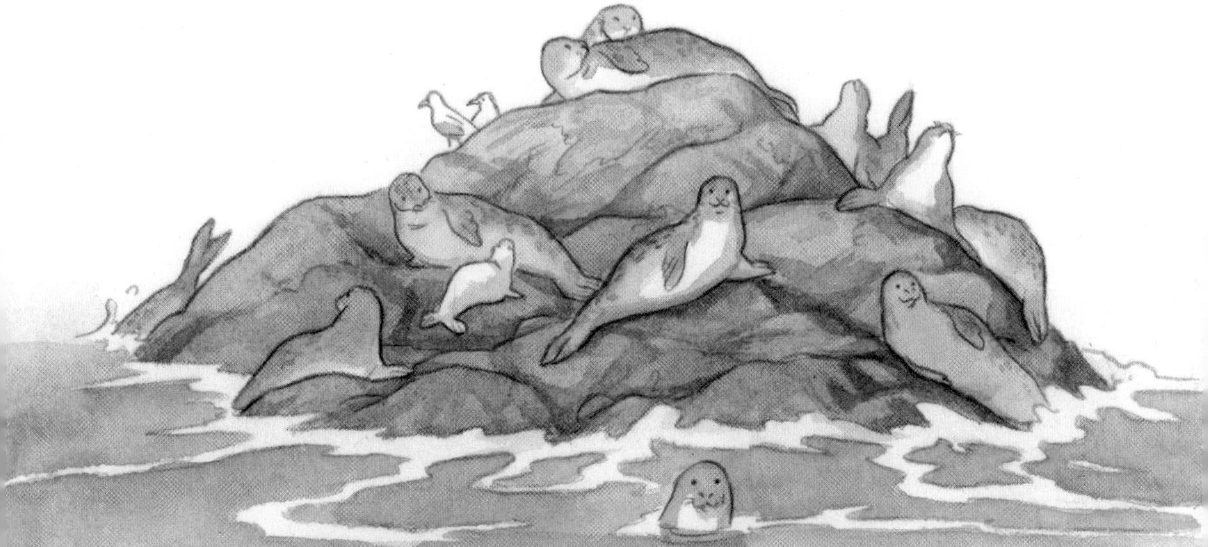

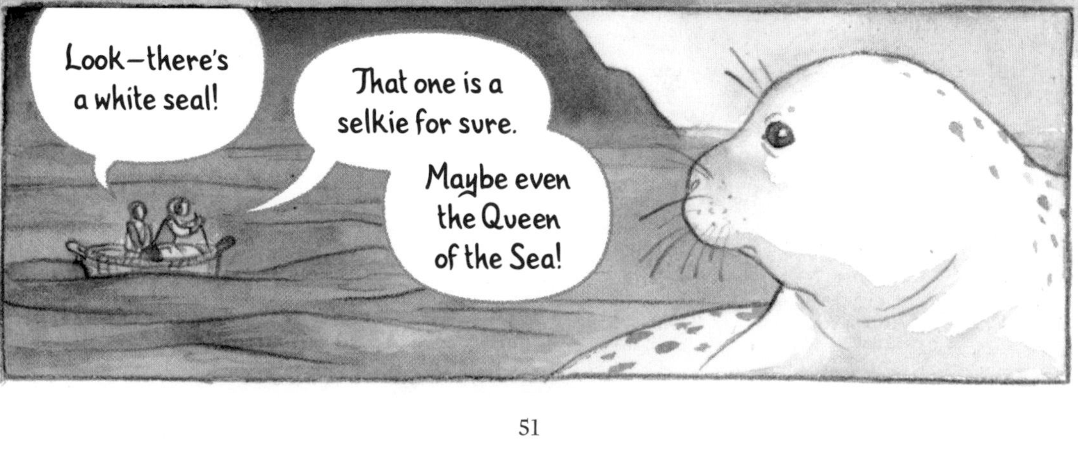
Look—there's a white seal!
That one is a selkie for sure.
Maybe even the Queen of the Sea!

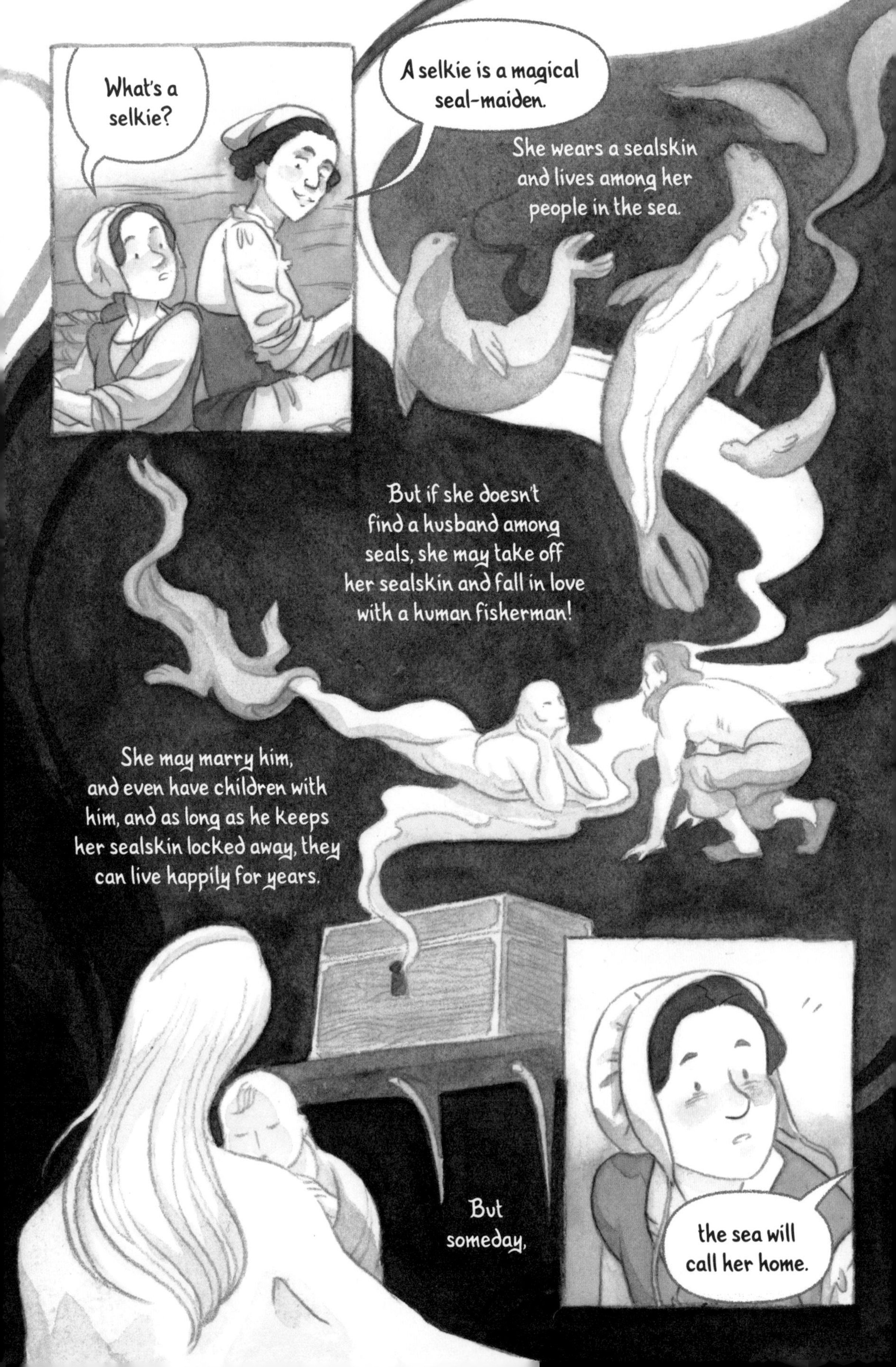
What's a selkie?
A selkie is a magical seal-maiden.
She wears a sealskin and lives among her people in the sea.
But if she doesn't find a husband among seals, she may take off her sealskin and fall in love with a human fisherman!
She may marry him, and even have children with him, and as long as he keeps her sealskin locked away, they can live happily for years.
But someday,
the sea will call her home.

When the long month was over, and Lady Cameron finally let William come outside with me again, I told him all about the white seal and the legend of the selkie.

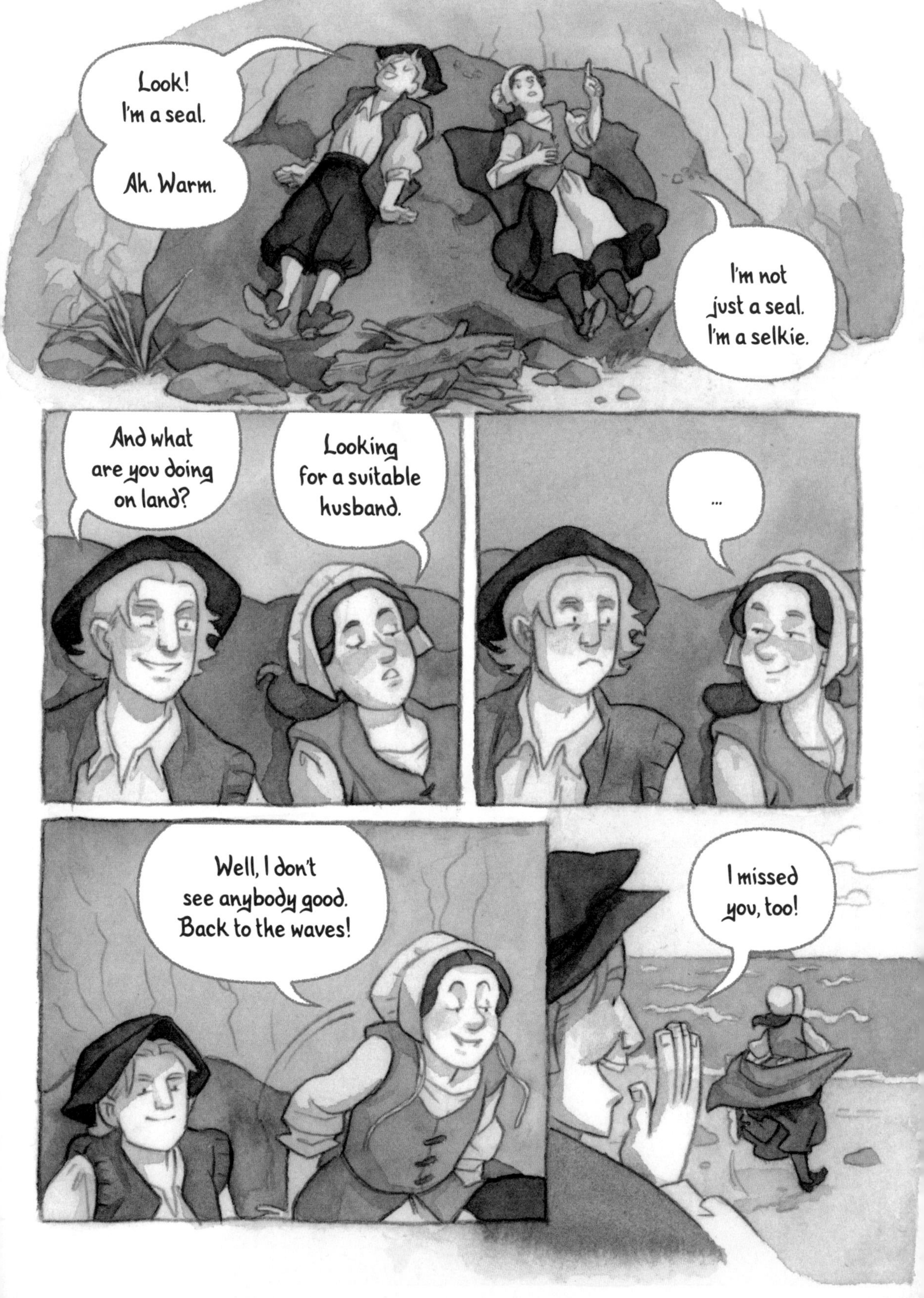
Look!
I'm a seal.
Ah. Warm.
I'm not just a seal. I'm a selkie.
And what are you doing on land?
Looking for a suitable husband.
...
Well, I don't see anybody good. Back to the waves!
I missed you, too!

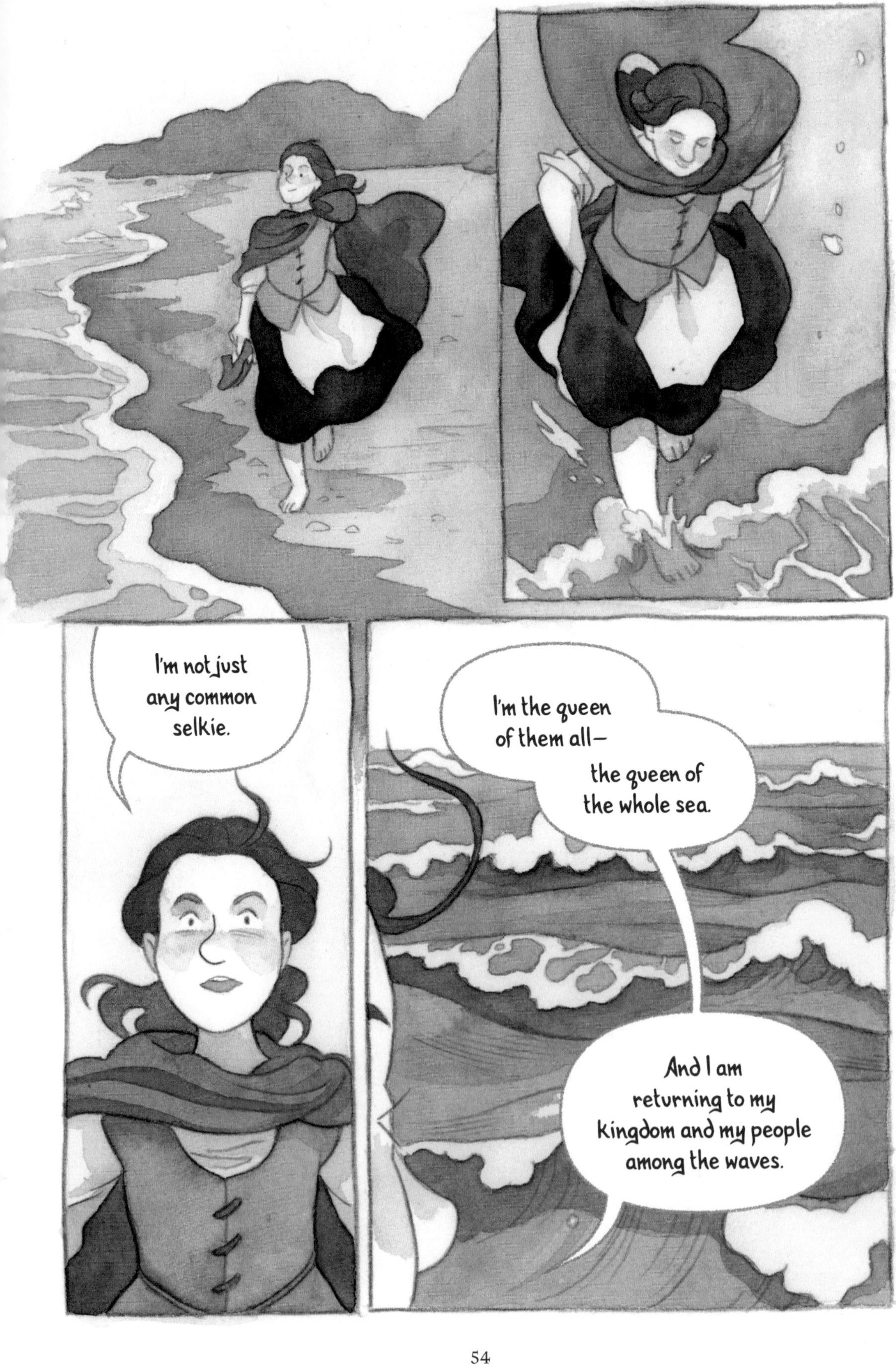
I'm not just any common selkie.
I'm the queen of them all—
the queen of the whole sea.
And I am returning to my kingdom and my people among the waves.

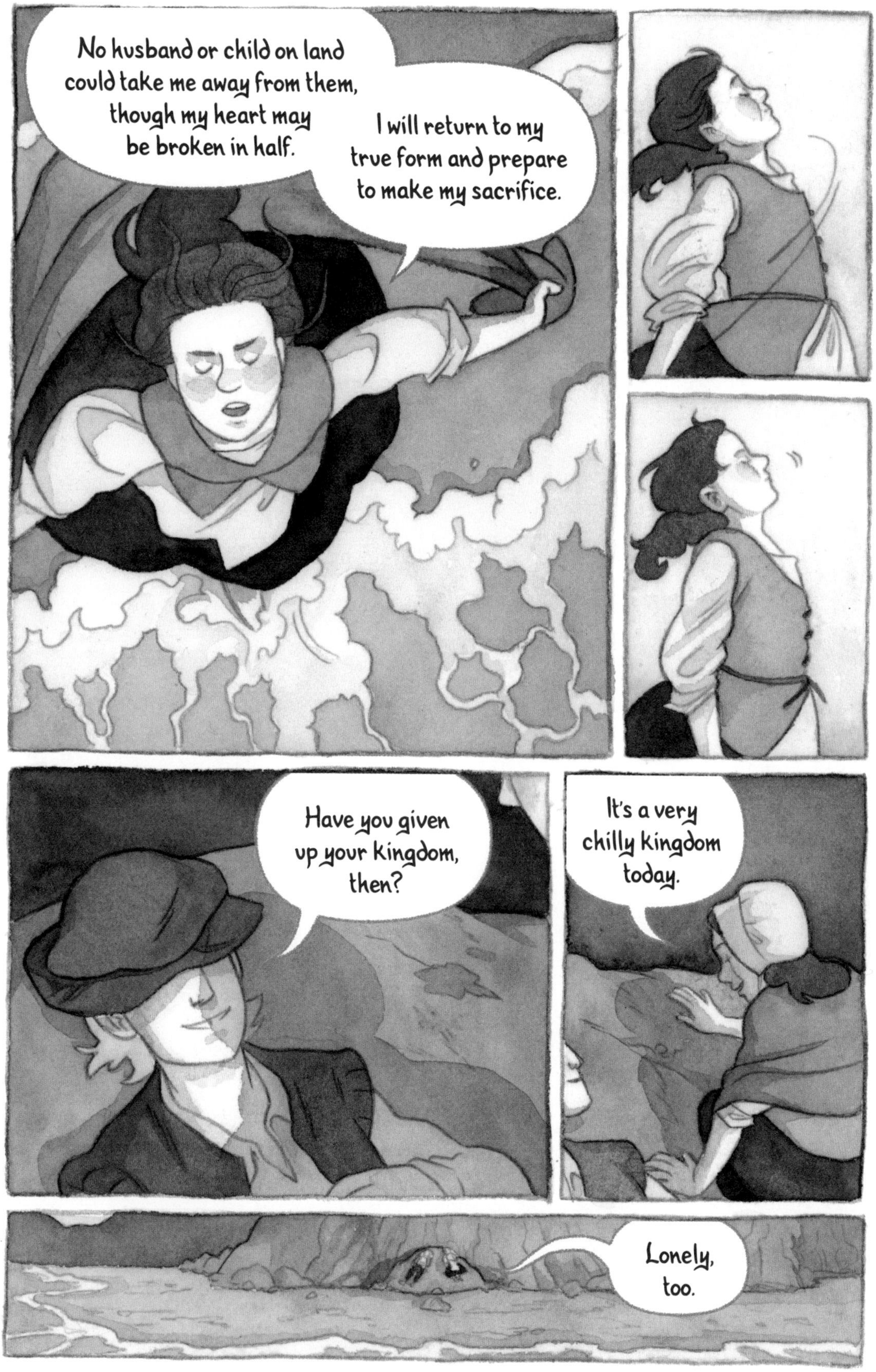
No husband or child on land could take me away from them, though my heart may be broken in half.
I will return to my true form and prepare to make my sacrifice.
Have you given up your kingdom, then?
It's a very chilly kingdom today.
Lonely, too.

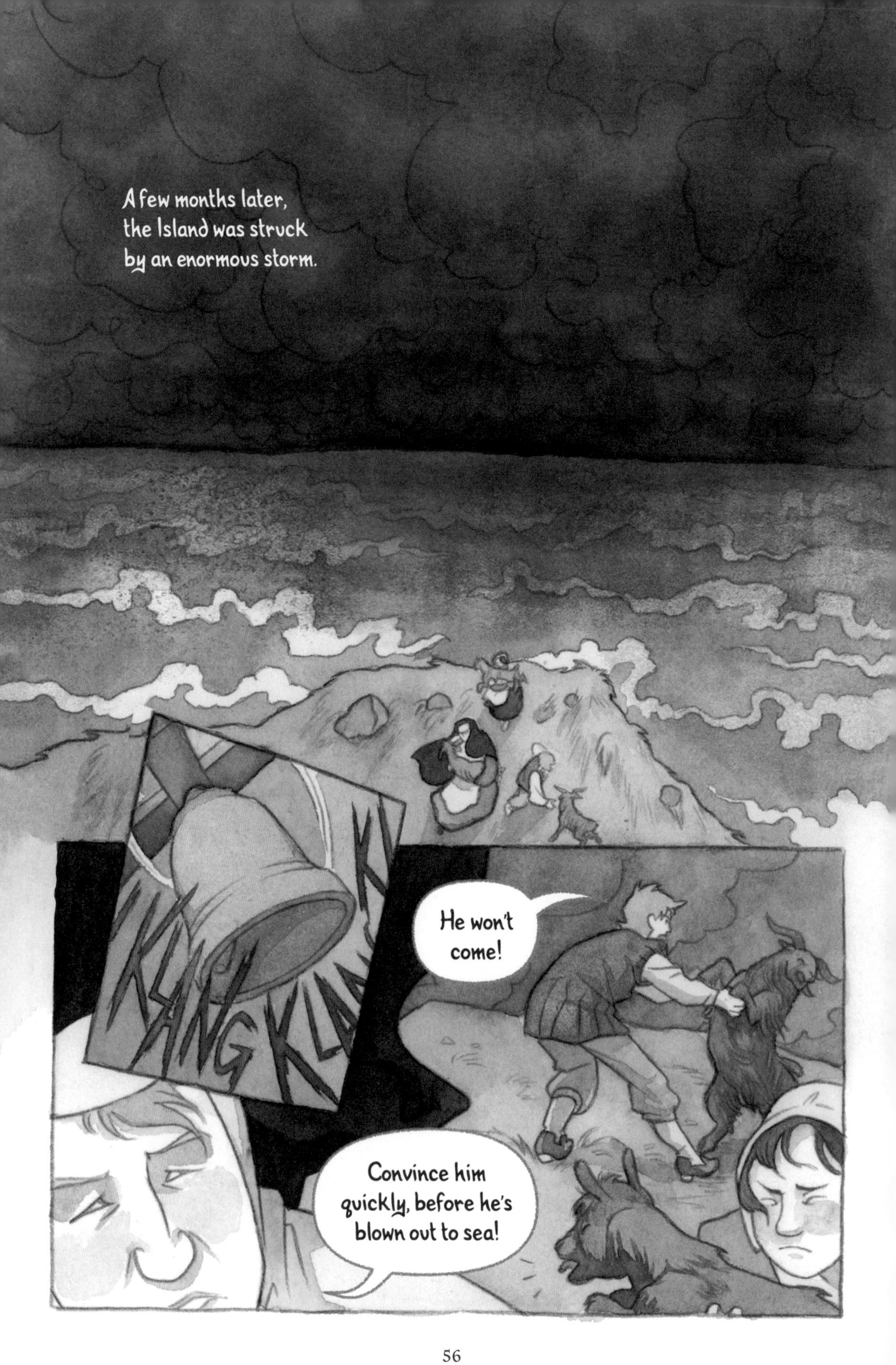
A few months later, the Island was struck by an enormous storm.
KLANG KLANG KLA
He won't come!
Convince him quickly, before he's blown out to sea!

We all waited in the church for the storm to pass. Everybody prayed. The wind made a horrible noise.

HWHEEEEUUUUWHHEUOWWHEE

SKASH!

Oh!

It's only a tile coming off the roof!

Margaret, would you recite the story of Saint Elysia's revelation for us all?

I believe Sister Sybil taught it to you recently.

It would be calming to hear.

Yes.

Elysia had no brothers or sisters and she hadn't married anybody yet.

Her father sailed ships full of valuable spices to faraway ports.

He would be gone for months at a time.

Elysia stayed home because the sea is a dangerous place, especially for a maiden.

One day news came that her father's ship had been sunk by *Rolf the Pirate King*

and her father had drowned.

Elysia was left alone and with no means of support.

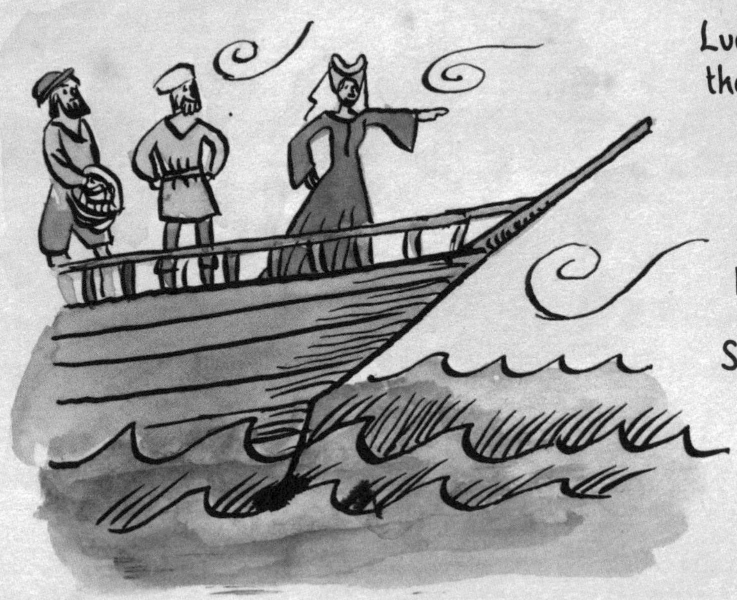

Luckily, Elysia wasn't the sort of person to give up.

She decided to run her father's business herself.

Some of the sailors thought she was

crazy!

Elysia didn't care. She sailed across the sea five times without any trouble. But on her sixth voyage, her ship was captured...

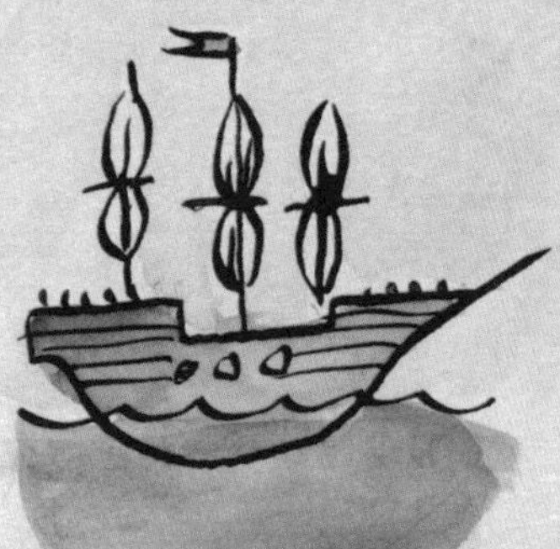

by Rolf the Pirate King

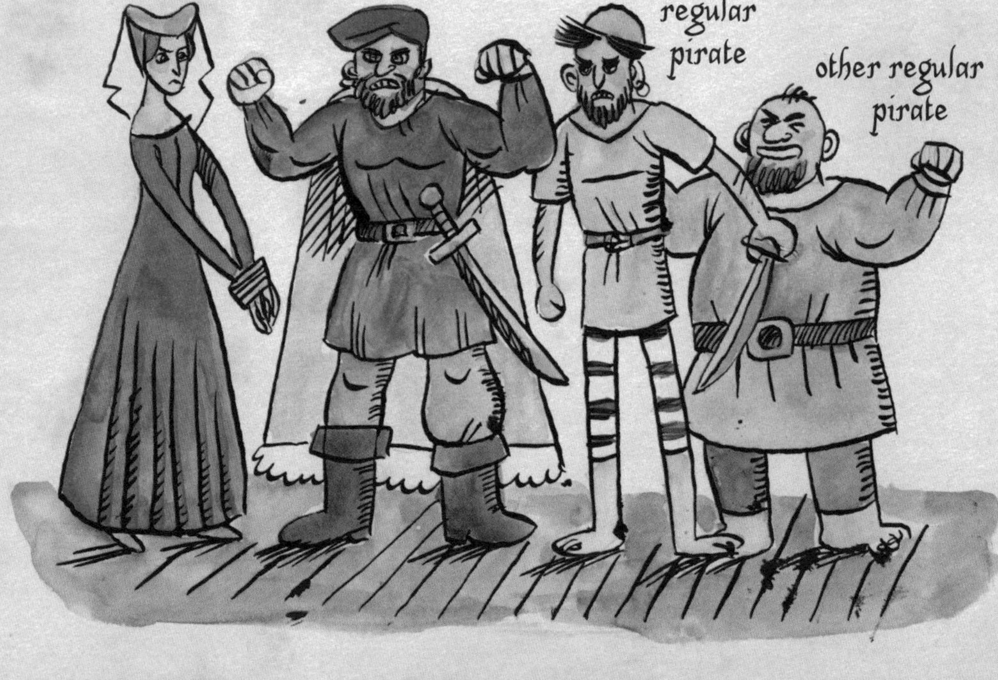
This one is Rolf.
regular pirate
other regular pirate

But even pirates couldn't frighten Elysia.

Elysia was very faithful and always said her prayers. Before long she had converted the whole crew and convinced them to give up piracy!

Rolf the Pirate King was NOT happy about this.

He thought Elysia was a *witch* and that she had cast a spell on his crew.

That was bad, but he decided that having a witch around could be pretty useful in the pirate business.

So he told Elysia,

Marry me!

...or else!

But Elysia said,

NO

Which was very brave,
but since she said her prayers
so often, Elysia knew it was
the right thing to do.

So Rolf threw her overboard.

I warned you!

Elysia sank and sank. (She didn't know how to swim.)

She thought she would probably drown.

But she wasn't scared.

When you've done the right thing, dying doesn't seem so bad. Elysia knew she would go to heaven.

So she said her prayers all the way to the bottom of the sea.

The fish heard her praying!

Then something
amazing
happened.

All the fish in the sea rose up and carried Elysia to the surface. Then they told her to stand on their backs, and they took her all the way home to Albion.

It was a miracle!

Elysia was so grateful for her miracle that as soon as she got home, she decided to take up the holy life and become a nun.

She sold her father's business and gave all the money to the widows and daughters of sailors lost at sea.

Many of them decided they wanted to become nuns, too. So Elysia founded her very own order!

Elysian sisters live in convents by the shore or on islands, like ours.

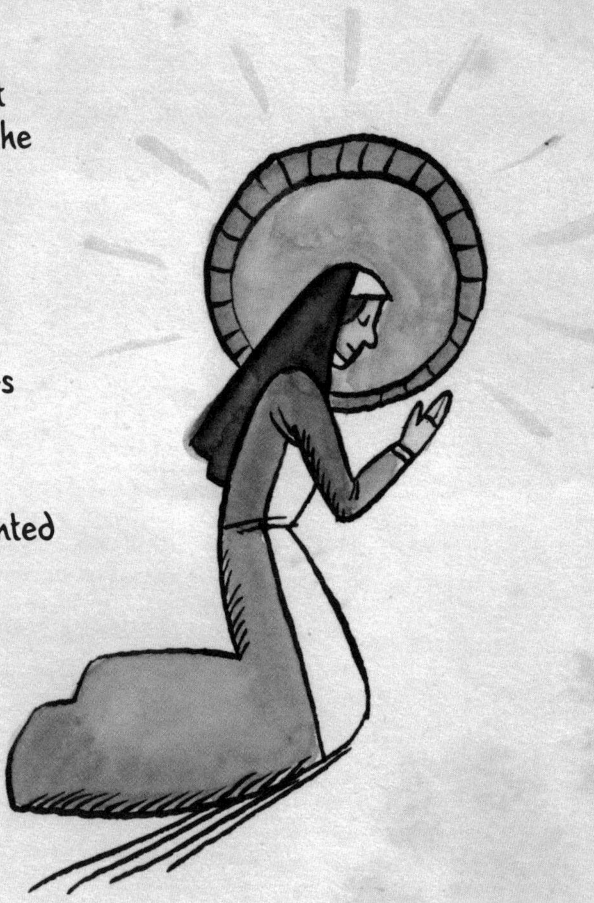

And Saint Elysia is the patron saint of anybody whose life or love is at the mercy of the sea.

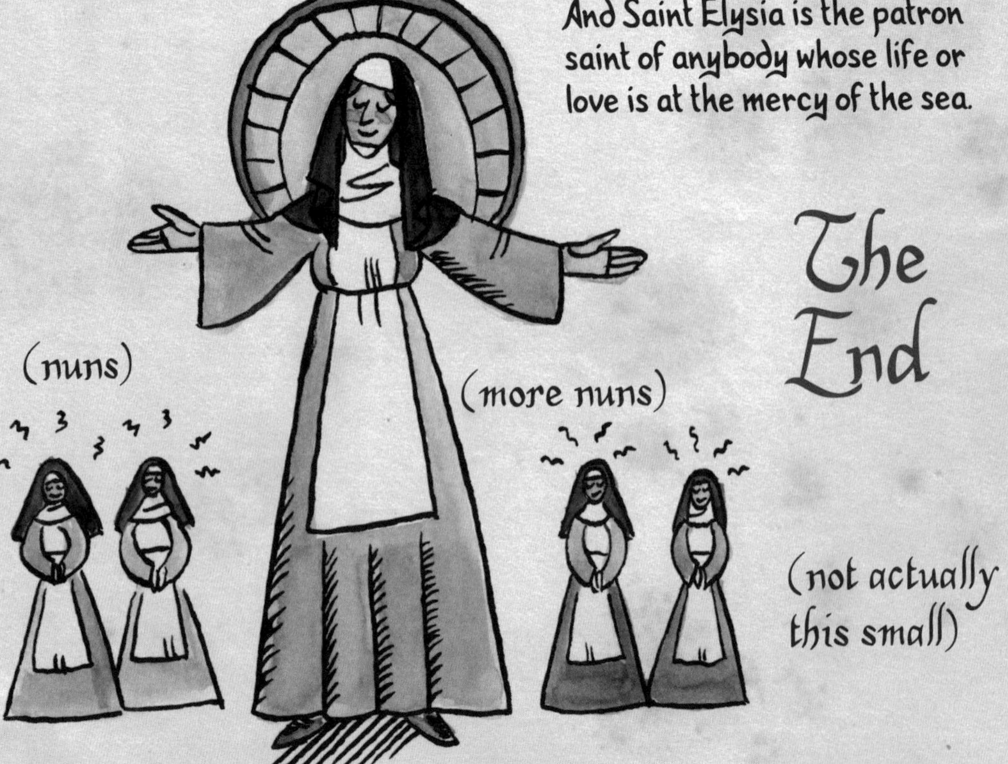
(nuns)
(more nuns)
The End
(not actually this small)

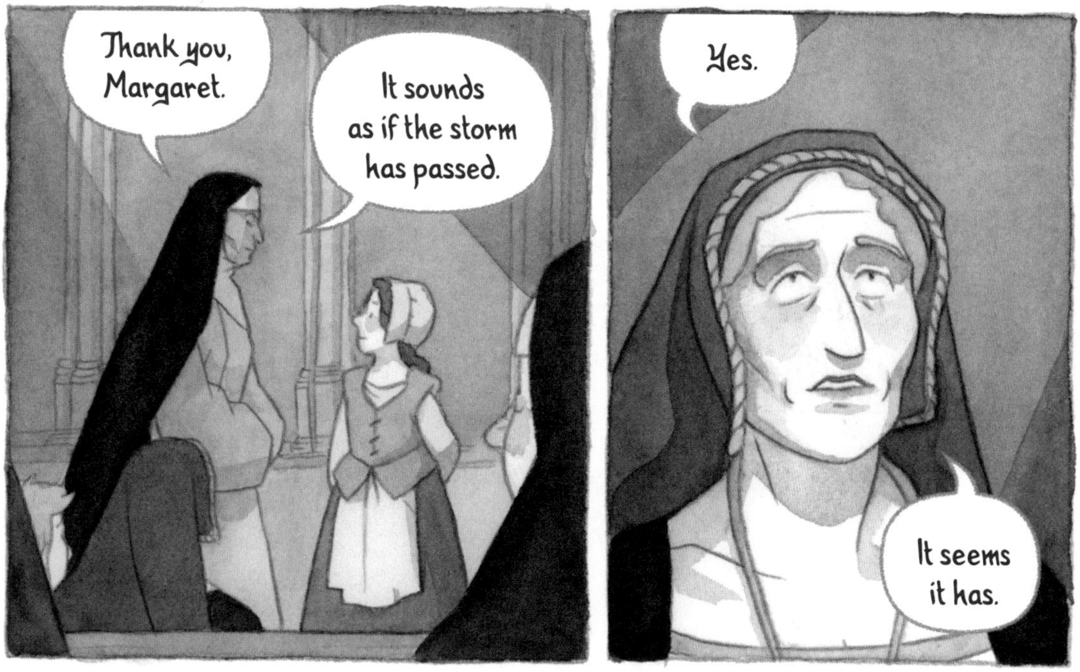
Thank you, Margaret.
It sounds as if the storm has passed.
Yes.
It seems it has.

The next morning we all went outside to see what other damage the storm had done. Normally the sisters are silent for most of the day, but Sister Agnes lifted the vow so everybody could discuss the repairs. The roof of the church had lost plenty of tiles, and two of the apple trees had been torn up. A window in the Guest House was broken. The kitchen had lost its chimney pot. The chicken house was leaning to the side.

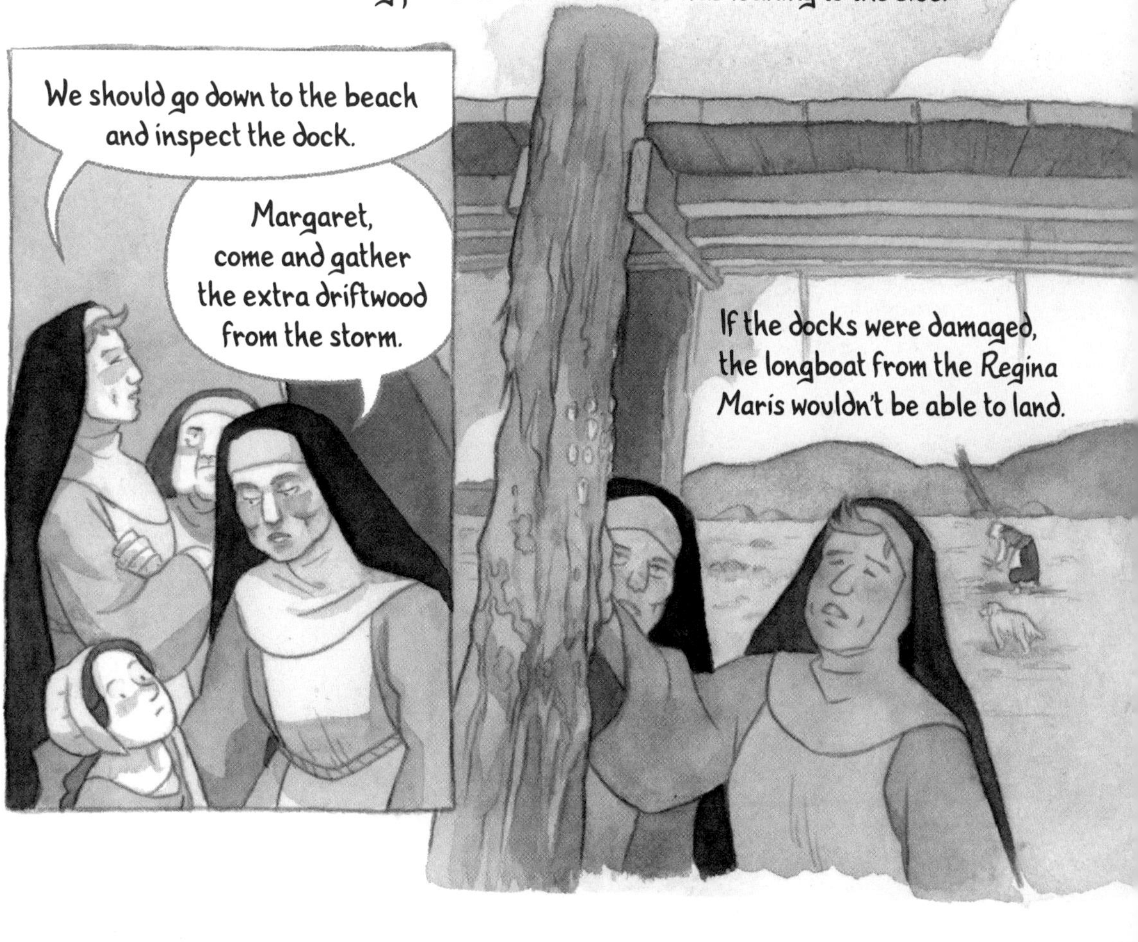
We should go down to the beach and inspect the dock.
Margaret, come and gather the extra driftwood from the storm.
If the docks were damaged, the longboat from the *Regina Maris* wouldn't be able to land.

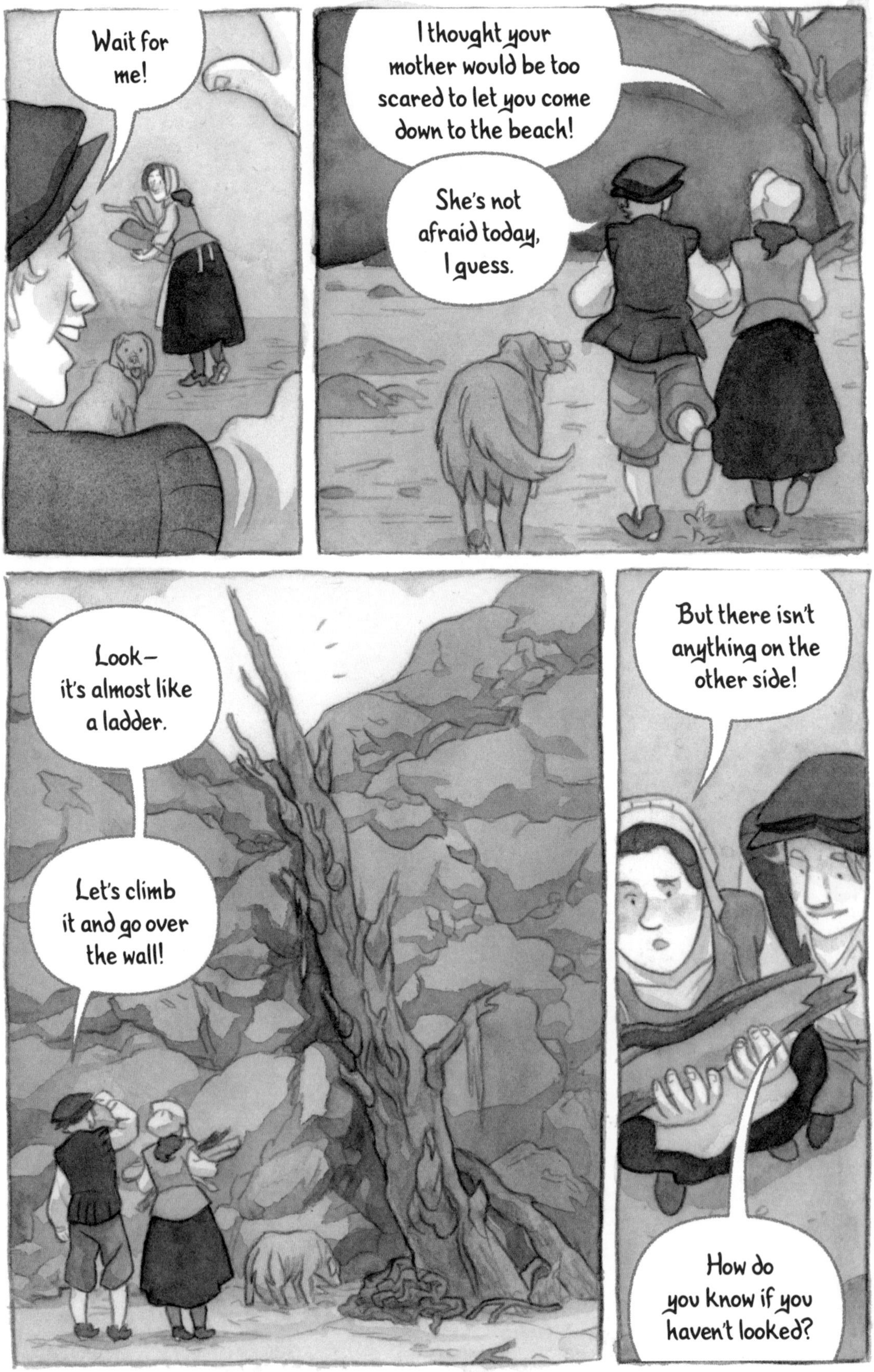
Wait for me!
I thought your mother would be too scared to let you come down to the beach!
She's not afraid today, I guess.
Look— it's almost like a ladder.
Let's climb it and go over the wall!
But there isn't anything on the other side!
How do you know if you haven't looked?

Do you think the sisters would let us?

They won't even notice we're gone!

Come up! It's easy!

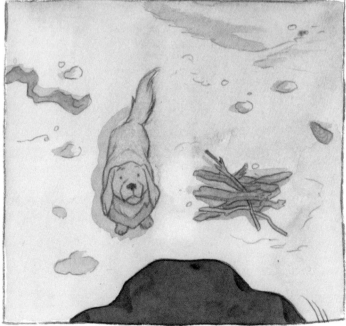

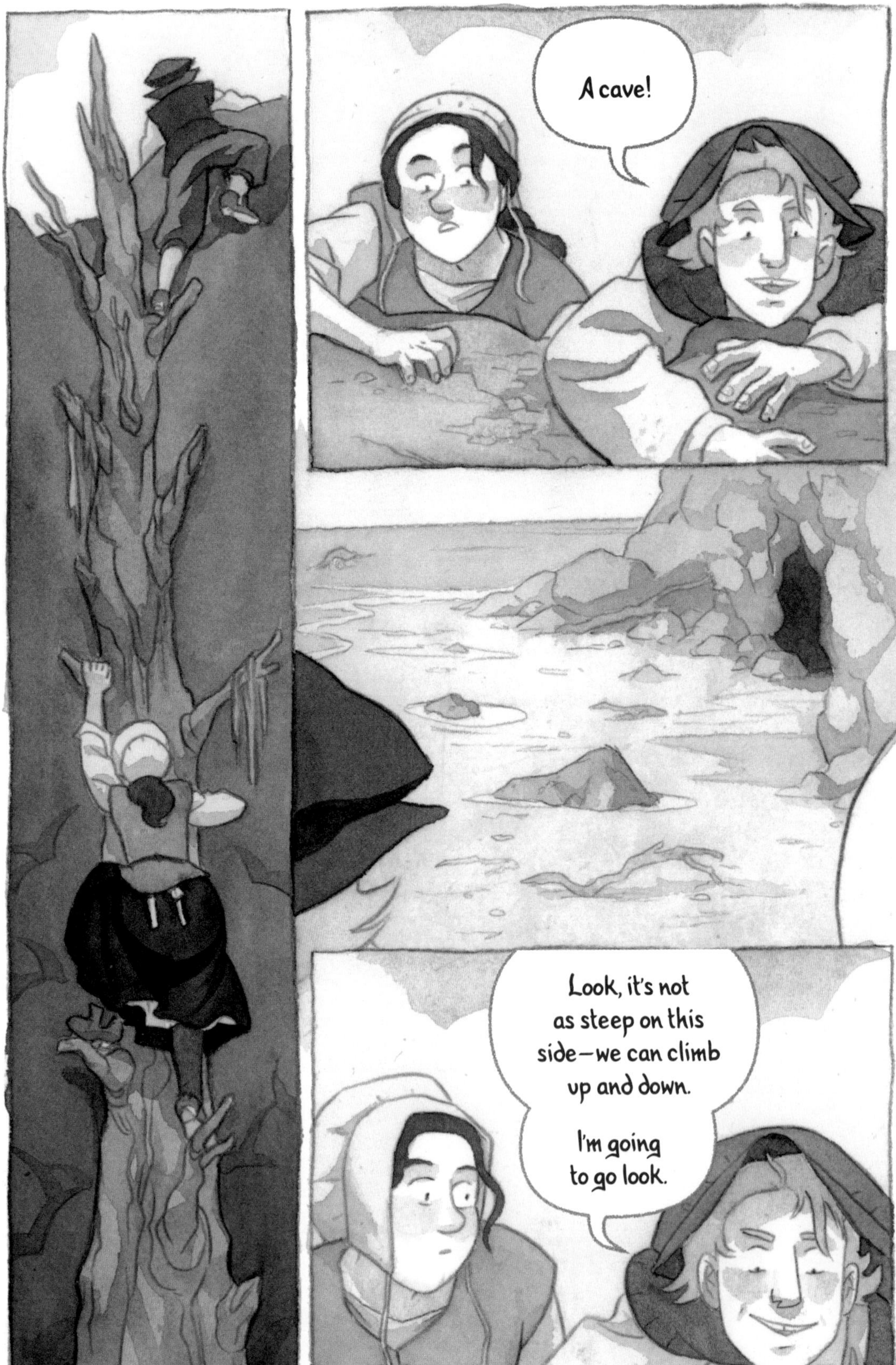
A cave!
Look, it's not as steep on this side—we can climb up and down.
I'm going to go look.

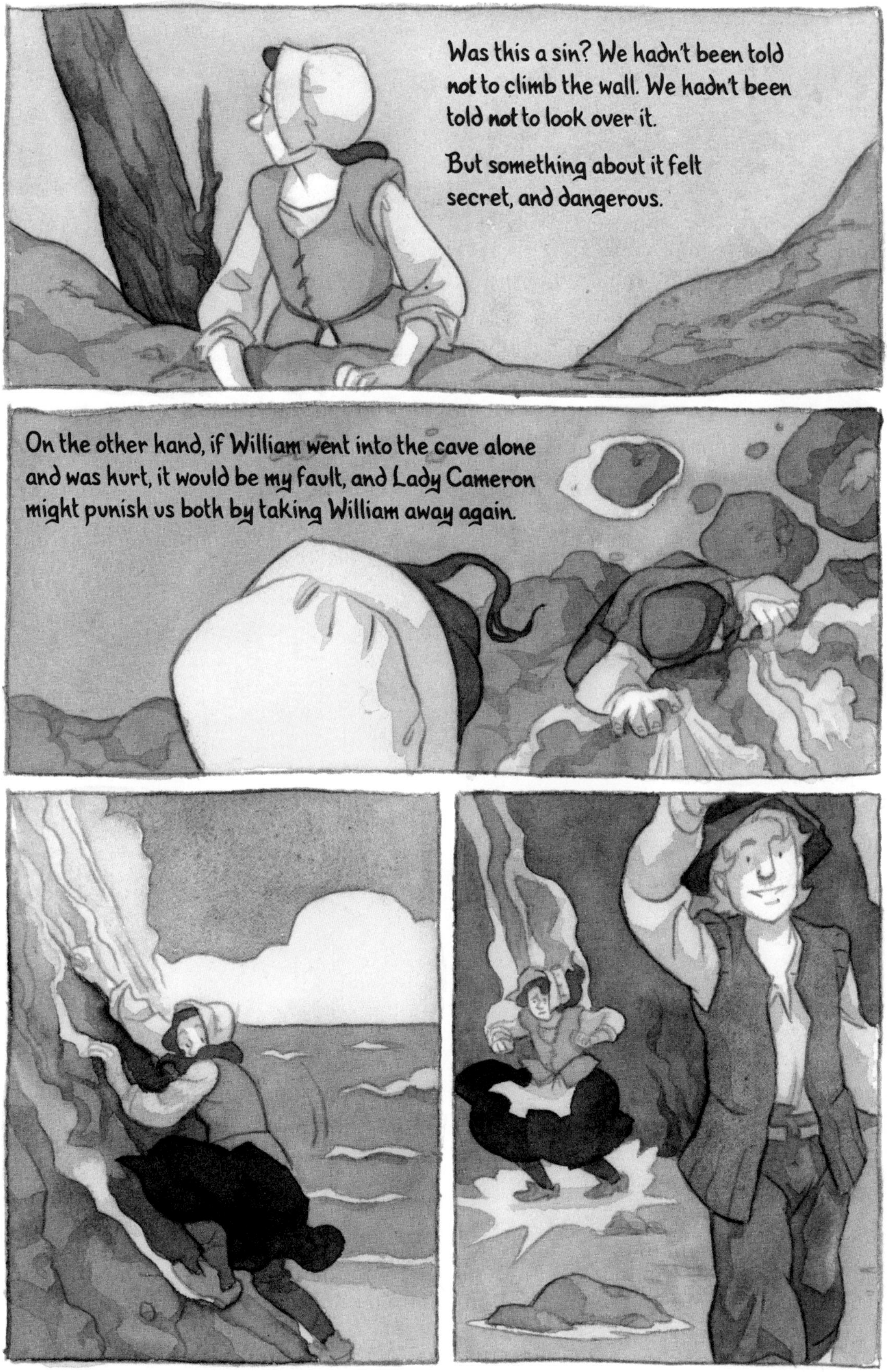
Was this a sin? We hadn't been told not to climb the wall. We hadn't been told not to look over it.
But something about it felt secret, and dangerous.
On the other hand, if William went into the cave alone and was hurt, it would be my fault, and Lady Cameron might punish us both by taking William away again.

Barnacles! The water must reach here at high tide.

You couldn't get inside the cave at all then.

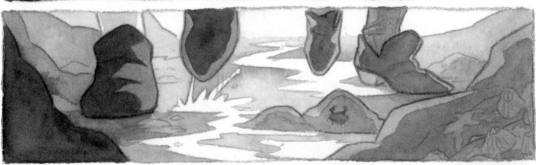

I wonder how far it goes.

Maybe forever!

There's sunlight!

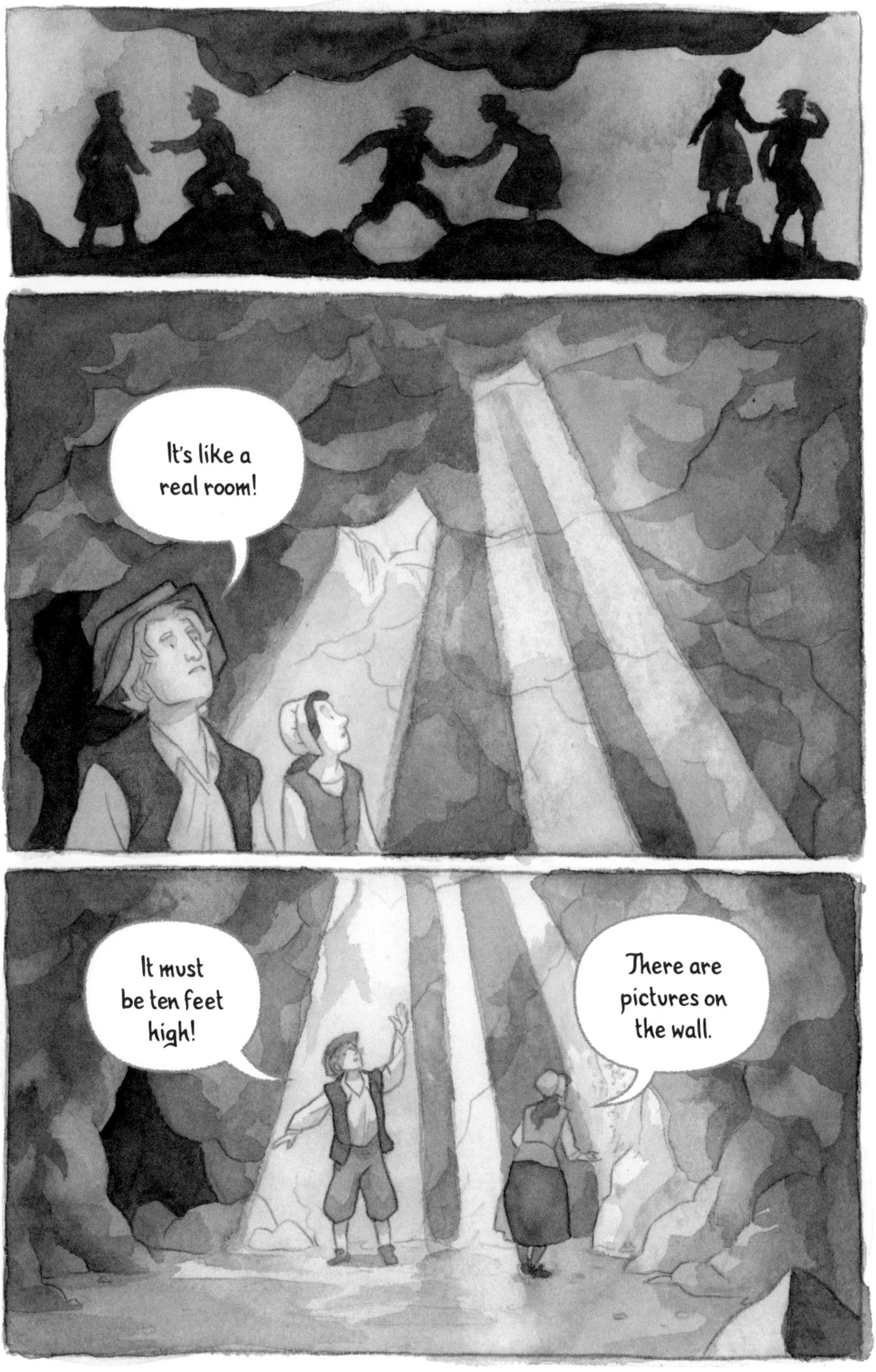
It's like a real room!
It must be ten feet high!
There are pictures on the wall.

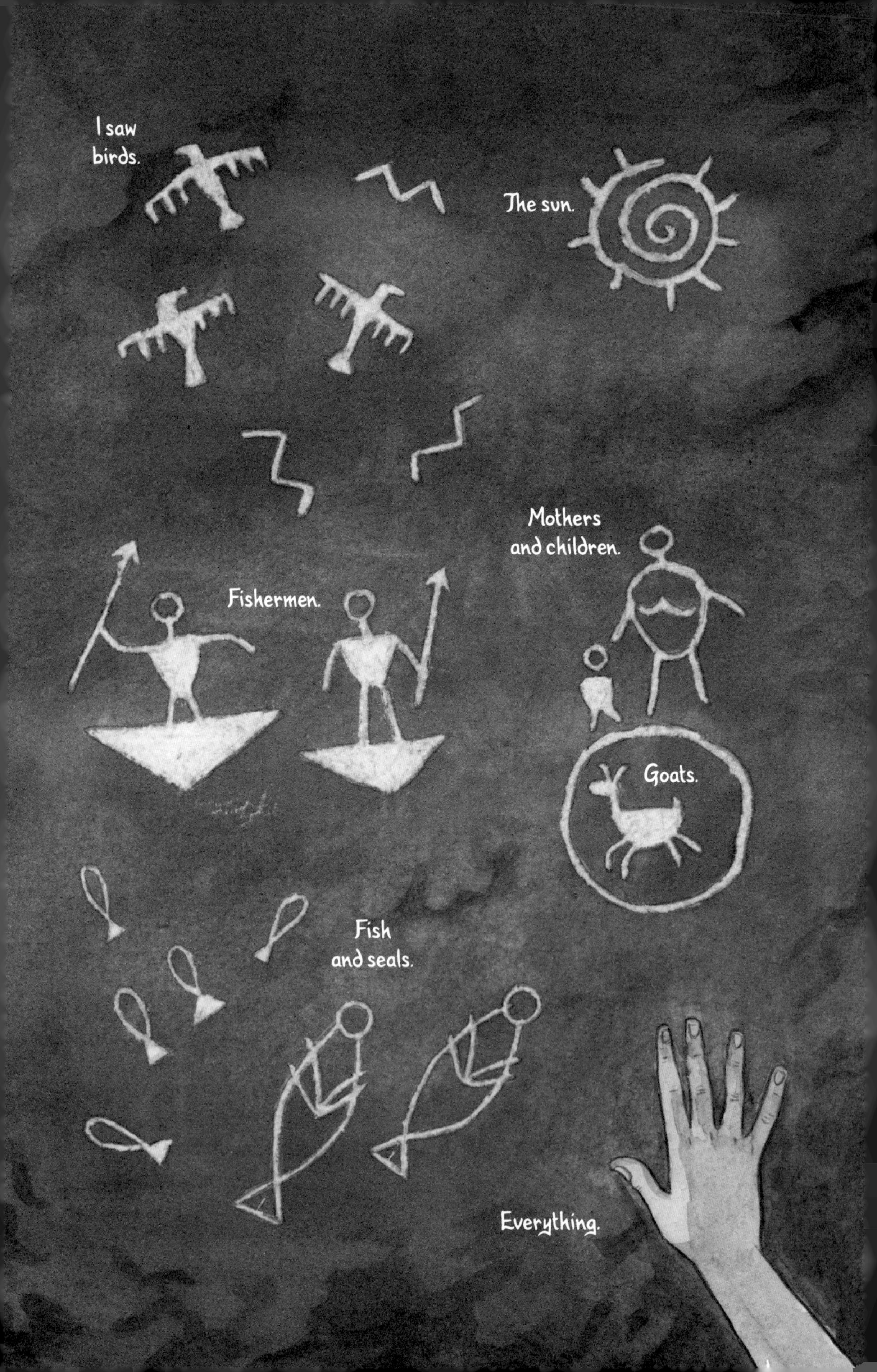
I saw birds.
The sun.
Mothers and children.
Fishermen.
Goats.
Fish and seals.
Everything.

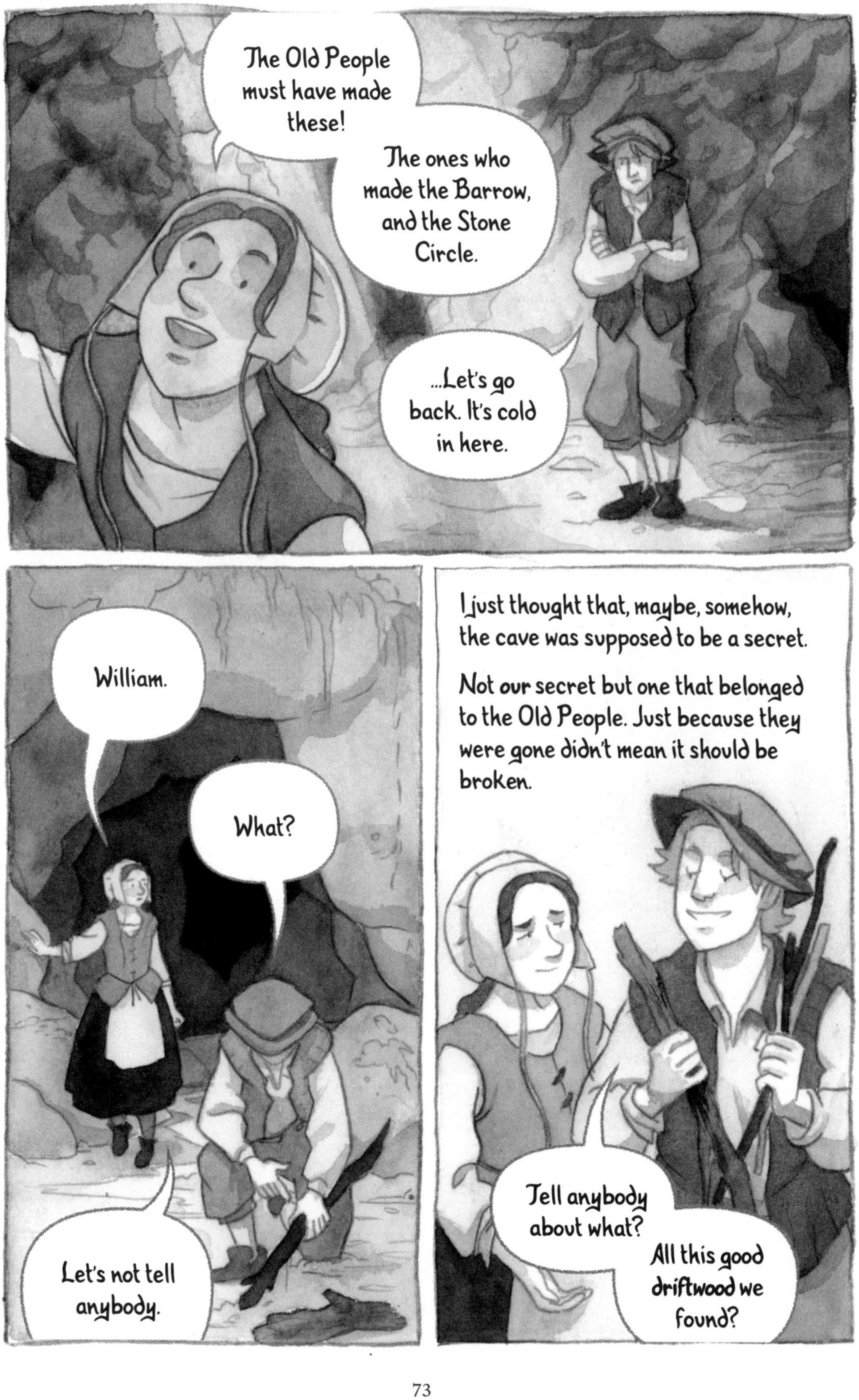

The Old People must have made these!
The ones who made the Barrow, and the Stone Circle.
...Let's go back. It's cold in here.
William.
What?
Let's not tell anybody.
I just thought that, maybe, somehow, the cave was supposed to be a secret.
Not our secret but one that belonged to the Old People. Just because they were gone didn't mean it should be broken.
Tell anybody about what?
All this good driftwood we found?

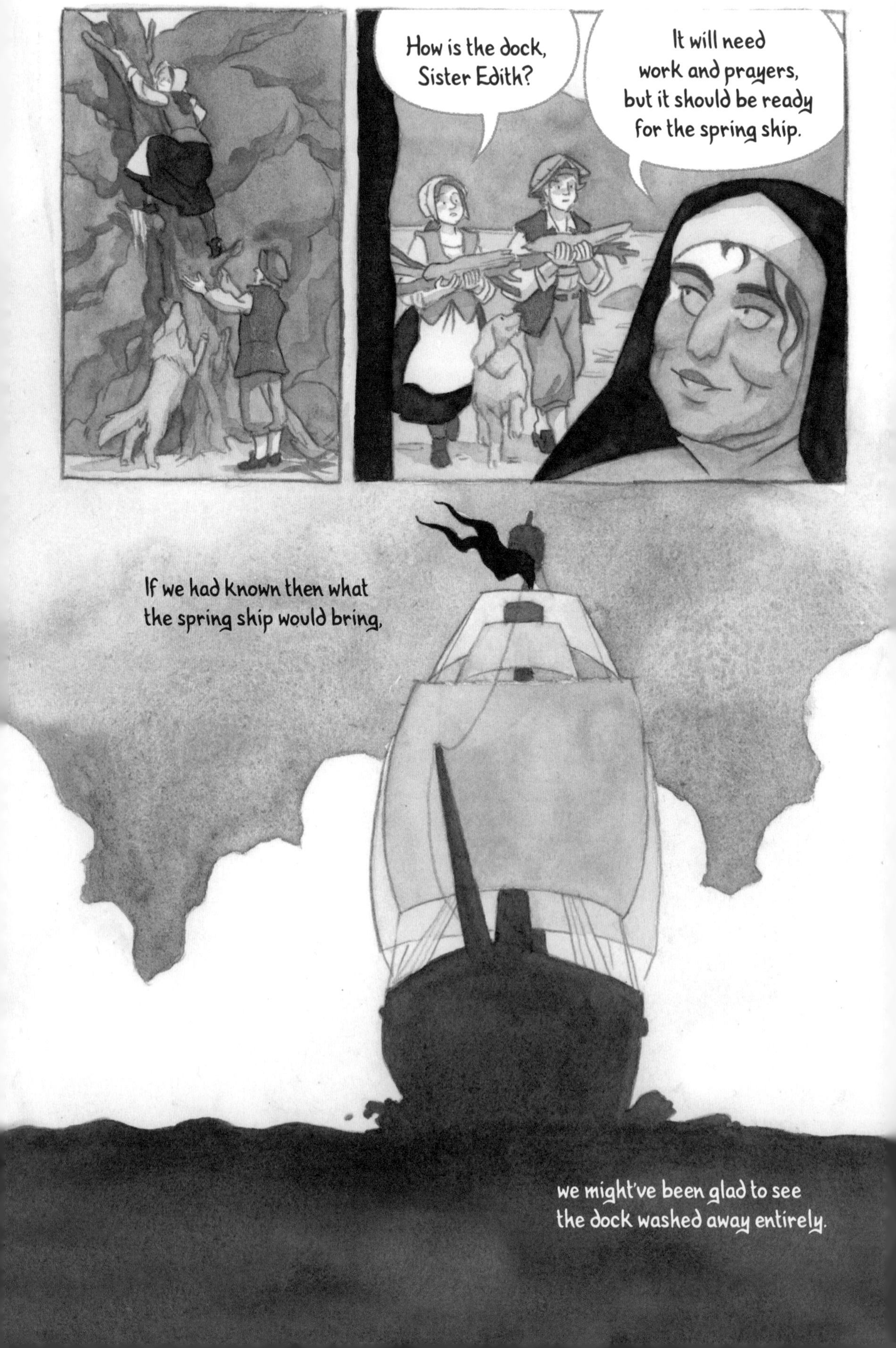
How is the dock, Sister Edith?
It will need work and prayers, but it should be ready for the spring ship.
If we had known then what the spring ship would bring,
we might've been glad to see the dock washed away entirely.

The storm had rearranged *many* things on the Island. The sisters had to set aside most of their usual work to fix it all. Sister Sybil left William and me to do our lessons on our own while she helped Sister Barbara make repairs to the church roof.

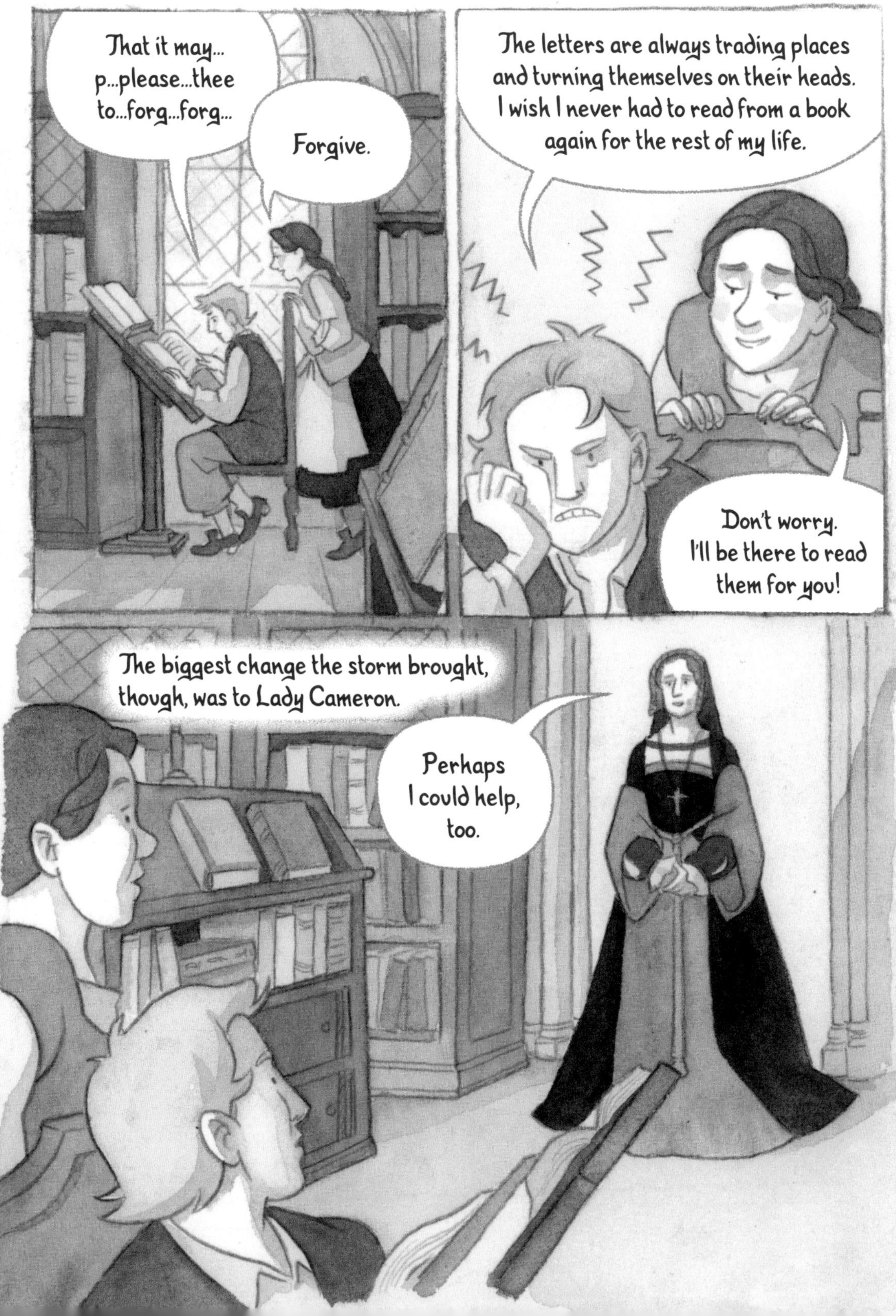
That it may... p...please...thee to...forg...forg...
Forgive.
The letters are always trading places and turning themselves on their heads. I wish I never had to read from a book again for the rest of my life.
Don't worry. I'll be there to read them for *you*!
The biggest change the storm brought, though, was to Lady Cameron.
Perhaps I could help, too.

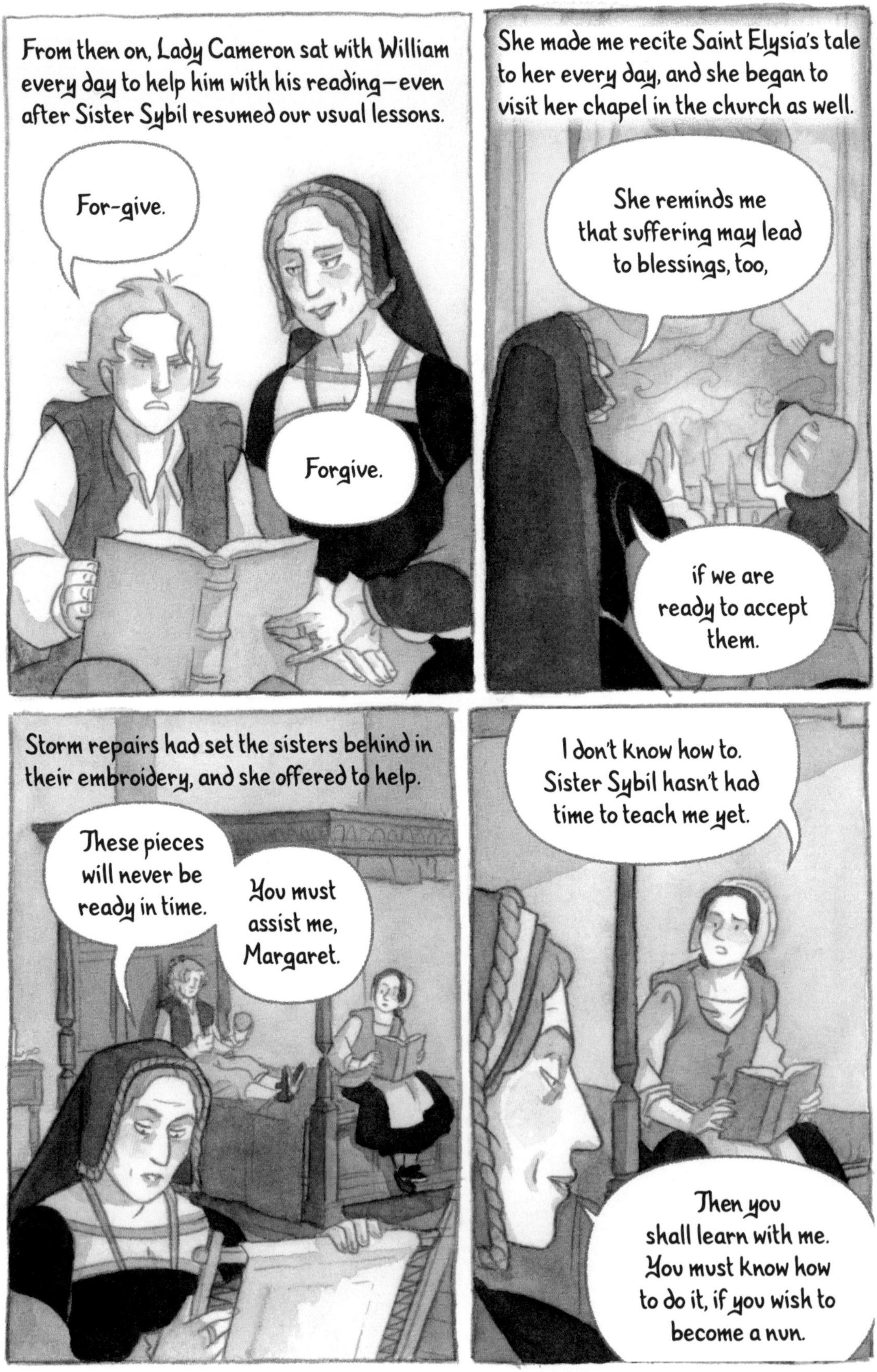
From then on, Lady Cameron sat with William every day to help him with his reading—even after Sister Sybil resumed our usual lessons.
For-give.
Forgive.
She made me recite Saint Elysia's tale to her every day, and she began to visit her chapel in the church as well.
She reminds me that suffering may lead to blessings, too,
if we are ready to accept them.
Storm repairs had set the sisters behind in their embroidery, and she offered to help.
These pieces will never be ready in time.
You must assist me, Margaret.
I don't know how to. Sister Sybil hasn't had time to teach me yet.
Then you shall learn with me. You must know how to do it, if you wish to become a nun.

Embroidery **seems** easy. You put the cloth in a frame to hold it tight, then you put thread on the needle, and then you sew it onto the cloth until it makes a picture. But there's much more to it than that! First you need the supplies.

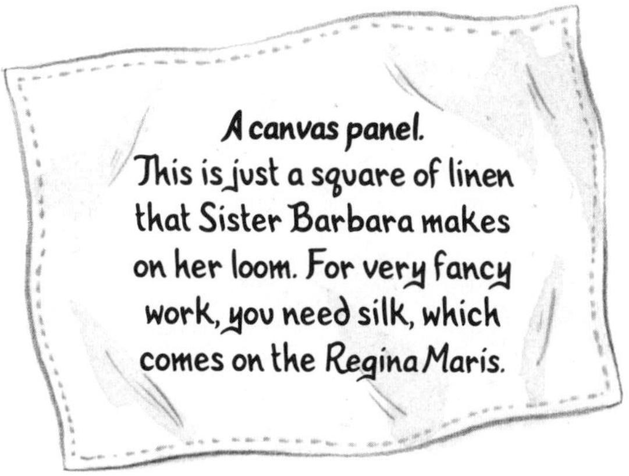

A canvas panel.
This is just a square of linen that Sister Barbara makes on her loom. For very fancy work, you need silk, which comes on the *Regina Maris*.

Silk thread, called **floss.**

Dyes, if you want to change any colors.

If you want the floss to be gold or silver, you'll need real gold or silver wire, very fine.

You wrap the wire around and around and around the floss, until it's covered.

And, of course, needles, needles, **needles!**

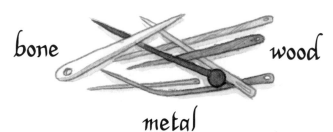

bone

wood

metal

(And a **thimble** to protect your finger from them.)

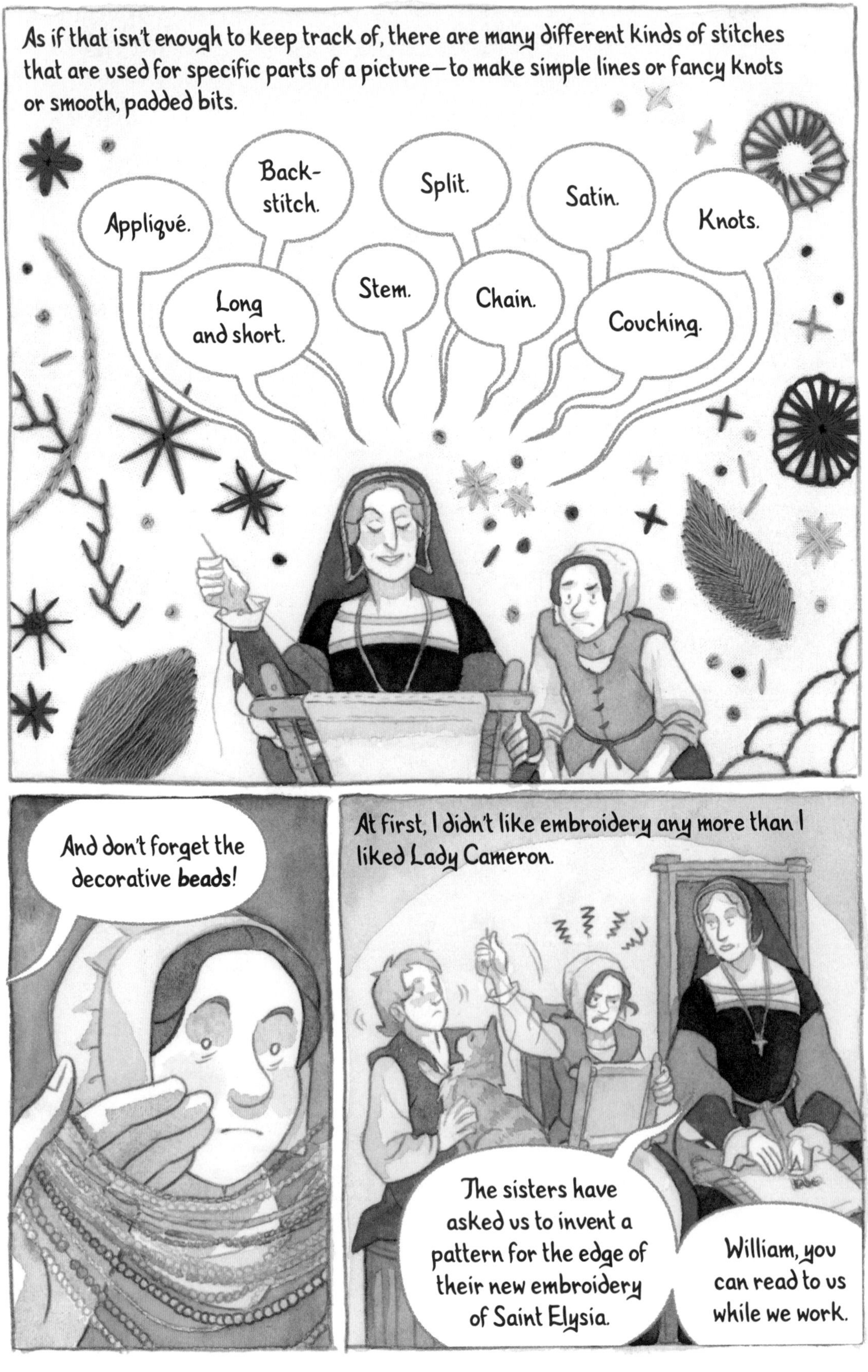
As if that isn't enough to keep track of, there are many different kinds of stitches that are used for specific parts of a picture—to make simple lines or fancy knots or smooth, padded bits.
Appliqué.
Back-stitch.
Long and short.
Stem.
Split.
Chain.
Satin.
Couching.
Knots.
And don't forget the decorative **beads**!
At first, I didn't like embroidery any more than I liked Lady Cameron.
The sisters have asked us to invent a pattern for the edge of their new embroidery of Saint Elysia.
William, you can read to us while we work.

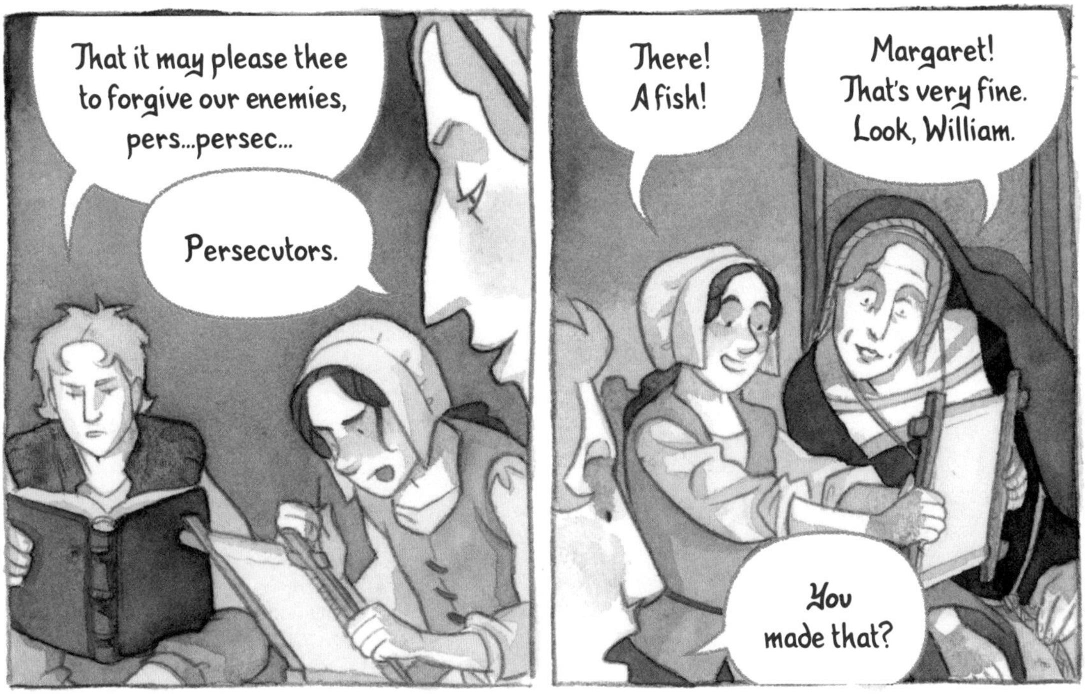
That it may please thee to forgive our enemies, pers...persec...
Persecutors.
There! A fish!
Margaret! That's very fine. Look, William.
You made that?

I gradually realized there were a few good things about embroidery and Lady Cameron.

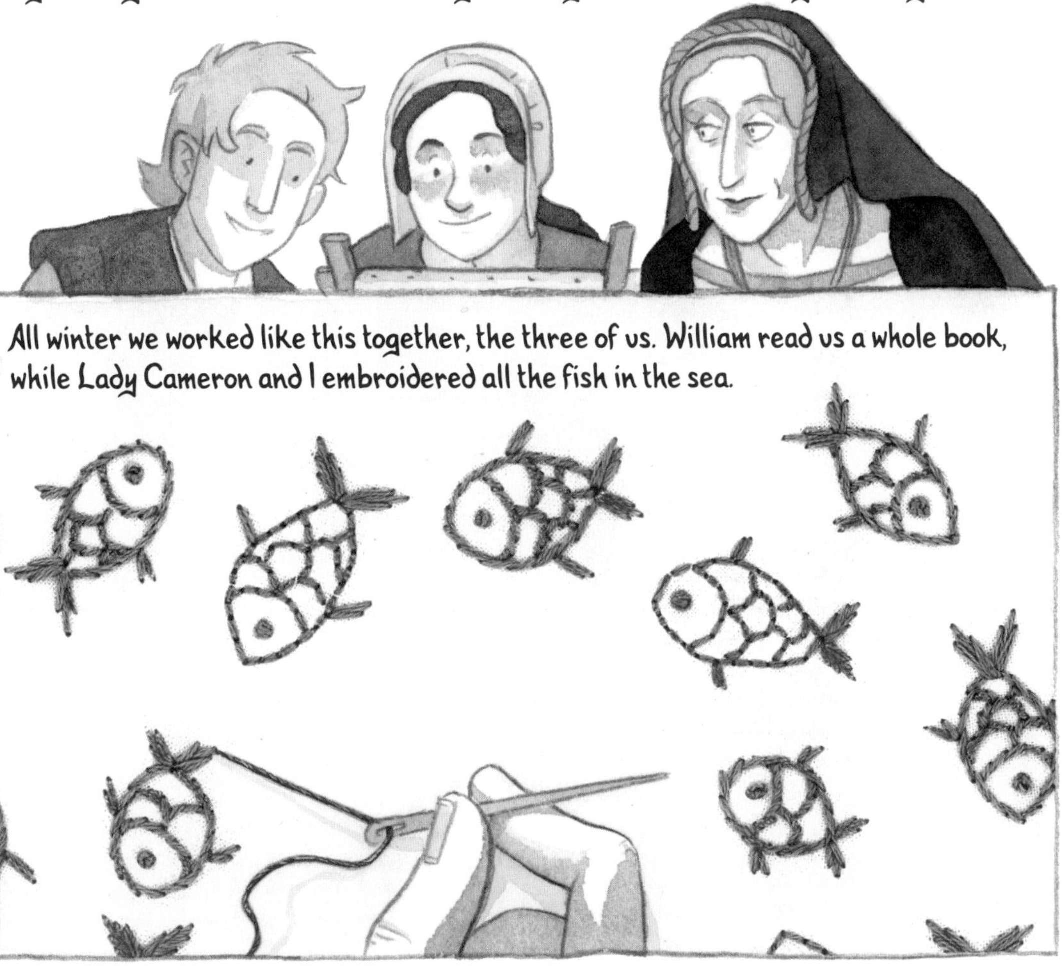
All winter we worked like this together, the three of us. William read us a whole book, while Lady Cameron and I embroidered all the fish in the sea.

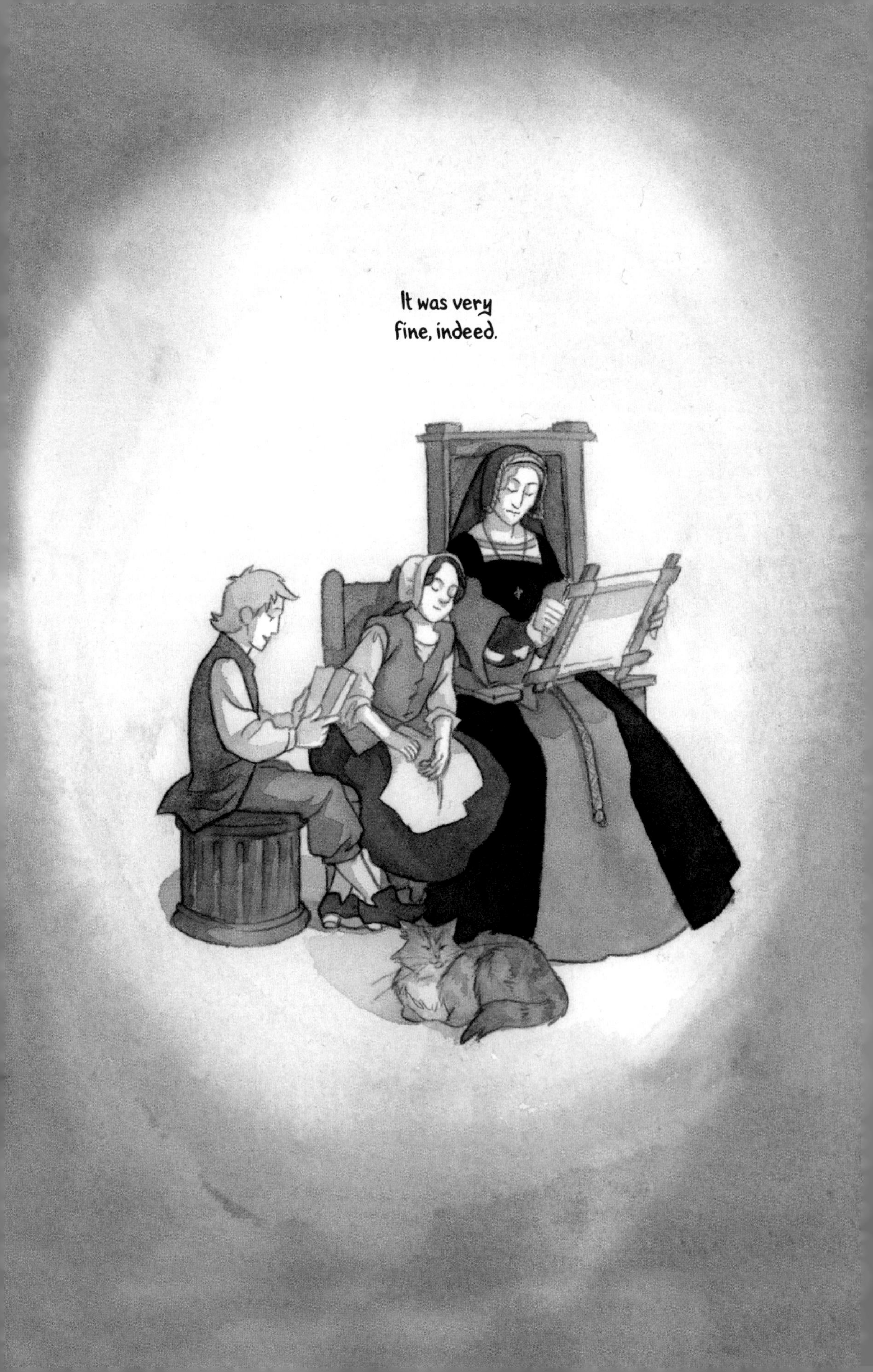
It was very fine, indeed.

And then, all of a sudden, it was spring,
Warm enough to have our lessons by
open windows instead of the hearth.

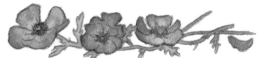

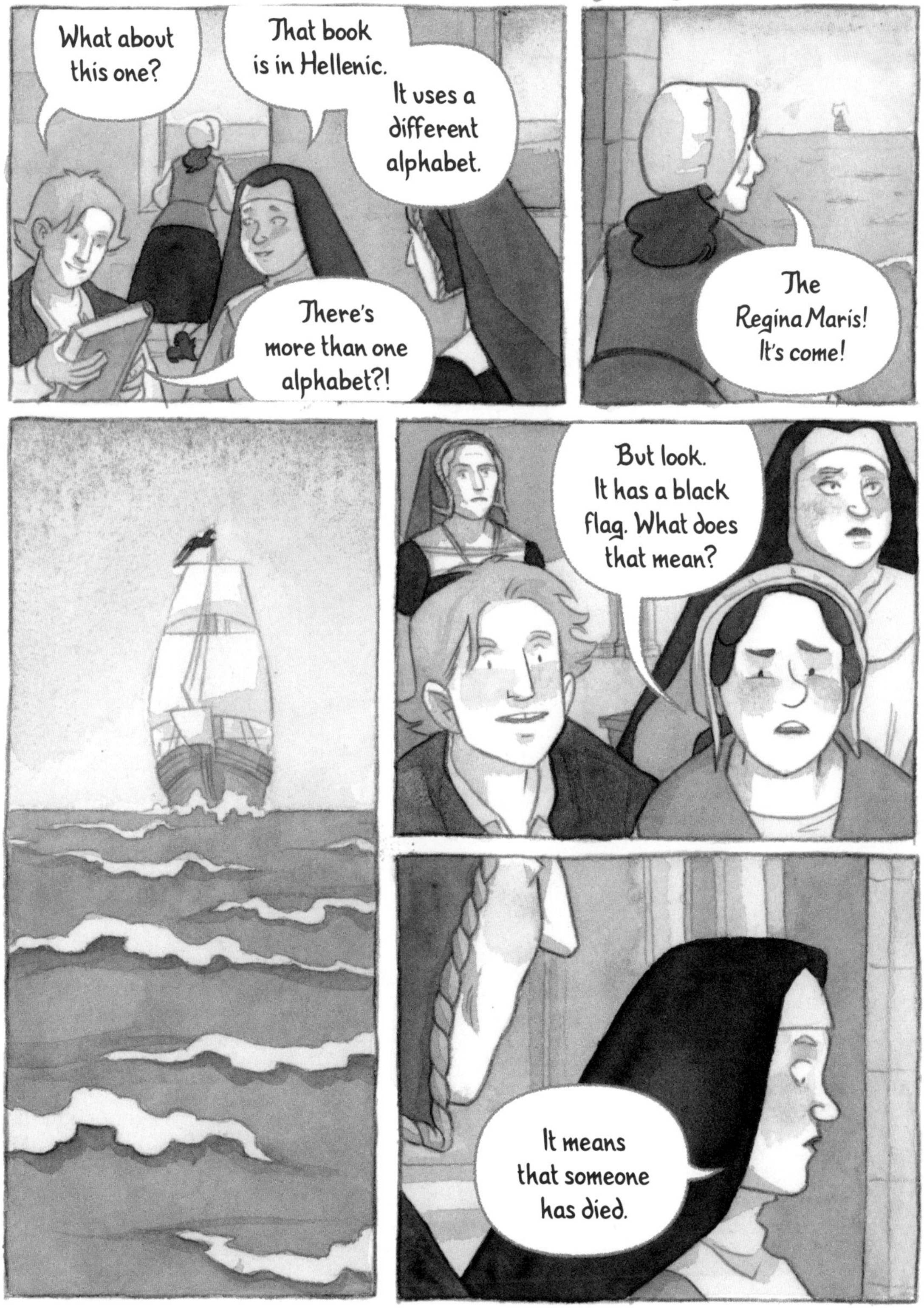
What about this one?
That book is in Hellenic.
It uses a different alphabet.
There's more than one alphabet?!
The Regina Maris! It's come!
But look. It has a black flag. What does that mean?
It means that someone has died.

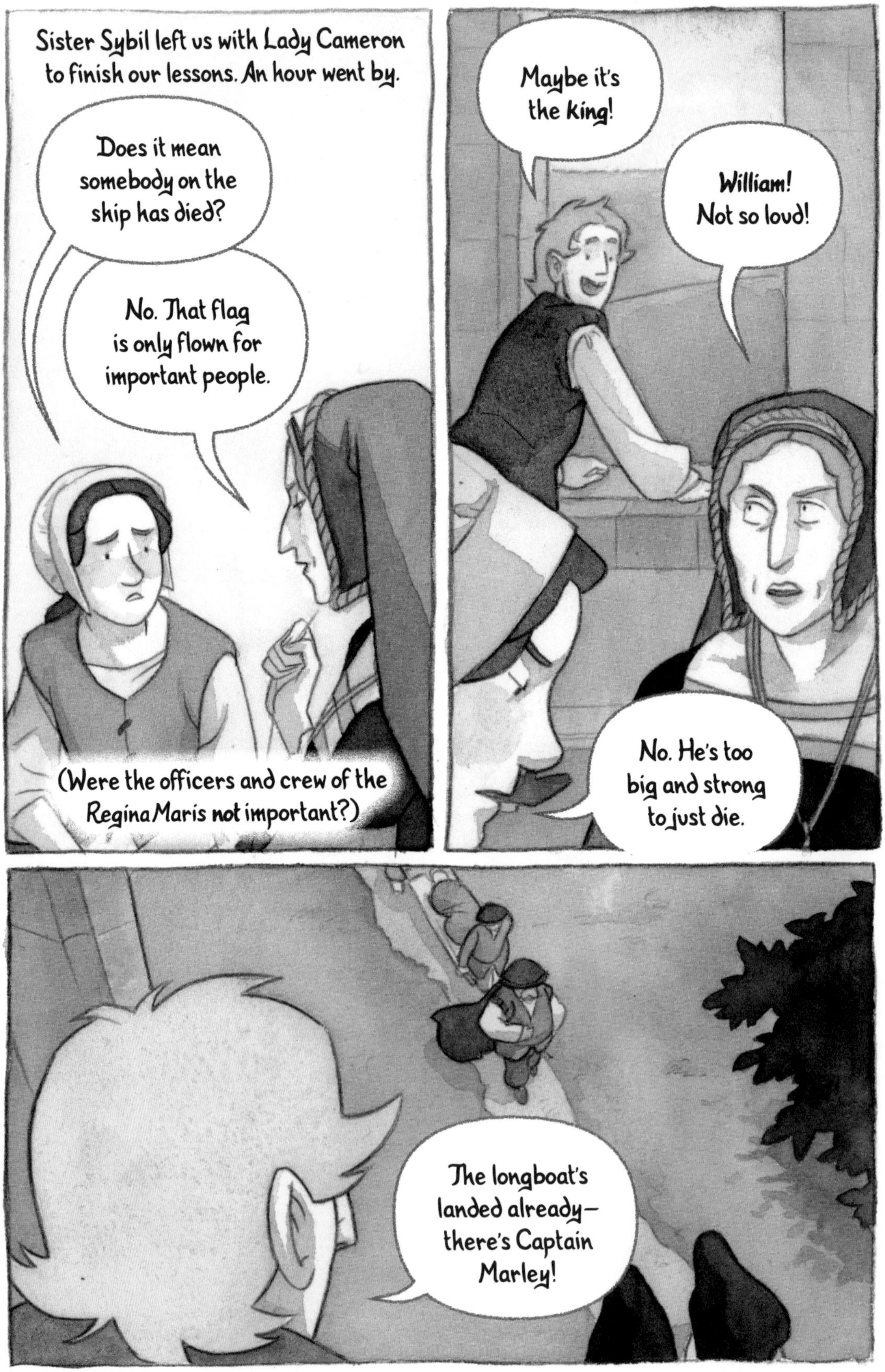
Sister Sybil left us with Lady Cameron to finish our lessons. An hour went by.
Does it mean somebody on the ship has died?
No. That flag is only flown for important people.
(Were the officers and crew of the Regina Maris not important?)
Maybe it's the king!
William! Not so loud!
No. He's too big and strong to just die.
The longboat's landed already— there's Captain Marley!

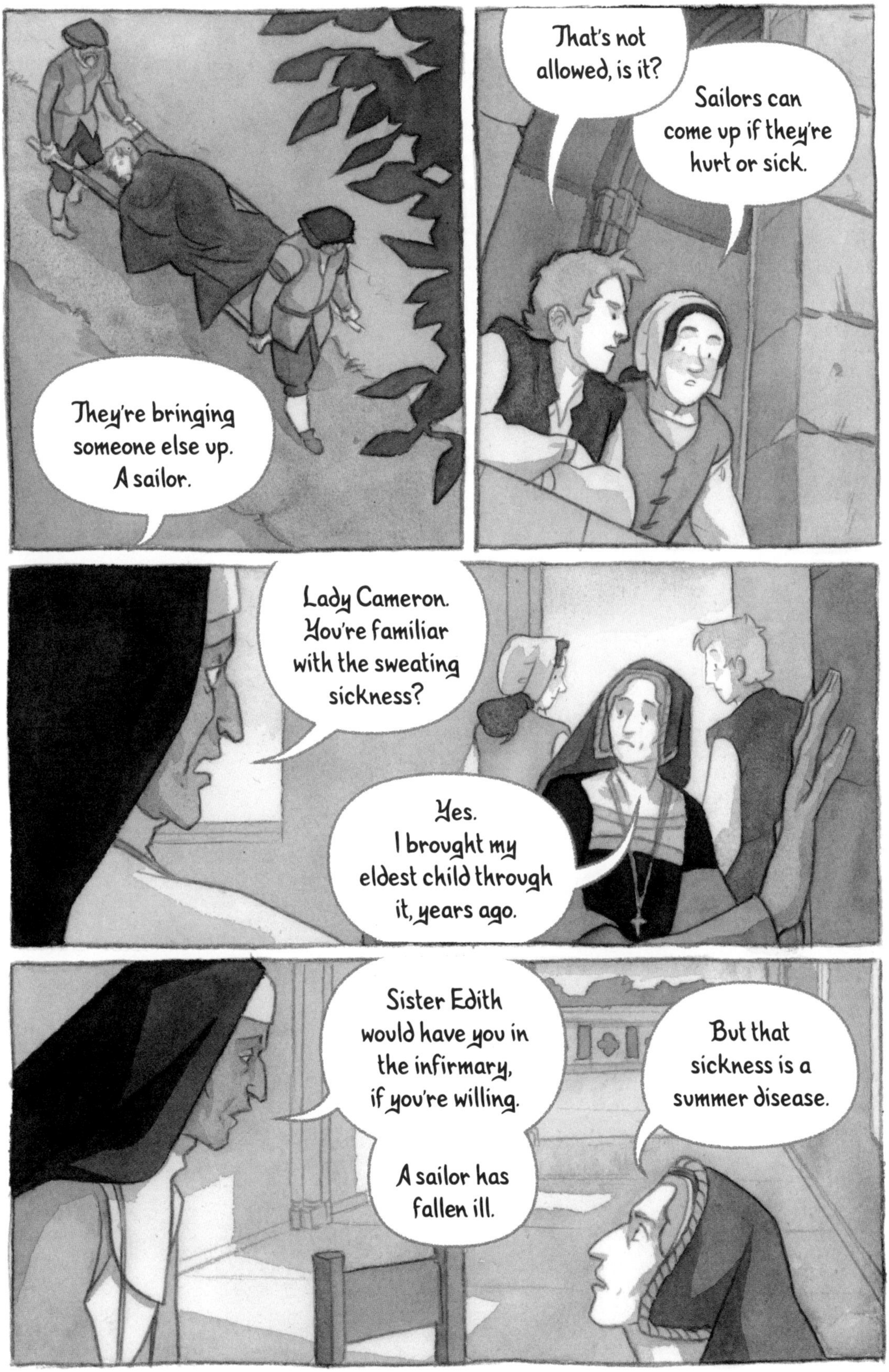
They're bringing someone else up. A sailor.
That's not allowed, is it?
Sailors can come up if they're hurt or sick.
Lady Cameron. You're familiar with the sweating sickness?
Yes. I brought my eldest child through it, years ago.
Sister Edith would have you in the infirmary, if you're willing.
A sailor has fallen ill.
But that sickness is a summer disease.

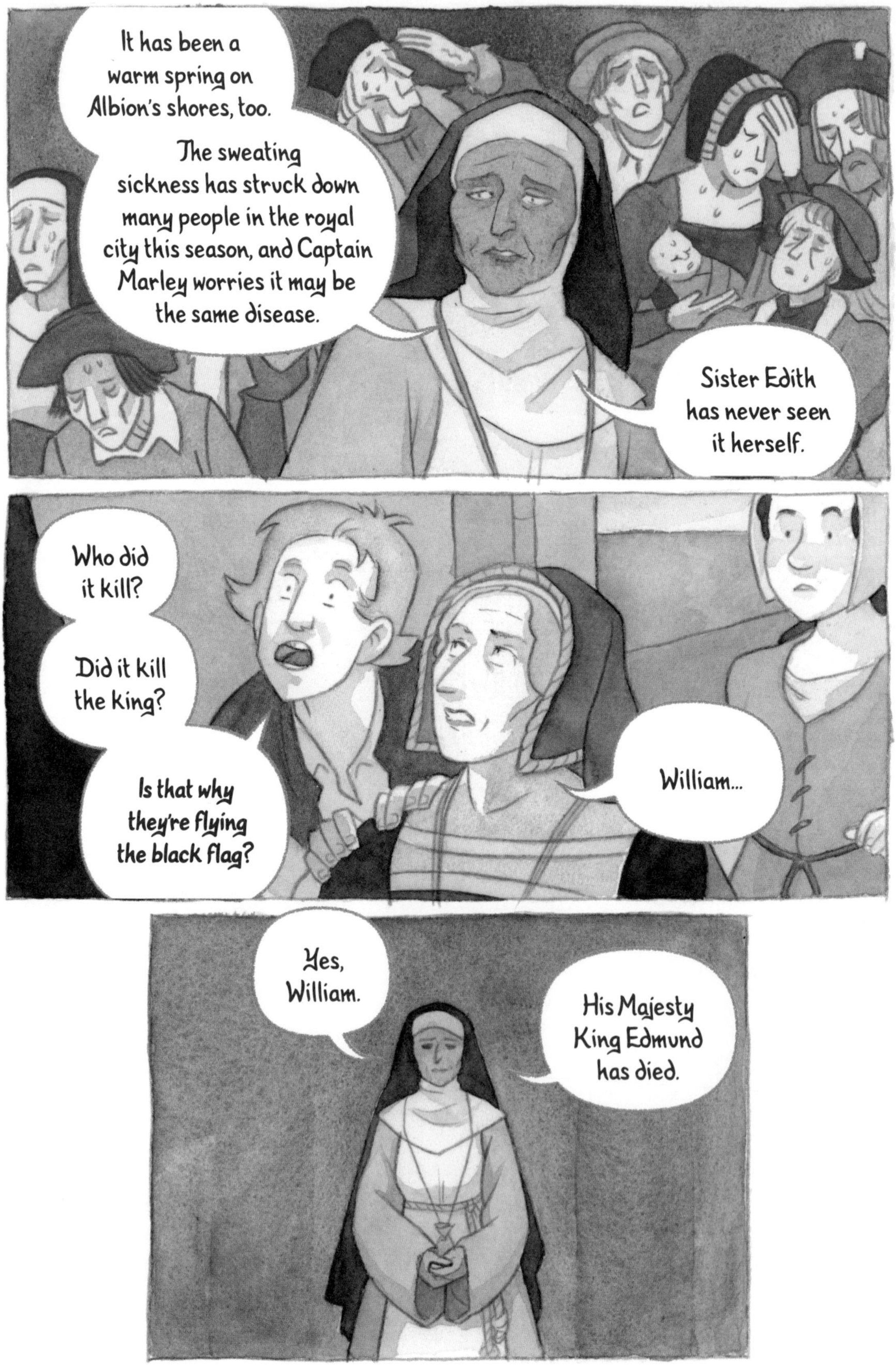
It has been a warm spring on Albion's shores, too.
The sweating sickness has struck down many people in the royal city this season, and Captain Marley worries it may be the same disease.
Sister Edith has never seen it herself.
Who did it kill?
Did it kill the king?
Is that why they're flying the black flag?
William...
Yes, William.
His Majesty King Edmund has died.

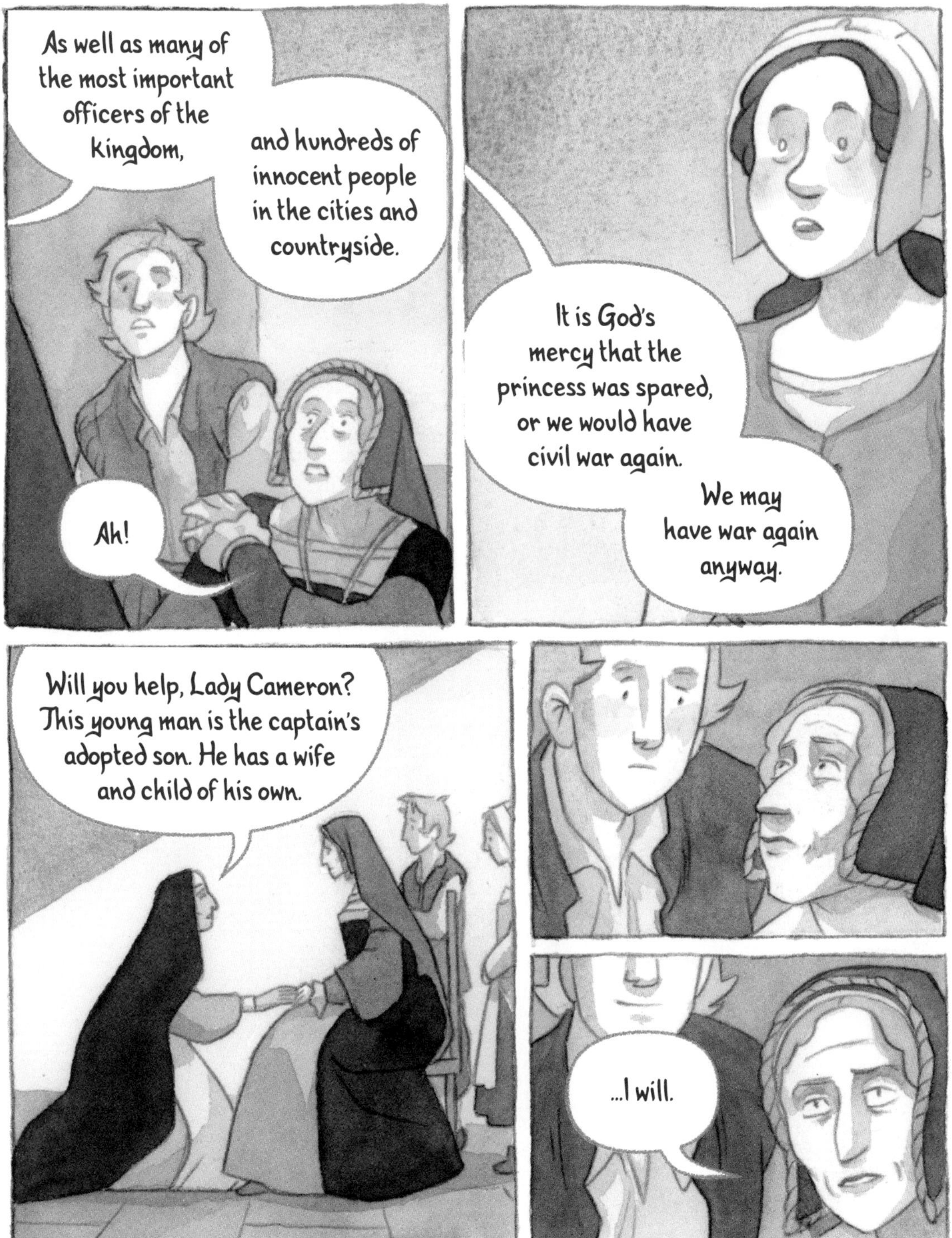

As well as many of the most important officers of the kingdom,
and hundreds of innocent people in the cities and countryside.
Ah!
It is God's mercy that the princess was spared, or we would have civil war again.
We may have war again anyway.
Will you help, Lady Cameron? This young man is the captain's adopted son. He has a wife and child of his own.
...I will.

William and I were sent down to the kitchen to help Maud and Jess and Bess with the food delivered by the *Regina Maris*. It was even more work than usual because all the sisters except for Sister Edith were saying special prayers for the soul of the king.

What would little Princess Eleanor do without her father's lap to sit in?

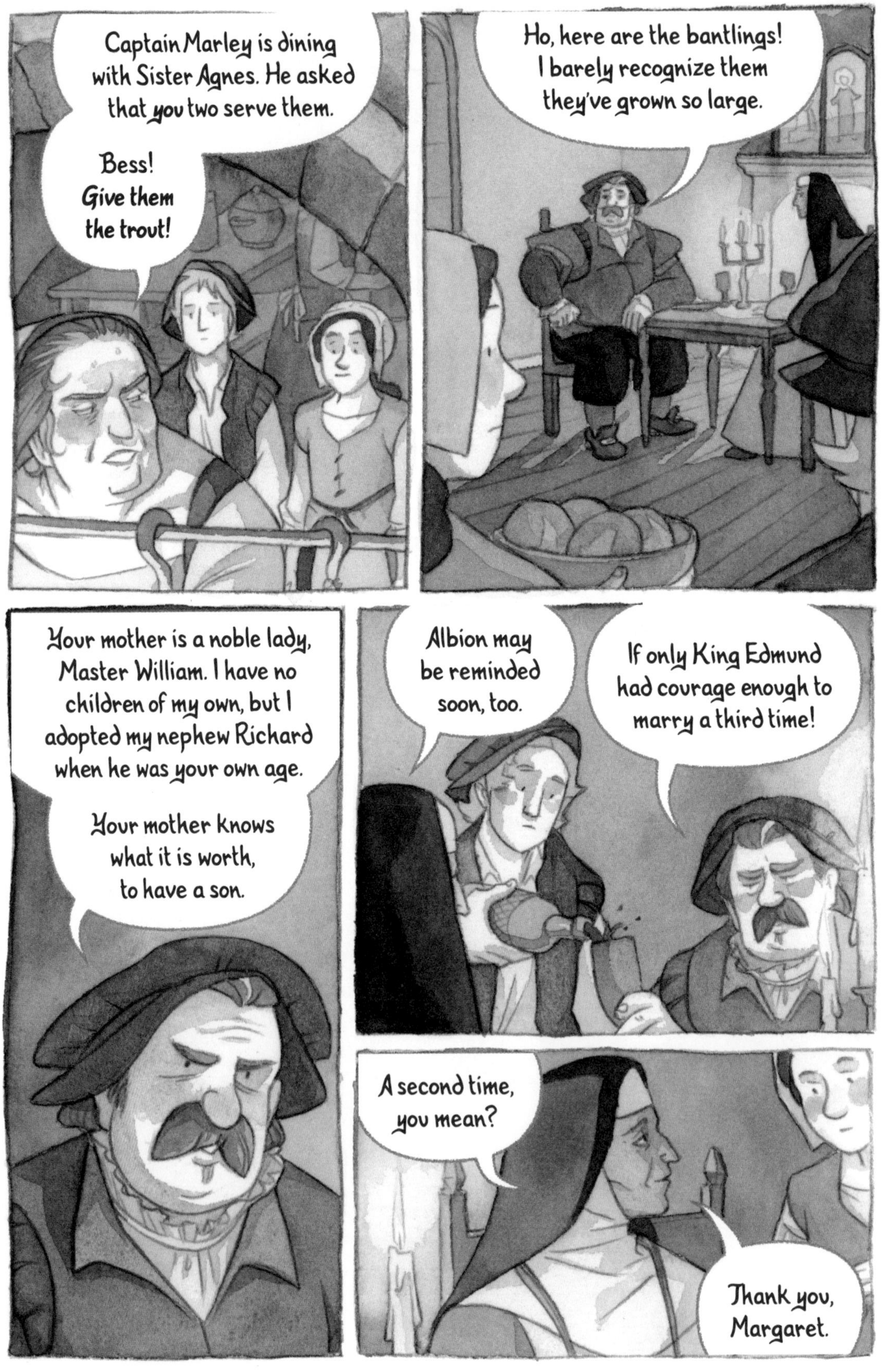
Captain Marley is dining with Sister Agnes. He asked that *you* two serve them.
Bess! **Give them the trout!**
Ho, here are the bantlings! I barely recognize them they've grown so large.
Your mother is a noble lady, Master William. I have no children of my own, but I adopted my nephew Richard when he was *your* own age.
Your mother knows what it is worth, to have a son.
Albion may be reminded soon, too.
If only King Edmund had courage enough to marry a third time!
A second time, you mean?
Thank you, Margaret.

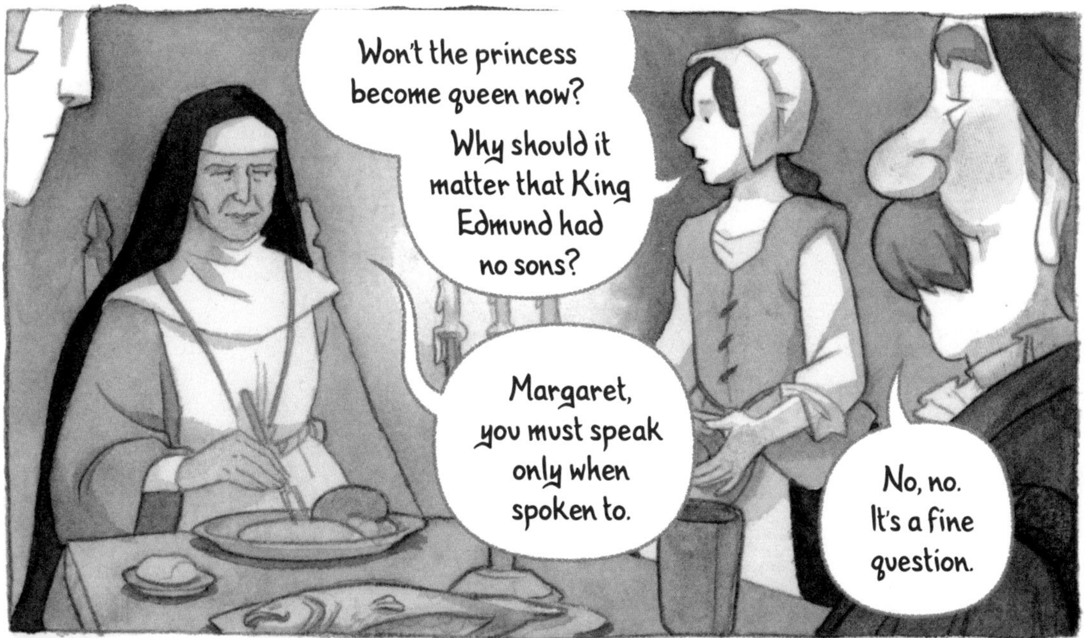
Won't the princess become queen now?
Why should it matter that King Edmund had no sons?
Margaret, you must speak only when spoken to.
No, no. It's a fine question.

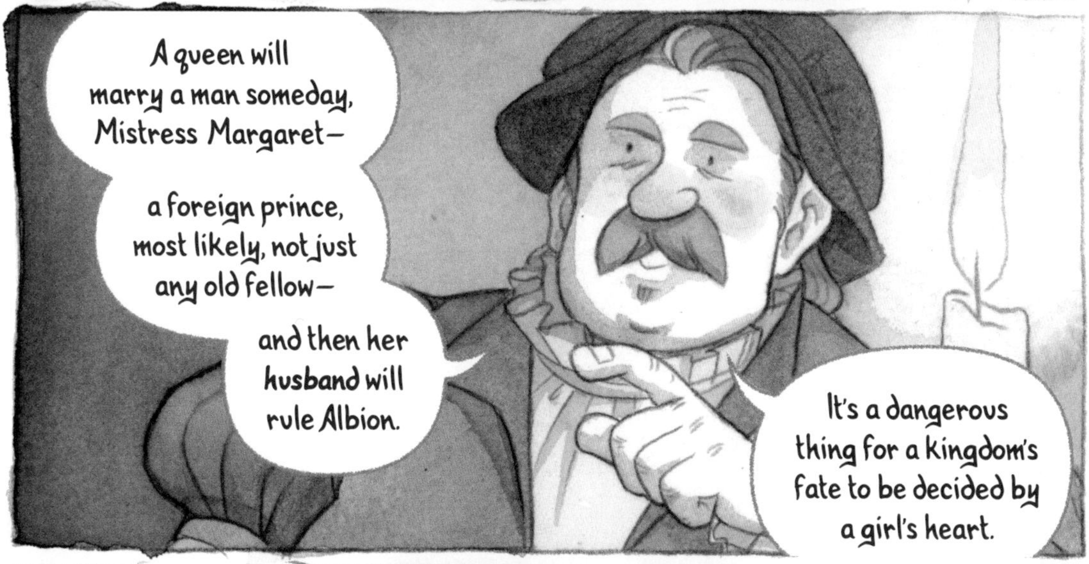
A queen will marry a man someday, Mistress Margaret—
a foreign prince, most likely, not just any old fellow—
and then her **husband** will rule Albion.
It's a dangerous thing for a kingdom's fate to be decided by a girl's heart.

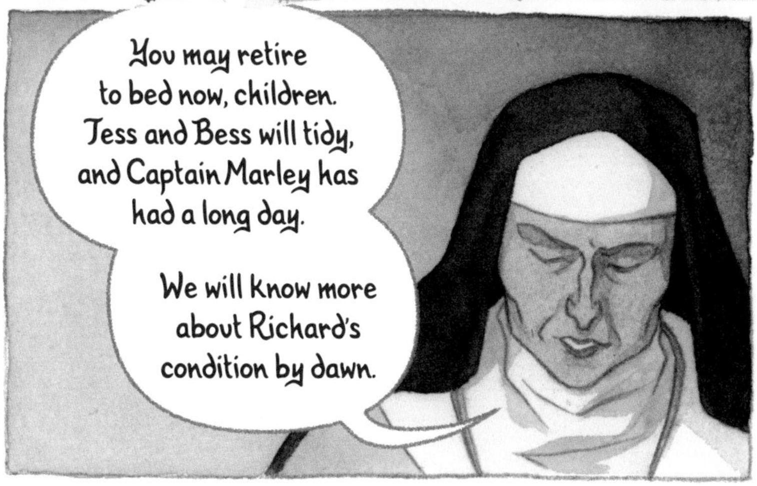
You may retire to bed now, children. Jess and Bess will tidy, and Captain Marley has had a long day.
We will know more about Richard's condition by dawn.

Lady Cameron could not come to bed yet, so I stayed with William in their chamber.

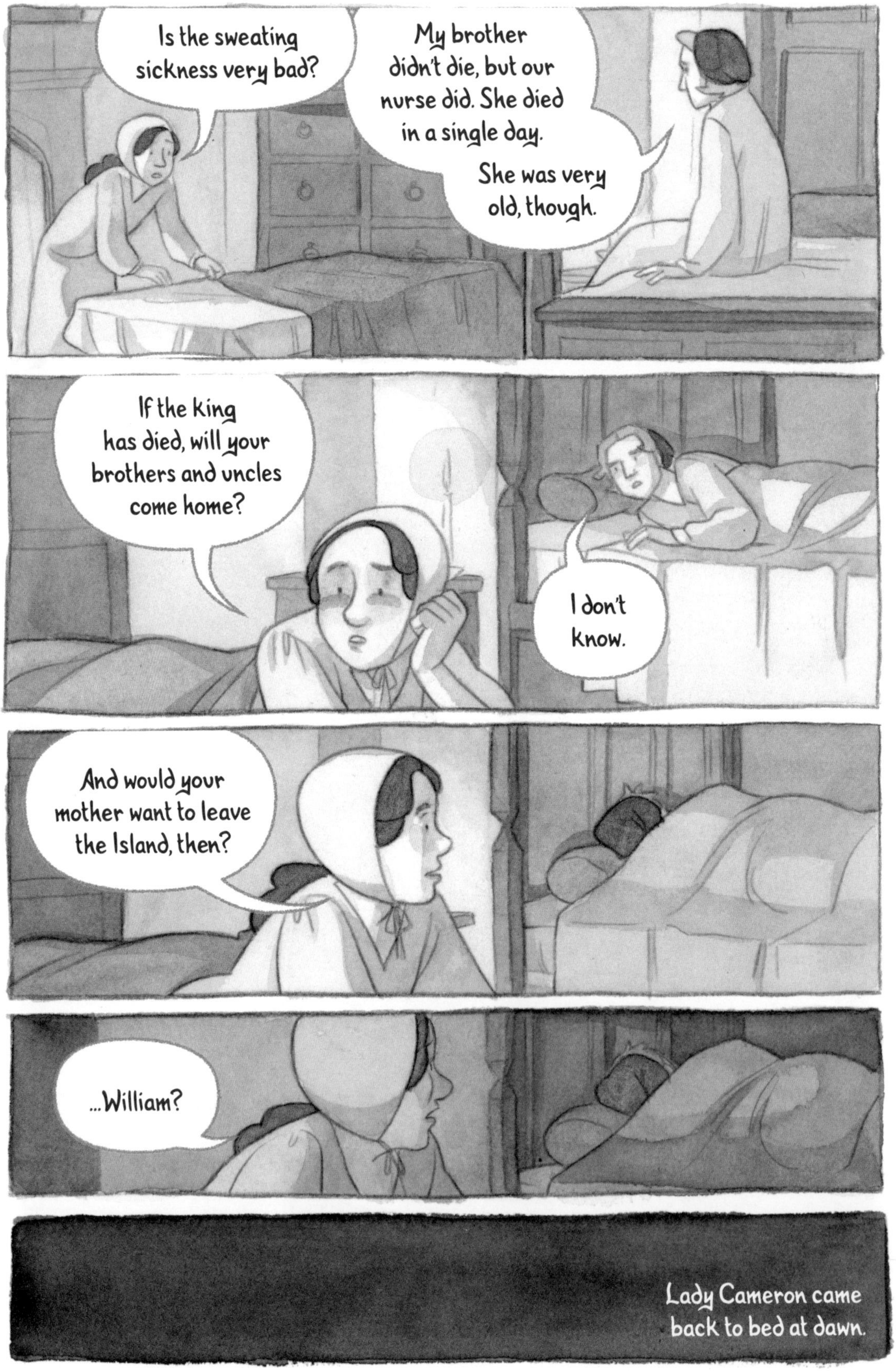
Is the sweating sickness very bad?
My brother didn't die, but our nurse did. She died in a single day.
She was very old, though.
If the king has died, will your brothers and uncles come home?
I don't know.
And would your mother want to leave the Island, then?
...William?
Lady Cameron came back to bed at dawn.

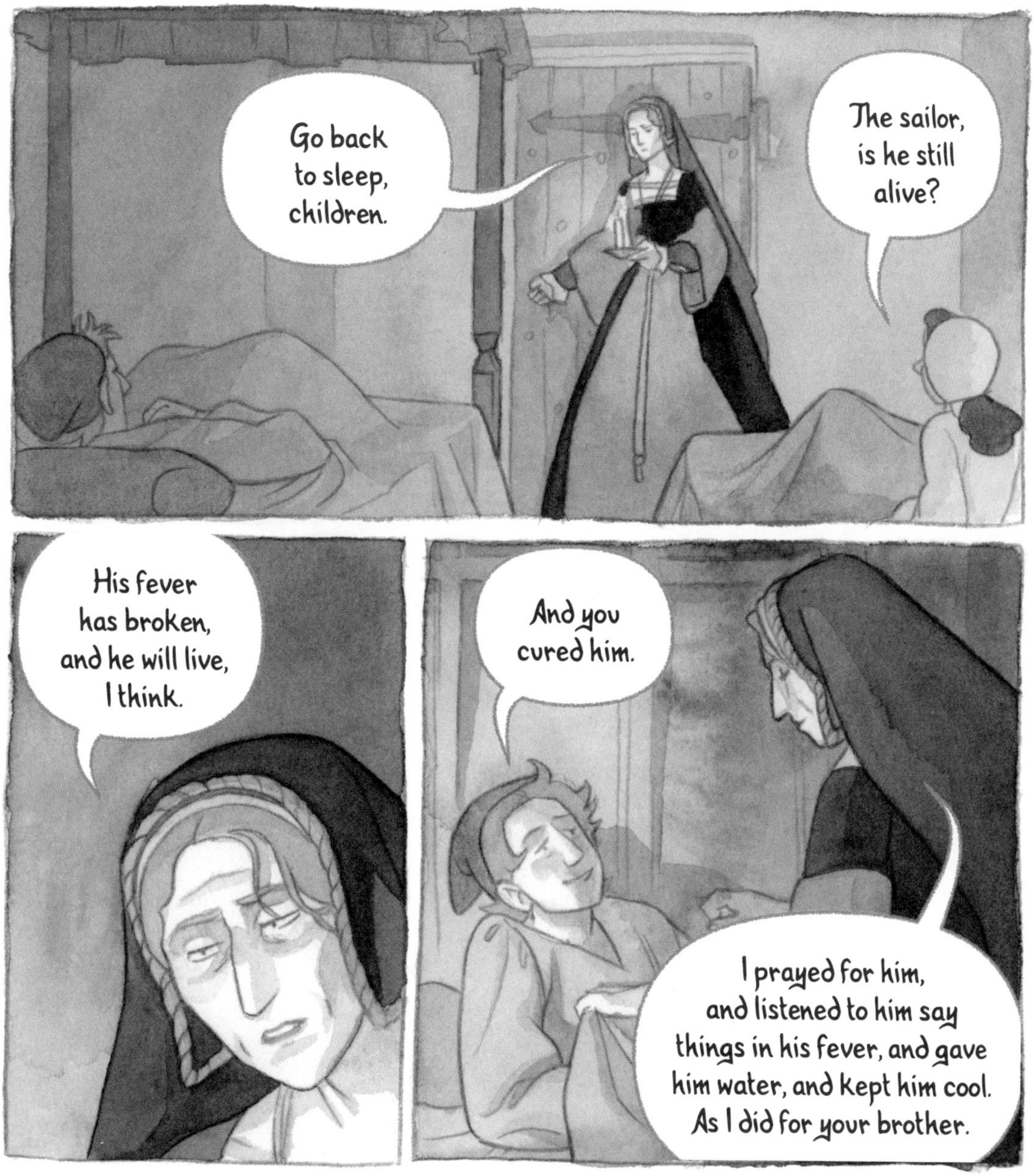
Go back to sleep, children.
The sailor, is he still alive?
His fever has broken, and he will live, I think.
And you cured him.
I prayed for him, and listened to him say things in his fever, and gave him water, and kept him cool. As I did for your brother.

In the morning we crept out of the bedchamber to the kitchen so Lady Cameron could sleep.

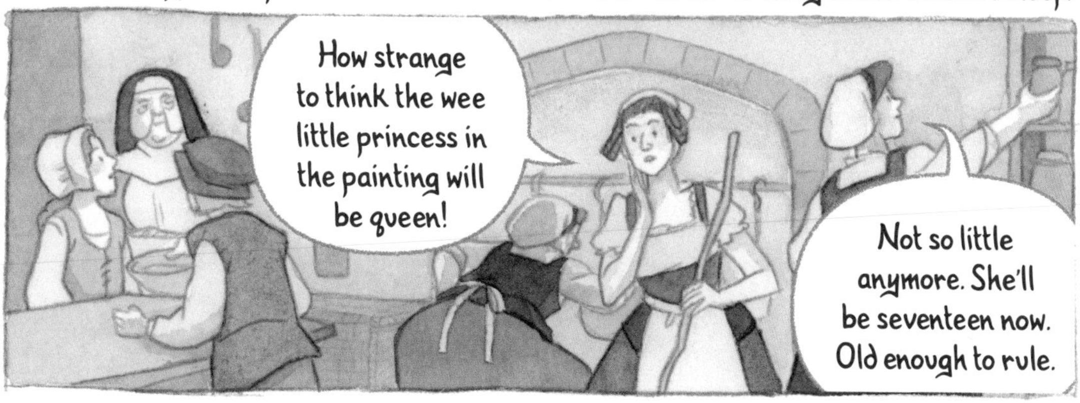
How strange to think the wee little princess in the painting will be queen!
Not so little anymore. She'll be seventeen now. Old enough to rule.

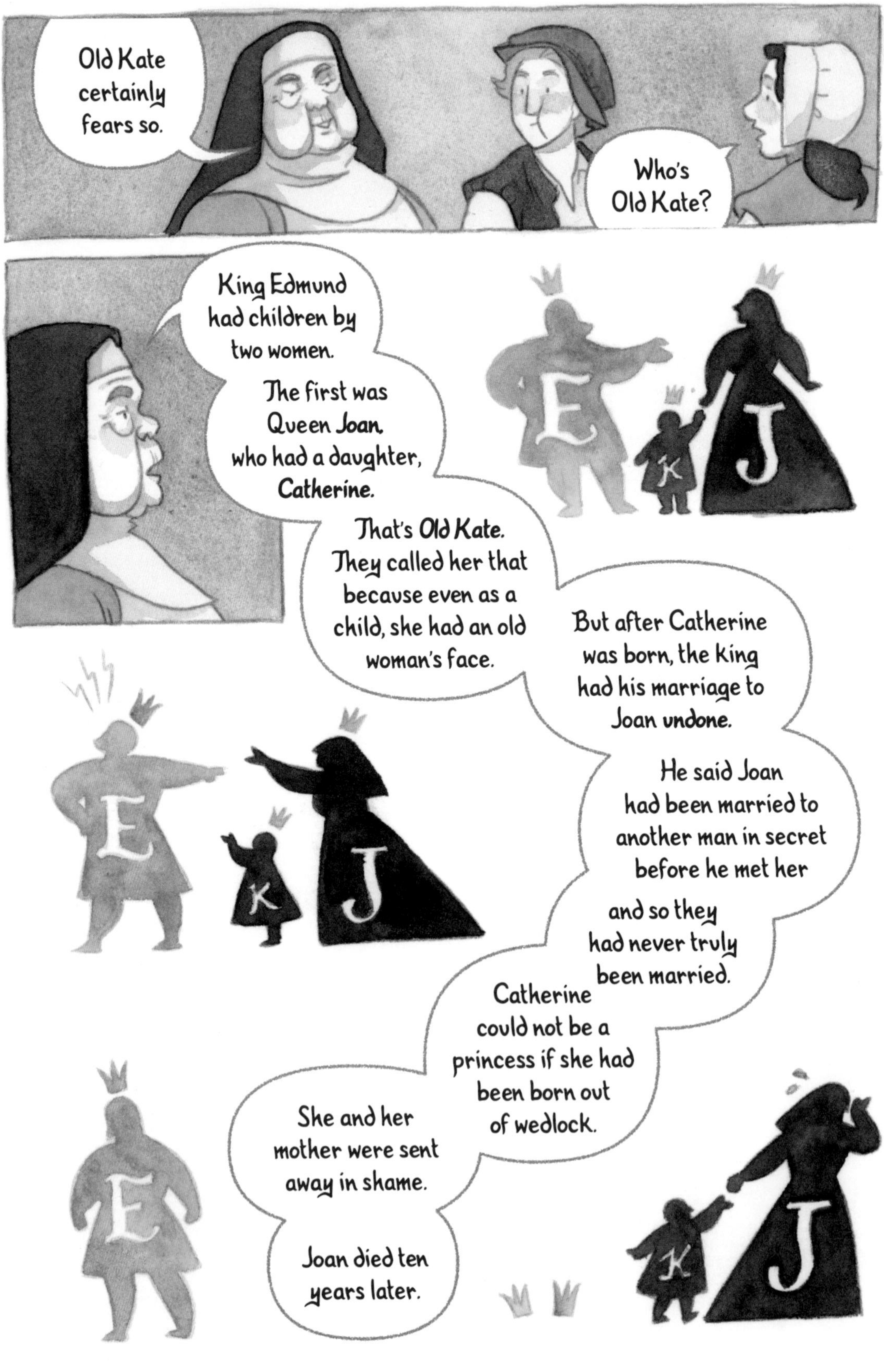

Old Kate certainly fears so.
Who's Old Kate?
King Edmund had children by two women.
The first was Queen Joan who had a daughter, Catherine.
E
K
J
That's Old Kate. They called her that because even as a child, she had an old woman's face.
But after Catherine was born, the king had his marriage to Joan undone.
He said Joan had been married to another man in secret before he met her
and so they had never truly been married.
E
K
J
Catherine could not be a princess if she had been born out of wedlock.
She and her mother were sent away in shame.
Joan died ten years later.
E
K
J

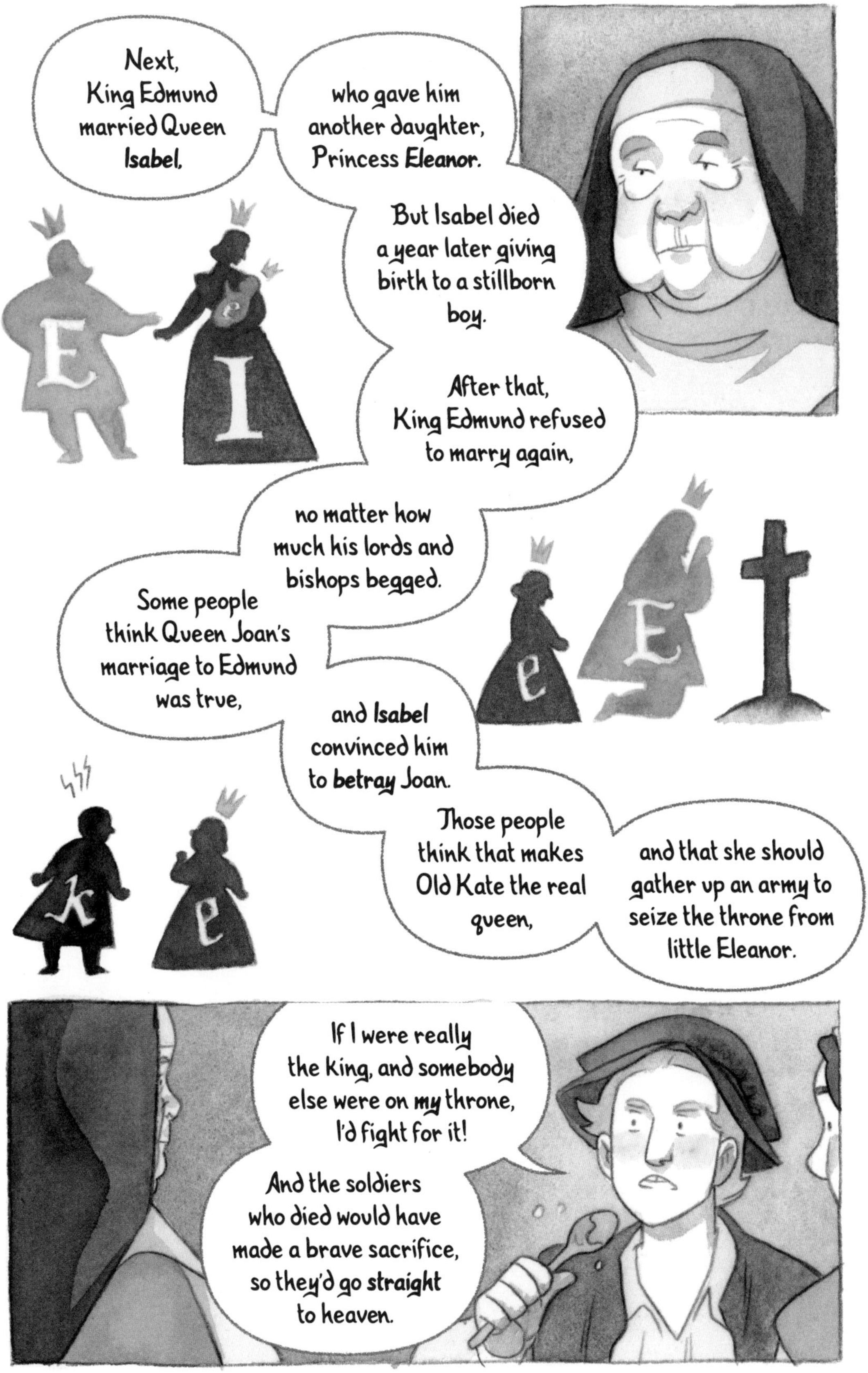
Next, King Edmund married Queen Isabel,
who gave him another daughter, Princess Eleanor.
But Isabel died a year later giving birth to a stillborn boy.
After that, King Edmund refused to marry again,
no matter how much his lords and bishops begged.
Some people think Queen Joan's marriage to Edmund was true,
and Isabel convinced him to betray Joan.
Those people think that makes Old Kate the real queen,
and that she should gather up an army to seize the throne from little Eleanor.
If I were really the king, and somebody else were on my throne, I'd fight for it!
And the soldiers who died would have made a brave sacrifice, so they'd go straight to heaven.

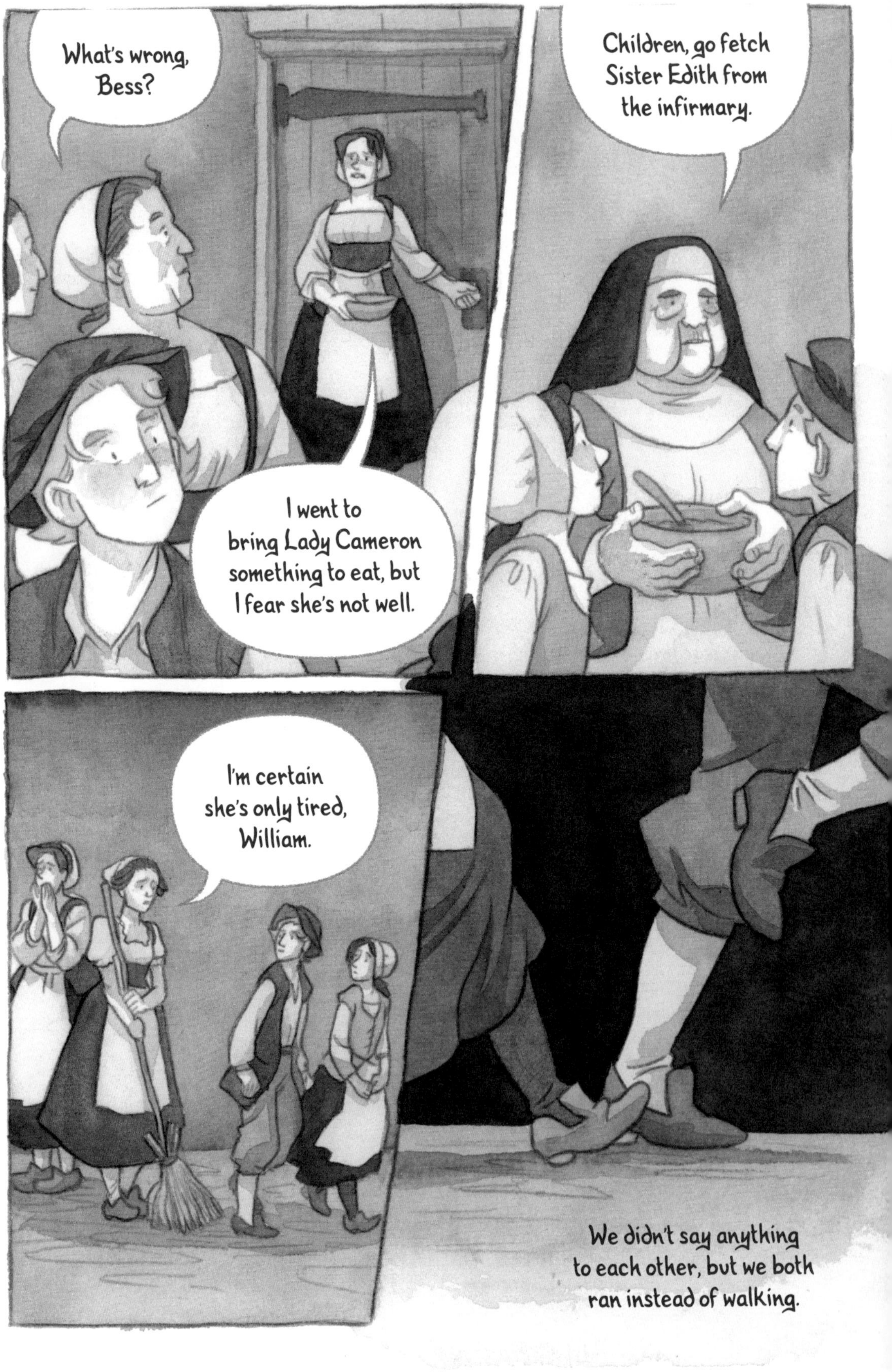
What's wrong, Bess?
I went to bring Lady Cameron something to eat, but I fear she's not well.
Children, go fetch Sister Edith from the infirmary.
I'm certain she's only tired, William.
We didn't say anything to each other, but we both ran instead of walking.

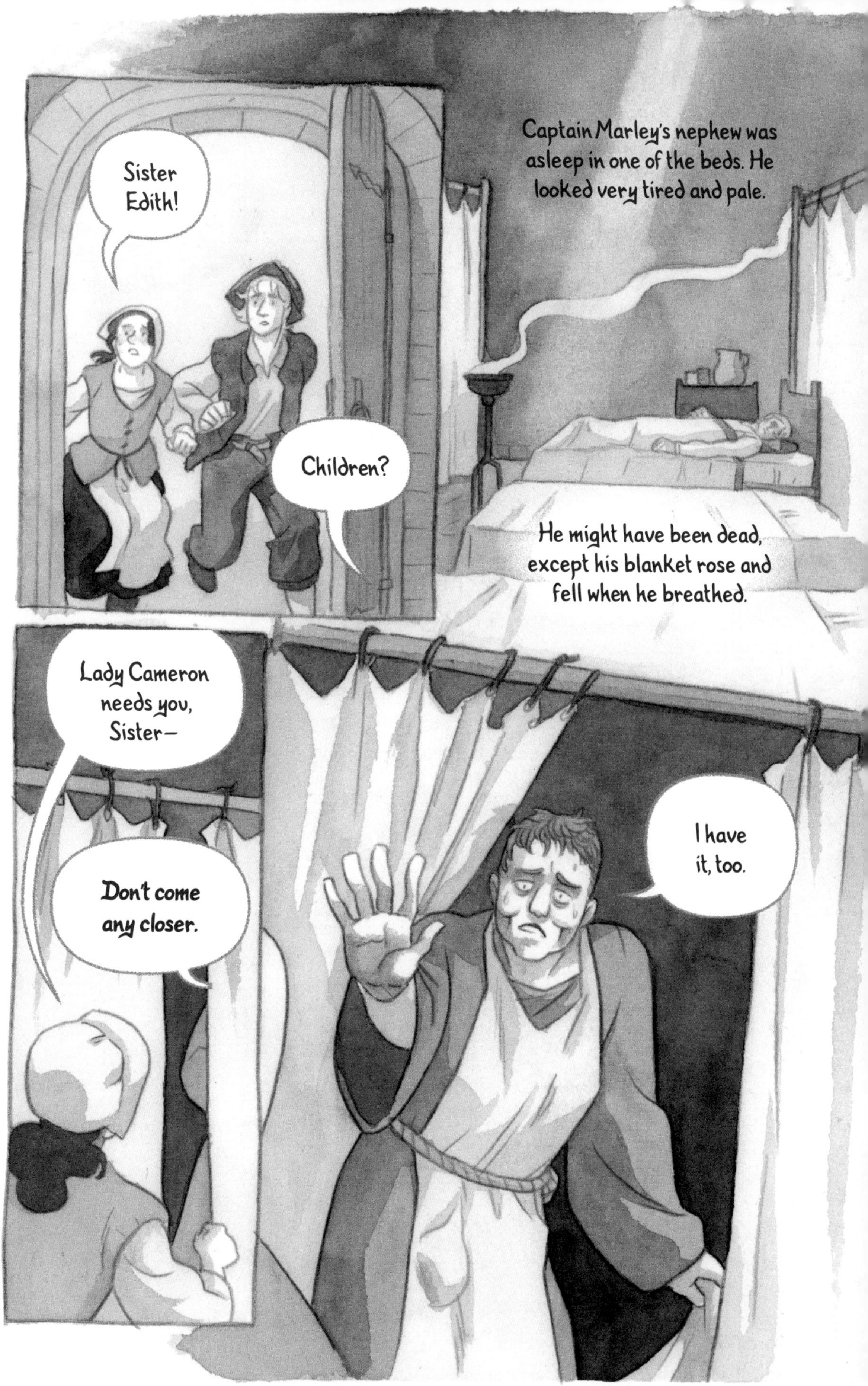
Sister Edith!
Children?
Captain Marley's nephew was asleep in one of the beds. He looked very tired and pale.
He might have been dead, except his blanket rose and fell when he breathed.
Lady Cameron needs you, Sister—
Don't come any closer.
I have it, too.

Sister Agnes wouldn't let us back into the infirmary, or into our bedchamber.
She and Sister Philippa would care for Lady Cameron and Sister Edith on their own.

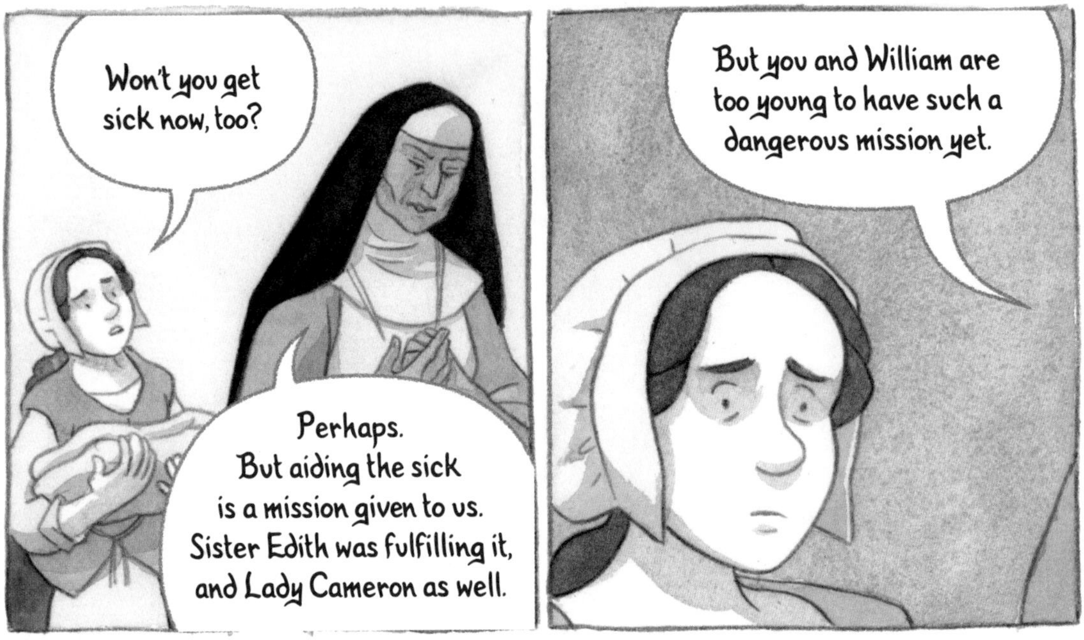
Won't you get sick now, too?
Perhaps. But aiding the sick is a mission given to us. Sister Edith was fulfilling it, and Lady Cameron as well.
But you and William are too young to have such a dangerous mission yet.

If we were too young to help the sick, we were old enough to help with everything else. We did every chore we could on the farm. We did every chore we could in the kitchen. We even swept the church; we found a nest of mice and let them all go without giving them to the cat, because Jess told us it was bad luck when somebody nearby was sick.

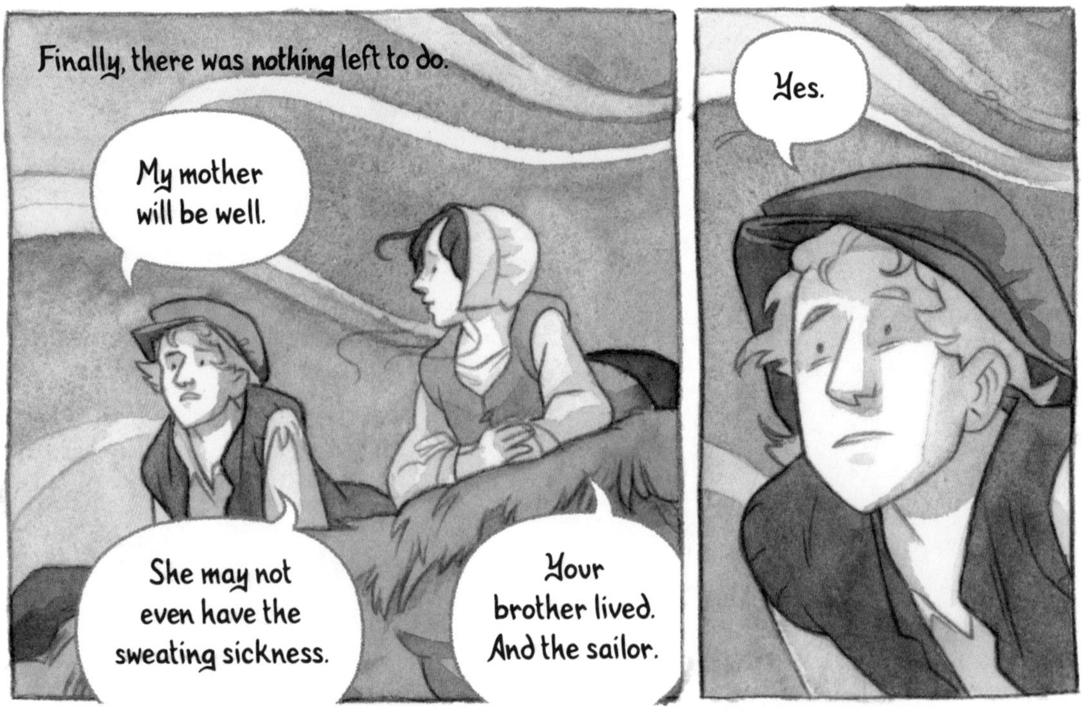
Finally, there was nothing left to do.
My mother will be well.
She may not even have the sweating sickness.
Your brother lived. And the sailor.
Yes.

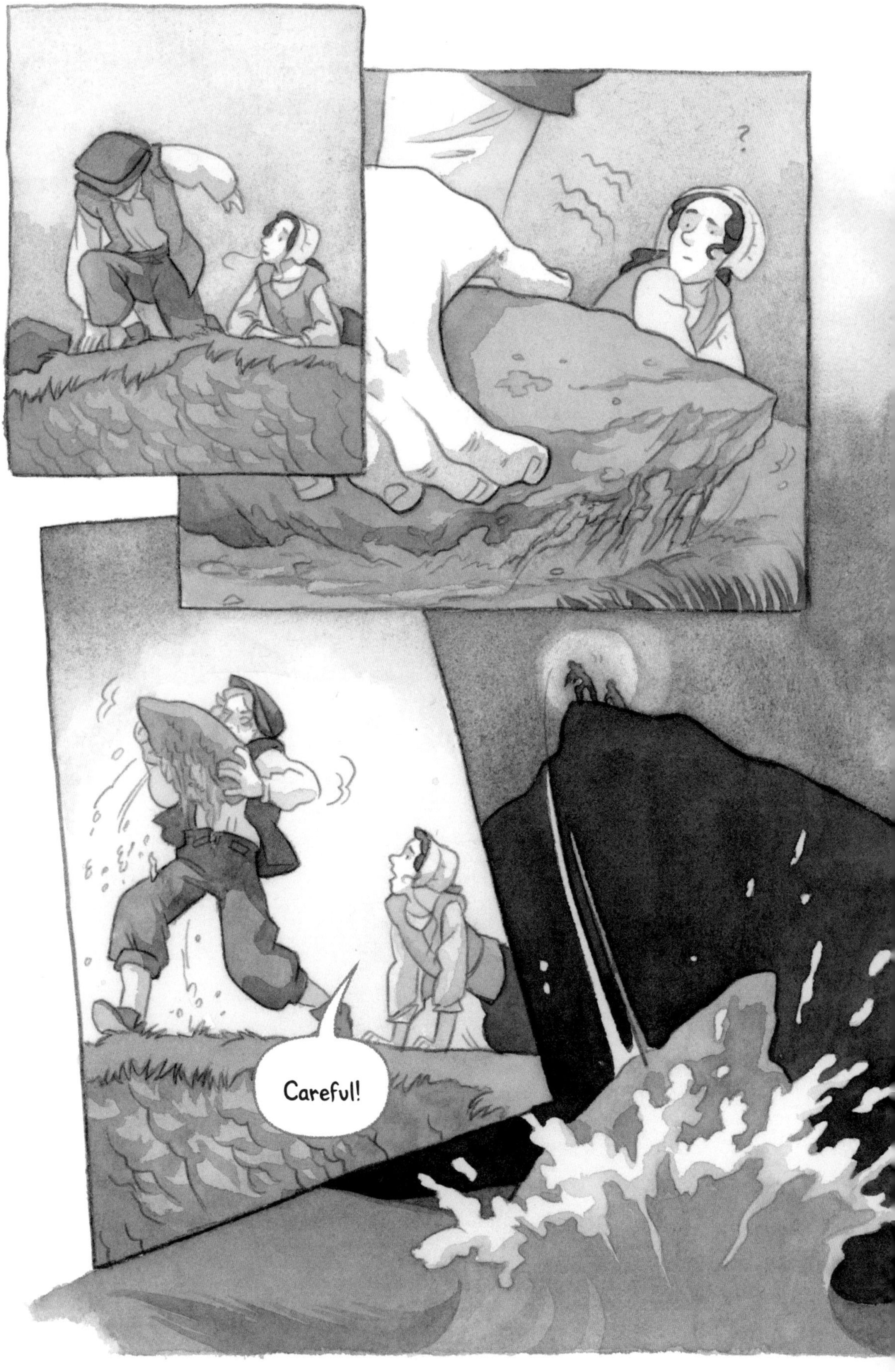
?
Careful!

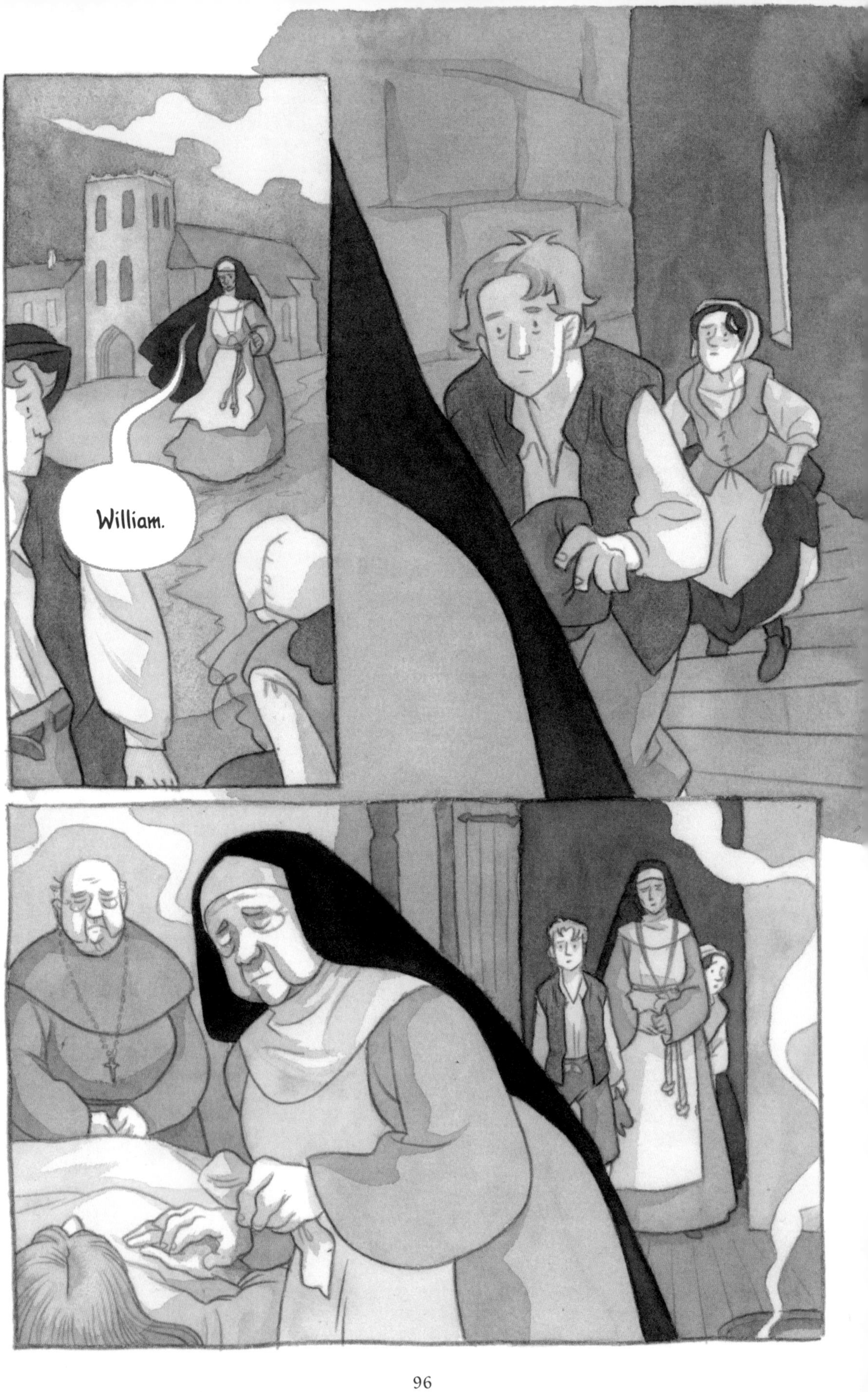
William.

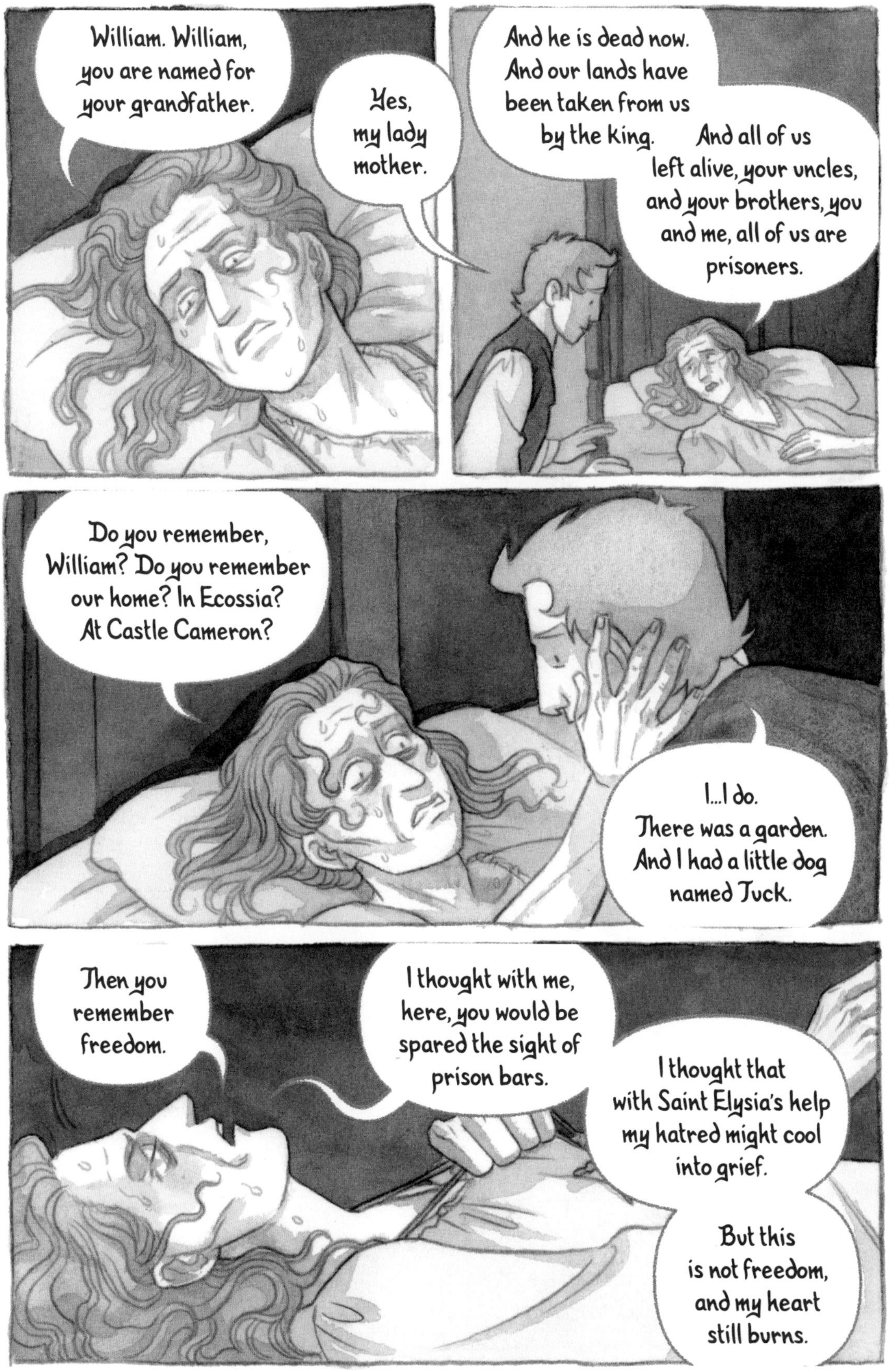
William. William, you are named for your grandfather.
Yes, my lady mother.
And he is dead now. And our lands have been taken from us by the king.
And all of us left alive, your uncles, and your brothers, you and me, all of us are prisoners.
Do you remember, William? Do you remember our home? In Ecossia? At Castle Cameron?
I...I do. There was a garden. And I had a little dog named Tuck.
Then you remember freedom.
I thought with me, here, you would be spared the sight of prison bars.
I thought that with Saint Elysia's help my hatred might cool into grief.
But this is not freedom, and my heart still burns.

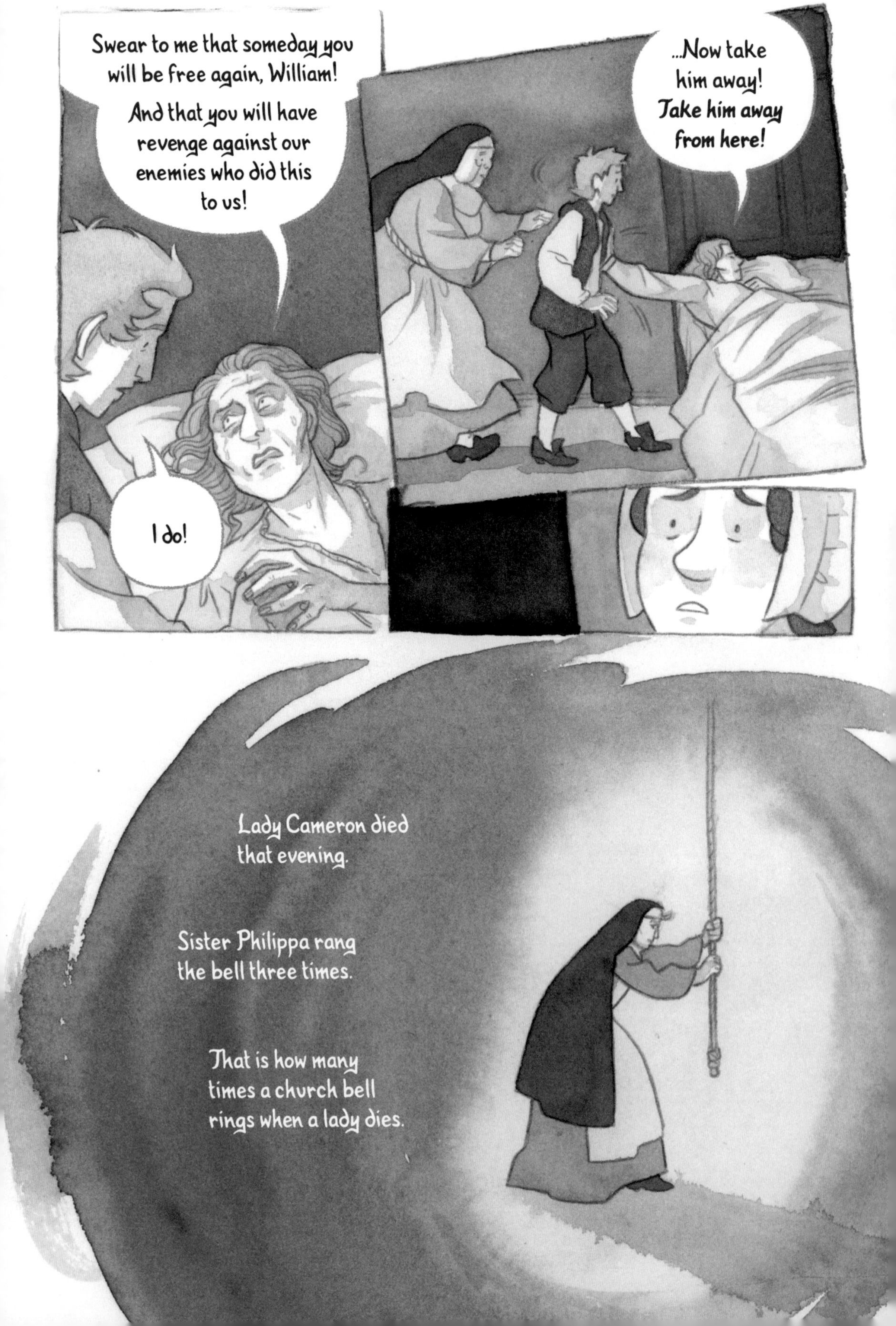
Swear to me that someday you will be free again, William!
And that you will have revenge against our enemies who did this to us!
I do!
...Now take him away! Take him away from here!
Lady Cameron died that evening.
Sister Philippa rang the bell three times.
That is how many times a church bell rings when a lady dies.

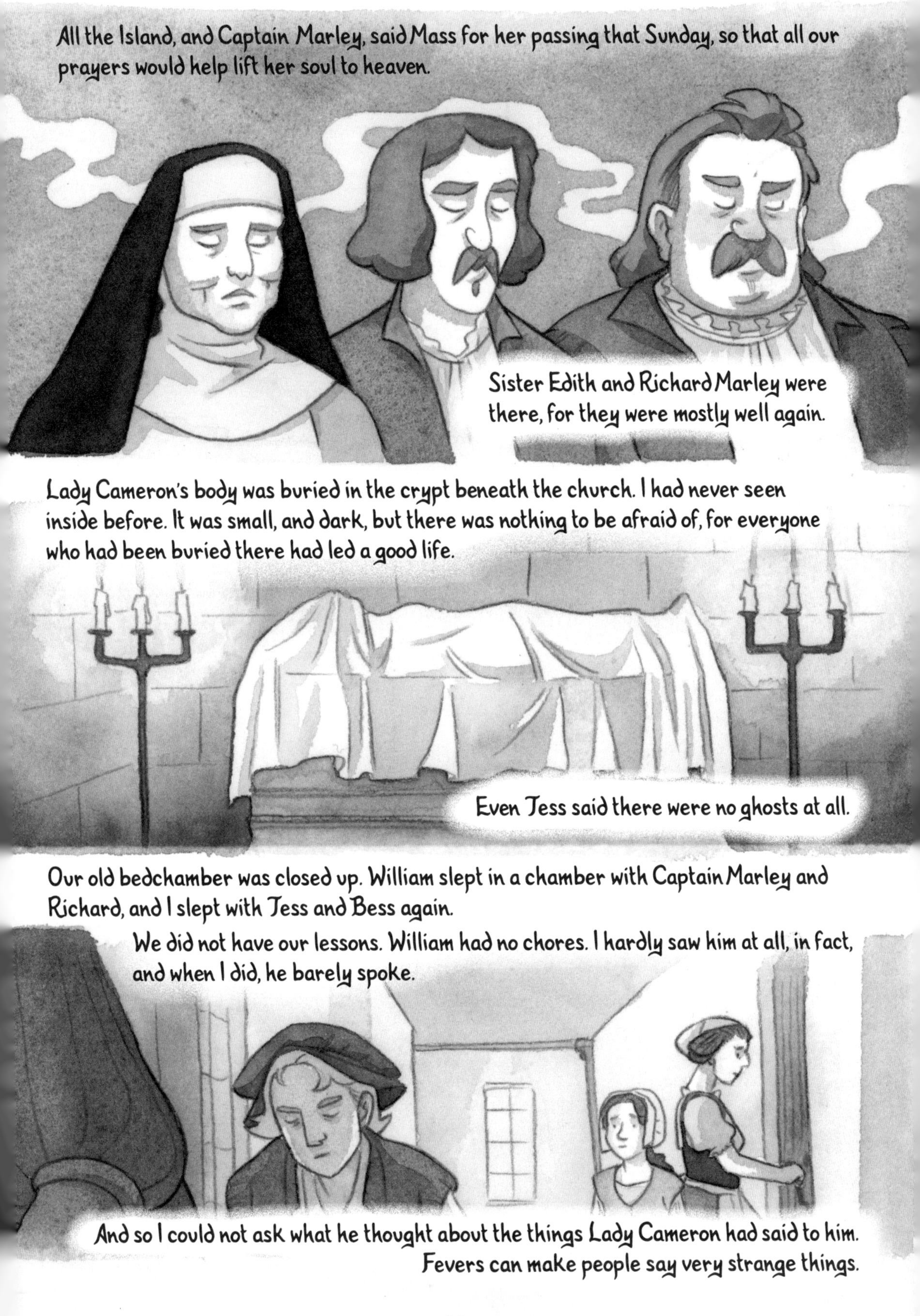
All the Island, and Captain Marley, said Mass for her passing that Sunday, so that all our prayers would help lift her soul to heaven.
Sister Edith and Richard Marley were there, for they were mostly well again.
Lady Cameron's body was buried in the crypt beneath the church. I had never seen inside before. It was small, and dark, but there was nothing to be afraid of, for everyone who had been buried there had led a good life.
Even Jess said there were no ghosts at all.
Our old bedchamber was closed up. William slept in a chamber with Captain Marley and Richard, and I slept with Jess and Bess again.
We did not have our lessons. William had no chores. I hardly saw him at all, in fact, and when I did, he barely spoke.
And so I could not ask what he thought about the things Lady Cameron had said to him.
Fevers can make people say very strange things.

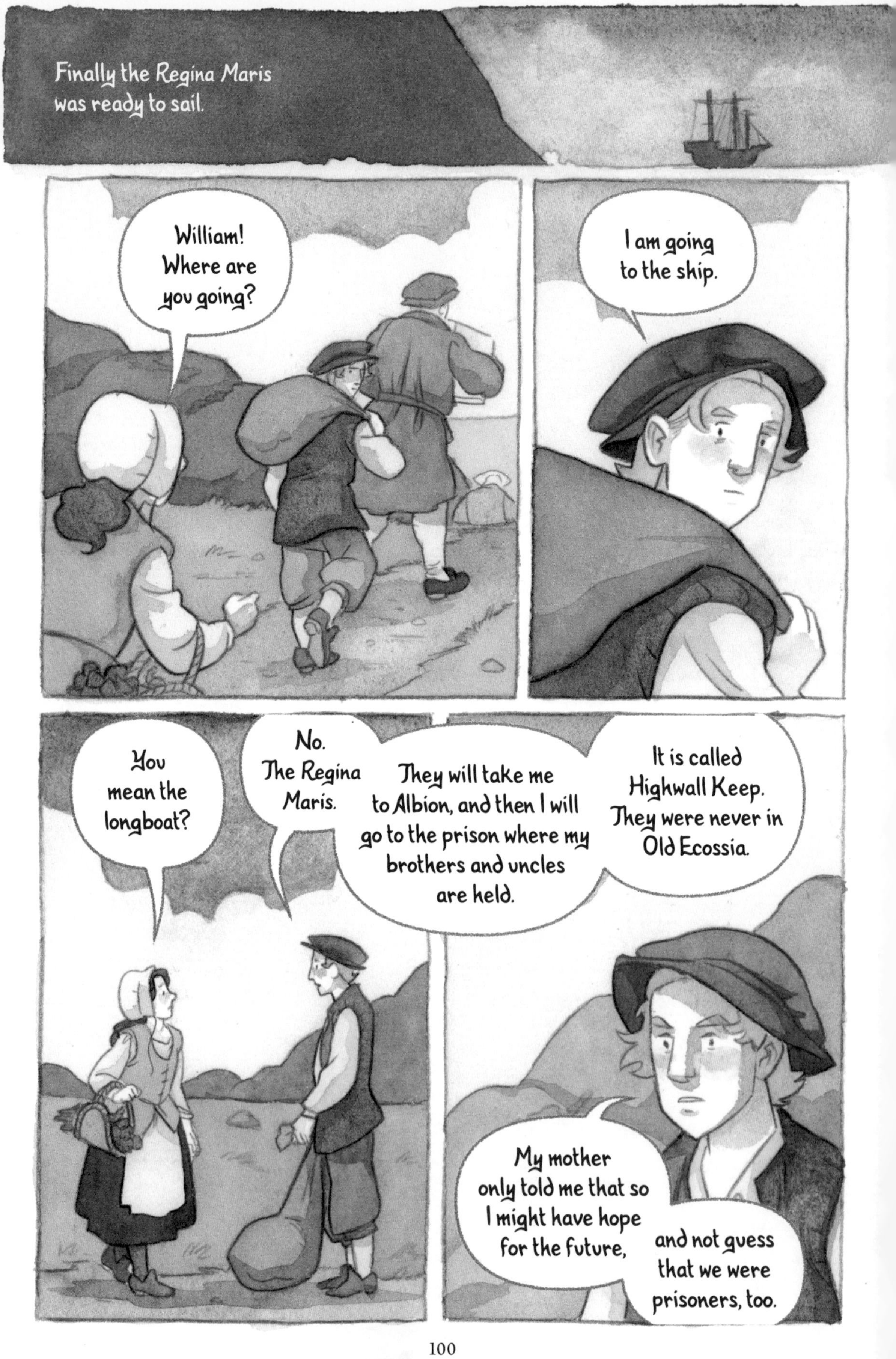

Finally the Regina Maris was ready to sail.
William! Where are you going?
I am going to the ship.
You mean the longboat?
No. The Regina Maris.
They will take me to Albion, and then I will go to the prison where my brothers and uncles are held.
It is called Highwall Keep. They were never in Old Ecossia.
My mother only told me that so I might have hope for the future,
and not guess that we were prisoners, too.

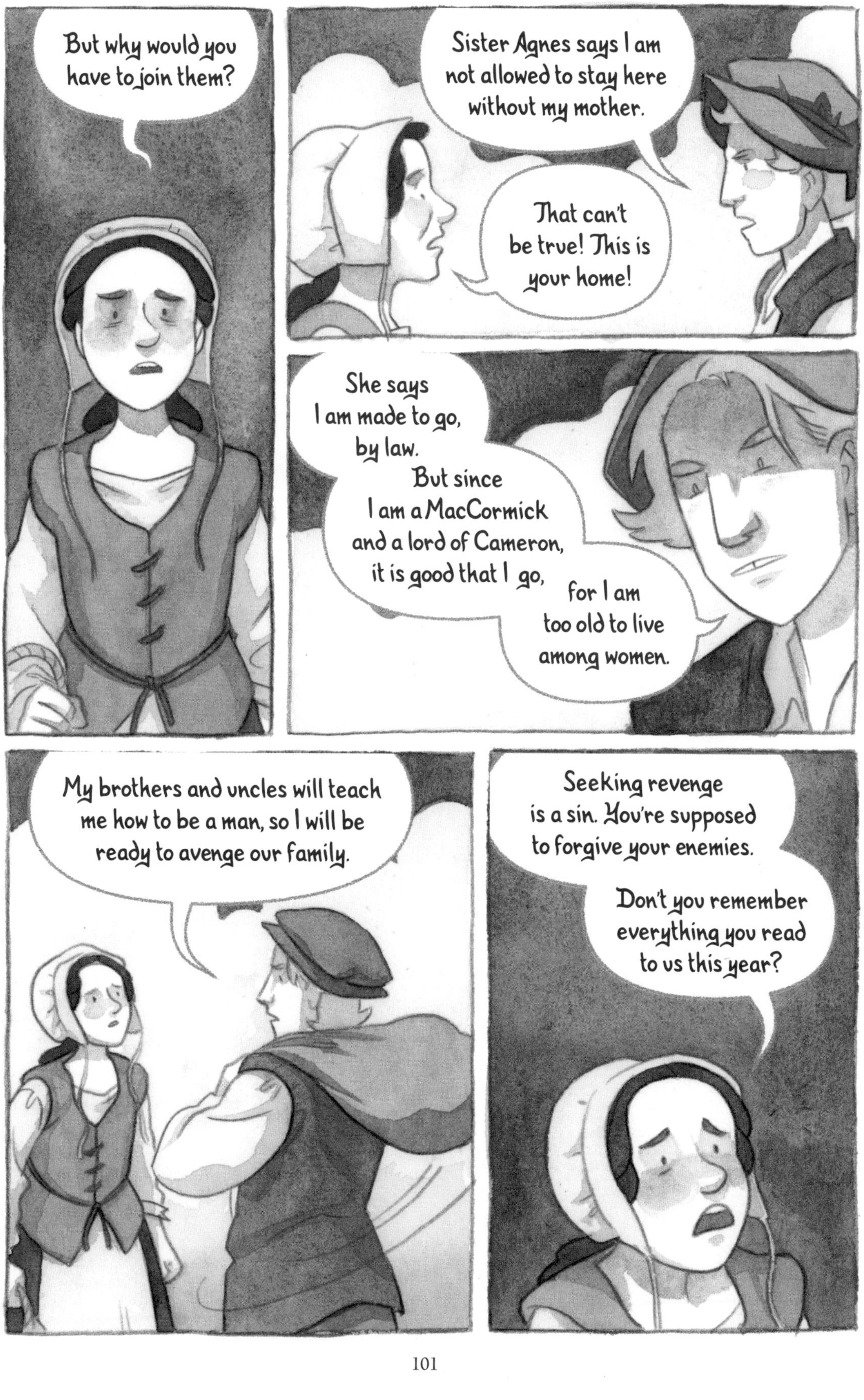
But why would you have to join them?
Sister Agnes says I am not allowed to stay here without my mother.
That can't be true! This is your home!
She says I am made to go, by law.
But since I am a MacCormick and a lord of Cameron, it is good that I go,
for I am too old to live among women.
My brothers and uncles will teach me how to be a man, so I will be ready to avenge our family.
Seeking revenge is a sin. You're supposed to forgive your enemies.
Don't you remember everything you read to us this year?

If there is a war in Albion, I may be free again soon.

Then I will come and rescue you.

Rescue me? You're the one going to prison!

I should rescue you!

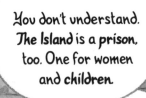

You don't understand. The Island is a prison, too. One for women and children.

Just because you and Lady Cameron were sent here doesn't make it a—

Ask Sister Agnes. Ask her who's allowed to leave the Island!

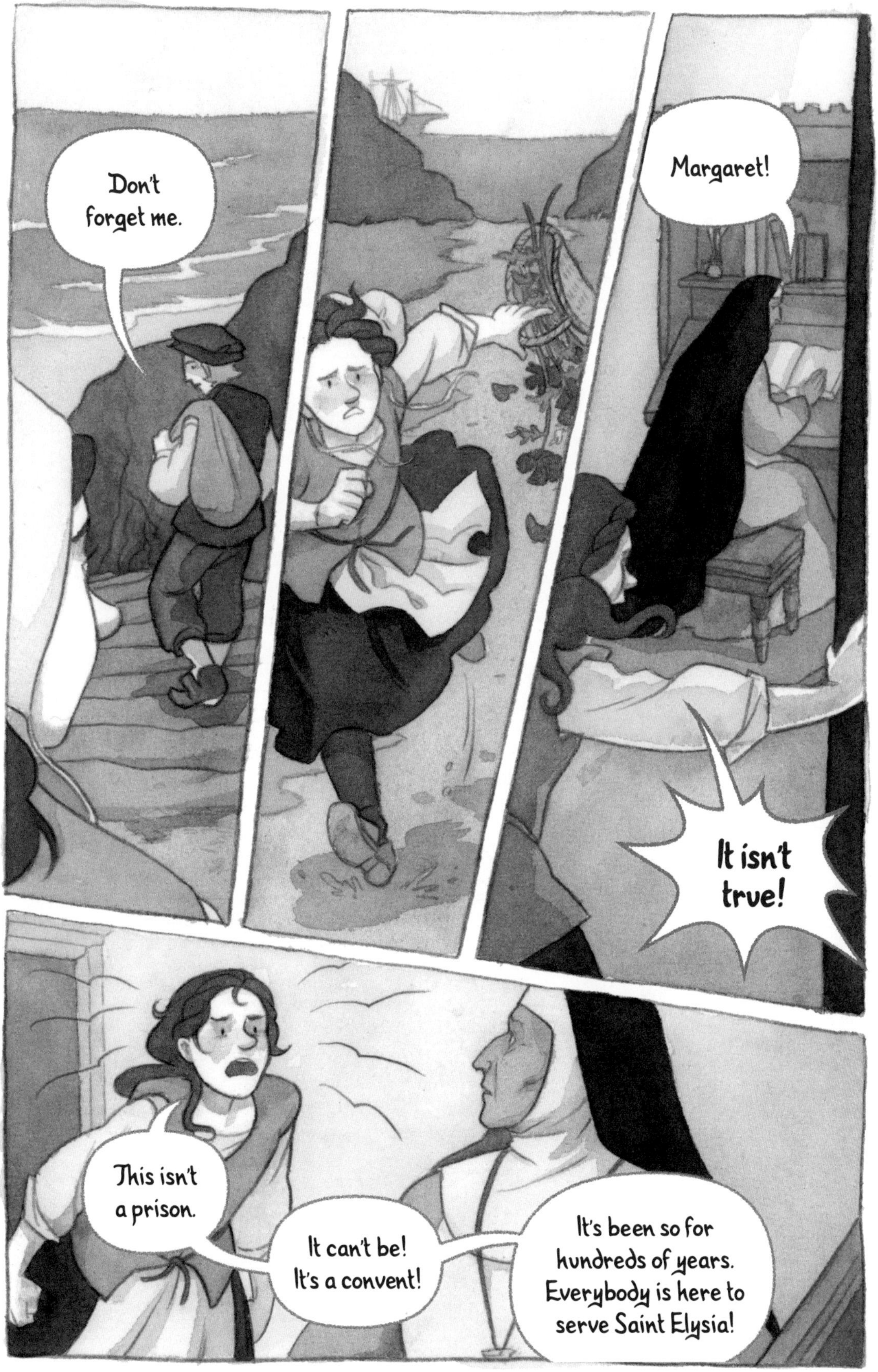
Don't forget me.
Margaret!
It isn't true!
This isn't a prison.
It can't be! It's a convent!
It's been so for hundreds of years. Everybody is here to serve Saint Elysia!

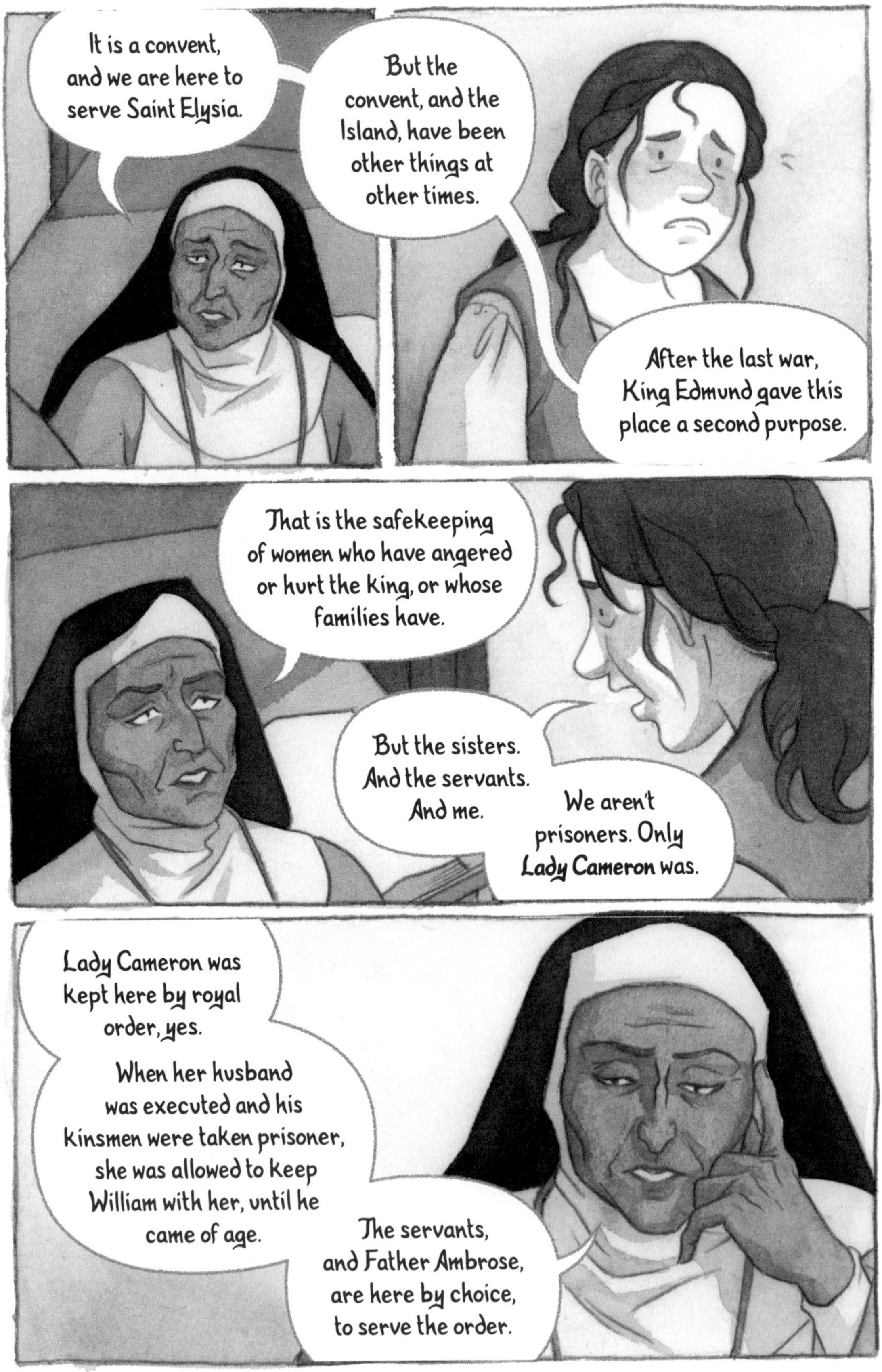
It is a convent, and we are here to serve Saint Elysia.
But the convent, and the Island, have been other things at other times.
After the last war, King Edmund gave this place a second purpose.
That is the safekeeping of women who have angered or hurt the king, or whose families have.
But the sisters. And the servants. And me.
We aren't prisoners. Only Lady Cameron was.
Lady Cameron was kept here by royal order, yes.
When her husband was executed and his kinsmen were taken prisoner, she was allowed to keep William with her, until he came of age.
The servants, and Father Ambrose, are here by choice, to serve the order.

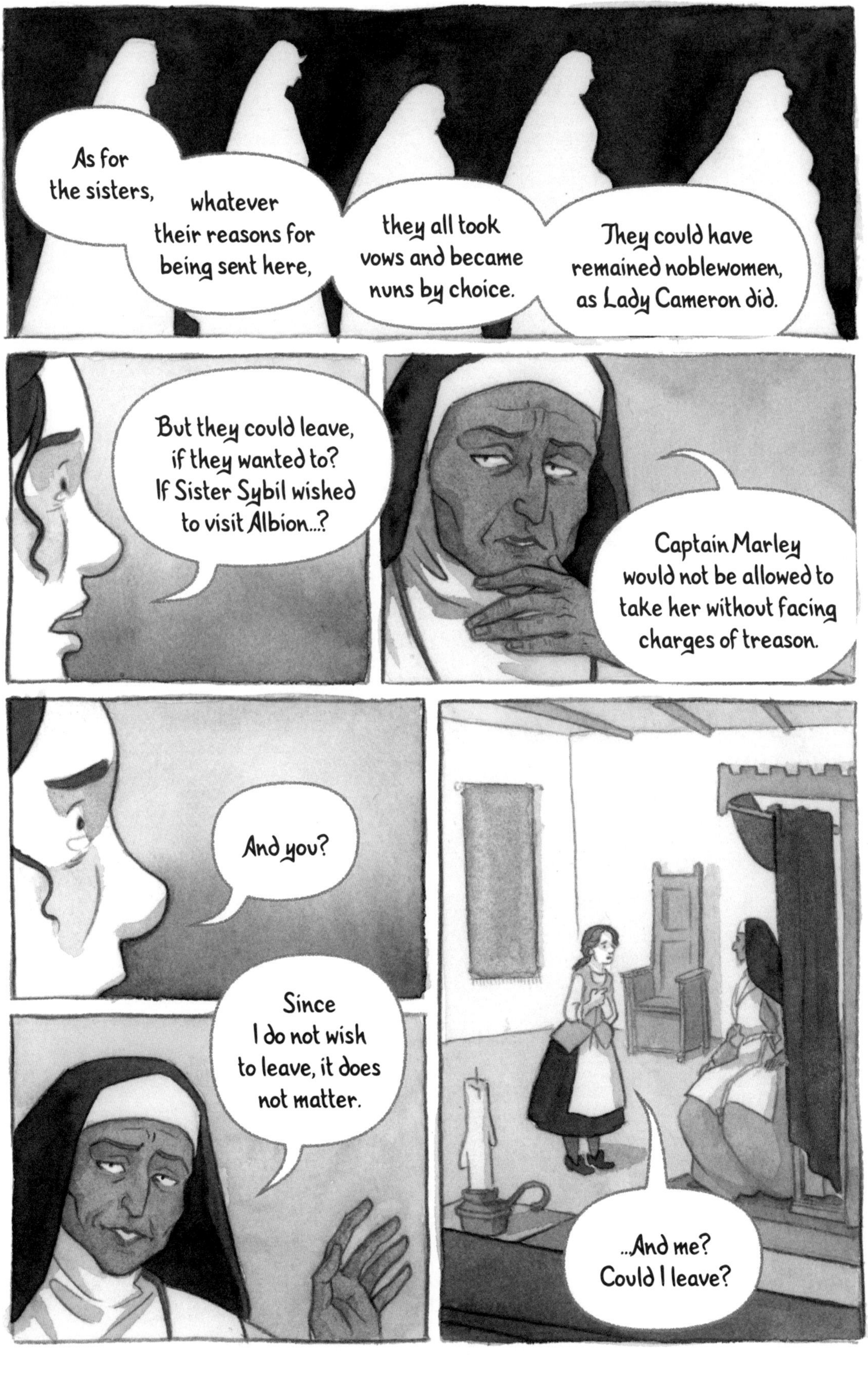
As for the sisters,
whatever their reasons for being sent here,
they all took vows and became nuns by choice.
They could have remained noblewomen, as Lady Cameron did.
But they could leave, if they wanted to? If Sister Sybil wished to visit Albion...?
Captain Marley would not be allowed to take her without facing charges of treason.
And you?
Since I do not wish to leave, it does not matter.
...And me? Could I leave?

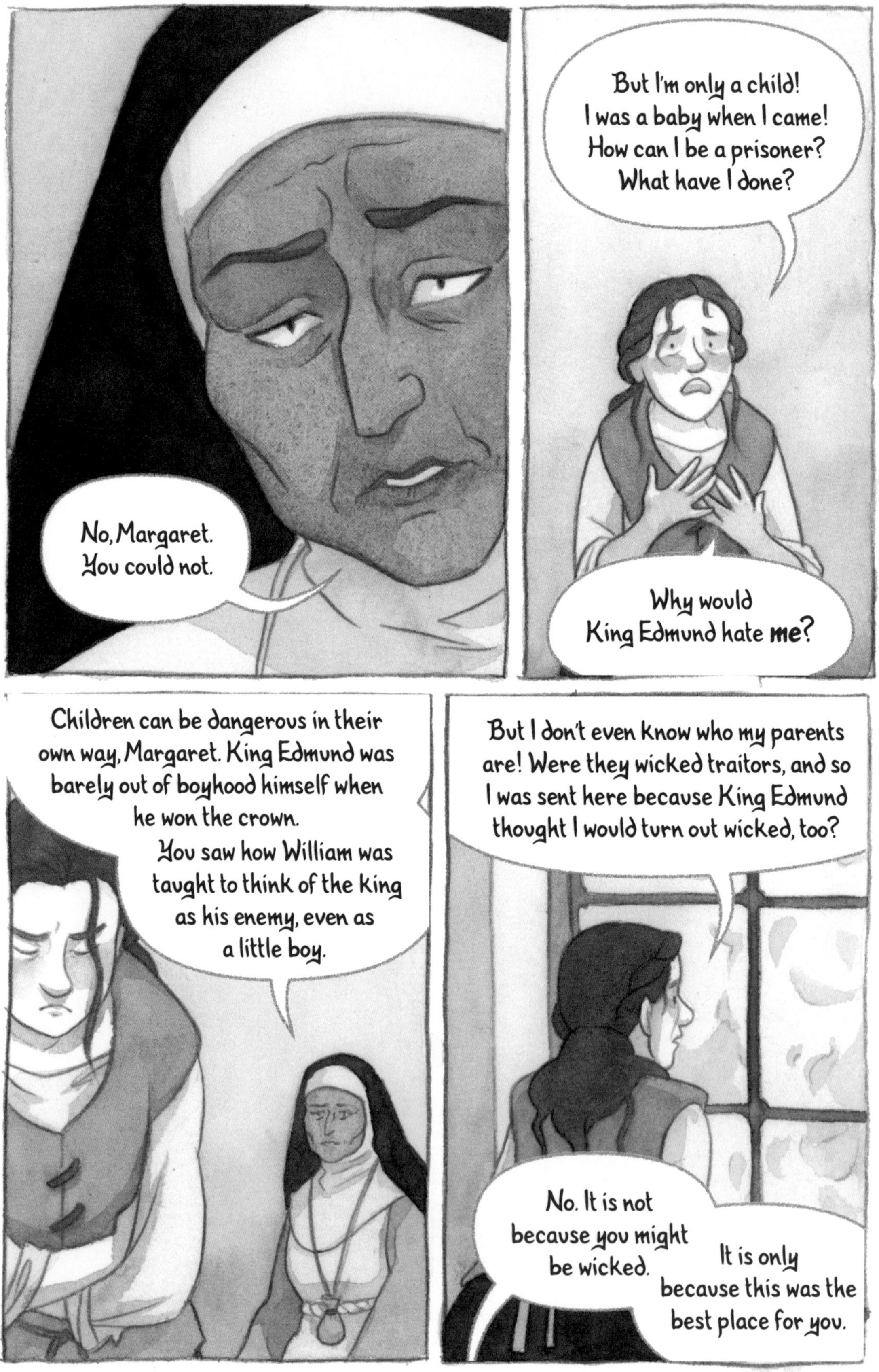

No, Margaret. You could not.
But I'm only a child! I was a baby when I came! How can I be a prisoner? What have I done?
Why would King Edmund hate **me**?
Children can be dangerous in their own way, Margaret. King Edmund was barely out of boyhood himself when he won the crown.
You saw how William was taught to think of the king as his enemy, even as a little boy.
But I don't even know who my parents are! Were they wicked traitors, and so I was sent here because King Edmund thought I would turn out wicked, too?
No. It is not because you might be wicked.
It is only because this was the best place for you.

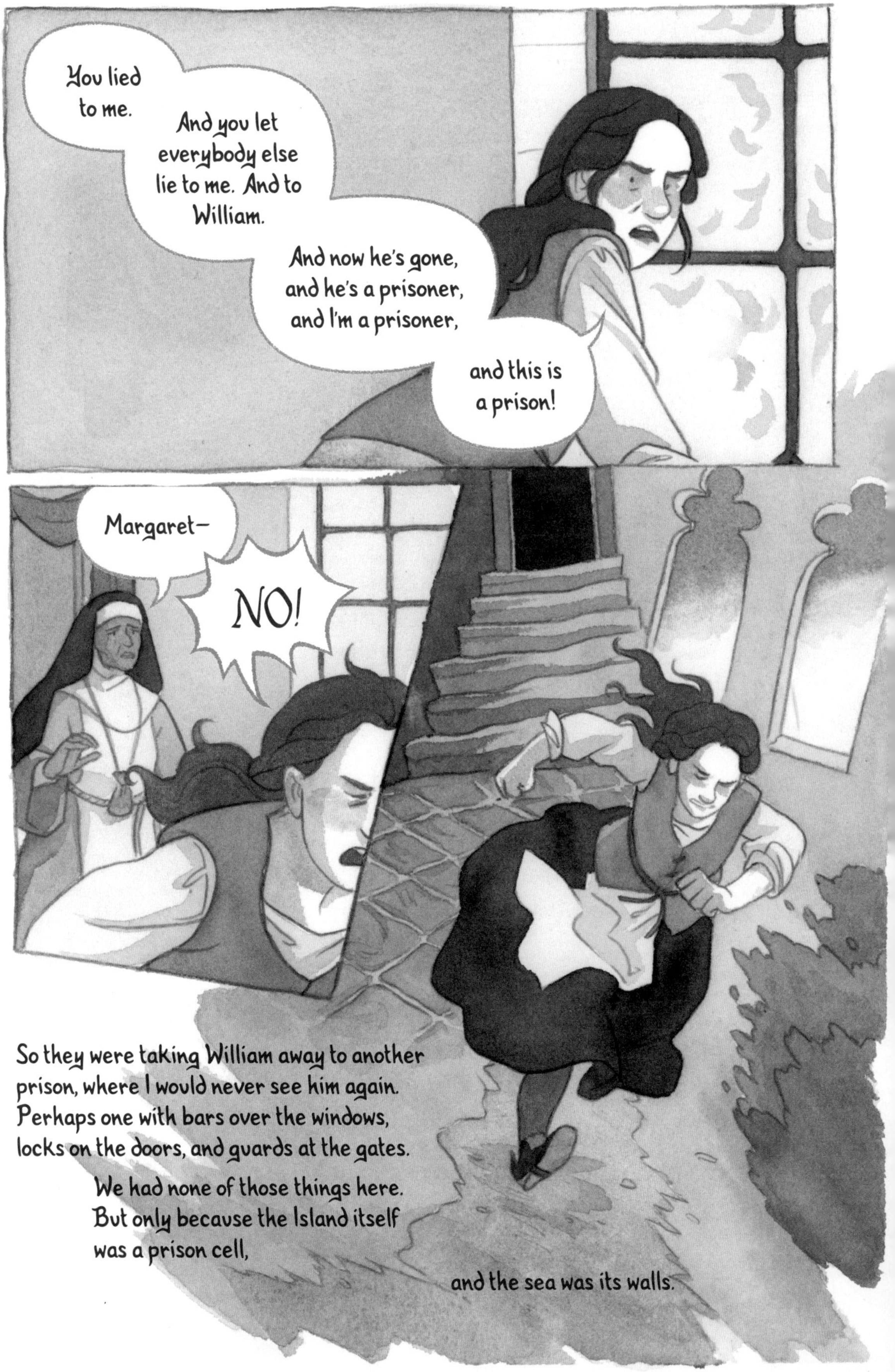
You lied to me.
And you let everybody else lie to me. And to William.
And now he's gone, and he's a prisoner, and I'm a prisoner,
and this is a prison!
Margaret—
NO!
So they were taking William away to another prison, where I would never see him again. Perhaps one with bars over the windows, locks on the doors, and guards at the gates.
We had none of those things here. But only because the Island itself was a prison cell,
and the sea was its walls.

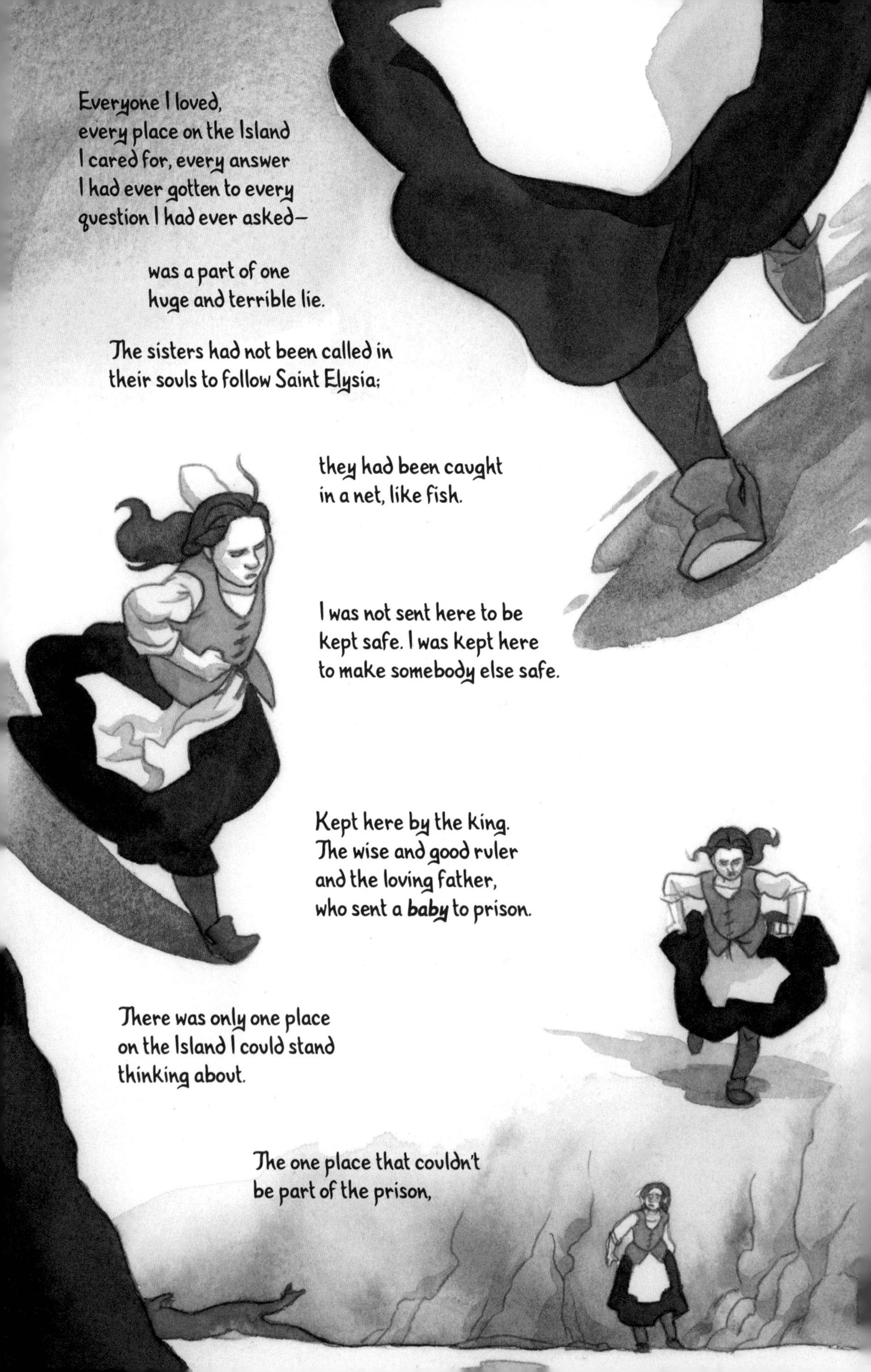
Everyone I loved,
every place on the Island
I cared for, every answer
I had ever gotten to every
question I had ever asked—
was a part of one
huge and terrible lie.
The sisters had not been called in
their souls to follow Saint Elysia;
they had been caught
in a net, like fish.
I was not sent here to be
kept safe. I was kept here
to make somebody else safe.
Kept here by the king.
The wise and good ruler
and the loving father,
who sent a ***baby*** to prison.
There was only one place
on the Island I could stand
thinking about.
The one place that couldn't
be part of the prison,

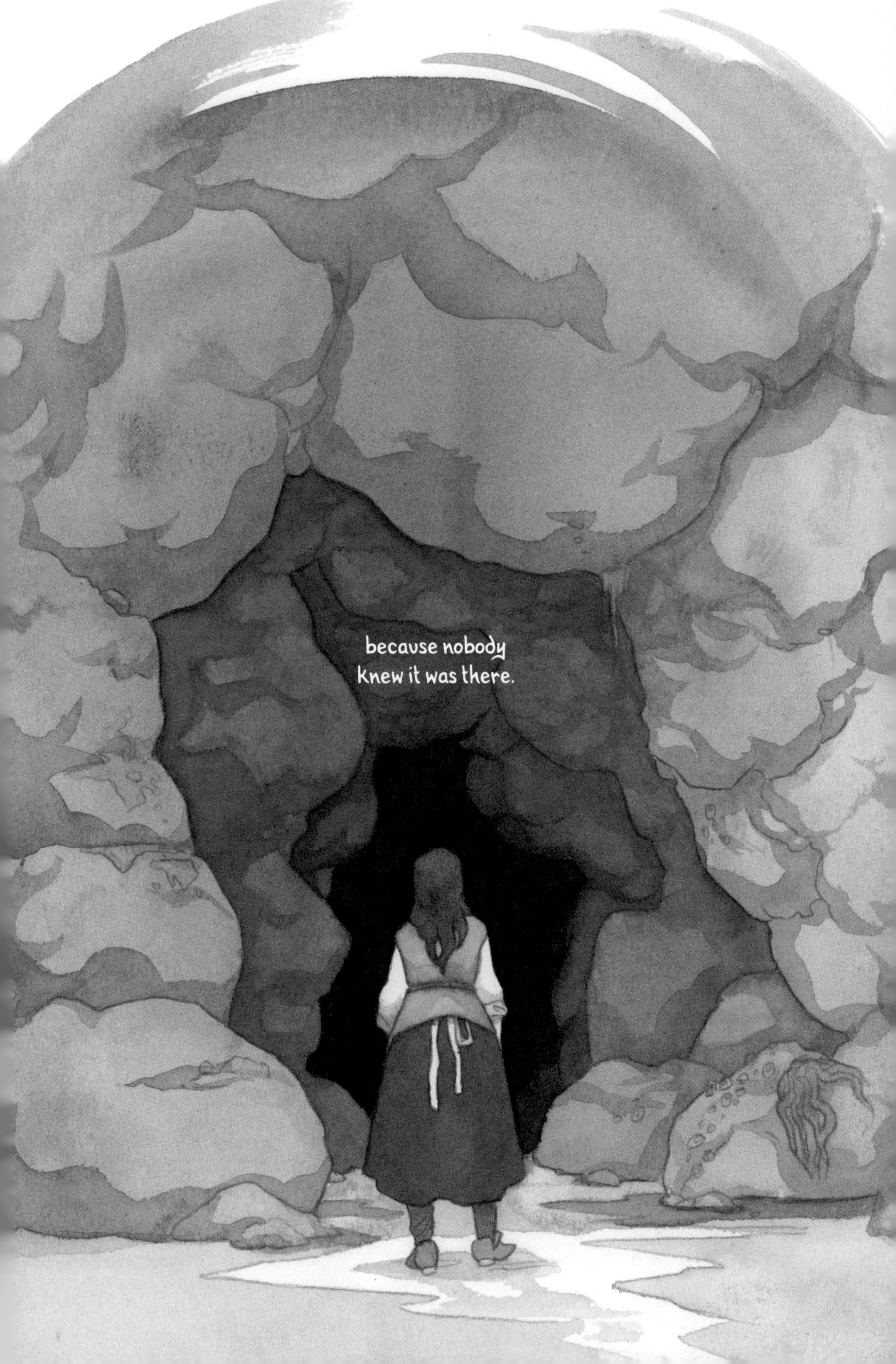
because nobody
knew it was there.

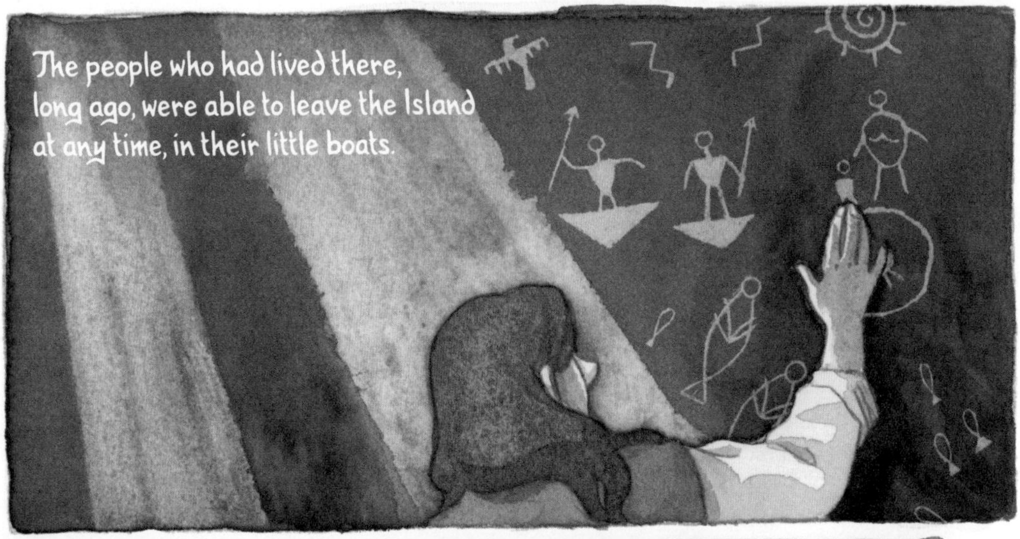
The people who had lived there, long ago, were able to leave the Island at any time, in their little boats.

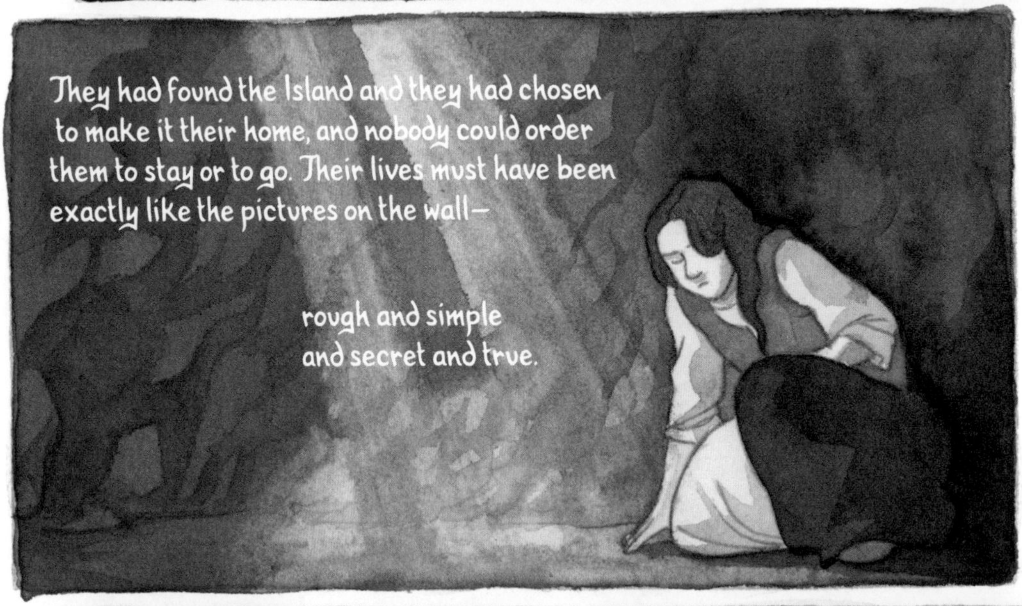
They had found the Island and they had chosen to make it their home, and nobody could order them to stay or to go. Their lives must have been exactly like the pictures on the wall—
rough and simple and secret and true.

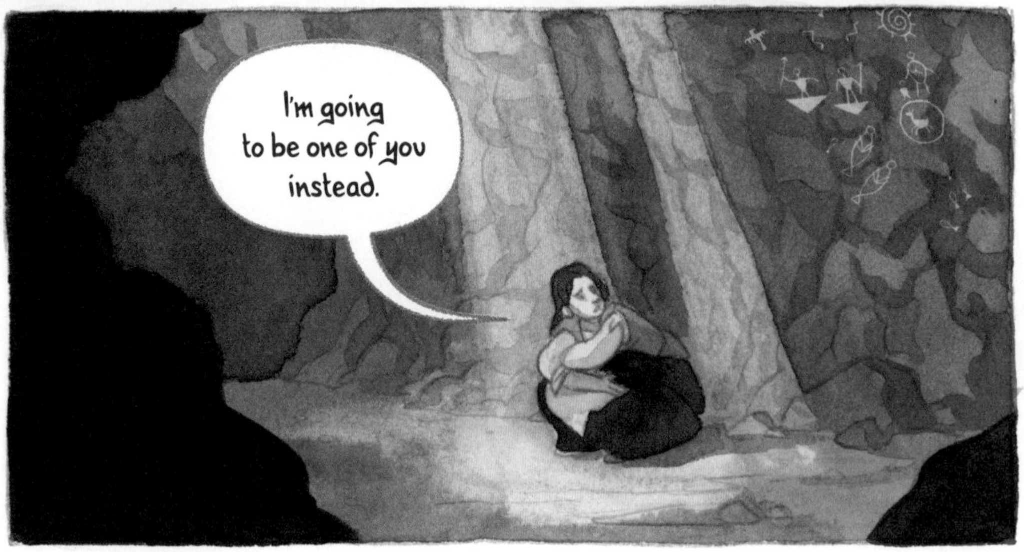
I'm going to be one of you instead.

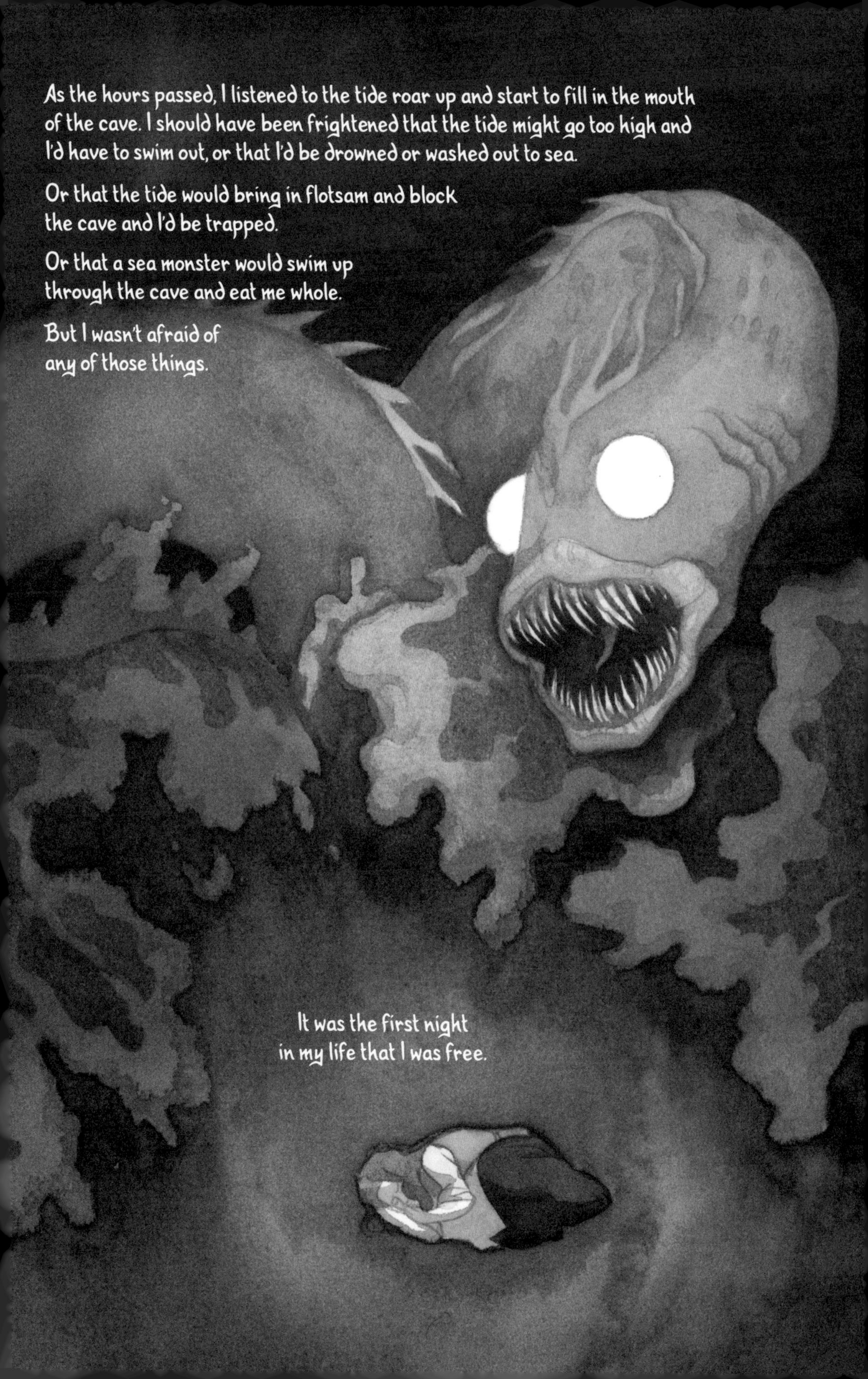
As the hours passed, I listened to the tide roar up and start to fill in the mouth of the cave. I should have been frightened that the tide might go too high and I'd have to swim out, or that I'd be drowned or washed out to sea.
Or that the tide would bring in flotsam and block the cave and I'd be trapped.
Or that a sea monster would swim up through the cave and eat me whole.
But I wasn't afraid of any of those things.
It was the first night in my life that I was free.

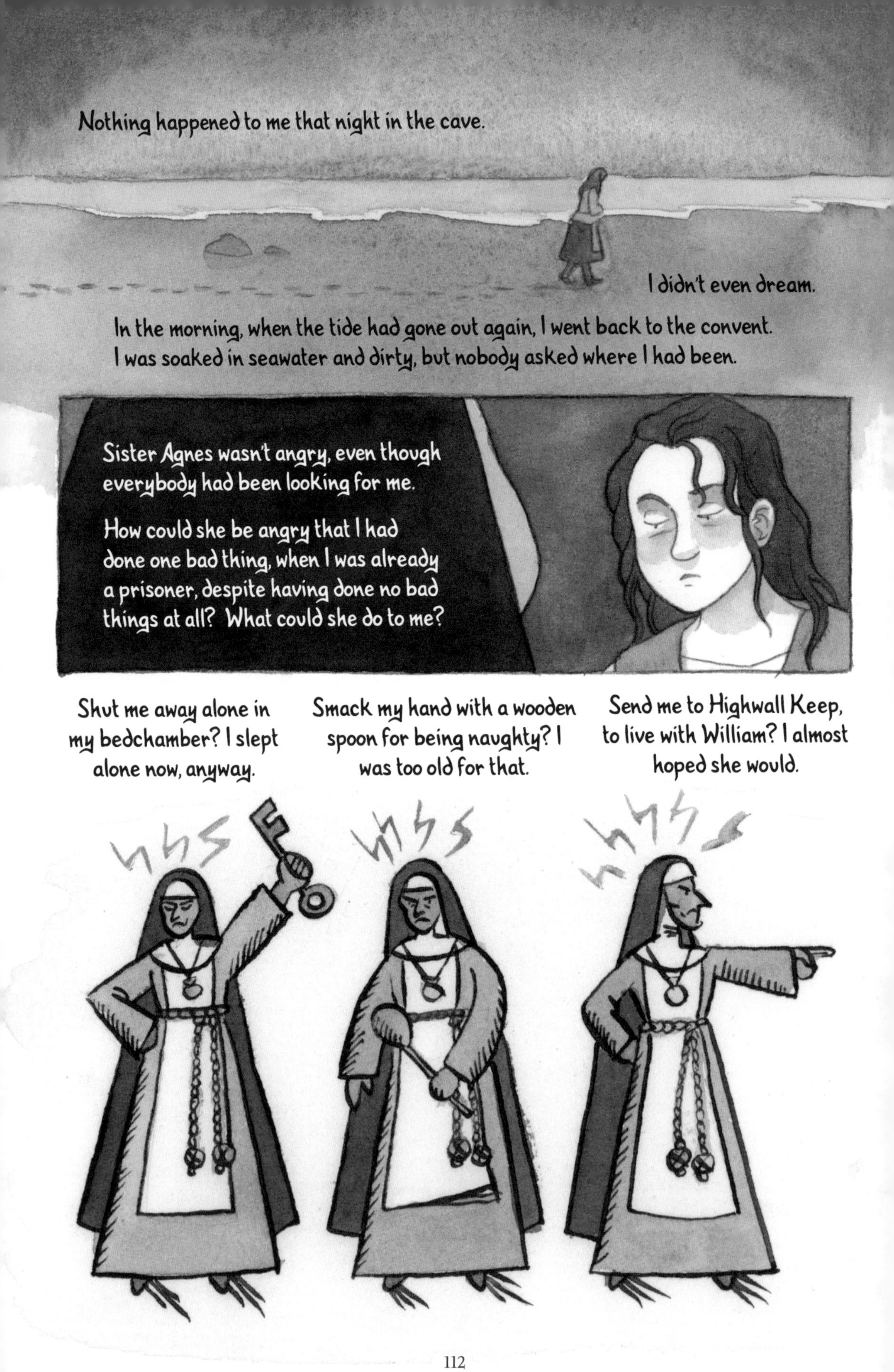
Nothing happened to me that night in the cave.
I didn't even dream.
In the morning, when the tide had gone out again, I went back to the convent. I was soaked in seawater and dirty, but nobody asked where I had been.
Sister Agnes wasn't angry, even though everybody had been looking for me.
How could she be angry that I had done one bad thing, when I was already a prisoner, despite having done no bad things at all? What could she do to me?
Shut me away alone in my bedchamber? I slept alone now, anyway.
Smack my hand with a wooden spoon for being naughty? I was too old for that.
Send me to Highwall Keep, to live with William? I almost hoped she would.

In the end, she made me apologize to
the sisters who went looking for me,
and say extra prayers, and do extra
chores, and read a long, boring book.

That was all.

She didn't even raise her voice.
Nuns aren't supposed to be angry.

But I wasn't a nun.

The days grew longer and
the nights grew shorter.

The rooster was let in
with one of the hens and
there were new chicks,
but I didn't visit them.

I embroidered a perfect rose.
Lady Cameron would have
been proud of me.

I threw it in the fire.

The Regina Maris
came on time, and left
again. Captain Marley
gave Sister Agnes news from the
wicked world. I didn't see him at all.

He snuck in and out, like a thief.

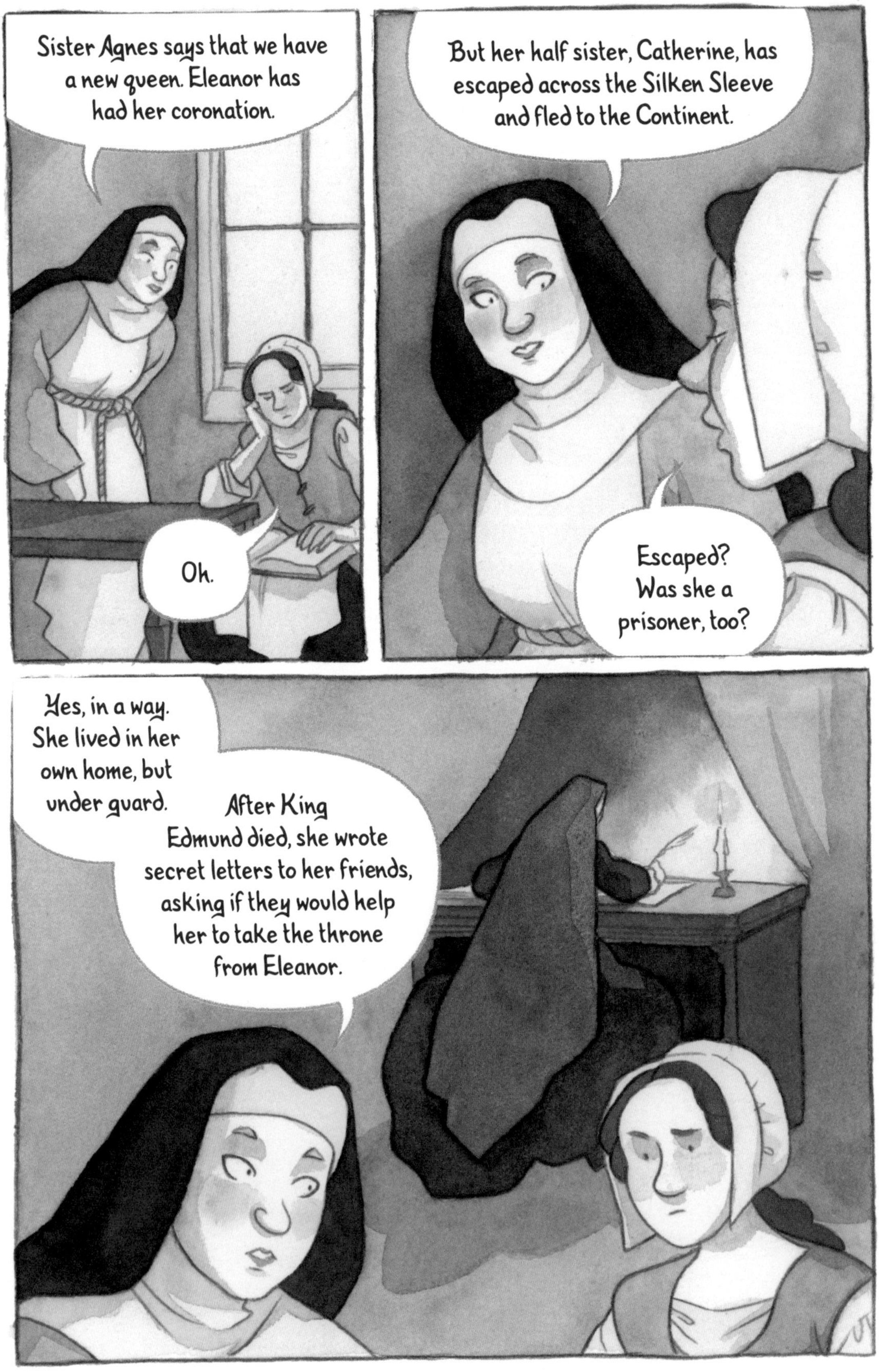
Sister Agnes says that we have a new queen. Eleanor has had her coronation.
Oh.
But her half sister, Catherine, has escaped across the Silken Sleeve and fled to the Continent.
Escaped? Was she a prisoner, too?
Yes, in a way. She lived in her own home, but under guard.
After King Edmund died, she wrote secret letters to her friends, asking if they would help her to take the throne from Eleanor.

I didn't know writing letters was a crime.

Just because a person has not yet done something wrong doesn't mean they have no plan to.

I began to wonder more about why each of the sisters had been sent to the Island. If I could find out what they had done wrong—or **thought** about doing wrong—

maybe I would have a better idea about why I was sent here.

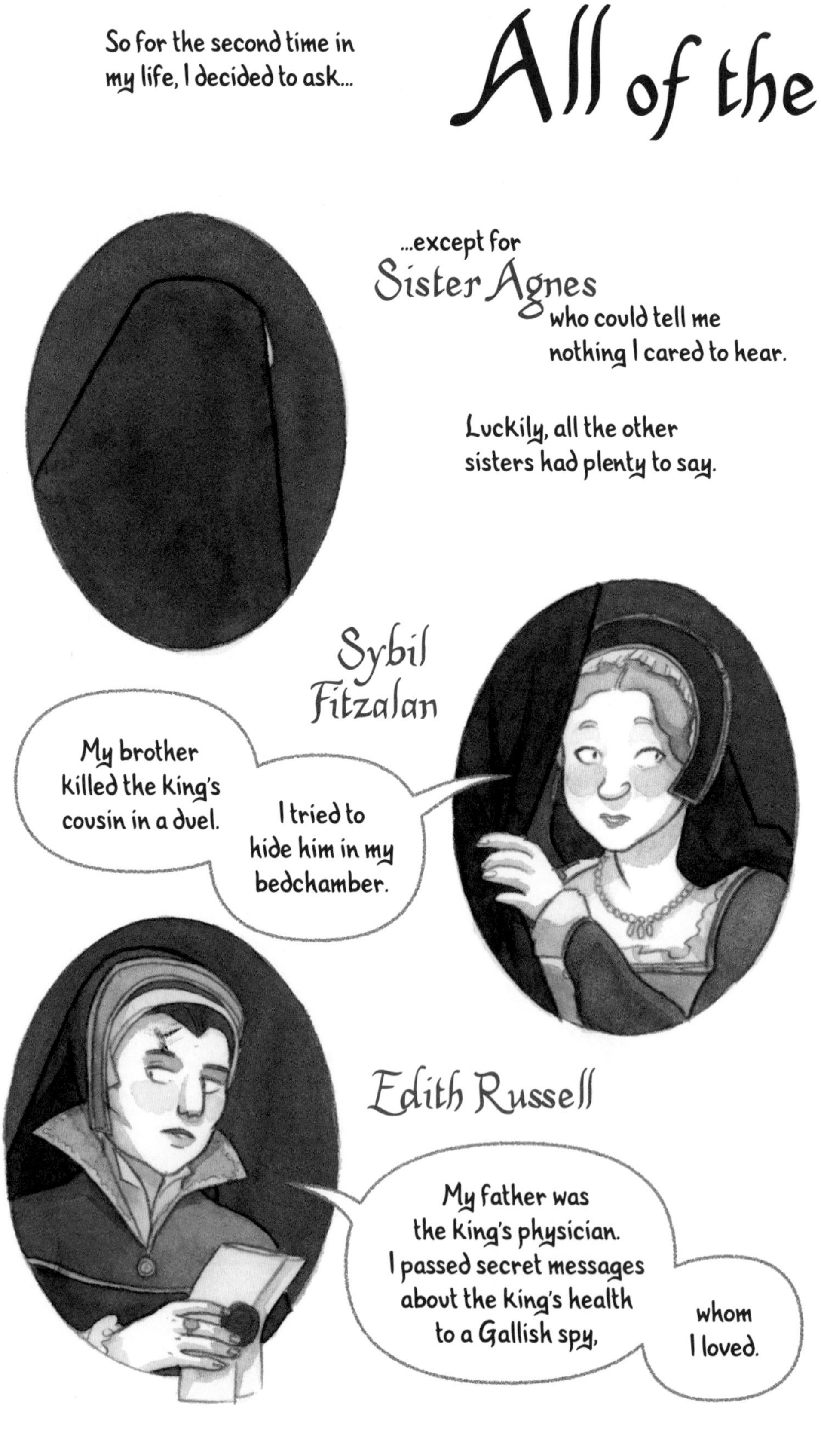
So for the second time in my life, I decided to ask...
All of the
...except for
Sister Agnes
who could tell me nothing I cared to hear.
Luckily, all the other sisters had plenty to say.
Sybil Fitzalan
My brother killed the king's cousin in a duel.
I tried to hide him in my bedchamber.
Edith Russell
My father was the king's physician. I passed secret messages about the king's health to a Gallish spy,
whom I loved.

Sisters

Barbara Chatwyn

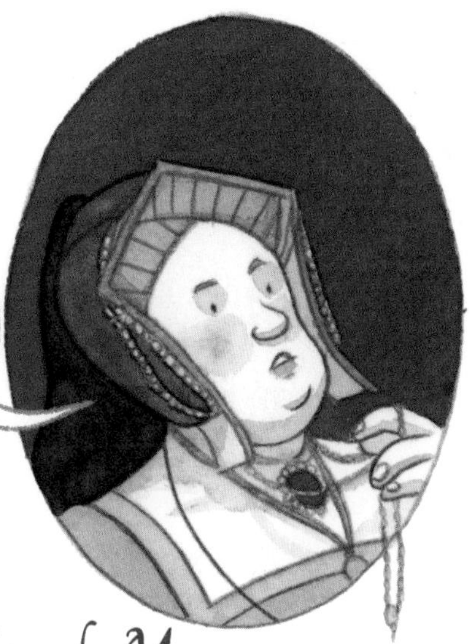
I was Lady of the Bedchamber to Queen Joan.
I stole jewels from her cabinet to pay off my family's debts.

Wynefreed More

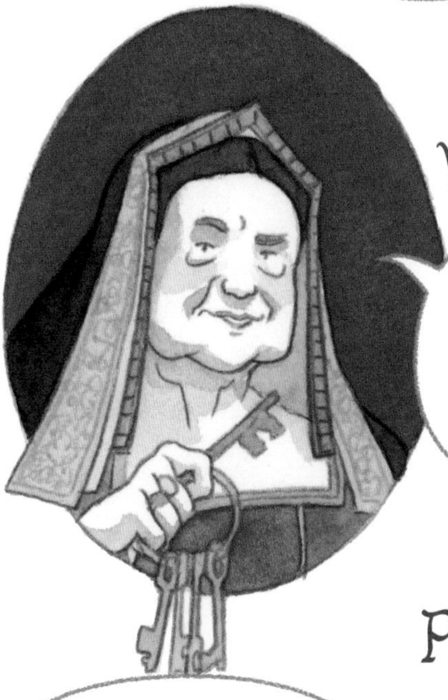
While he was fighting for the crown, Edmund tried to rest his troops at our manor.
I locked the door against him!

Philippa Cecil

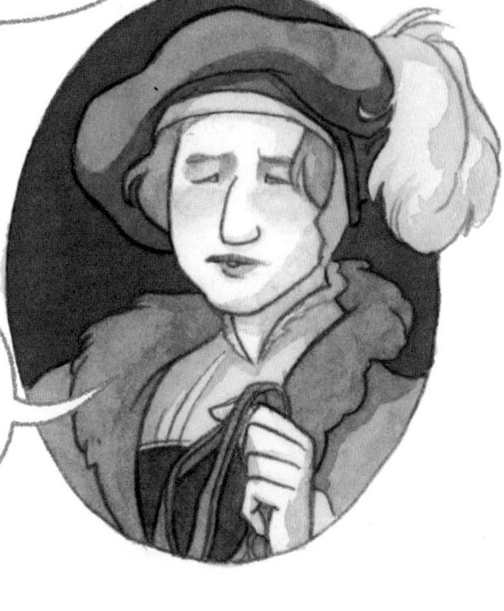
My husband was Master of the Horse. During a hunt, the king was thrown from his mare, and my husband was accused of plotting it.
I was sent here after his execution.

I certainly learned a great deal from this. Some of the sisters had been very wicked, indeed; some seemed guilty of nothing but bad luck.

I wasn't sure, though, that I had learned anything useful.

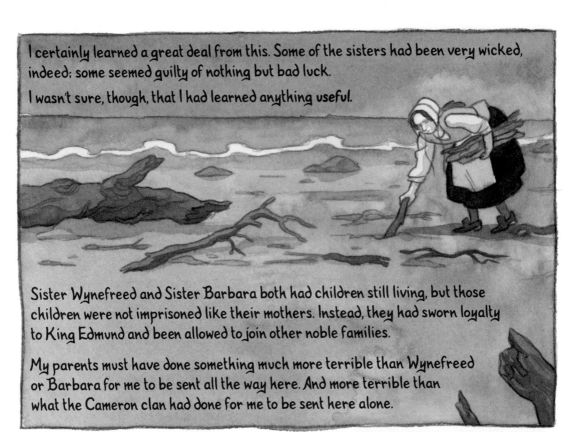

Sister Wynefreed and Sister Barbara both had children still living, but those children were not imprisoned like their mothers. Instead, they had sworn loyalty to King Edmund and been allowed to join other noble families.

My parents must have done something much more terrible than Wynefreed or Barbara for me to be sent all the way here. And more terrible than what the Cameron clan had done for me to be sent here alone.

Maybe my father had tried to murder the king.

Maybe my mother was a spy from Gallia or Hispania!

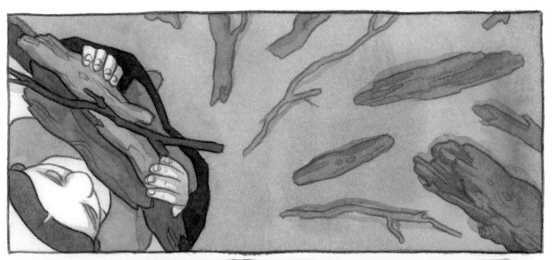

A ship.

It wasn't merely passing by on its way around Albion, or out to the sea.

It was coming toward the Island.

And it was not the Regina Maris.

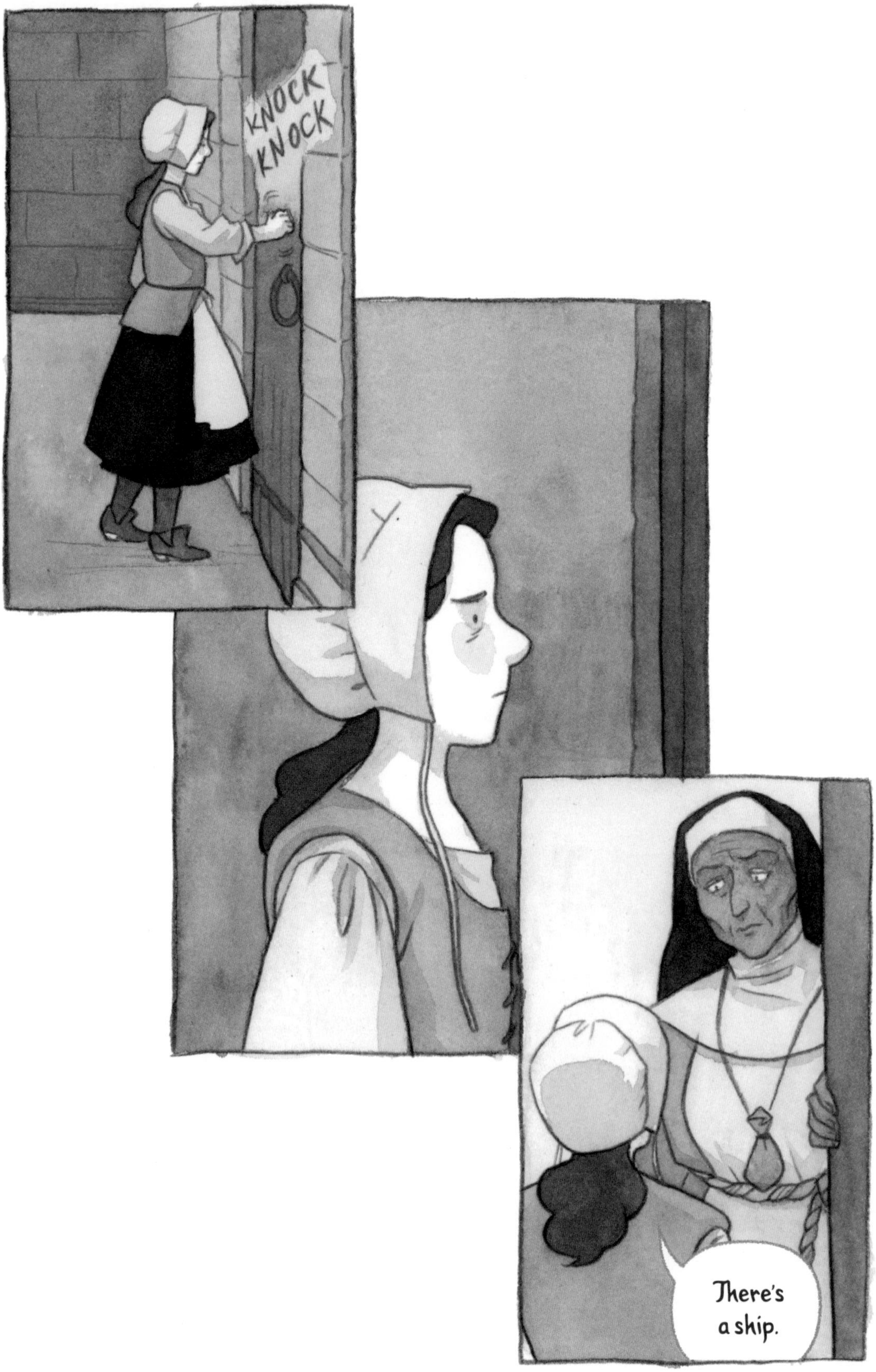
KNOCK KNOCK
There's a ship.

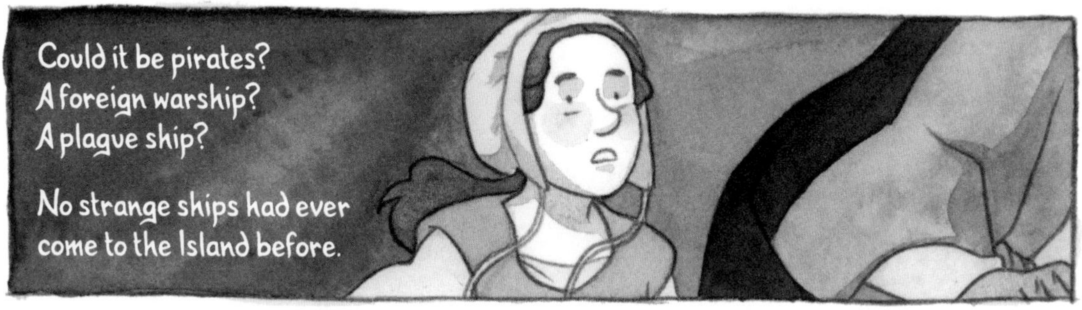
Could it be pirates?
A foreign warship?
A plague ship?
No strange ships had ever come to the Island before.

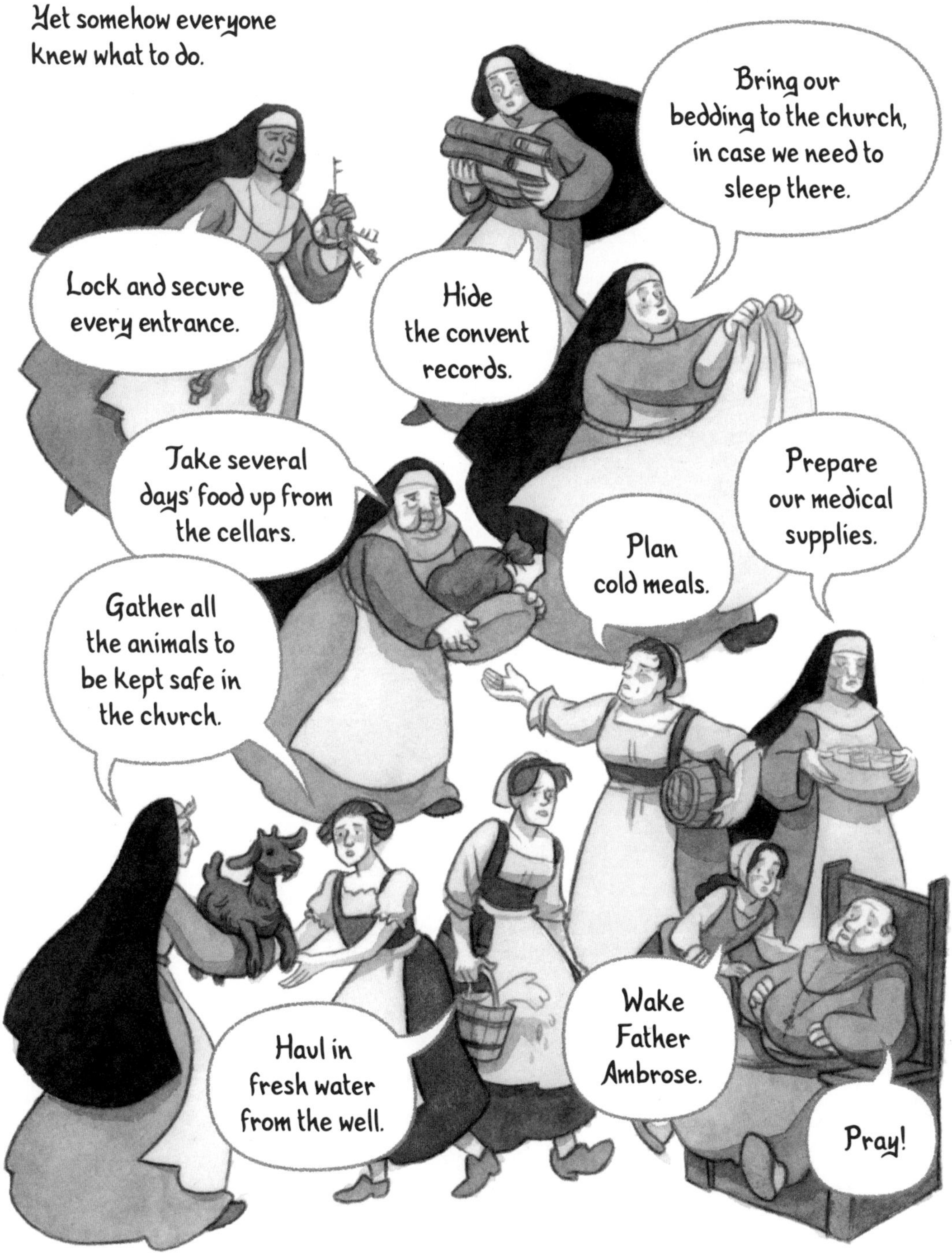
Yet somehow everyone knew what to do.
Bring our bedding to the church, in case we need to sleep there.
Lock and secure every entrance.
Hide the convent records.
Take several days' food up from the cellars.
Prepare our medical supplies.
Plan cold meals.
Gather all the animals to be kept safe in the church.
Haul in fresh water from the well.
Wake Father Ambrose.
Pray!

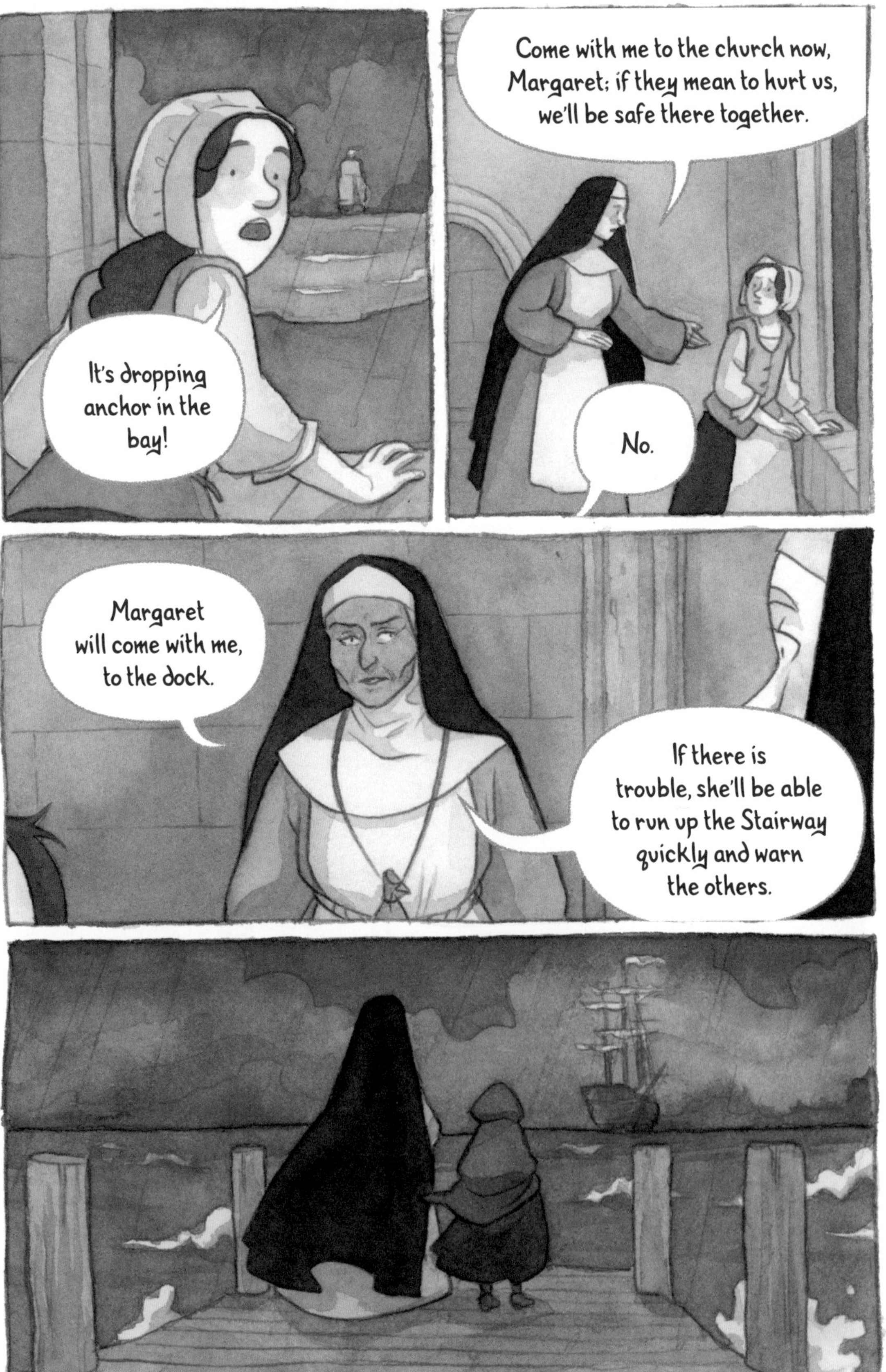

It's dropping anchor in the bay!
Come with me to the church now, Margaret; if they mean to hurt us, we'll be safe there together.
No.
Margaret will come with me, to the dock.
If there is trouble, she'll be able to run up the Stairway quickly and warn the others.

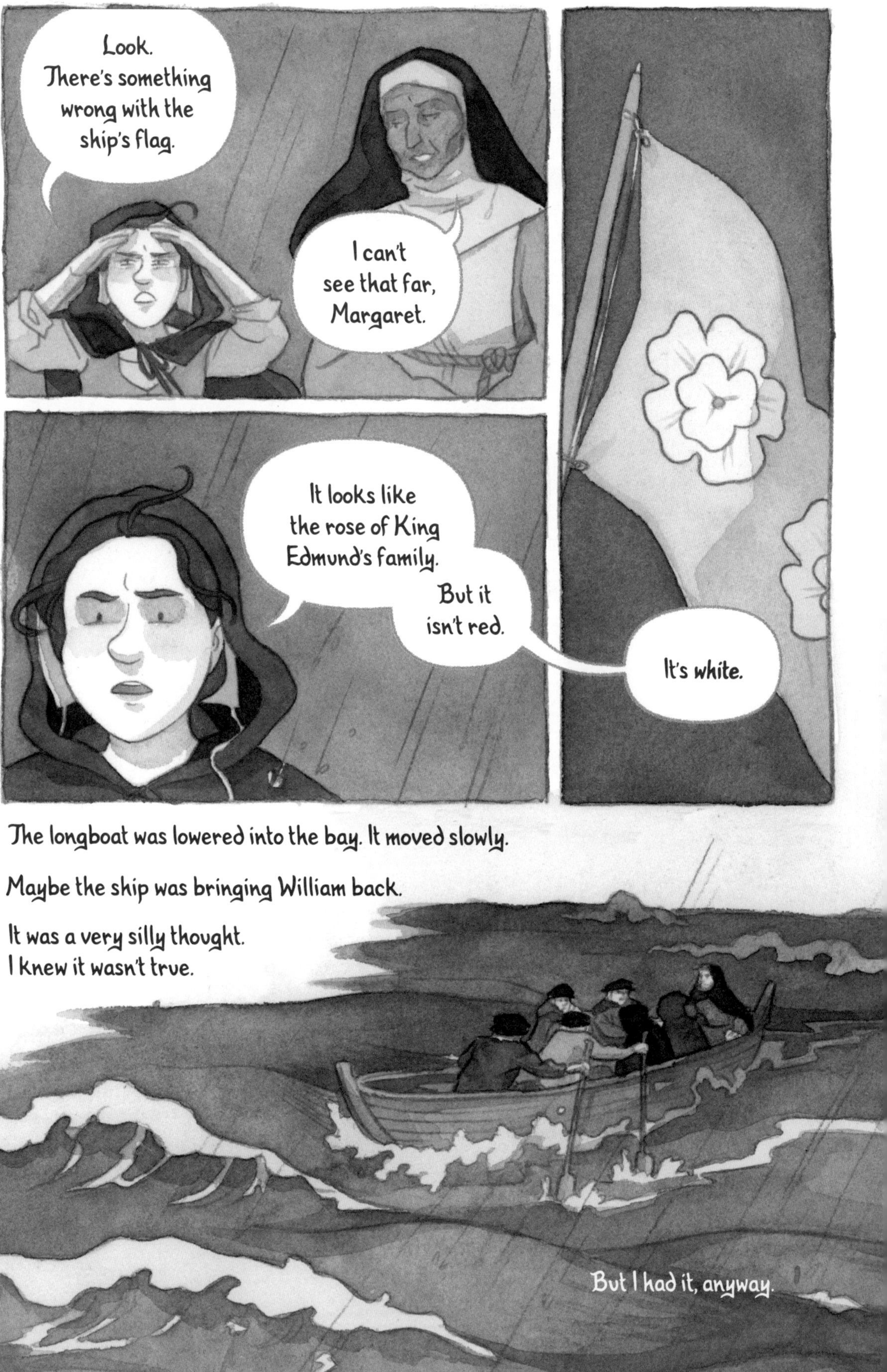
Look. There's something wrong with the ship's flag.
I can't see that far, Margaret.
It looks like the rose of King Edmund's family.
But it isn't red.
It's white.
The longboat was lowered into the bay. It moved slowly.
Maybe the ship was bringing William back.
It was a very silly thought.
I knew it wasn't true.
But I had it, anyway.

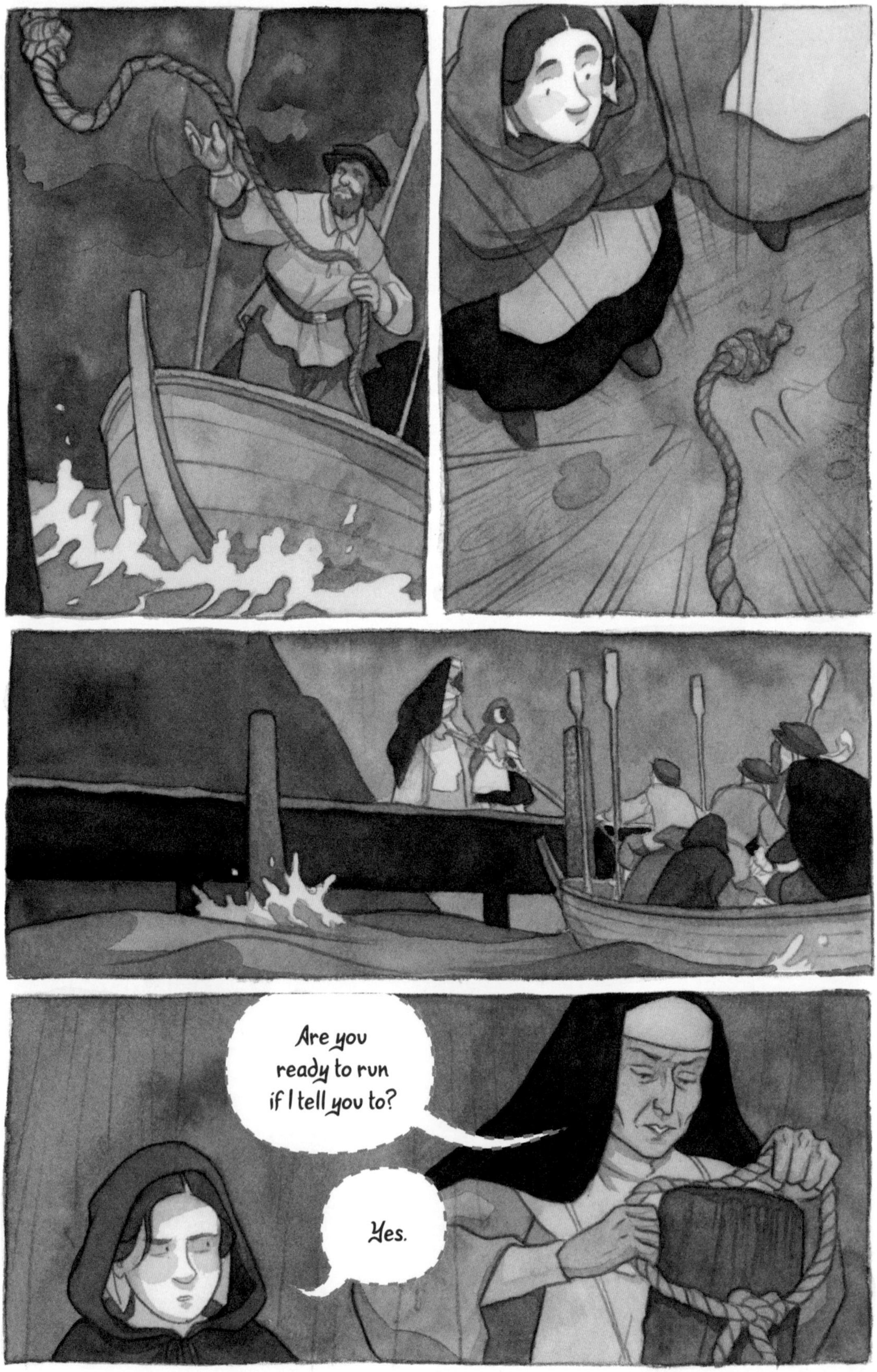
Are you ready to run if I tell you to?
Yes.

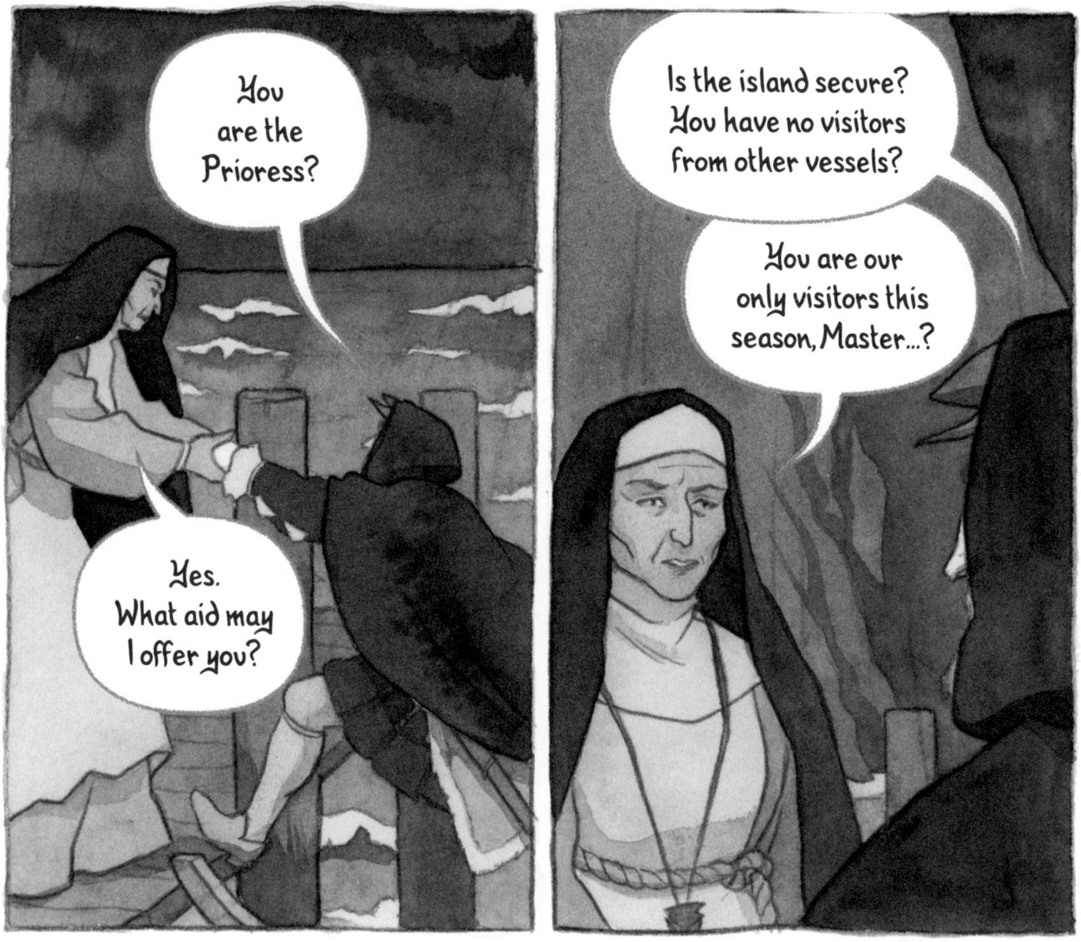
You are the Prioress?
Yes. What aid may I offer you?
Is the island secure? You have no visitors from other vessels?
You are our only visitors this season, Master...?

I am *Sir John Worsley, Baron Hapsworth.*

It falls to me to tell you that the pretender to the throne, *Lady Eleanor*, has been captured at sea, and Her Majesty Queen Catherine has begun her rightful reign.

We sail under Her pennant, and I serve at Her Majesty's pleasure.

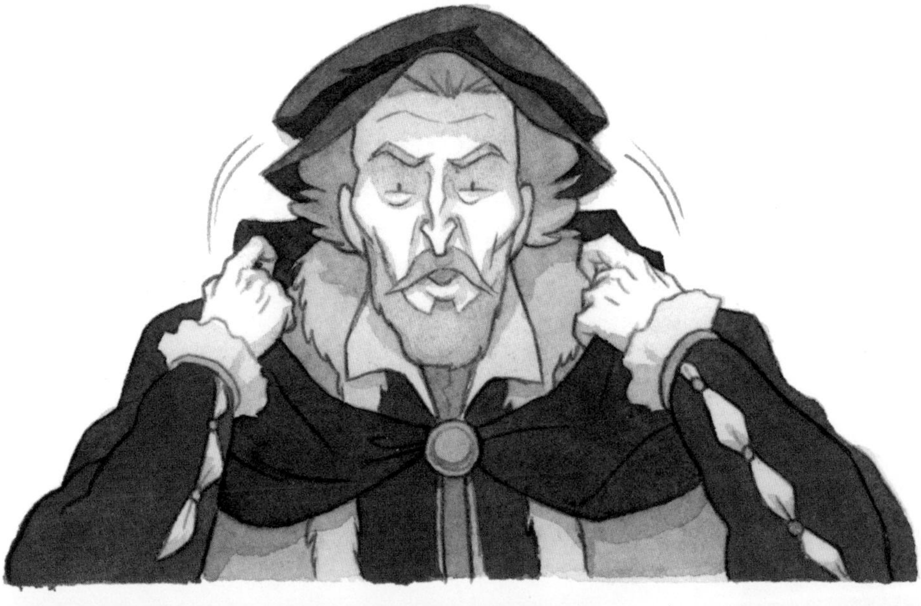

Old Kate was queen!

Would she be more forgiving than her father, after all the terrible things that had happened to her? She had lost her title and her mother and her freedom. Surely she wouldn't want to cause those same things to happen to anybody else.

Maybe Sir John had come to tell us
that everybody on the Island was—

Pardoned
and free!

It was not that I didn't love the Island.

But knowing that I had no choice in living
there had changed it from a wonderful place—
the *only* place—

to a grim one.

I did not want to go to Albion, where it seemed
even an innocent baby could be hated.

I only wanted to be free so that
I would have the Island, **my** Island—

back again.

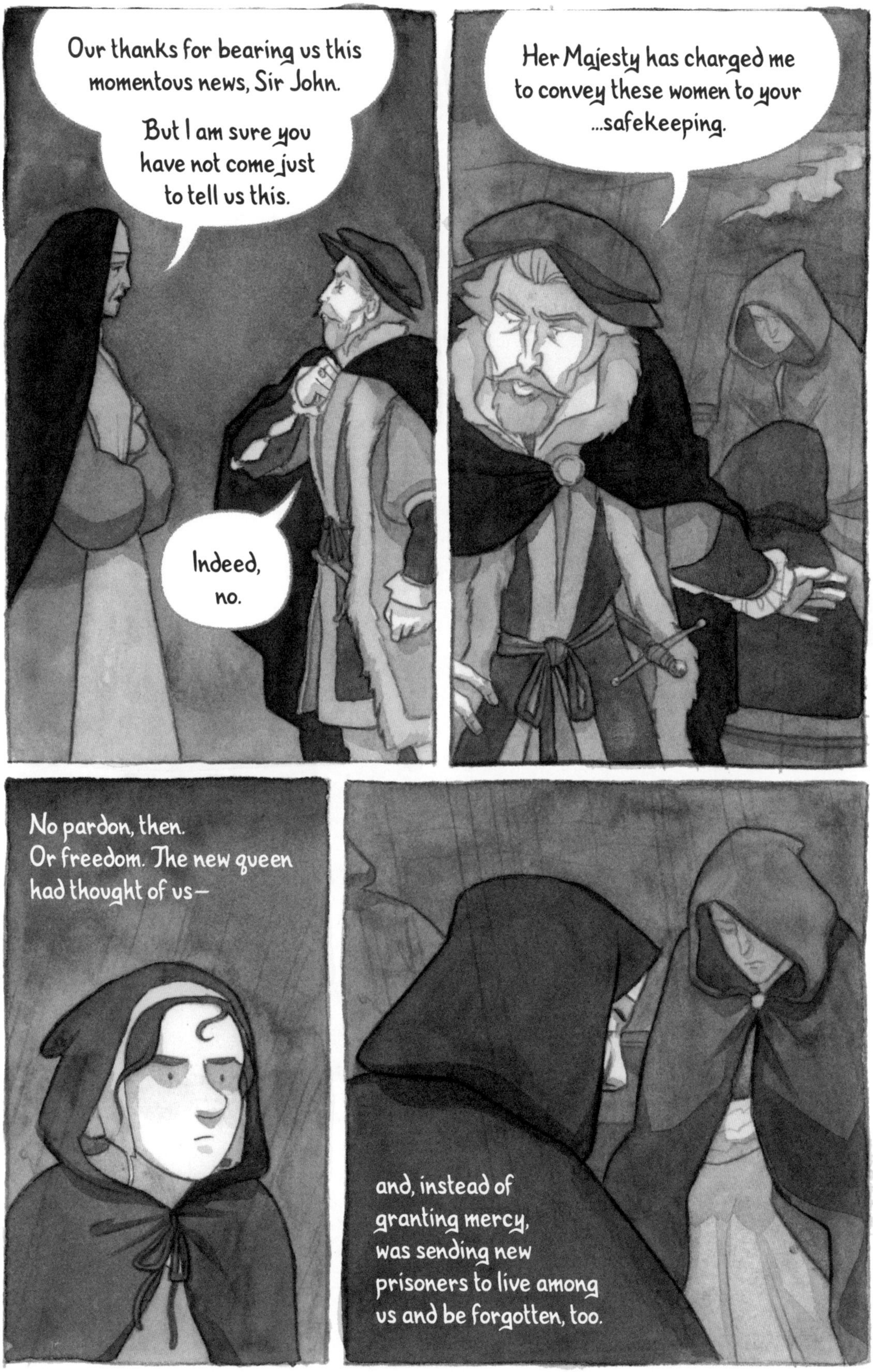
Our thanks for bearing us this momentous news, Sir John.
But I am sure you have not come just to tell us this.
Indeed, no.
Her Majesty has charged me to convey these women to your ...safekeeping.
No pardon, then. Or freedom. The new queen had thought of us—
and, instead of granting mercy, was sending new prisoners to live among us and be forgotten, too.

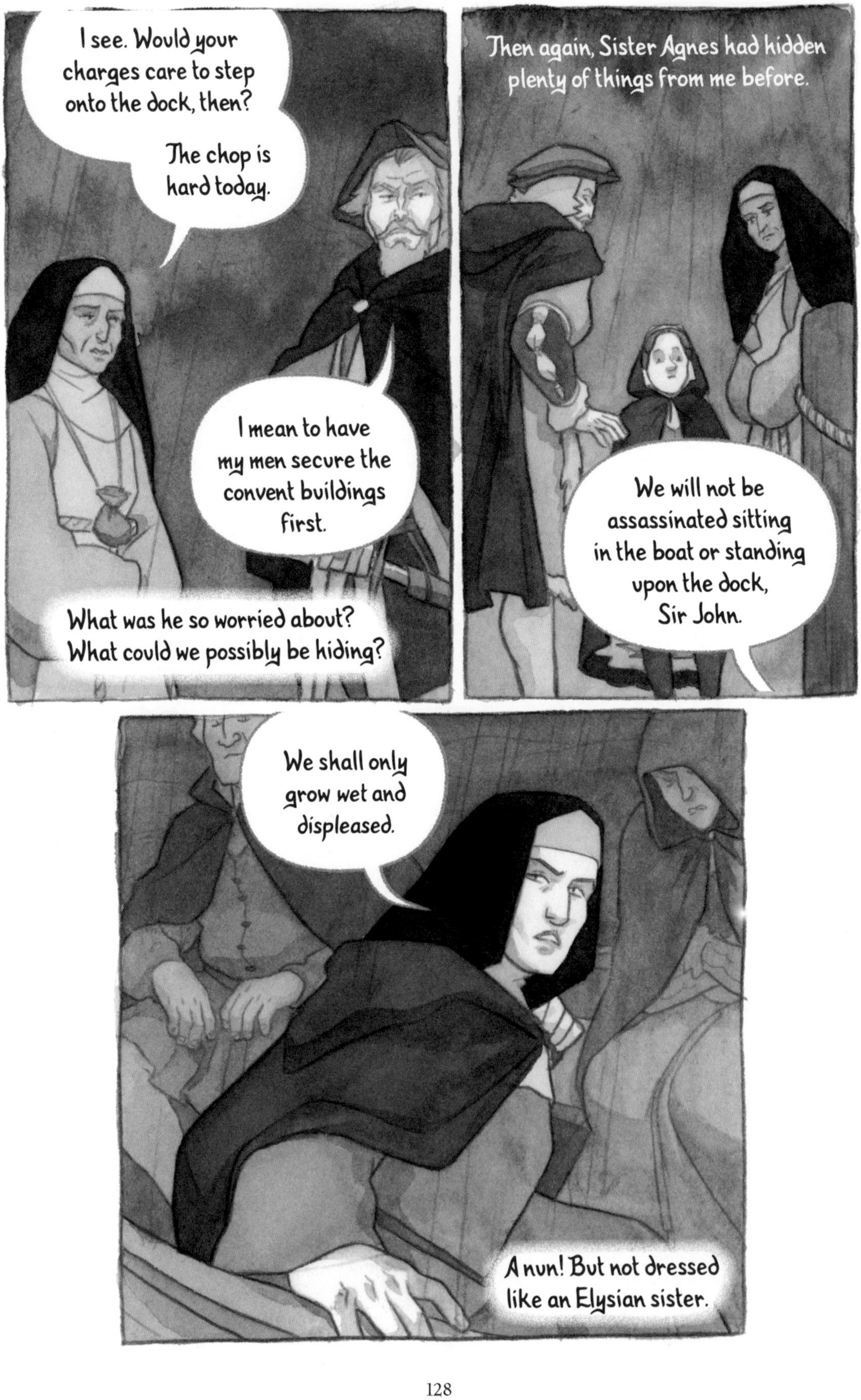
I see. Would your charges care to step onto the dock, then?
The chop is hard today.
I mean to have my men secure the convent buildings first.
What was he so worried about? What could we possibly be hiding?
Then again, Sister Agnes had hidden plenty of things from me before.
We will not be assassinated sitting in the boat or standing upon the dock, Sir John.
We shall only grow wet and displeased.
A nun! But not dressed like an Elysian sister.

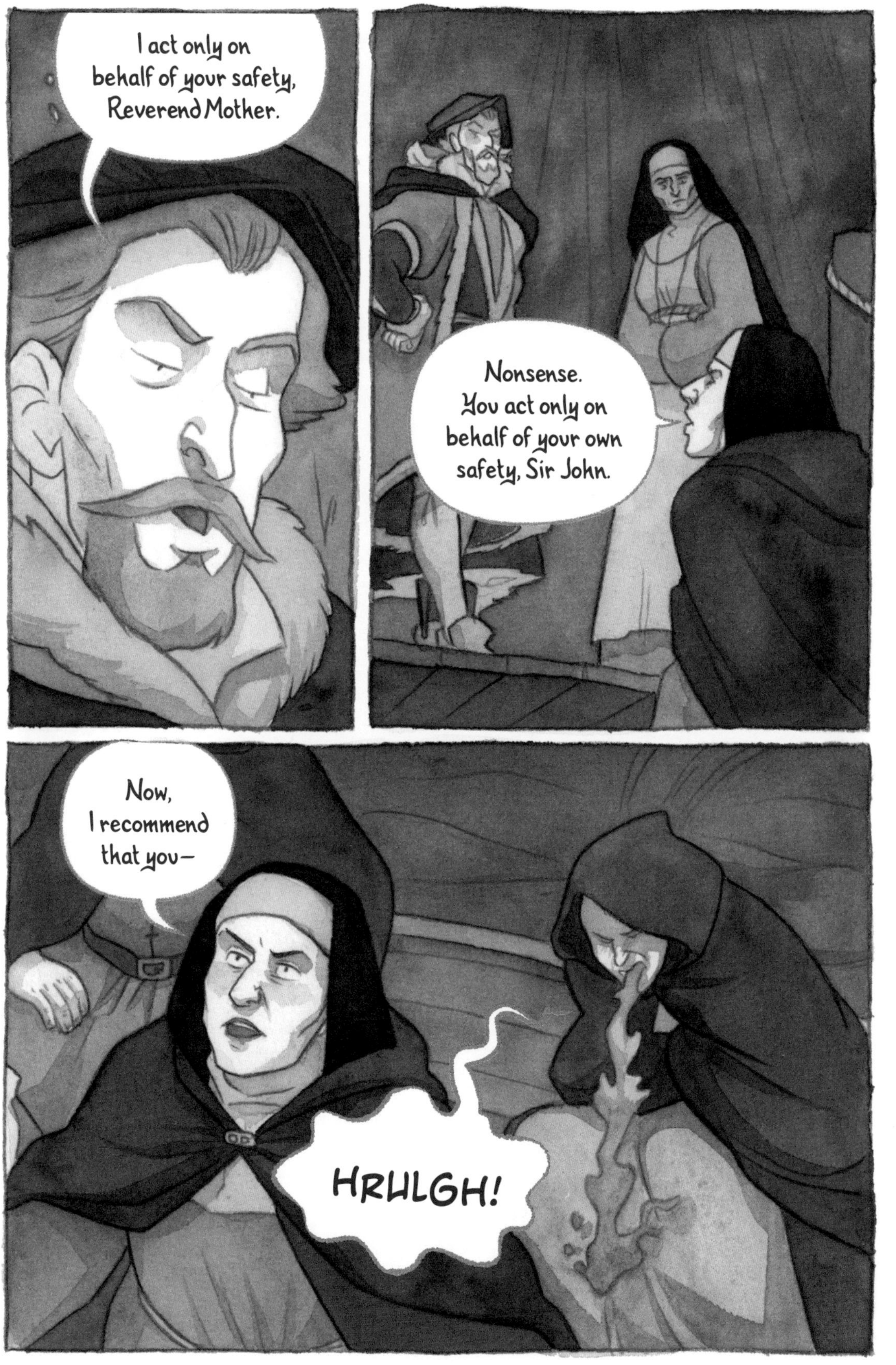
I act only on behalf of your safety, Reverend Mother.
Nonsense. You act only on behalf of your own safety, Sir John.
Now, I recommend that you—
HRULGH!

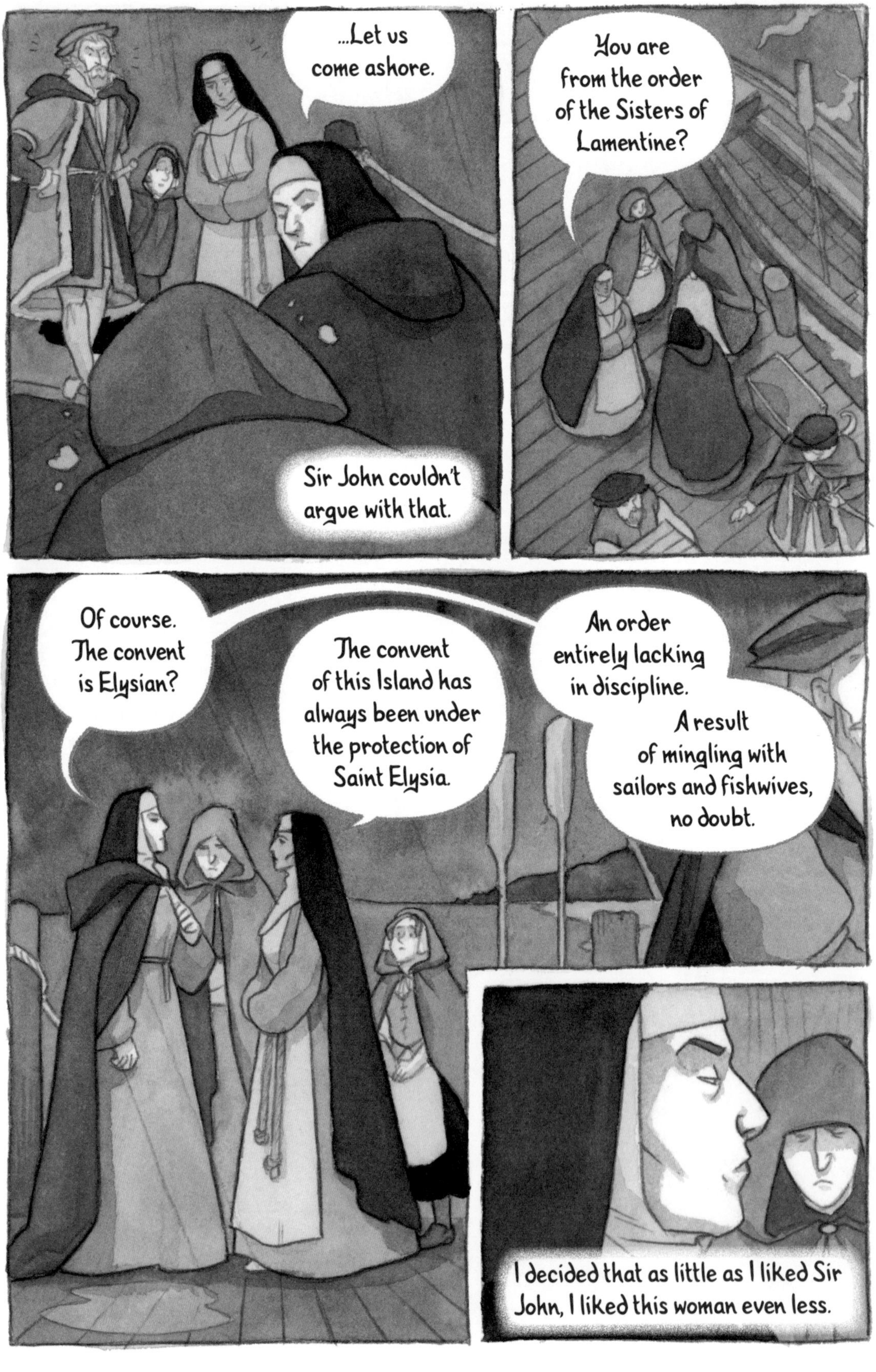
...Let us come ashore.
Sir John couldn't argue with that.
You are from the order of the Sisters of Lamentine?
Of course. The convent is Elysian?
The convent of this Island has always been under the protection of Saint Elysia.
An order entirely lacking in discipline.
A result of mingling with sailors and fishwives, no doubt.
I decided that as little as I liked Sir John, I liked this woman even less.

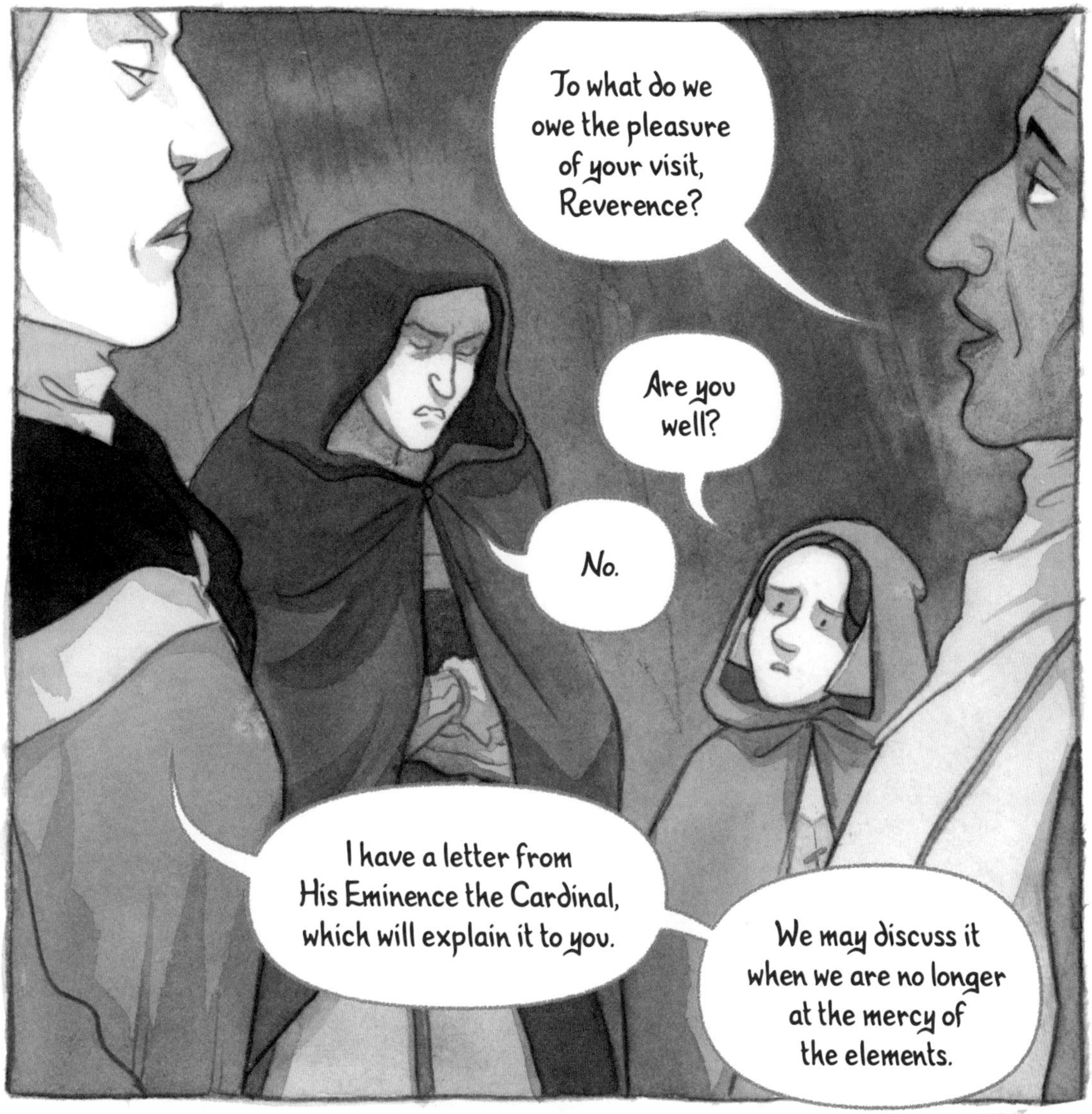
To what do we owe the pleasure of your visit, Reverence?
Are you well?
No.
I have a letter from His Eminence the Cardinal, which will explain it to you.
We may discuss it when we are no longer at the mercy of the elements.

I knew that the Cardinal was the most important priest in Albion. Just like Sister Agnes was the head of our little convent, the Cardinal was the head of all the churches, convents, and monasteries of Albion. And he answered to only two other people on earth:

His Holiness the Pope, who is a bit like a king who rules all the world's churches—

and the King...or Queen...of Albion.

Just meeting the Cardinal would be a great honor. Being sent a letter from him was nearly as important.

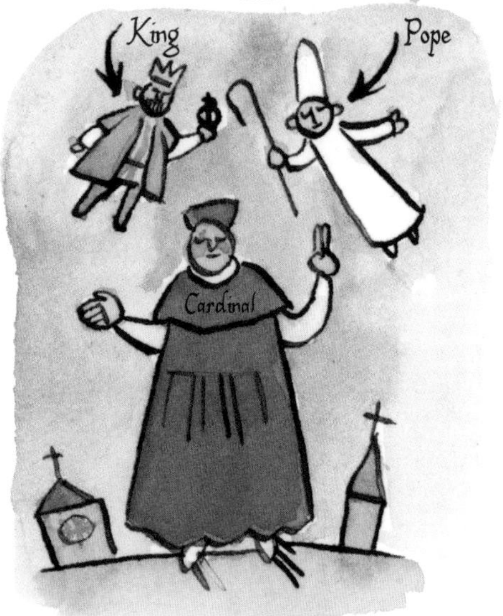
King
Pope
Cardinal

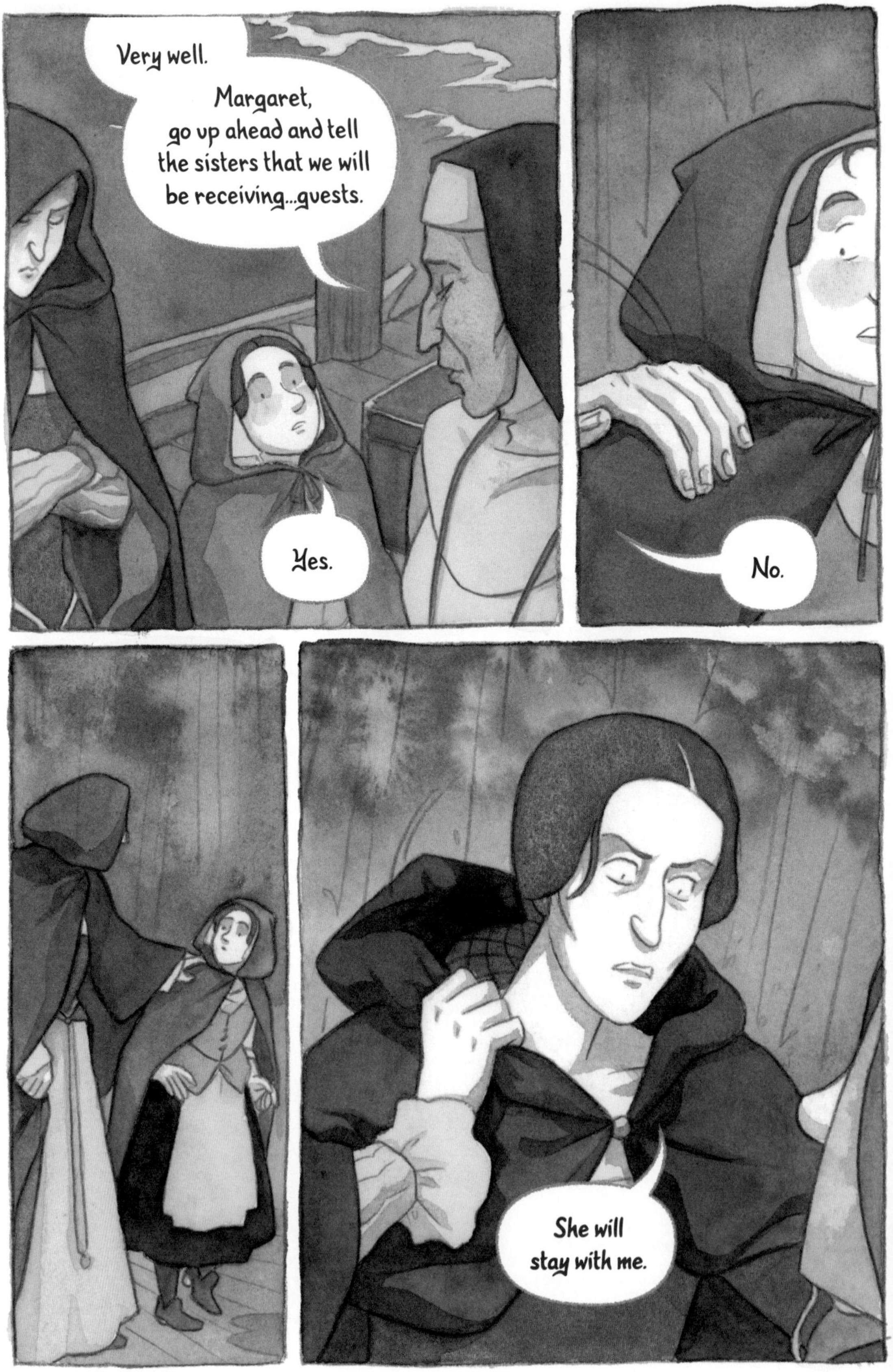
Very well.
Margaret, go up ahead and tell the sisters that we will be receiving...guests.
Yes.
No.
She will stay with me.

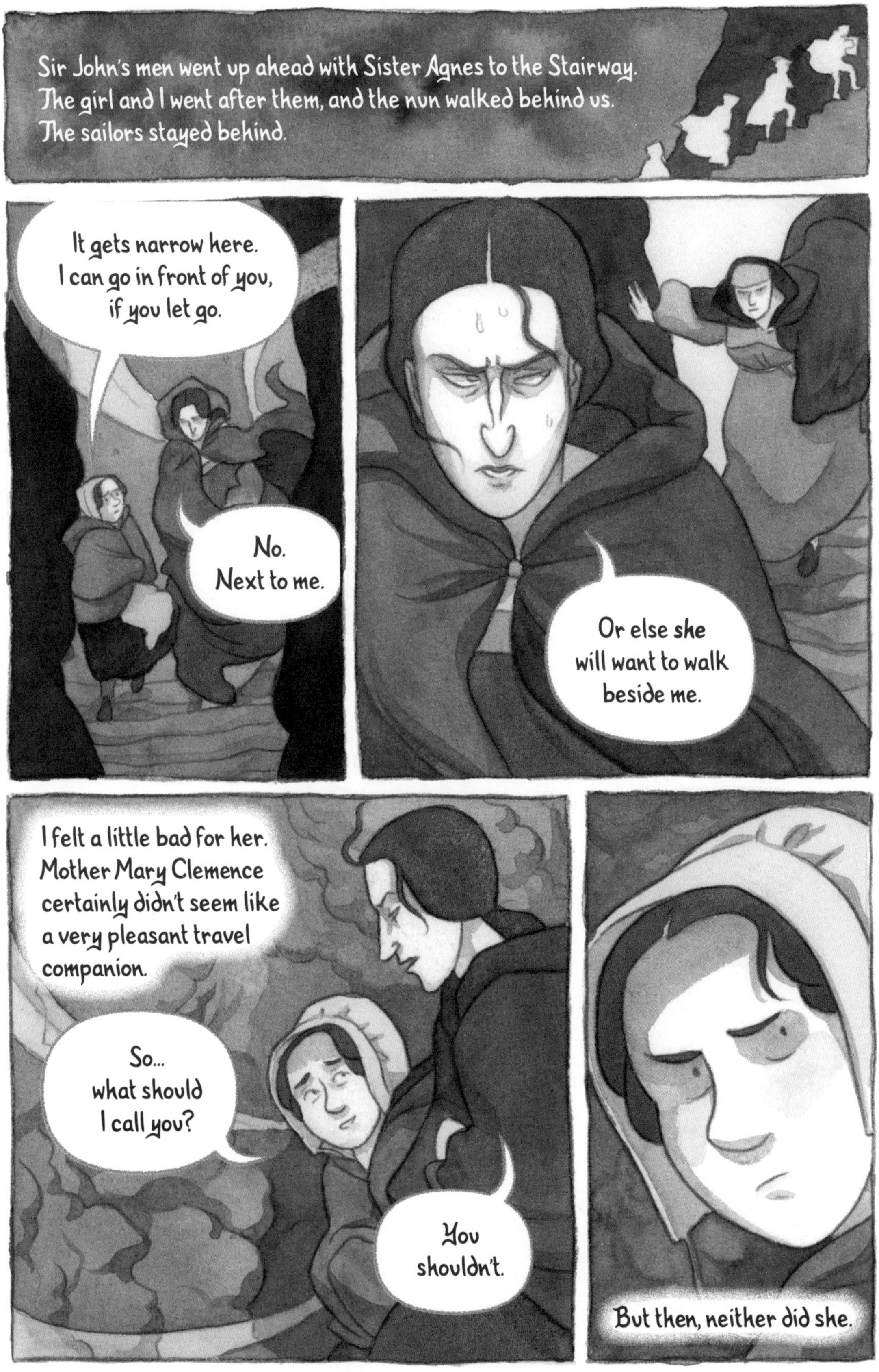

Sir John's men went up ahead with Sister Agnes to the Stairway. The girl and I went after them, and the nun walked behind us. The sailors stayed behind.
It gets narrow here. I can go in front of you, if you let go.
No. Next to me.
Or else she will want to walk beside me.
I felt a little bad for her. Mother Mary Clemence certainly didn't seem like a very pleasant travel companion.
So... what should I call you?
You shouldn't.
But then, neither did she.

We all went to the Warming House to dry off—the only room where the hearth is kept lit all day and night in the cold months.

Sir John and his two men went off to look into all the other chambers, with Sister Barbara and Sister Wynefreed following after them. Sister Agnes read the Cardinal's letter.

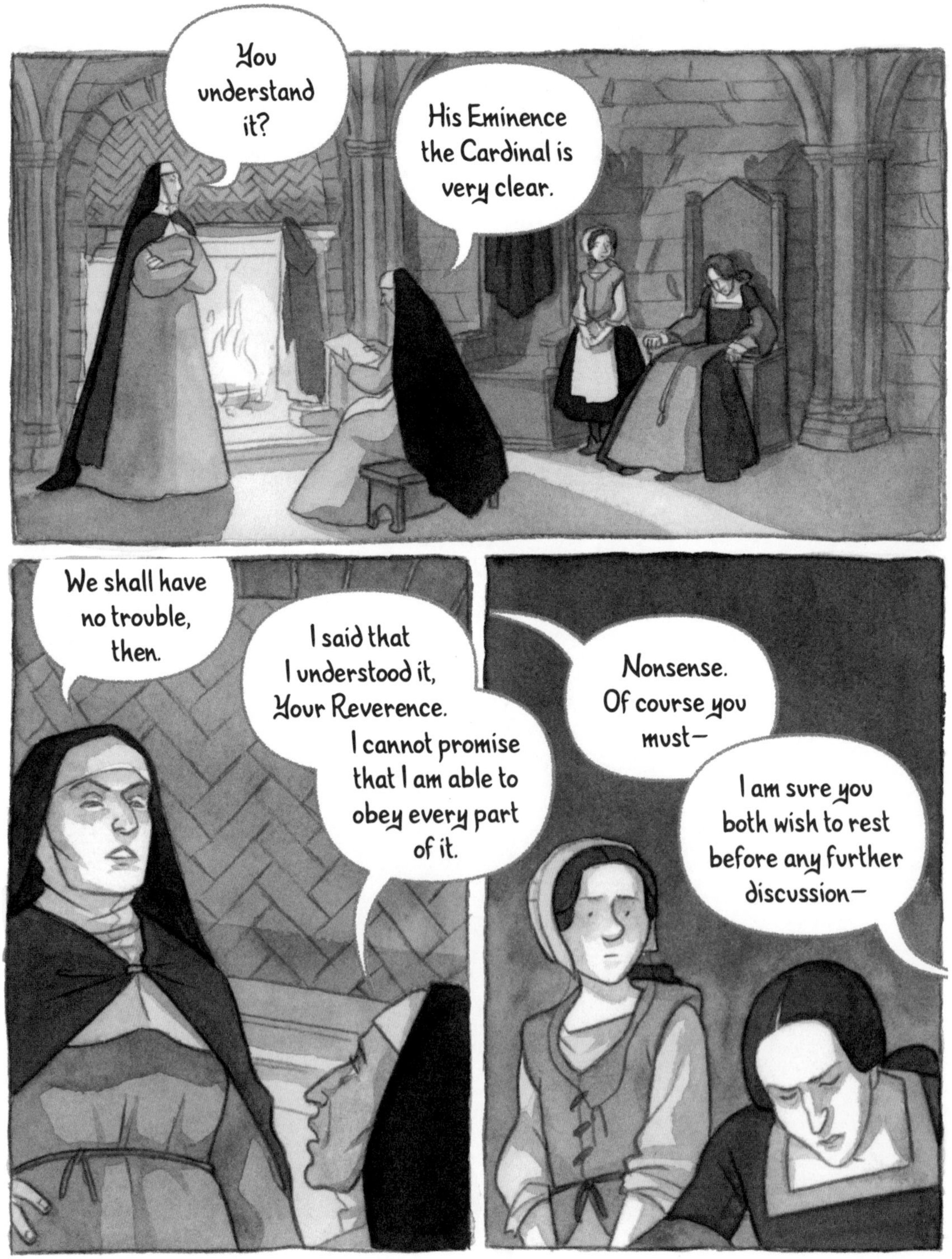
You understand it?
His Eminence the Cardinal is very clear.
We shall have no trouble, then.
I said that I understood it, Your Reverence.
I cannot promise that I am able to obey every part of it.
Nonsense. Of course you must—
I am sure you both wish to rest before any further discussion—

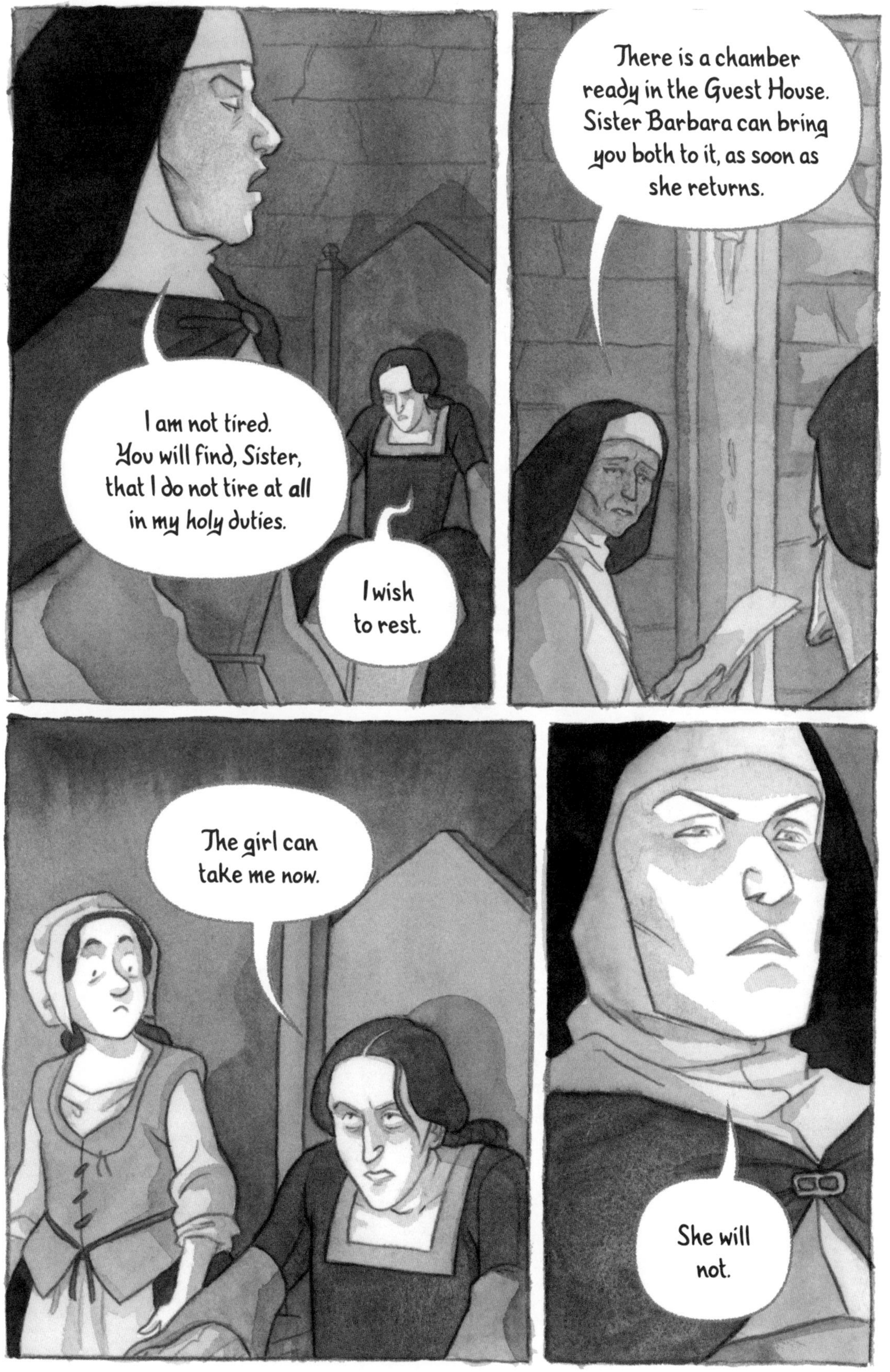
I am not tired. You will find, Sister, that I do not tire at all in my holy duties.
I wish to rest.
There is a chamber ready in the Guest House. Sister Barbara can bring you both to it, as soon as she returns.
The girl can take me now.
She will not.

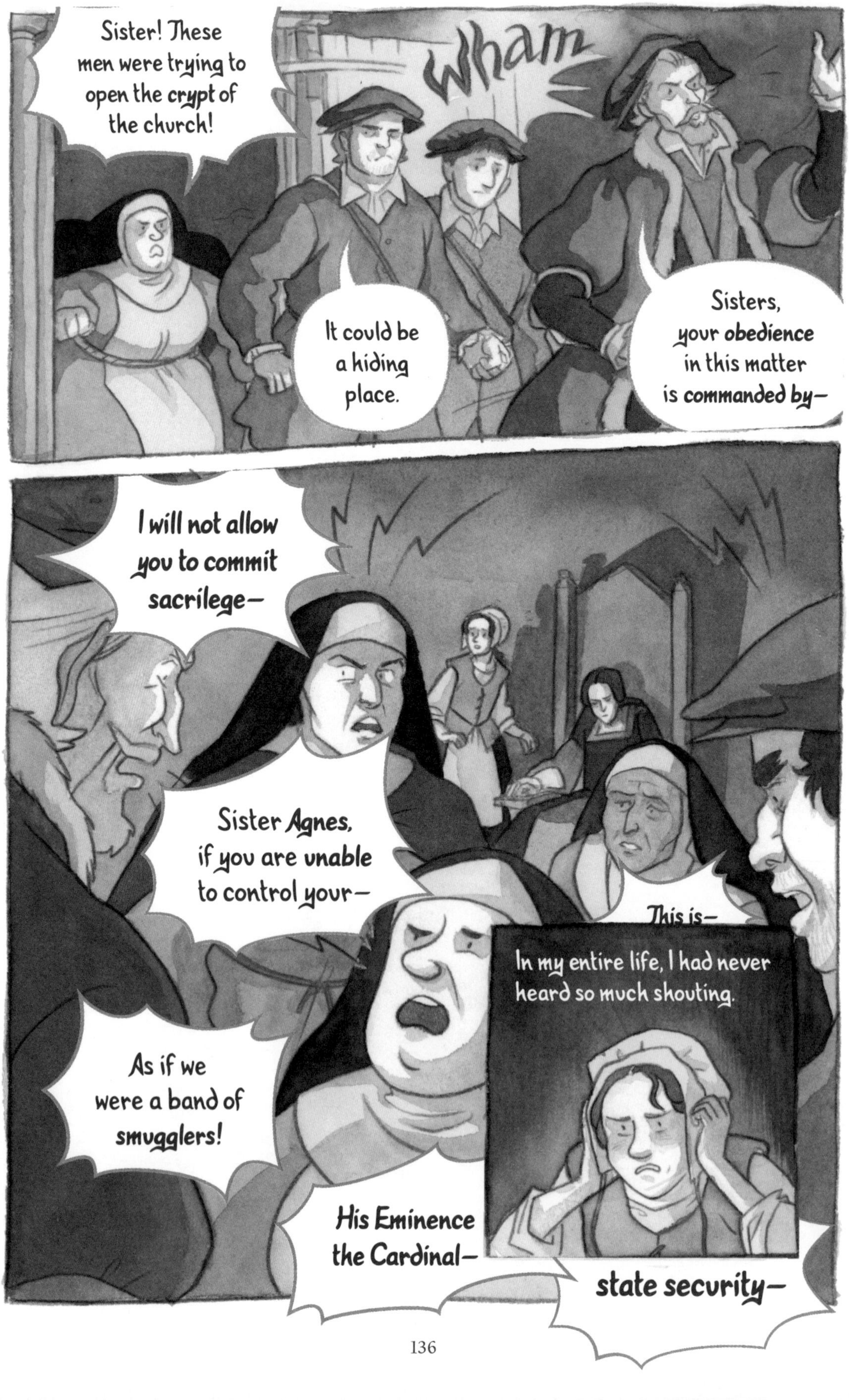
Sister! These men were trying to open the crypt of the church!
Wham
It could be a hiding place.
Sisters, your obedience in this matter is commanded by—
I will not allow you to commit sacrilege—
Sister Agnes, if you are unable to control your—
This is—
In my entire life, I had never heard so much shouting.
As if we were a band of smugglers!
His Eminence the Cardinal—
state security—

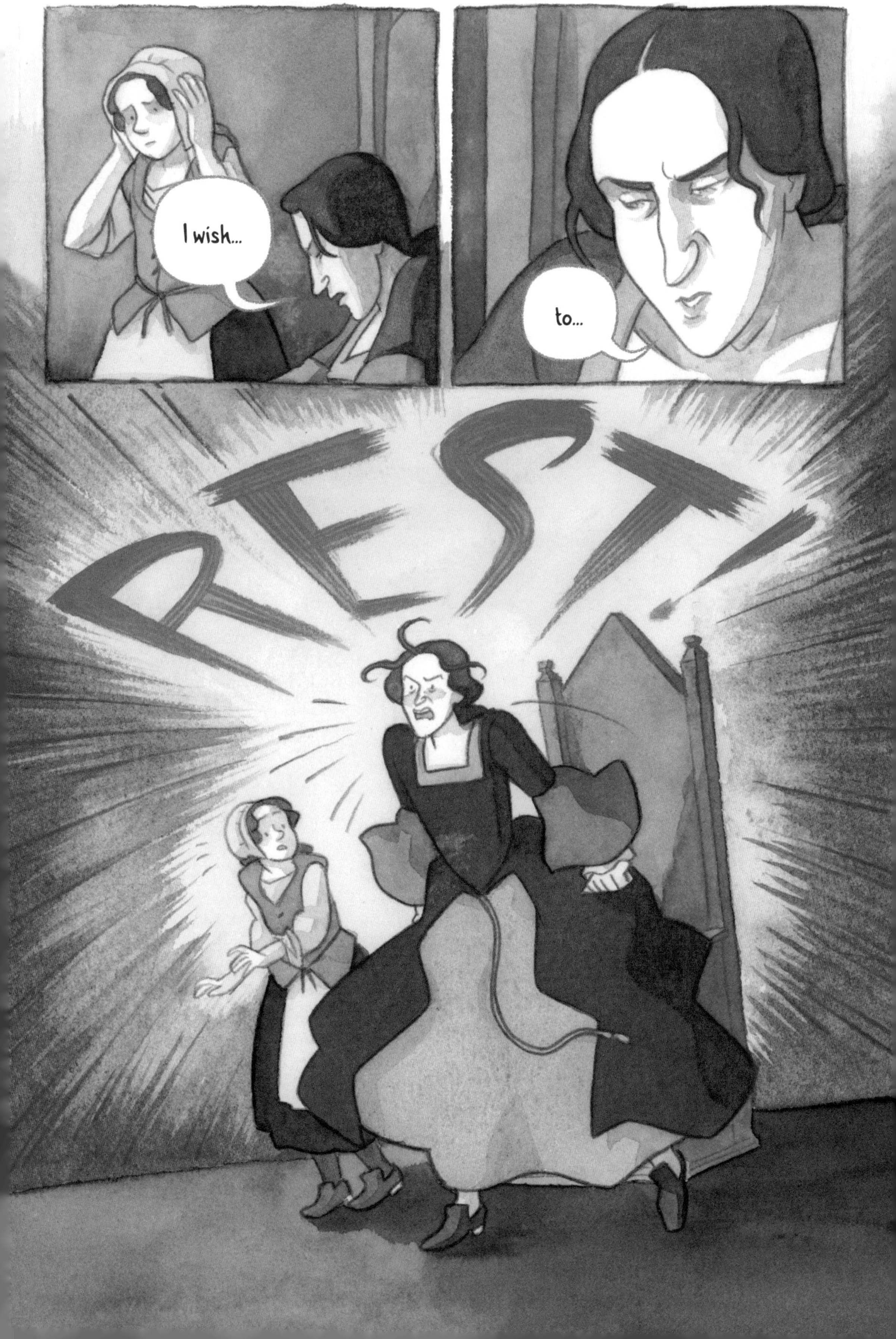
I wish...
to...
REST!

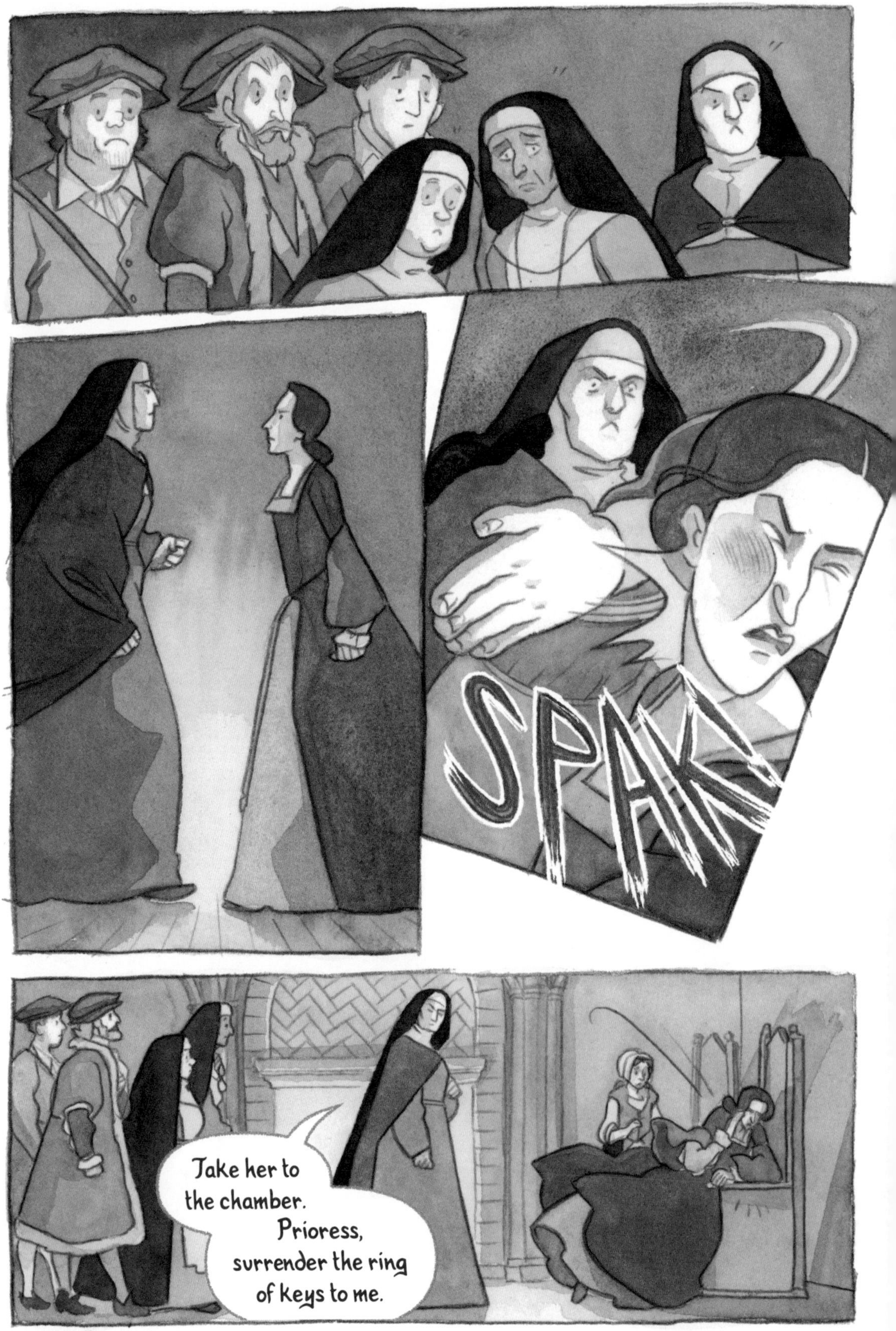
SPAK
Take her to the chamber. Prioress, surrender the ring of keys to me.

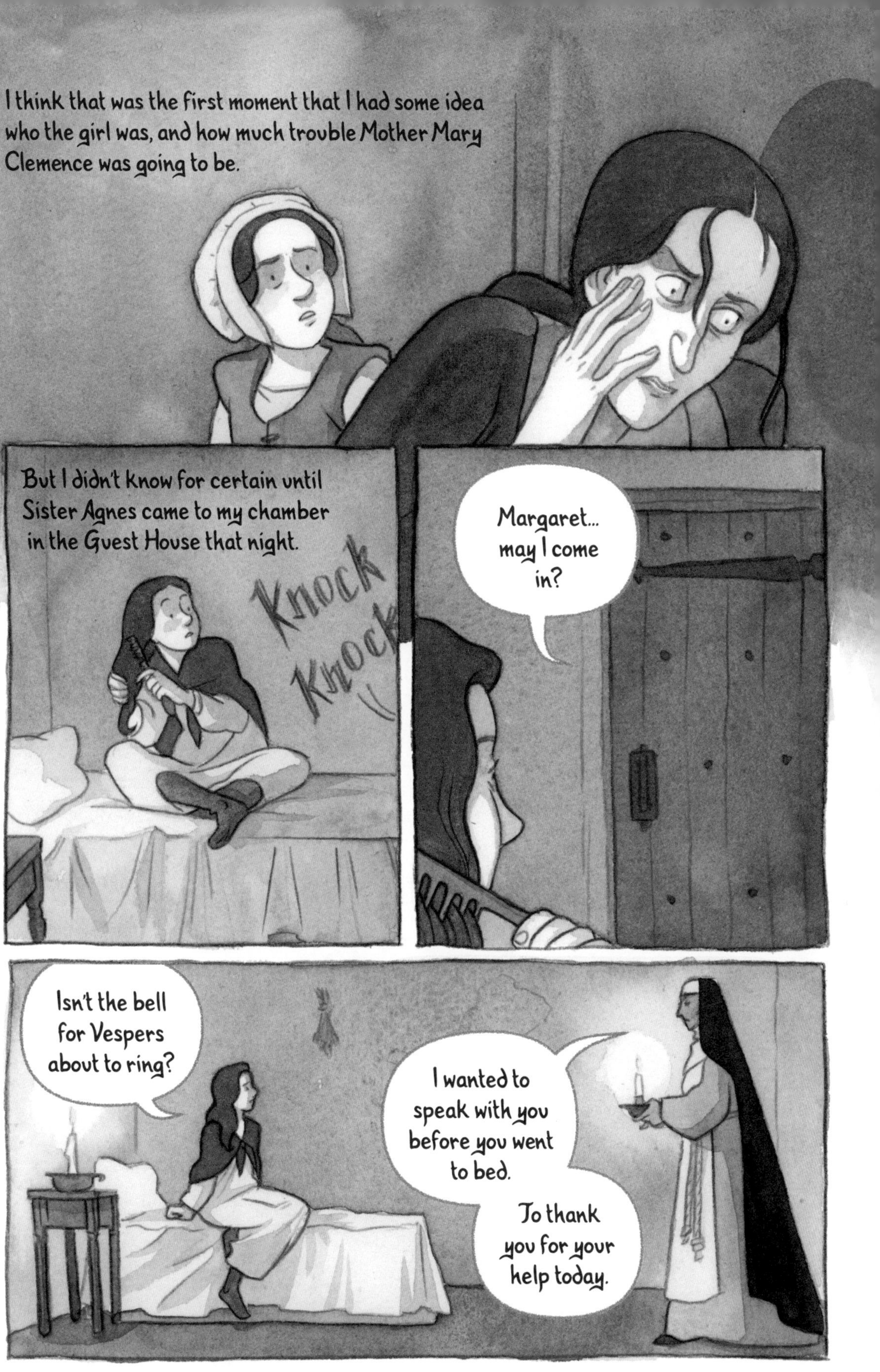
I think that was the first moment that I had some idea who the girl was, and how much trouble Mother Mary Clemence was going to be.
But I didn't know for certain until Sister Agnes came to my chamber in the Guest House that night.
Knock Knock
Margaret... may I come in?
Isn't the bell for Vespers about to ring?
I wanted to speak with you before you went to bed.
To thank you for your help today.

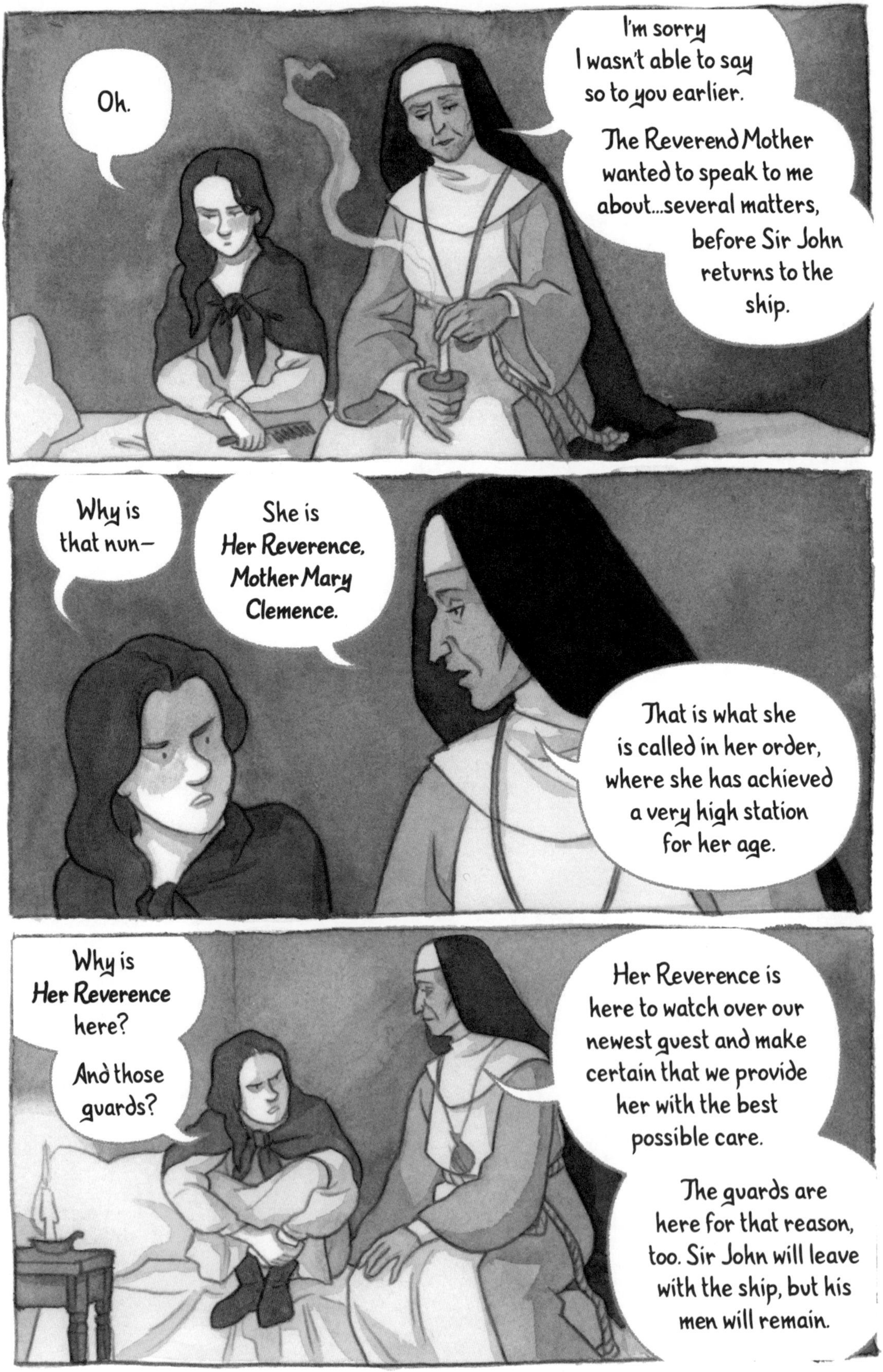
Oh.
I'm sorry I wasn't able to say so to you earlier.
The Reverend Mother wanted to speak to me about...several matters, before Sir John returns to the ship.
Why is that nun—
She is Her Reverence, Mother Mary Clemence.
That is what she is called in her order, where she has achieved a very high station for her age.
Why is Her Reverence here?
And those guards?
Her Reverence is here to watch over our newest guest and make certain that we provide her with the best possible care.
The guards are here for that reason, too. Sir John will leave with the ship, but his men will remain.

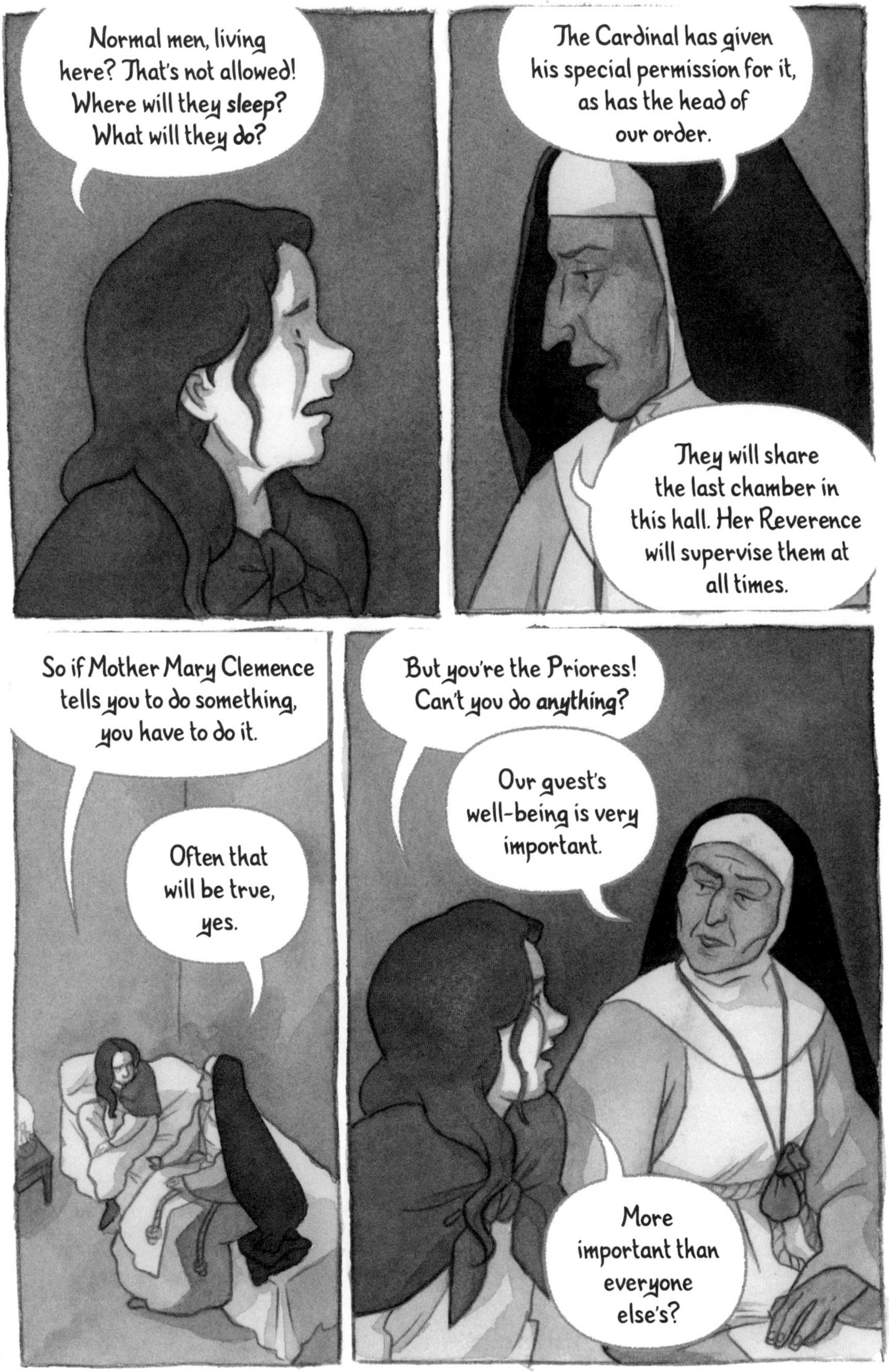
Normal men, living here? That's not allowed! Where will they *sleep*? What will they *do*?
The Cardinal has given his special permission for it, as has the head of our order.
They will share the last chamber in this hall. Her Reverence will supervise them at all times.
So if Mother Mary Clemence tells *you* to do something, *you* have to do it.
Often that will be true, *yes*.
But *you're* the Prioress! Can't *you* do *anything*?
Our guest's well-being is very important.
More important than everyone else's?

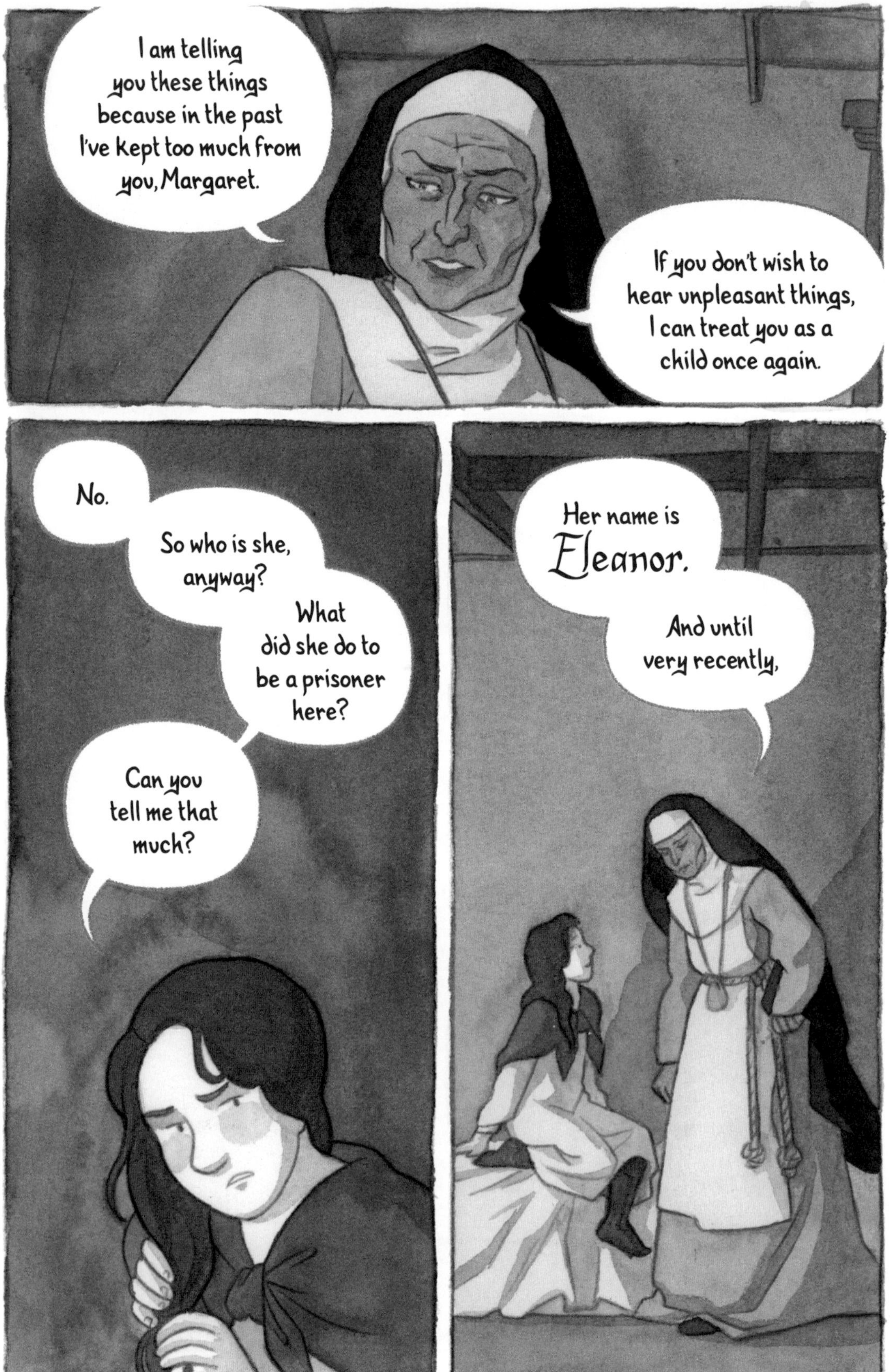

I am telling you these things because in the past I've kept too much from you, Margaret.
If you don't wish to hear unpleasant things, I can treat you as a child once again.
No.
So who is she, anyway?
What did she do to be a prisoner here?
Can you tell me that much?
Her name is Eleanor.
And until very recently,

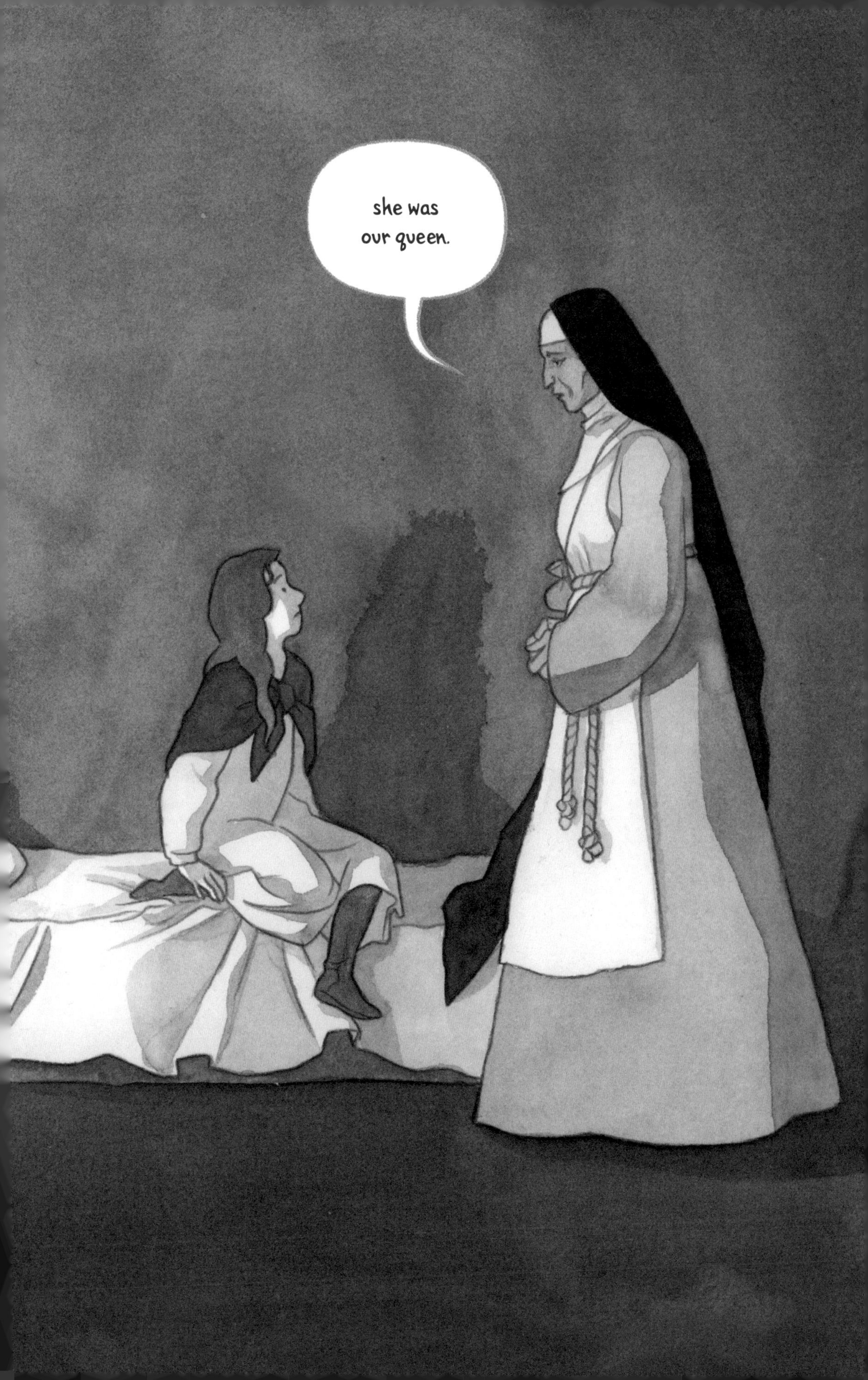
she was our queen.

Time works differently inside a convent than it does on regular land, or even the way it works at sea.

It's not that it goes faster or slower (although it might seem slower to some people). We just have our very own set of hours. They're religious hours.

Captain Marley had a wonderful thing called a watch. It's a clock small enough to fit in his hand, not like the big hourglass in Sister Agnes's study, or the notched candles that Sister Barbara makes, and certainly smaller than the stone circle.

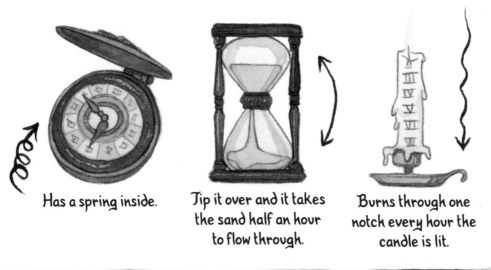

Has a spring inside.

Tip it over and it takes the sand half an hour to flow through.

Burns through one notch every hour the candle is lit.

The first time I saw the watch, I asked,
What do all the numbers mean?
Captain Marley answered,
Why, those are the hours of the day.
But where are their names?

I had never known that hours could be reduced to simple **numbers**—

as if they were the hens
we counted each night before
closing the coop!

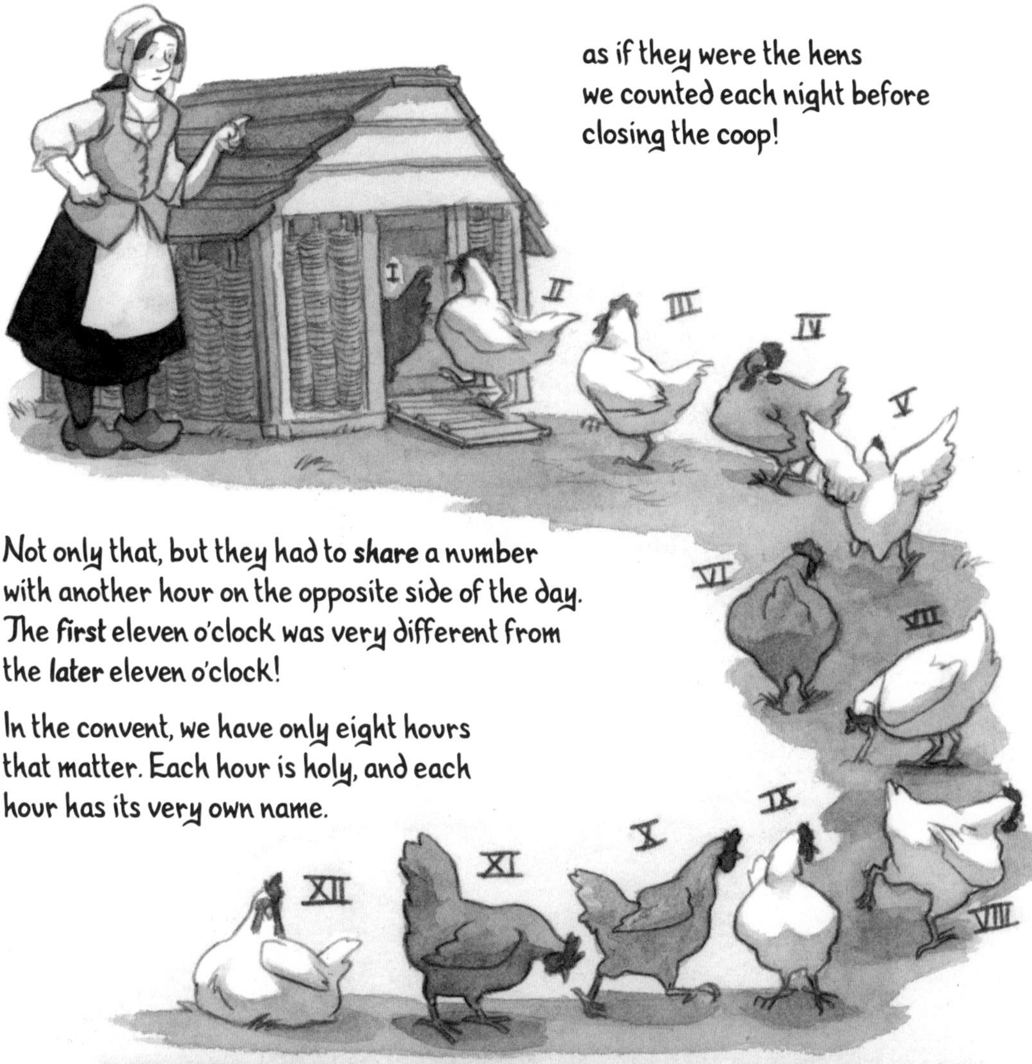
I
II
III
IV
V
VI
VII
VIII
IX
X
XI
XII

Not only that, but they had to ***share*** a number with another hour on the opposite side of the day. The ***first*** eleven o'clock was very different from the ***later*** eleven o'clock!

In the convent, we have only eight hours that matter. Each hour is holy, and each hour has its very own name.

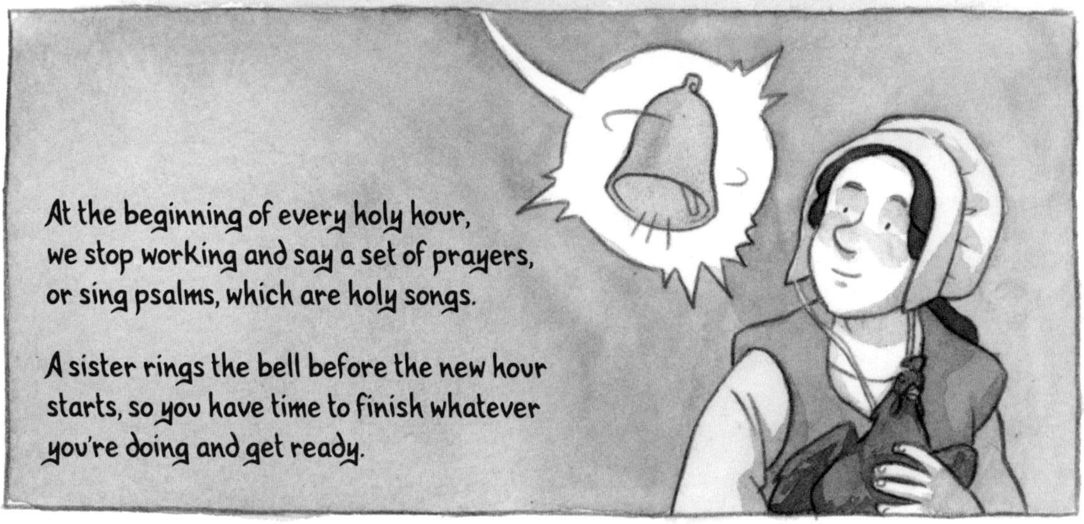
At the beginning of every holy hour,
we stop working and say a set of prayers,
or sing psalms, which are holy songs.
A sister rings the bell before the new hour
starts, so you have time to finish whatever
you're doing and get ready.

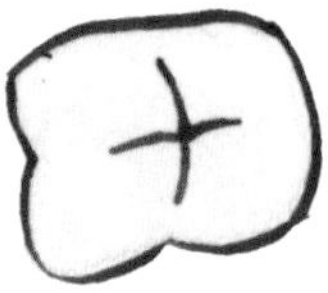

NOCTURNS happens at midnight. This hour makes you ready for the end of the world coming someday, which is supposed to be like being woken up in the middle of the night. I'm asleep for it, or I should be.

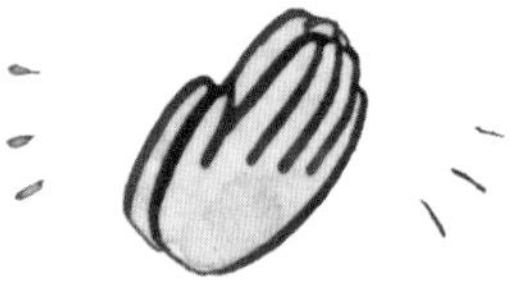

COMPLINE is when I go to bed. Some of the saints thought that going to sleep is a little like dying (!), so this is the time to think about people who have died and to pray for their souls.

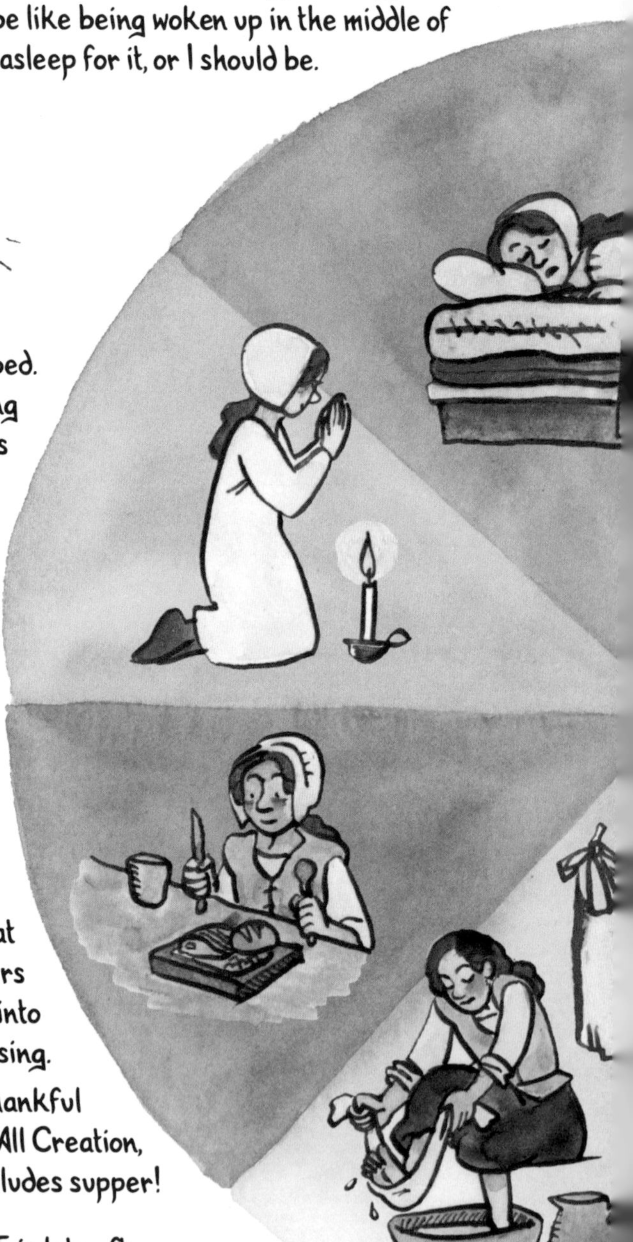

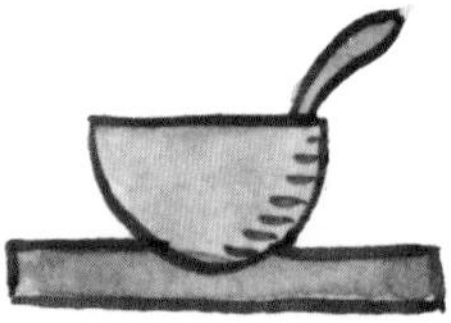

VESPERS is at sunset. It's a Major Hour, which means that everybody, not just the sisters and Father Ambrose, goes into the church to pray and sing.

This is the time to be thankful for the Glory of All Creation, which luckily includes supper!

NONE is late afternoon. This is the hour of day that the Sorrowful Son died. It wouldn't be very kind to keep working after that happened, so instead it's time to rest or bathe.

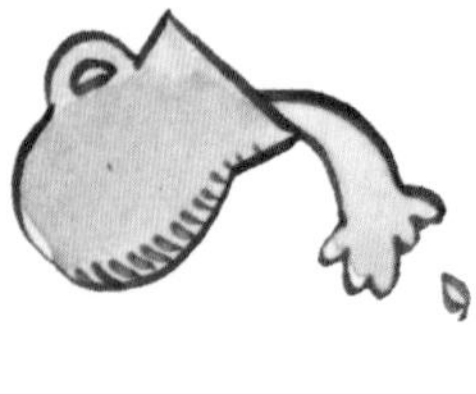

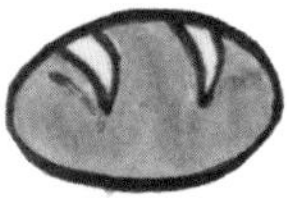

LAUDS is a Major Hour. Most times it's right before dawn, and we all wake up and go straight into the church. LAUDS is when you give thanks for light, not just from the sun, but also the light from God.

Maud gets up even before Lauds to bake bread. I like to call that time MAUDS.

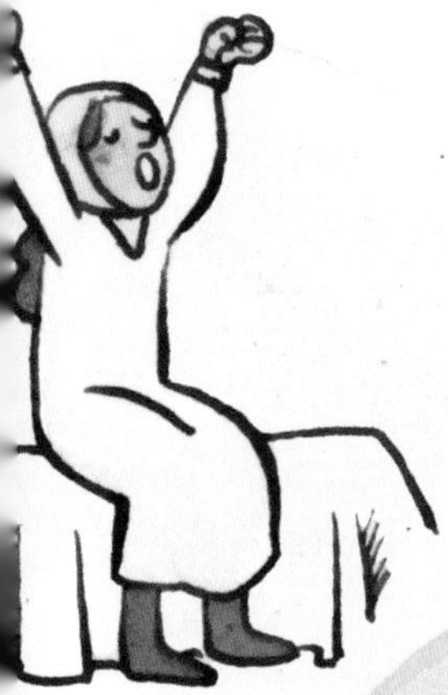

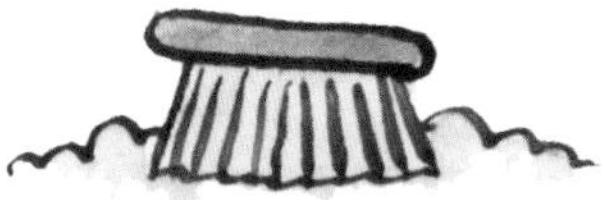

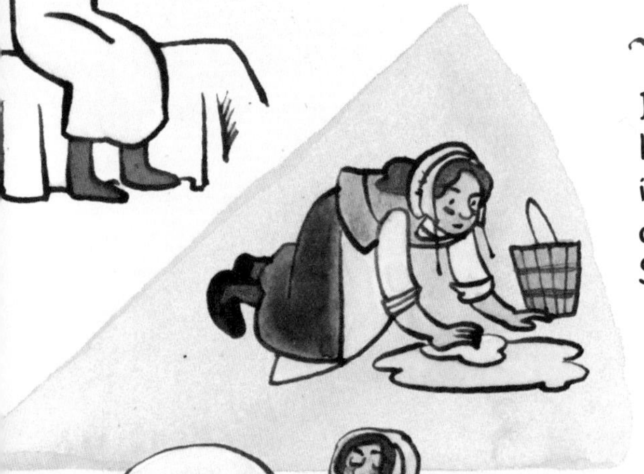

PRIME is the time before we eat breakfast. I spend it doing chores in the kitchen with Jess if it's a cold month, or at the farm with Sister Philippa if it's warm.

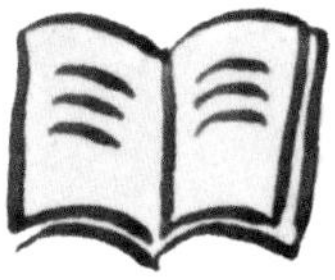

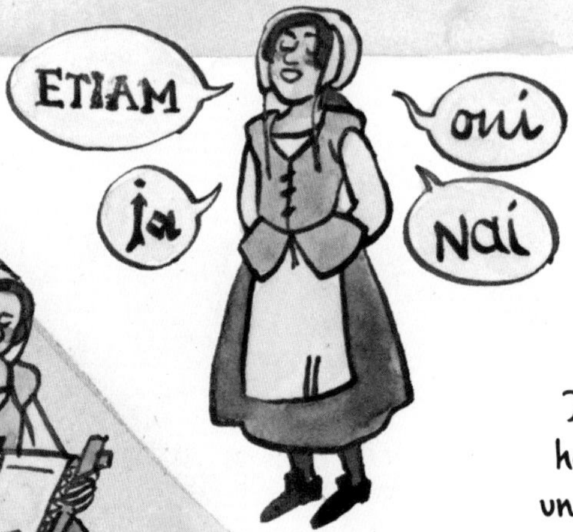
ETIAM
oui
ja
Nai

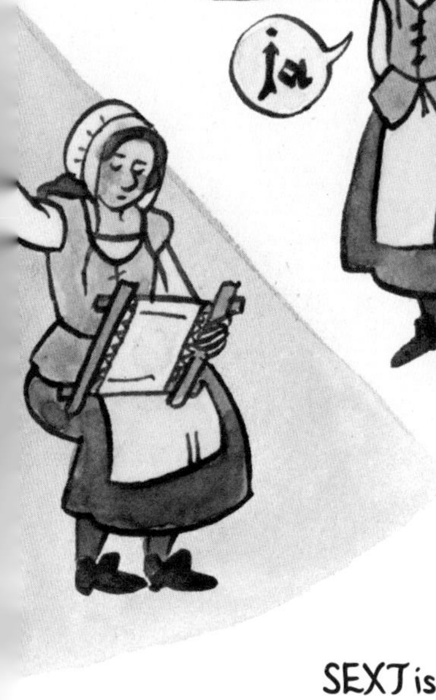

TERCE is mid-morning.

This is the hour that the Sorrowful Son's followers discovered a miracle. Tongues of flame floated over their heads that allowed them to speak and understand any language!

Unfortunately it hasn't happened to me, so I spend this time learning languages from Sister Sybil.

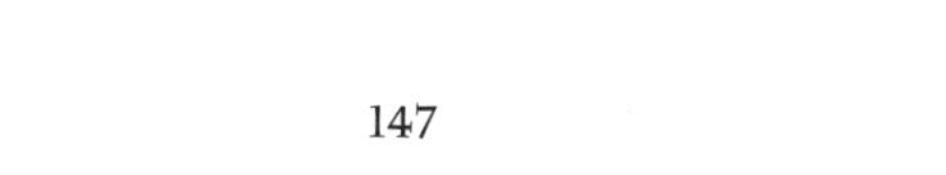

SEXT is in the exact middle of the day. I work on my embroidery with the sisters.

Whenever anybody came to visit the convent, they were supposed to come pray in the church at Lauds and Vespers. Even Sir John's awful guards came. (Their names were Harold Carpenter and Peter Yarrow.)

But Eleanor—Queen Eleanor or Lady Eleanor or whatever she was—did not. Neither did Mother Mary Clemence.

Instead, Father Ambrose was sent up to the Guest House (wheezing all the way) to give them a private service.

And while Mother Mary Clemence came to breakfast and supper with us—and stuck her nose in every other part of the convent—

I must taste the food first, to be certain it is not poisoned.

Or oversalted.

The foul odors of the farm are a disturbance to us as we rest in our chamber. The animals will be moved.

I correspond with many important members of the church in Albion, and my reports must remain secret. You will give up your study to me.

Eleanor did not leave the chamber at all. It was the chamber I had shared with William and Lady Cameron, and where Lady Cameron had died. I wondered if anybody had told Mother Mary Clemence that or if she had simply picked out the biggest room.

Mother Mary Clemence slept there as well, instead of in the dorter with the other sisters.

At Lauds, Jess would take away their chamber pot and last night's supper dishes.
At Prime, Father Ambrose came to say a private Mass for them.
At Terce, Bess would bring up their breakfasts.
At Sext, I would bring up a washbasin of rosewater and take the breakfast dishes.
At None, Father Ambrose returned to lead them in evening prayers,
And at Vespers, Bess brought their supper and took away the wash water.

Either Mother Mary Clemence would open the door, or, if she was out (pestering the sisters, or writing letters to Very Important People who would not receive them for months and months), we would leave anything we brought on a little stool by the door.

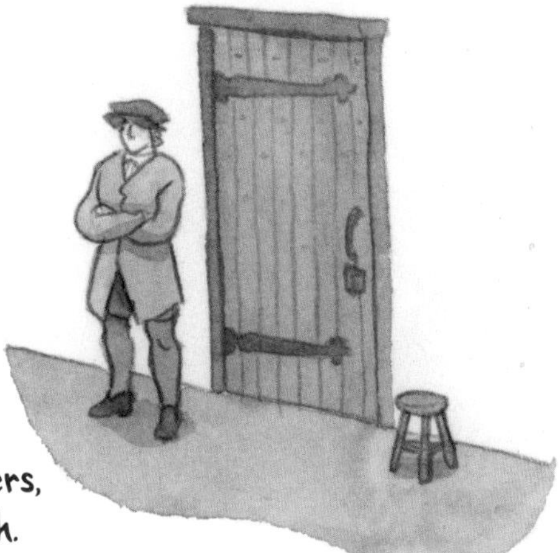

One of the guards was always standing by the door. The other would go around with **Her Reverence**—except during Lauds and Vespers, when both men went to join prayers in the church.

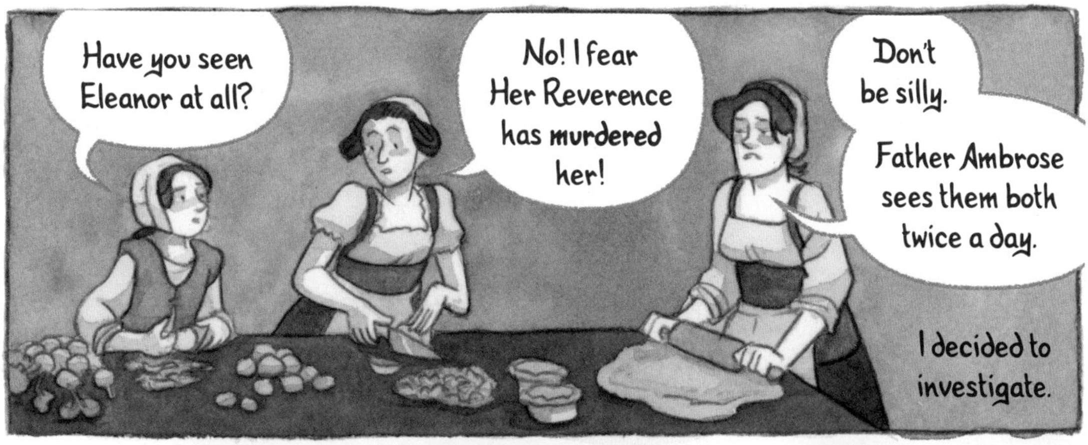
Have you seen Eleanor at all?
No! I fear Her Reverence has **murdered** her!
Don't be silly.
Father Ambrose sees them both twice a day.
I decided to investigate.

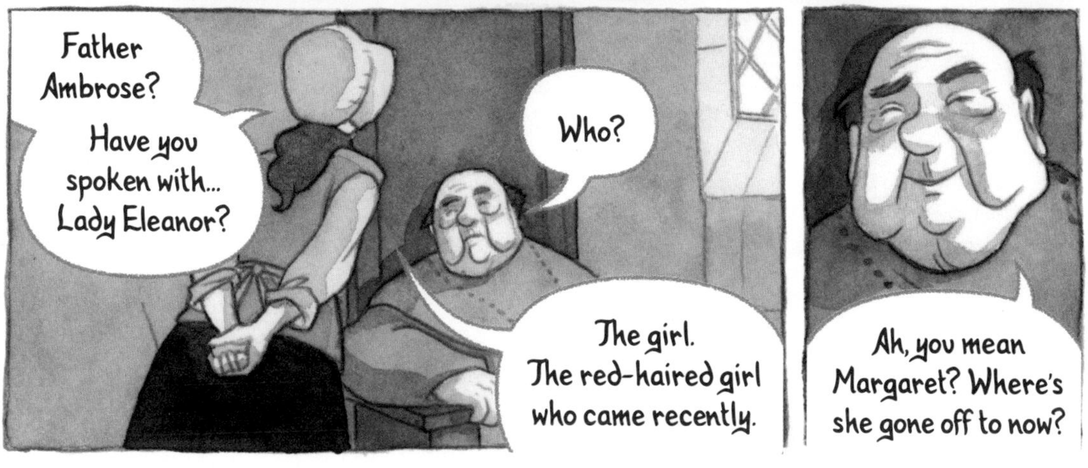
Father Ambrose?
Have you spoken with... Lady Eleanor?
Who?
The girl. The red-haired girl who came recently.
Ah, you mean Margaret? Where's she gone off to now?

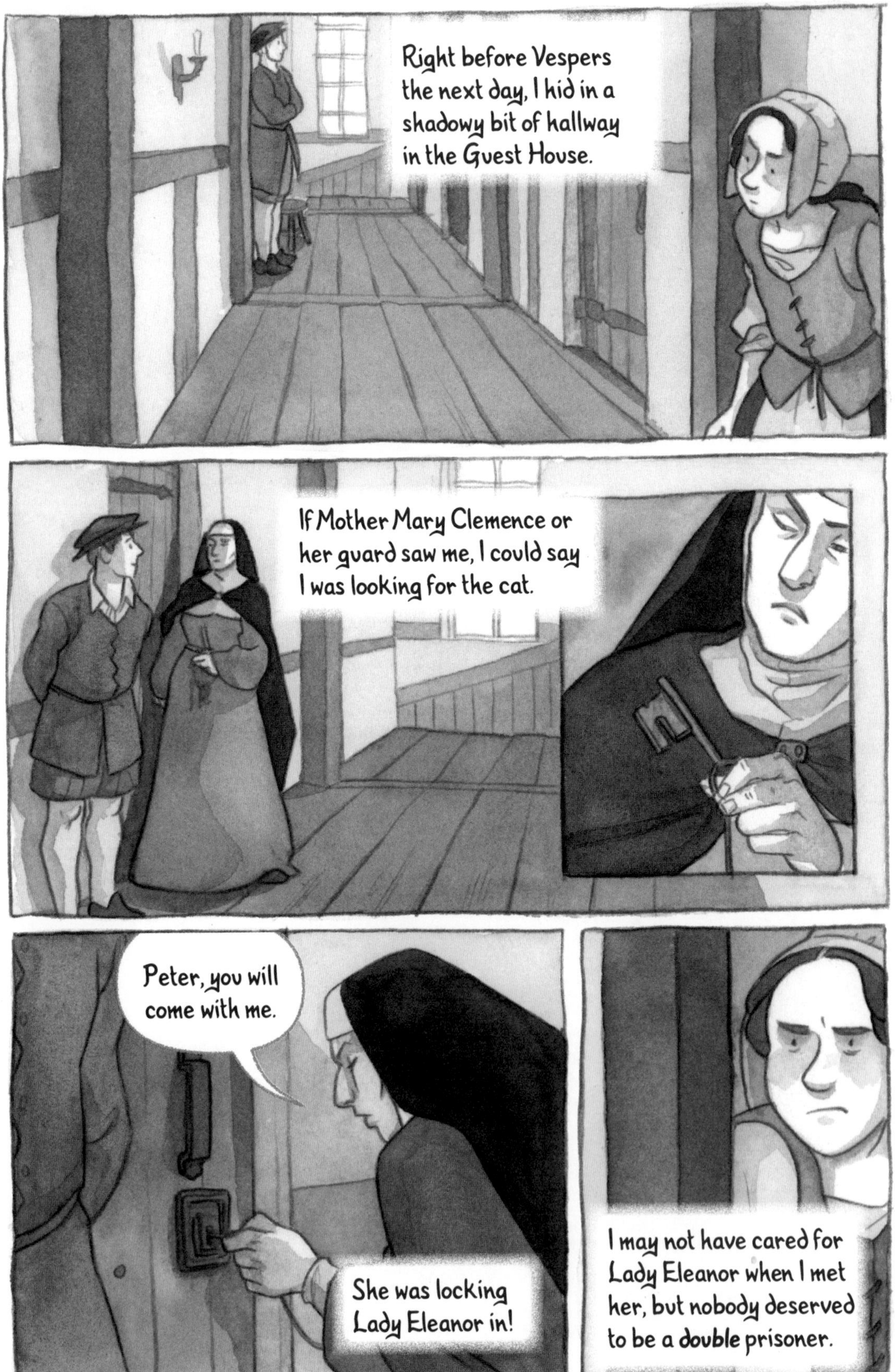
Right before Vespers the next day, I hid in a shadowy bit of hallway in the Guest House.
If Mother Mary Clemence or her guard saw me, I could say I was looking for the cat.
Peter, you will come with me.
She was locking Lady Eleanor in!
I may not have cared for Lady Eleanor when I met her, but nobody deserved to be a double prisoner.

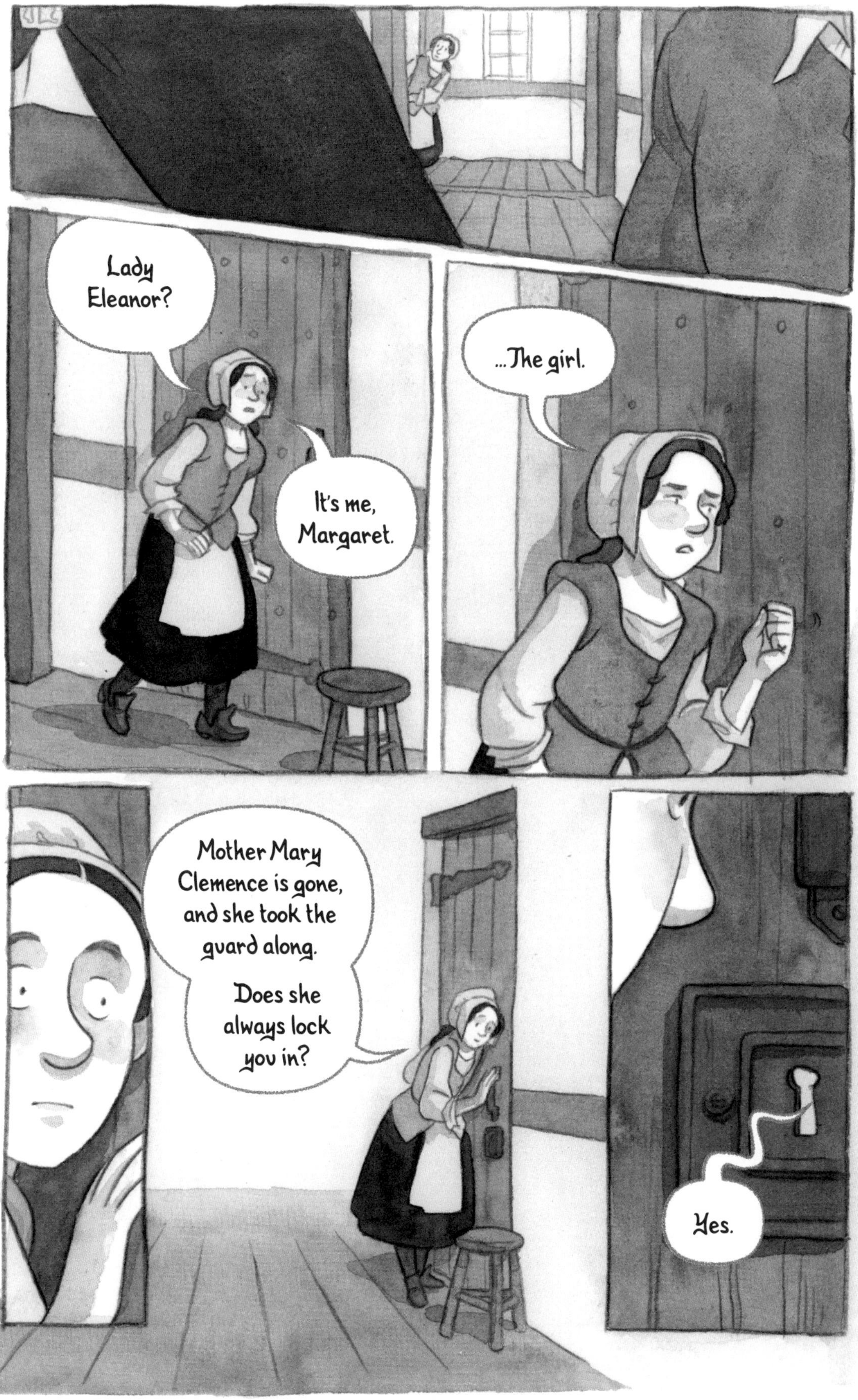

Lady Eleanor?
It's me, Margaret.
...The girl.
Mother Mary Clemence is gone, and she took the guard along.
Does she always lock you in?
Yes.

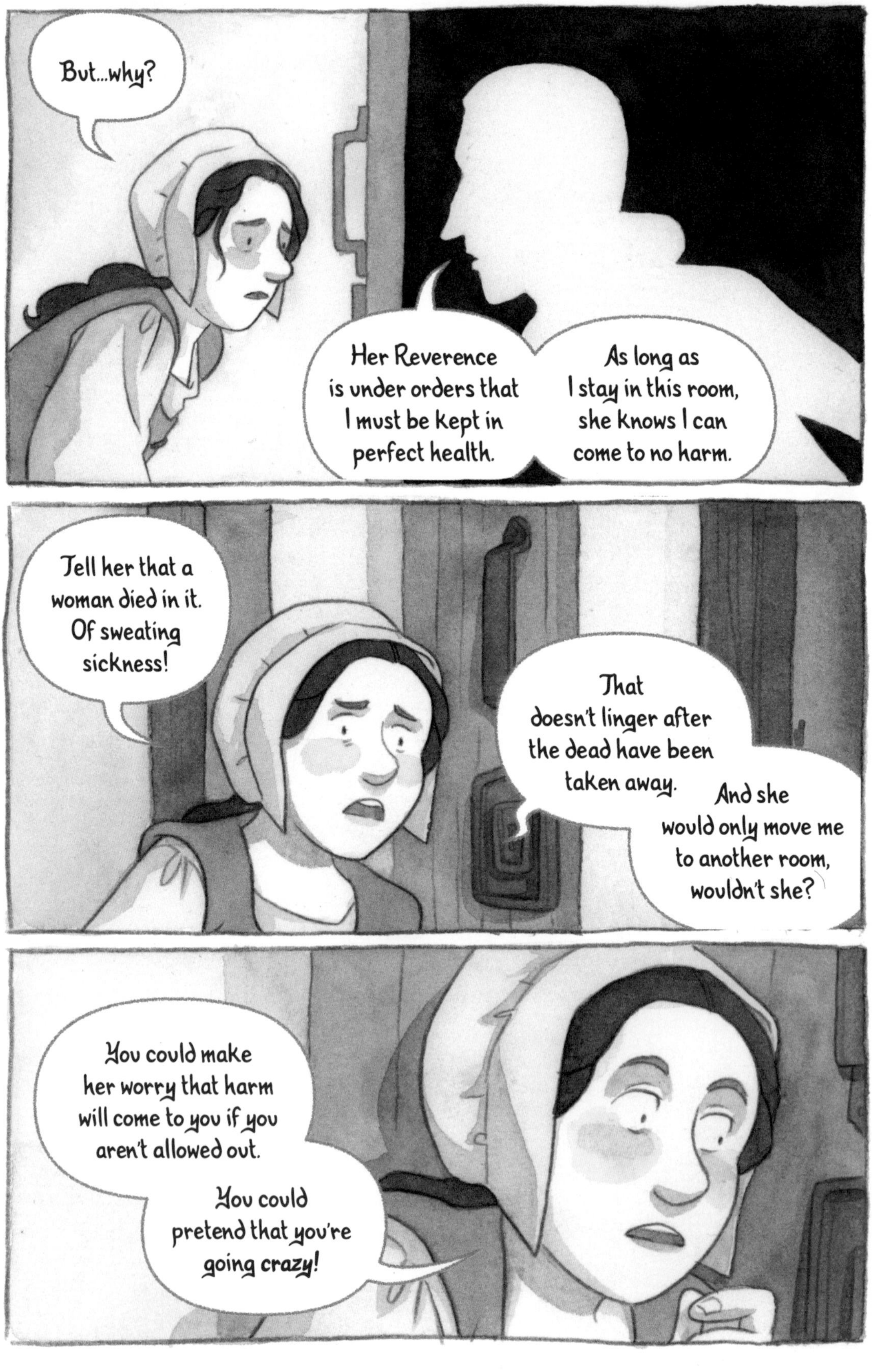
But...why?
Her Reverence is under orders that I must be kept in perfect health.
As long as I stay in this room, she knows I can come to no harm.
Tell her that a woman died in it. Of sweating sickness!
That doesn't linger after the dead have been taken away.
And she would only move me to another room, wouldn't she?
You could make her worry that harm will come to you if you aren't allowed out.
You could pretend that you're going crazy!

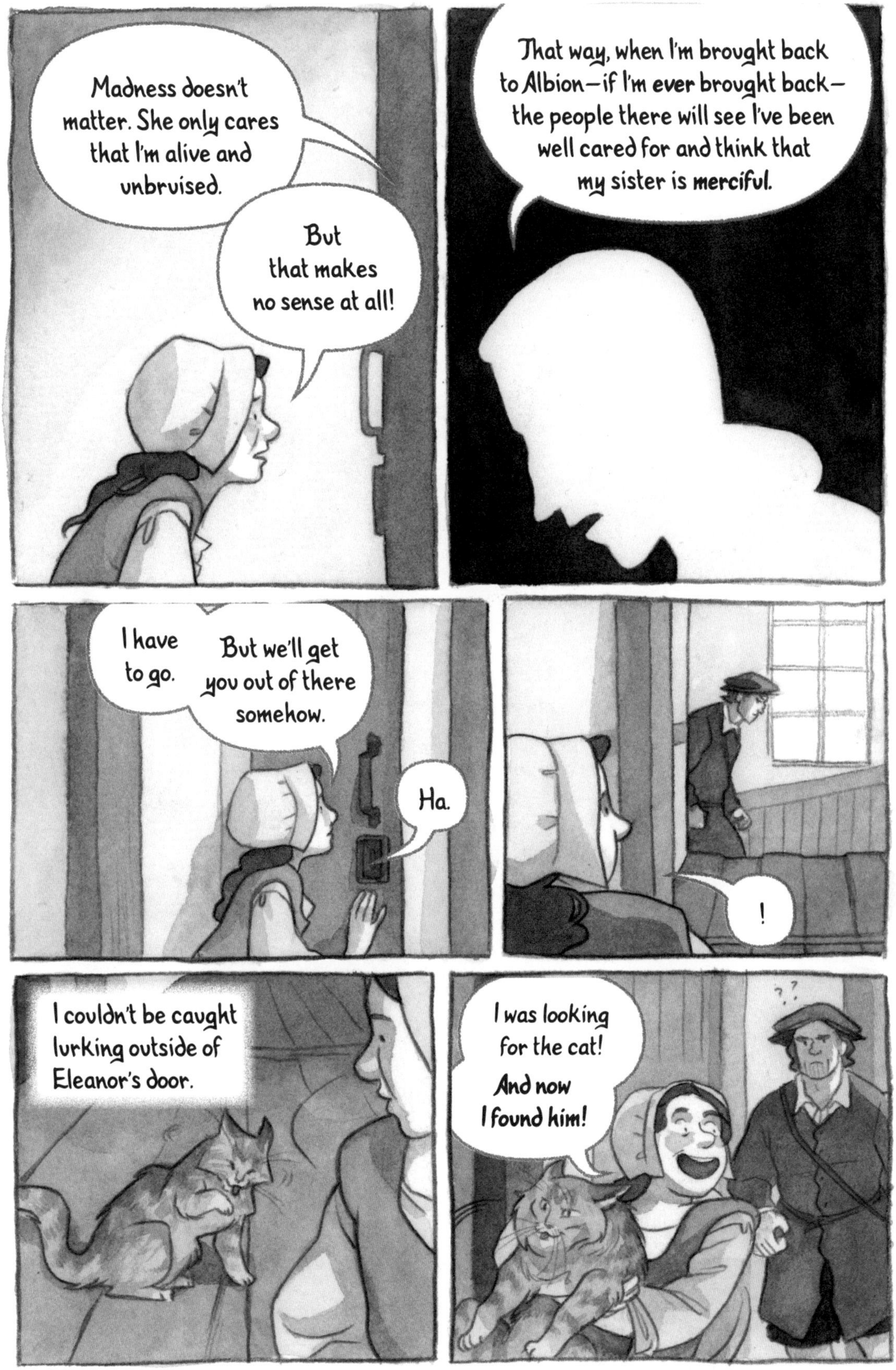
Madness doesn't matter. She only cares that I'm alive and unbruised.
But that makes no sense at all!
That way, when I'm brought back to Albion—if I'm ever brought back—the people there will see I've been well cared for and think that my sister is merciful.
I have to go.
But we'll get you out of there somehow.
Ha.
!
I couldn't be caught lurking outside of Eleanor's door.
I was looking for the cat!
And now I found him!

I couldn't think of a way to convince Mother Mary Clemence to let Eleanor out of her chamber, or to let me in. And of course Sister Agnes couldn't (or wouldn't) do anything. I shouldn't have worried, though. Eleanor had her own idea almost right away.

Although now I know that that should have worried me even more.

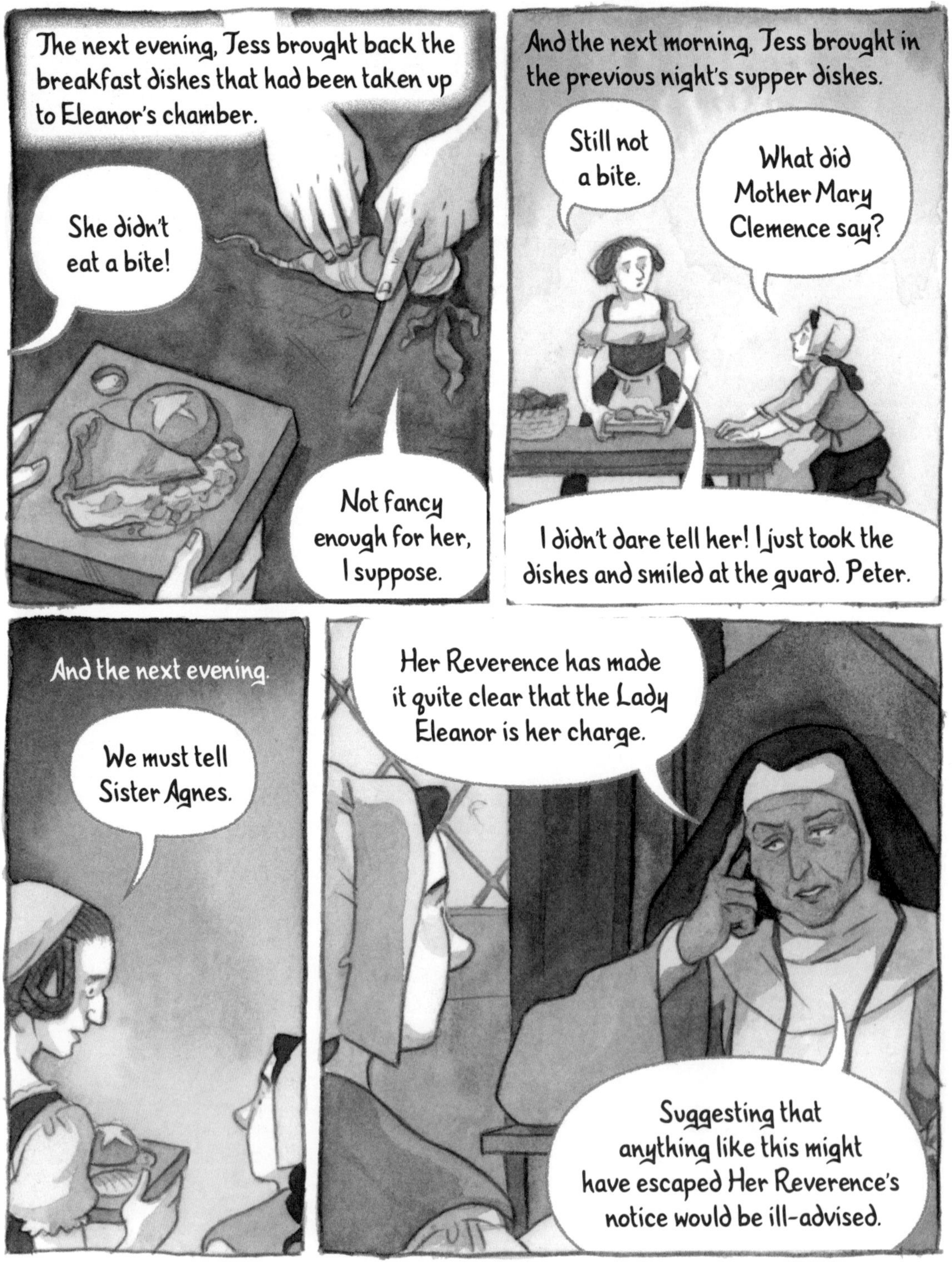

The next evening, Jess brought back the breakfast dishes that had been taken up to Eleanor's chamber.
She didn't eat a bite!
Not fancy enough for her, I suppose.
And the next morning, Jess brought in the previous night's supper dishes.
Still not a bite.
What did Mother Mary Clemence say?
I didn't dare tell her! I just took the dishes and smiled at the guard. Peter.
And the next evening.
We must tell Sister Agnes.
Her Reverence has made it quite clear that the Lady Eleanor is her charge.
Suggesting that anything like this might have escaped Her Reverence's notice would be ill-advised.

I didn't understand at all. Was Eleanor sick? Was Mother Mary Clemence starving her? It was two days before I had another chance to talk to Eleanor. This time I went with Jess.

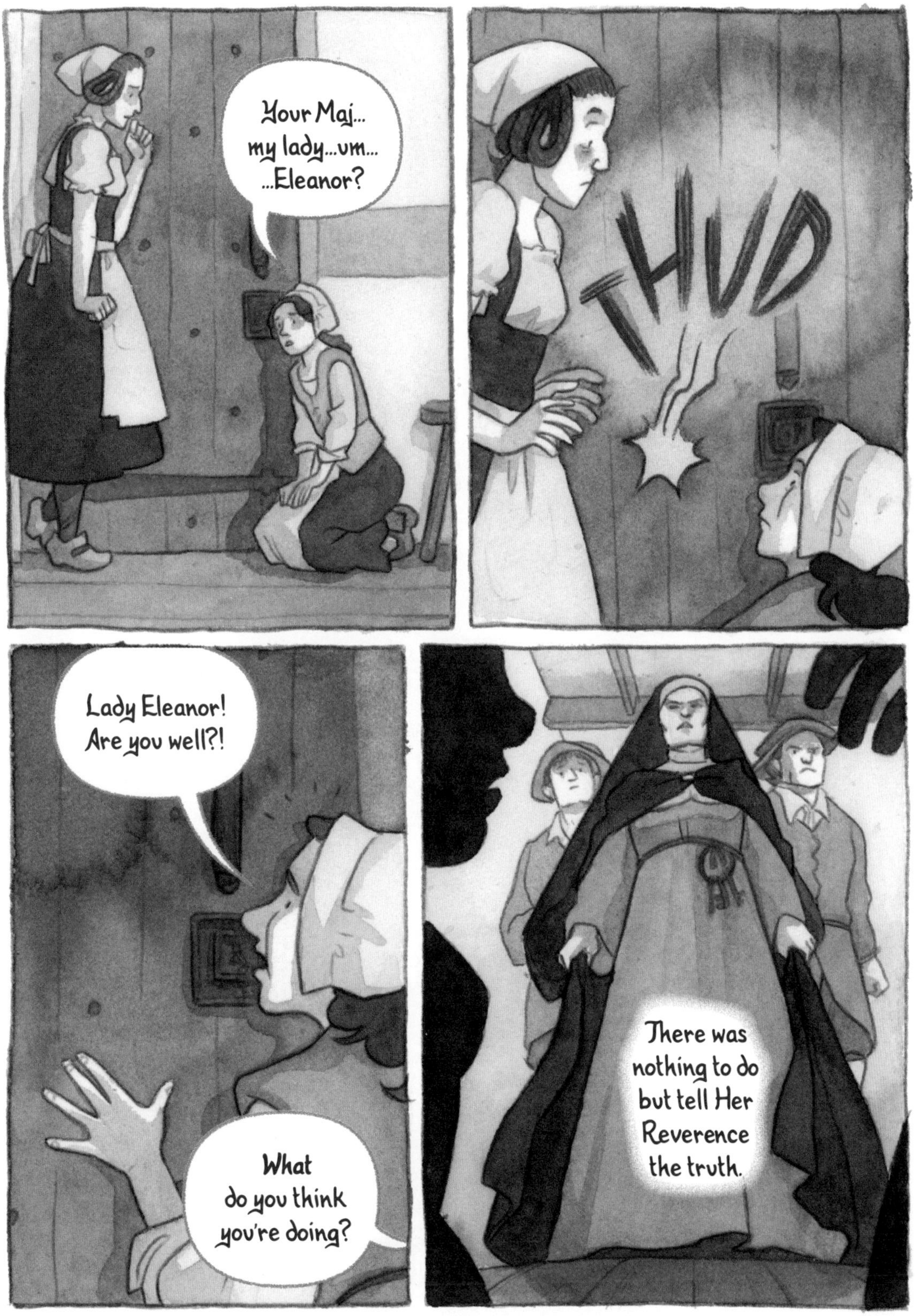
Your Maj...
my lady...um...
...Eleanor?
THUD
Lady Eleanor! Are you well?!
What do you think you're doing?
There was nothing to do but tell Her Reverence the truth.

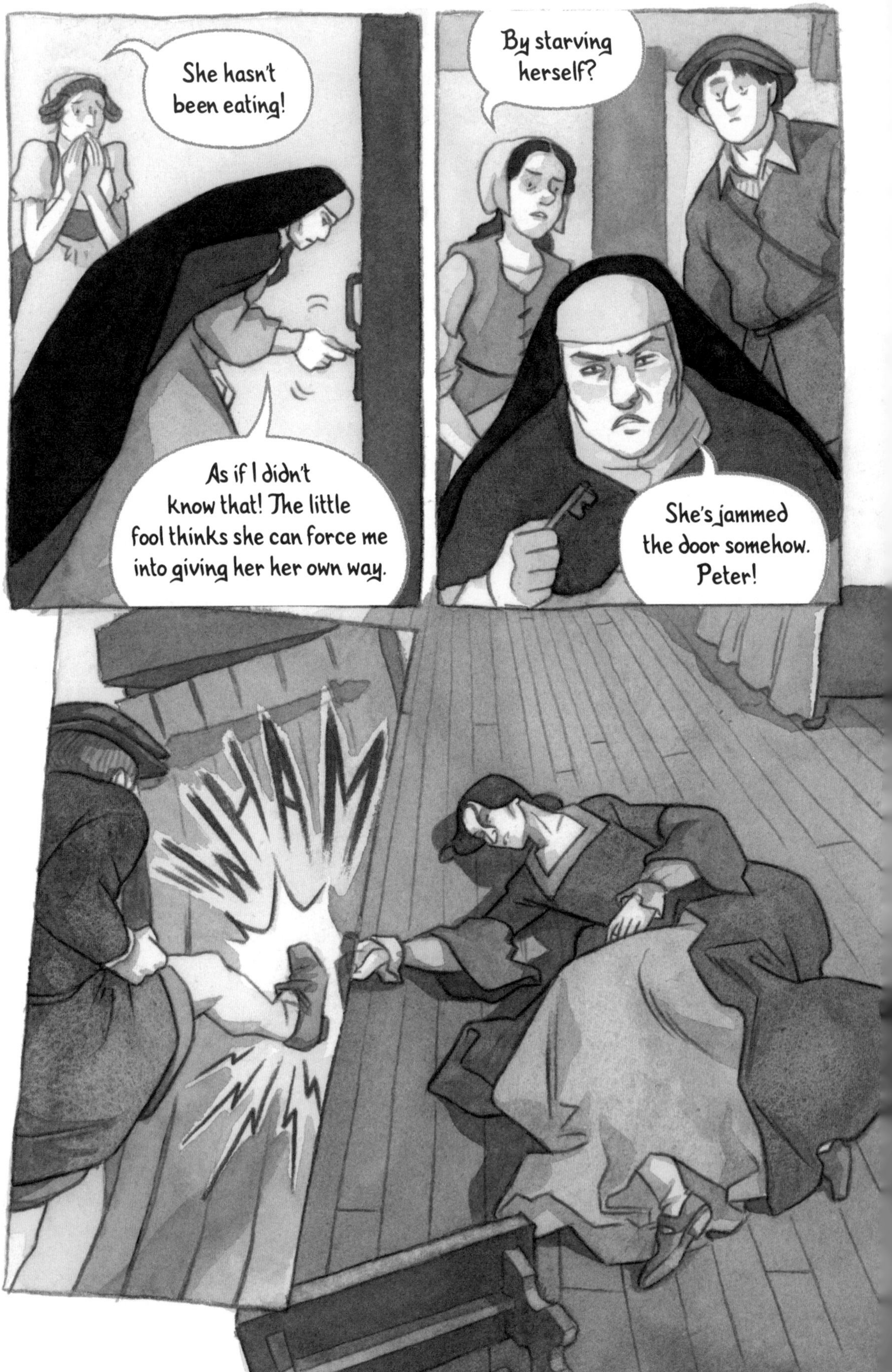
She hasn't been eating!
As if I didn't know that! The little fool thinks she can force me into giving her her own way.
By starving herself?
She's jammed the door somehow. Peter!
WHAM

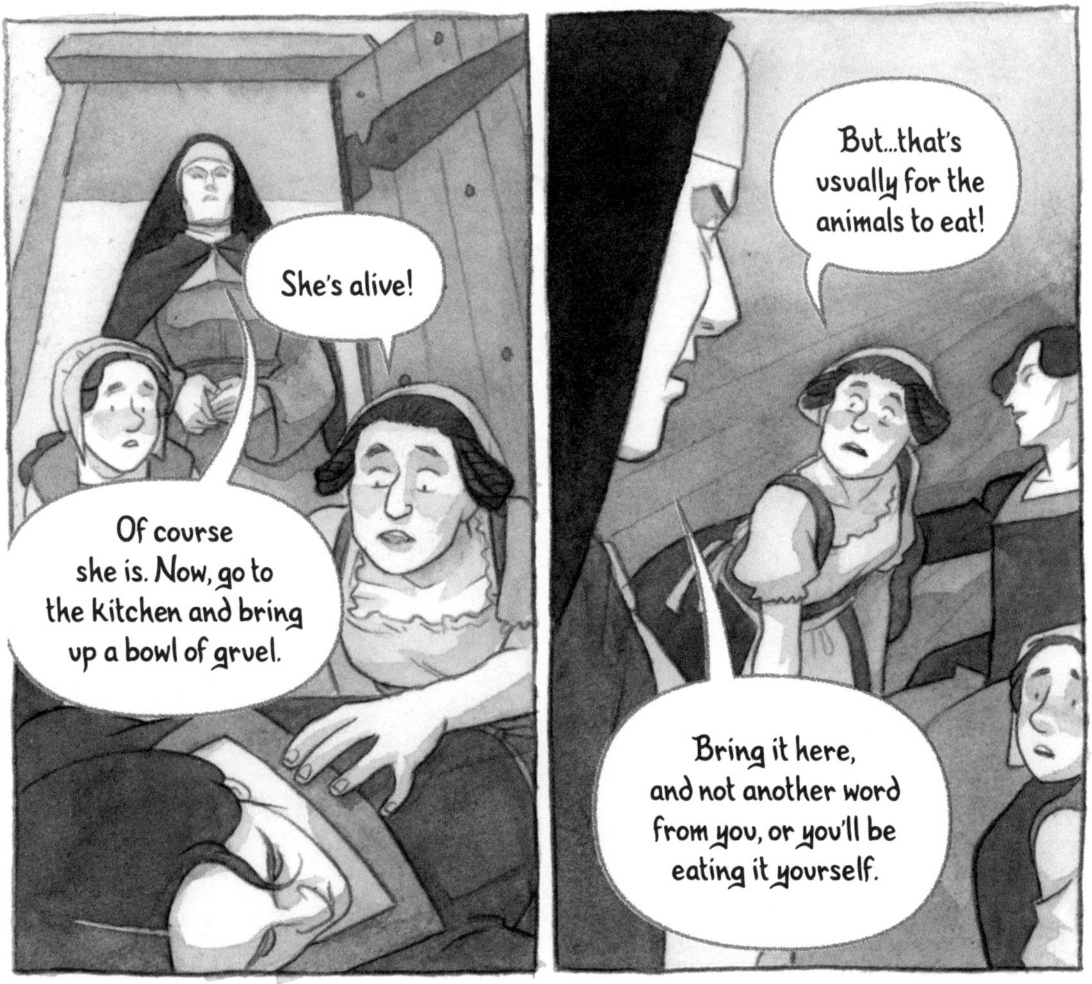
She's alive!
Of course she is. Now, go to the kitchen and bring up a bowl of gruel.
But...that's usually for the animals to eat!
Bring it here, and not another word from you, or you'll be eating it yourself.

Gruel is a kind of porridge, but not the good kind.

A Terrible Recipe for Terrible Gruel

(it's terrible!)

- 1 part OATS (normally for the horse)
- 1 part DRIED PEAS (normally for the chickens)
- 1 part WARM WATER or SKIMMED MILK

Directions: Soak everything until soft. Then mash with a spoon until disgusting. Do not sweeten or season. Eat with caution.

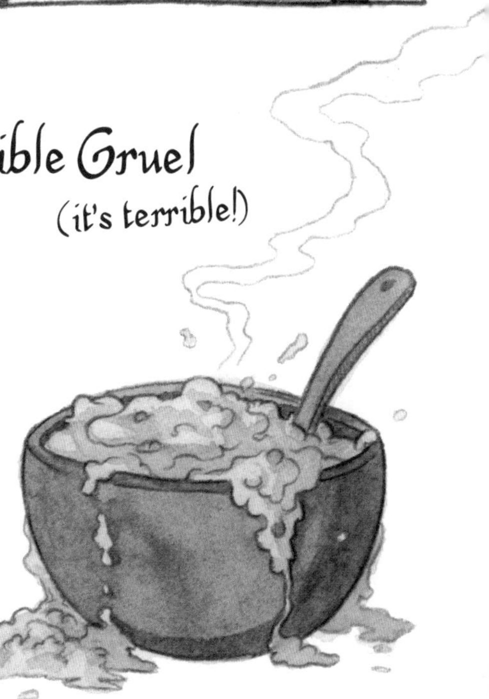

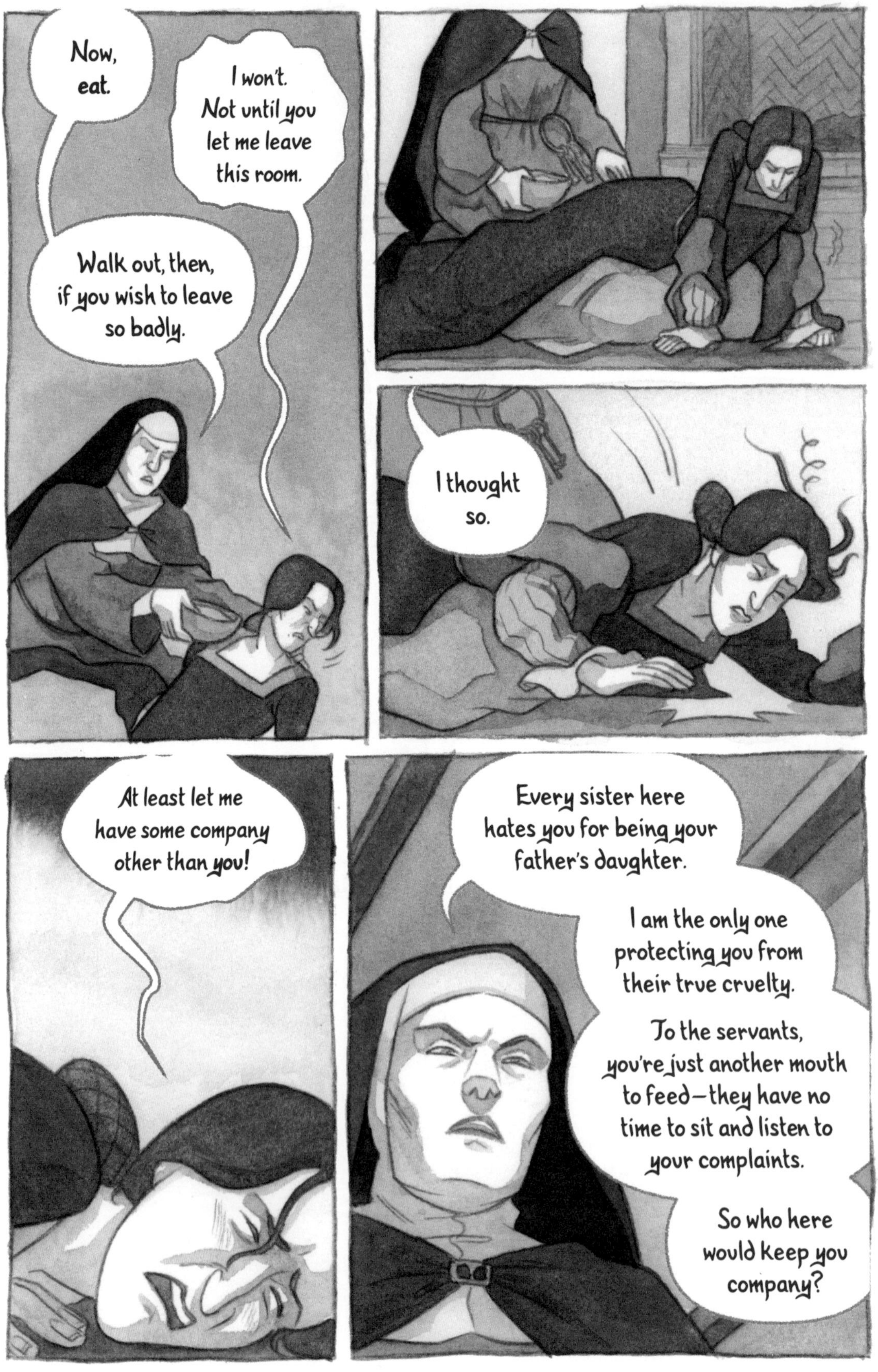

Now, eat.
I won't. Not until you let me leave this room.
Walk out, then, if you wish to leave so badly.
I thought so.
At least let me have some company other than you!
Every sister here hates you for being your father's daughter.
I am the only one protecting you from their true cruelty.
To the servants, you're just another mouth to feed—they have no time to sit and listen to your complaints.
So who here would keep you company?

The rats?

I'll do it.

I'll visit her.

Hmh. What do you say to that?

You would have your chambermaid after all.

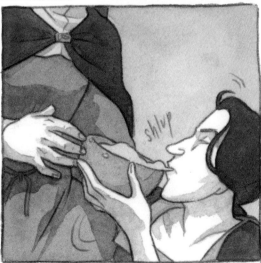

shlup

159

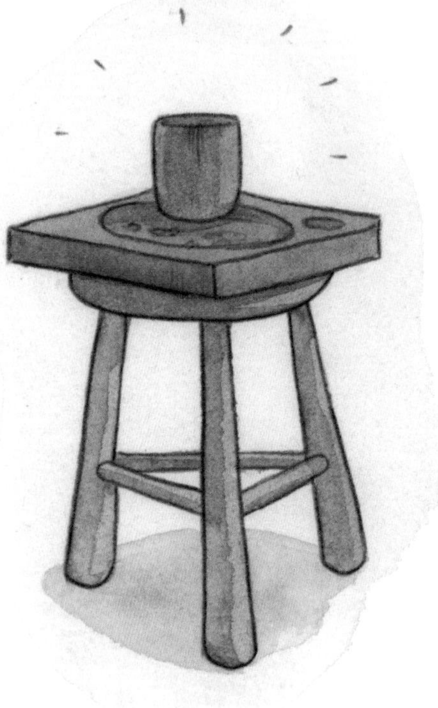

Mother Mary Clemence made us watch as Lady Eleanor ate the rest of the gruel, then sent us away.

That night Eleanor's supper dishes came back without a scrap left on them.

Over the next two days, Eleanor stayed in the chamber and continued to eat her food. But nobody sent for me. I knocked on the door, once, but nobody answered.

Maybe Eleanor had changed her mind about needing company.

Or about needing my company, anyway.

On the third morning, I woke up at sunrise for Lauds, as always.

I dressed and went to church and then helped Sister Philippa milk the goats.

I had breakfast in the kitchen and did some chores there, then went to change my clothes for lessons—

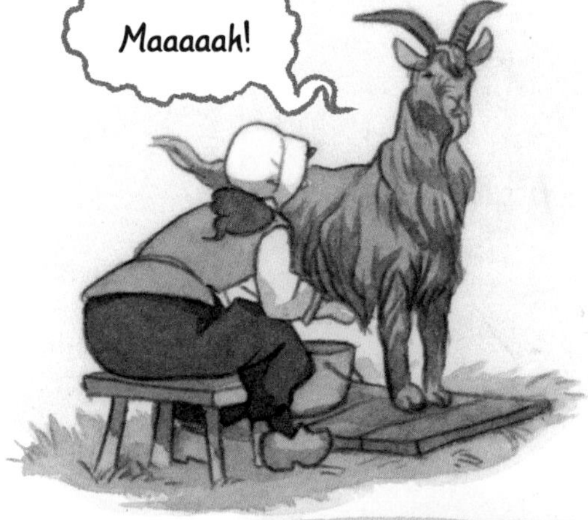

Maaaaah!

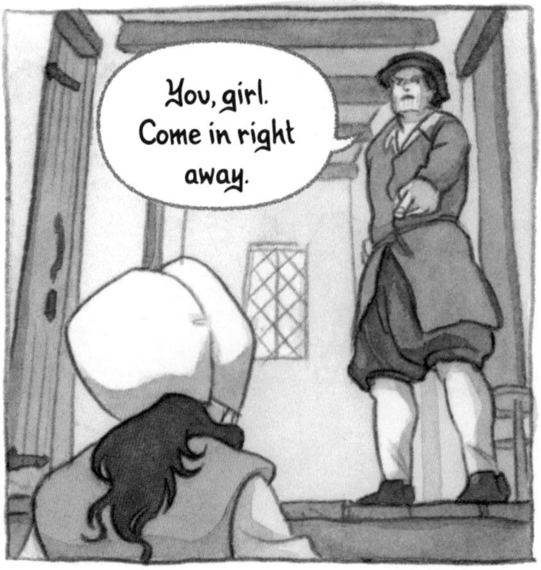

You, girl. Come in right away.

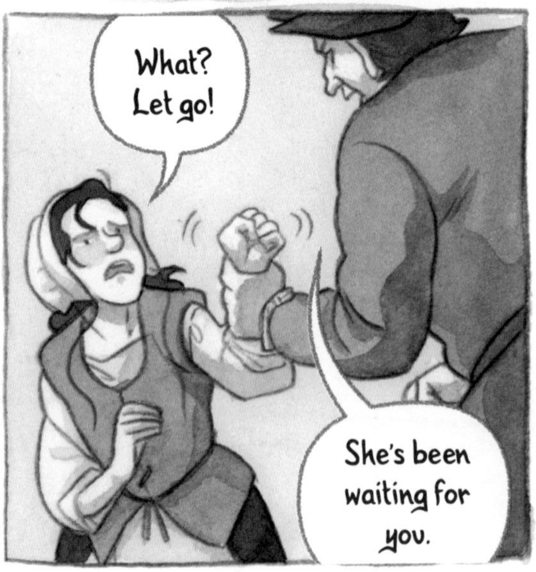

What? Let go!
She's been waiting for you.

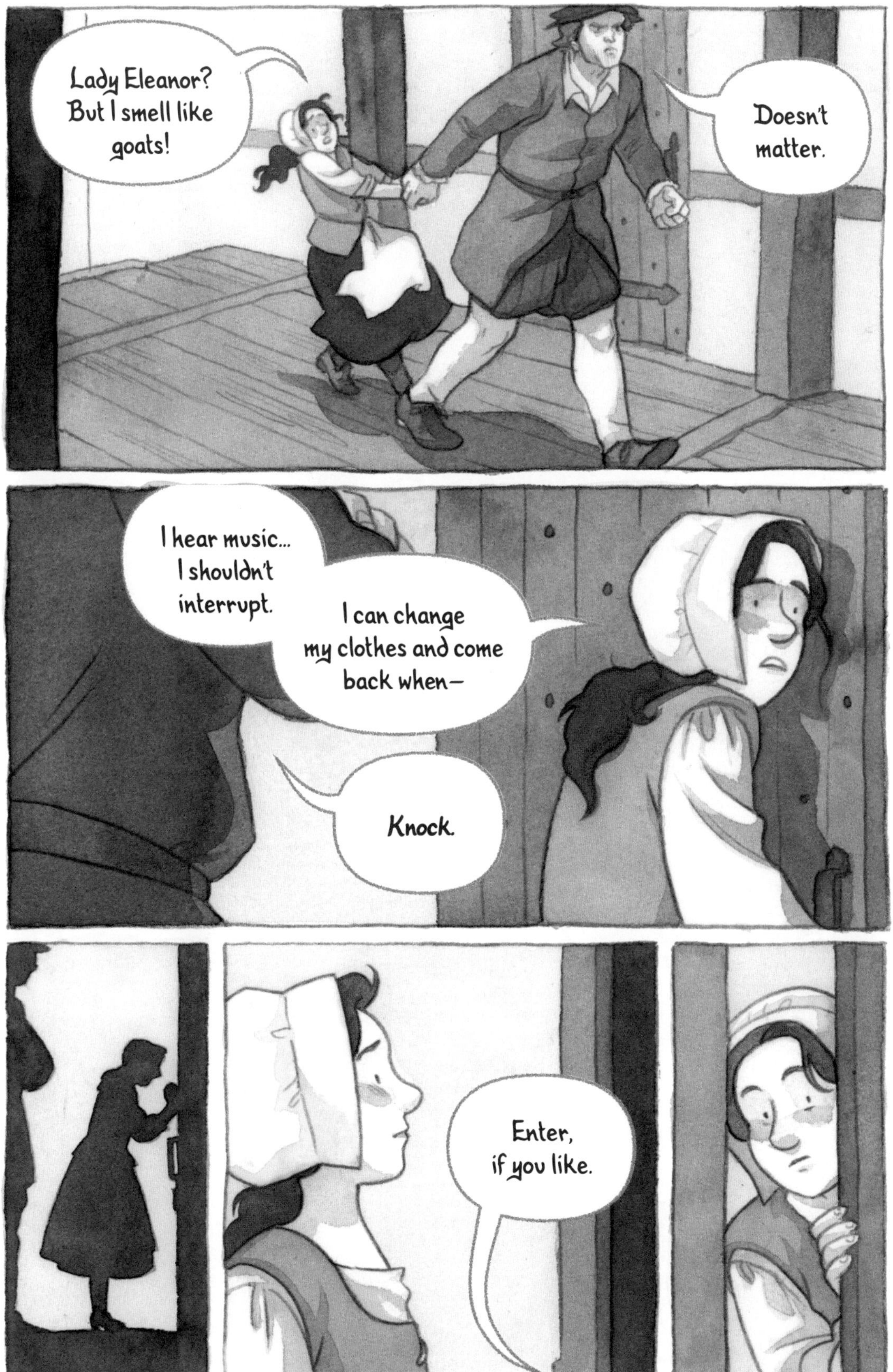
Lady Eleanor? But I smell like goats!
Doesn't matter.
I hear music... I shouldn't interrupt.
I can change my clothes and come back when—
Knock.
Enter, if you like.

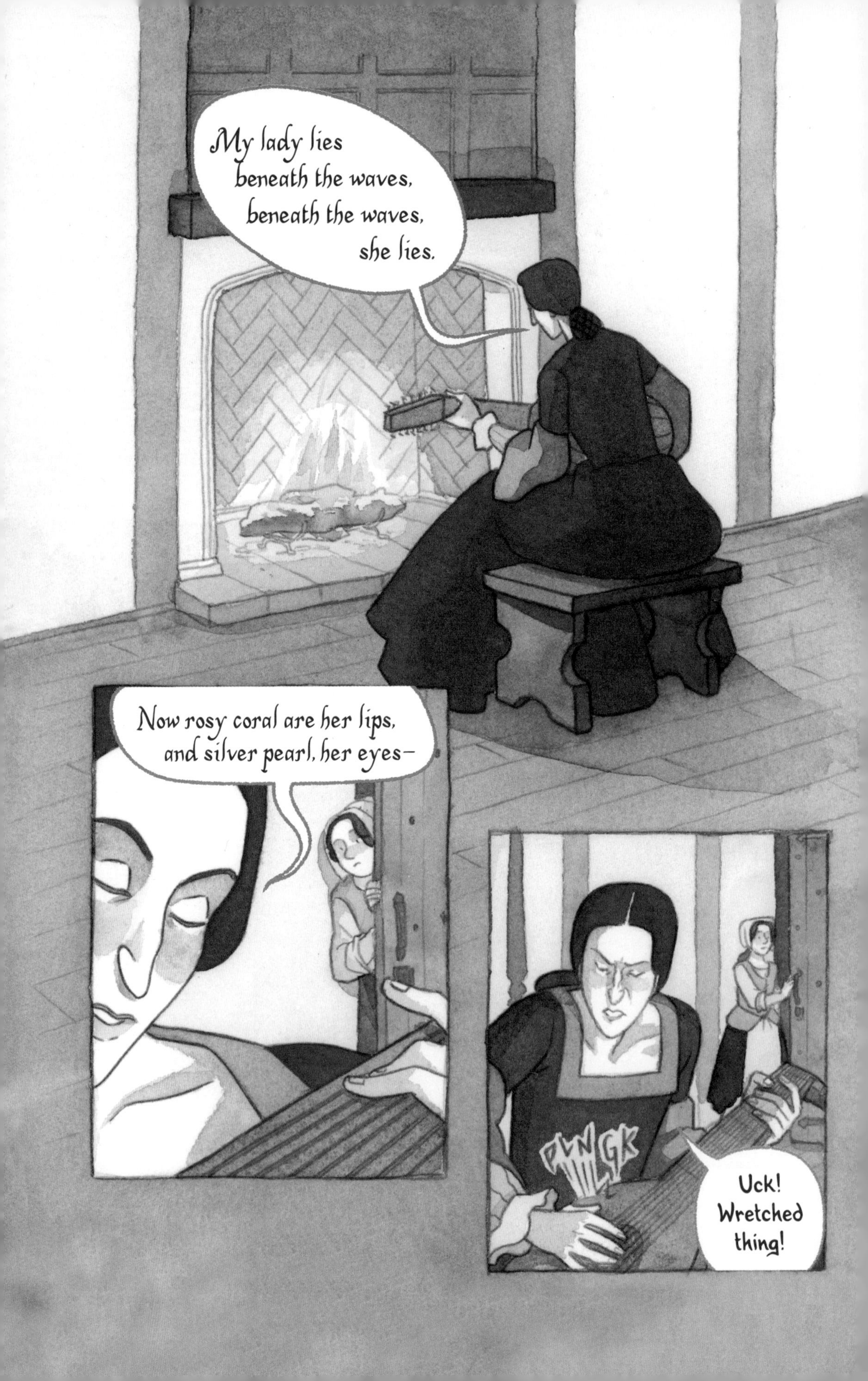
My lady lies beneath the waves, beneath the waves, she lies.
Now rosy coral are her lips, and silver pearl, her eyes–
PWNGK
Uck! Wretched thing!

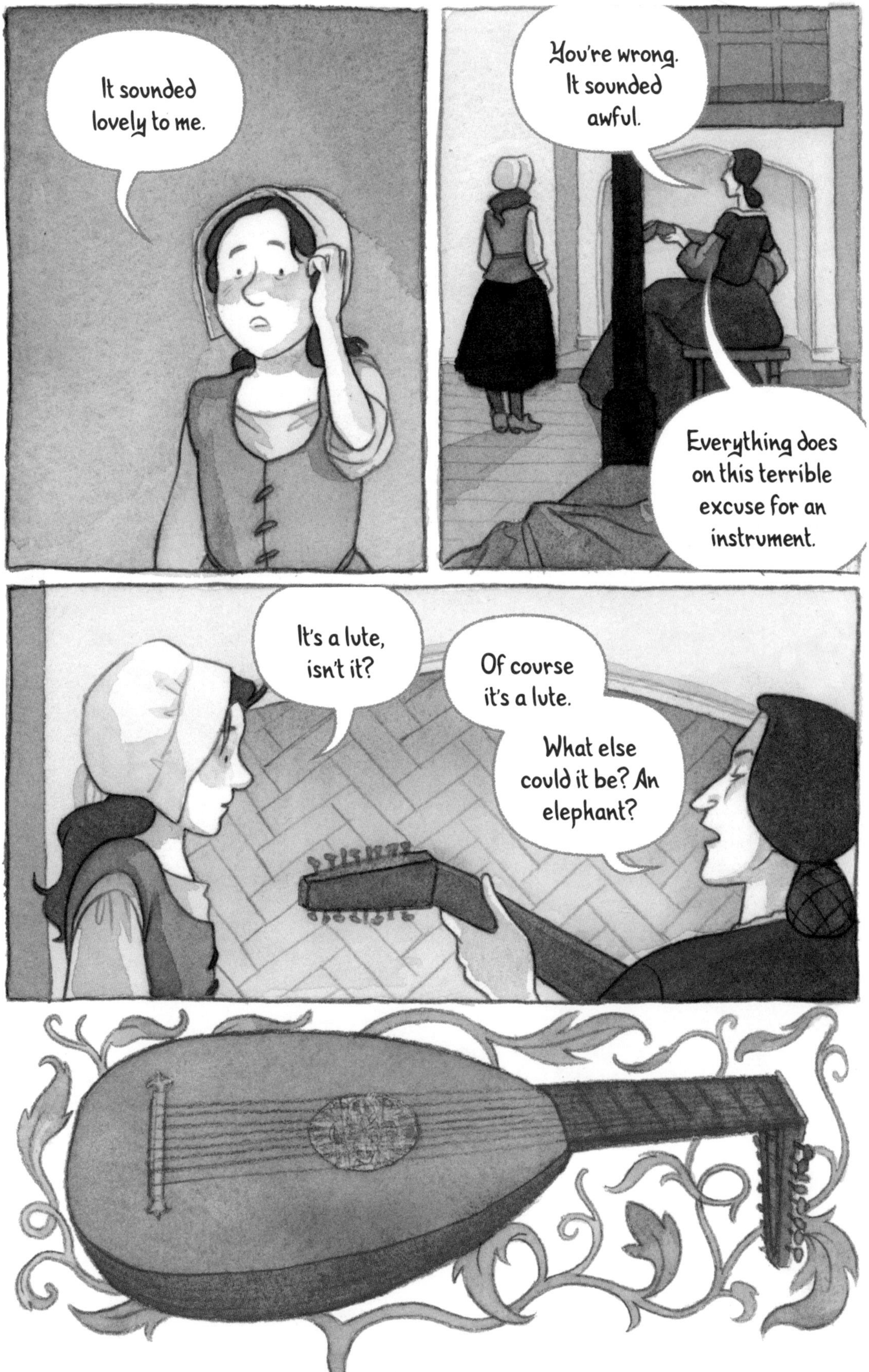
It sounded lovely to me.
You're wrong. It sounded awful.
Everything does on this terrible excuse for an instrument.
It's a lute, isn't it?
Of course it's a lute.
What else could it be? An elephant?

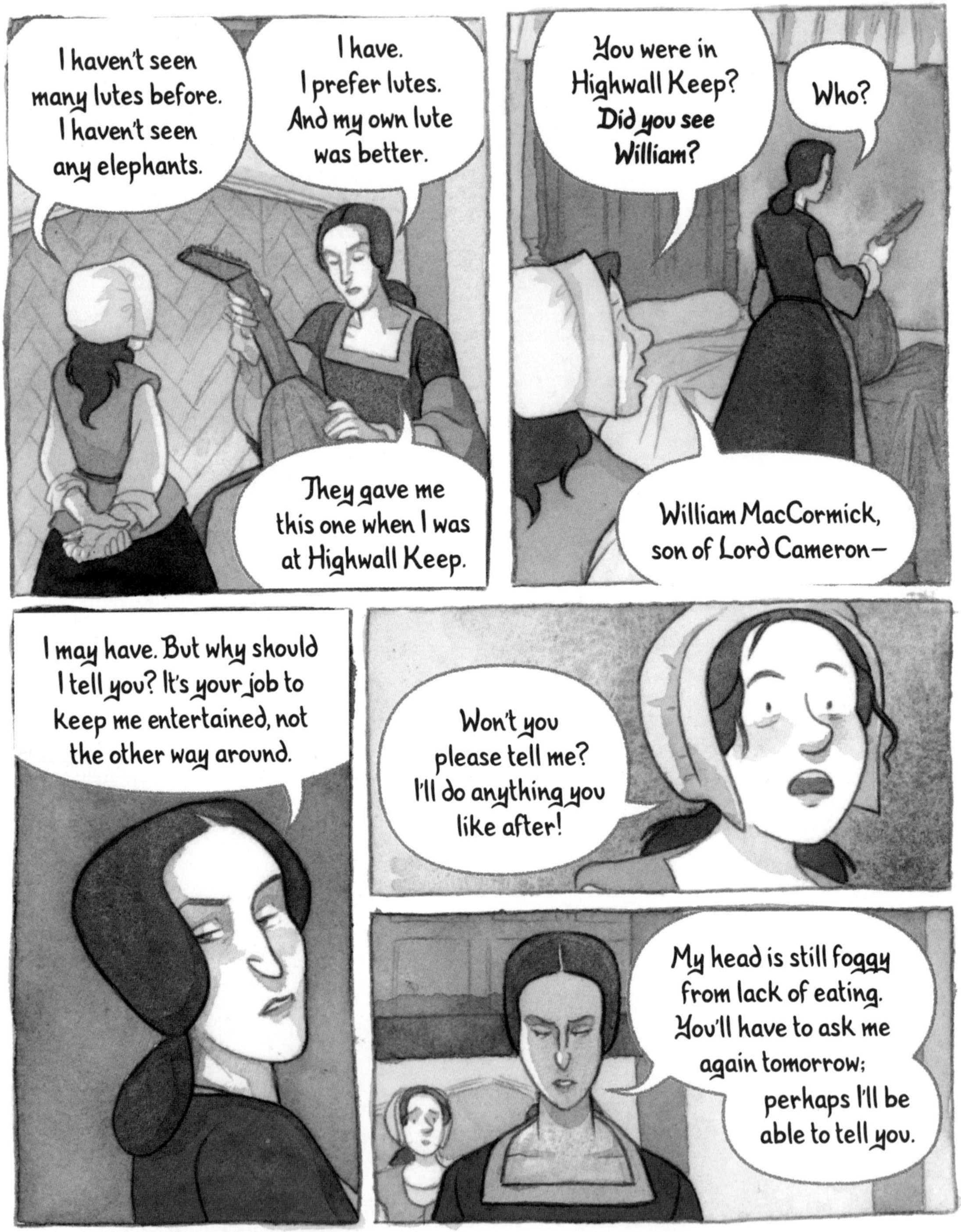
I haven't seen many lutes before. I haven't seen any elephants.
I have. I prefer lutes. And my own lute was better.
They gave me this one when I was at Highwall Keep.
You were in Highwall Keep? Did you see William?
Who?
William MacCormick, son of Lord Cameron—
I may have. But why should I tell you? It's your job to keep me entertained, not the other way around.
Won't you please tell me? I'll do anything you like after!
My head is still foggy from lack of eating. You'll have to ask me again tomorrow; perhaps I'll be able to tell you.

Now I know that she was lonely, and afraid I wouldn't come back if she didn't have an important secret to tempt me with.

But right then I only thought that she was very strange and a little cruel and I almost regretted agreeing to visit her.

When I was brought to the chamber the next day, Mother Mary Clemence was there.

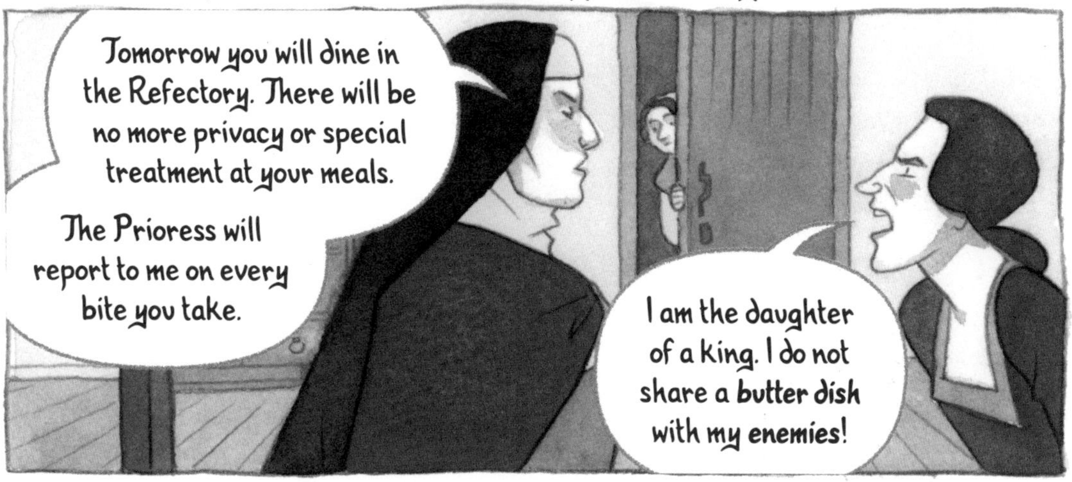
Tomorrow you will dine in the Refectory. There will be no more privacy or special treatment at your meals.
The Prioress will report to me on every bite you take.
I am the daughter of a king. I do not share a **butter dish** with **my enemies**!

Eleanor didn't say much more than that, and soon Her Reverence left us, looking very satisfied. Had Mother Mary Clemence truly broken Eleanor's spirit? Or was Eleanor secretly pleased that, in the end, she was being allowed out of the chamber?

Maybe that had been her plan all along. I wasn't foolish enough to ask her.

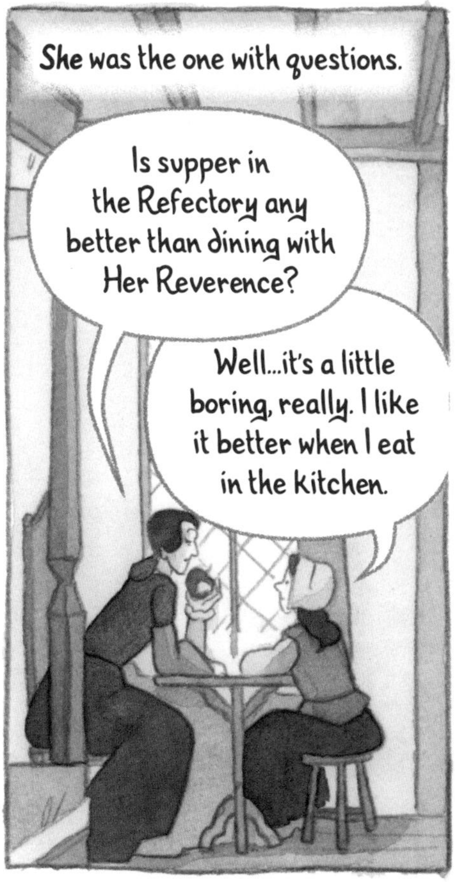
She was the one with questions.
Is supper in the Refectory any better than dining with Her Reverence?
Well...it's a little boring, really. I like it better when I eat in the kitchen.

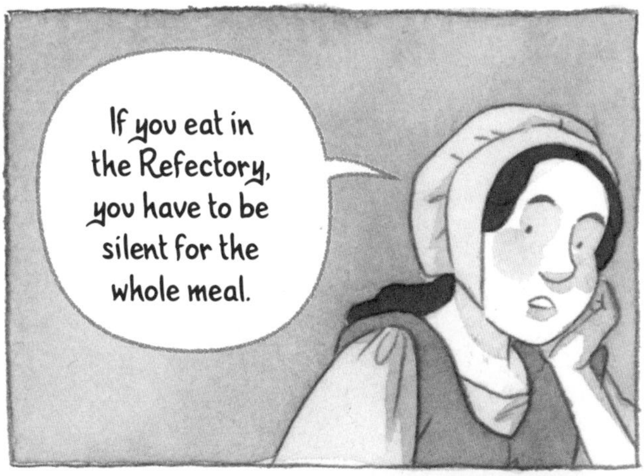
If you eat in the Refectory, you have to be silent for the whole meal.

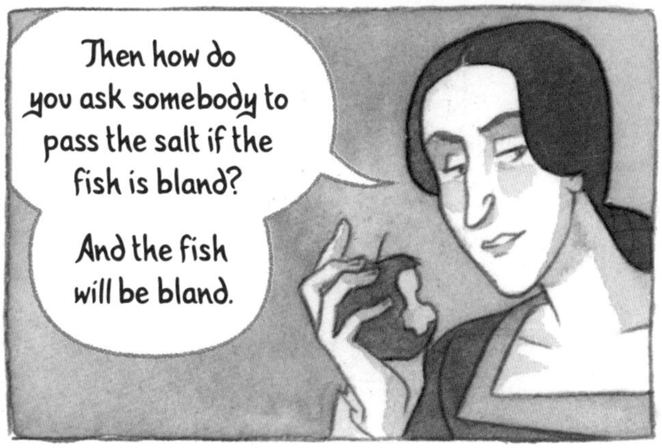
Then how do you ask somebody to pass the salt if the fish is bland?
And the fish will be bland.

Table

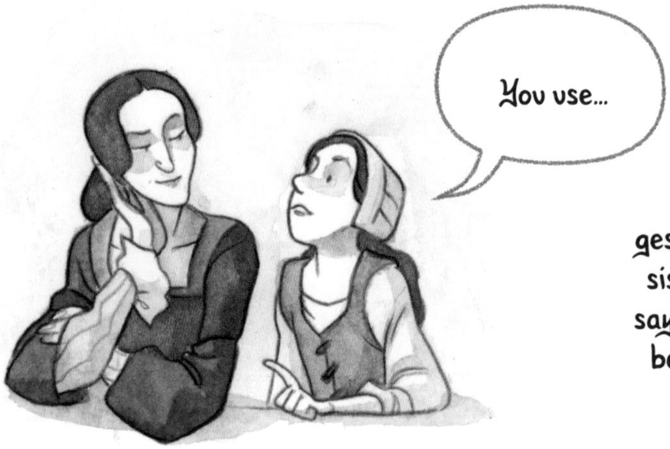
You use...

These are silent hand gestures that every Elysian sister learns! Sister Sybil says some of them may even be hundreds of years old.

For **honey**, pretend you have some stuck on your thumb, and then lick it away. (Mmm.)

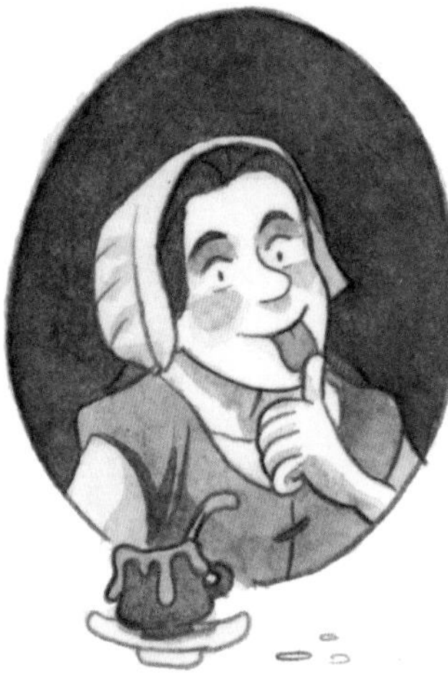

Our **bread** loaves are round, so make a circle with your thumb and forefinger.

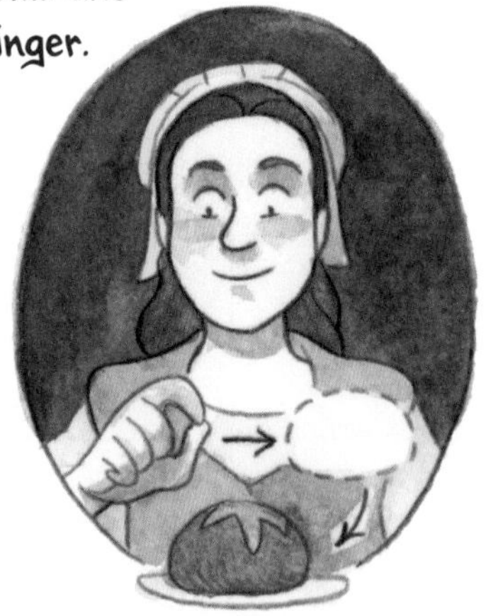

If you want **vinegar**, make a sour face—just as sour as vinegar tastes!

This one can be easy to mix up with the sign for honey, so look out.

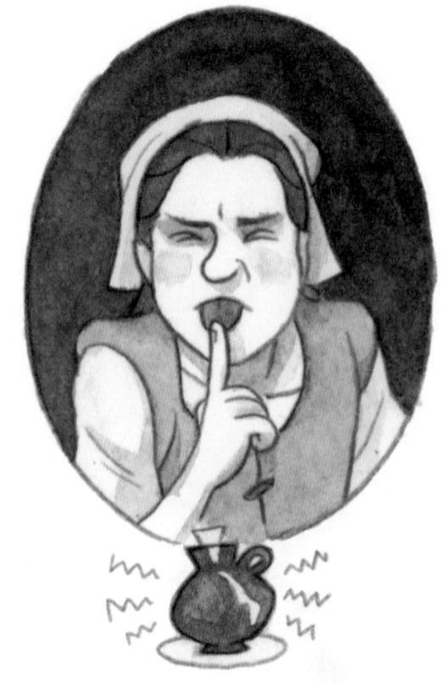

Signs!

Does the food need any salt?
Just pretend to sprinkle some.

If you'd like some fish,
all you have to do is hold
your breath and swim for it!

Who loves cheese
more than a mouse?

We have to milk the goats
every morning, so it isn't hard
to do it again at the table.

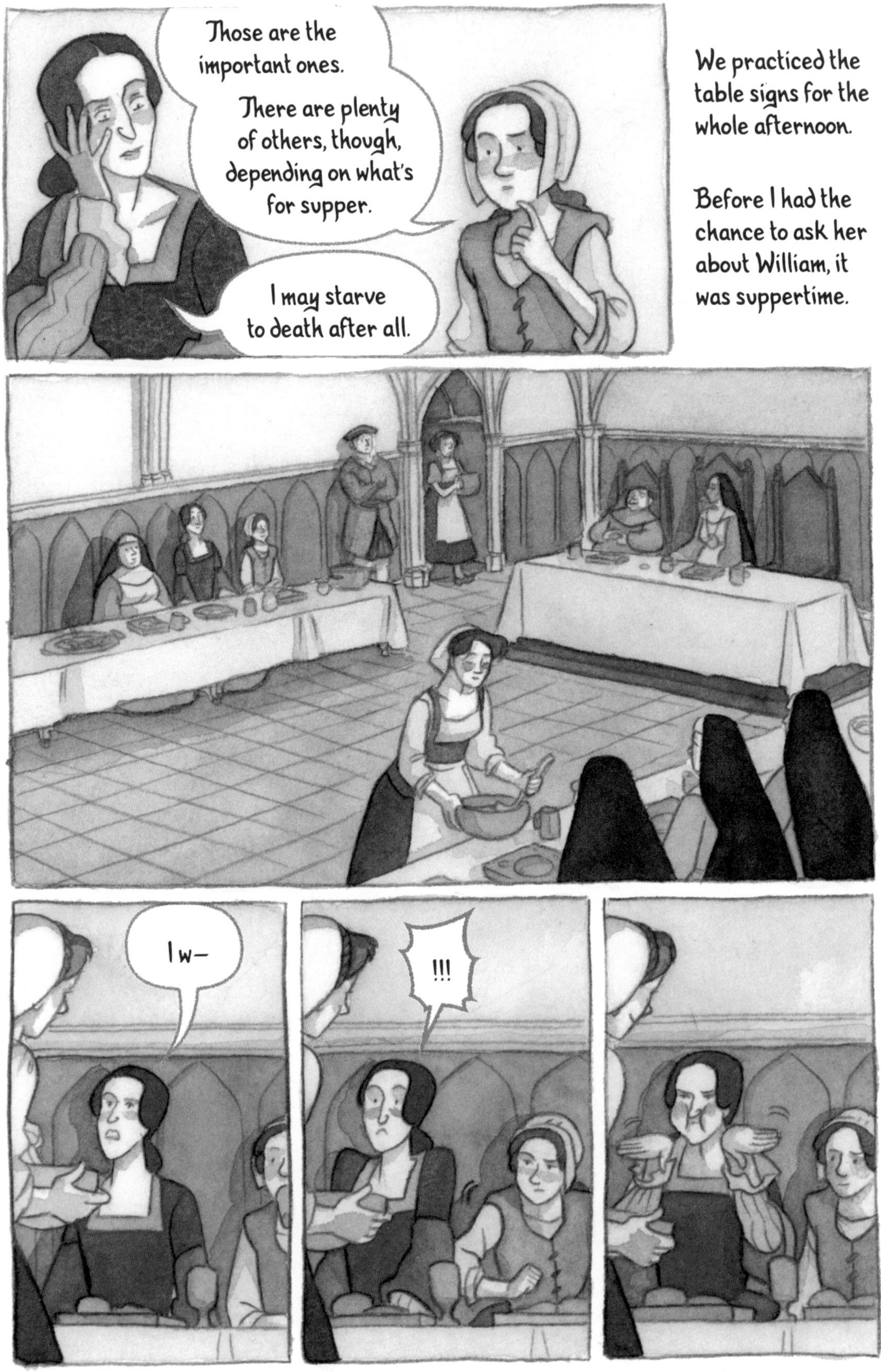
Those are the important ones.
There are plenty of others, though, depending on what's for supper.
I may starve to death after all.
We practiced the table signs for the whole afternoon.
Before I had the chance to ask her about William, it was suppertime.
I w–
!!!

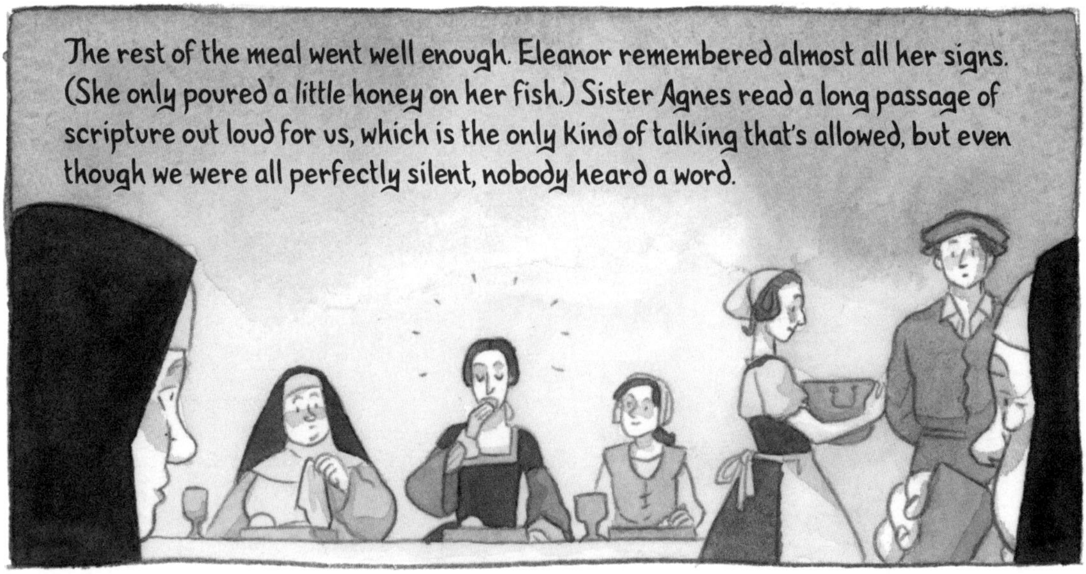
The rest of the meal went well enough. Eleanor remembered almost all her signs. (She only poured a little honey on her fish.) Sister Agnes read a long passage of scripture out loud for us, which is the only kind of talking that's allowed, but even though we were all perfectly silent, nobody heard a word.

Supper seemed as though it lasted for hours. Finally the dishes were cleared away, and the sisters went off to say their Compline prayers. Peter Yarrow took us back upstairs.

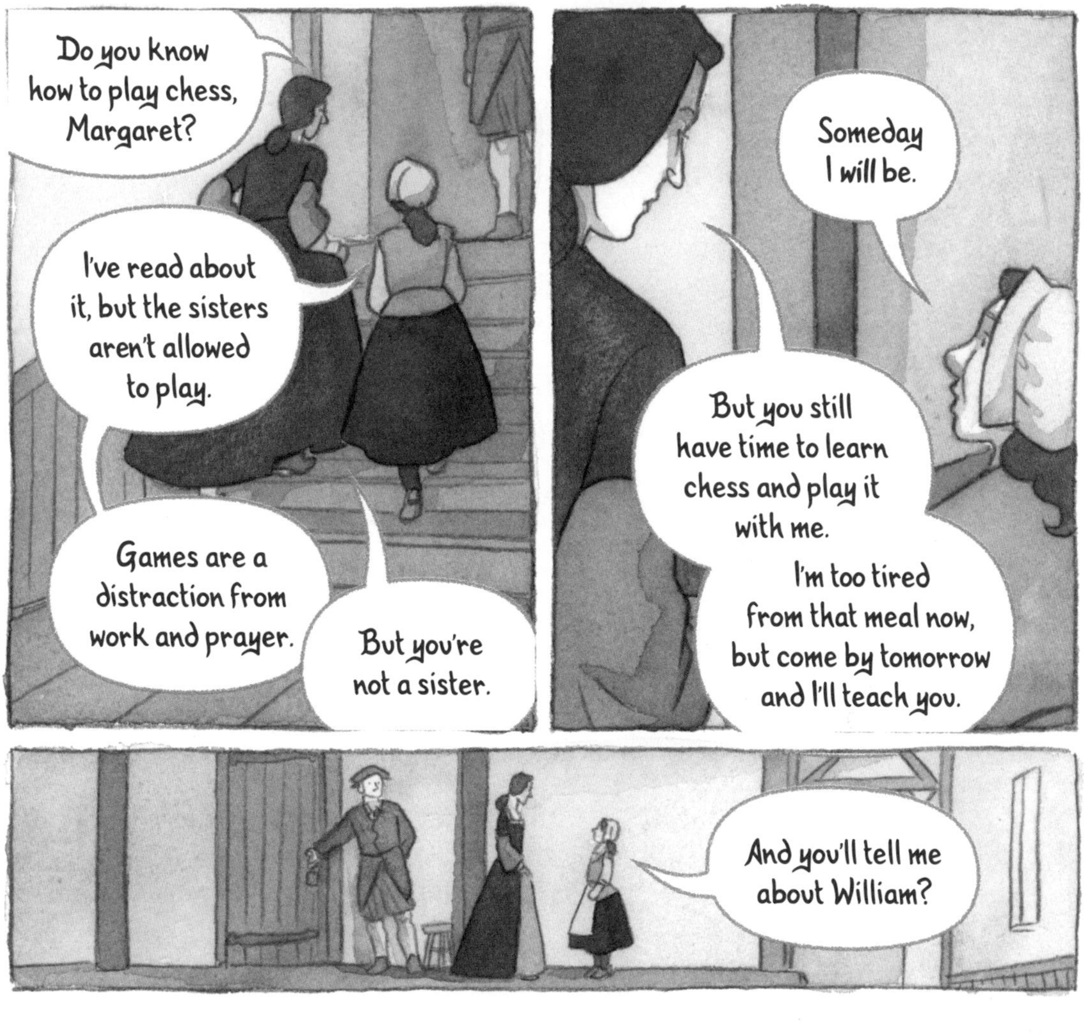
Do you know how to play chess, Margaret?
I've read about it, but the sisters aren't allowed to play.
Games are a distraction from work and prayer.
But you're not a sister.
Someday I will be.
But you still have time to learn chess and play it with me.
I'm too tired from that meal now, but come by tomorrow and I'll teach you.
And you'll tell me about William?

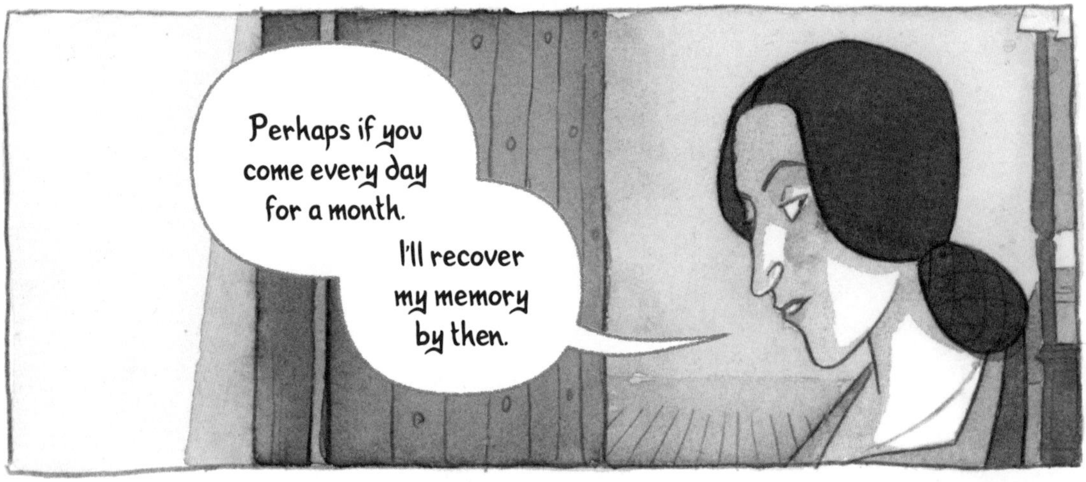
Perhaps if you come every day for a month.
I'll recover my memory by then.

After that, the hours of my day were never the same.

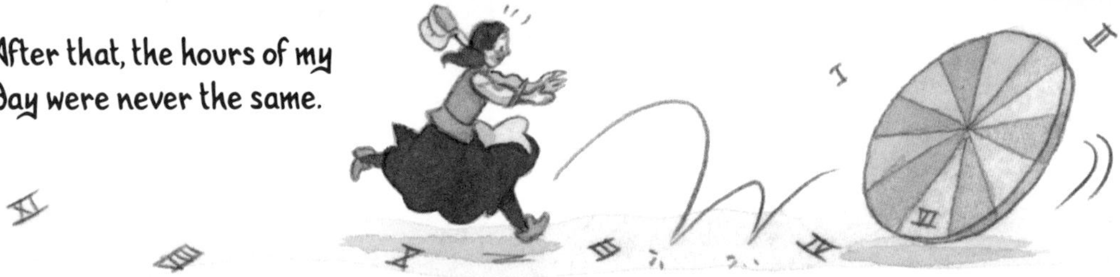

Some days I wasn't sent for at all, and I only saw Eleanor in the Refectory. Other days, Harold Carpenter or Peter Yarrow would fetch me from the kitchen before Terce, and instead of going to study with Sister Sybil, I would stay in Eleanor's chamber all day.

The next several times I was brought to the chamber, Mother Mary Clemence was there—and she did not leave us alone at all except to use the necessarium. She read us very boring things she had written, mostly about—

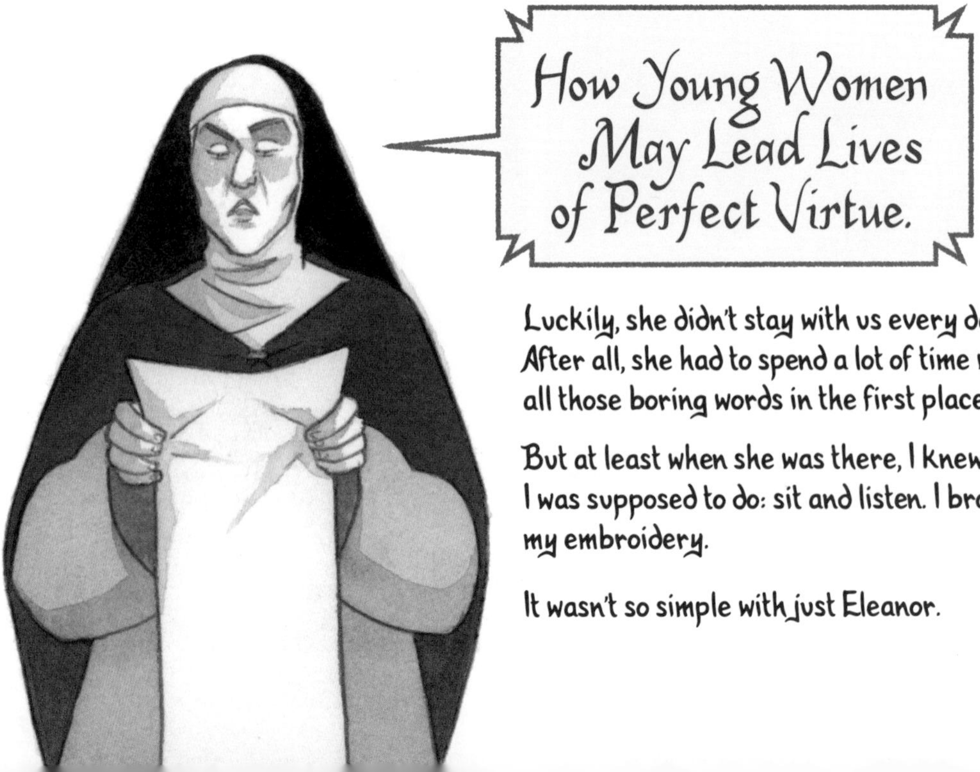
How Young Women May Lead Lives of Perfect Virtue.

Luckily, she didn't stay with us every day. After all, she had to spend a lot of time writing all those boring words in the first place.

But at least when she was there, I knew what I was supposed to do: sit and listen. I brought my embroidery.

It wasn't so simple with just Eleanor.

The first day that we had to ourselves, Eleanor played the lute and told me funny stories about a duchess's pet monkey at the royal court in Albion.

It would hop on ladies' shoulders and steal their earrings, and then hide them inside an old boot.

When a servant found his little treasure trove, all the noble children at court held a trial for the monkey. They found him guilty and sentenced him to death.

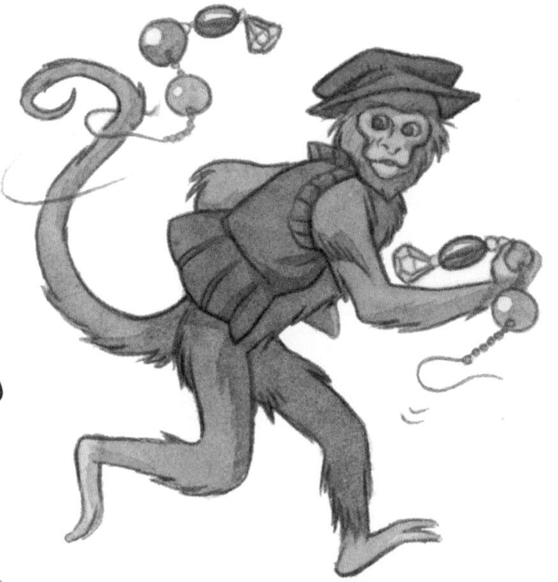

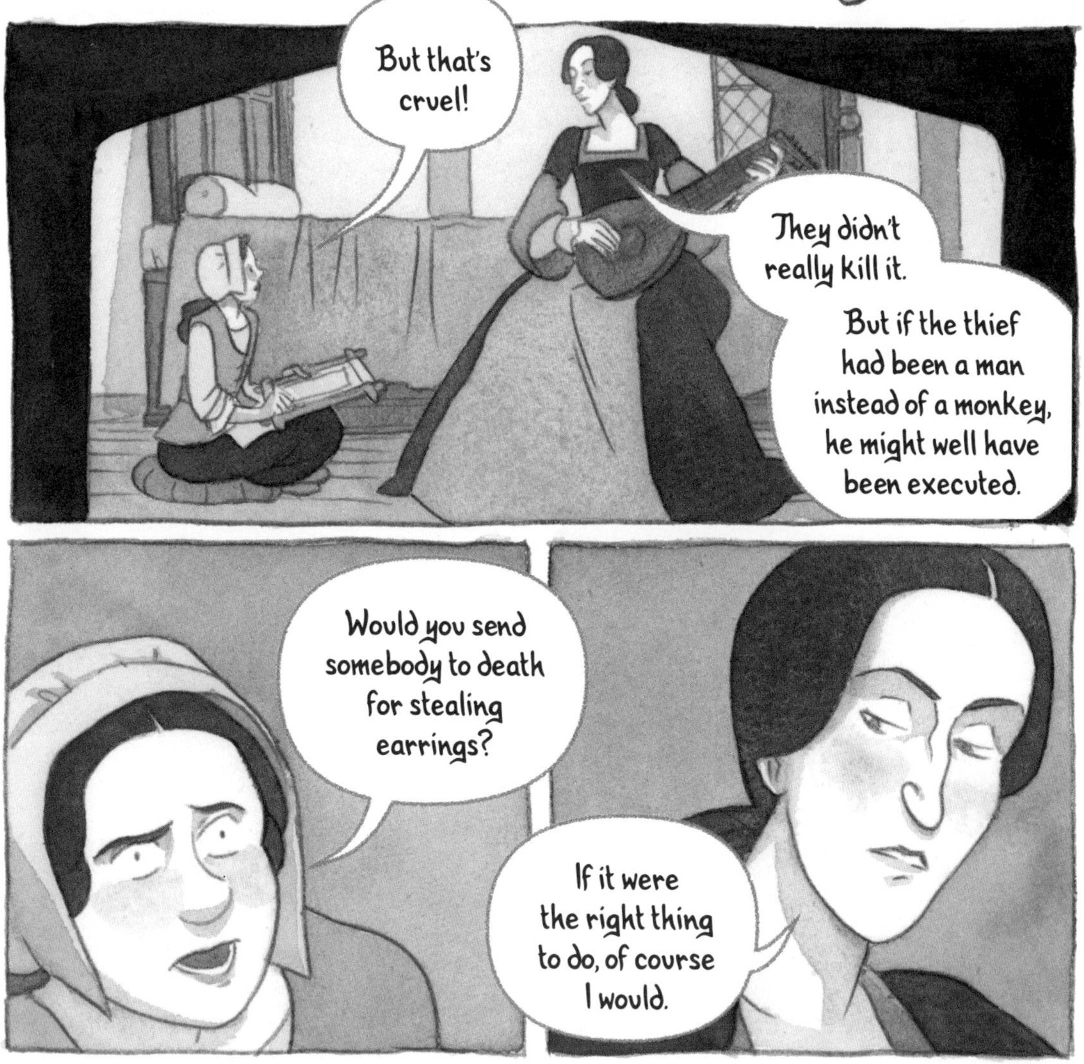

But that's cruel!
They didn't really kill it.
But if the thief had been a man instead of a monkey, he might well have been executed.
Would you send somebody to death for stealing earrings?
If it were the right thing to do, of course I would.

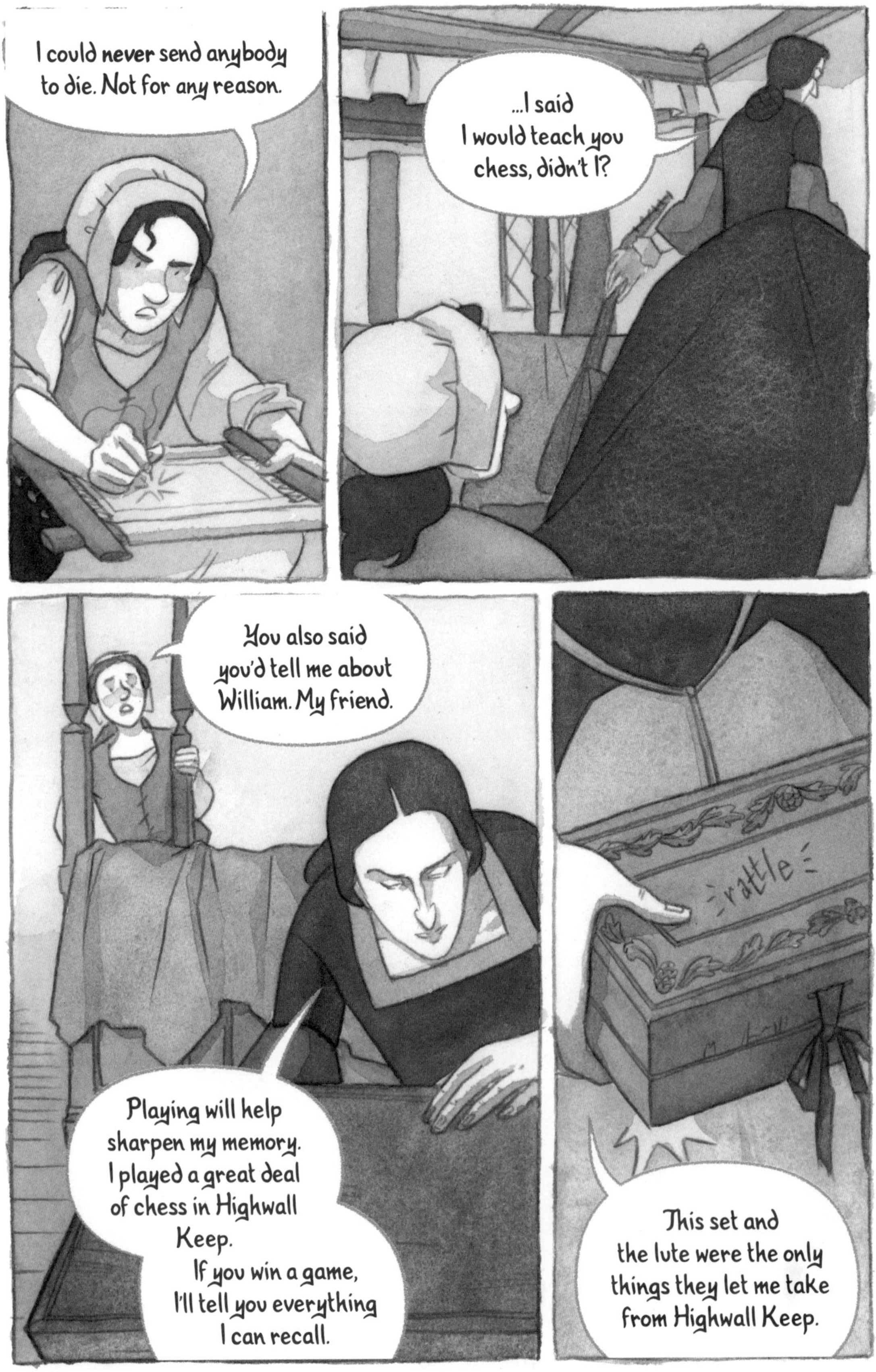
I could never send anybody to die. Not for any reason.
...I said I would teach you chess, didn't I?
You also said you'd tell me about William. My friend.
Playing will help sharpen my memory. I played a great deal of chess in Highwall Keep.
If you win a game, I'll tell you everything I can recall.
rattle
This set and the lute were the only things they let me take from Highwall Keep.

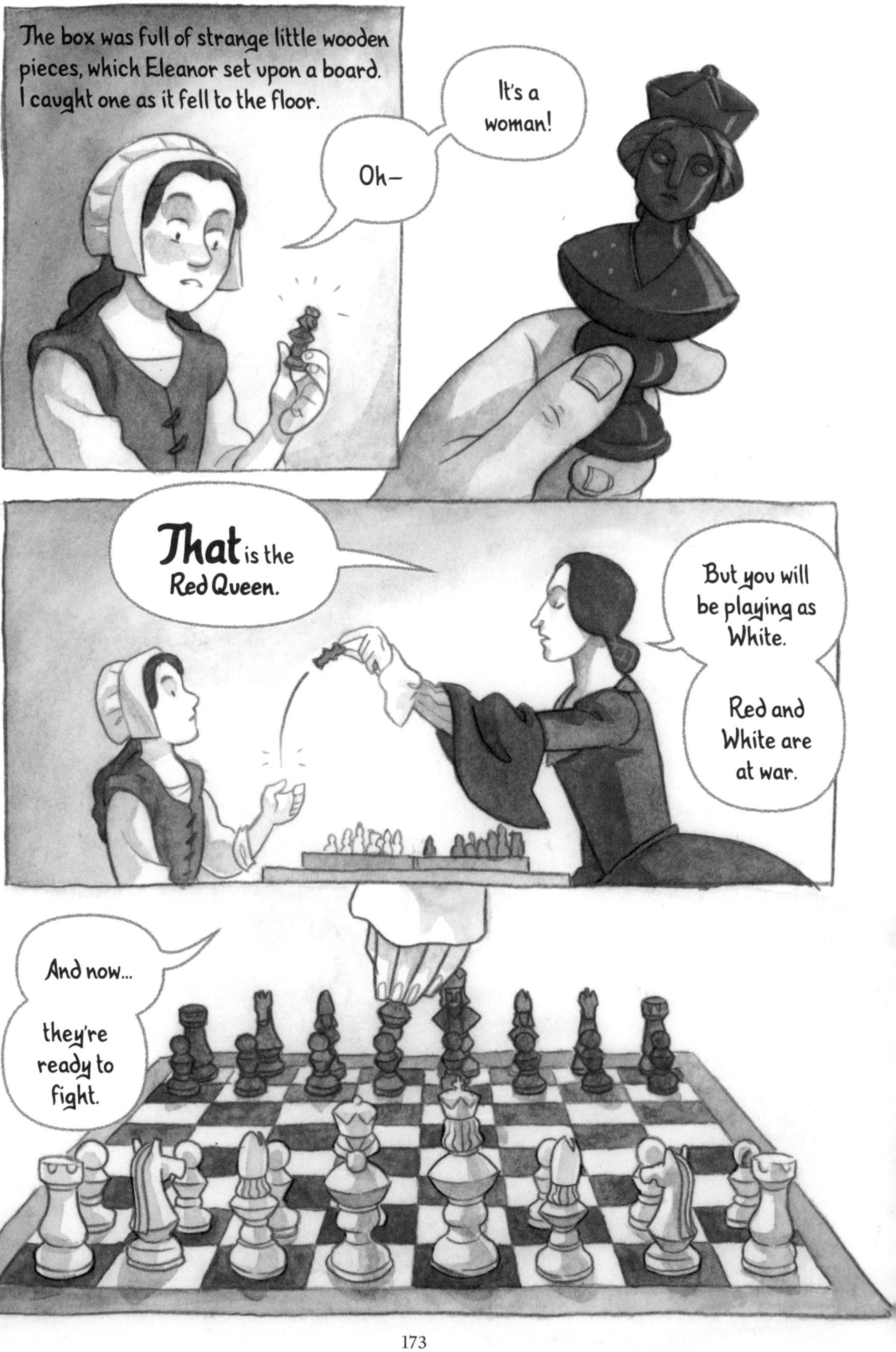
The box was full of strange little wooden pieces, which Eleanor set upon a board. I caught one as it fell to the floor.
Oh–
It's a woman!
That is the Red Queen.
But you will be playing as White.
Red and White are at war.
And now...
they're ready to fight.

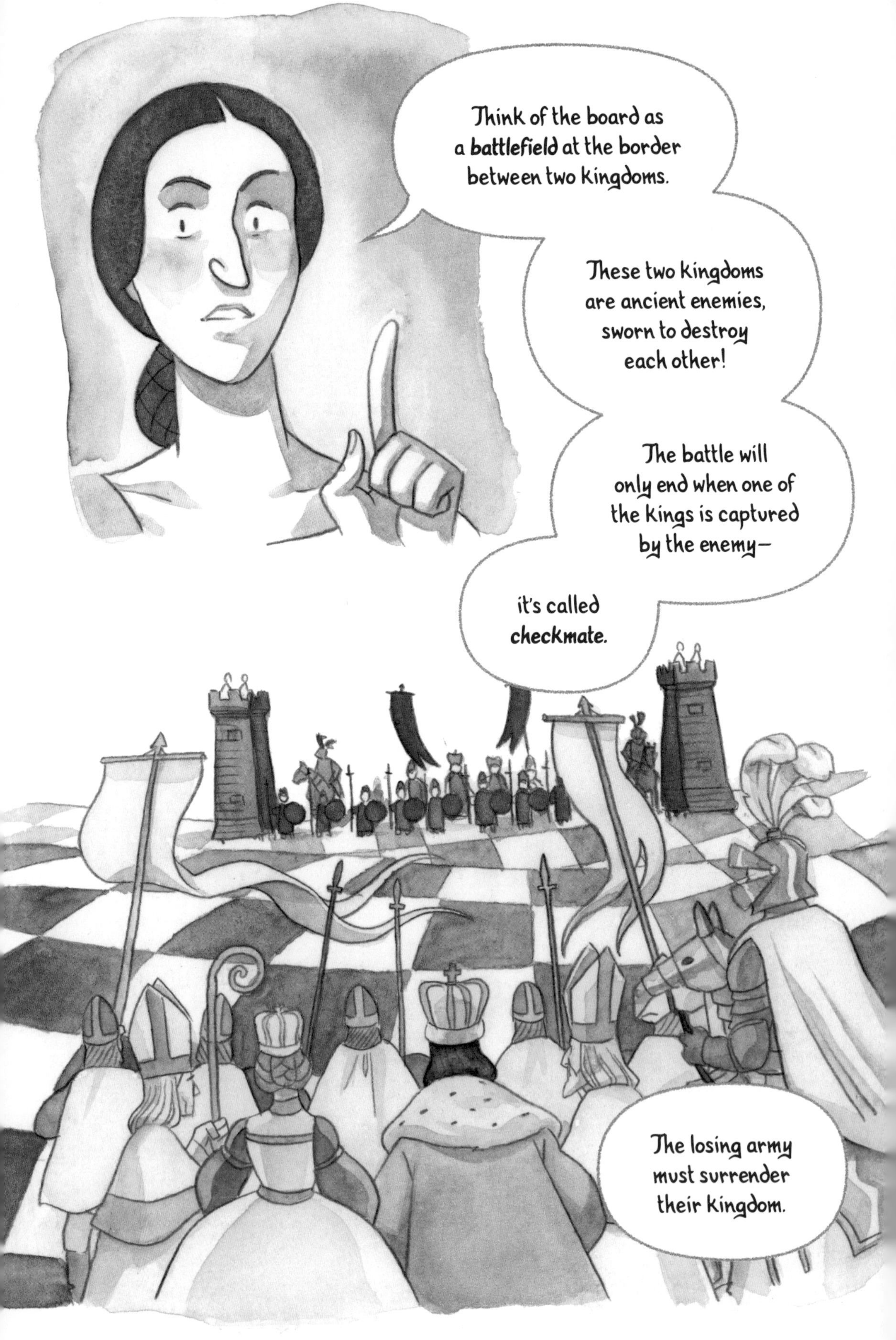
Think of the board as a battlefield at the border between two kingdoms.
These two kingdoms are ancient enemies, sworn to destroy each other!
The battle will only end when one of the kings is captured by the enemy—
it's called checkmate.
The losing army must surrender their kingdom.

the Pawn

A foot soldier who has left his farm and family to fight for his kingdom. At the start of the battle, he will charge two spaces, but then he becomes more cautious and only moves **one**.

His pike is long but his arms are short, so he can only defeat a piece in the space across from him.

Each side has eight.

the Rook

Not a single soldier—but a **siege tower**, made of wood and set on iron wheels.

Archers at the top fire arrows over the enemy's walls

or throw down a plank and climb across them.

Because of its wheels, a rook can only move in straight lines.

Each side has two.

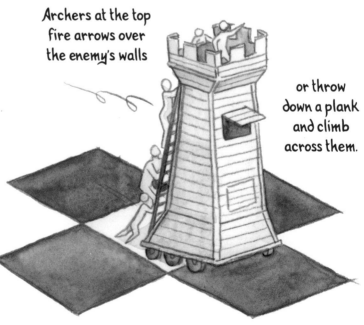

the Bishop

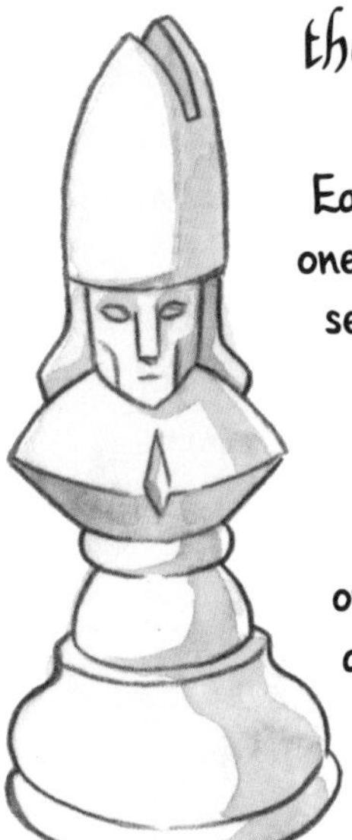

Each kingdom has one bishop who only sets foot on white spaces...

and one who only travels across red.

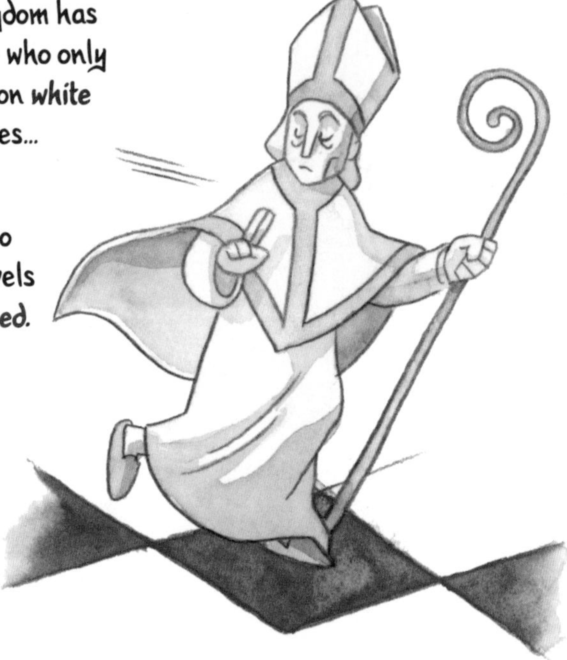

Perhaps they've quarreled over a church matter.

the Knight

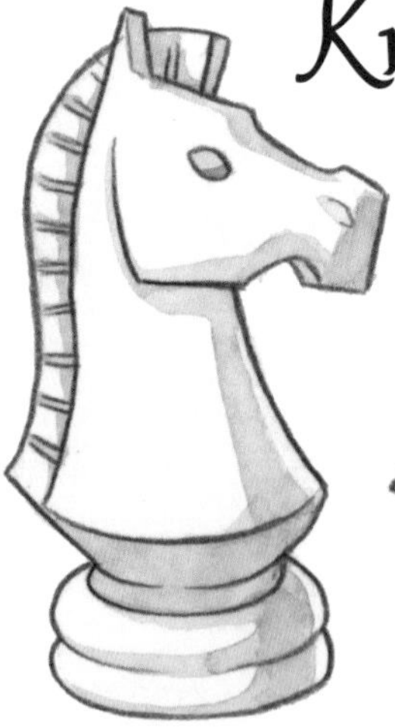

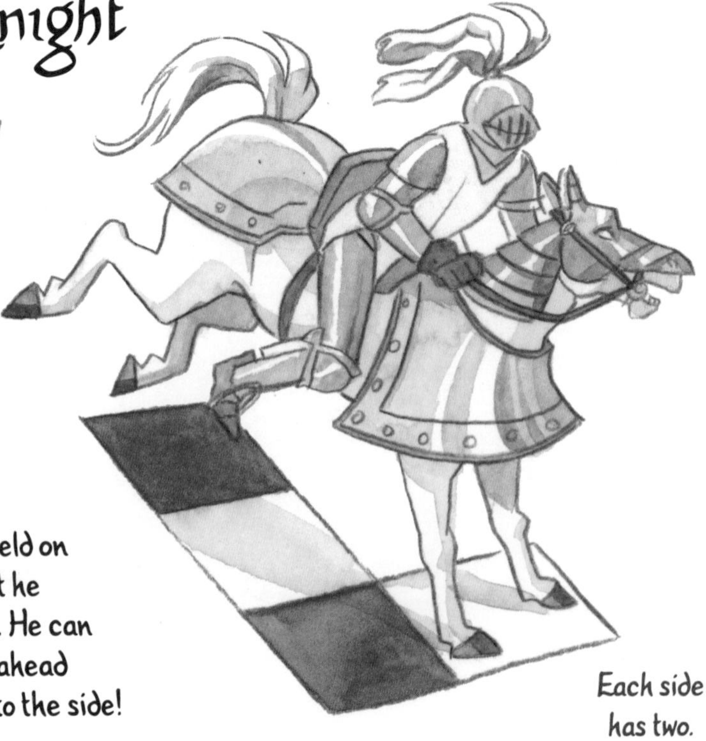

He gallops around the field on his mighty warhorse, but he often yanks at the reins. He can only charge two spaces ahead before his steed bucks to the side!

Each side has two.

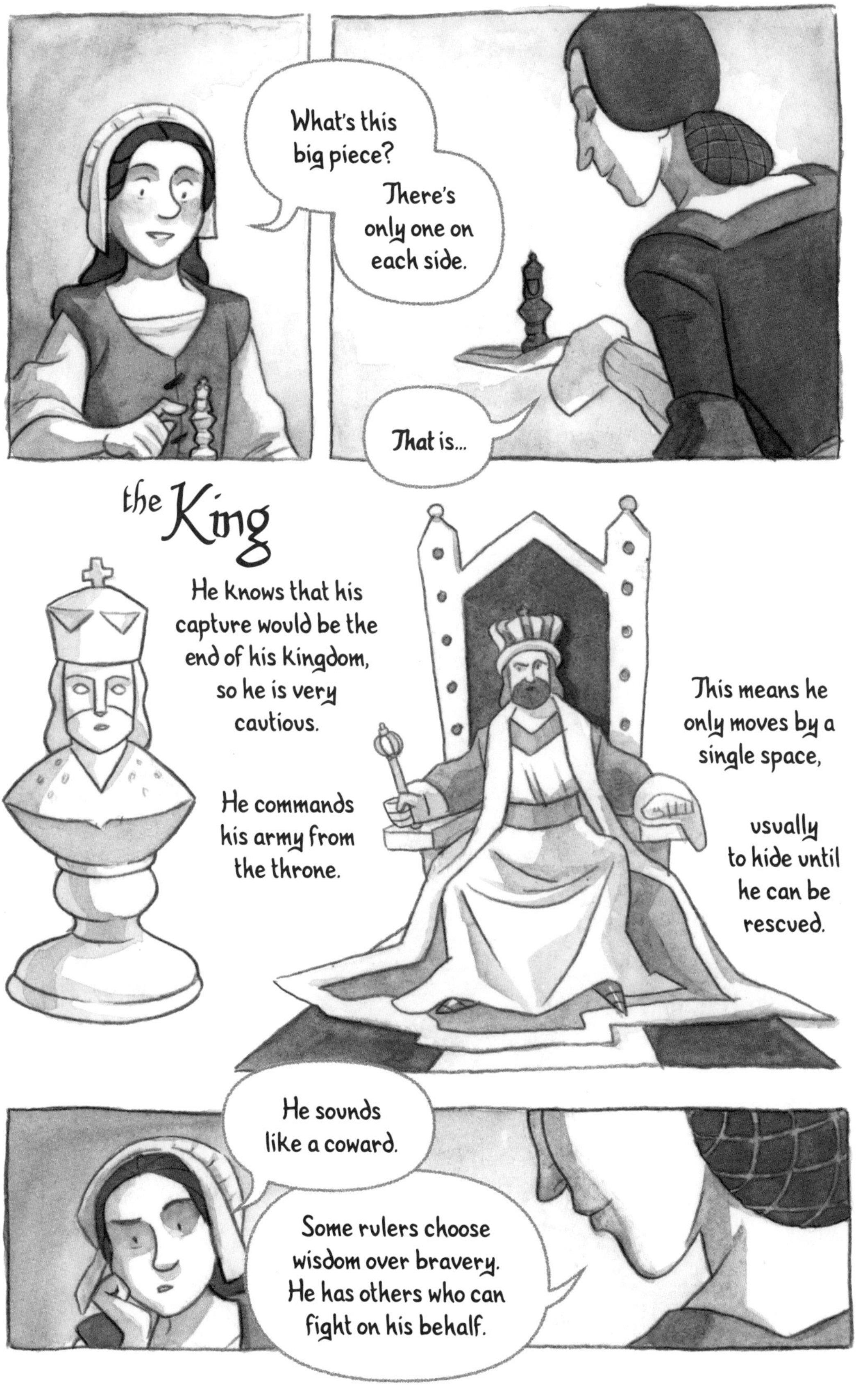
What's this big piece?
There's only one on each side.
That is...
the King
He knows that his capture would be the end of his kingdom, so he is very cautious.
He commands his army from the throne.
This means he only moves by a single space,
usually to hide until he can be rescued.
He sounds like a coward.
Some rulers choose wisdom over bravery. He has others who can fight on his behalf.

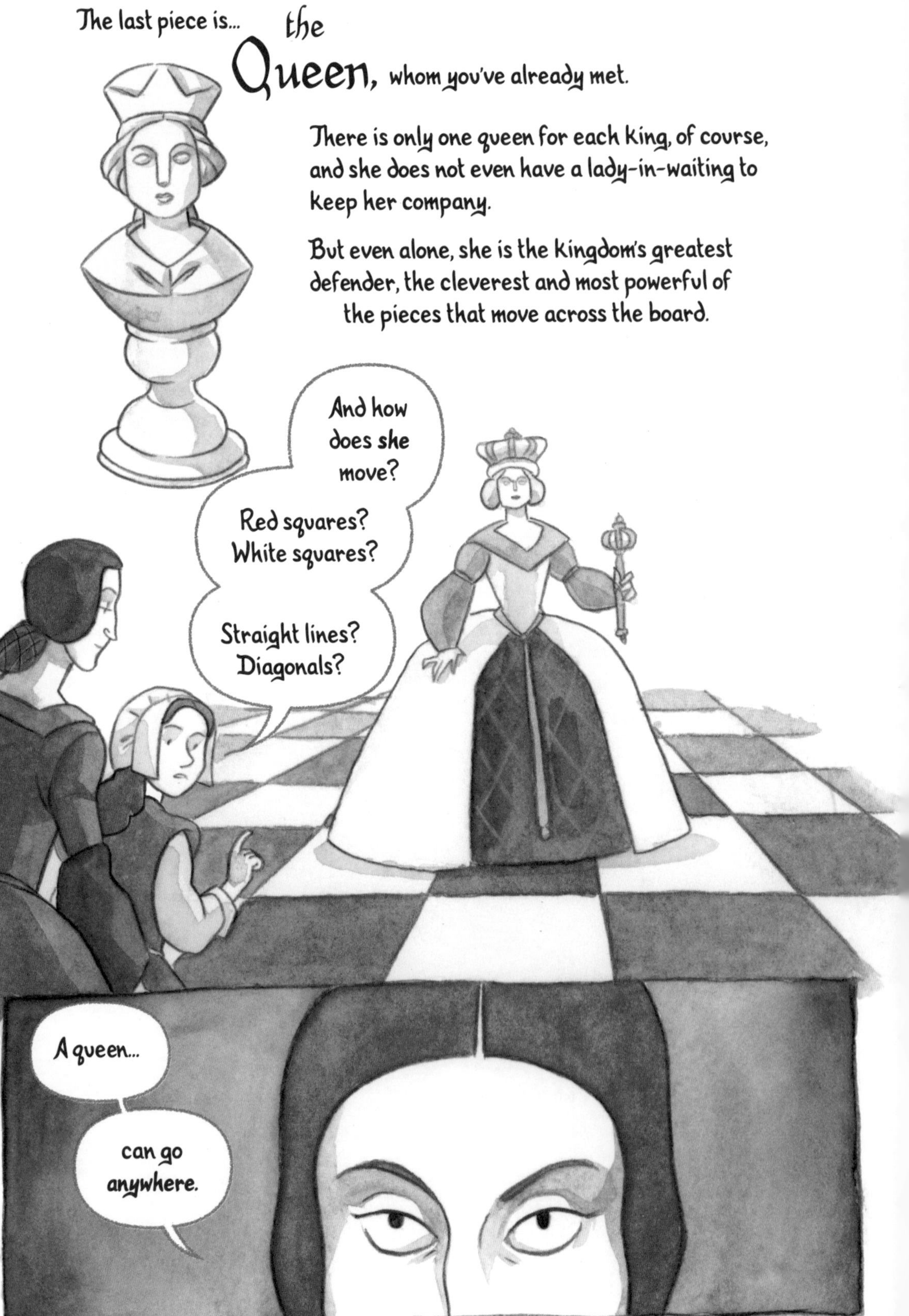
The last piece is... the Queen, whom you've already met.
There is only one queen for each King, of course, and she does not even have a lady-in-waiting to keep her company.
But even alone, she is the kingdom's greatest defender, the cleverest and most powerful of the pieces that move across the board.
And how does she move?
Red squares? White squares?
Straight lines? Diagonals?
A queen...
can go anywhere.

So we played chess, every day.

I tried to keep my pieces out of danger. Eleanor said that whenever one piece defeated another, the losing piece was taken prisoner and executed. I decided that my pieces were more merciful than that. They simply convinced them that it was wrong to fight.

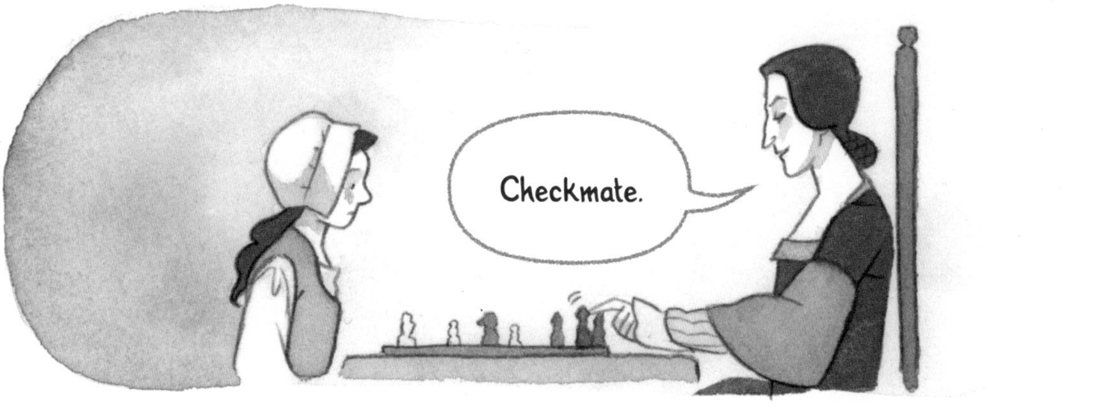
Checkmate.

I lost the first few games, but that wasn't unexpected, since I was still only learning. But after a week, I still lost every game. And Eleanor still told me nothing about William. It was the same the week after that.

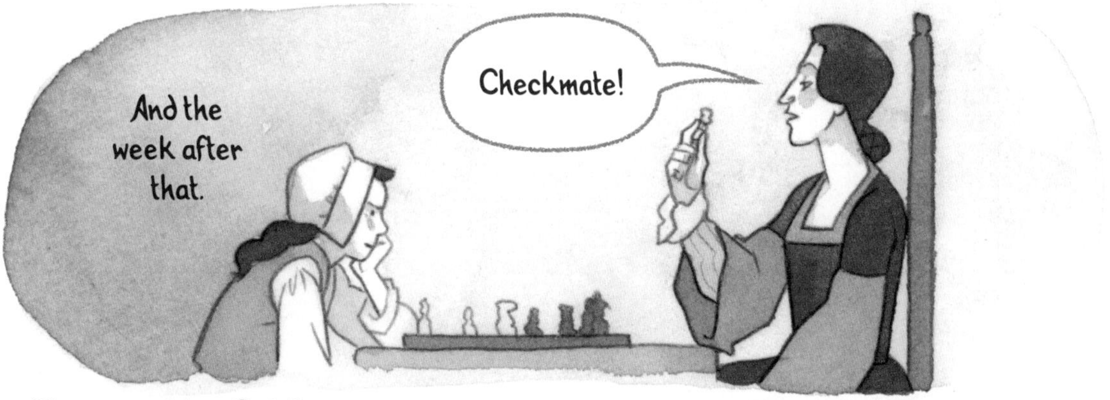
And the week after that.
Checkmate!

Eleanor and her Red Queen were very good at setting traps. I thought about all the pawns and knights and bishops and queens and kings she had taken. They had all died because I couldn't play well enough.

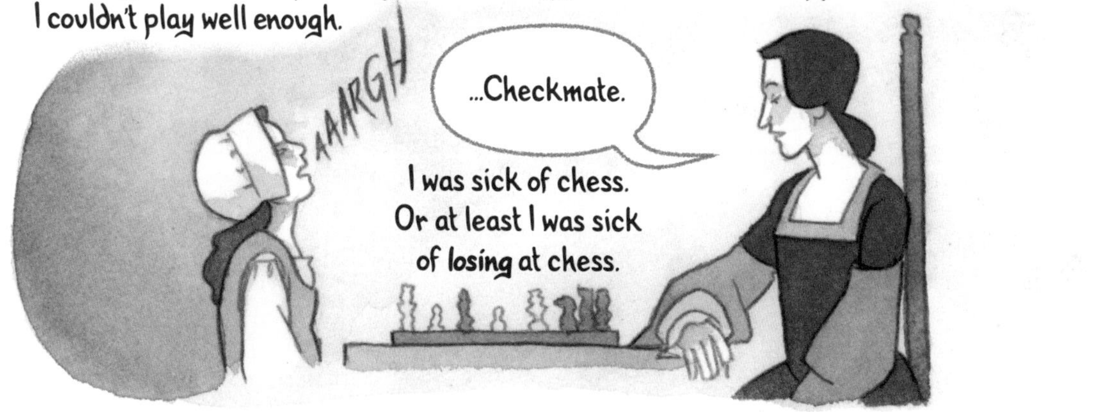
AAARGH
...Checkmate.
I was sick of chess. Or at least I was sick of *losing* at chess.

But Eleanor refused to do anything else with me until I won a game.

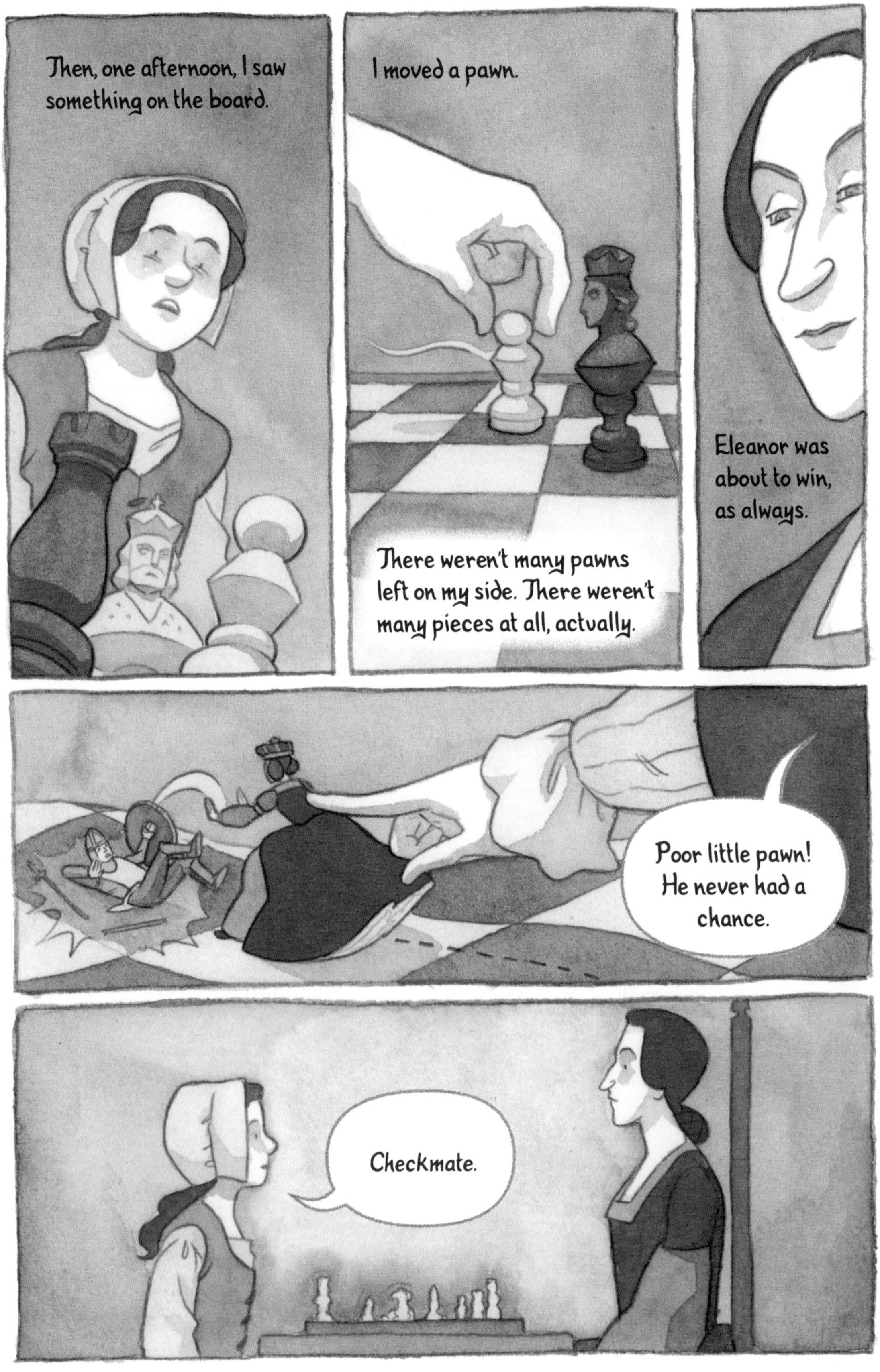
Then, one afternoon, I saw something on the board.
I moved a pawn.
There weren't many pawns left on my side. There weren't many pieces at all, actually.
Eleanor was about to win, as always.
Poor little pawn! He never had a chance.
Checkmate.

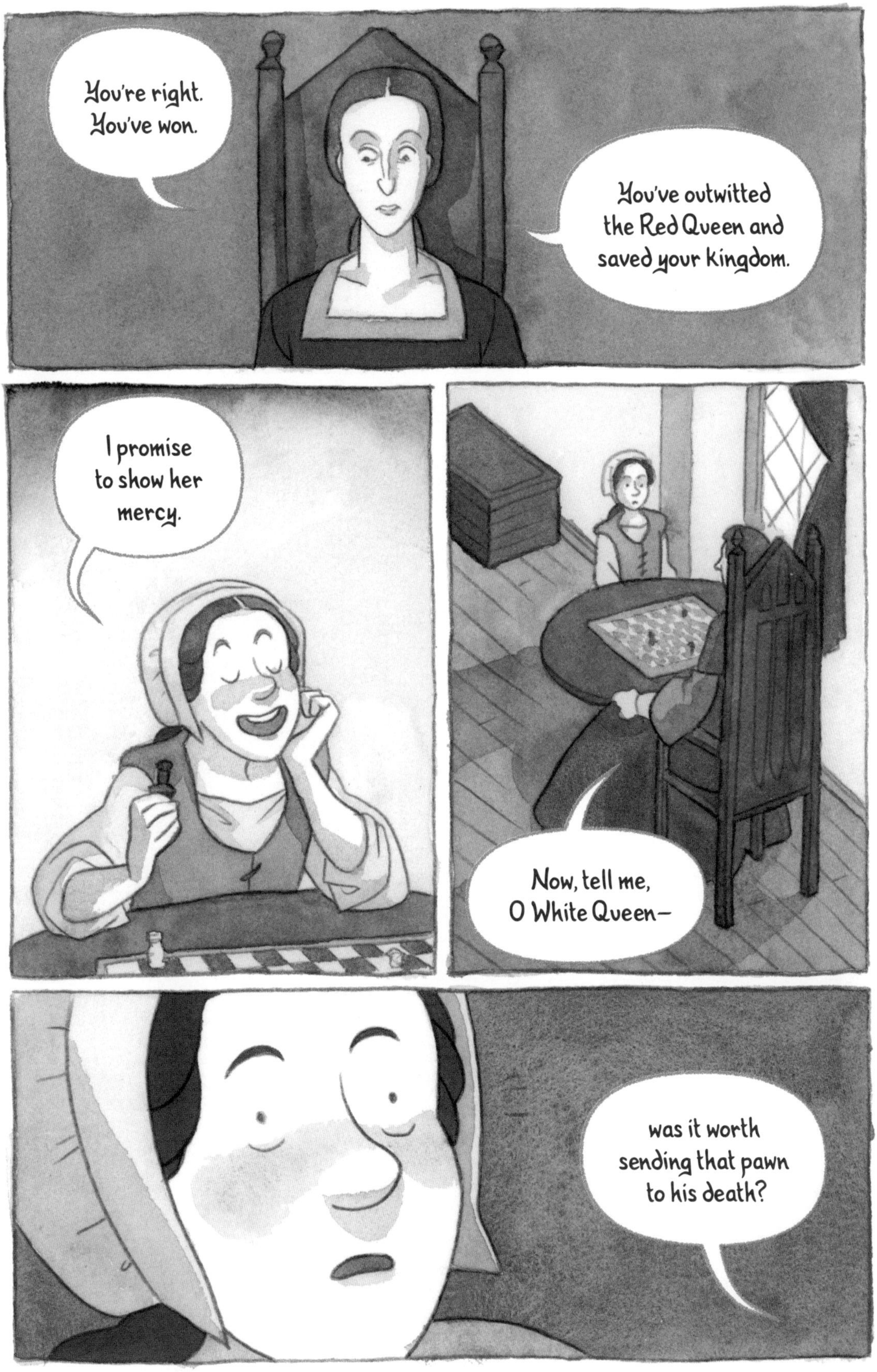
You're right. You've won.
You've outwitted the Red Queen and saved your kingdom.
I promise to show her mercy.
Now, tell me, O White Queen—
was it worth sending that pawn to his death?

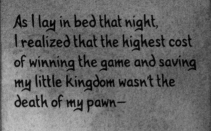

As I lay in bed that night, I realized that the highest cost of winning the game and saving my little kingdom wasn't the death of my pawn—

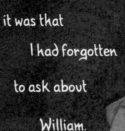

it was that

I had forgotten

to ask about

William.

I decided I would ask Eleanor about him the next morning.

But the next day, Mother Mary Clemence was in the chamber. She had an illness called gout, which makes your foot hurt and, in her case, makes you even more awful than usual.

Oh! Quiet your voice, child. I feel it down to my toes when you speak.

But I didn't say anything yet.

Perhaps Her Reverence will be more comfortable if we leave her and take a walk around the convent.

182

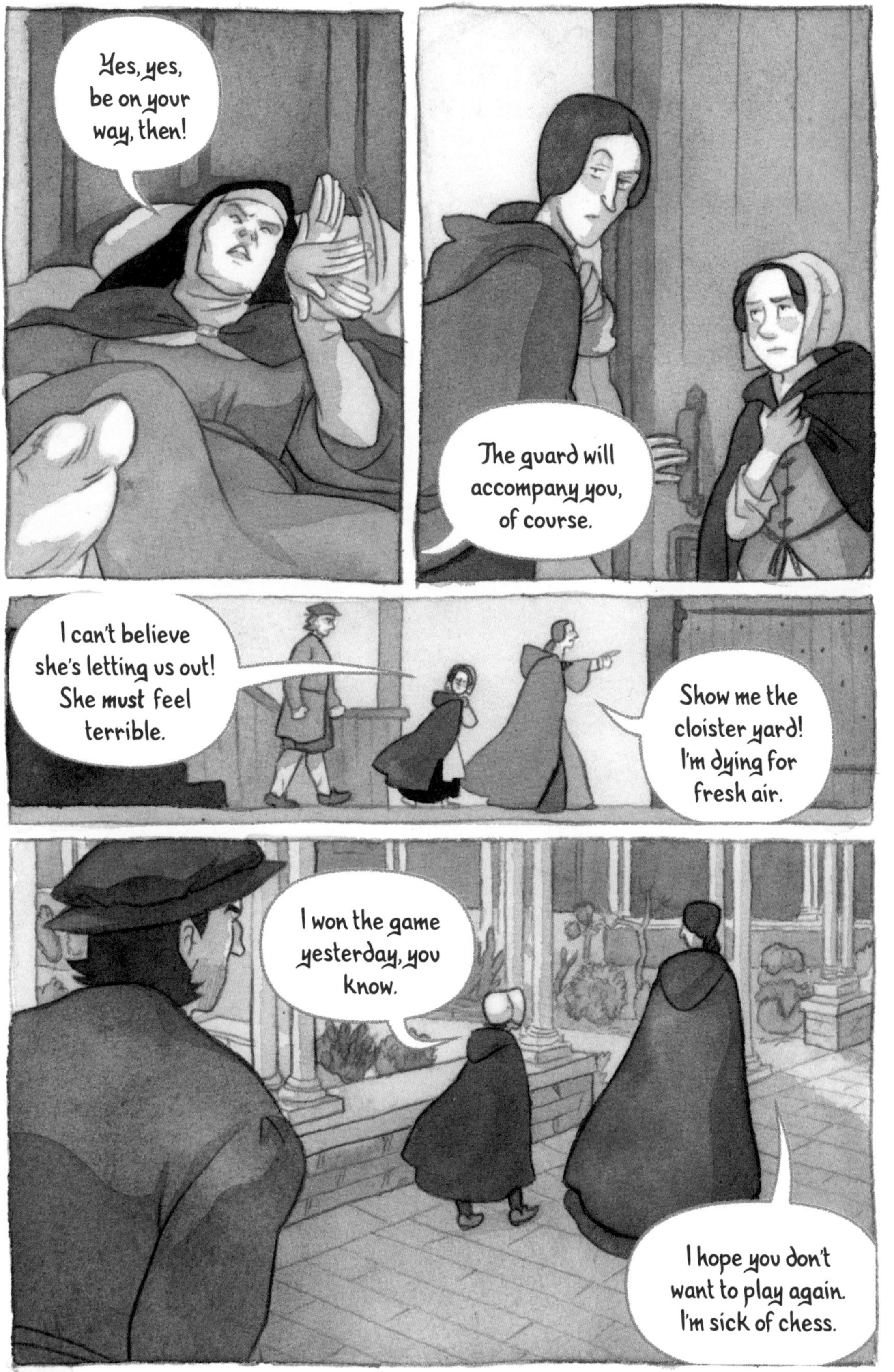

Yes, yes, be on your way, then!
The guard will accompany you, of course.
I can't believe she's letting us out! She must feel terrible.
Show me the cloister yard! I'm dying for fresh air.
I won the game yesterday, you know.
I hope you don't want to play again. I'm sick of chess.

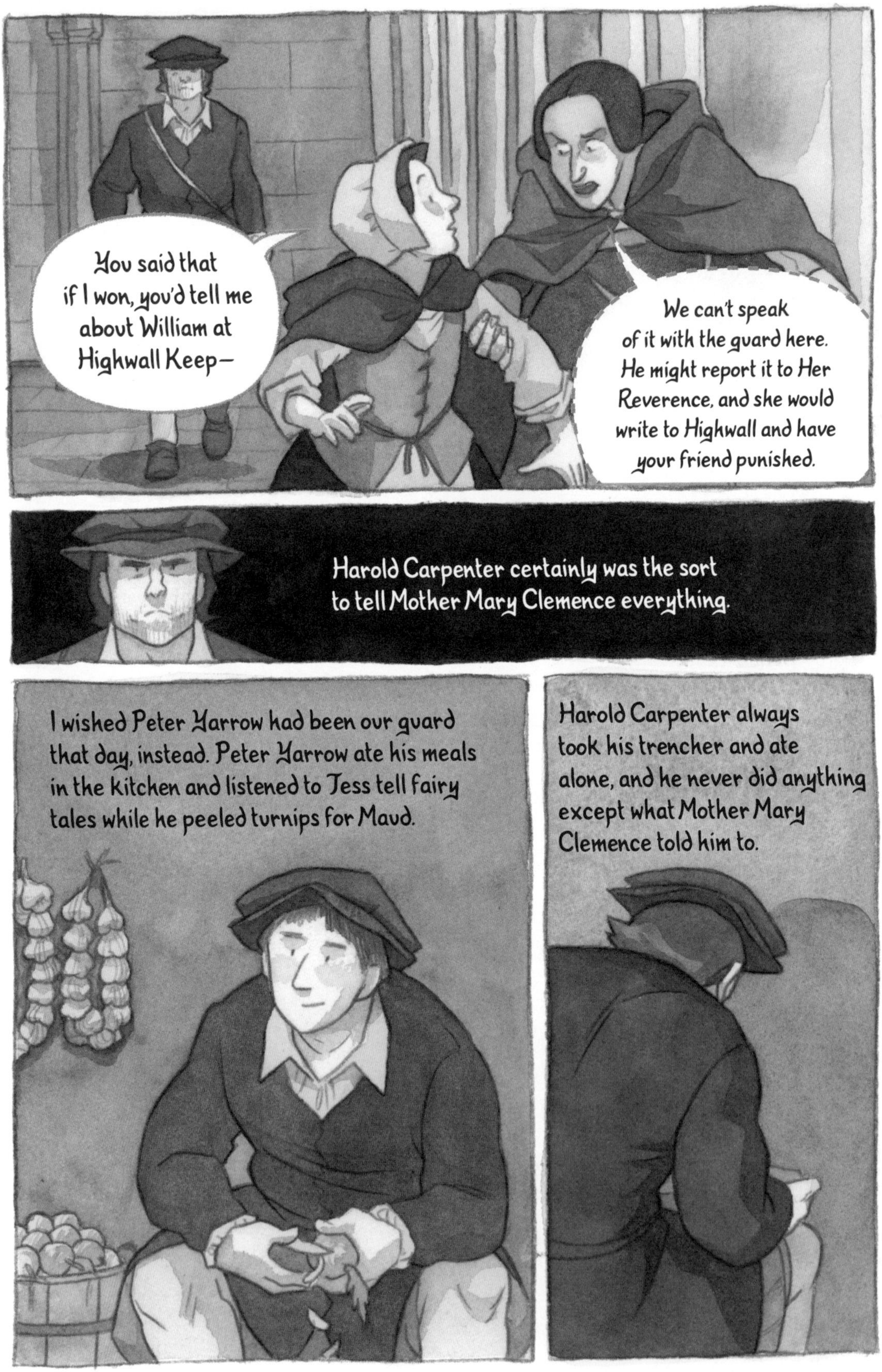
You said that if I won, you'd tell me about William at Highwall Keep—
We can't speak of it with the guard here. He might report it to Her Reverence, and she would write to Highwall and have your friend punished.
Harold Carpenter certainly was the sort to tell Mother Mary Clemence everything.
I wished Peter Yarrow had been our guard that day, instead. Peter Yarrow ate his meals in the kitchen and listened to Jess tell fairy tales while he peeled turnips for Maud.
Harold Carpenter always took his trencher and ate alone, and he never did anything except what Mother Mary Clemence told him to.

Why don't you describe your friend to me, as if you were simply telling me about him.
That's safe enough, and that way I can be certain if I met him.
He's...hmm.

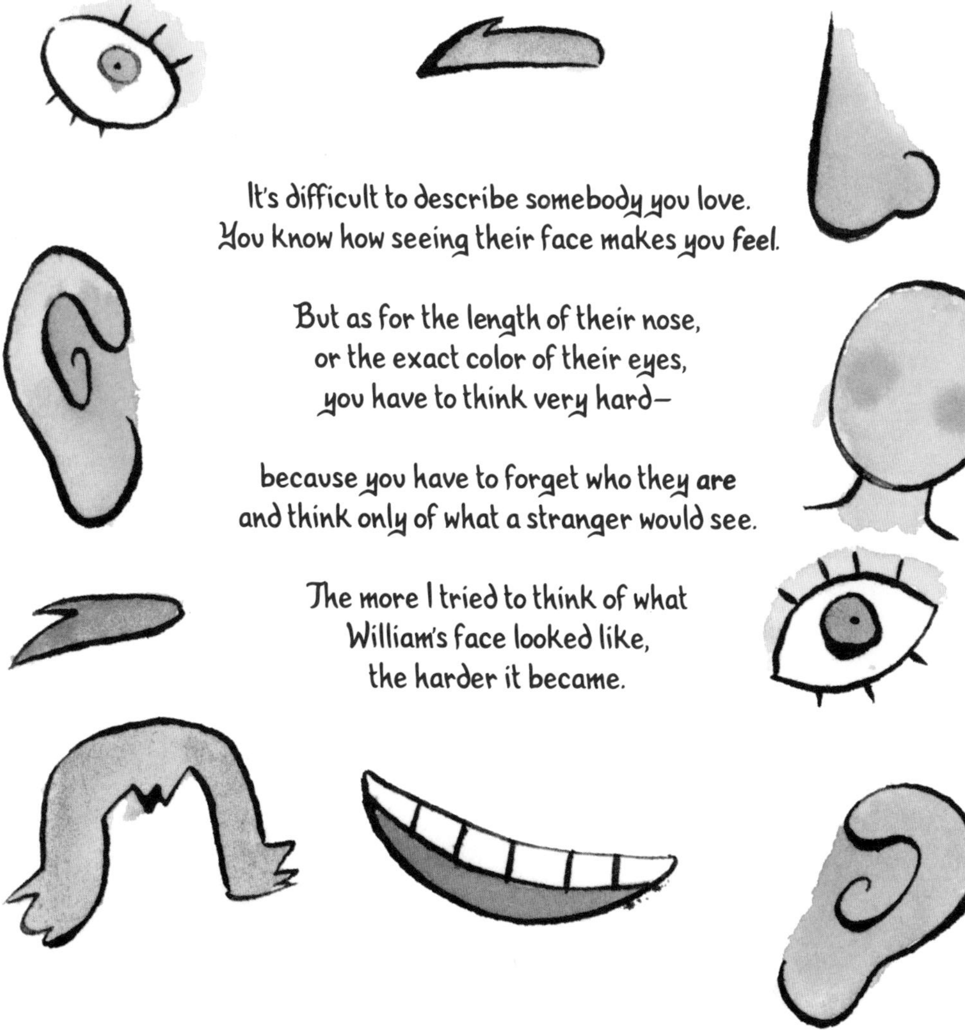

It's difficult to describe somebody you love.
You know how seeing their face makes you feel.
But as for the length of their nose,
or the exact color of their eyes,
you have to think very hard—
because you have to forget who they are
and think only of what a stranger would see.
The more I tried to think of what
William's face looked like,
the harder it became.

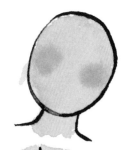

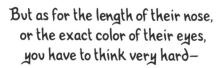

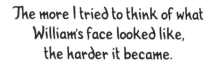

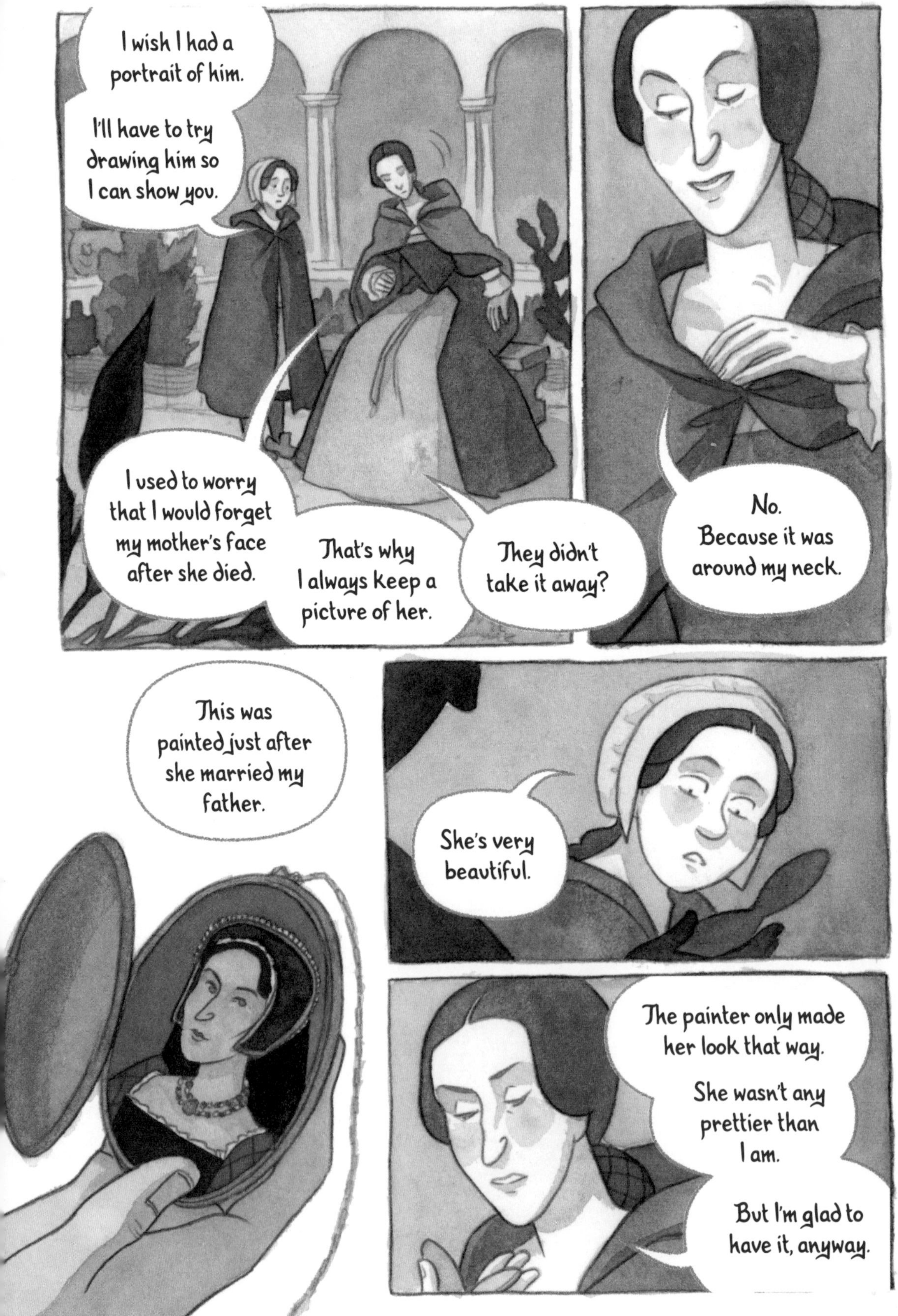
I wish I had a portrait of him.
I'll have to try drawing him so I can show you.
I used to worry that I would forget my mother's face after she died.
That's why I always keep a picture of her.
They didn't take it away?
No. Because it was around my neck.
This was painted just after she married my father.
She's very beautiful.
The painter only made her look that way.
She wasn't any prettier than I am.
But I'm glad to have it, anyway.

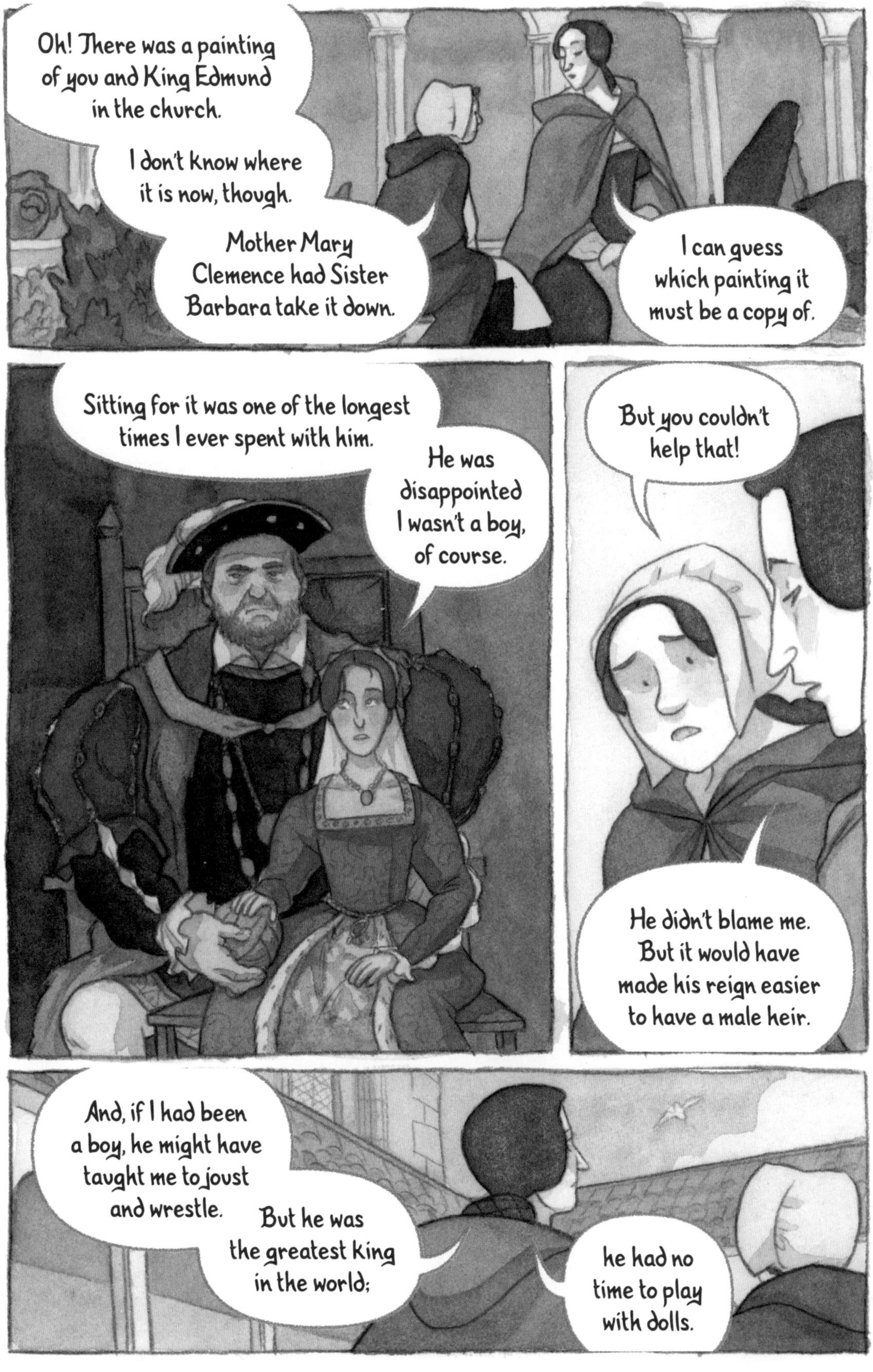
Oh! There was a painting of you and King Edmund in the church.
I don't know where it is now, though.
Mother Mary Clemence had Sister Barbara take it down.
I can guess which painting it must be a copy of.
Sitting for it was one of the longest times I ever spent with him.
He was disappointed I wasn't a boy, of course.
But you couldn't help that!
He didn't blame me. But it would have made his reign easier to have a male heir.
And, if I had been a boy, he might have taught me to joust and wrestle.
But he was the greatest king in the world;
he had no time to play with dolls.

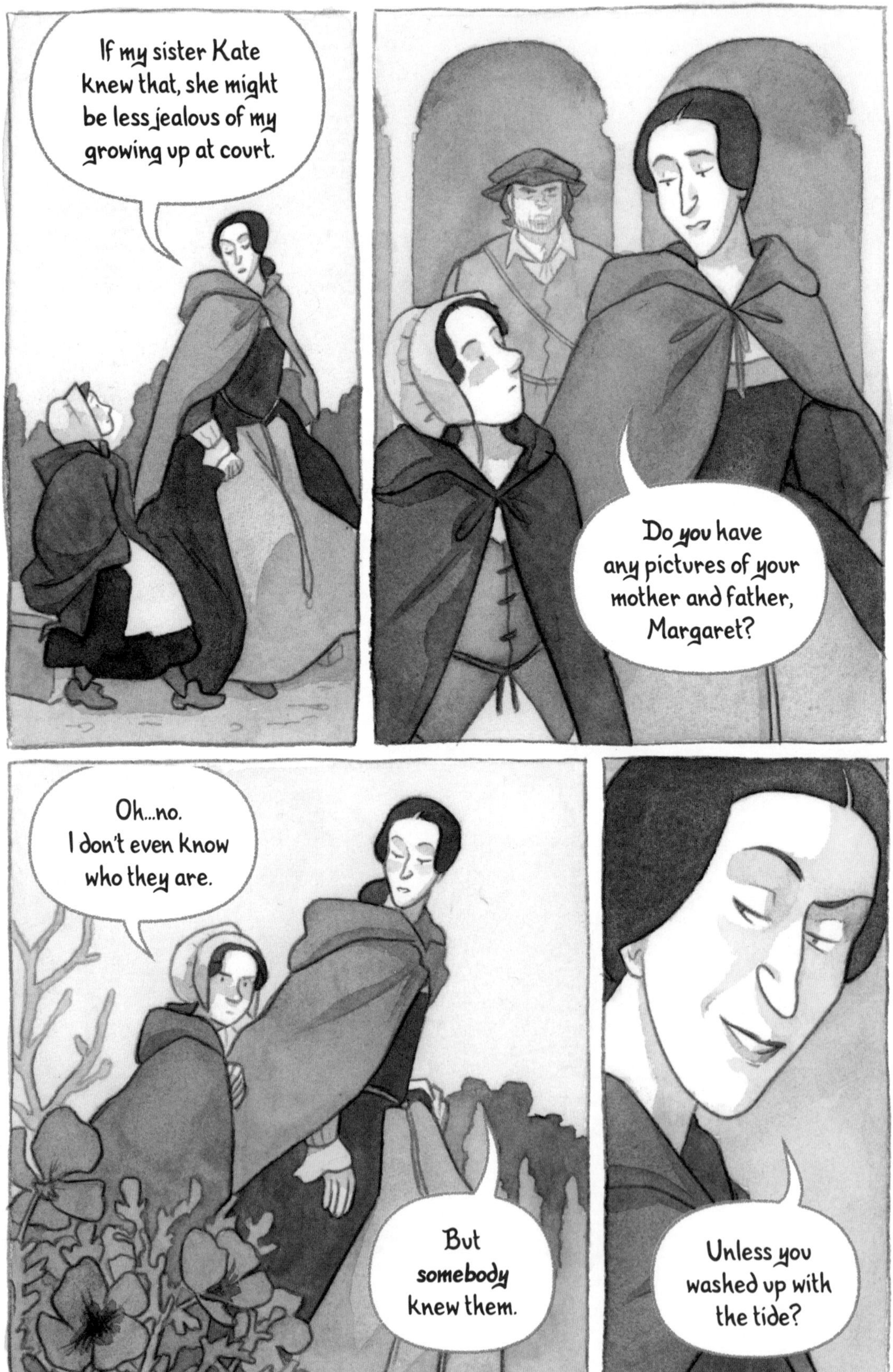
If my sister Kate knew that, she might be less jealous of my growing up at court.
Do you have any pictures of your mother and father, Margaret?
Oh...no. I don't even know who they are.
But somebody knew them.
Unless you washed up with the tide?

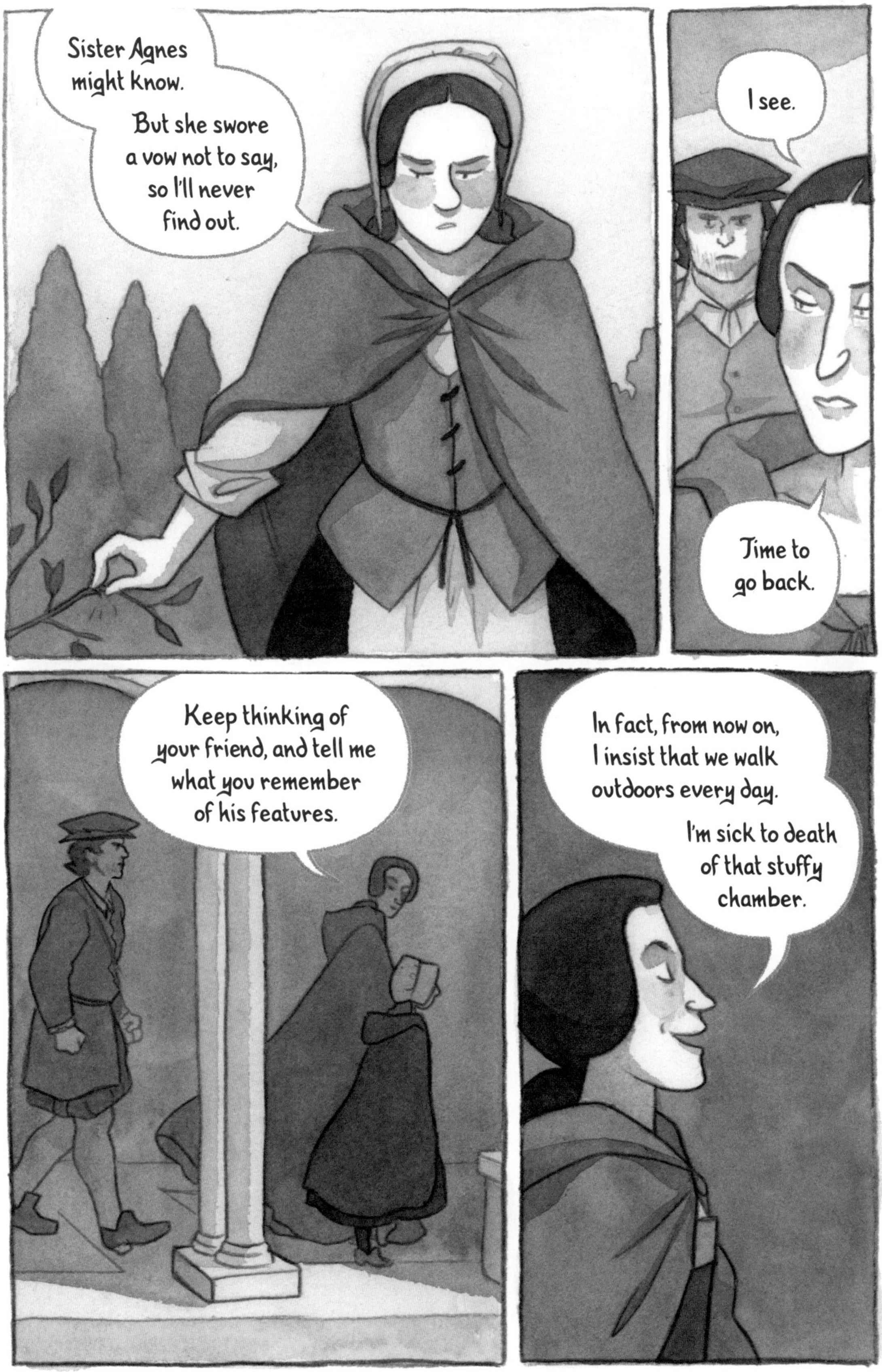
Sister Agnes might know.
But she swore a vow not to say, so I'll never find out.
I see.
Time to go back.
Keep thinking of your friend, and tell me what you remember of his features.
In fact, from now on, I insist that we walk outdoors every day.
I'm sick to death of that stuffy chamber.

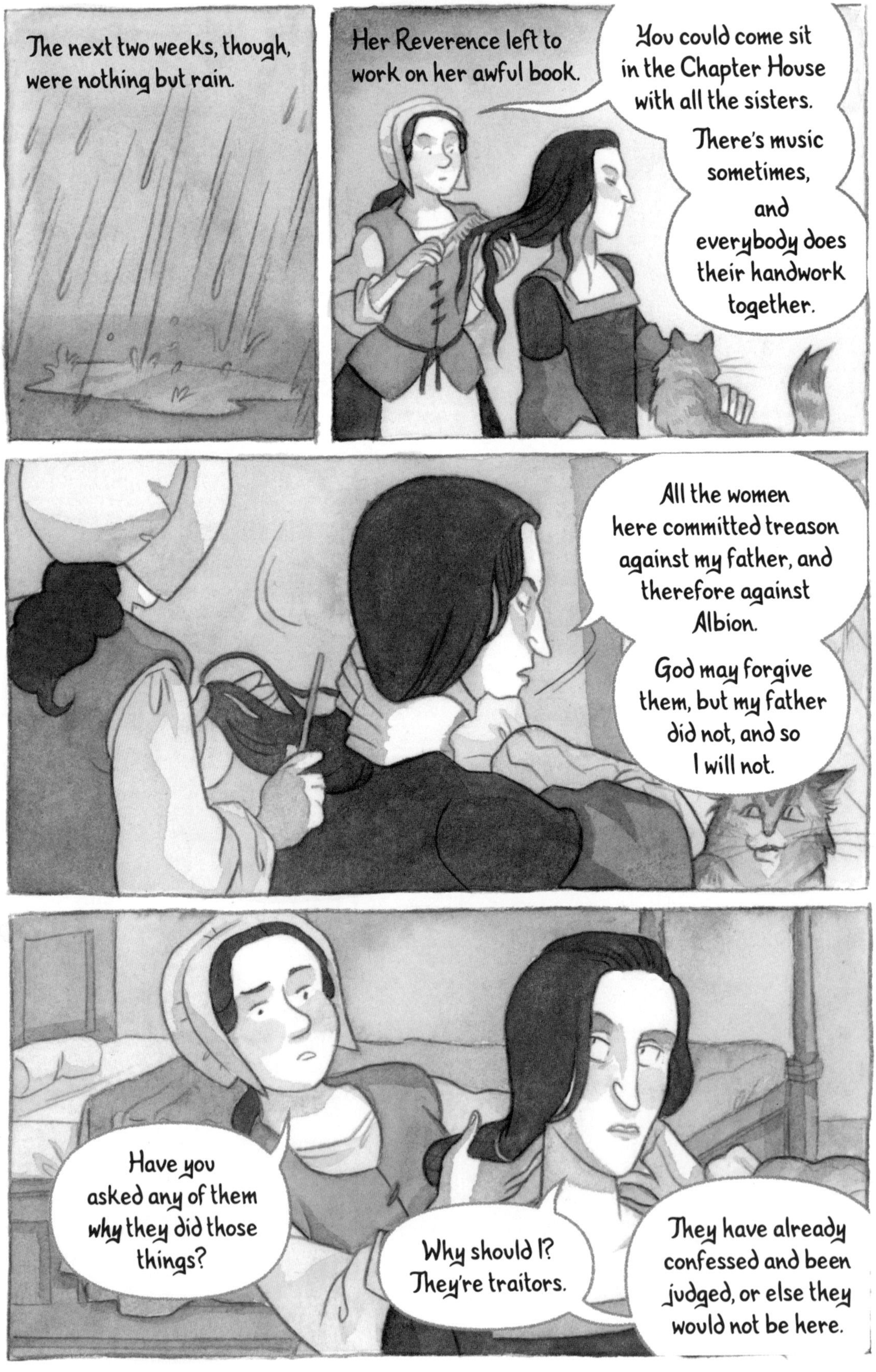
The next two weeks, though, were nothing but rain.
Her Reverence left to work on her awful book.
You could come sit in the Chapter House with all the sisters.
There's music sometimes,
and everybody does their handwork together.
All the women here committed treason against my father, and therefore against Albion.
God may forgive them, but my father did not, and so I will not.
Have you asked any of them why they did those things?
Why should I? They're traitors.
They have already confessed and been judged, or else they would not be here.

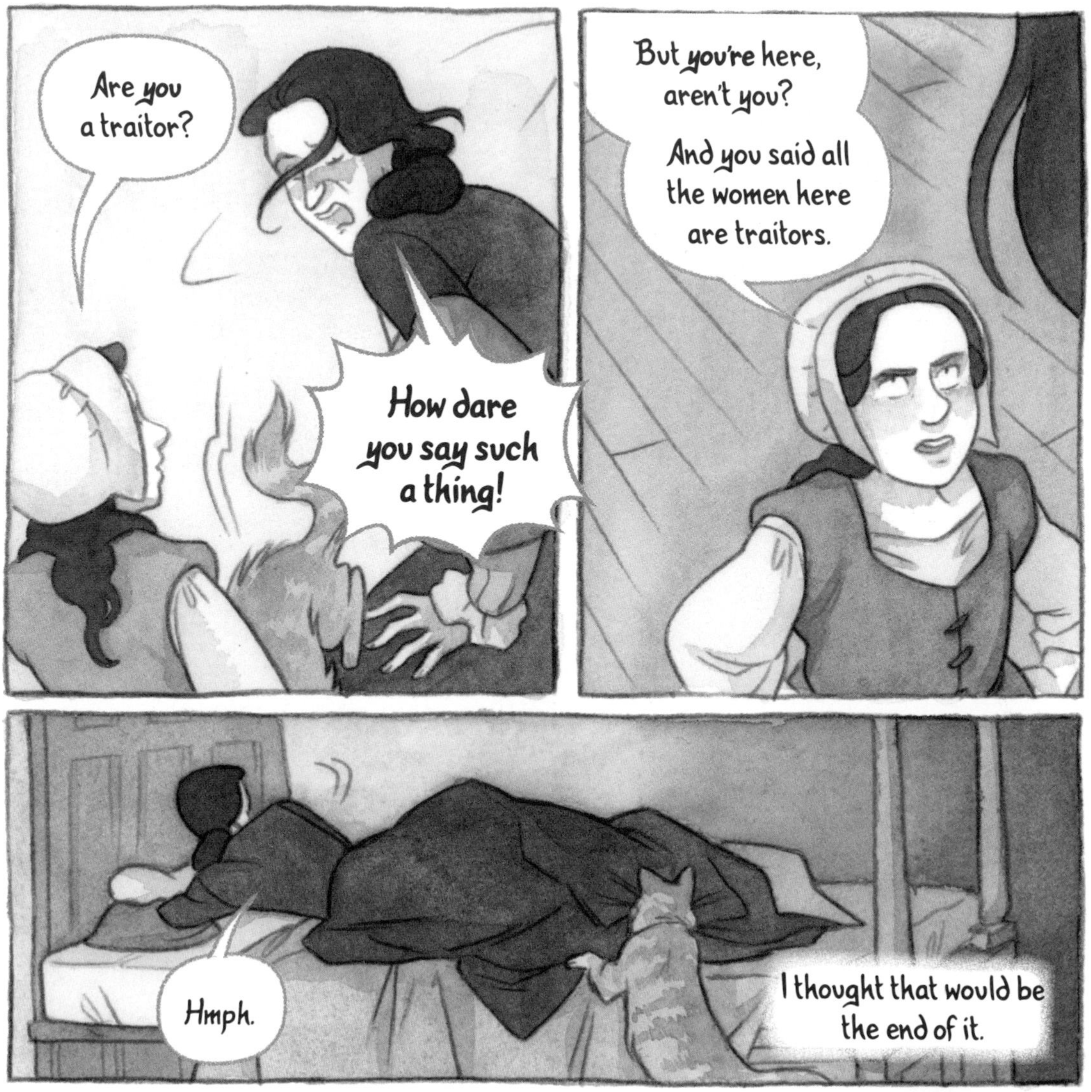
Are you a traitor?
How dare you say such a thing!
But you're here, aren't you?
And you said all the women here are traitors.
Hmph.
I thought that would be the end of it.

But the next day, Eleanor invited Sister Sybil to visit us in the chamber; the day after that, Sister Edith; and eventually all the other sisters, too.

Eleanor told Mother Mary Clemence that these were prayer lessons. We would all say a prayer together, so it wasn't really a lie.

And then Eleanor would ask each sister,

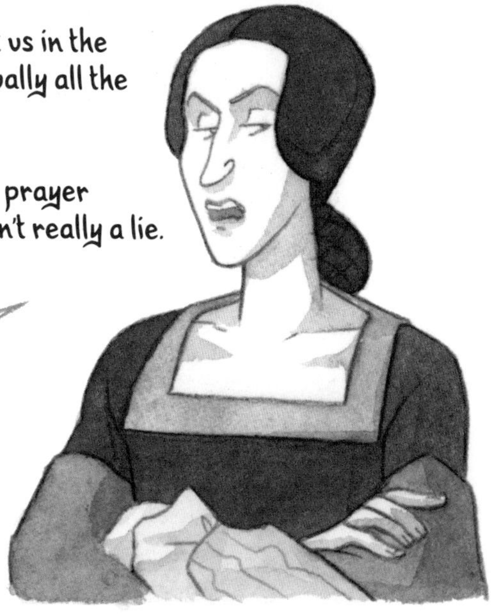
Tell me about your crimes against the crown.

They told her the same stories they had told me. The difference was that they told her about King Edmund, too.

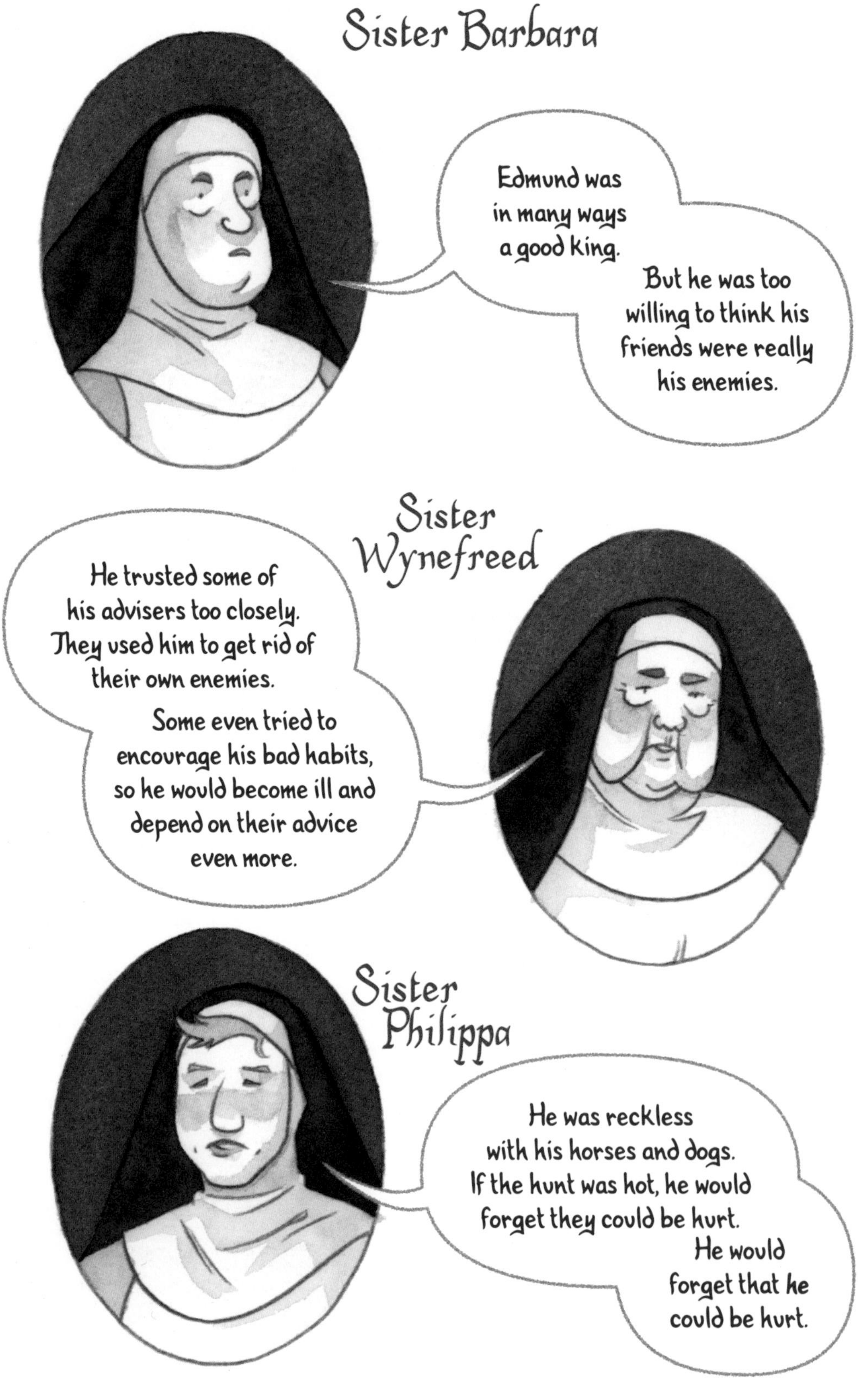
Sister Barbara
Edmund was in many ways a good king.
But he was too willing to think his friends were really his enemies.
Sister Wynefreed
He trusted some of his advisers too closely. They used him to get rid of their own enemies.
Some even tried to encourage his bad habits, so he would become ill and depend on their advice even more.
Sister Philippa
He was reckless with his horses and dogs. If the hunt was hot, he would forget they could be hurt.
He would forget that he could be hurt.

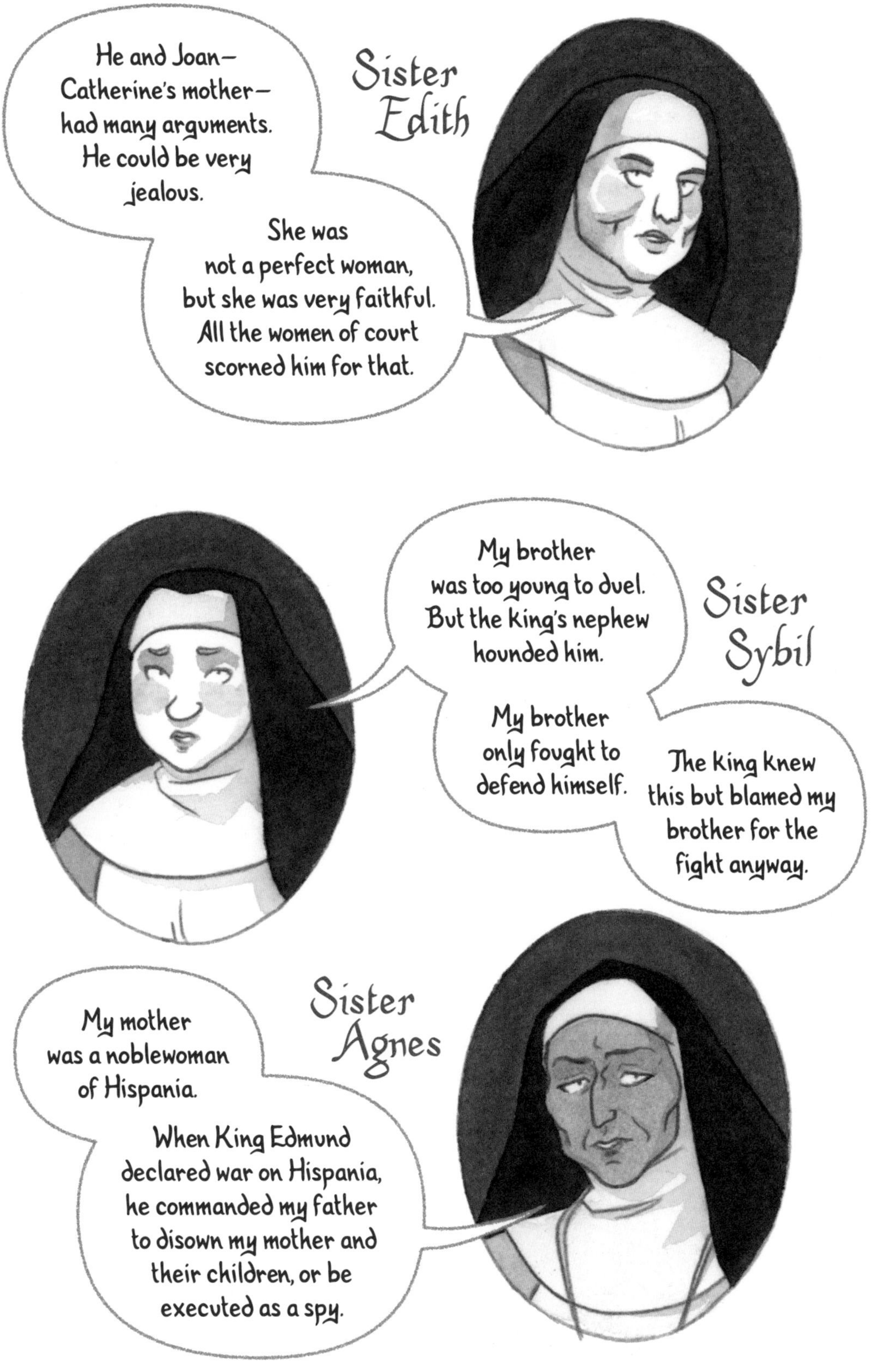
He and Joan—Catherine's mother—had many arguments. He could be very jealous.
Sister Edith
She was not a perfect woman, but she was very faithful. All the women of court scorned him for that.
My brother was too young to duel. But the king's nephew hounded him.
Sister Sybil
My brother only fought to defend himself.
The king knew this but blamed my brother for the fight anyway.
Sister Agnes
My mother was a noblewoman of Hispania.
When King Edmund declared war on Hispania, he commanded my father to disown my mother and their children, or be executed as a spy.

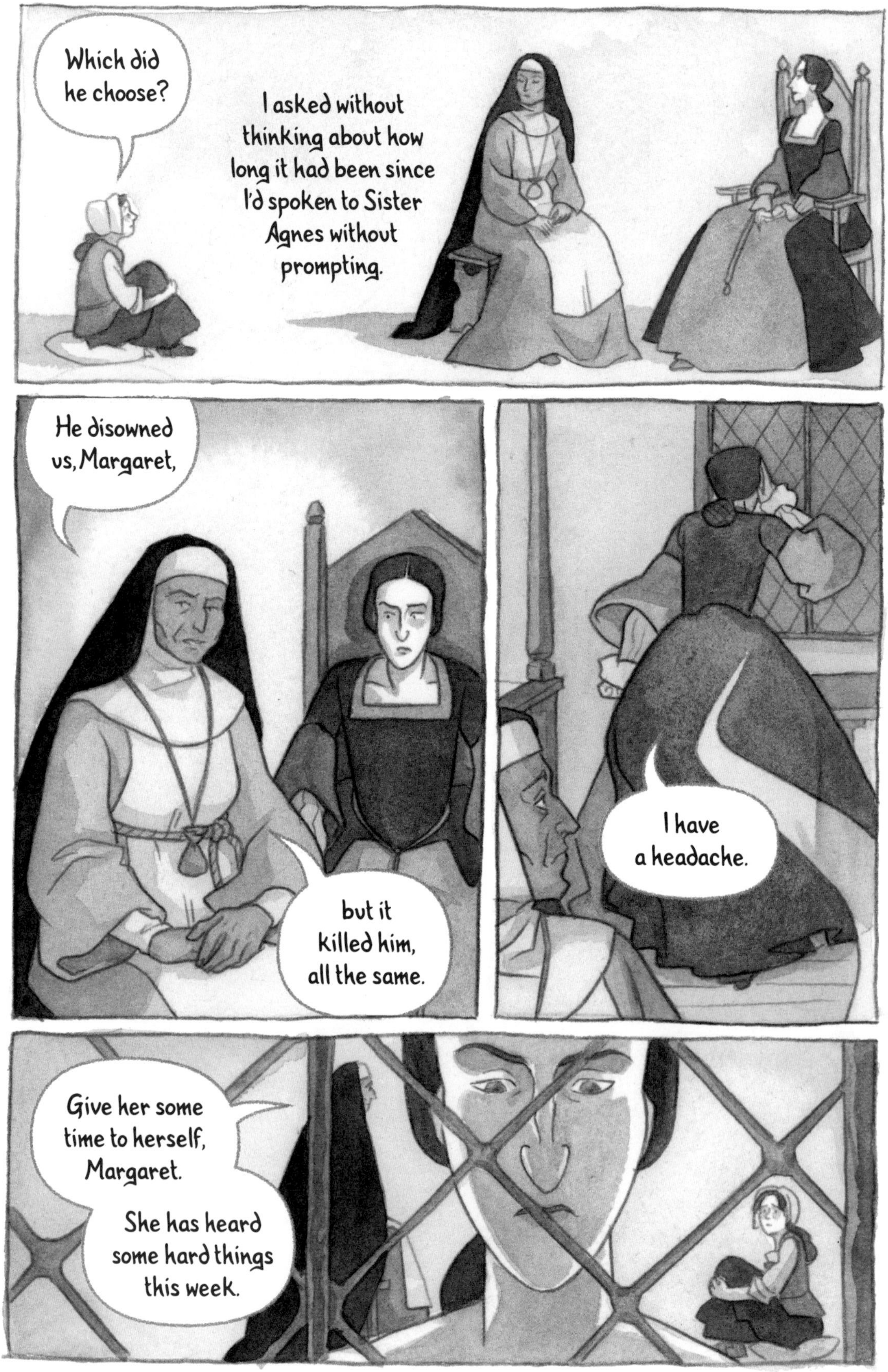
Which did he choose?
I asked without thinking about how long it had been since I'd spoken to Sister Agnes without prompting.
He disowned us, Margaret,
but it killed him, all the same.
I have a headache.
Give her some time to herself, Margaret.
She has heard some hard things this week.

Eleanor didn't ask to see me for a while after that.
I caught up on my lessons with Sister Sybil, and I worked on my portrait of William.
The sisters and the servants did their best to help.

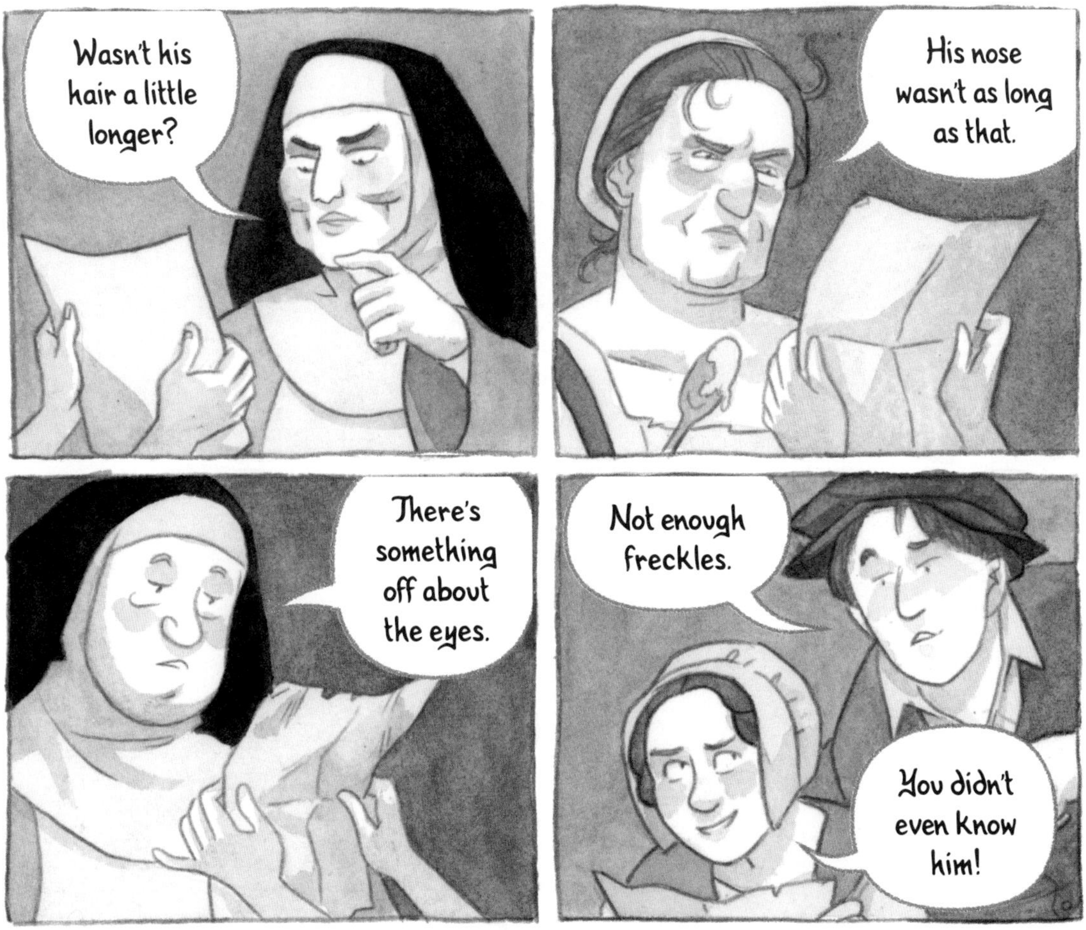
Wasn't his hair a little longer?
His nose wasn't as long as that.
There's something off about the eyes.
Not enough freckles.
You didn't even know him!

Before it was finished, Eleanor sent for me again, and we started to walk outside every day. If her feelings had been hurt by everything the sisters had said, it didn't show—or maybe she was just tired of sitting with Mother Mary Clemence.

Walking was a very good idea because Mother Mary Clemence, even when she had set aside her writing and her foot wasn't hurting her, never followed us for long.

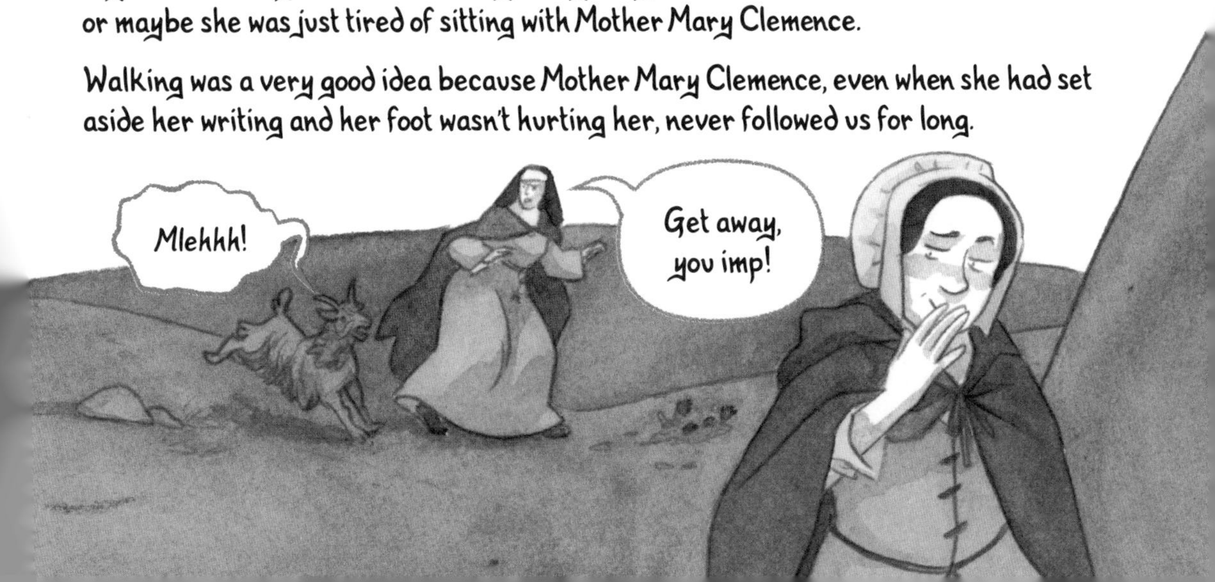
Mlehhh!
Get away, you imp!

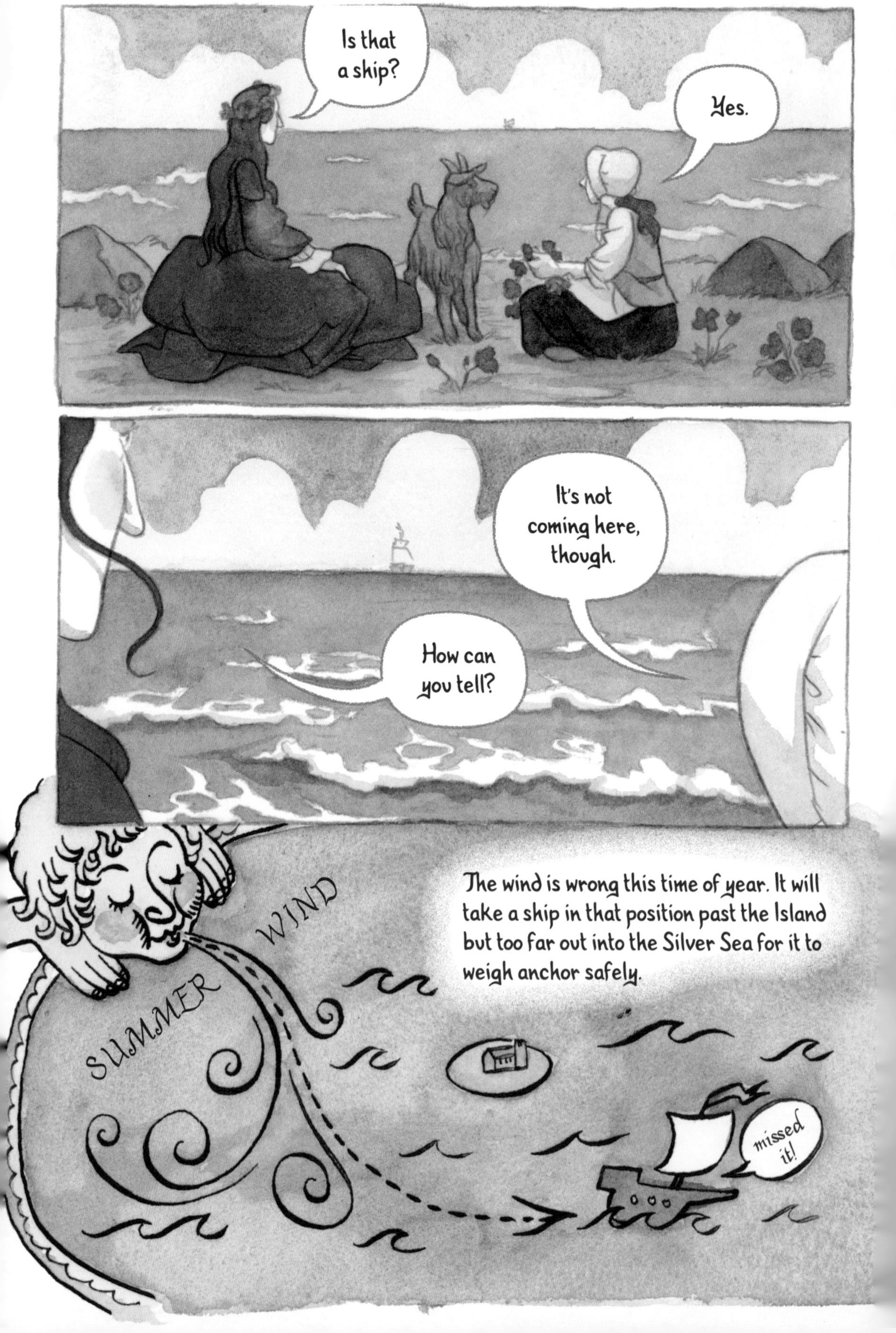
Is that a ship?
Yes.
It's not coming here, though.
How can you tell?
The wind is wrong this time of year. It will take a ship in that position past the Island but too far out into the Silver Sea for it to weigh anchor safely.
SUMMER WIND
missed it!

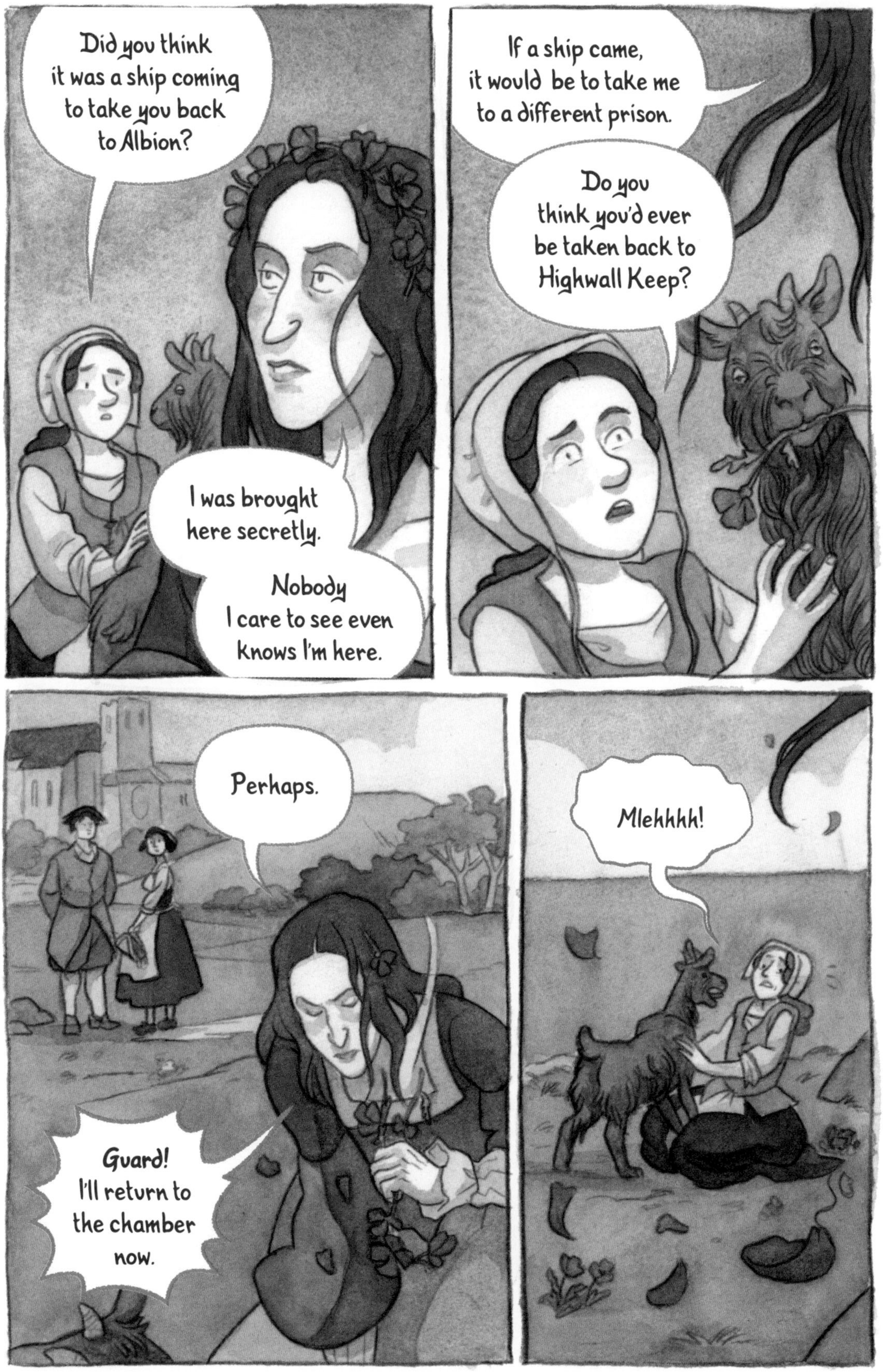
Did you think it was a ship coming to take you back to Albion?
I was brought here secretly.
Nobody I care to see even knows I'm here.
If a ship came, it would be to take me to a different prison.
Do you think you'd ever be taken back to Highwall Keep?
Perhaps.
Guard! I'll return to the chamber now.
Mlehhhh!

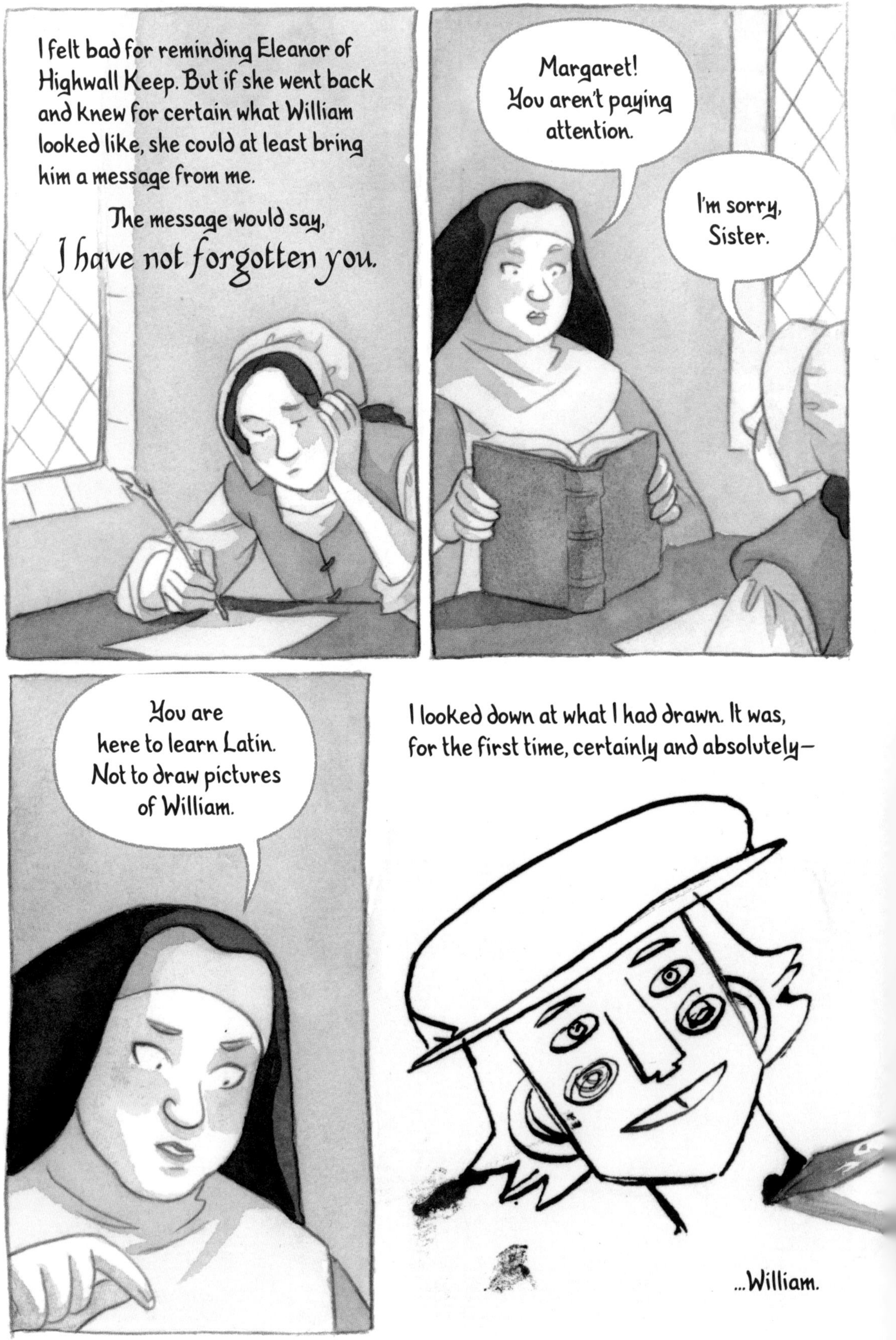
I felt bad for reminding Eleanor of Highwall Keep. But if she went back and knew for certain what William looked like, she could at least bring him a message from me.
The message would say,
I have not forgotten you.
Margaret! You aren't paying attention.
I'm sorry, Sister.
You are here to learn Latin. Not to draw pictures of William.
I looked down at what I had drawn. It was, for the first time, certainly and absolutely—
...William.

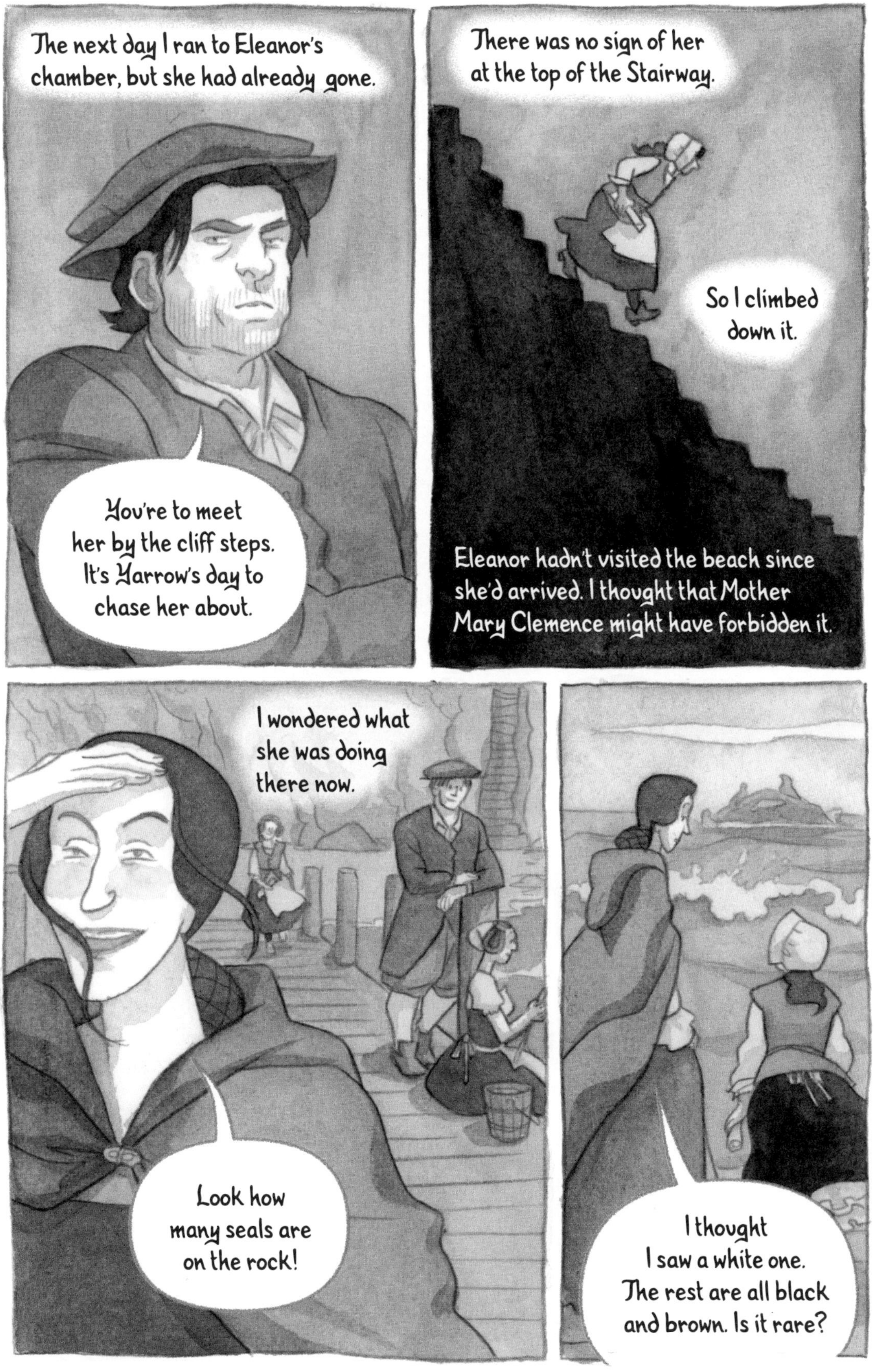

The next day I ran to Eleanor's chamber, but she had already gone.
You're to meet her by the cliff steps. It's Yarrow's day to chase her about.
There was no sign of her at the top of the Stairway.
So I climbed down it.
Eleanor hadn't visited the beach since she'd arrived. I thought that Mother Mary Clemence might have forbidden it.
I wondered what she was doing there now.
Look how many seals are on the rock!
I thought I saw a white one. The rest are all black and brown. Is it rare?

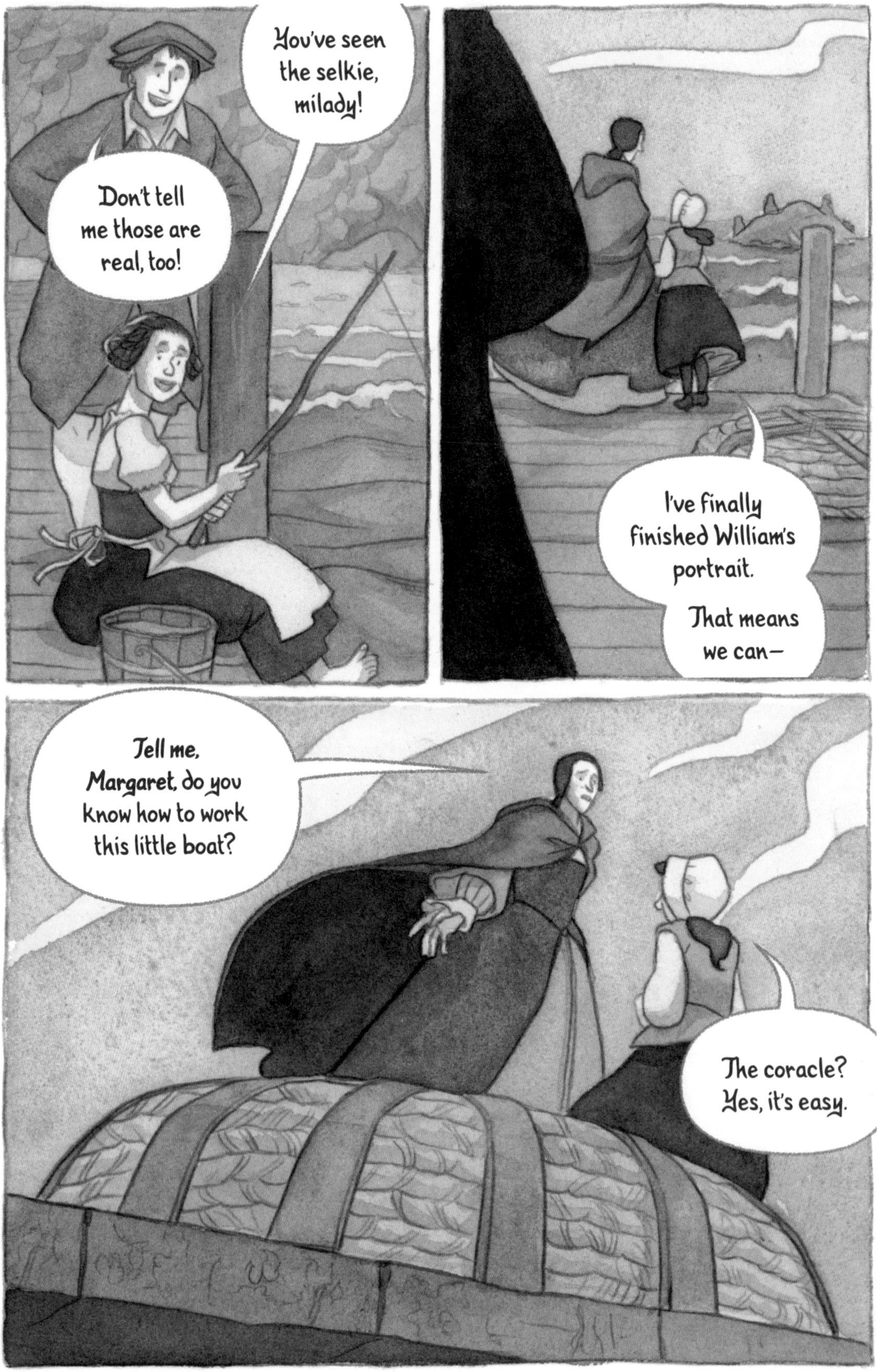
Don't tell me those are real, too!
You've seen the selkie, milady!
I've finally finished William's portrait.
That means we can—
Tell me, Margaret, do you know how to work this little boat?
The coracle? Yes, it's easy.

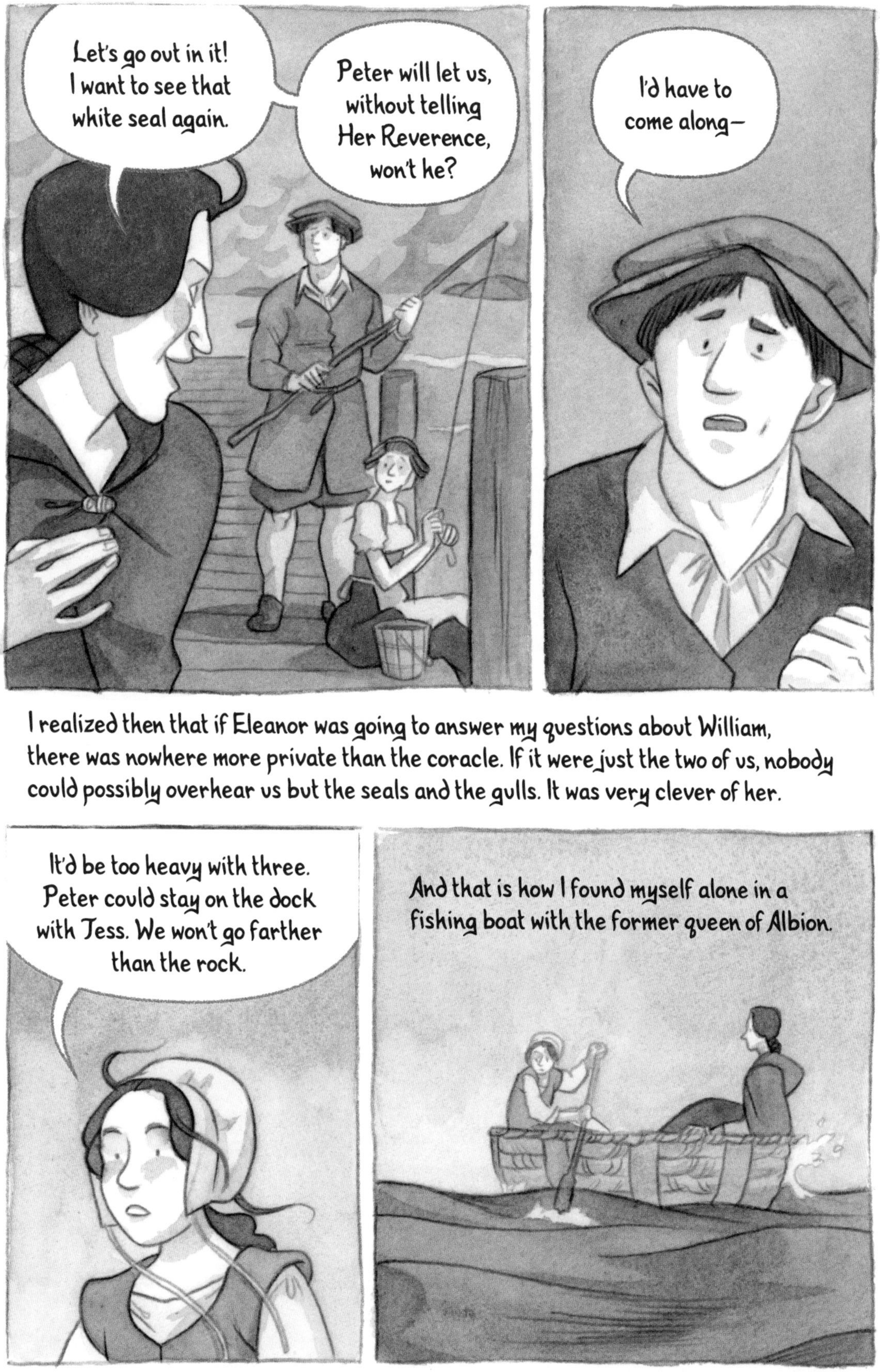
Let's go out in it! I want to see that white seal again.
Peter will let us, without telling Her Reverence, won't he?
I'd have to come along—
I realized then that if Eleanor was going to answer my questions about William, there was nowhere more private than the coracle. If it were just the two of us, nobody could possibly overhear us but the seals and the gulls. It was very clever of her.
It'd be too heavy with three. Peter could stay on the dock with Jess. We won't go farther than the rock.
And that is how I found myself alone in a fishing boat with the former queen of Albion.

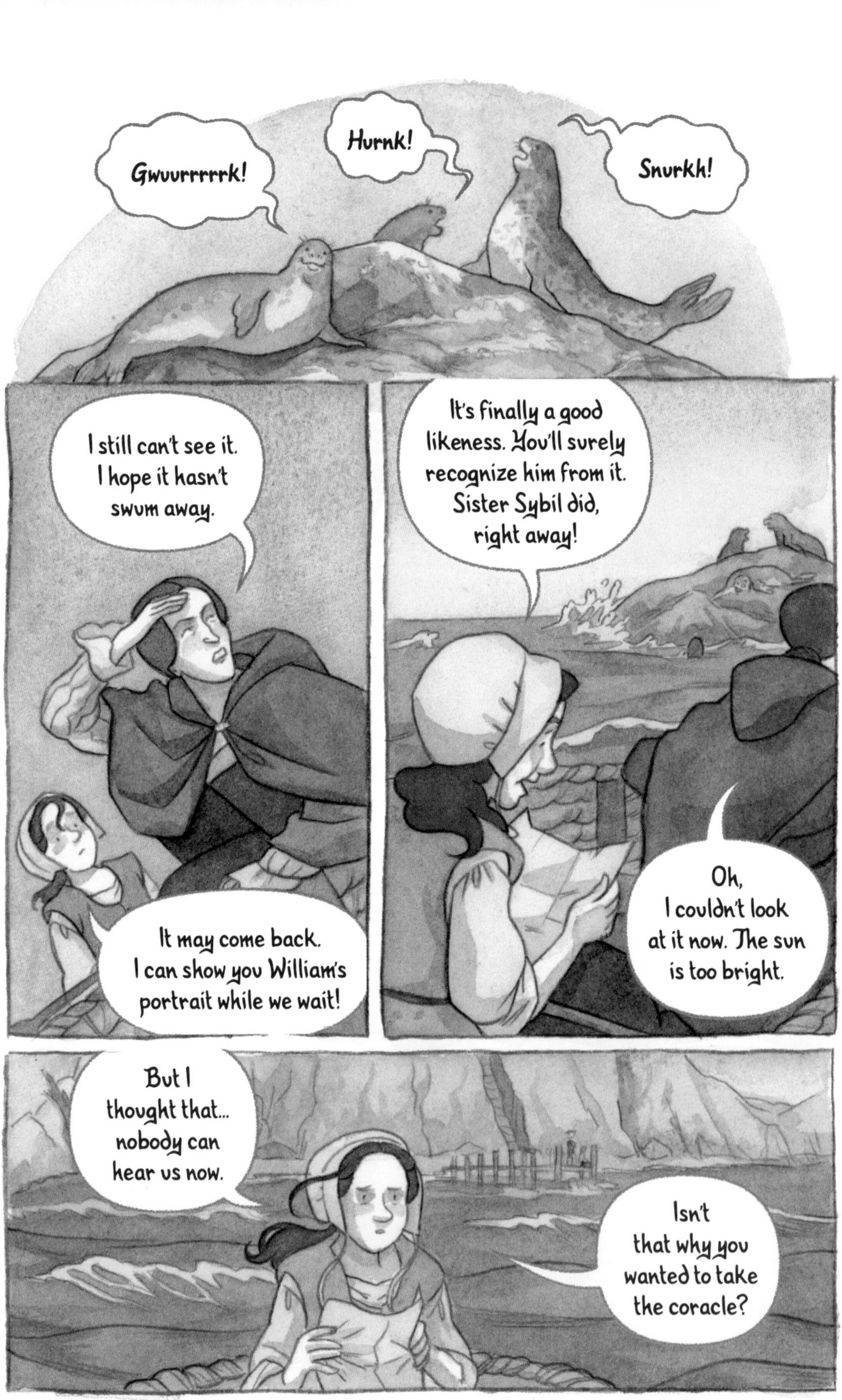
Gwuurrrrrk!
Hurnk!
Snurkh!
I still can't see it. I hope it hasn't swum away.
It may come back. I can show you William's portrait while we wait!
It's finally a good likeness. You'll surely recognize him from it. Sister Sybil did, right away!
Oh, I couldn't look at it now. The sun is too bright.
But I thought that... nobody can hear us now.
Isn't that why you wanted to take the coracle?

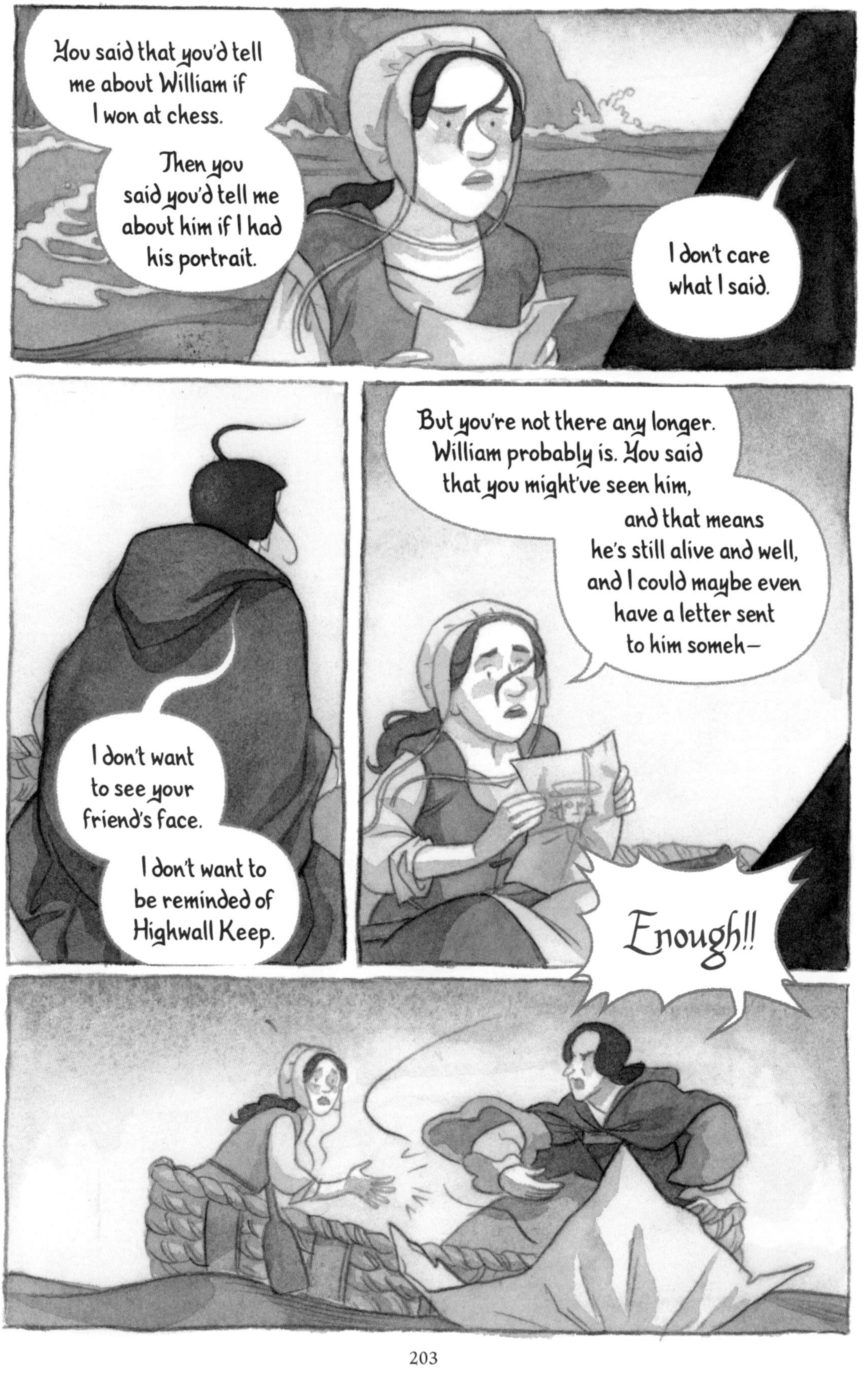
You said that you'd tell me about William if I won at chess.
Then you said you'd tell me about him if I had his portrait.
I don't care what I said.
I don't want to see your friend's face.
I don't want to be reminded of Highwall Keep.
But you're not there any longer. William probably is. You said that you might've seen him,
and that means he's still alive and well, and I could maybe even have a letter sent to him someh—
Enough!!

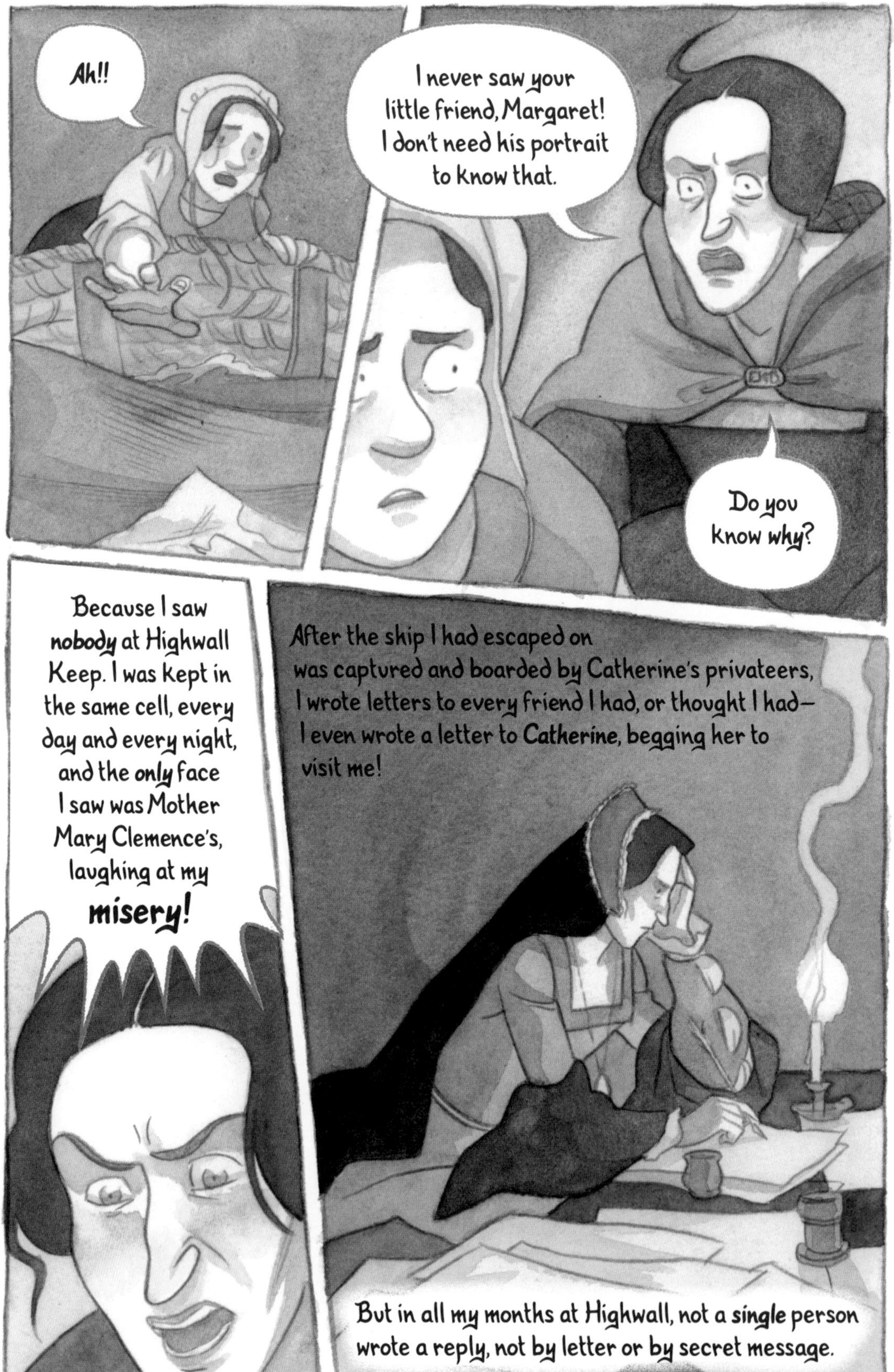
Ah!!
I never saw your little friend, Margaret! I don't need his portrait to know that.
Do you know why?
Because I saw nobody at Highwall Keep. I was kept in the same cell, every day and every night, and the only face I saw was Mother Mary Clemence's, laughing at my misery!
After the ship I had escaped on was captured and boarded by Catherine's privateers, I wrote letters to every friend I had, or thought I had— I even wrote a letter to Catherine, begging her to visit me!
But in all my months at Highwall, not a single person wrote a reply, not by letter or by secret message.

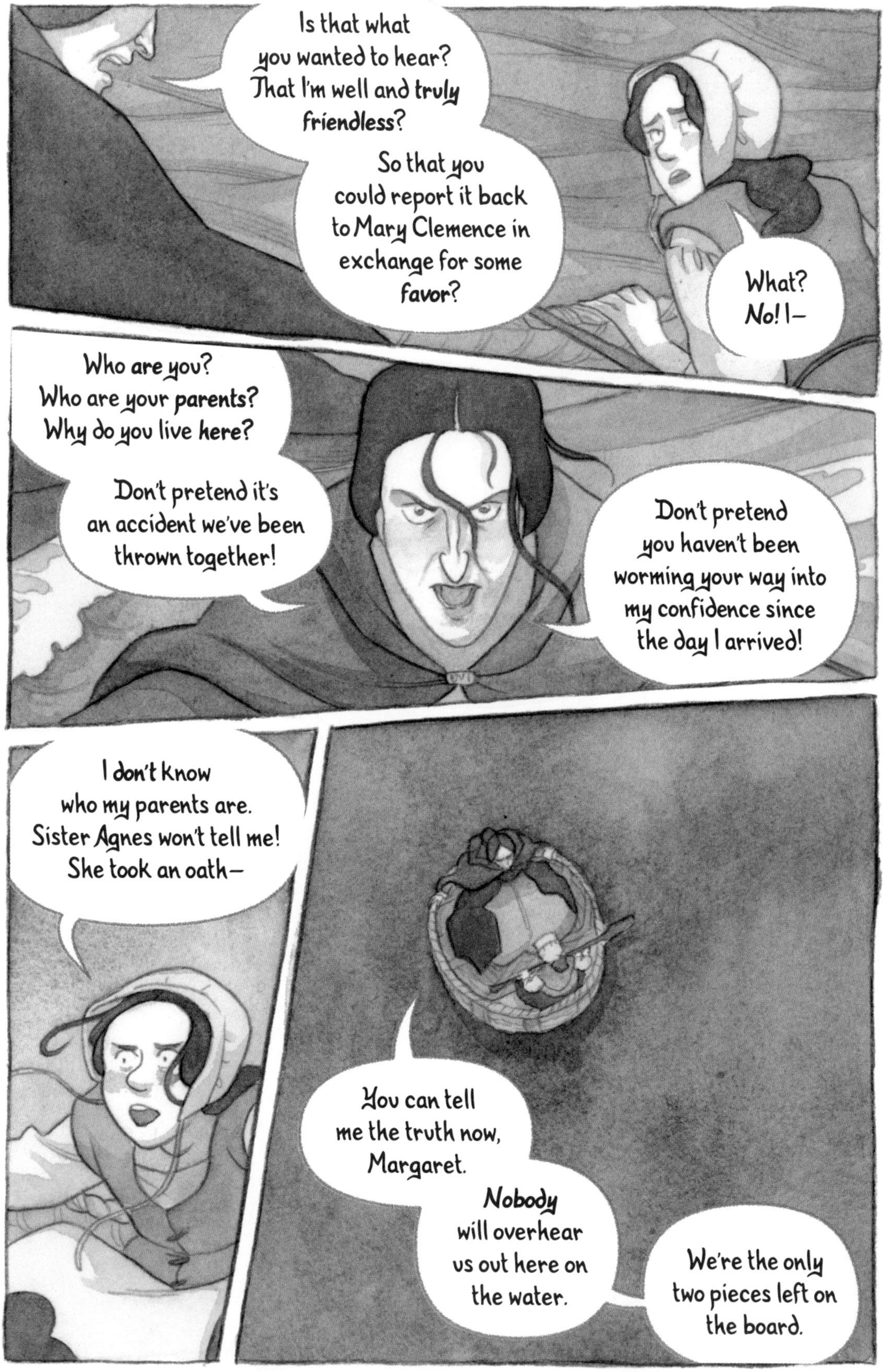
Is that what you wanted to hear? That I'm well and truly friendless?
So that you could report it back to Mary Clemence in exchange for some favor?
What? No! I—
Who are you? Who are your parents? Why do you live here?
Don't pretend it's an accident we've been thrown together!
Don't pretend you haven't been worming your way into my confidence since the day I arrived!
I don't know who my parents are. Sister Agnes won't tell me! She took an oath—
You can tell me the truth now, Margaret.
Nobody will overhear us out here on the water.
We're the only two pieces left on the board.

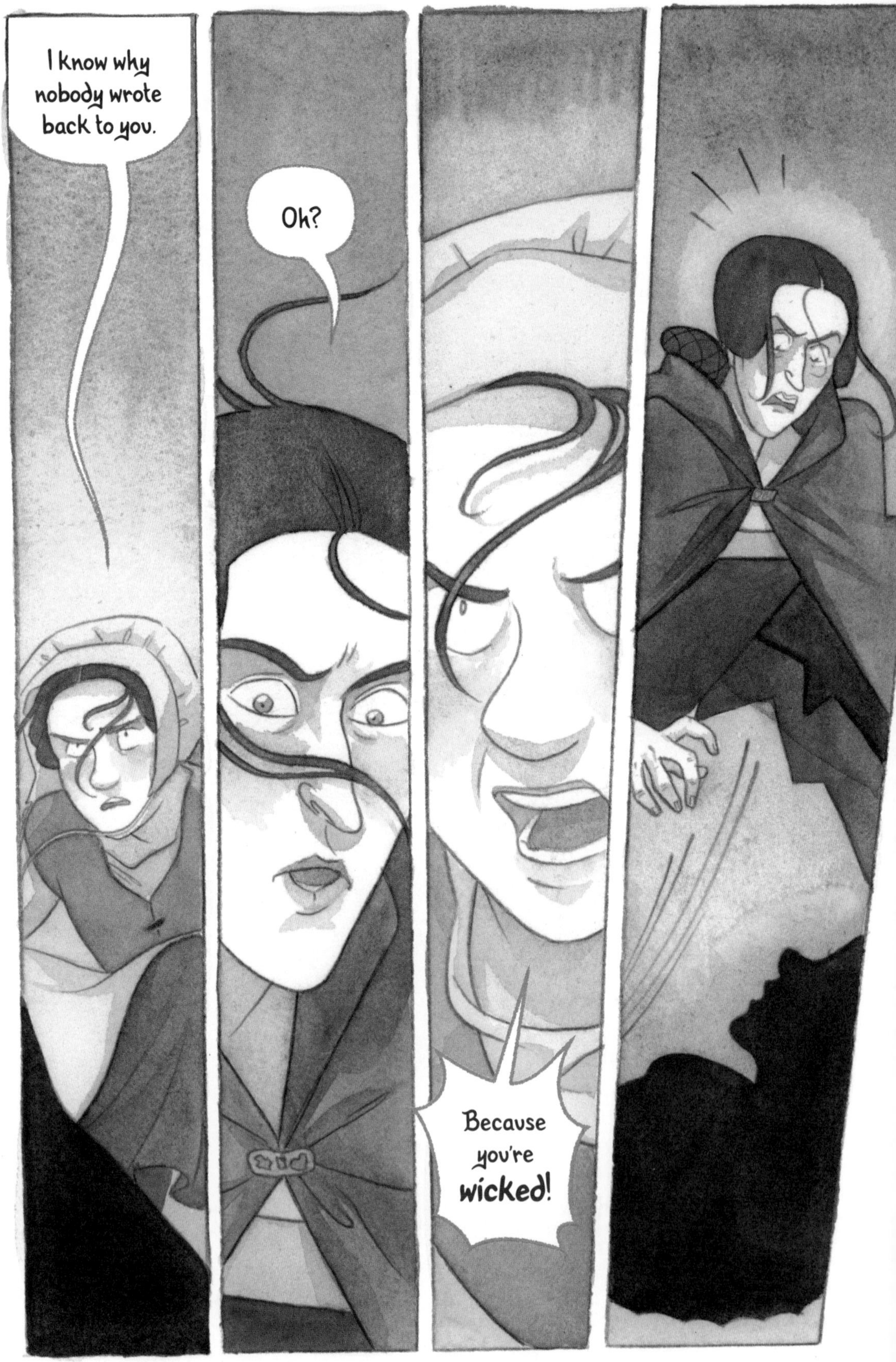
I know why nobody wrote back to you.
Oh?
Because you're wicked!

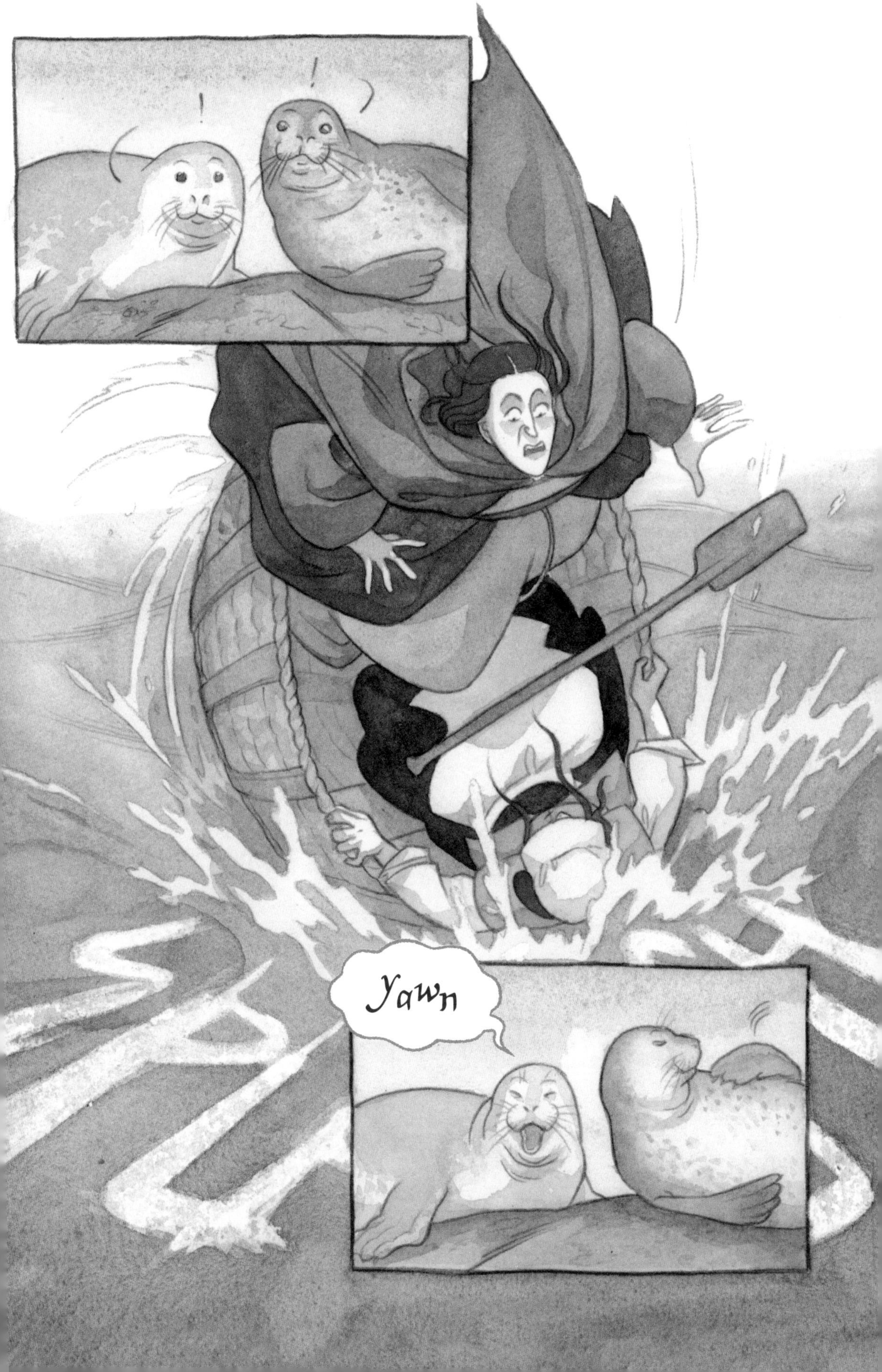
!
!
Yawn

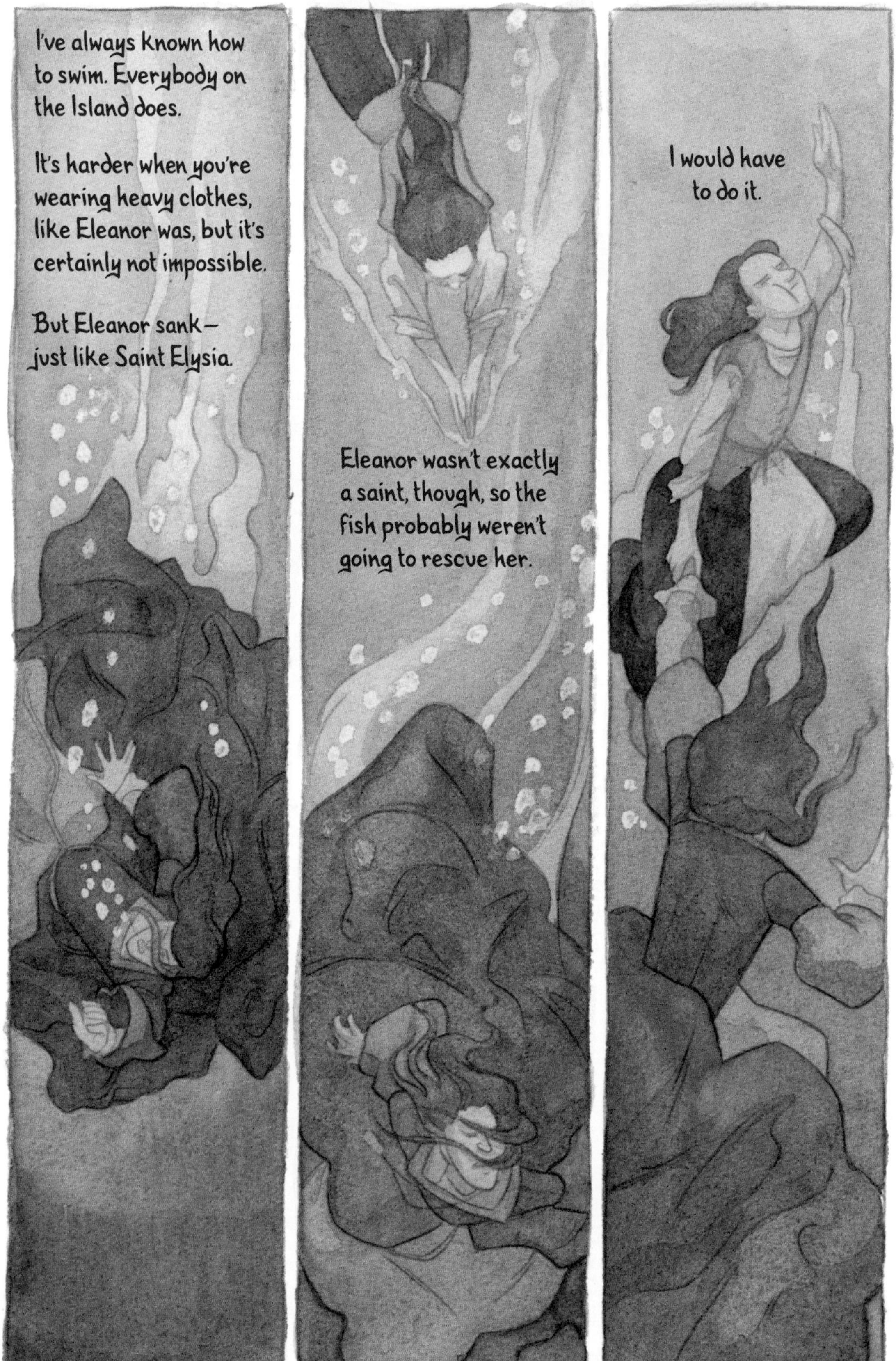
I've always known how to swim. Everybody on the Island does.
It's harder when you're wearing heavy clothes, like Eleanor was, but it's certainly not impossible.
But Eleanor sank—just like Saint Elysia.
Eleanor wasn't exactly a saint, though, so the fish probably weren't going to rescue her.
I would have to do it.

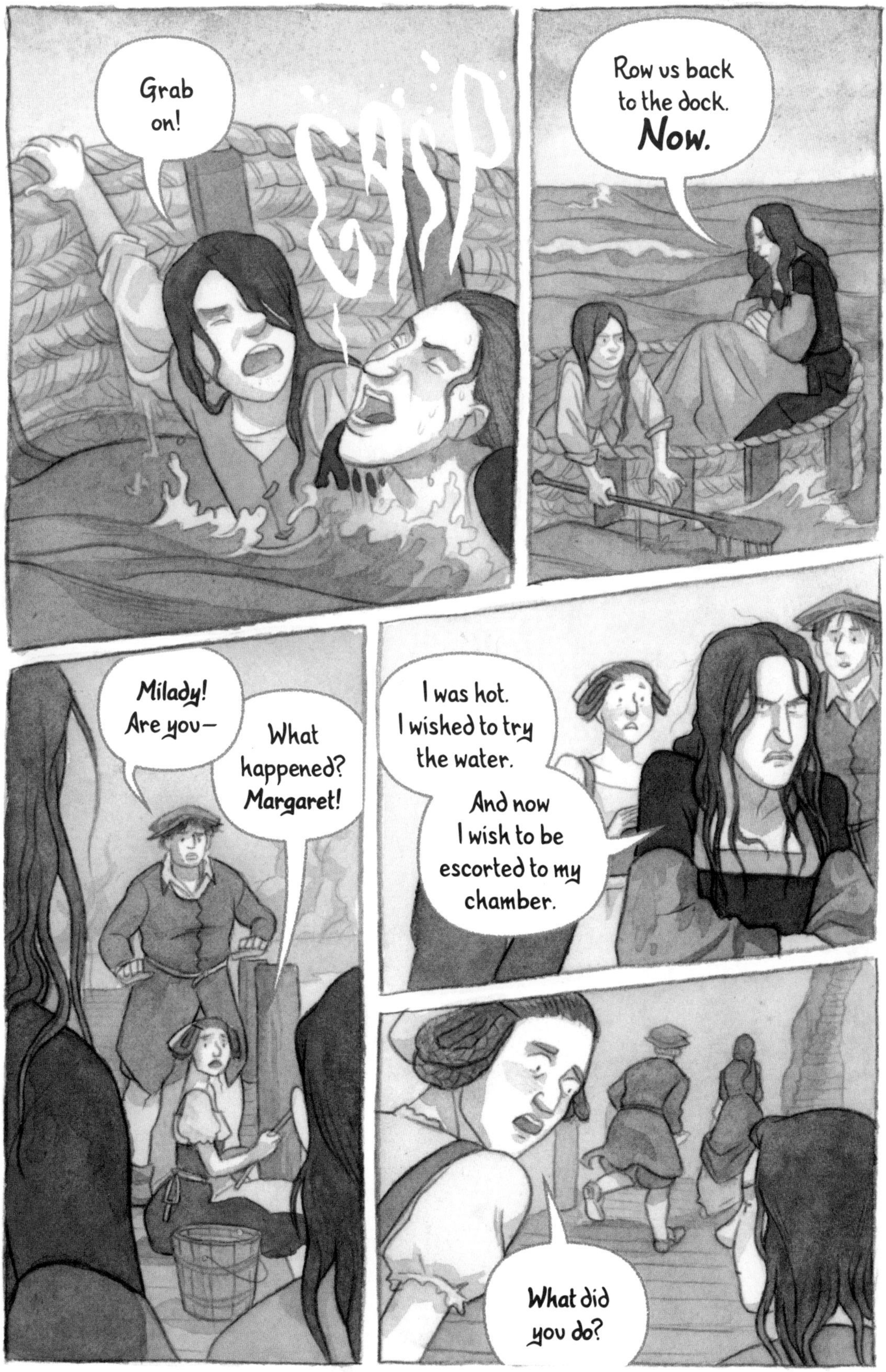
Grab on!
GASP
Row us back to the dock. Now.
Milady! Are you—
What happened? Margaret!
I was hot. I wished to try the water.
And now I wish to be escorted to my chamber.
What did you do?

I went to dry off in front of the kitchen fire—if I went to the Guest House I might run into Eleanor again or, worse, Mother Mary Clemence.

Jess was worried that Peter Yarrow would be blamed for letting Eleanor go out in the coracle, and Mother Mary Clemence would—

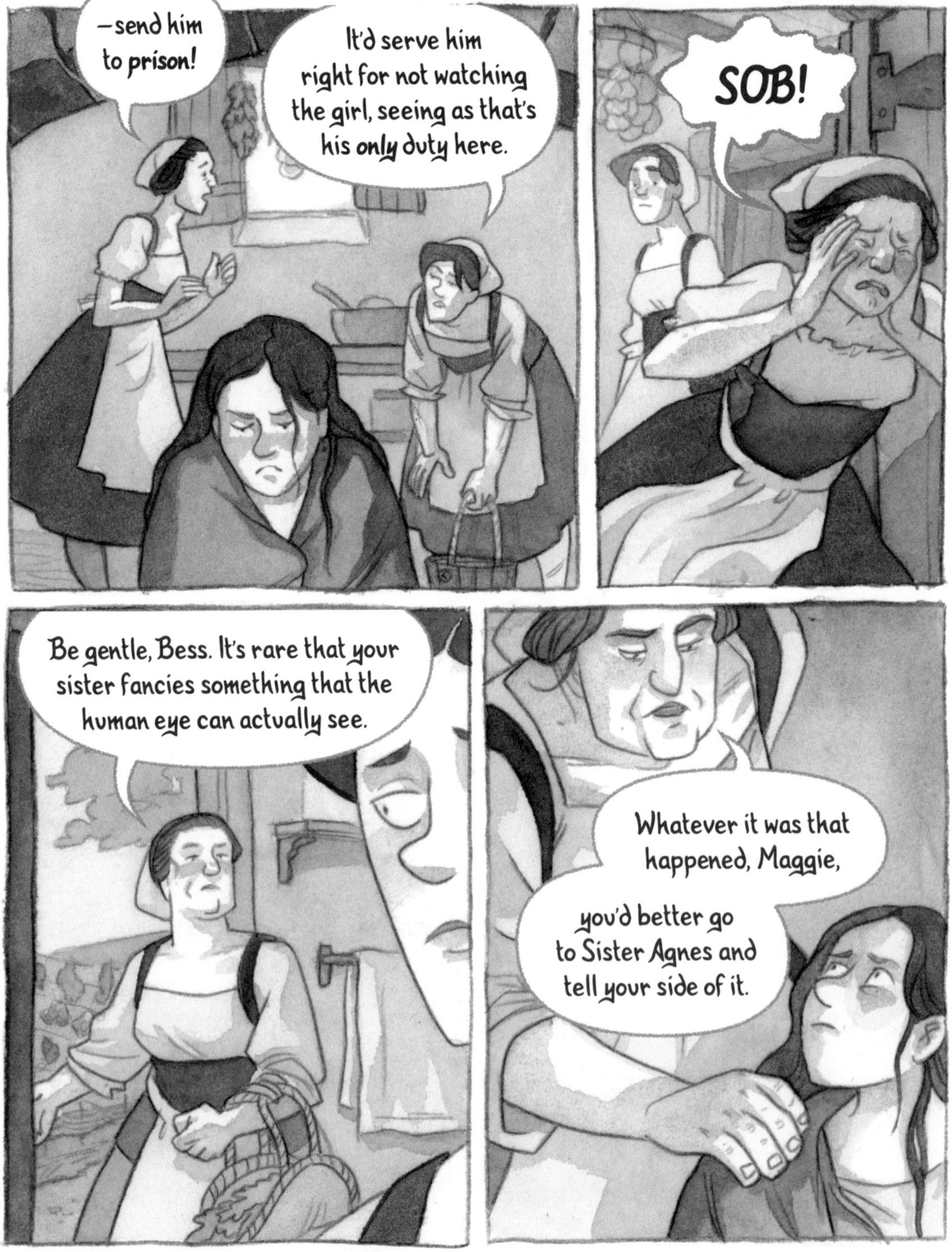
—send him to *prison!*
It'd serve him right for not watching the girl, seeing as that's his *only* duty here.
SOB!
Be gentle, Bess. It's rare that your sister fancies something that the human eye can actually see.
Whatever it was that happened, Maggie,
you'd better go to Sister Agnes and tell your side of it.

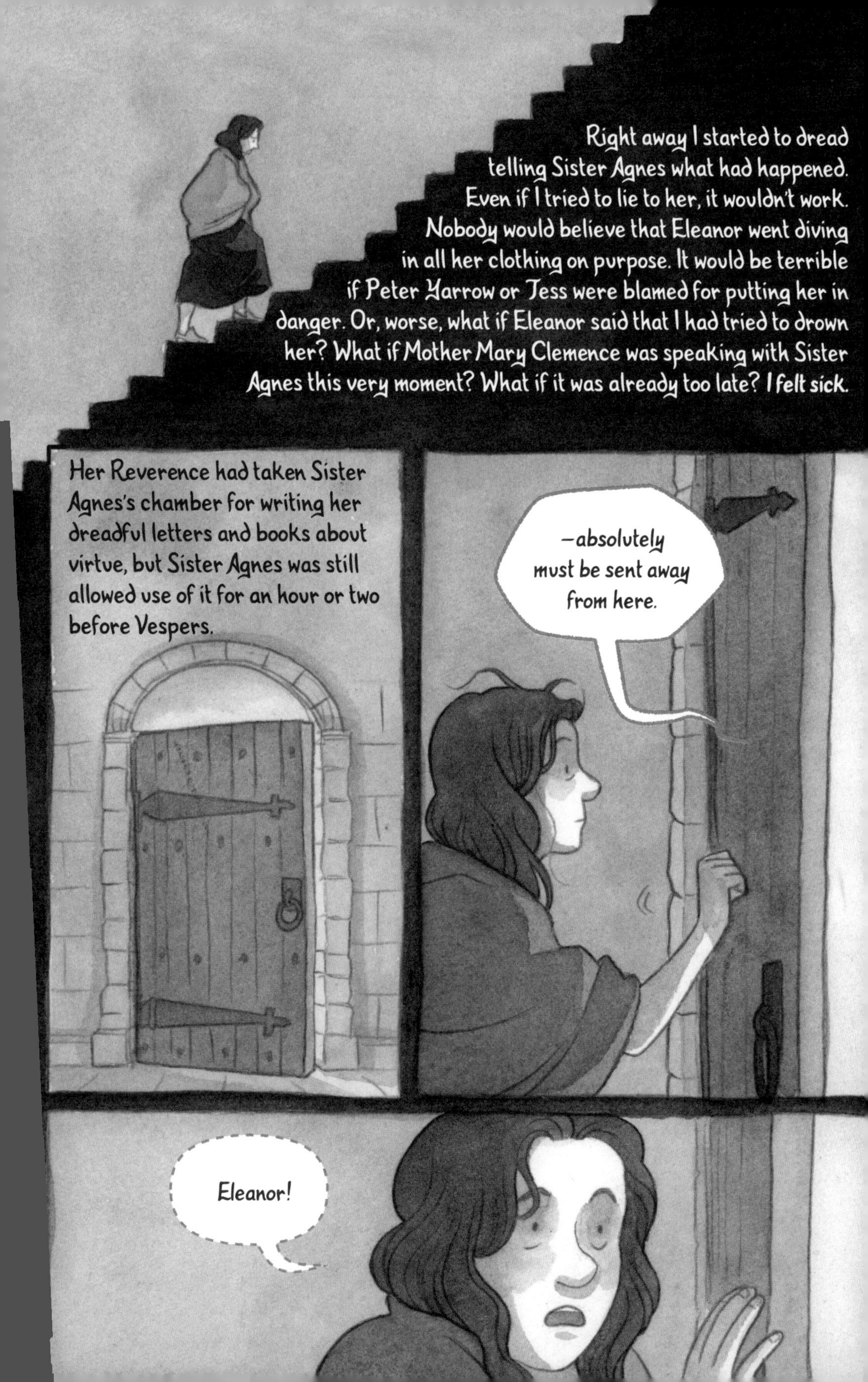

Right away I started to dread telling Sister Agnes what had happened. Even if I tried to lie to her, it wouldn't work. Nobody would believe that Eleanor went diving in all her clothing on purpose. It would be terrible if Peter Yarrow or Jess were blamed for putting her in danger. Or, worse, what if Eleanor said that I had tried to drown her? What if Mother Mary Clemence was speaking with Sister Agnes this very moment? What if it was already too late? I felt sick.
Her Reverence had taken Sister Agnes's chamber for writing her dreadful letters and books about virtue, but Sister Agnes was still allowed use of it for an hour or two before Vespers.
—absolutely must be sent away from here.
Eleanor!

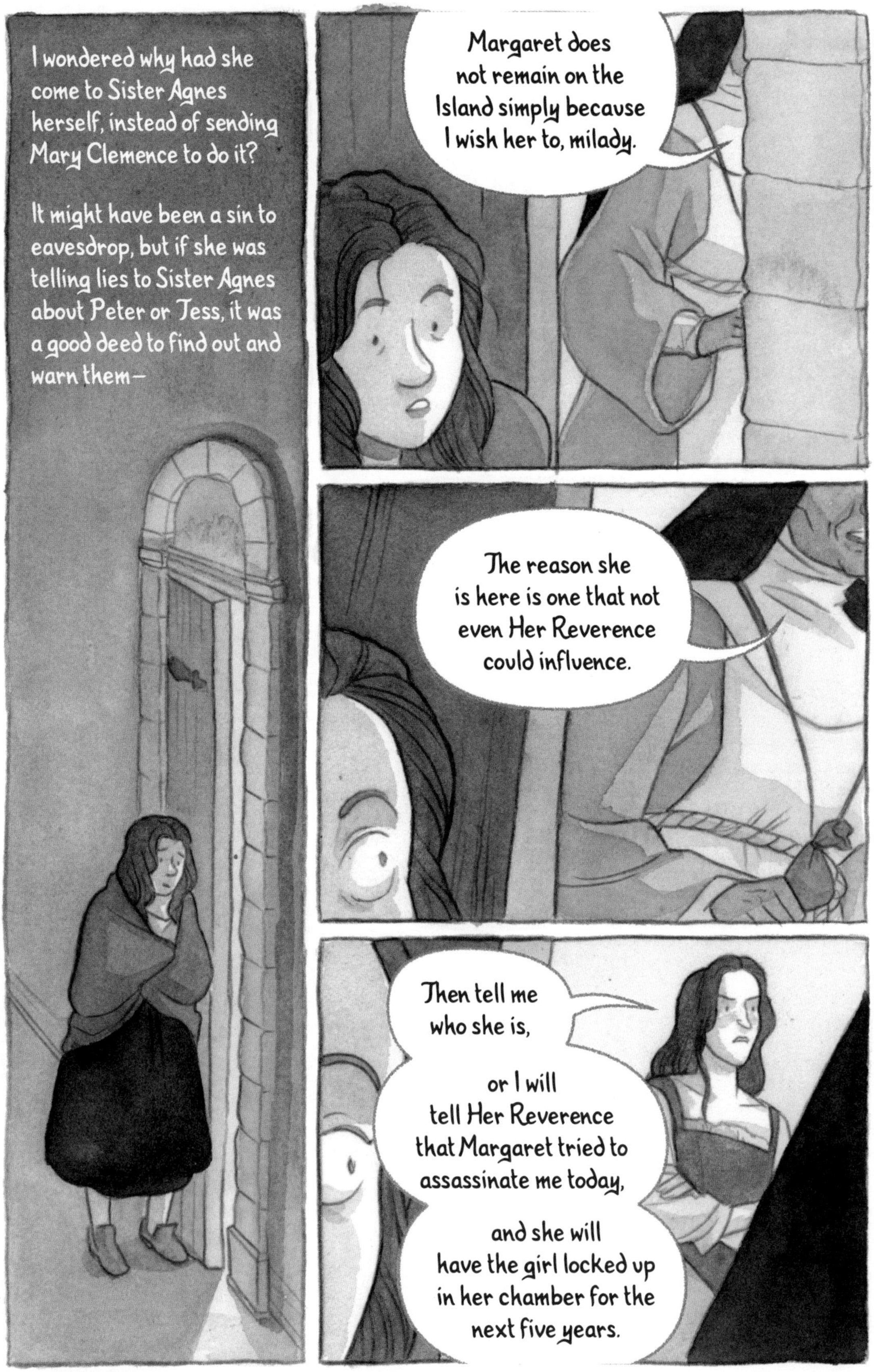
I wondered why had she come to Sister Agnes herself, instead of sending Mary Clemence to do it?
It might have been a sin to eavesdrop, but if she was telling lies to Sister Agnes about Peter or Jess, it was a good deed to find out and warn them—
Margaret does not remain on the Island simply because I wish her to, milady.
The reason she is here is one that not even Her Reverence could influence.
Then tell me who she is,
or I will tell Her Reverence that Margaret tried to assassinate me today,
and she will have the girl locked up in her chamber for the next five years.

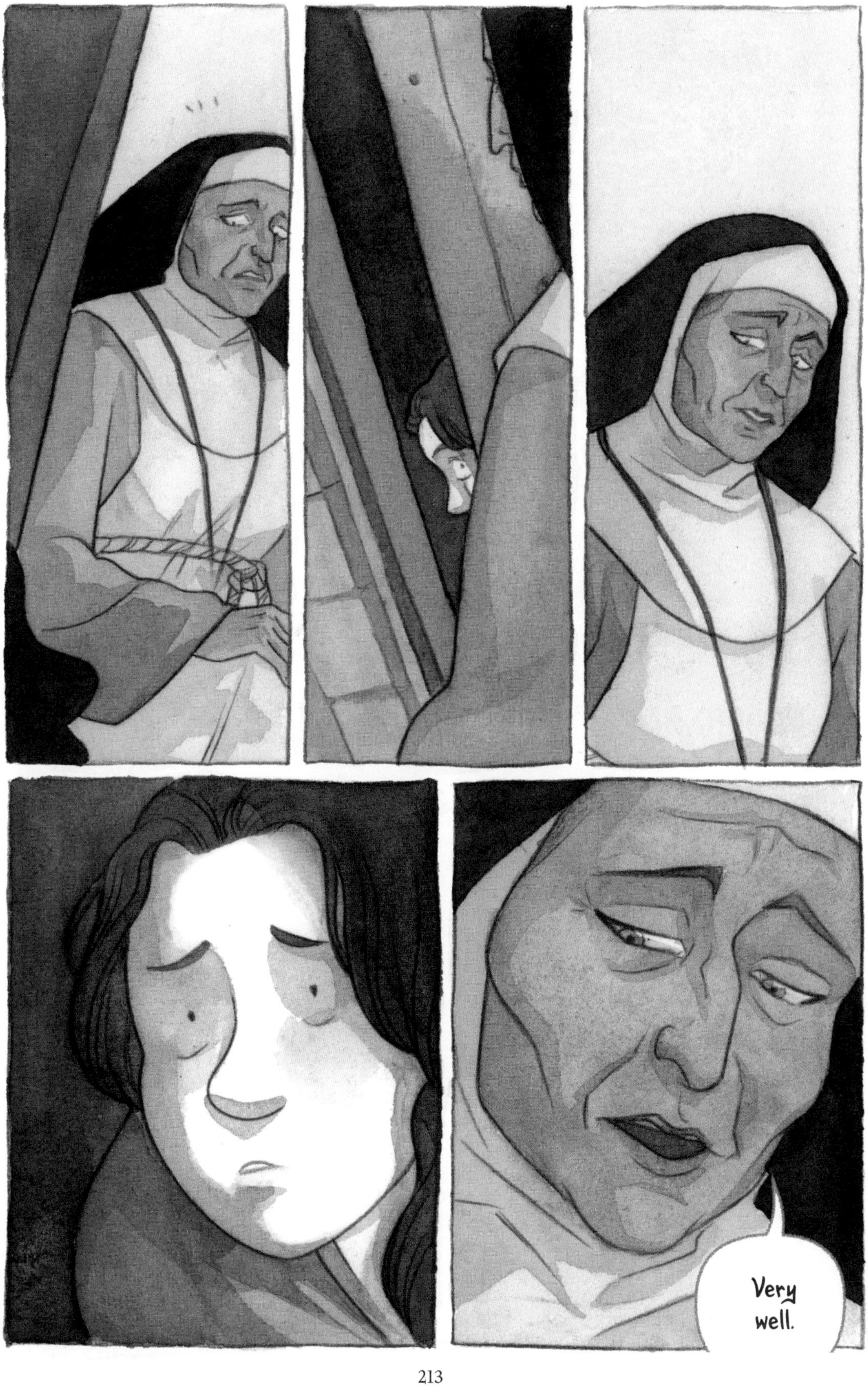
Very well.

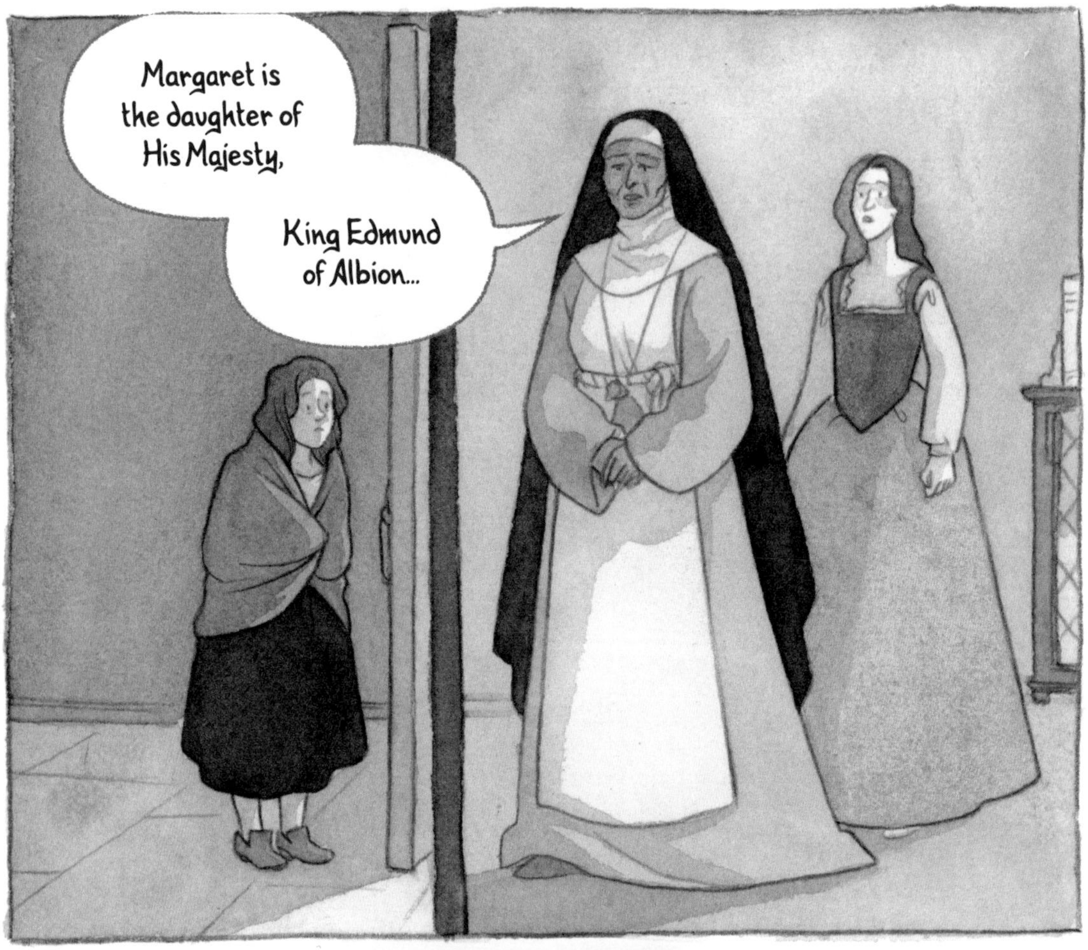
Margaret is the daughter of His Majesty,
King Edmund of Albion...

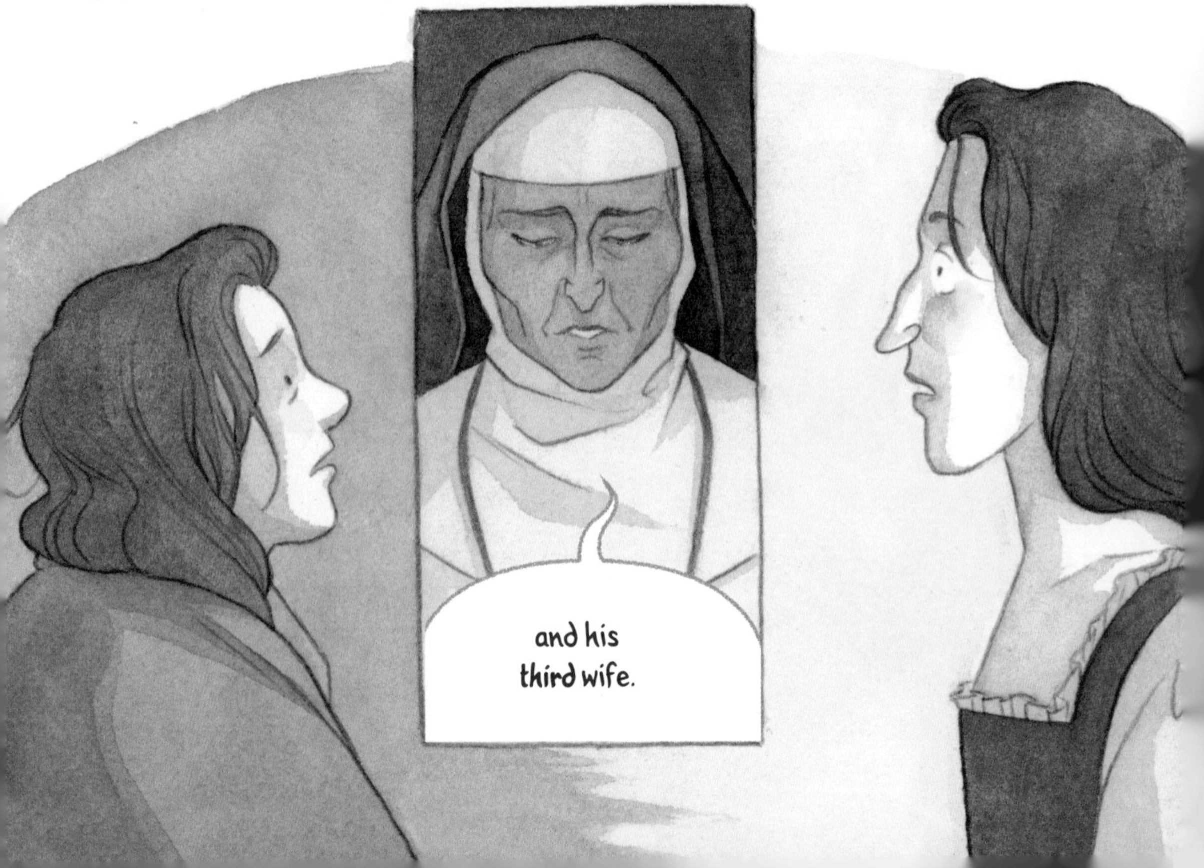
and his third wife.

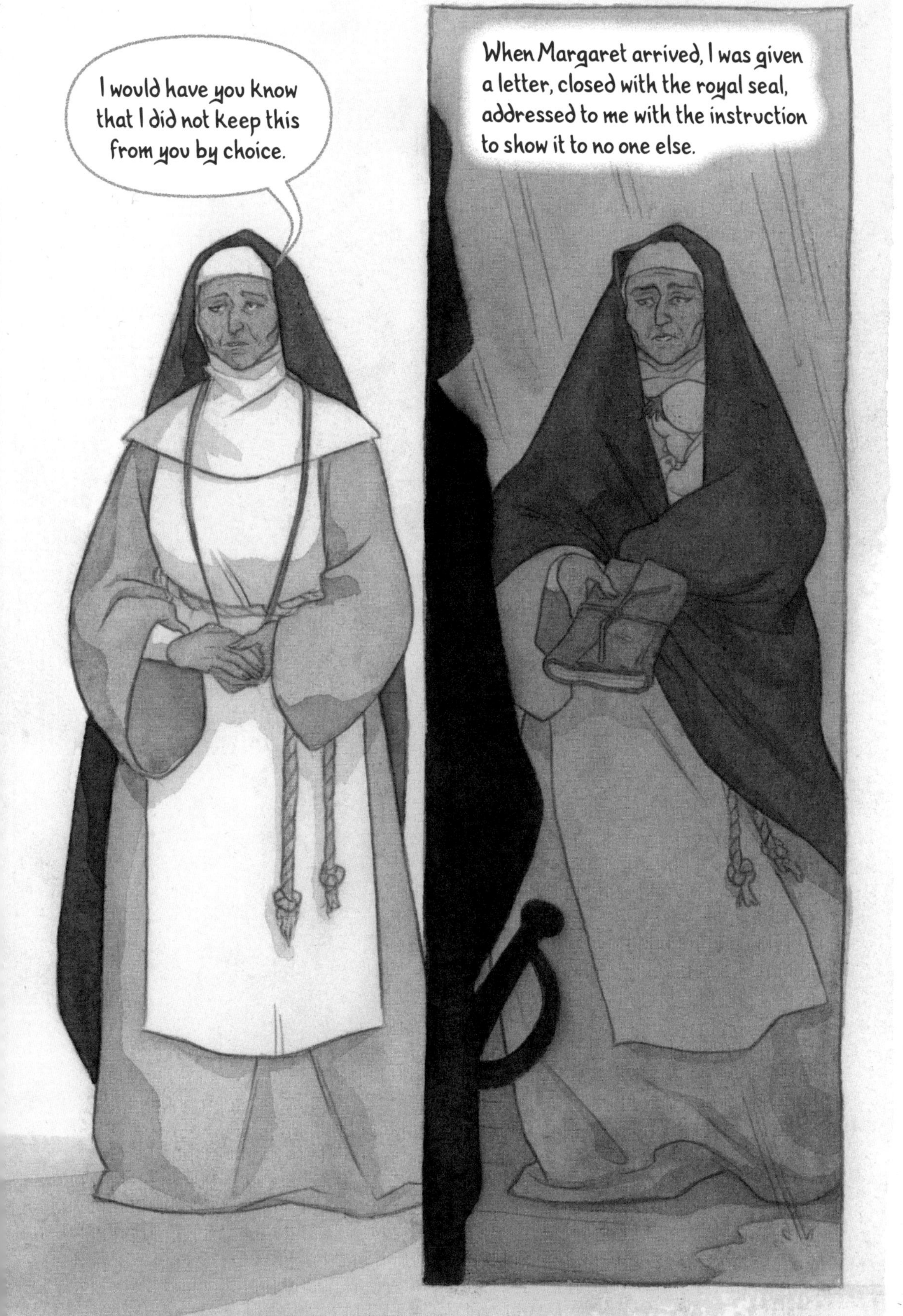
I would have you know that I did not keep this from you by choice.
When Margaret arrived, I was given a letter, closed with the royal seal, addressed to me with the instruction to show it to no one else.

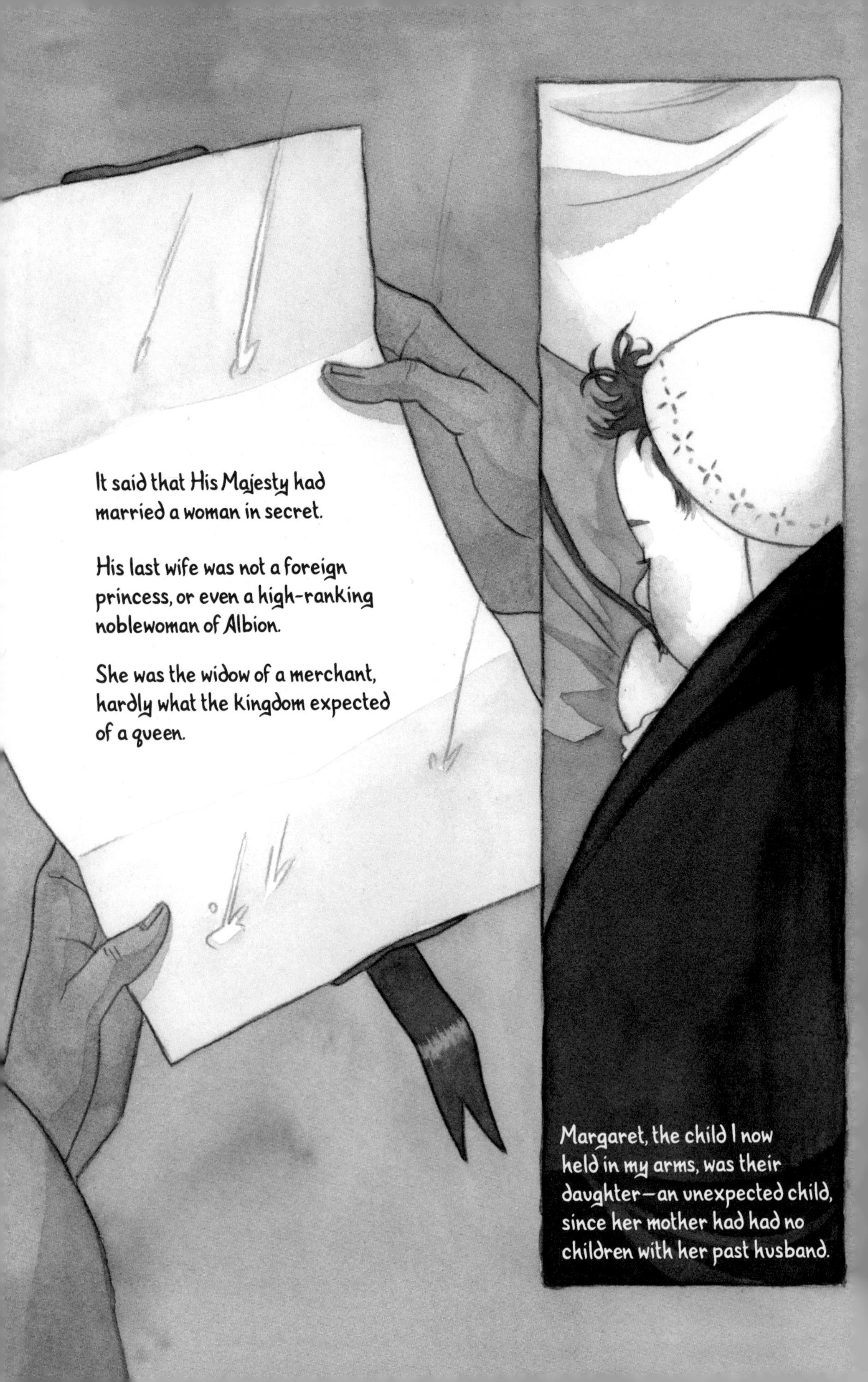
It said that His Majesty had married a woman in secret.
His last wife was not a foreign princess, or even a high-ranking noblewoman of Albion.
She was the widow of a merchant, hardly what the kingdom expected of a queen.
Margaret, the child I now held in my arms, was their daughter—an unexpected child, since her mother had had no children with her past husband.

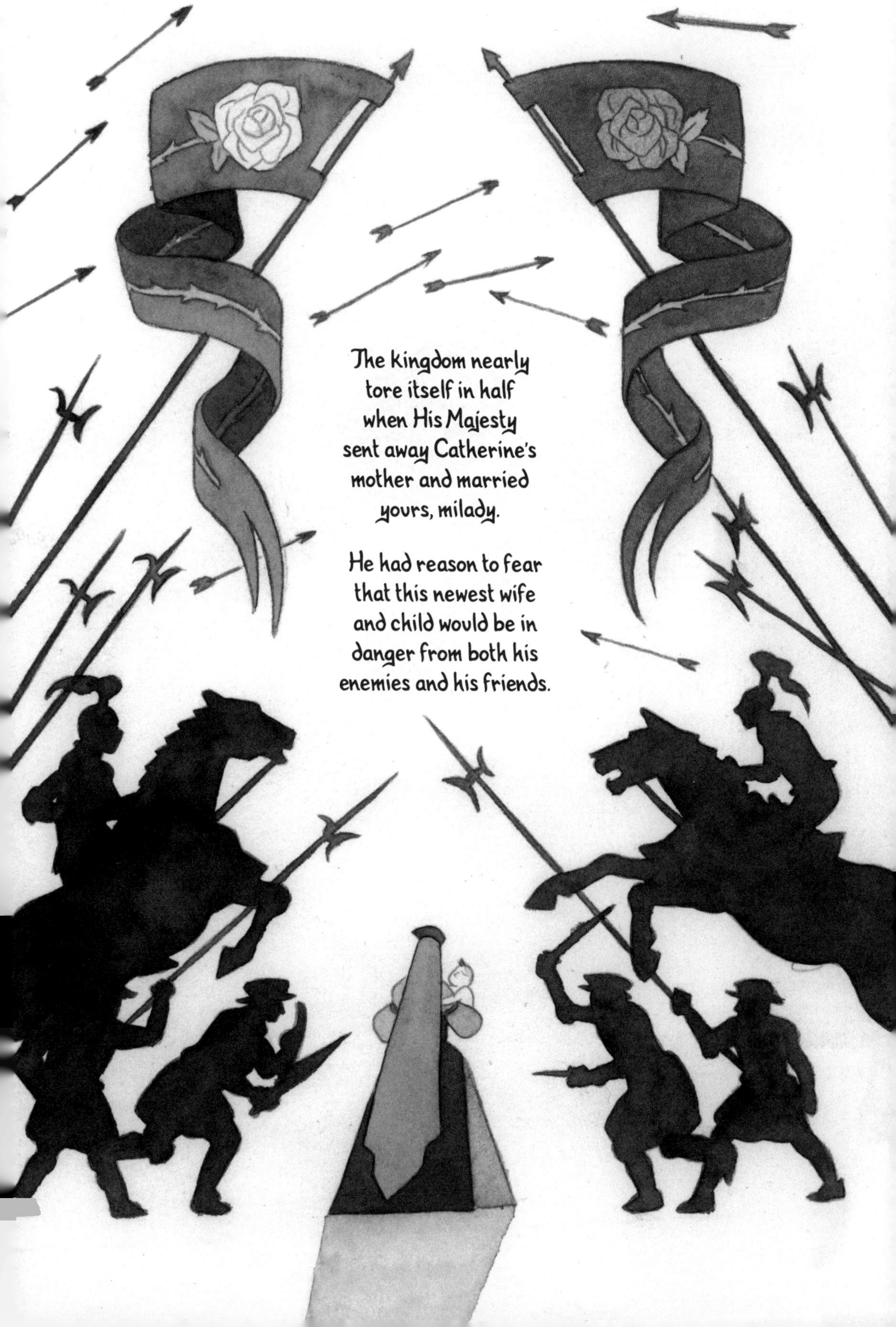
The kingdom nearly tore itself in half when His Majesty sent away Catherine's mother and married yours, milady.
He had reason to fear that this newest wife and child would be in danger from both his enemies and his friends.

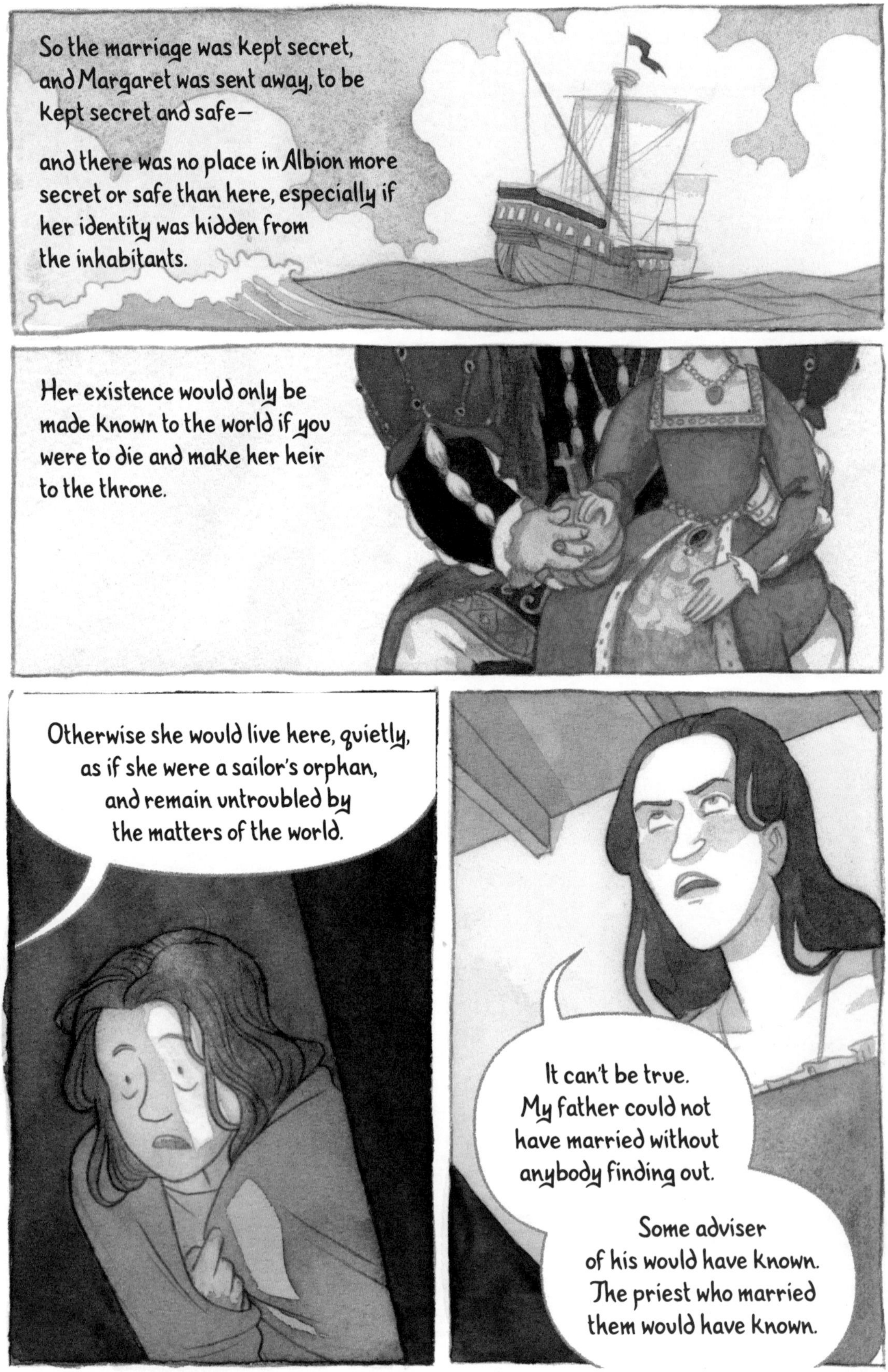
So the marriage was kept secret, and Margaret was sent away, to be kept secret and safe—
and there was no place in Albion more secret or safe than here, especially if her identity was hidden from the inhabitants.
Her existence would only be made known to the world if you were to die and make her heir to the throne.
Otherwise she would live here, quietly, as if she were a sailor's orphan, and remain untroubled by the matters of the world.
It can't be true. My father could not have married without anybody finding out.
Some adviser of his would have known. The priest who married them would have known.

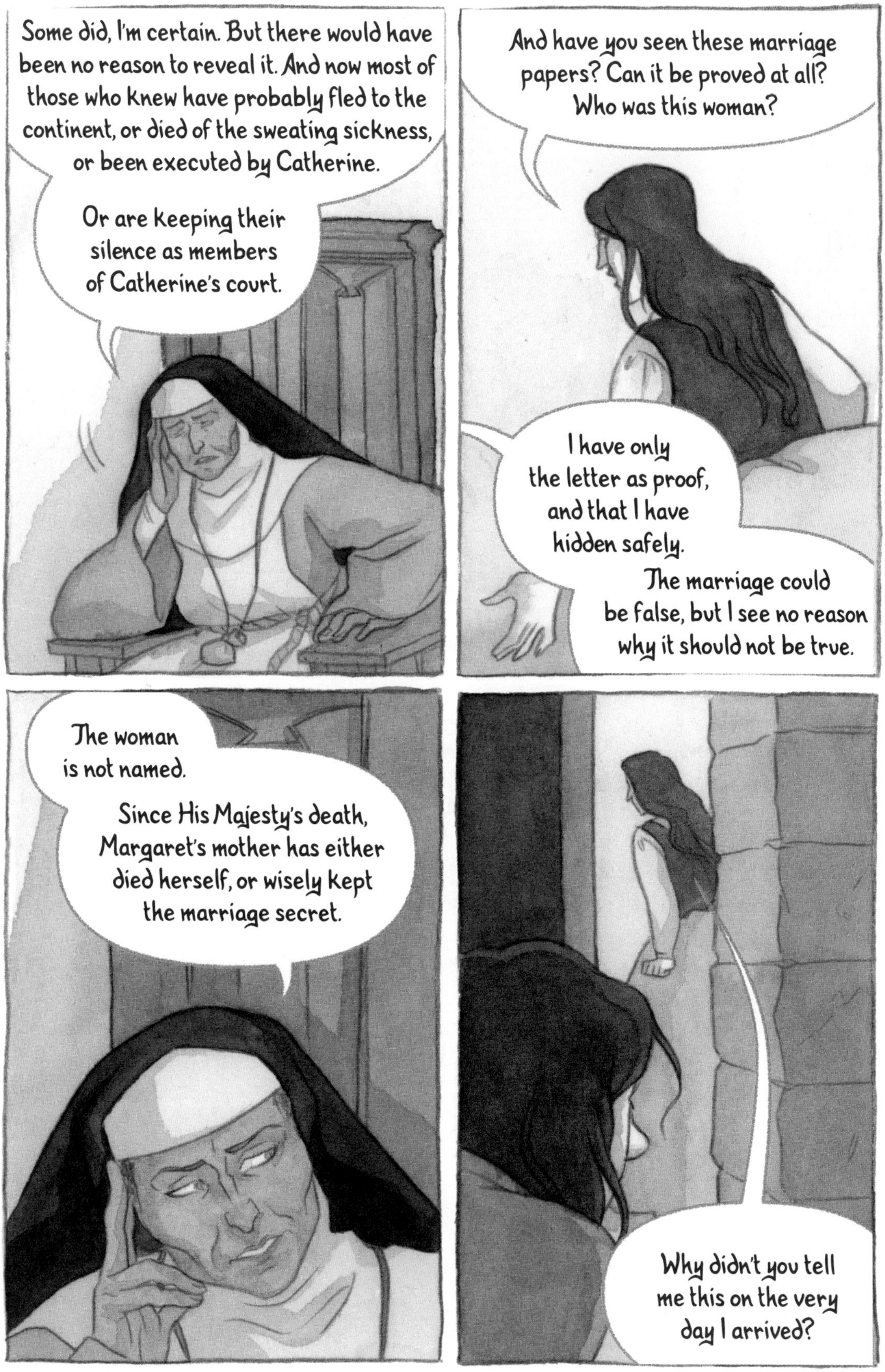
Some did, I'm certain. But there would have been no reason to reveal it. And now most of those who knew have probably fled to the continent, or died of the sweating sickness, or been executed by Catherine.
Or are keeping their silence as members of Catherine's court.
And have you seen these marriage papers? Can it be proved at all? Who was this woman?
I have only the letter as proof, and that I have hidden safely.
The marriage could be false, but I see no reason why it should not be true.
The woman is not named.
Since His Majesty's death, Margaret's mother has either died herself, or wisely kept the marriage secret.
Why didn't you tell me this on the very day I arrived?

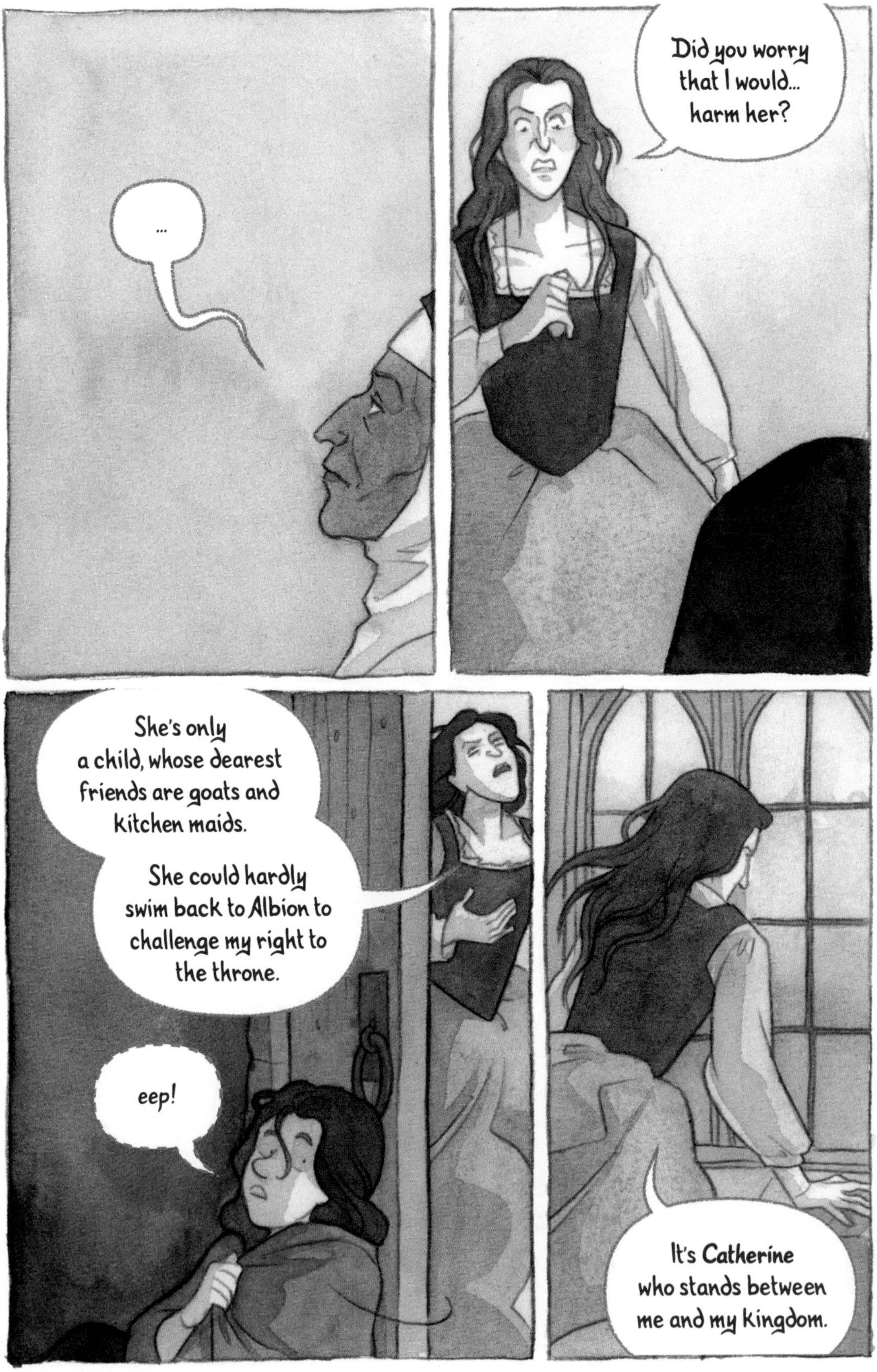

...
Did you worry that I would... harm her?
She's only a child, whose dearest friends are goats and kitchen maids.
She could hardly swim back to Albion to challenge my right to the throne.
eep!
It's Catherine who stands between me and my kingdom.

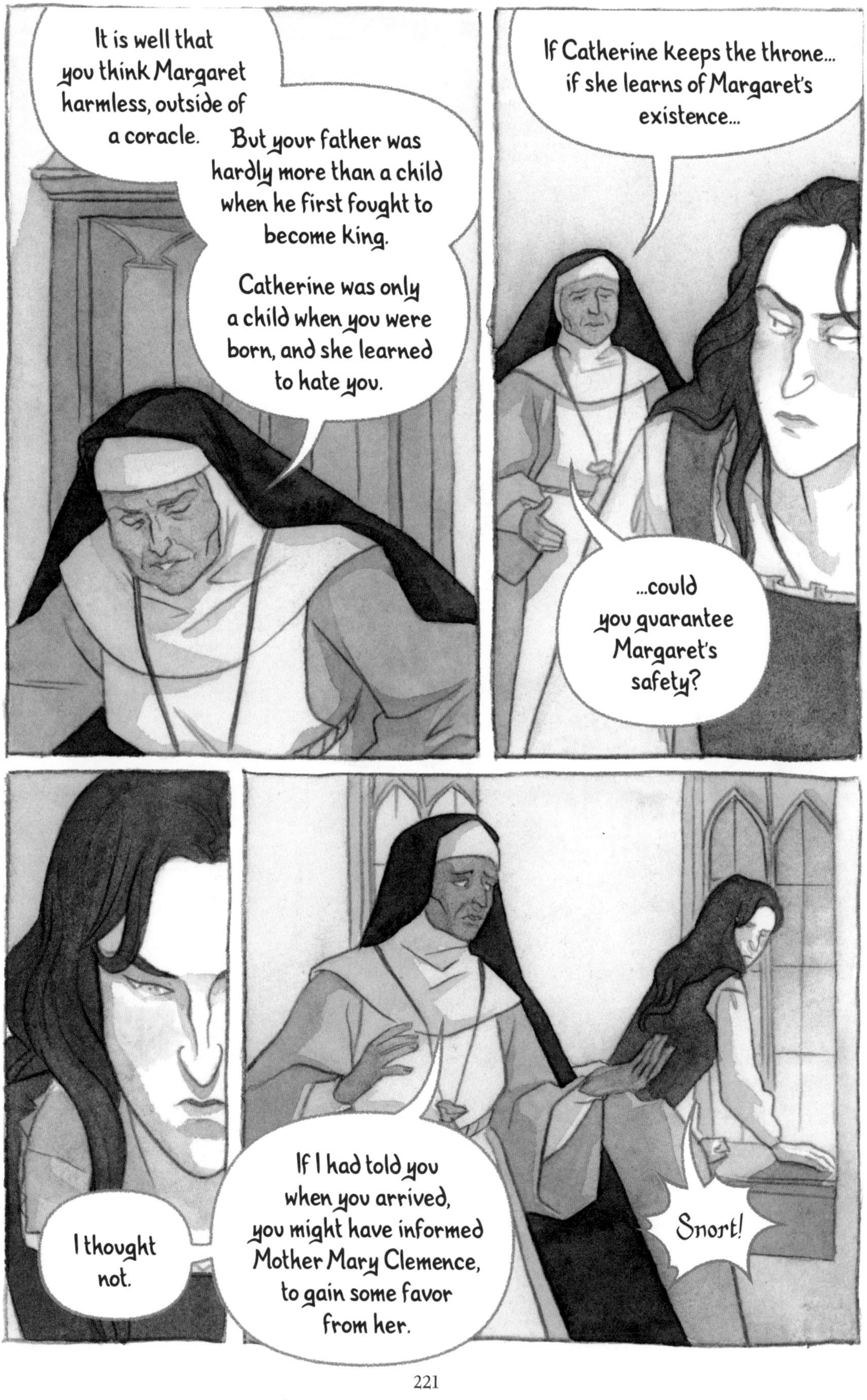
It is well that you think Margaret harmless, outside of a coracle.
But your father was hardly more than a child when he first fought to become king.
Catherine was only a child when you were born, and she learned to hate you.
If Catherine keeps the throne... if she learns of Margaret's existence...
...could you guarantee Margaret's safety?
I thought not.
If I had told you when you arrived, you might have informed Mother Mary Clemence, to gain some favor from her.
Snort!

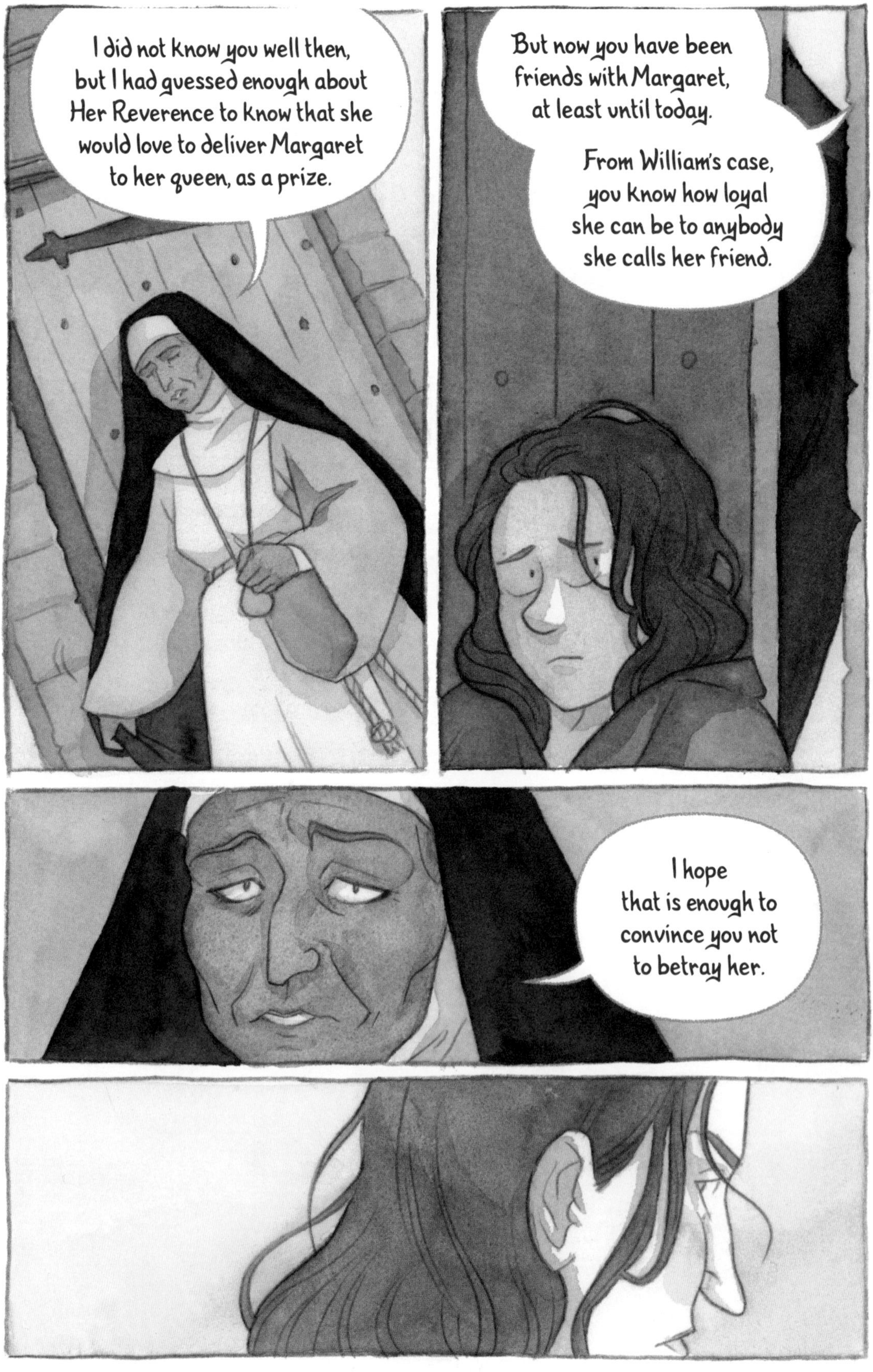
I did not know you well then, but I had guessed enough about Her Reverence to know that she would love to deliver Margaret to her queen, as a prize.
But now you have been friends with Margaret, at least until today.
From William's case, you know how loyal she can be to anybody she calls her friend.
I hope that is enough to convince you not to betray her.

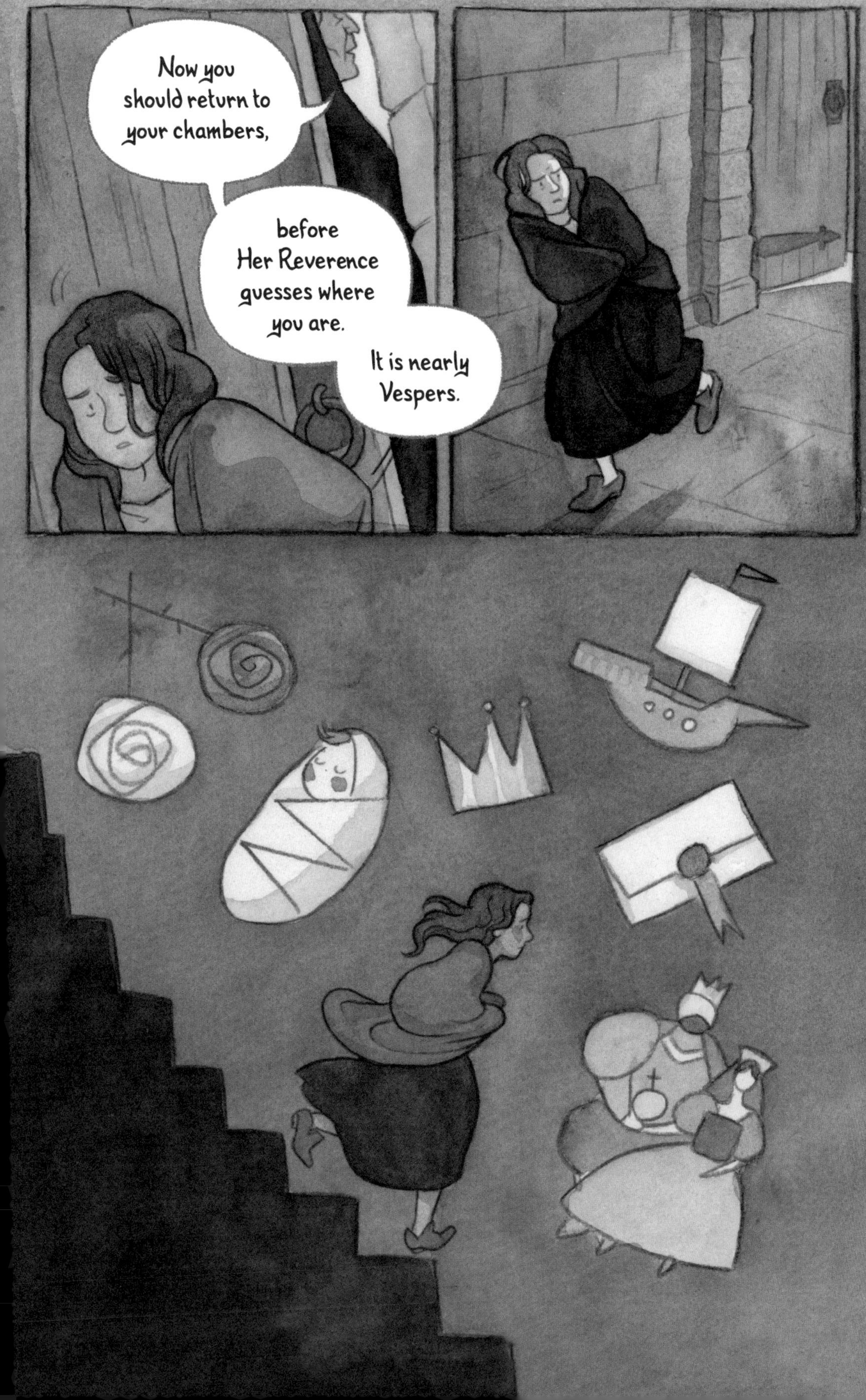
Now you should return to your chambers,
before Her Reverence guesses where you are.
It is nearly Vespers.

Eleanor didn't call for me to visit her after that. She even took her meals in her chamber. She must have told Mother Mary Clemence that she was unwell. Maybe she really was. I was not certain I would have gone to visit her even if she had asked.

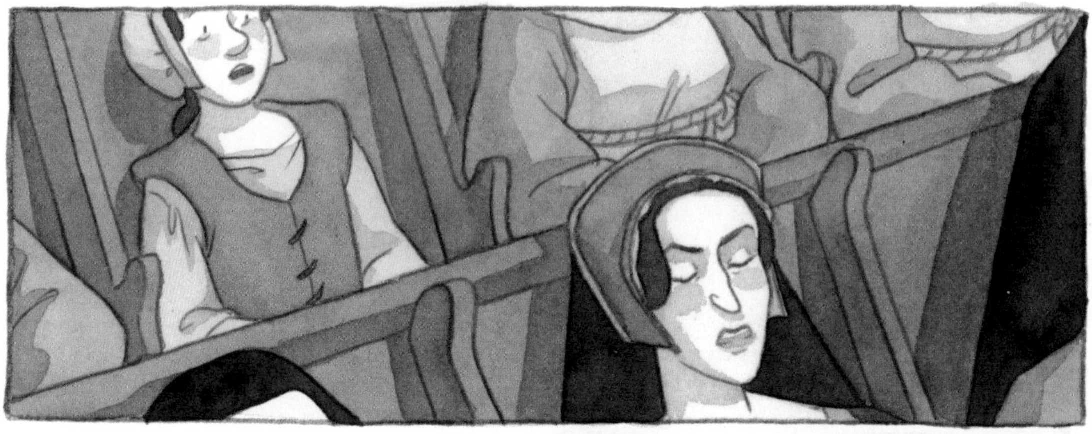

Perhaps she would change her mind about my being a threat to her crown, and push me down the stairs!

Her own sister!

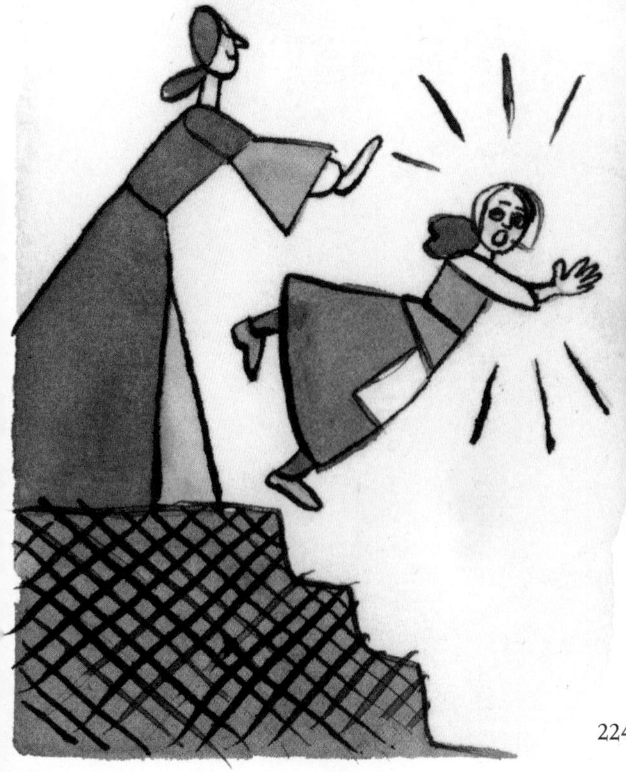

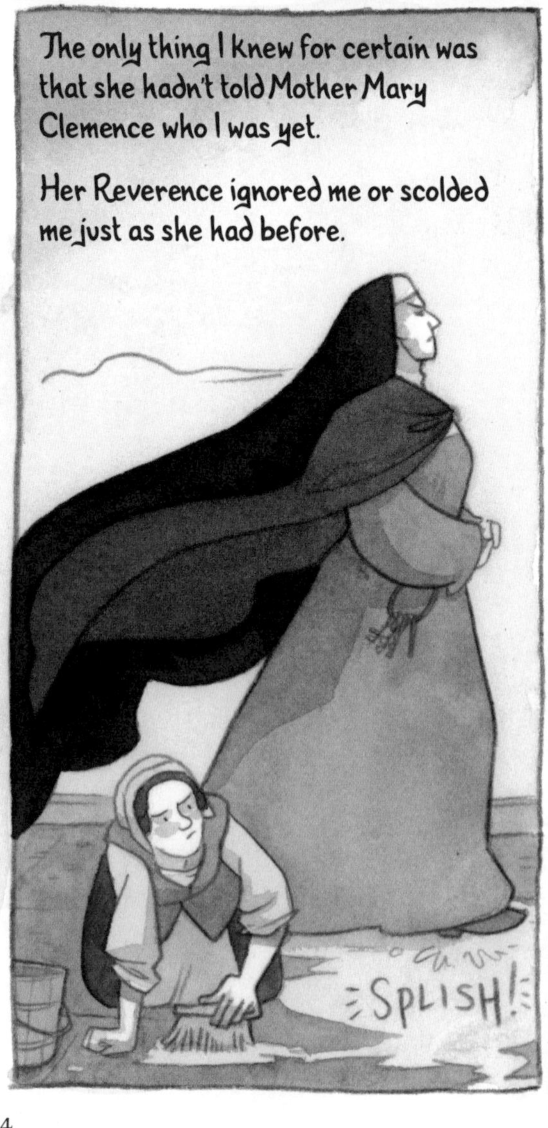
The only thing I knew for certain was that she hadn't told Mother Mary Clemence who I was yet.
Her Reverence ignored me or scolded me just as she had before.
SPLISH!

Sister Agnes also behaved as if nothing had happened, even though she knew that I had heard the entire conversation. I had so many questions I wanted to ask her:

Where was the letter hidden? Had she really told Eleanor everything that was in it, or did it say who my mother was? Did it say why my mother didn't come to the Island with me? Why did Sister Agnes let me listen at all? Was it so I would know to be wary of Eleanor? Would Sister Agnes have ever told me any of those secrets if Eleanor hadn't made threats?

It had been so long since the two of us had truly spoken.

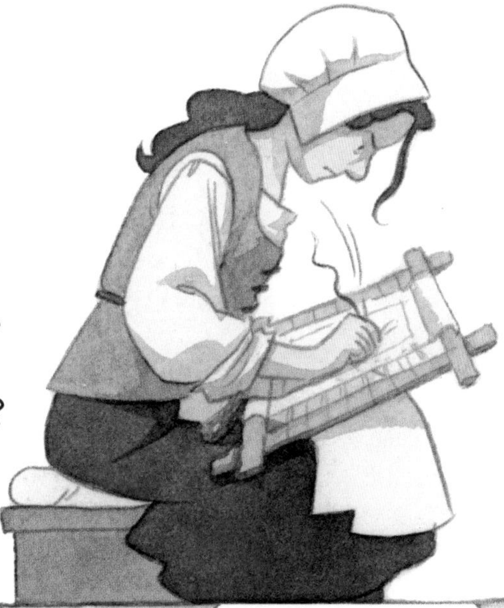

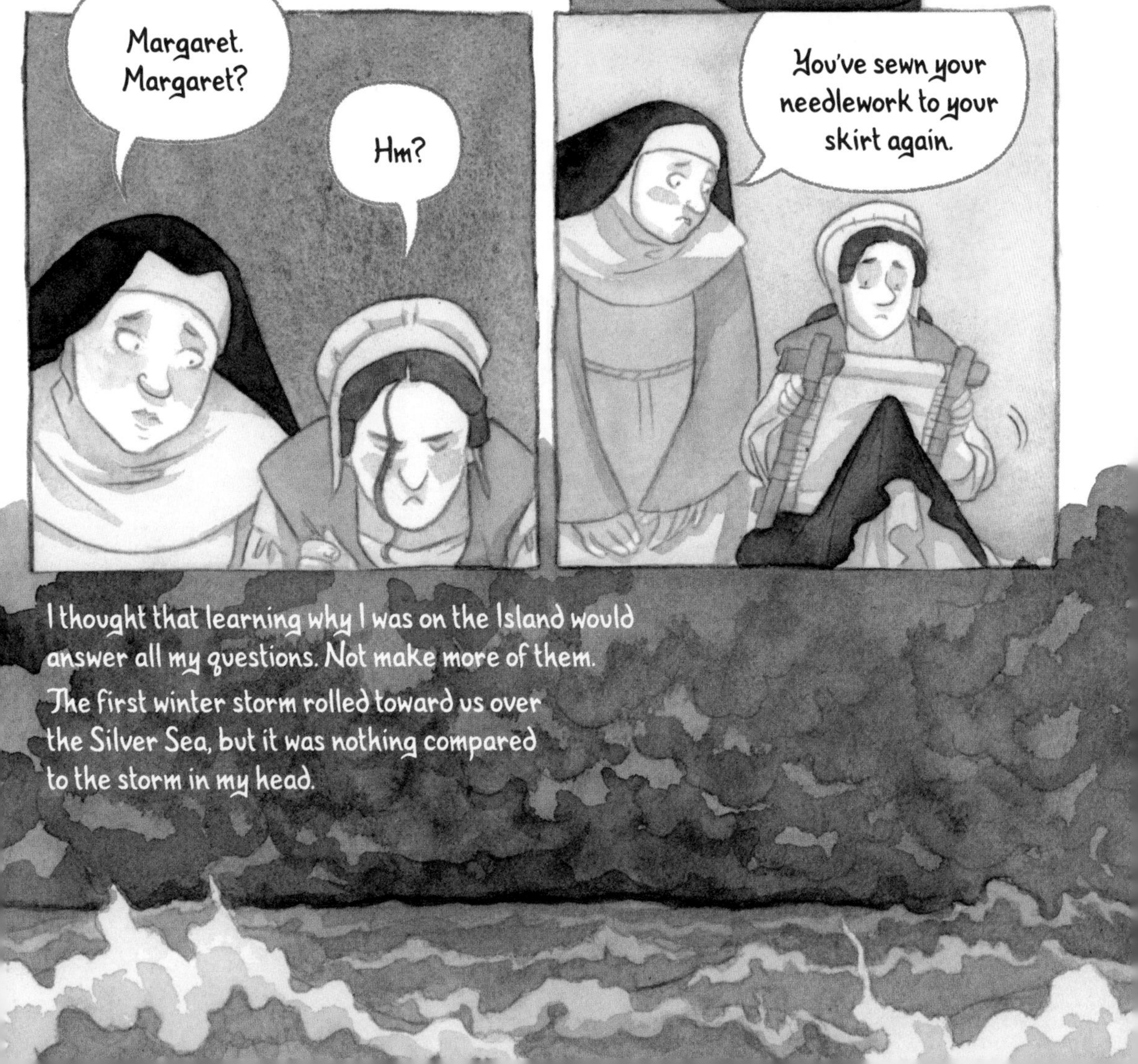
Margaret. Margaret?
Hm?
You've sewn your needlework to your skirt again.
I thought that learning why I was on the Island would answer all my questions. Not make more of them.
The first winter storm rolled toward us over the Silver Sea, but it was nothing compared to the storm in my head.

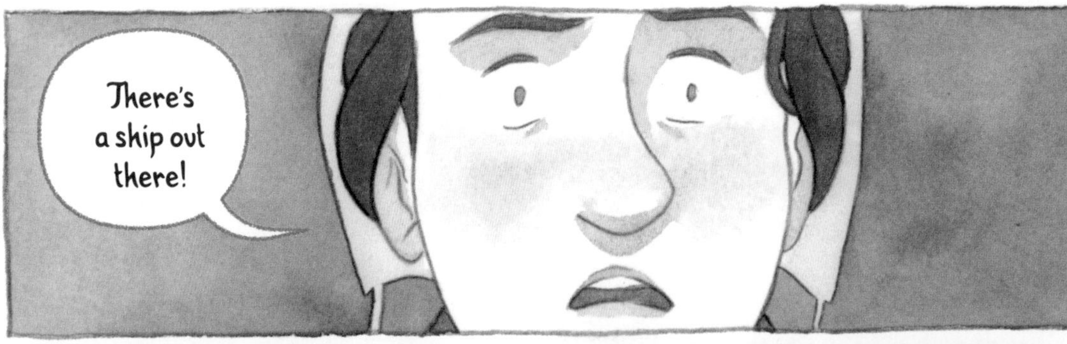
There's a ship out there!

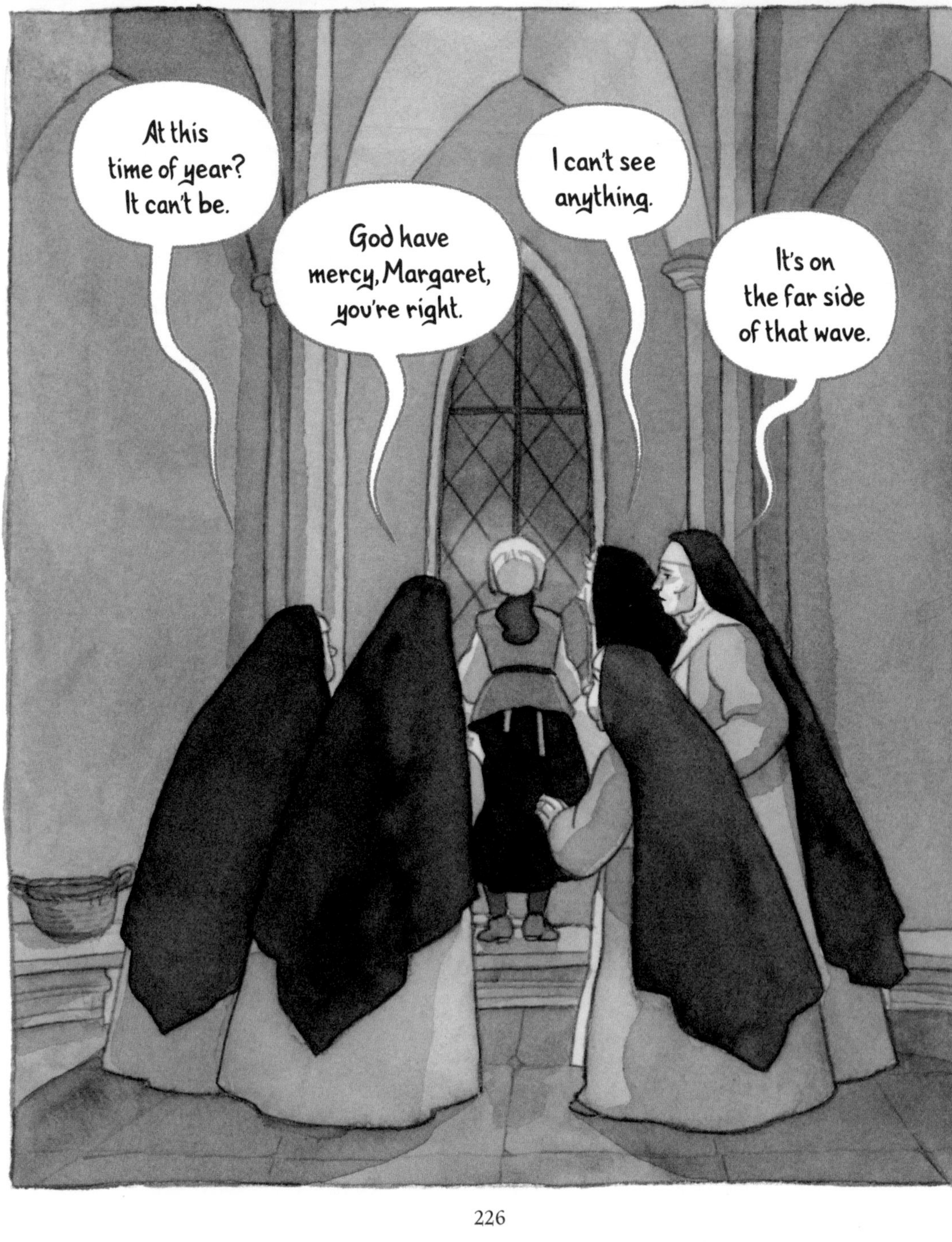
At this time of year? It can't be.
God have mercy, Margaret, you're right.
I can't see anything.
It's on the far side of that wave.

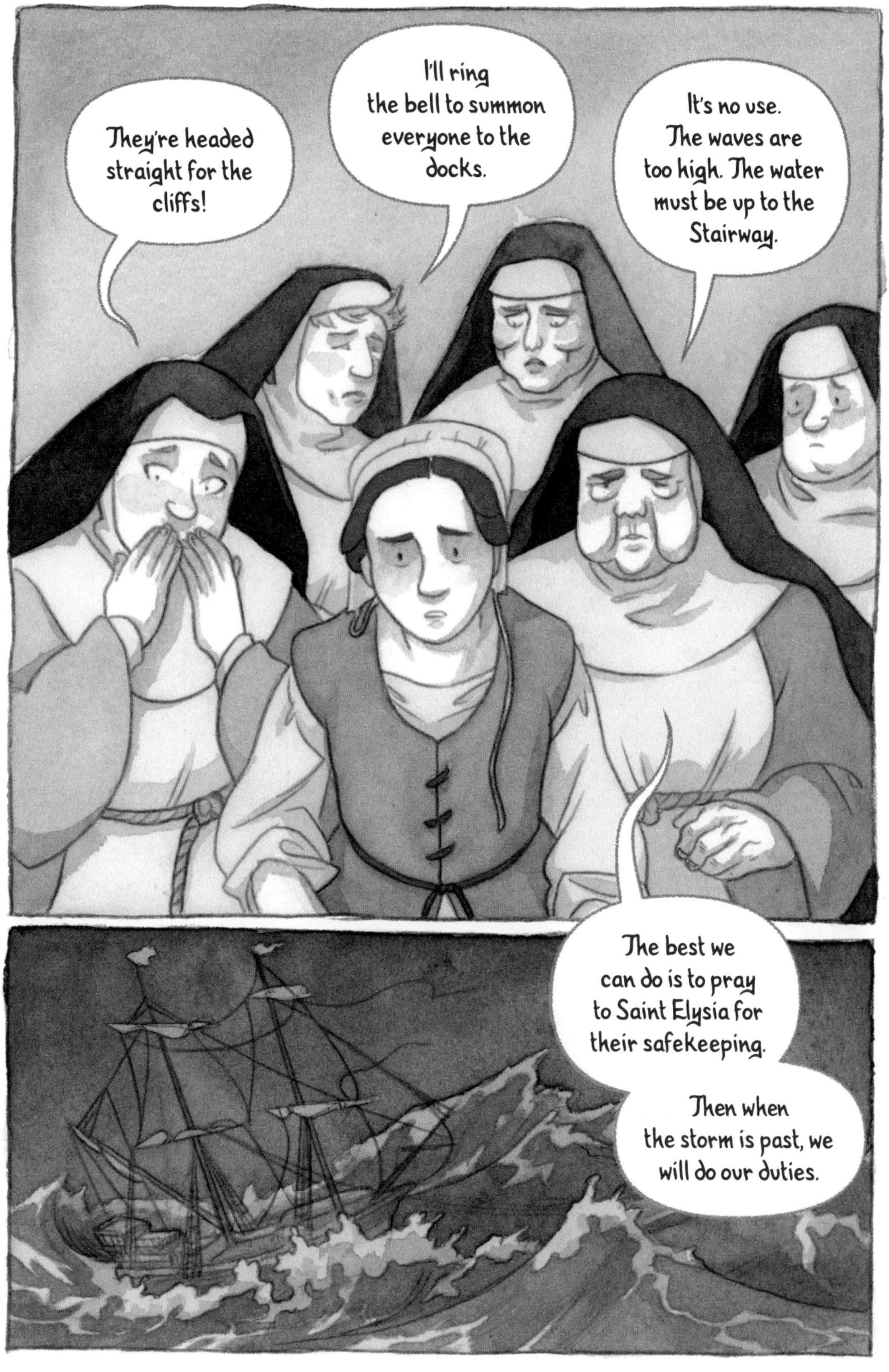
They're headed straight for the cliffs!
I'll ring the bell to summon everyone to the docks.
It's no use. The waves are too high. The water must be up to the Stairway.
The best we can do is to pray to Saint Elysia for their safekeeping.
Then when the storm is past, we will do our duties.

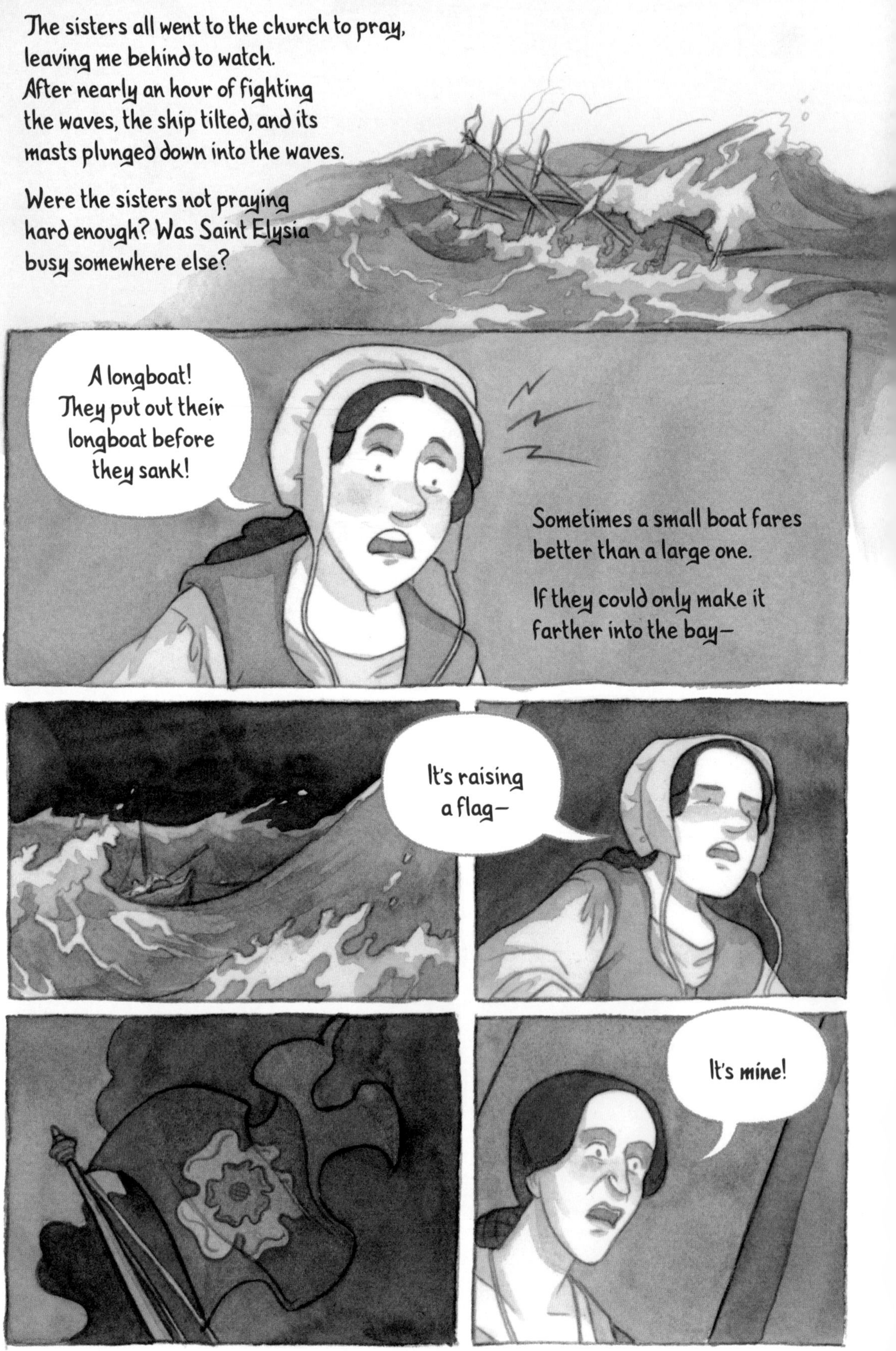

The sisters all went to the church to pray, leaving me behind to watch. After nearly an hour of fighting the waves, the ship tilted, and its masts plunged down into the waves.
Were the sisters not praying hard enough? Was Saint Elysia busy somewhere else?
A longboat! They put out their longboat before they sank!
Sometimes a small boat fares better than a large one.
If they could only make it farther into the bay—
It's raising a flag—
It's mine!

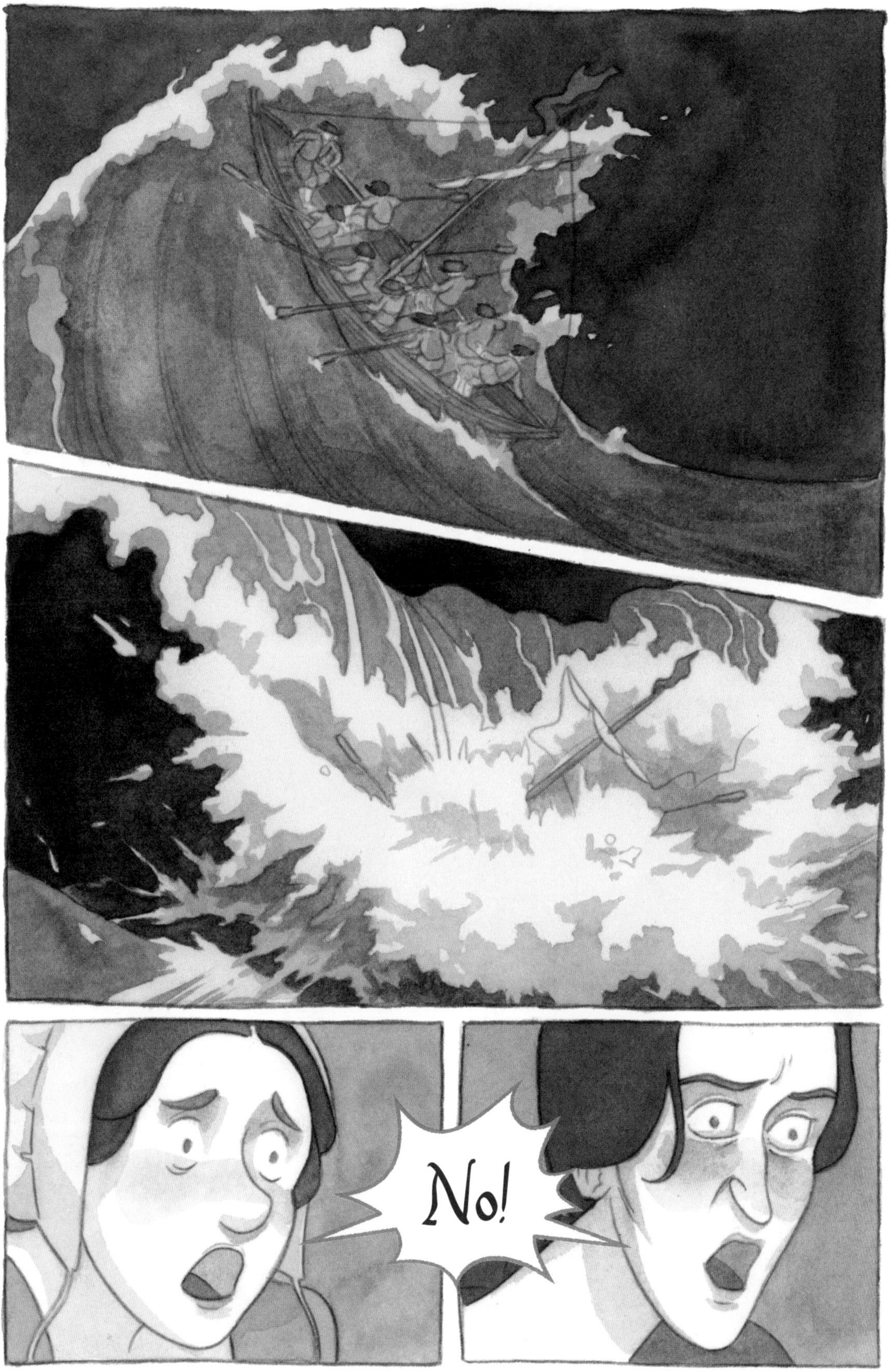
No!

After that, there was nothing left to see.

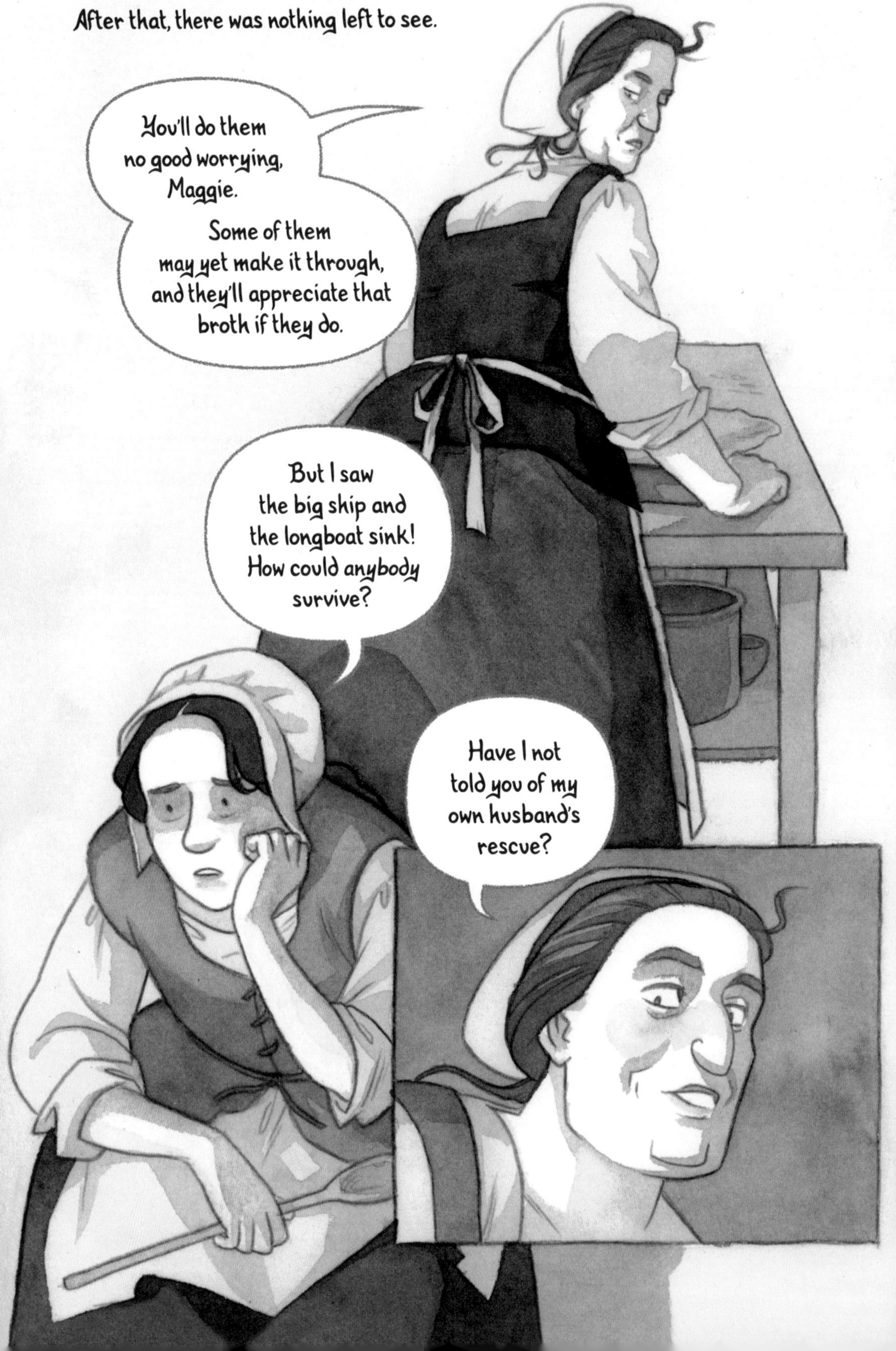
You'll do them no good worrying, Maggie.
Some of them may yet make it through, and they'll appreciate that broth if they do.
But I saw the big ship and the longboat sink! How could anybody survive?
Have I not told you of my own husband's rescue?

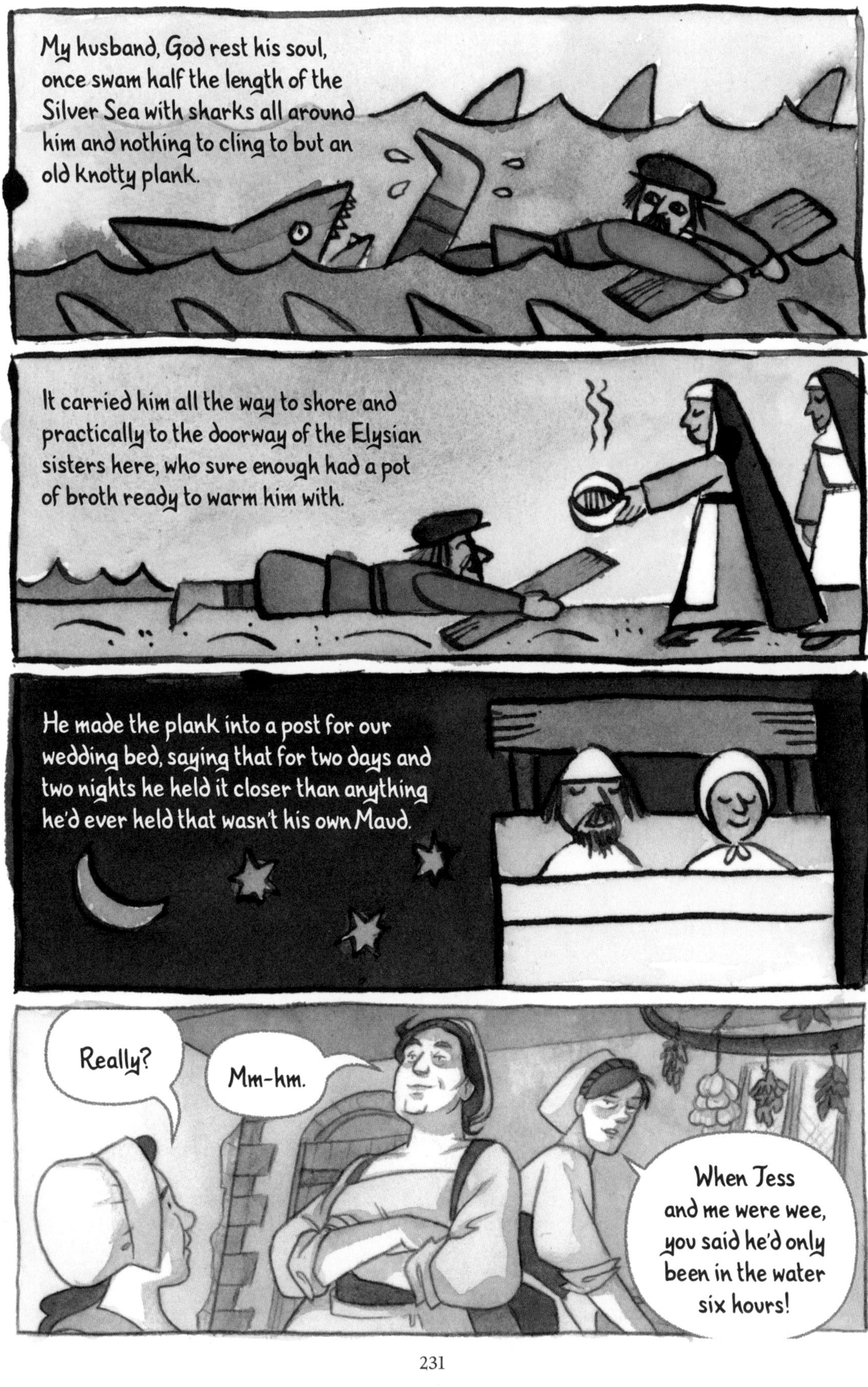
My husband, God rest his soul, once swam half the length of the Silver Sea with sharks all around him and nothing to cling to but an old knotty plank.
It carried him all the way to shore and practically to the doorway of the Elysian sisters here, who sure enough had a pot of broth ready to warm him with.
He made the plank into a post for our wedding bed, saying that for two days and two nights he held it closer than anything he'd ever held that wasn't his own Maud.
Really?
Mm-hm.
When Jess and me were wee, you said he'd only been in the water six hours!

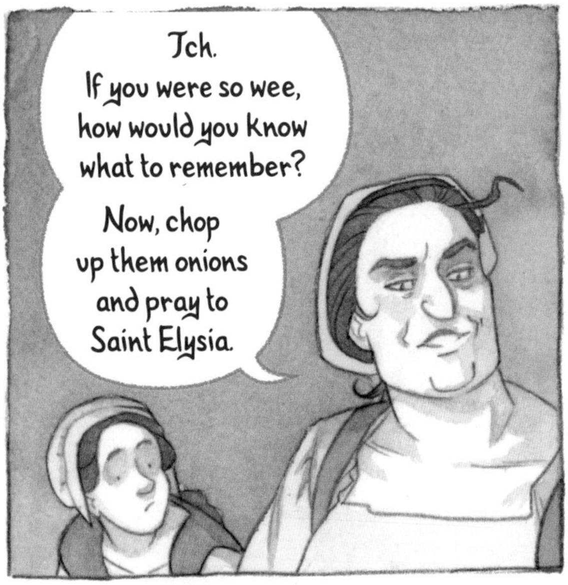
Tch.
If you were so wee, how would you know what to remember?
Now, chop up them onions and pray to Saint Elysia.

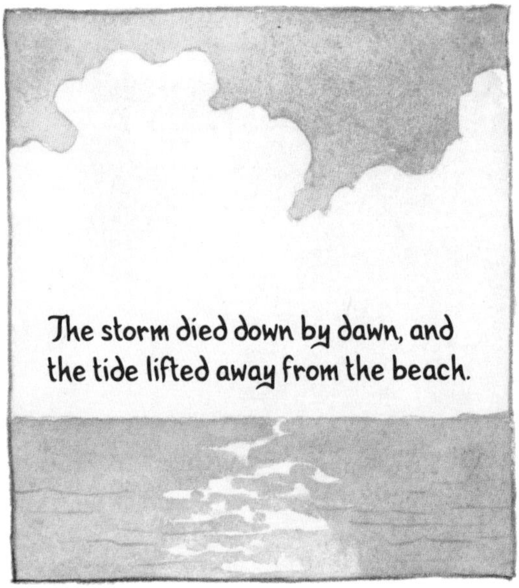
The storm died down by dawn, and the tide lifted away from the beach.

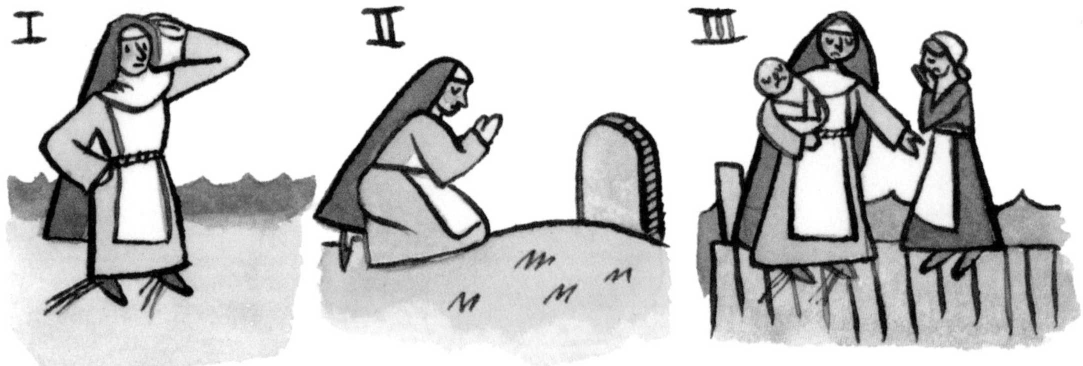
I
II
III

The Elysian order's duty, once a storm at sea has passed, is to search the shores and the harbor for any survivors in need of hospital care, to ***find, bury, and pray*** for the drowned, and to ***provide charity and shelter*** to any widows or orphans who remain.

We can't quite do that last part—instead, the sisters send their embroideries back to the order, which sells them and then gives the money to the grieving families.

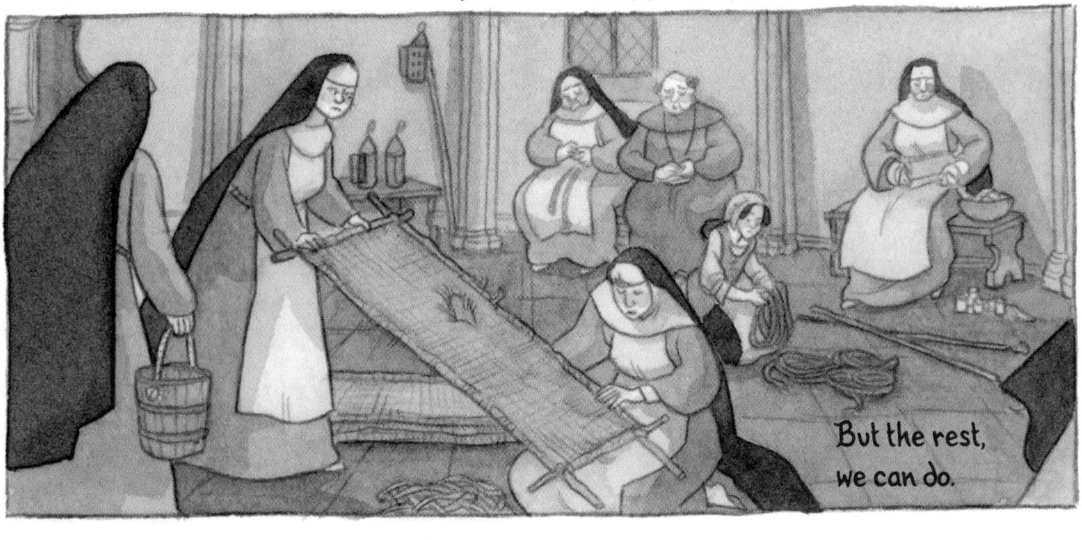
But the rest, we can do.

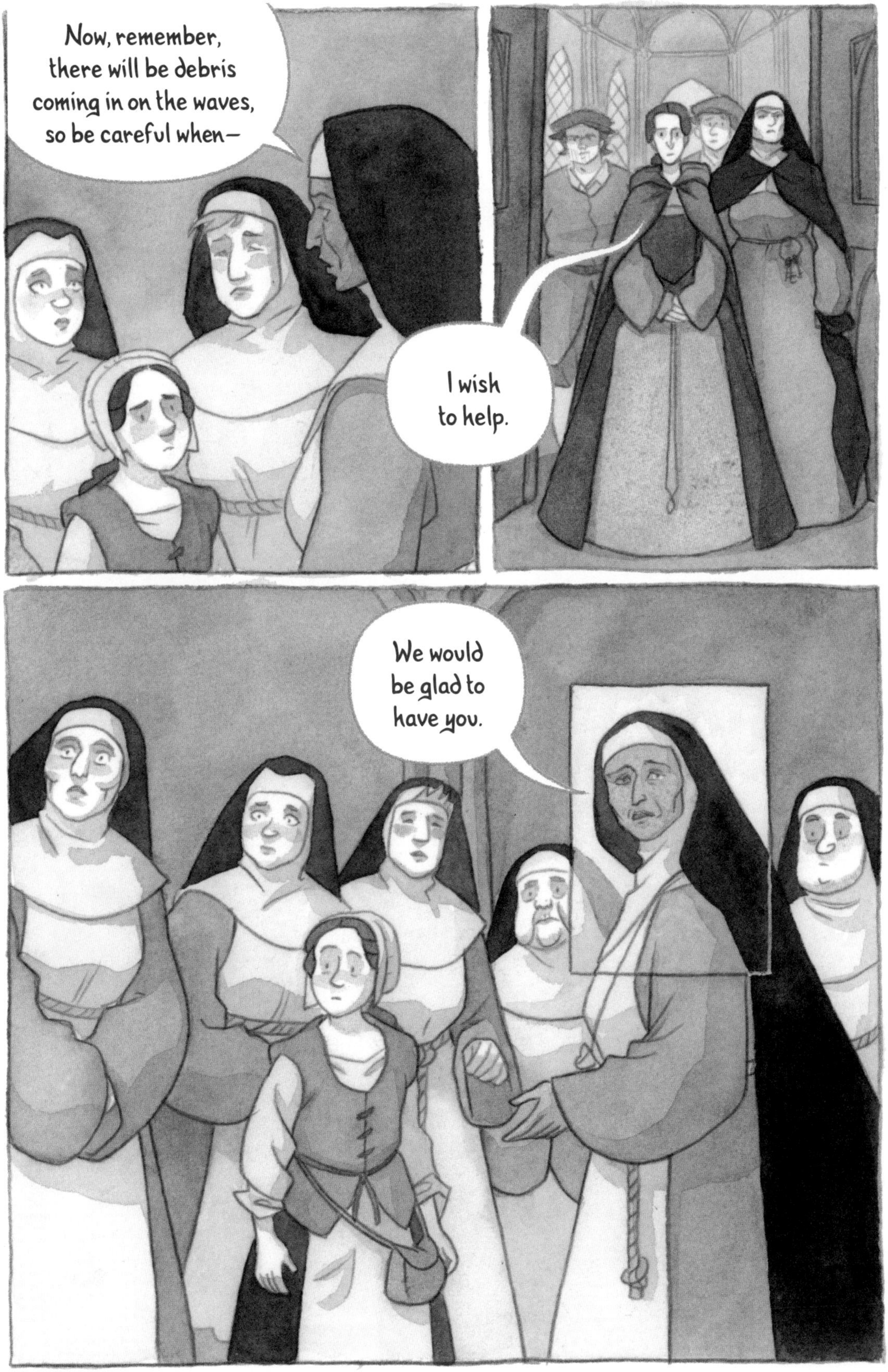
Now, remember, there will be debris coming in on the waves, so be careful when—
I wish to help.
We would be glad to have you.

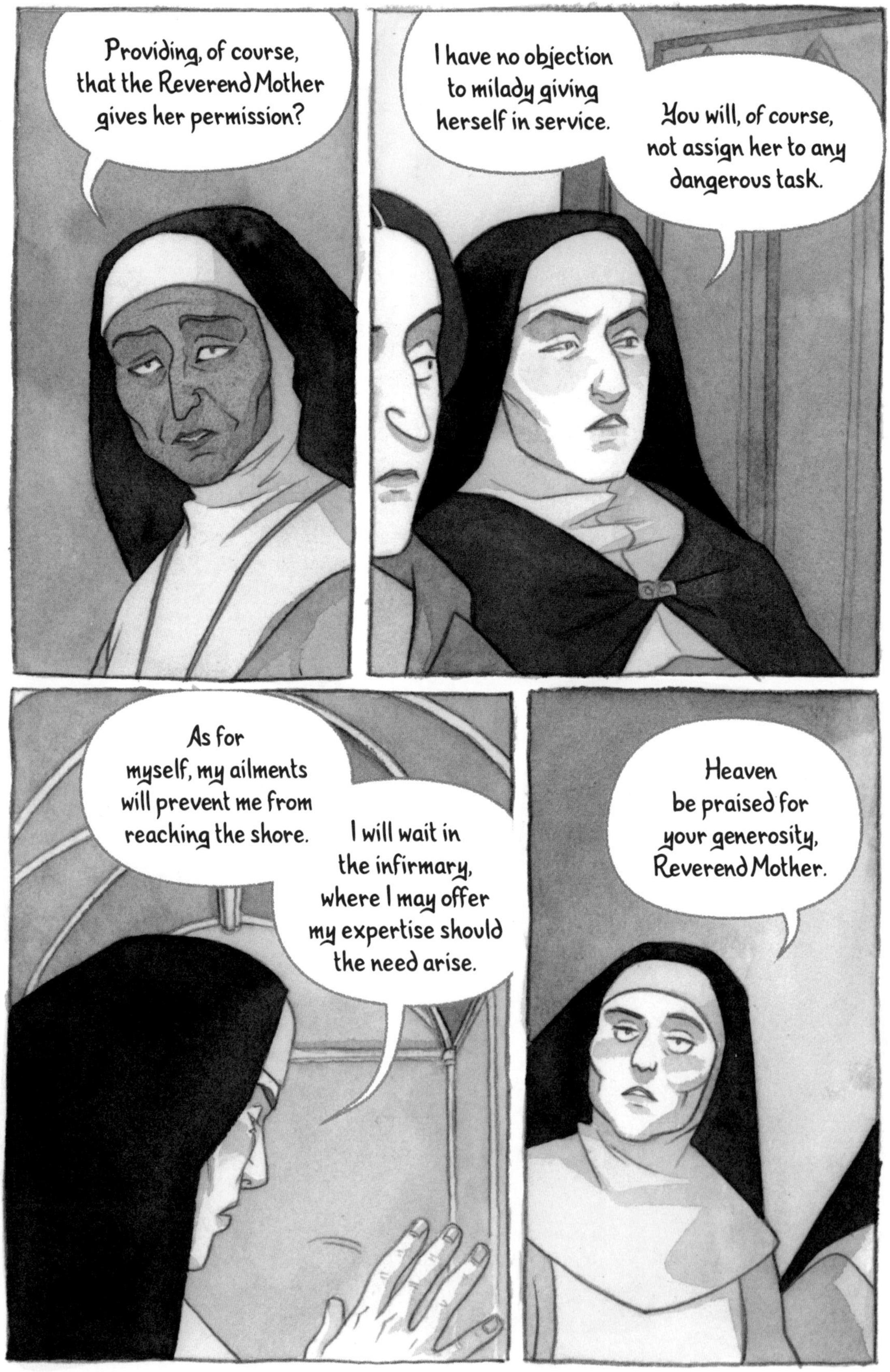
Providing, of course, that the Reverend Mother gives her permission?
I have no objection to milady giving herself in service.
You will, of course, not assign her to any dangerous task.
As for myself, my ailments will prevent me from reaching the shore.
I will wait in the infirmary, where I may offer my expertise should the need arise.
Heaven be praised for your generosity, Reverend Mother.

Sometimes storms will rake across the Silver Sea and bring more to the beach than just weathered logs and seaweed.

I had seen all sorts of things wash up that sailors may have lost overboard, or parts of ships knocked off in a storm.

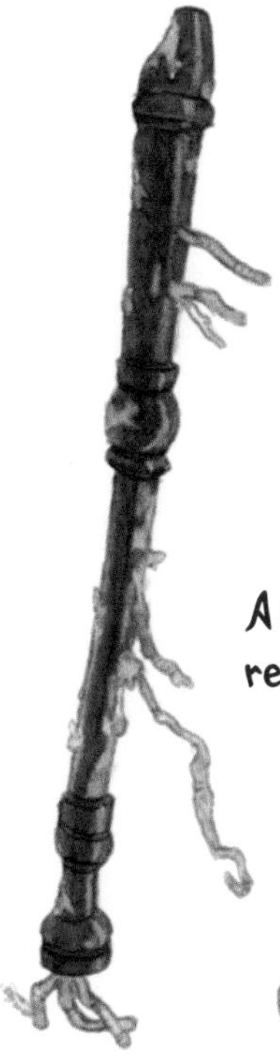

A wooden recorder.

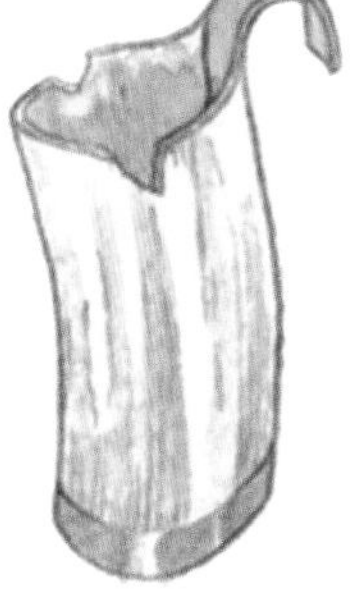

A drinking cup made of horn.

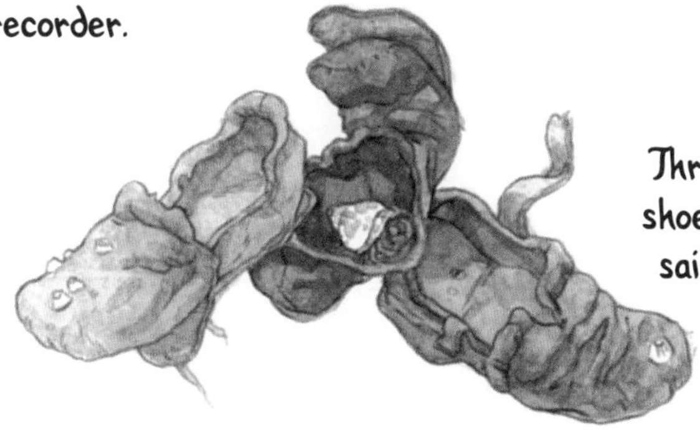

Three leather shoes, the kind sailors wear.

A glass flask, empty except for a little seawater.

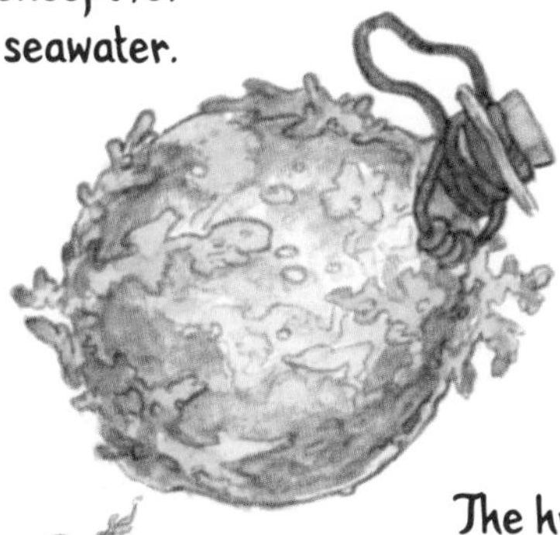

A funny necklace, strung with abalones.

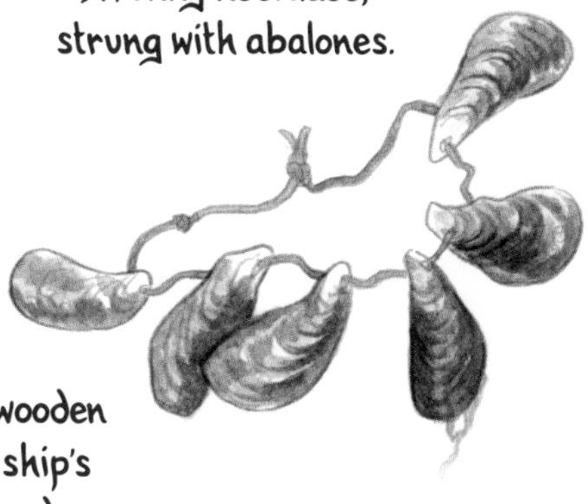

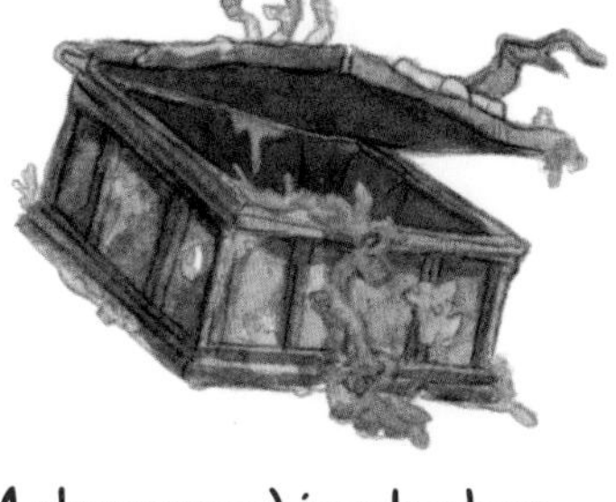

A cherrywood jewelry box, with no jewels left inside.

The huge wooden hand of a ship's figurehead.

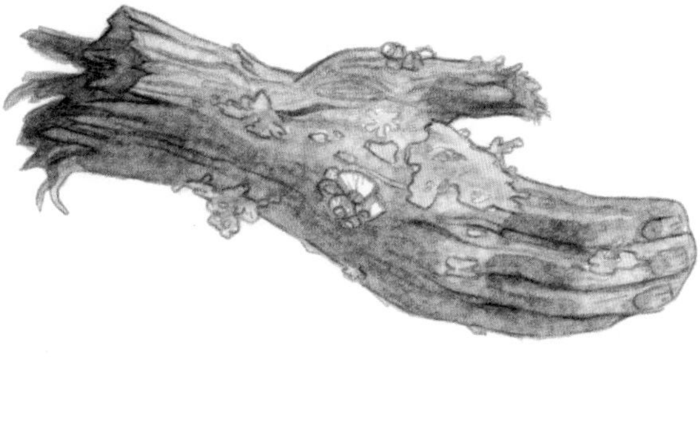

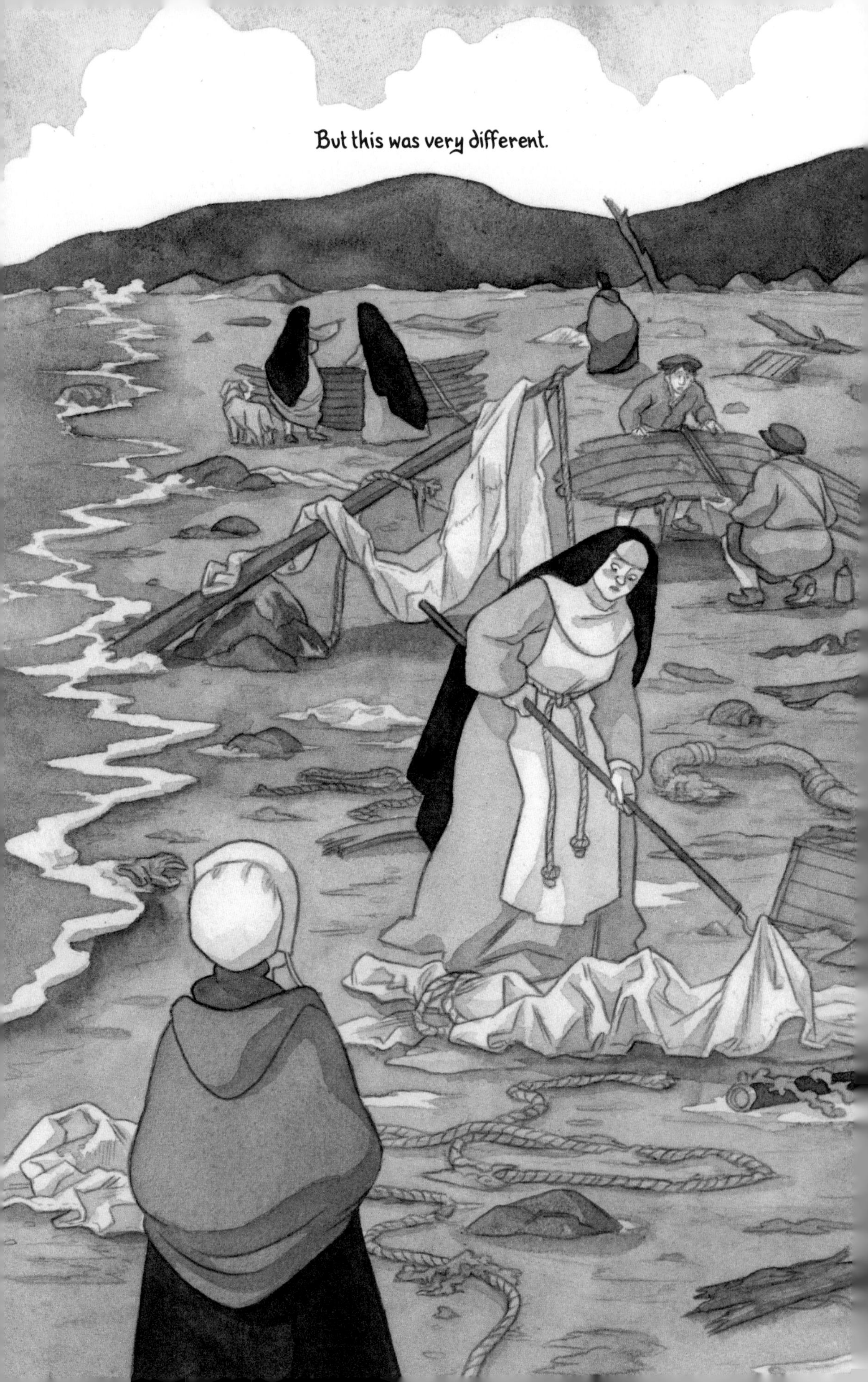
But this was very different.

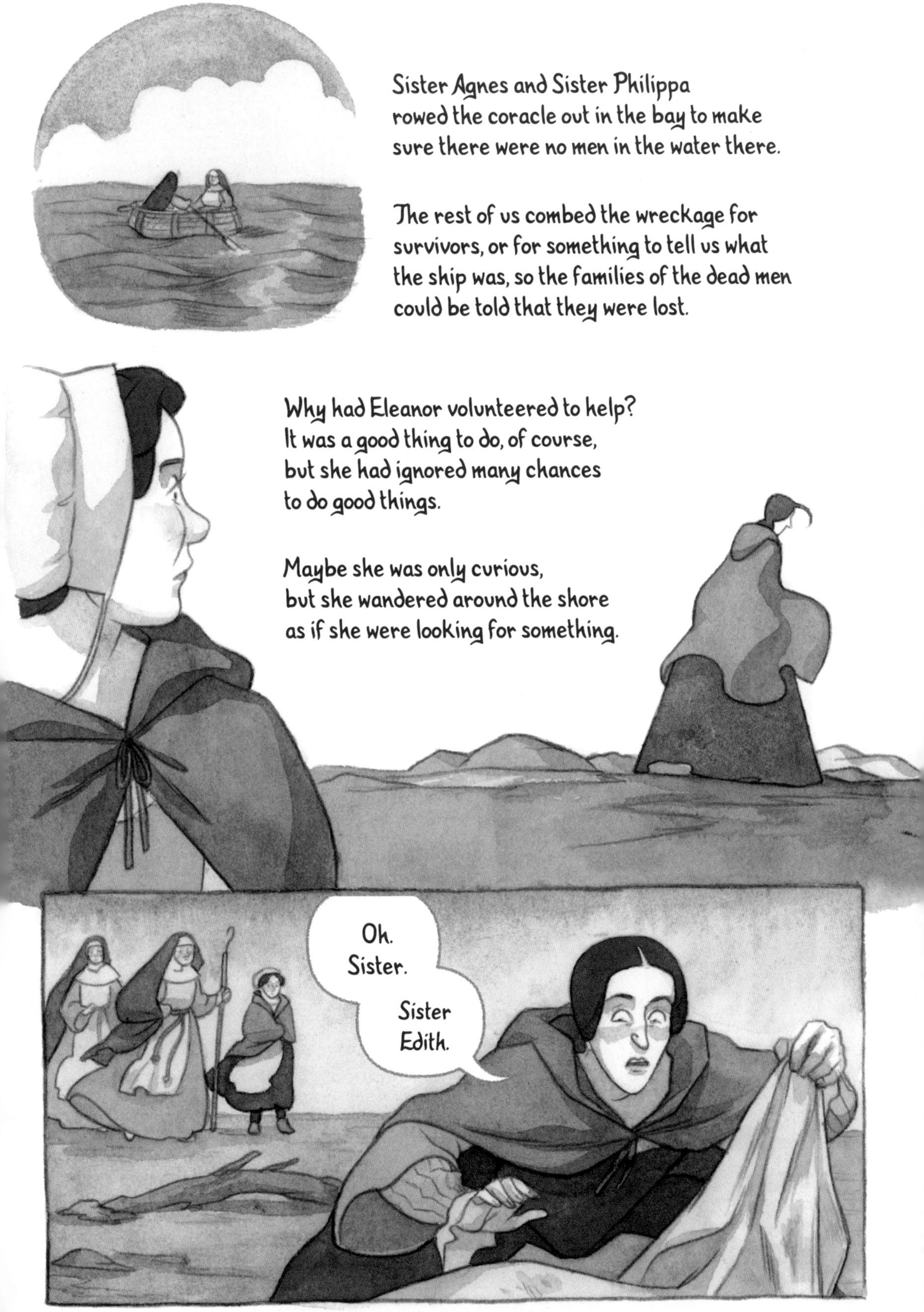
Sister Agnes and Sister Philippa rowed the coracle out in the bay to make sure there were no men in the water there.
The rest of us combed the wreckage for survivors, or for something to tell us what the ship was, so the families of the dead men could be told that they were lost.
Why had Eleanor volunteered to help? It was a good thing to do, of course, but she had ignored many chances to do good things.
Maybe she was only curious, but she wandered around the shore as if she were looking for something.
Oh. Sister.
Sister Edith.

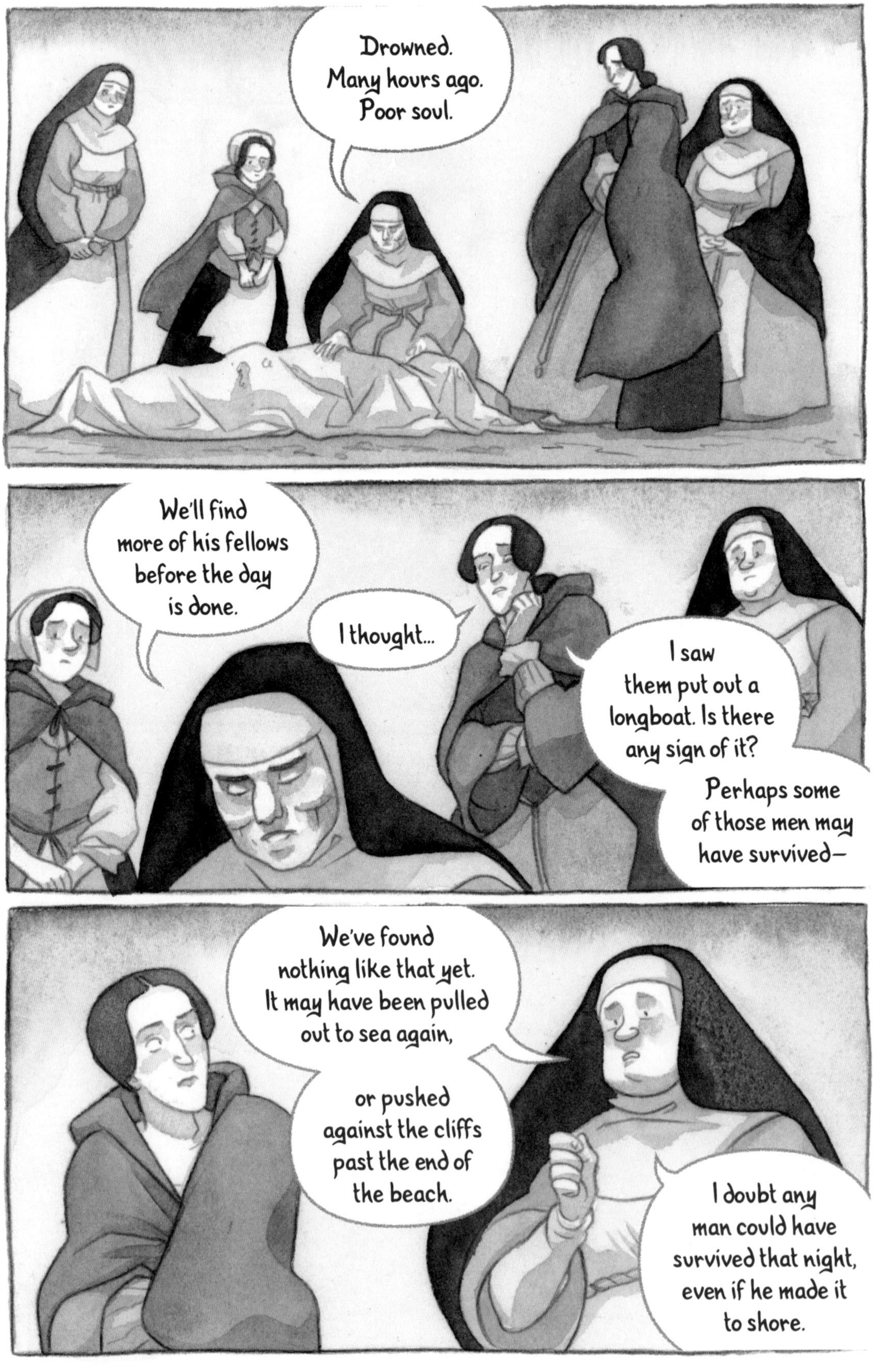

Drowned. Many hours ago. Poor soul.
We'll find more of his fellows before the day is done.
I thought...
I saw them put out a longboat. Is there any sign of it?
Perhaps some of those men may have survived—
We've found nothing like that yet. It may have been pulled out to sea again,
or pushed against the cliffs past the end of the beach.
I doubt any man could have survived that night, even if he made it to shore.

Eleanor had seen the longboat.

She had seen the flag as well, then.
That was why she had come down to the beach.

But she hadn't mentioned the flag at all.
She didn't want the sisters to know.

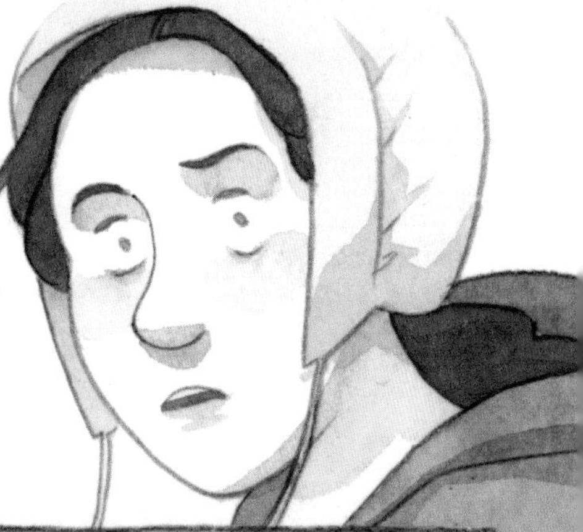

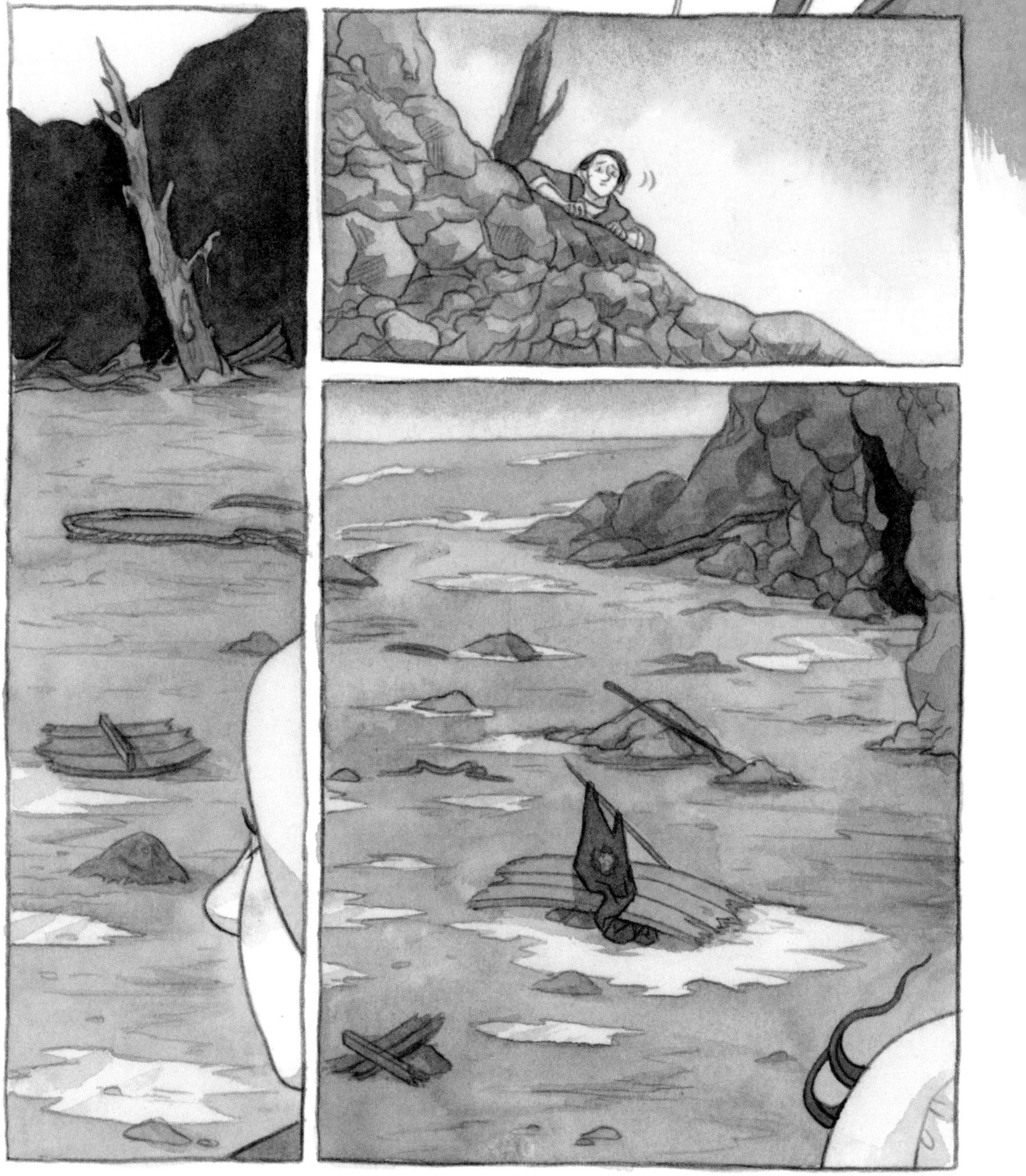

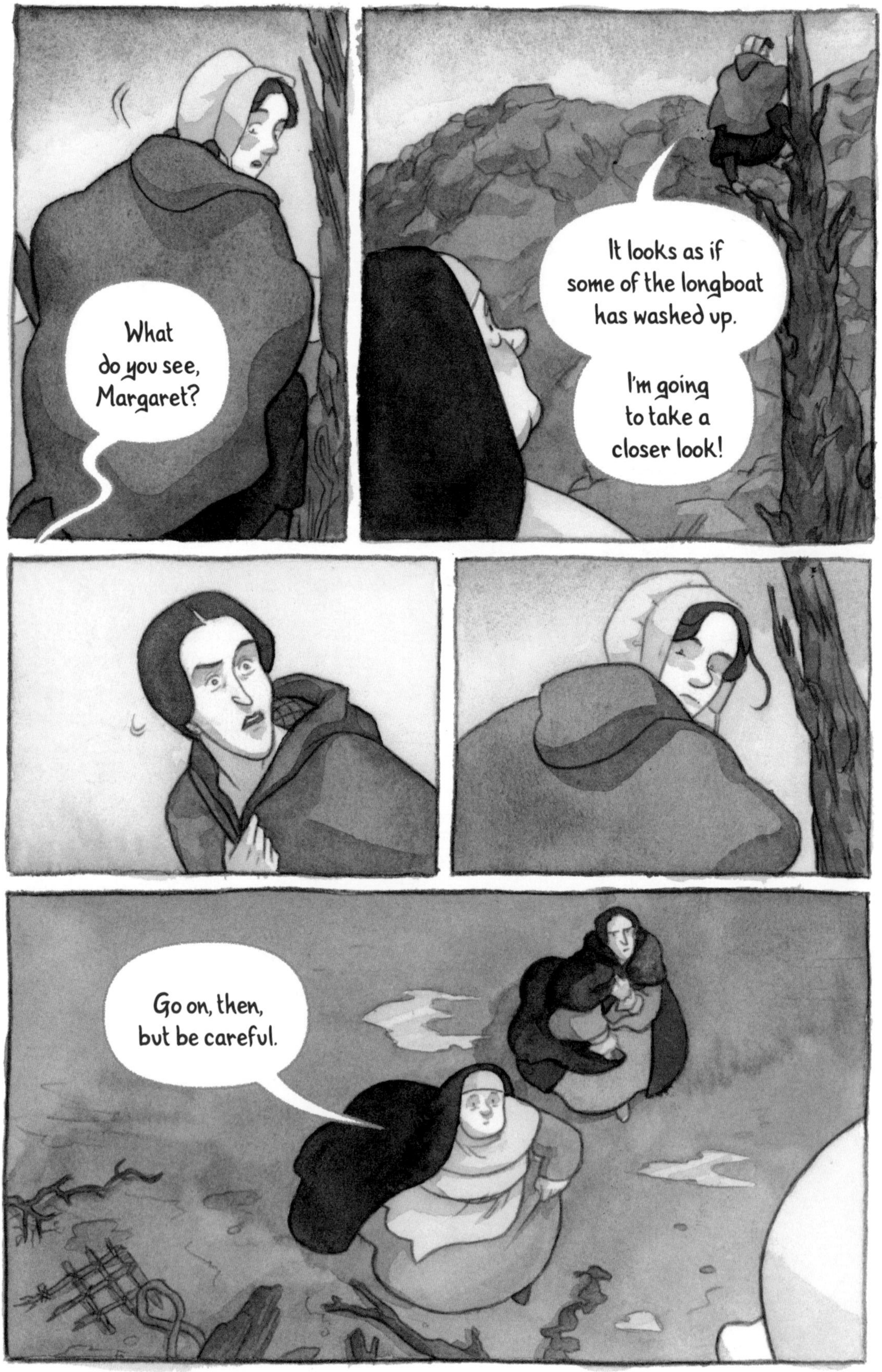
What do you see, Margaret?
It looks as if some of the longboat has washed up.
I'm going to take a closer look!
Go on, then, but be careful.

What would happen if the guards or the sisters found out that the ship was actually loyal to Eleanor?

She had been brought here secretly. Not even Captain Marley knew that his passenger used to be a queen.

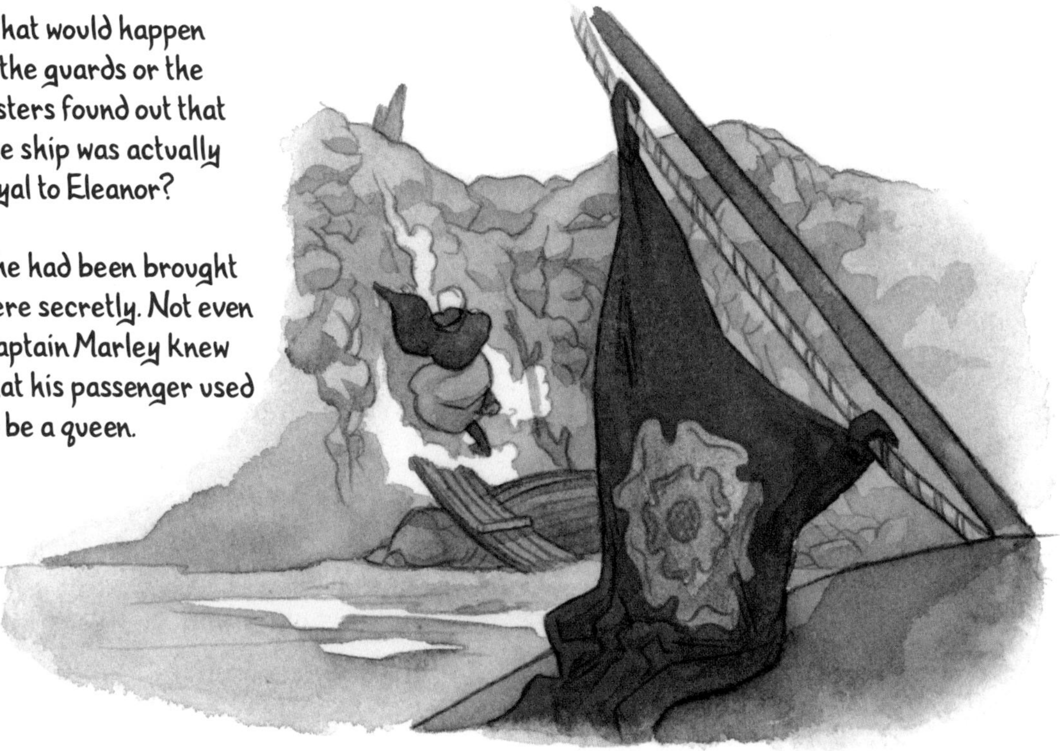

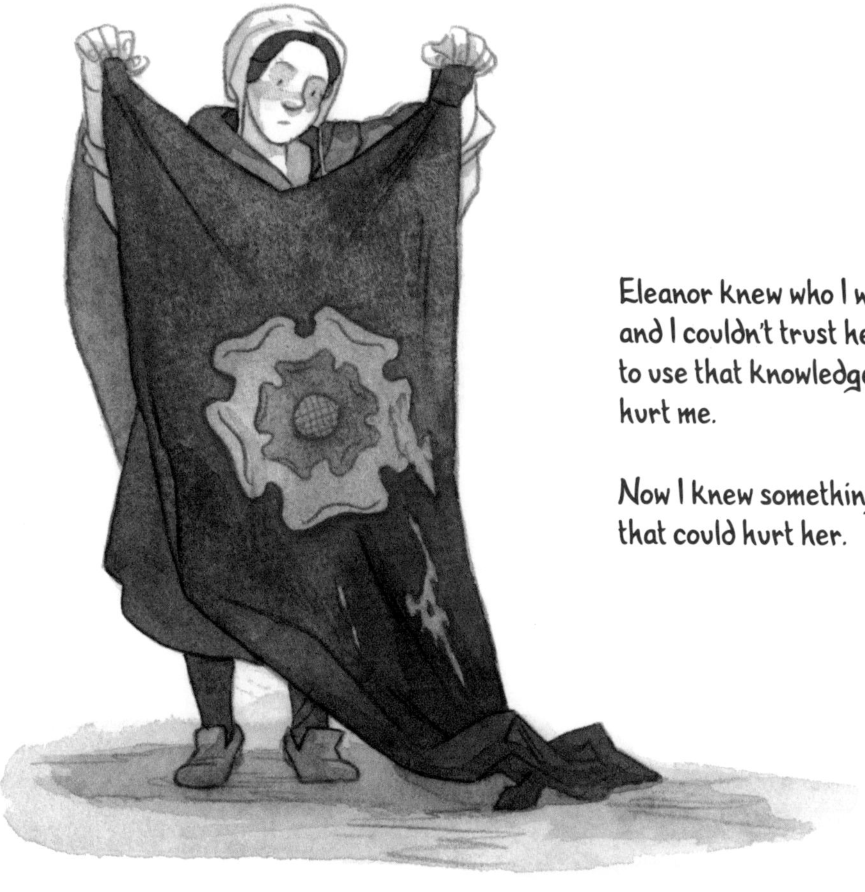

Eleanor knew who I was, and I couldn't trust her not to use that knowledge to hurt me.

Now I knew something that could hurt her.

Eleanor may have lied to me and then tried to have me sent away, but I didn't think she deserved to be *punished*. At least not in the ways Her Reverence or Her Majesty would think up.

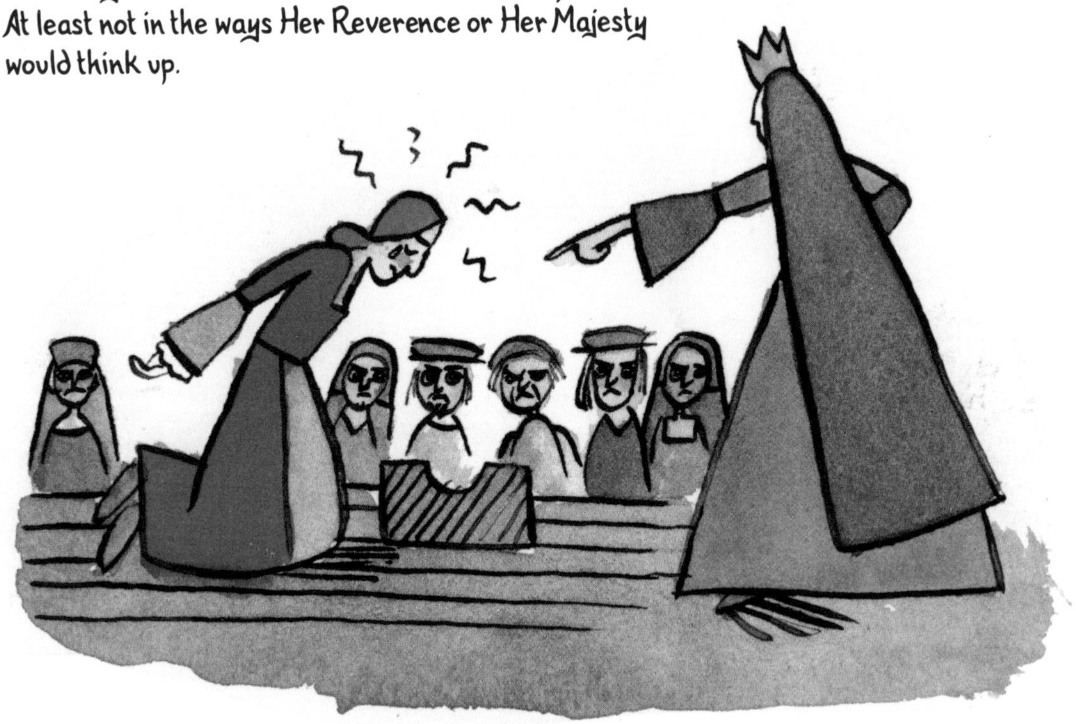

What if I told Eleanor about the flag but *hid* it? I could just *threaten* to expose the rescue attempt to Her Reverence unless she kept our sisterhood secret.

That would mean telling Eleanor that I knew we were sisters, though, and that might put me in even more danger from her.

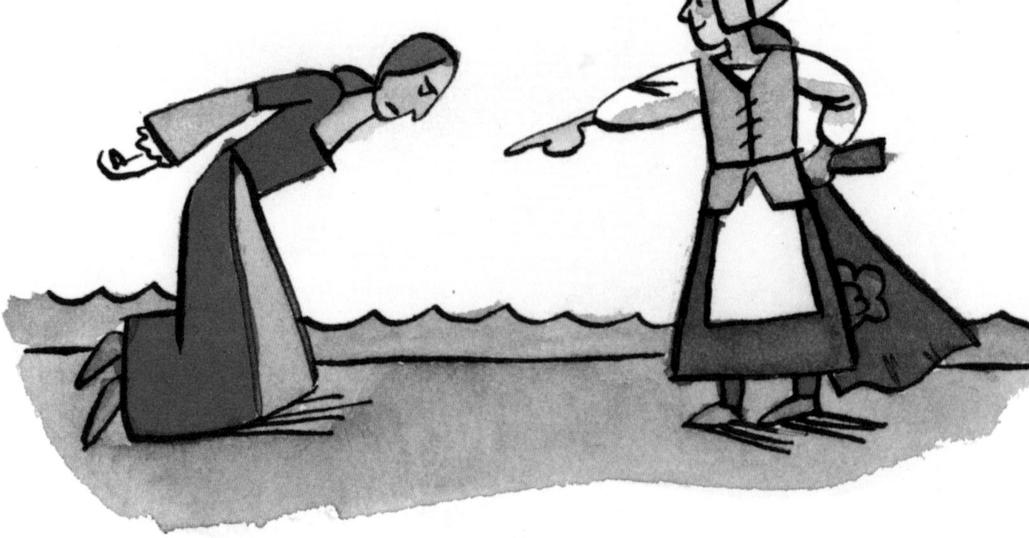

It had been less than a week since I'd learned that I had any sisters at all, and there were already so many ways we could hurt each other.

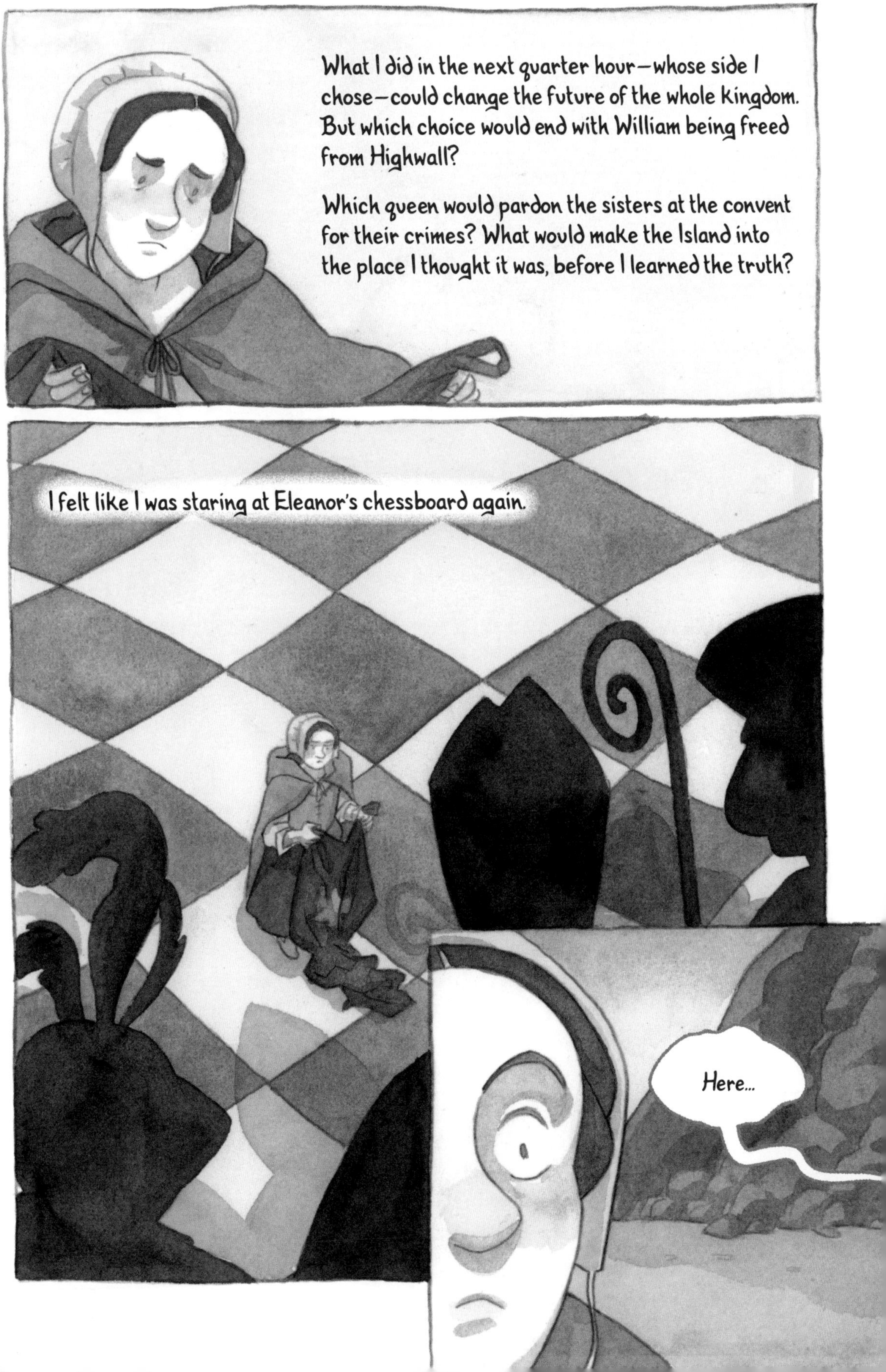
What I did in the next quarter hour—whose side I chose—could change the future of the whole kingdom. But which choice would end with William being freed from Highwall?
Which queen would pardon the sisters at the convent for their crimes? What would make the Island into the place I thought it was, before I learned the truth?
I felt like I was staring at Eleanor's chessboard again.
Here...

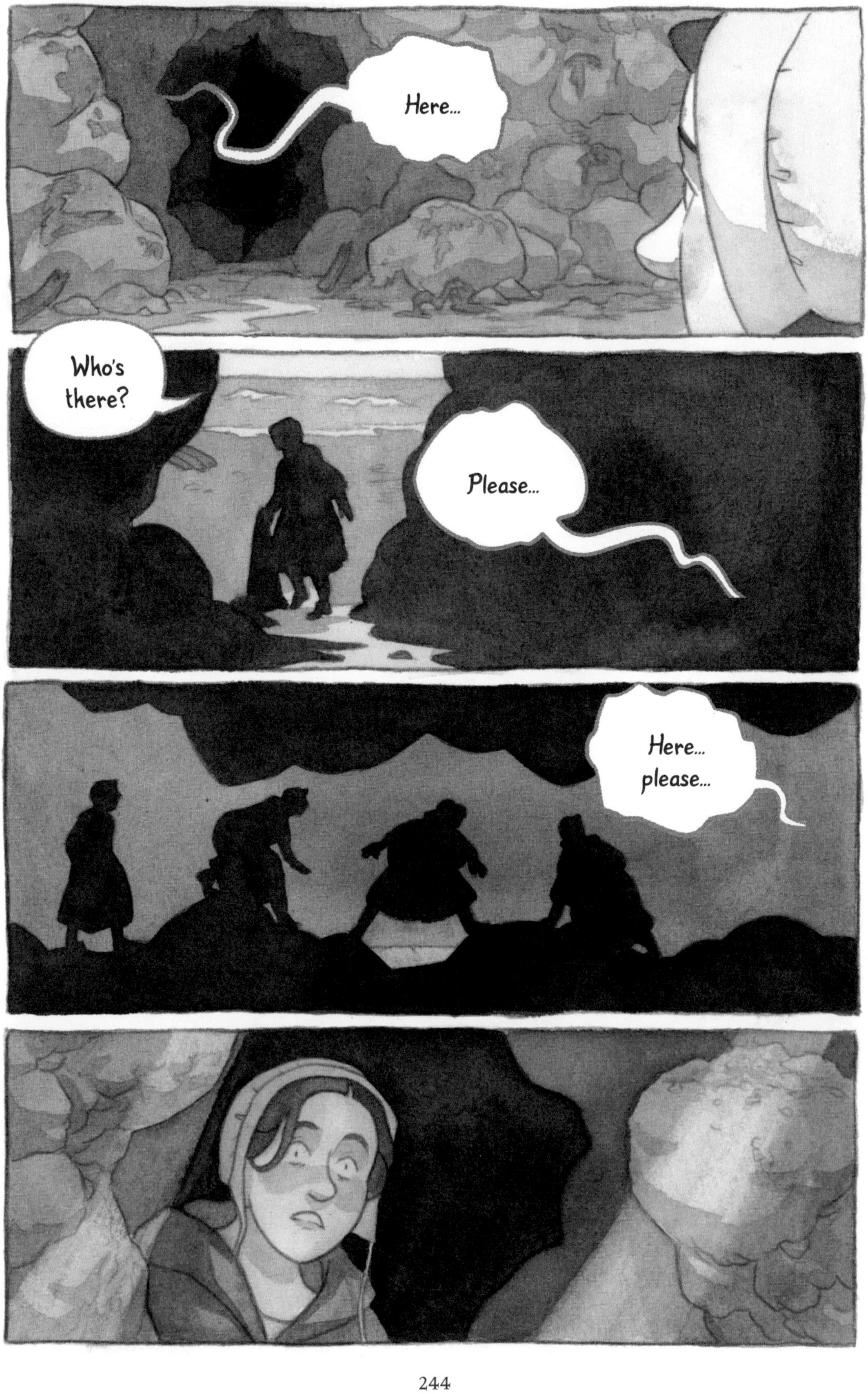
Here...
Who's there?
Please...
Here... please...

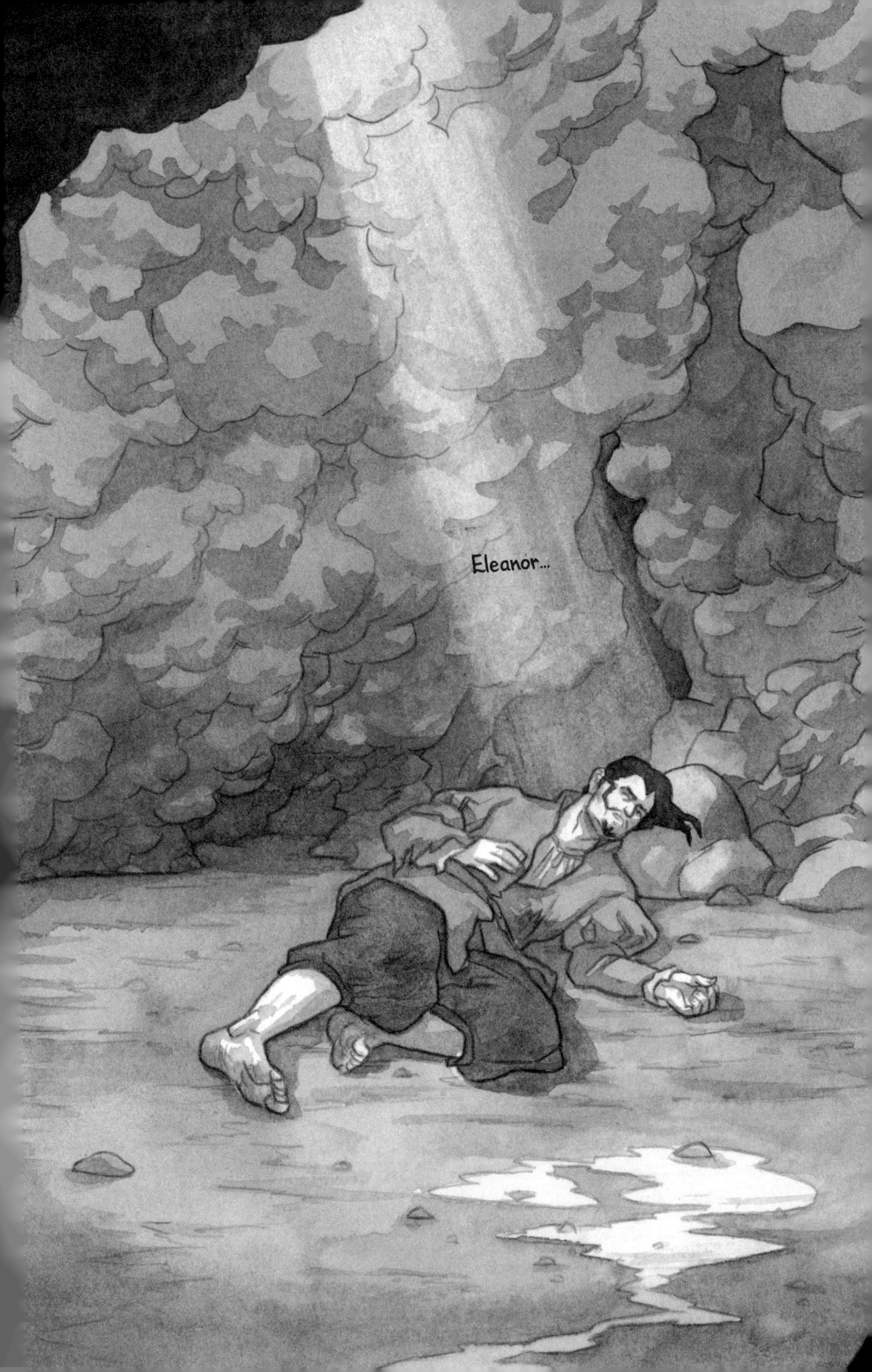
Eleanor...

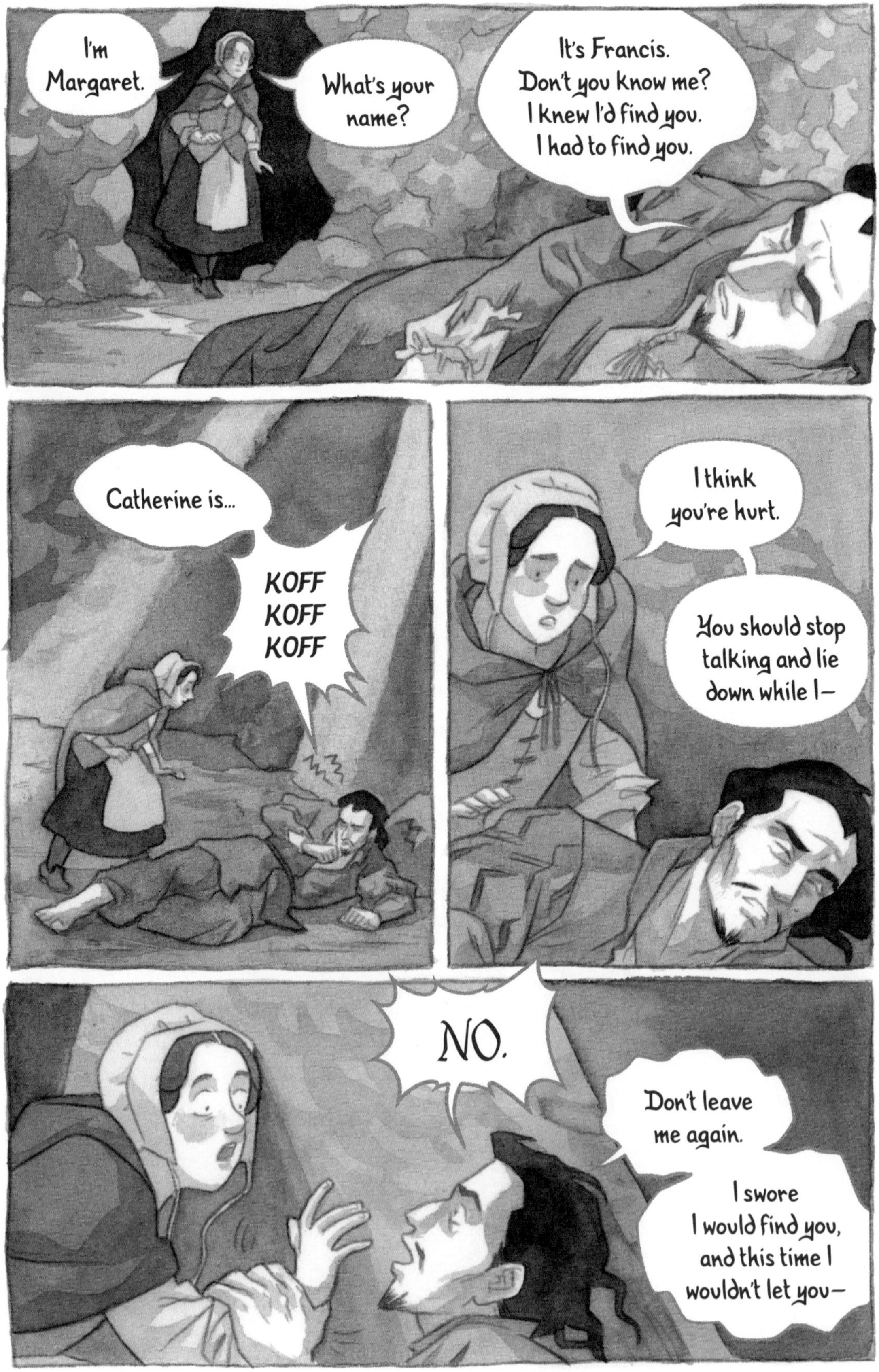
I'm Margaret.
What's your name?
It's Francis. Don't you know me? I knew I'd find you. I had to find you.
Catherine is...
KOFF KOFF KOFF
I think you're hurt.
You should stop talking and lie down while I—
NO.
Don't leave me again.
I swore I would find you, and this time I wouldn't let you—

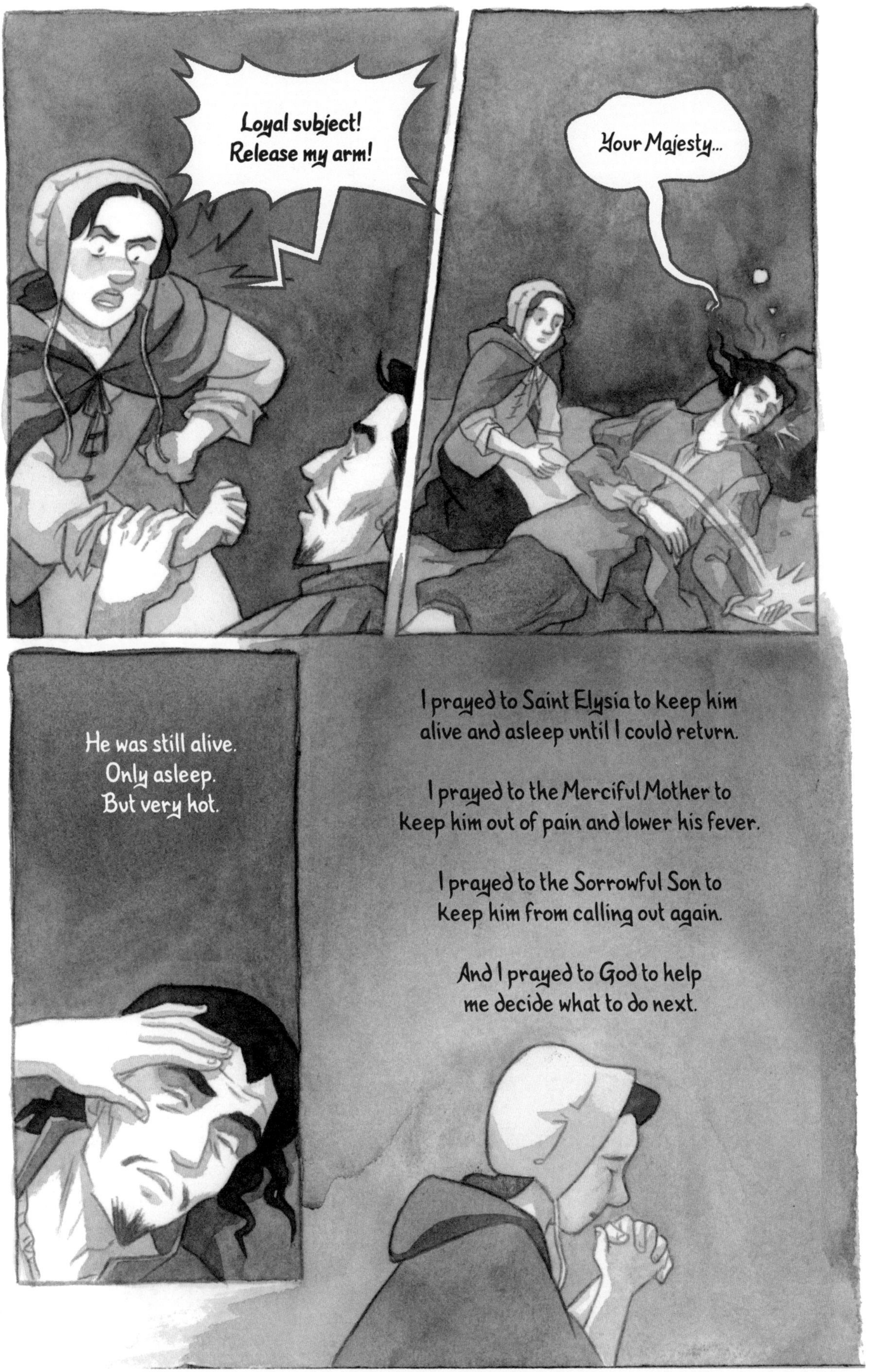
Loyal subject!
Release my arm!
Your Majesty...
He was still alive.
Only asleep.
But very hot.
I prayed to Saint Elysia to keep him alive and asleep until I could return.
I prayed to the Merciful Mother to keep him out of pain and lower his fever.
I prayed to the Sorrowful Son to keep him from calling out again.
And I prayed to God to help me decide what to do next.

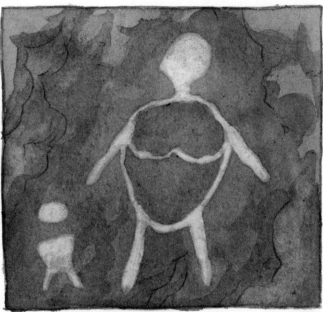

You look out for him, too.

Margaret! Margaret, can you hear me?

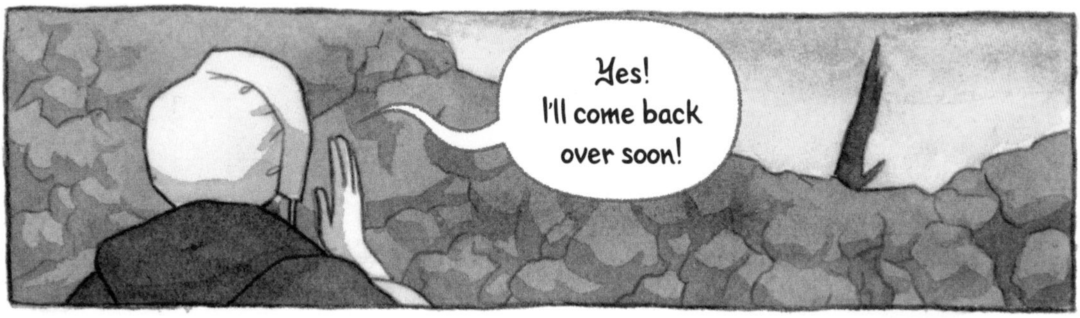
Yes!
I'll come back over soon!

I pulled the flag back into the sea cave, where it couldn't be seen, and tied it around a rock so the tide couldn't wash it out again.

If the man stumbled toward the outside, maybe he'd see it and guess that I had been real, and not some strange dream, and he would remember to stay in the cave.

I pushed as much of the wrecked longboat as I could down toward the waves, so the tide would take it away sooner.

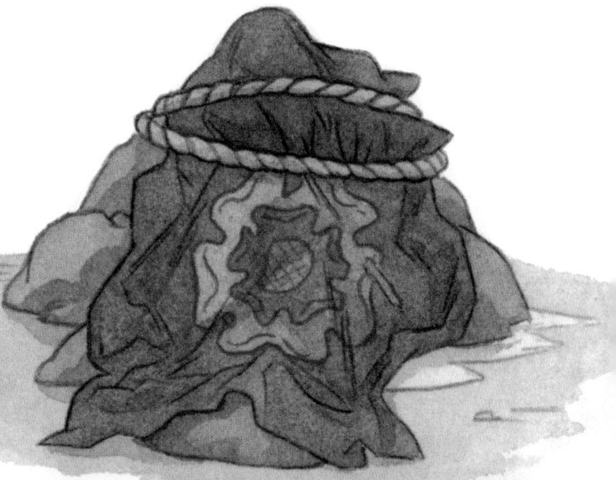

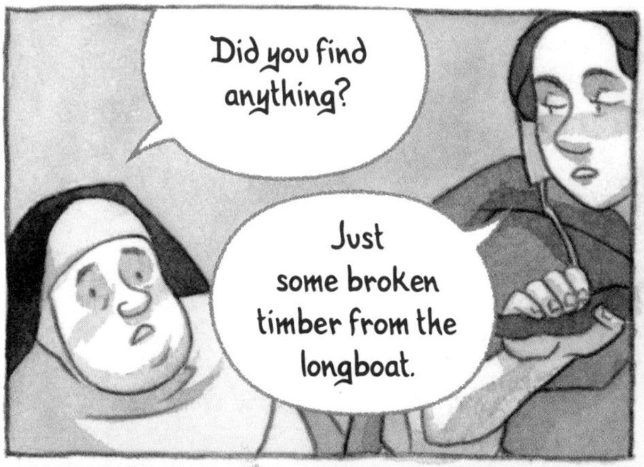
Did you find anything?
Just some broken timber from the longboat.

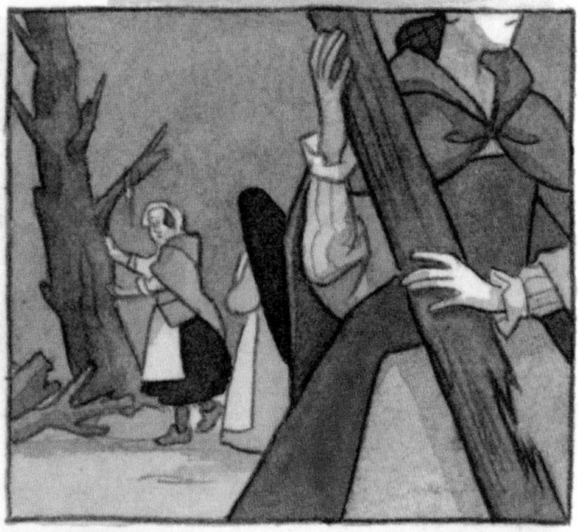

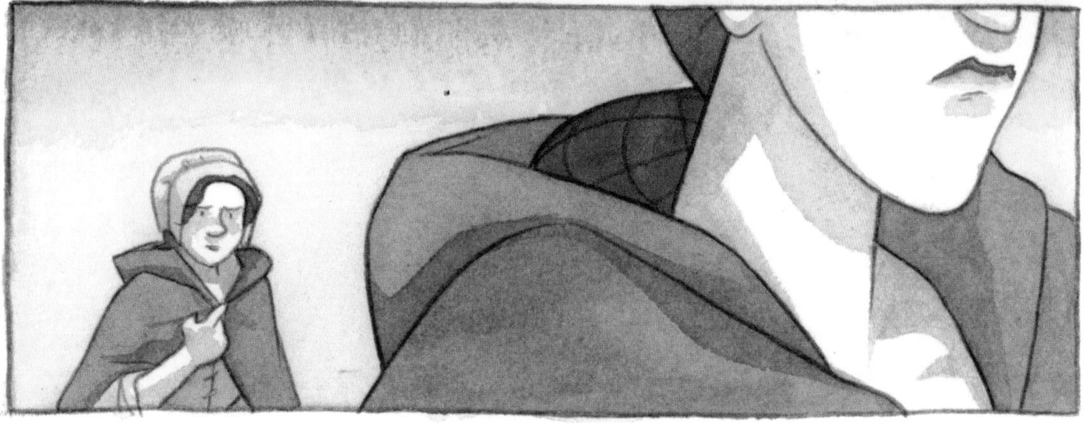

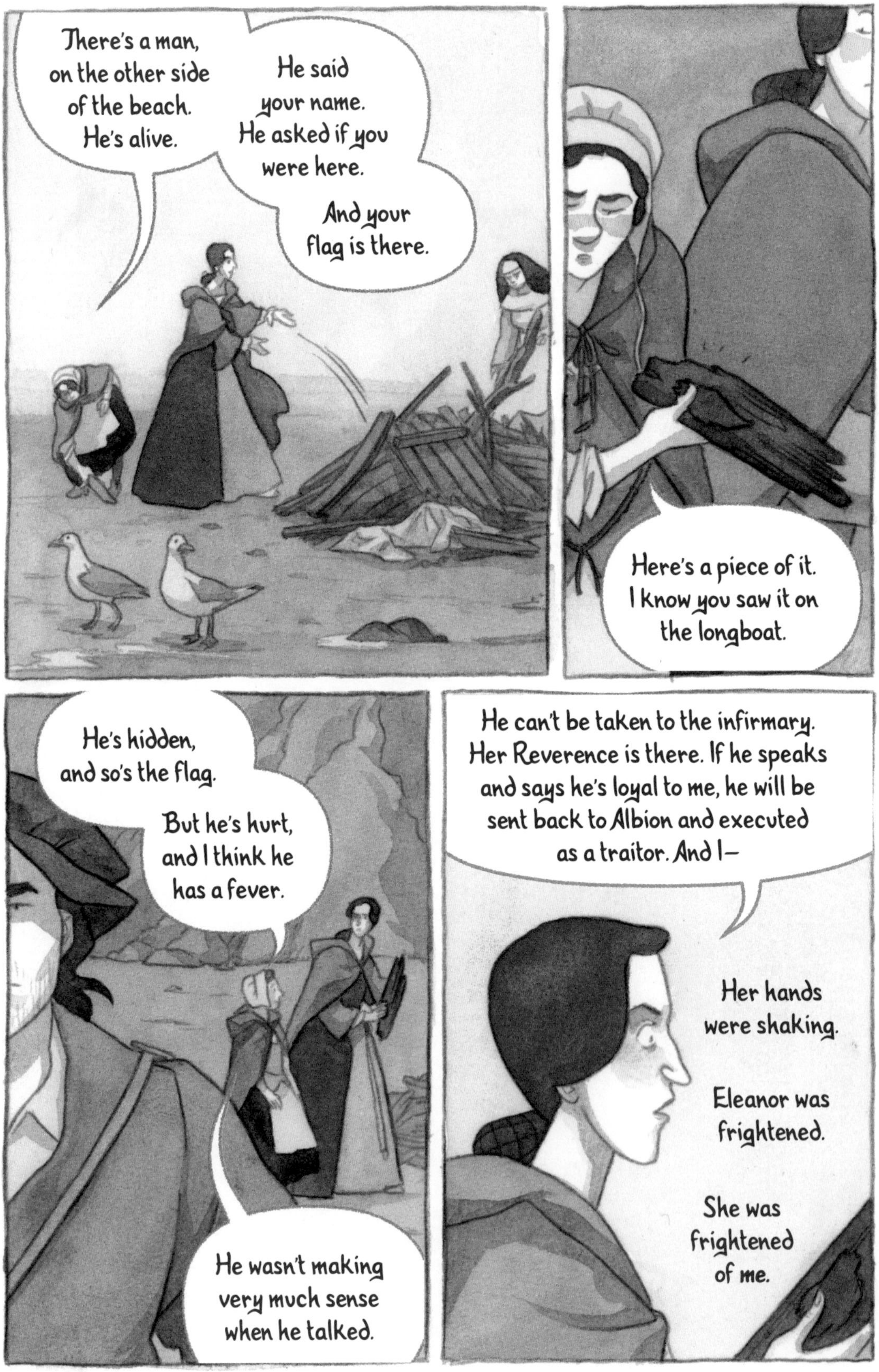
There's a man, on the other side of the beach. He's alive.
He said your name. He asked if you were here.
And your flag is there.
Here's a piece of it. I know you saw it on the longboat.
He's hidden, and so's the flag.
But he's hurt, and I think he has a fever.
He wasn't making very much sense when he talked.
He can't be taken to the infirmary. Her Reverence is there. If he speaks and says he's loyal to me, he will be sent back to Albion and executed as a traitor. And I—
Her hands were shaking.
Eleanor was frightened.
She was frightened of me.

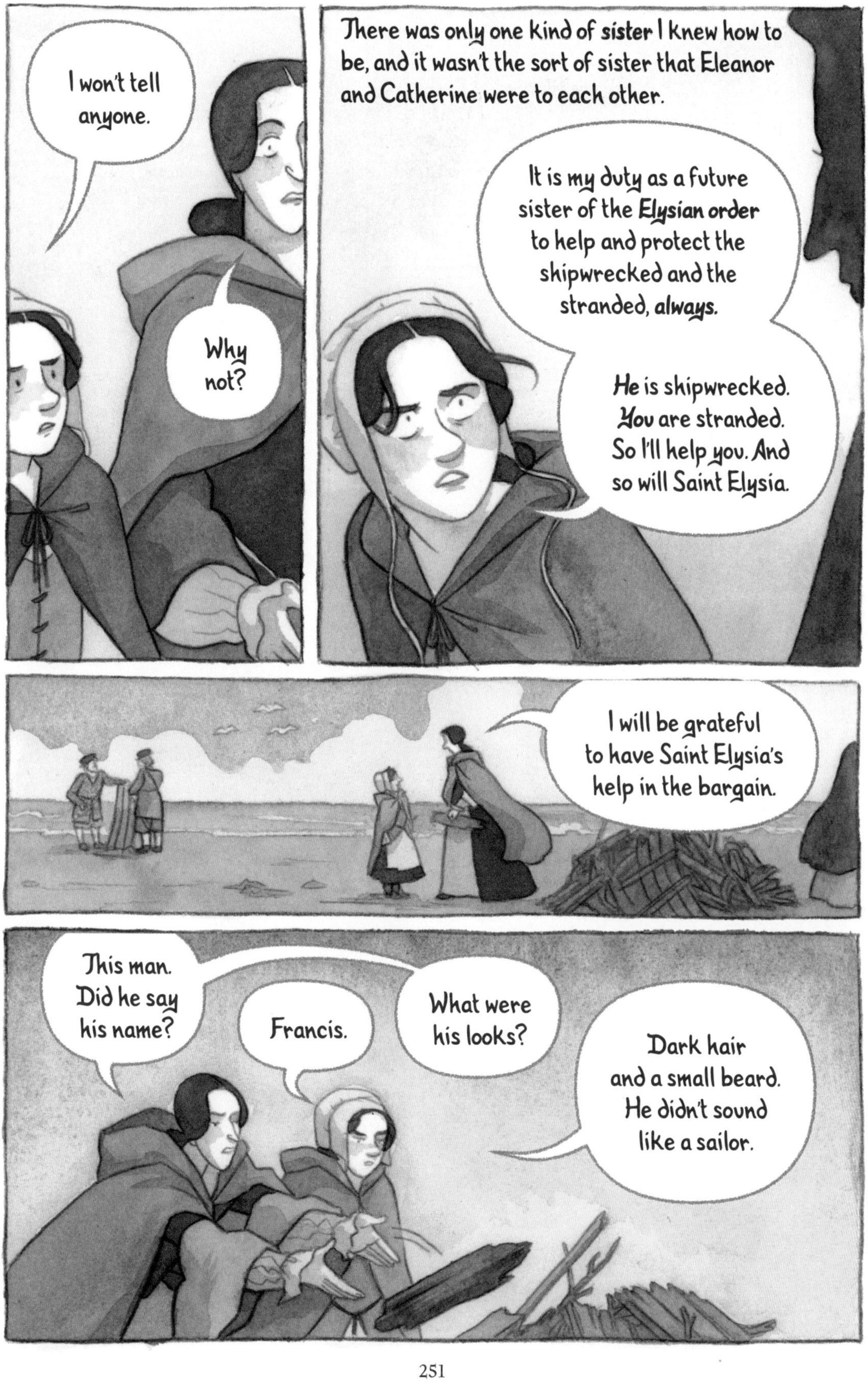

I won't tell anyone.
Why not?
There was only one kind of sister I knew how to be, and it wasn't the sort of sister that Eleanor and Catherine were to each other.
It is my duty as a future sister of the Elysian order to help and protect the shipwrecked and the stranded, always.
He is shipwrecked. You are stranded. So I'll help you. And so will Saint Elysia.
I will be grateful to have Saint Elysia's help in the bargain.
This man. Did he say his name?
Francis.
What were his looks?
Dark hair and a small beard. He didn't sound like a sailor.

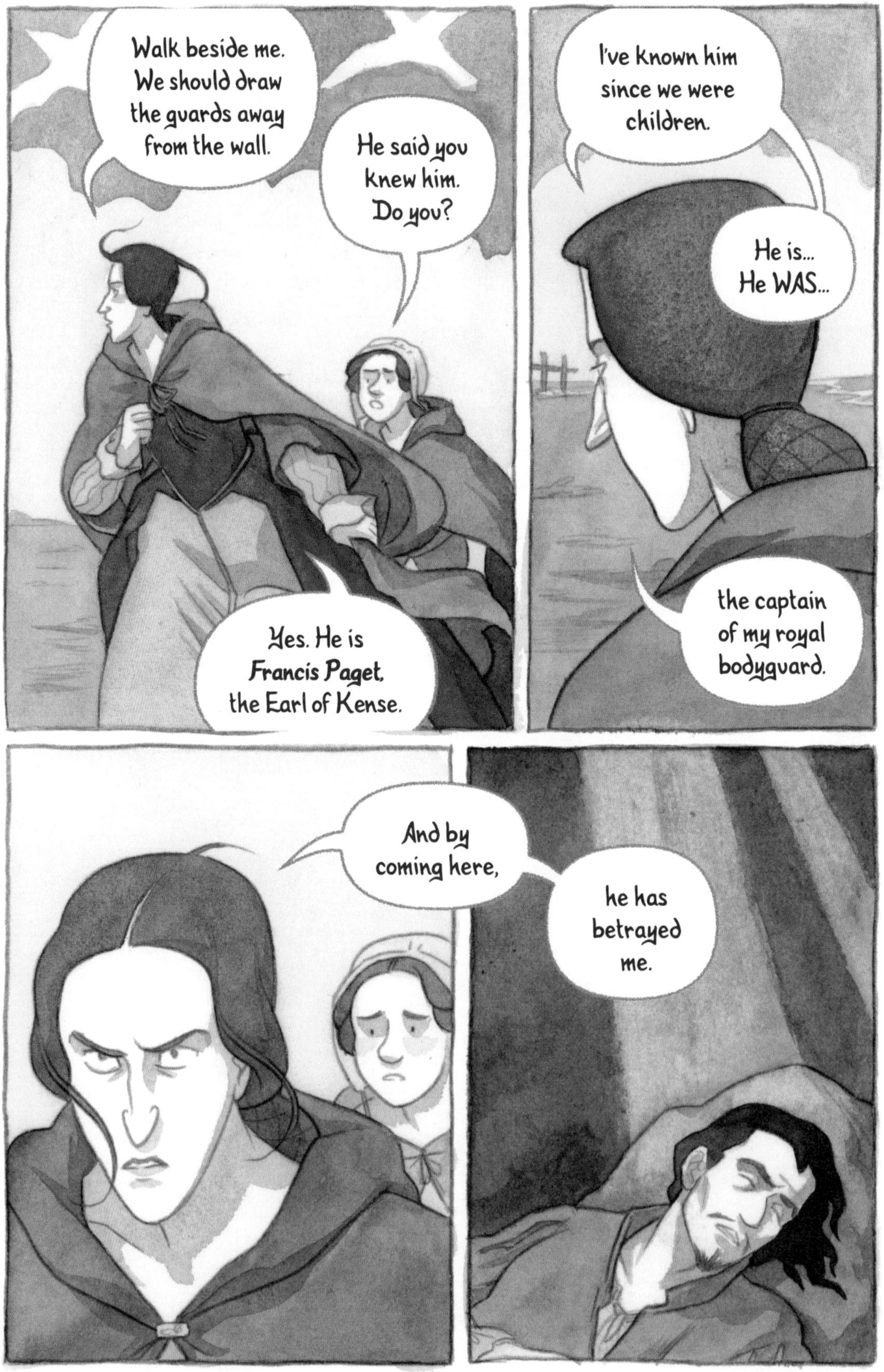
Walk beside me. We should draw the guards away from the wall.
He said you knew him. Do you?
Yes. He is Francis Paget, the Earl of Kense.
I've known him since we were children.
He is... He WAS...
the captain of my royal bodyguard.
And by coming here,
he has betrayed me.

The next few days were very strange.

The young man—*Francis Paget, the Earl of Kense*—would have to stay hidden in the cave until he was no longer so feverish that he might give himself away.

Eleanor could not get away from Mother Mary Clemence or the guards. After the coracle, even Peter Yarrow would not let her out of his sight.

So I was the only one who could go to the cave.

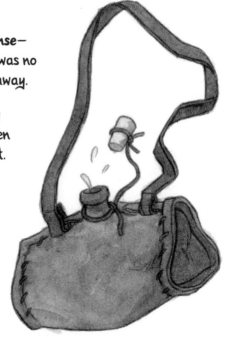

I could bring him fresh water without much trouble, but I couldn't get caught taking food from the kitchen, or sneaking bandages from the infirmary, or missing my lessons.

We tore up one of Eleanor's fine linen shifts into strips for bandages. She had the kitchen send food with me when I visited her chamber, and then I would hide it in my apron to take to the cave.

So Eleanor asked for me to keep her company every day, then would send me out on "errands" at low tide, when the mouth of the cave was open.

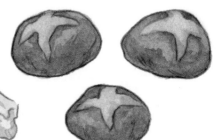

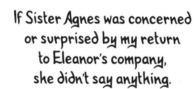

If Sister Agnes was concerned or surprised by my return to Eleanor's company, she didn't say anything.

253

Eleanor was *almost* sweet to me.

Whether she was *trying* to show her gratitude for my help, or fear that I might betray her and Francis to Mother Mary Clemence, I couldn't tell.

I kept the scrap of flag in my pocket, just in case.

It turned my fingers red.

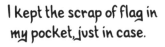

There was just one thing that I didn't understand at all.

You said that he betrayed you by coming here.

How?

He's put all three of us in danger, hasn't he?

Now, hurry out, before you miss the tide or *Her Reverence* returns.

Caring for him in secret was dangerous, but the storm was hardly his fault. The ship had come here under her flag, so surely he had come to rescue her.

How could that be a betrayal?

Francis gradually grew better. Once he was dried off, and his cuts and scrapes healed up, he was able to eat and drink a little more. His fever went down, though he was still very pale. He finally realized that I wasn't Eleanor.

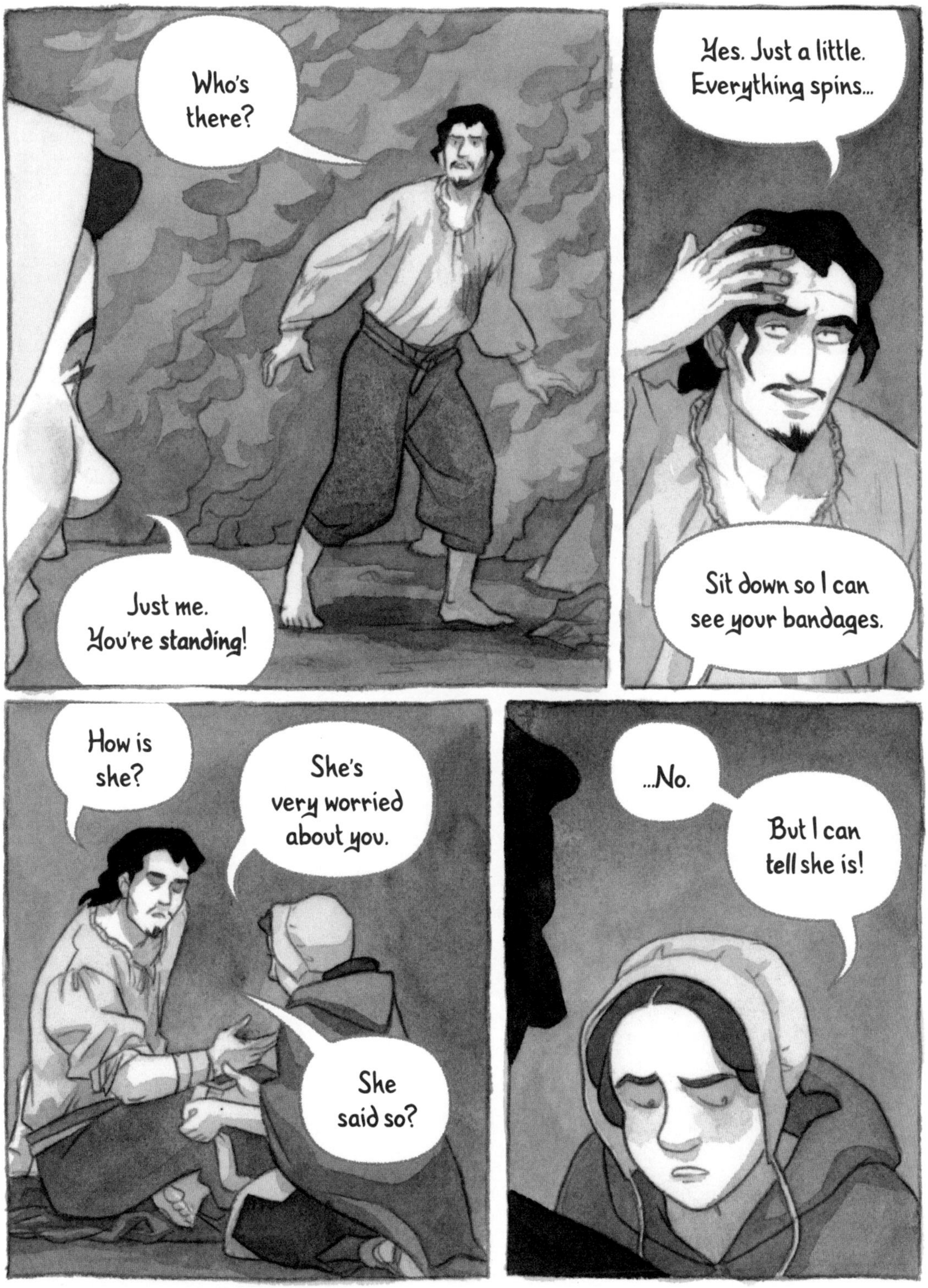

Who's there?
Just me. You're standing!
Yes. Just a little. Everything spins...
Sit down so I can see your bandages.
How is she?
She's very worried about you.
She said so?
...No.
But I can tell she is!

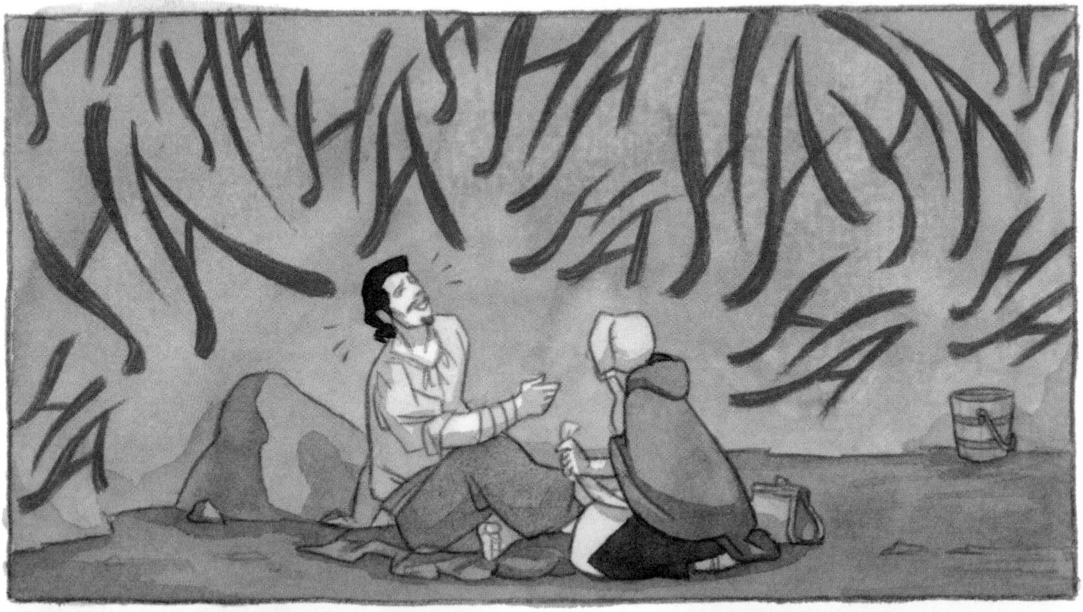
HA HA HA HA HA HA HA HA HA HA HA HA HA HA HA HA

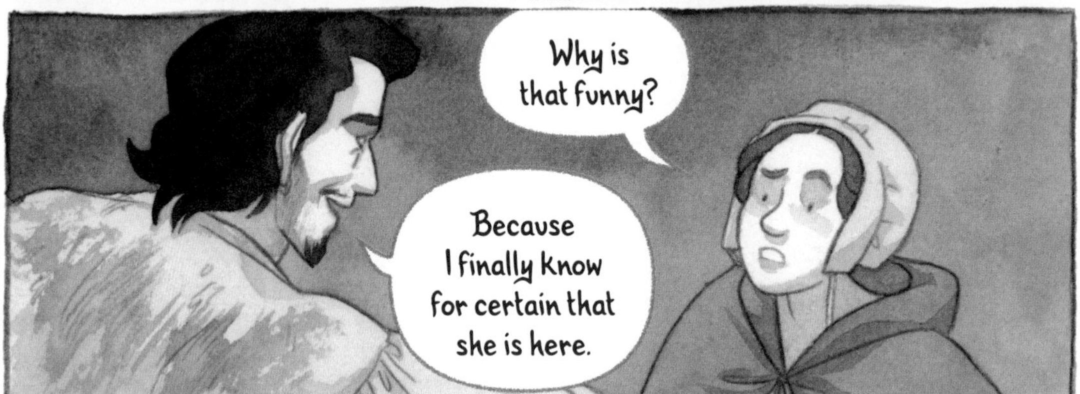
Why is that funny?
Because I finally know for certain that she is here.

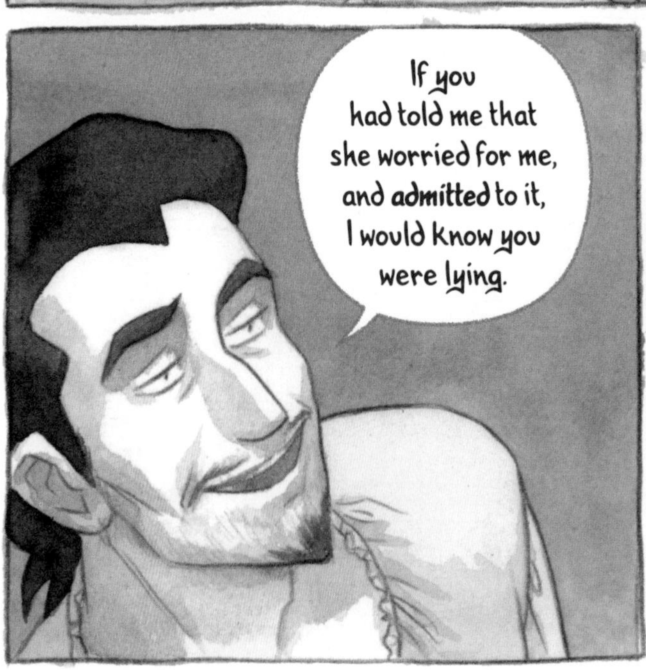
If you had told me that she worried for me, and admitted to it, I would know you were lying.

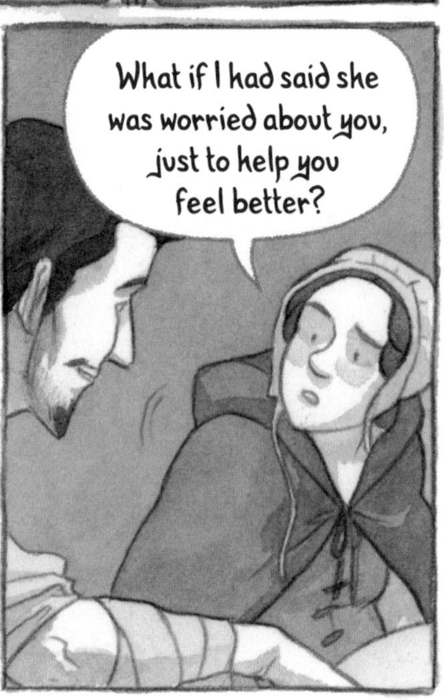
What if I had said she was worried about you, just to help you feel better?

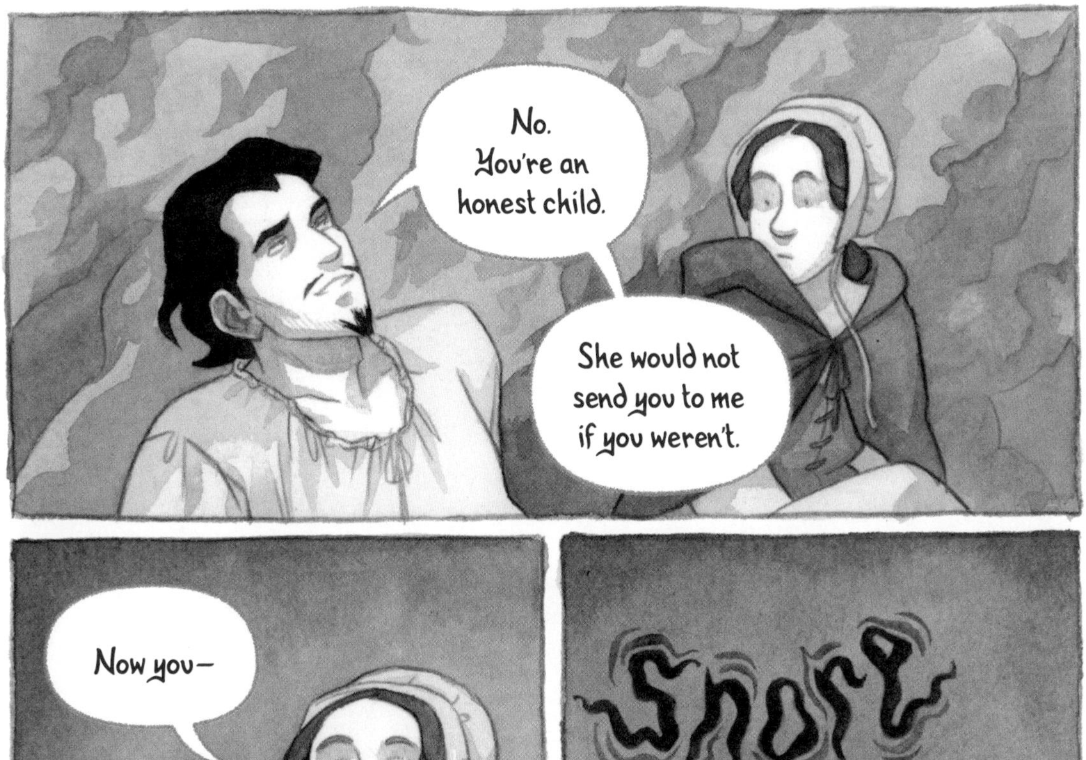
No.
You're an honest child.
She would not send you to me if you weren't.
Now you—
Snore
...

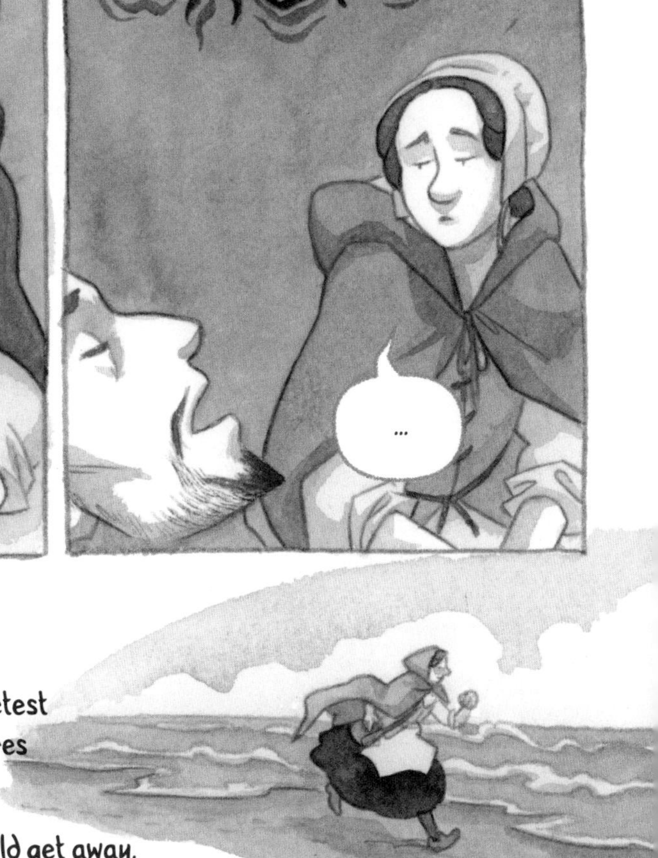

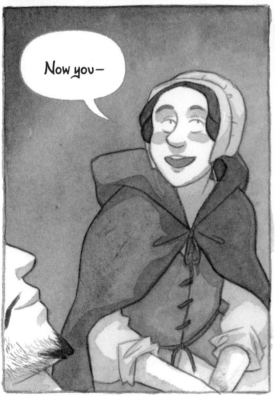

I didn't get to visit Francis the next day.

It was Sunday, and Sundays are the quietest day at the convent, when even most chores are set aside in favor of prayer.

The tide was too high the only time I could get away. When I saw him on Monday, something had changed.

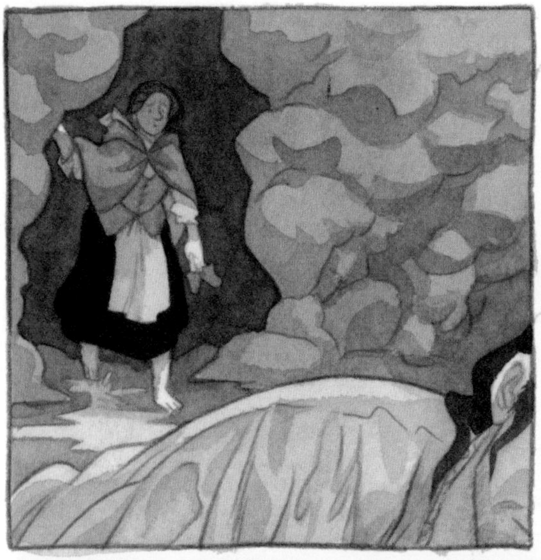

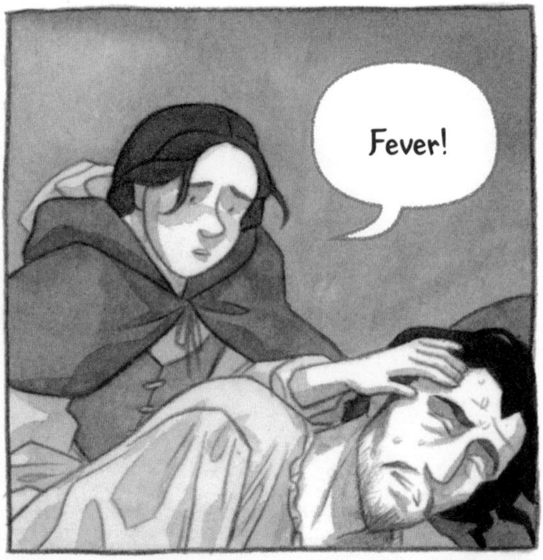
Fever!

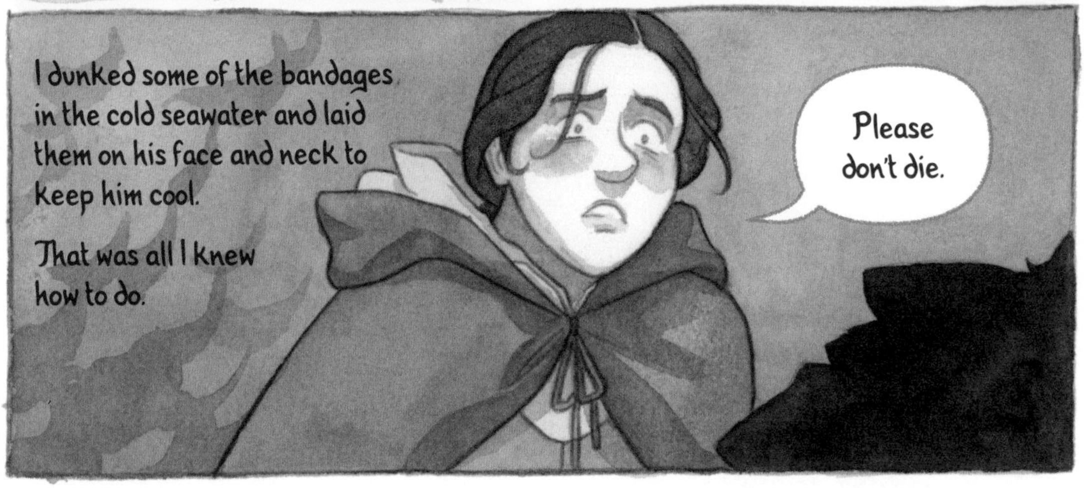
I dunked some of the bandages in the cold seawater and laid them on his face and neck to keep him cool.
That was all I knew how to do.
Please don't die.

I had a terrible feeling that he *would*, very soon, unless he had better help than me. The tide was coming in, and so was another storm. The water was already rushing up to my ankles at the mouth of the cave. Soon it would be up to my knees, and at the rock wall it would be up to my waist—too strong and cold and dangerous to wade through.

There wasn't time to run and get Eleanor, even if she were free to help me.

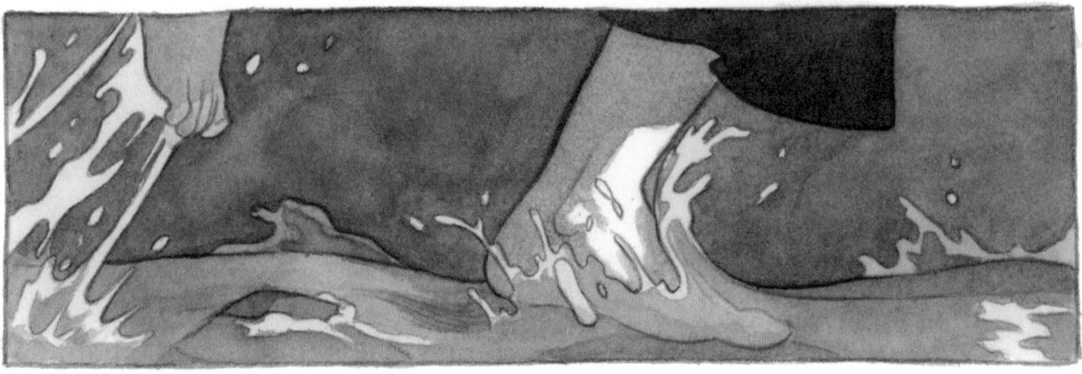

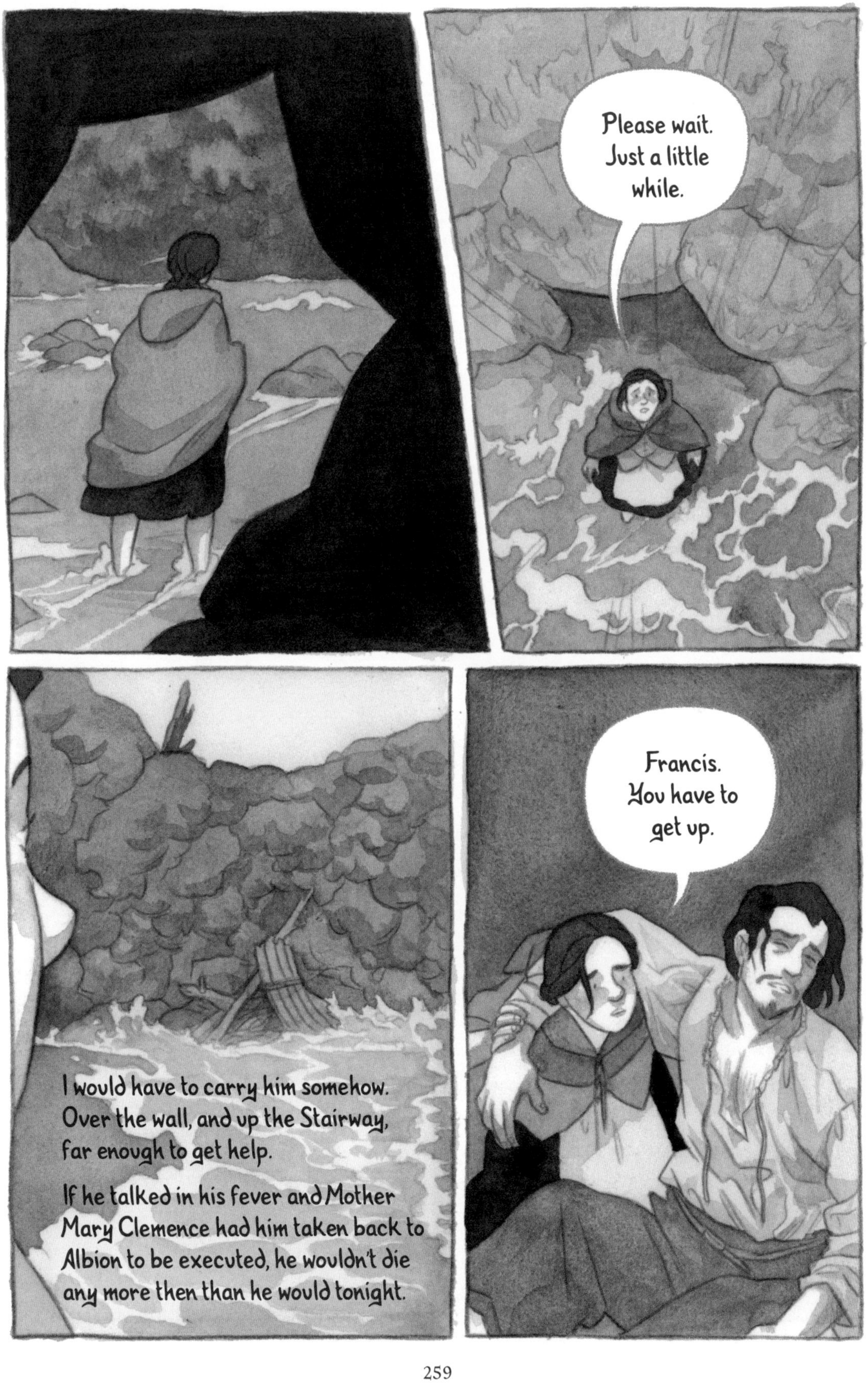
Please wait. Just a little while.
I would have to carry him somehow. Over the wall, and up the Stairway, far enough to get help.
If he talked in his fever and Mother Mary Clemence had him taken back to Albion to be executed, he wouldn't die any more then than he would tonight.
Francis. You have to get up.

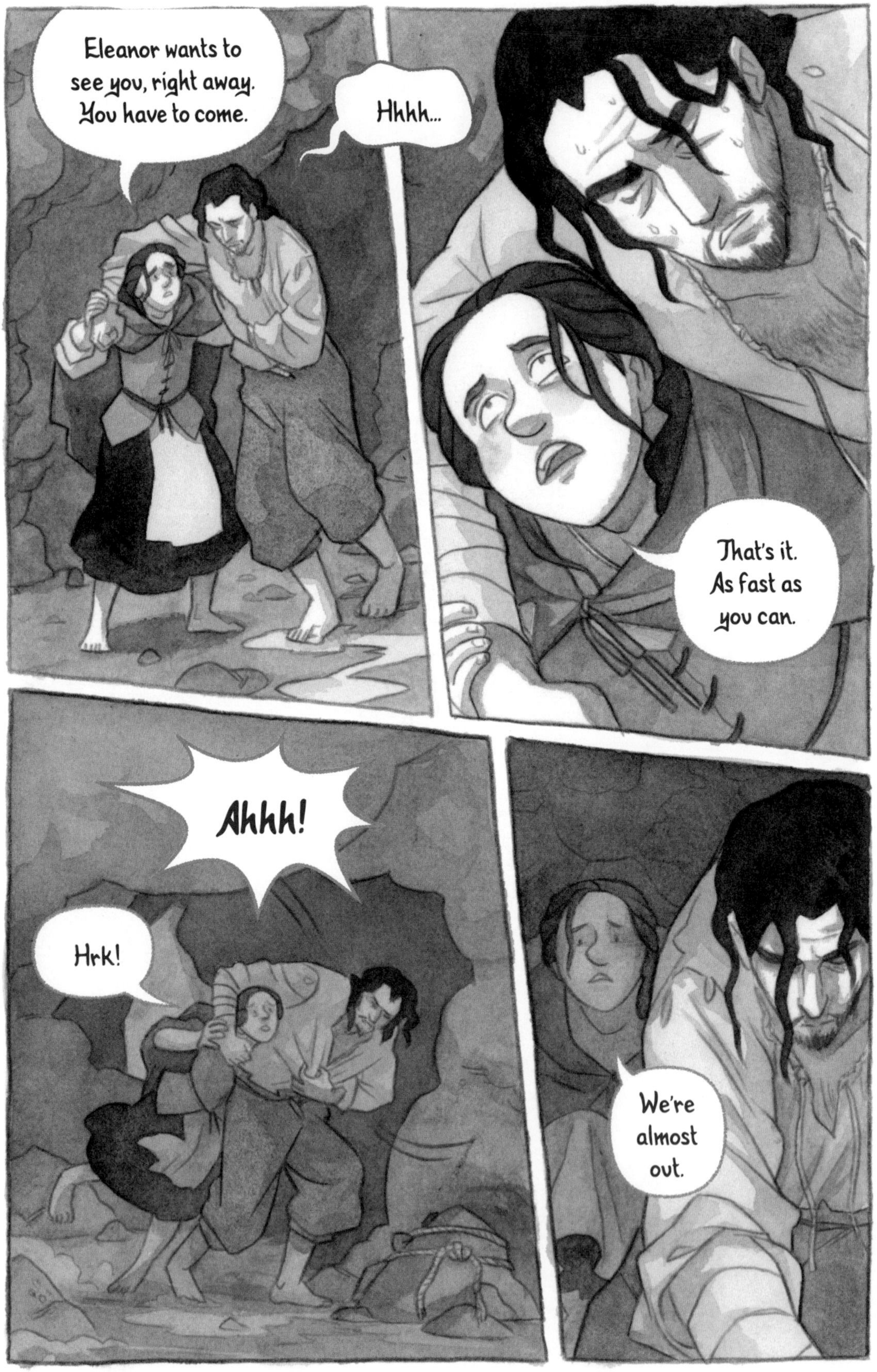
Eleanor wants to see you, right away. You have to come.
Hhhh...
That's it. As fast as you can.
Ahhh!
Hrk!
We're almost out.

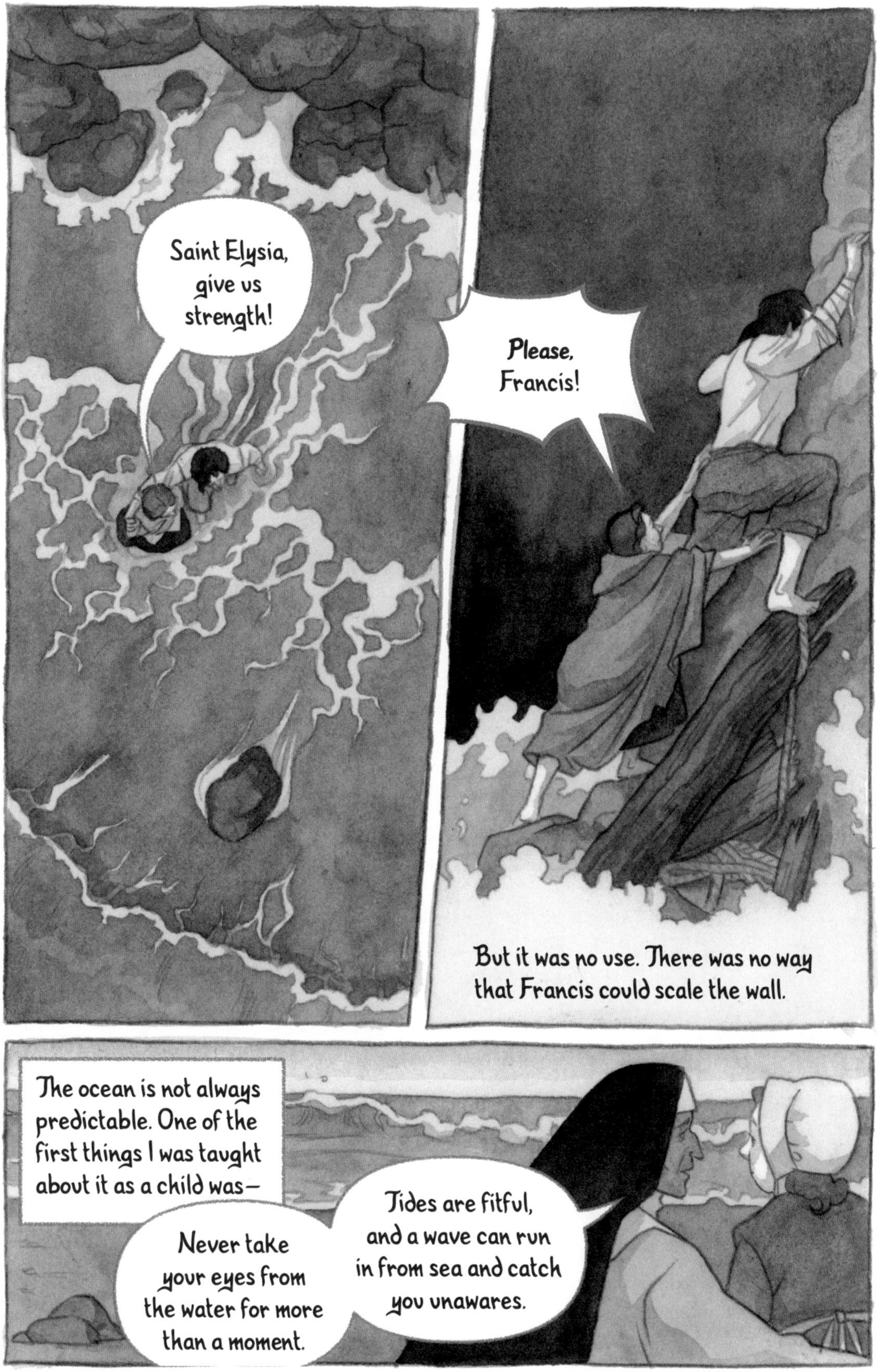
Saint Elysia, give us strength!
Please, Francis!
But it was no use. There was no way that Francis could scale the wall.
The ocean is not always predictable. One of the first things I was taught about it as a child was—
Never take your eyes from the water for more than a moment.
Tides are fitful, and a wave can run in from sea and catch you unawares.

Jess had a different explanation, which I liked much better,

although I also found it far more frightening.

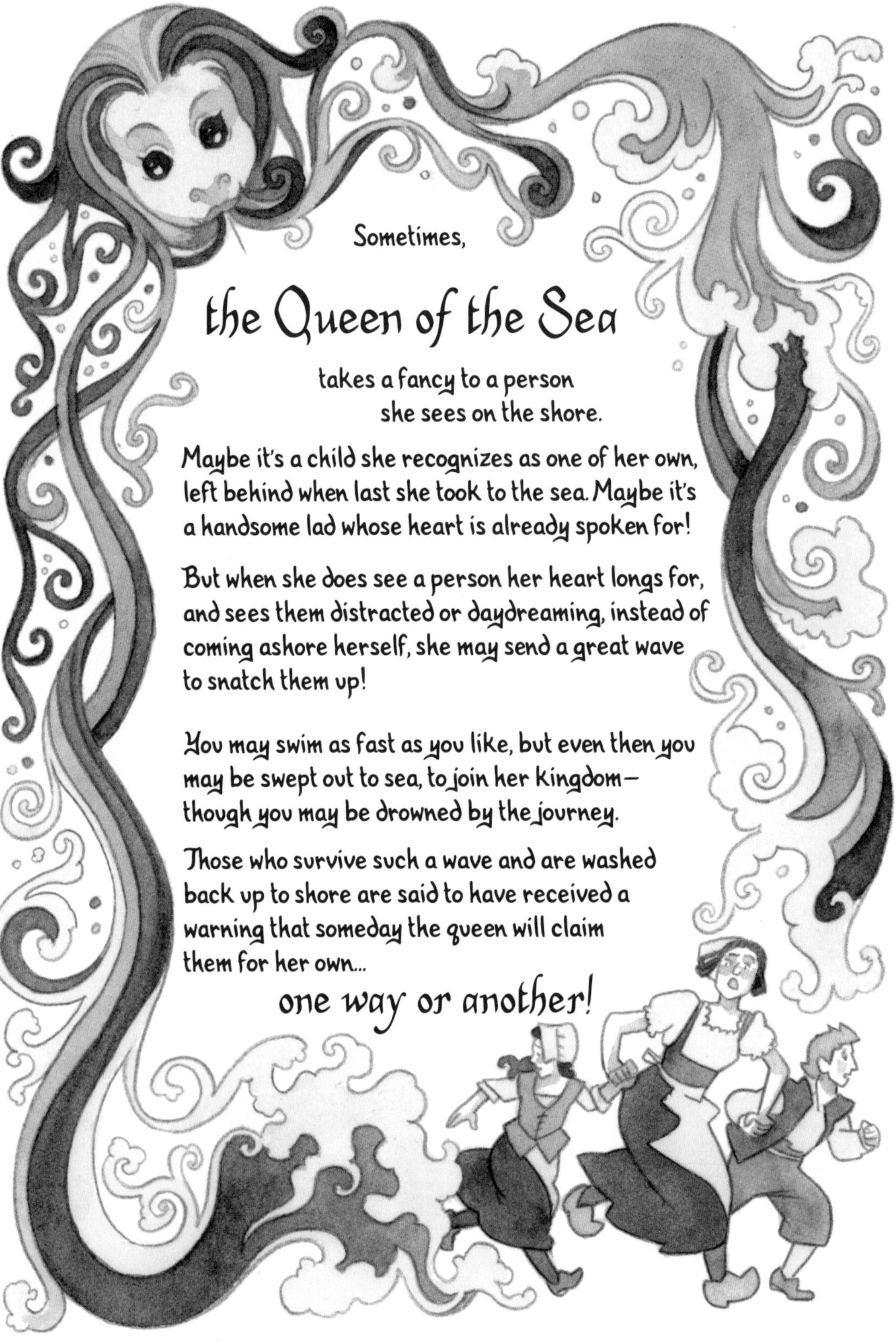

Sometimes,

the Queen of the Sea

takes a fancy to a person
she sees on the shore.

Maybe it's a child she recognizes as one of her own, left behind when last she took to the sea. Maybe it's a handsome lad whose heart is already spoken for!

But when she does see a person her heart longs for, and sees them distracted or daydreaming, instead of coming ashore herself, she may send a great wave to snatch them up!

You may swim as fast as you like, but even then you may be swept out to sea, to join her kingdom—though you may be drowned by the journey.

Those who survive such a wave and are washed back up to shore are said to have received a warning that someday the queen will claim them for her own...

one way or another!

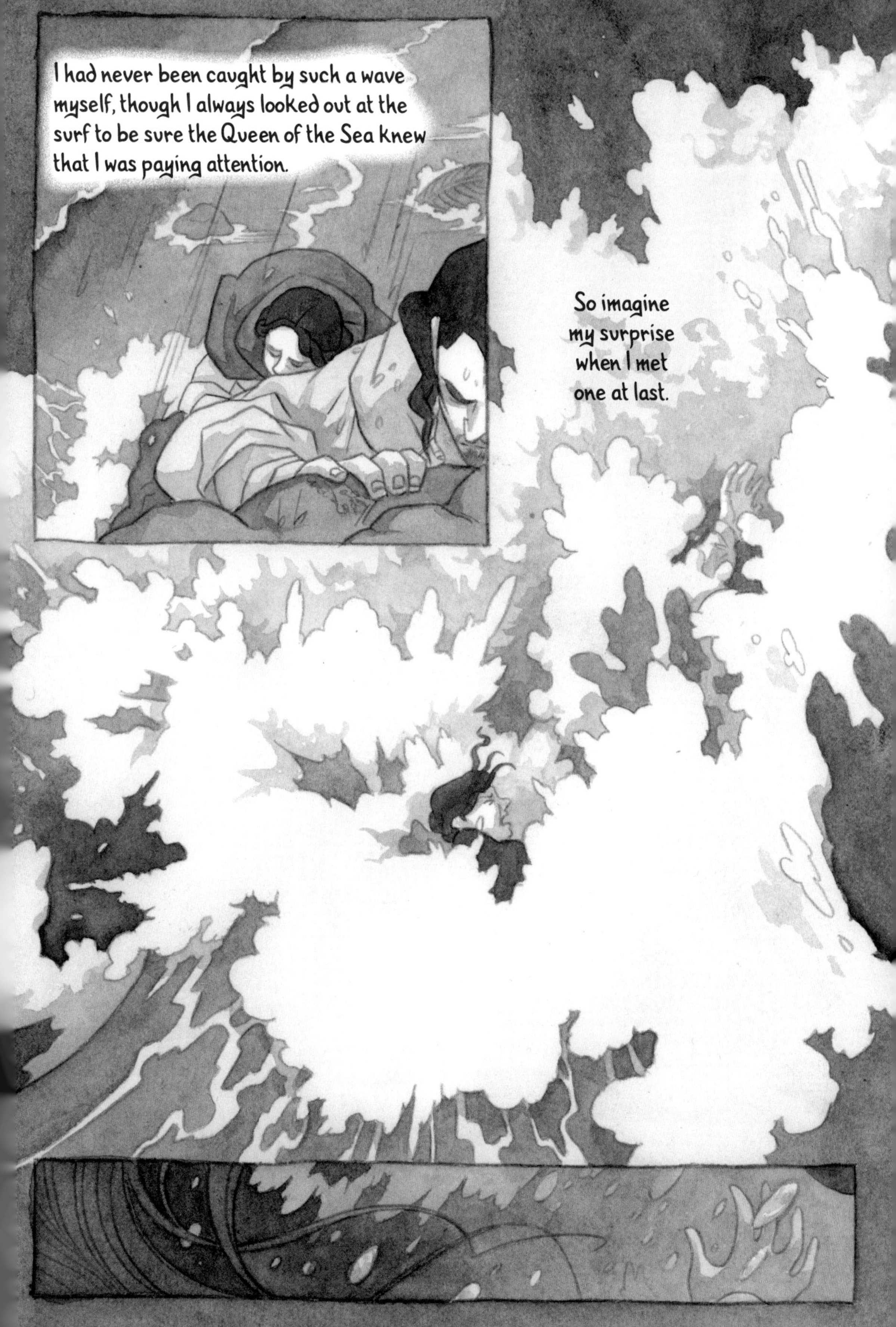
I had never been caught by such a wave myself, though I always looked out at the surf to be sure the Queen of the Sea knew that I was paying attention.
So imagine my surprise when I met one at last.

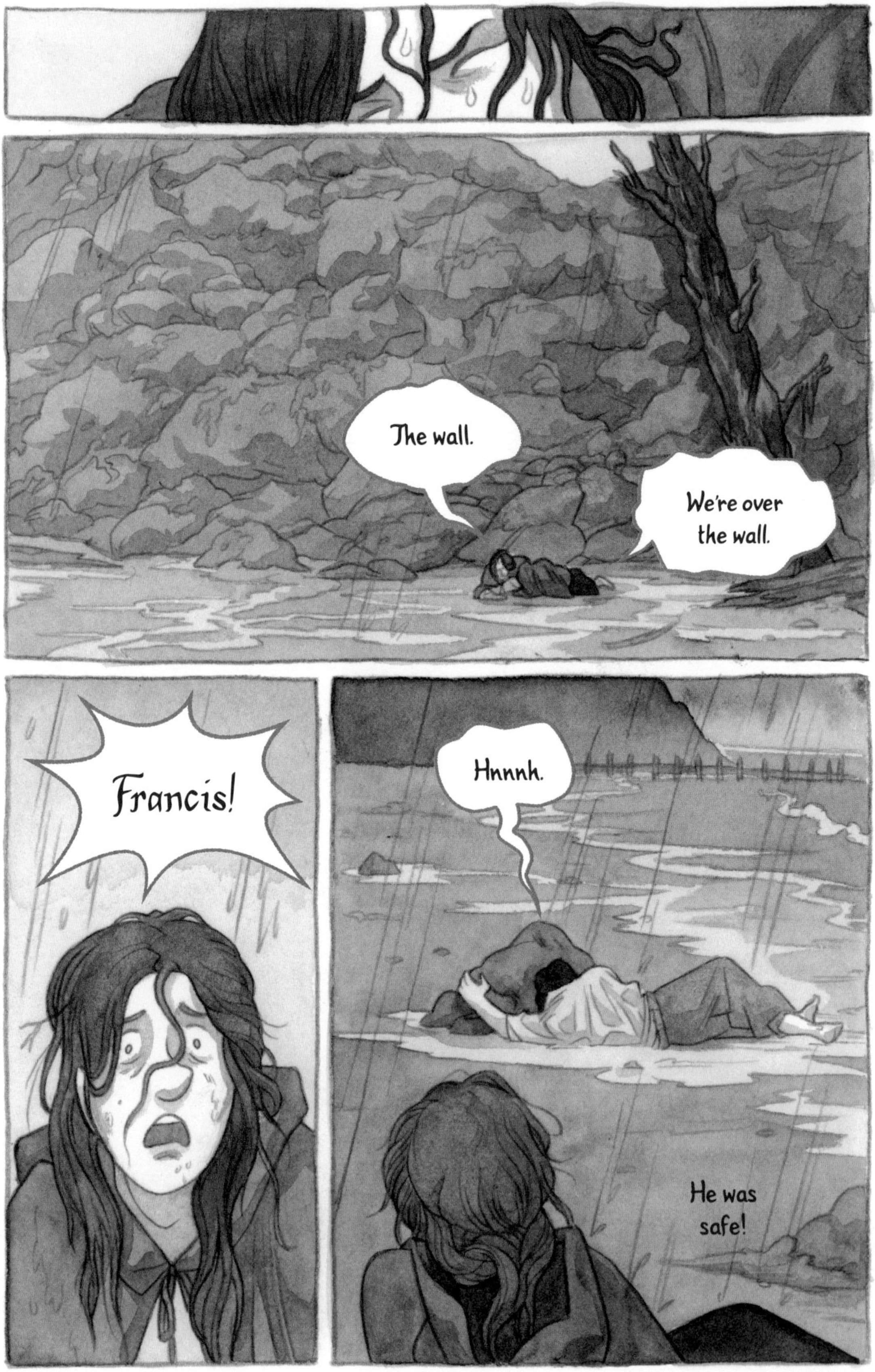
The wall.
We're over the wall.
Francis!
Hnnnh.
He was safe!

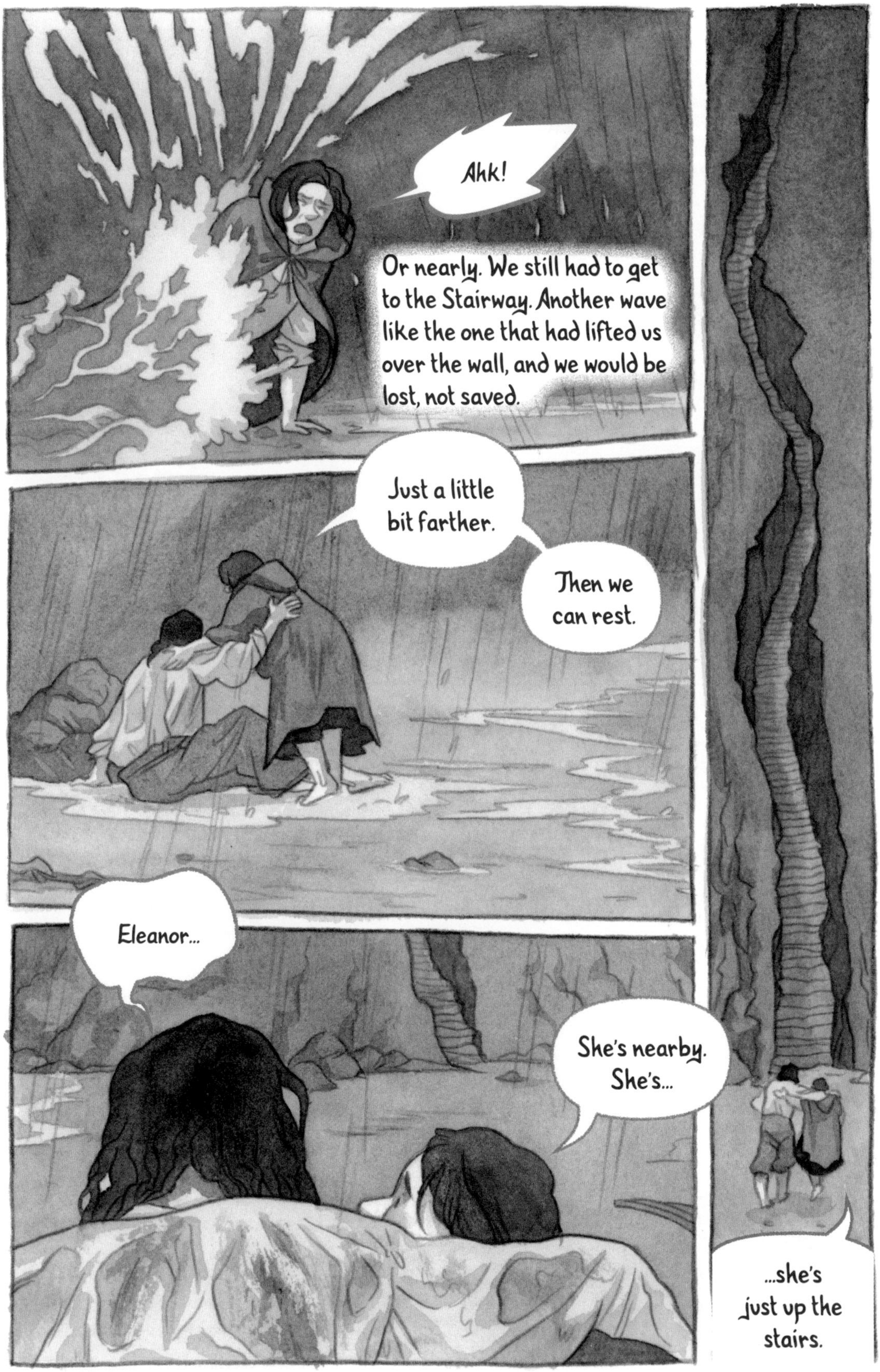
SLOSH
Ahk!
Or nearly. We still had to get to the Stairway. Another wave like the one that had lifted us over the wall, and we would be lost, not saved.
Just a little bit farther.
Then we can rest.
Eleanor...
She's nearby. She's...
...she's just up the stairs.

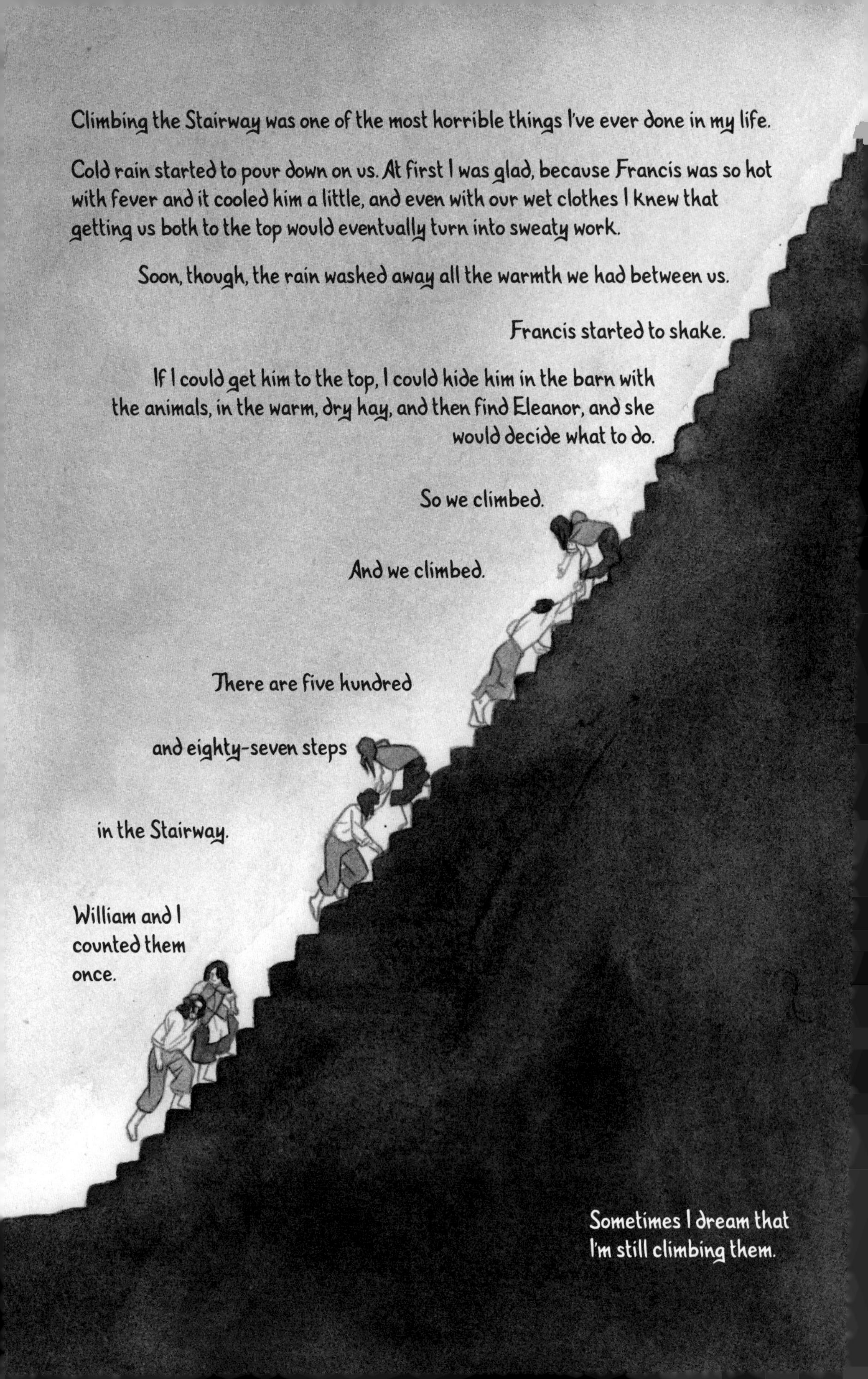

Climbing the Stairway was one of the most horrible things I've ever done in my life.
Cold rain started to pour down on us. At first I was glad, because Francis was so hot with fever and it cooled him a little, and even with our wet clothes I knew that getting us both to the top would eventually turn into sweaty work.
Soon, though, the rain washed away all the warmth we had between us.
Francis started to shake.
If I could get him to the top, I could hide him in the barn with the animals, in the warm, dry hay, and then find Eleanor, and she would decide what to do.
So we climbed.
And we climbed.
There are five hundred
and eighty-seven steps
in the Stairway.
William and I counted them once.
Sometimes I dream that I'm still climbing them.

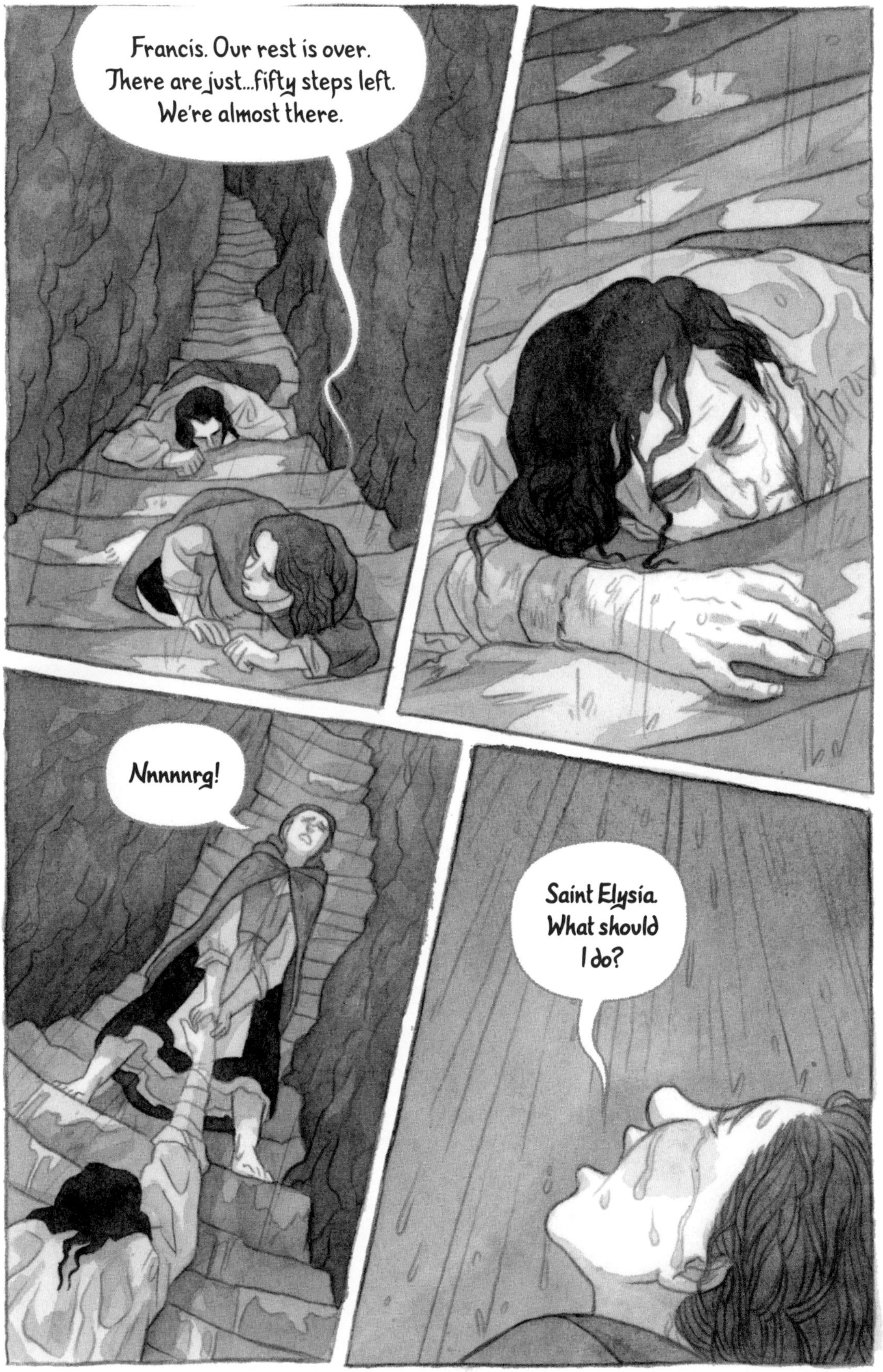
Francis. Our rest is over. There are just...fifty steps left. We're almost there.
Nnnnnrg!
Saint Elysia. What should I do?

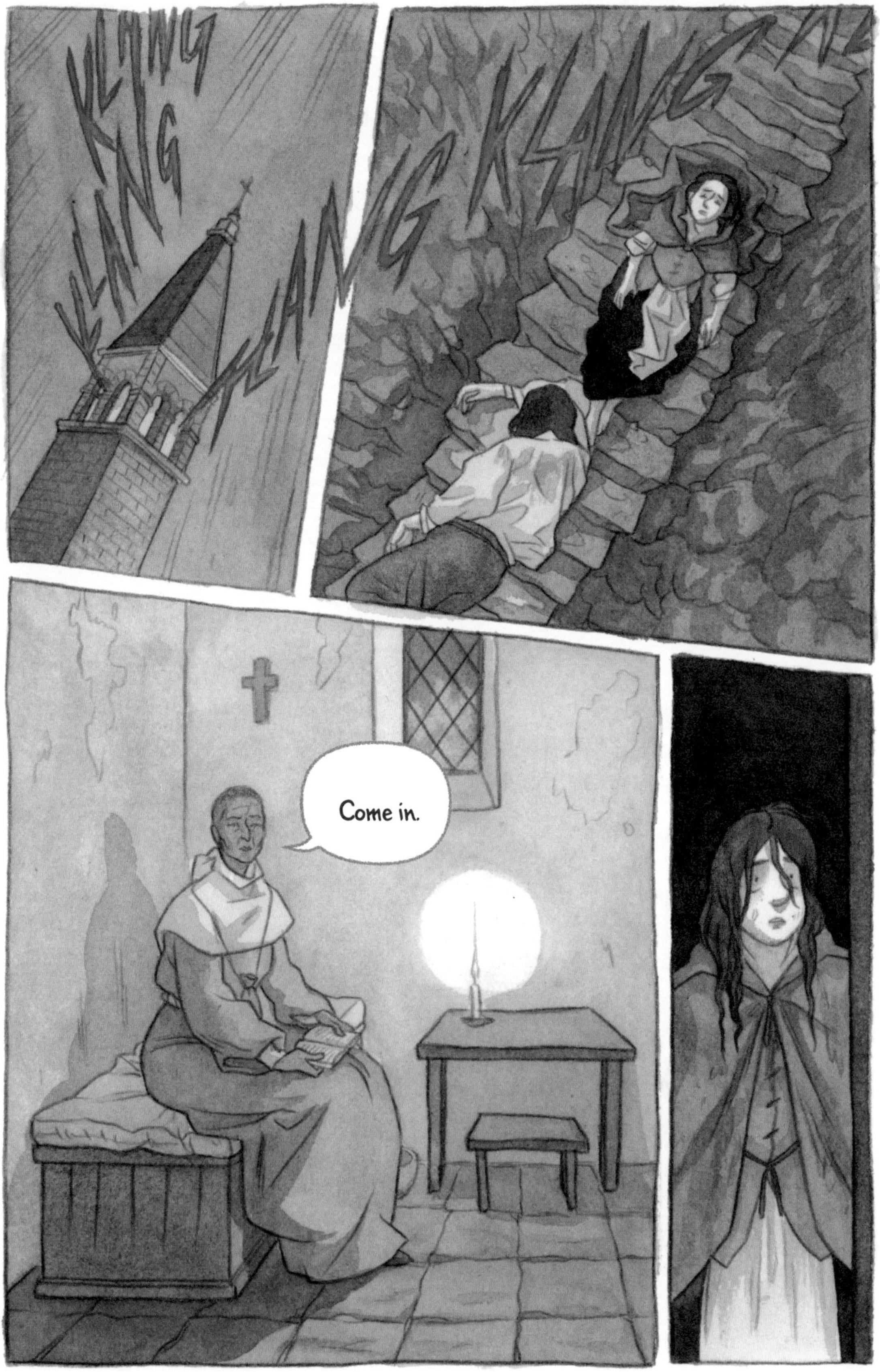
KLANG KLANG
KLANG KLANG
Come in.

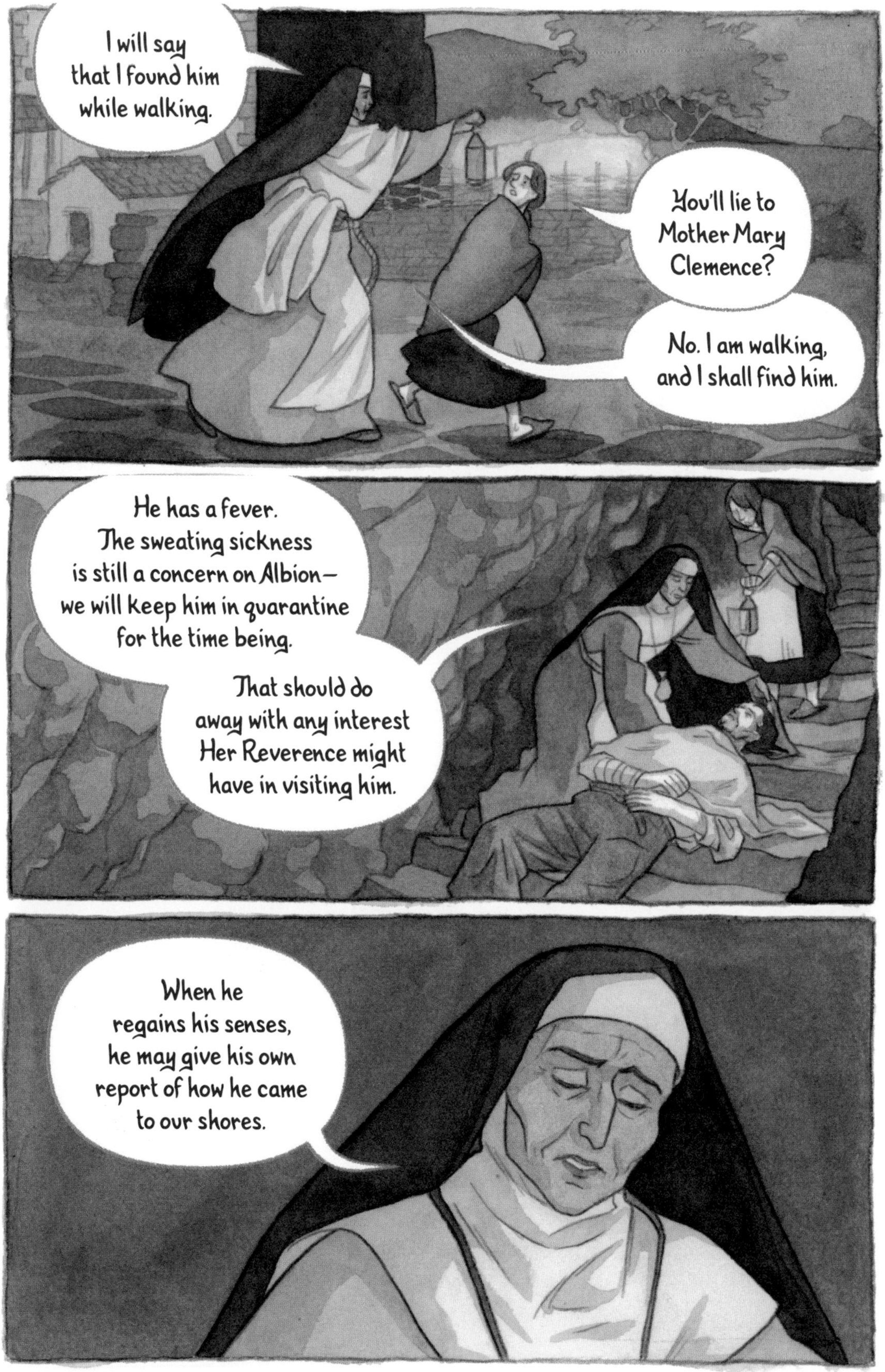

I will say that I found him while walking.
You'll lie to Mother Mary Clemence?
No. I am walking, and I shall find him.
He has a fever. The sweating sickness is still a concern on Albion— we will keep him in quarantine for the time being.
That should do away with any interest Her Reverence might have in visiting him.
When he regains his senses, he may give his own report of how he came to our shores.

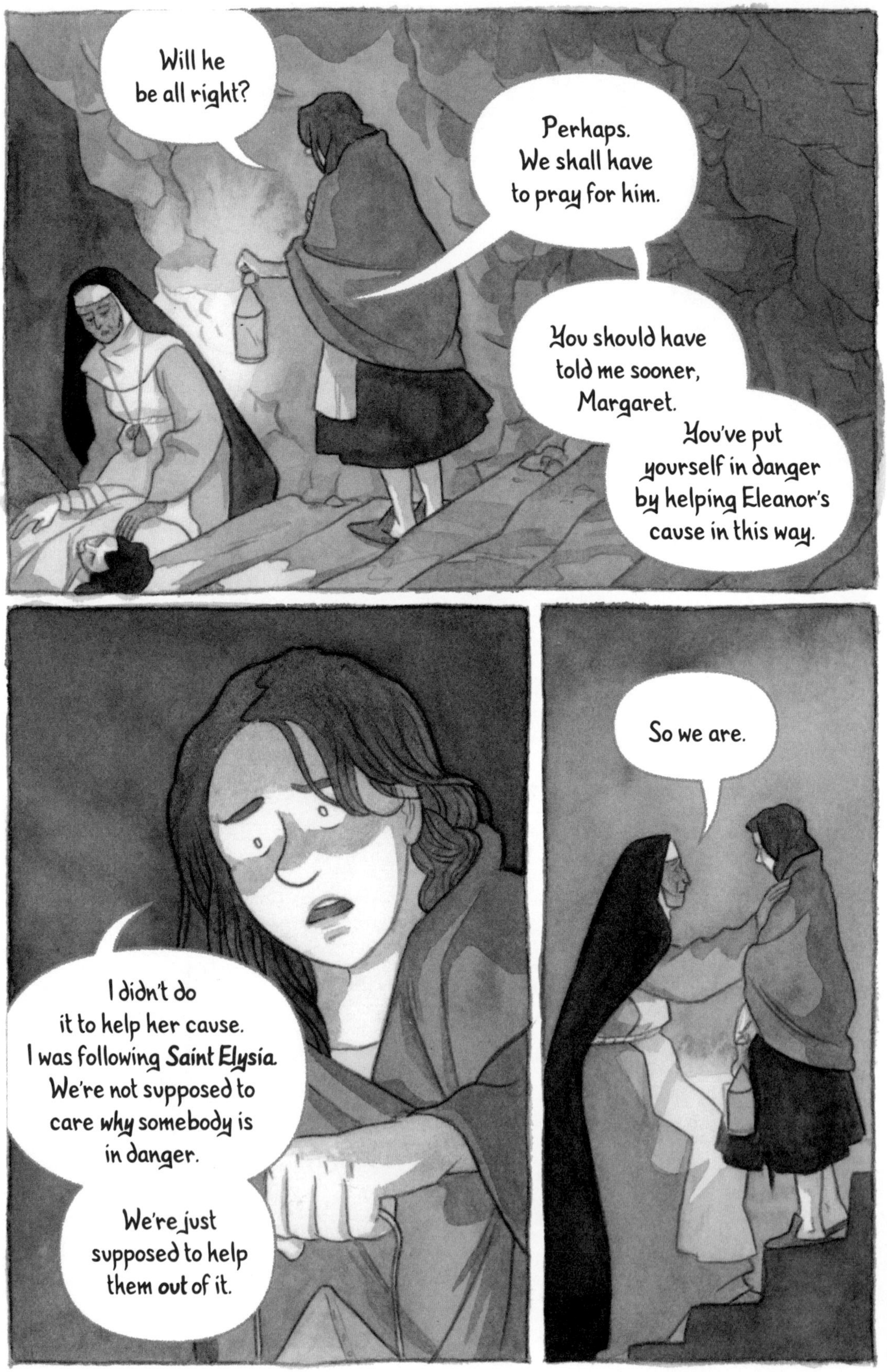
Will he be all right?
Perhaps. We shall have to pray for him.
You should have told me sooner, Margaret.
You've put yourself in danger by helping Eleanor's cause in this way.
I didn't do it to help her cause. I was following *Saint Elysia.* We're not supposed to care *why* somebody is in danger.
We're just supposed to help them out of it.
So we are.

Sister Agnes went to quietly fetch Sister Edith and the litter to bring Francis in with. I sat on the Stairway with him and held his hand, though I don't know if he could even feel it any longer.

The rain stopped, but it grew darker, and the wind made strange noises howling up the Stairway.

It took a little doing, but he was in the infirmary before dark, and nobody had breathed a word about our new patient to Mother Mary Clemence.

Or to Eleanor.

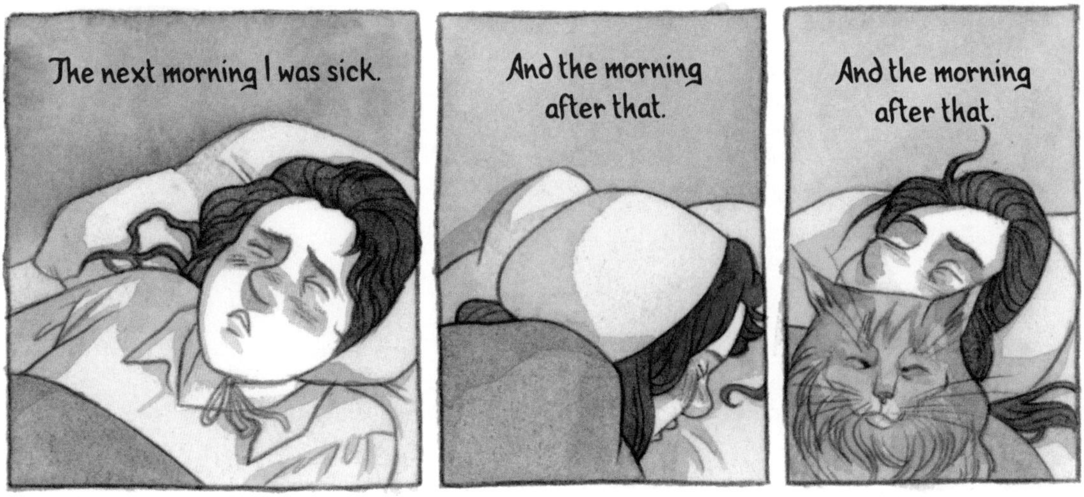
The next morning I was sick.
And the morning after that.
And the morning after that.

Sister Edith and Sister Agnes were both in the infirmary as part of Francis's "quarantine," so I heard no news from them. Eleanor didn't come to visit me.

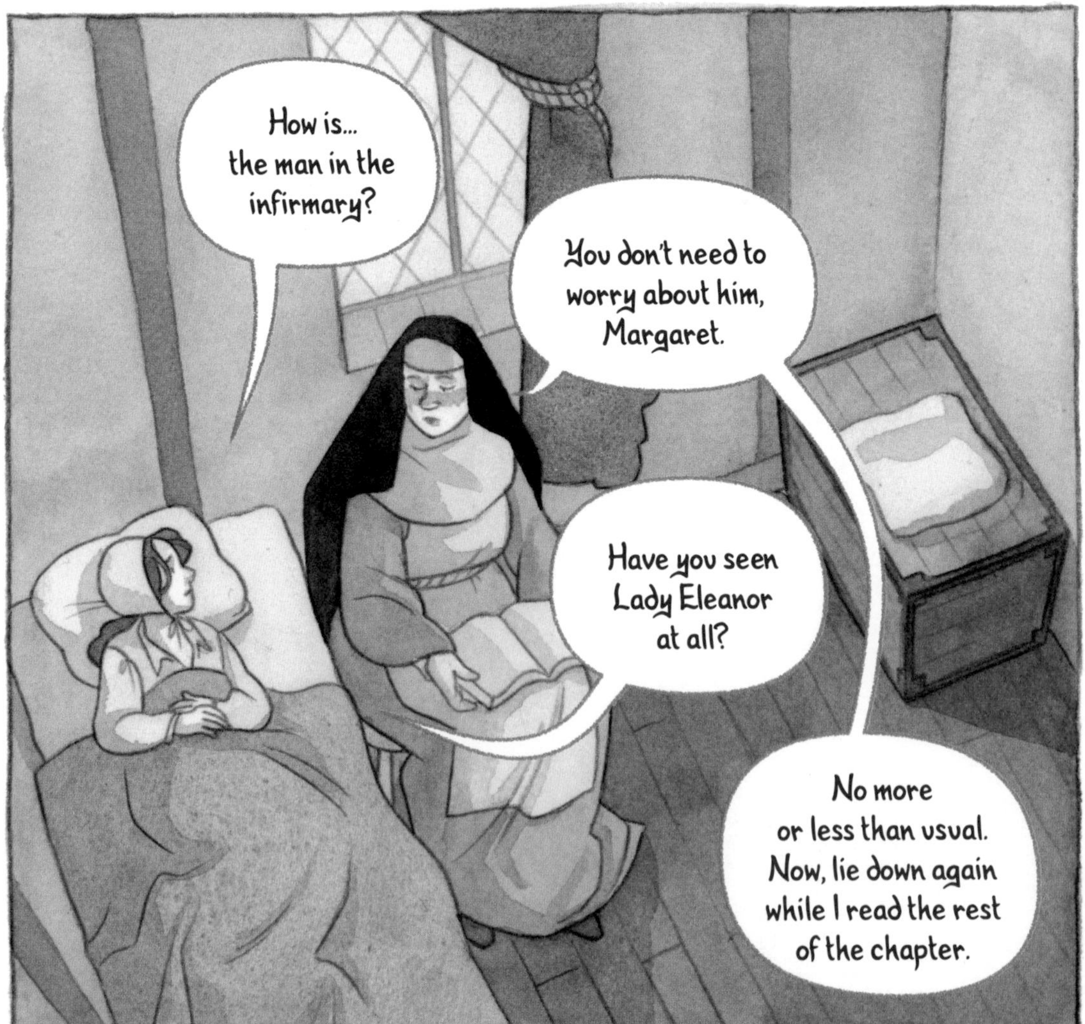
How is... the man in the infirmary?
You don't need to worry about him, Margaret.
Have you seen Lady Eleanor at all?
No more or less than usual. Now, lie down again while I read the rest of the chapter.

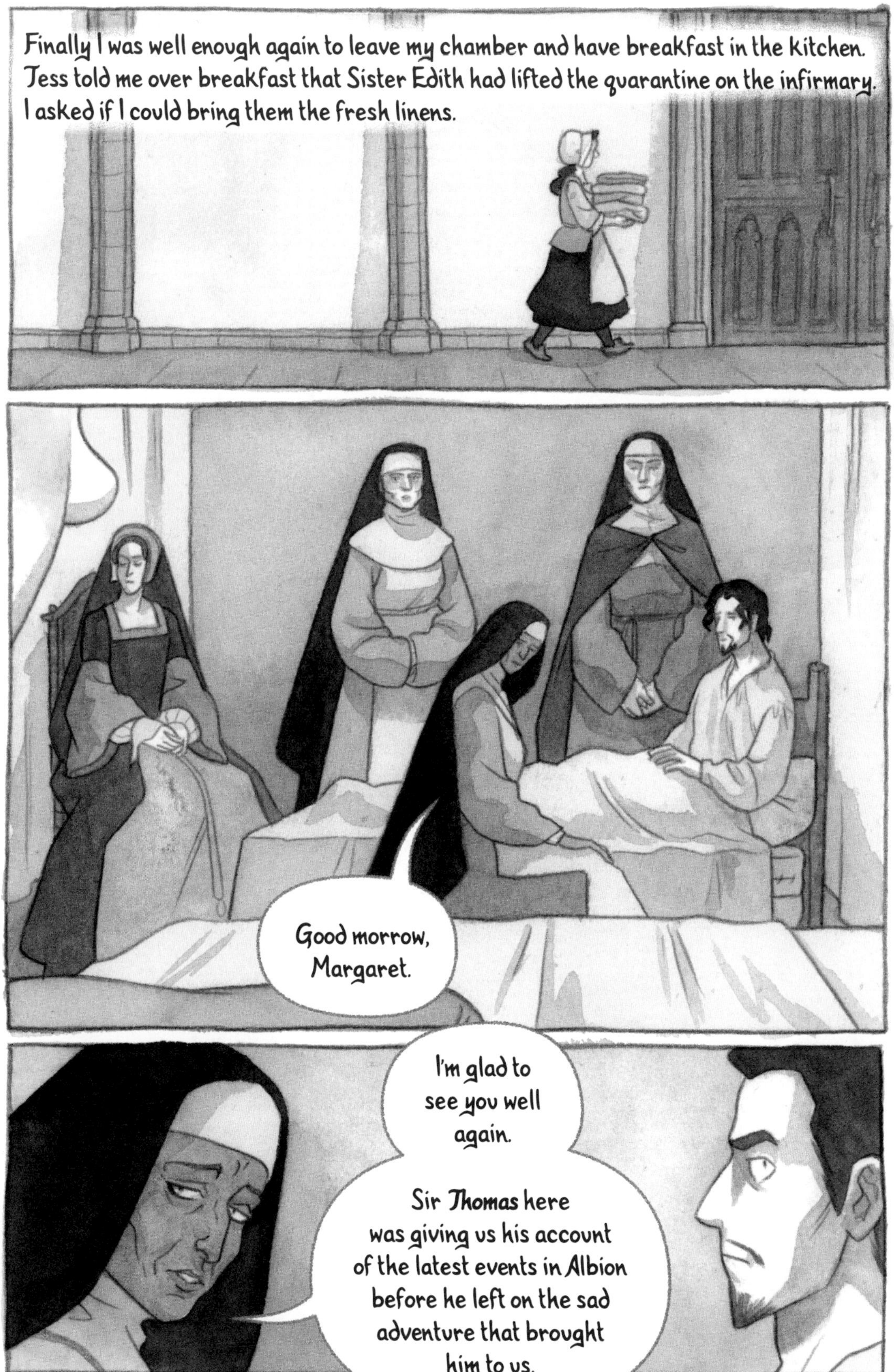

Finally I was well enough again to leave my chamber and have breakfast in the kitchen. Jess told me over breakfast that Sister Edith had lifted the quarantine on the infirmary. I asked if I could bring them the fresh linens.
Good morrow, Margaret.
I'm glad to see you well again.
Sir Thomas here was giving us his account of the latest events in Albion before he left on the sad adventure that brought him to us.

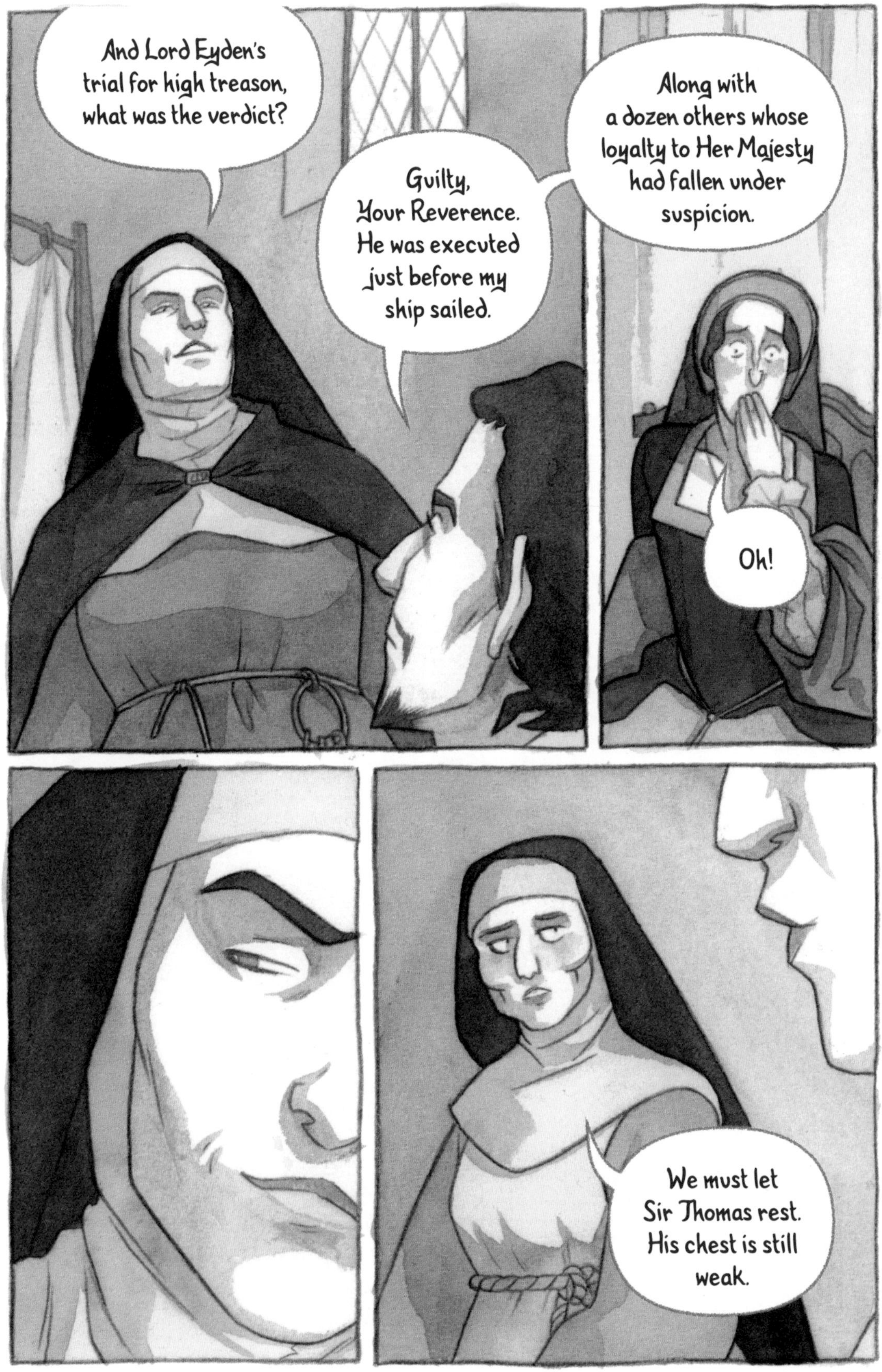
And Lord Eyden's trial for high treason, what was the verdict?
Guilty, Your Reverence. He was executed just before my ship sailed.
Along with a dozen others whose loyalty to Her Majesty had fallen under suspicion.
Oh!
We must let Sir Thomas rest. His chest is still weak.

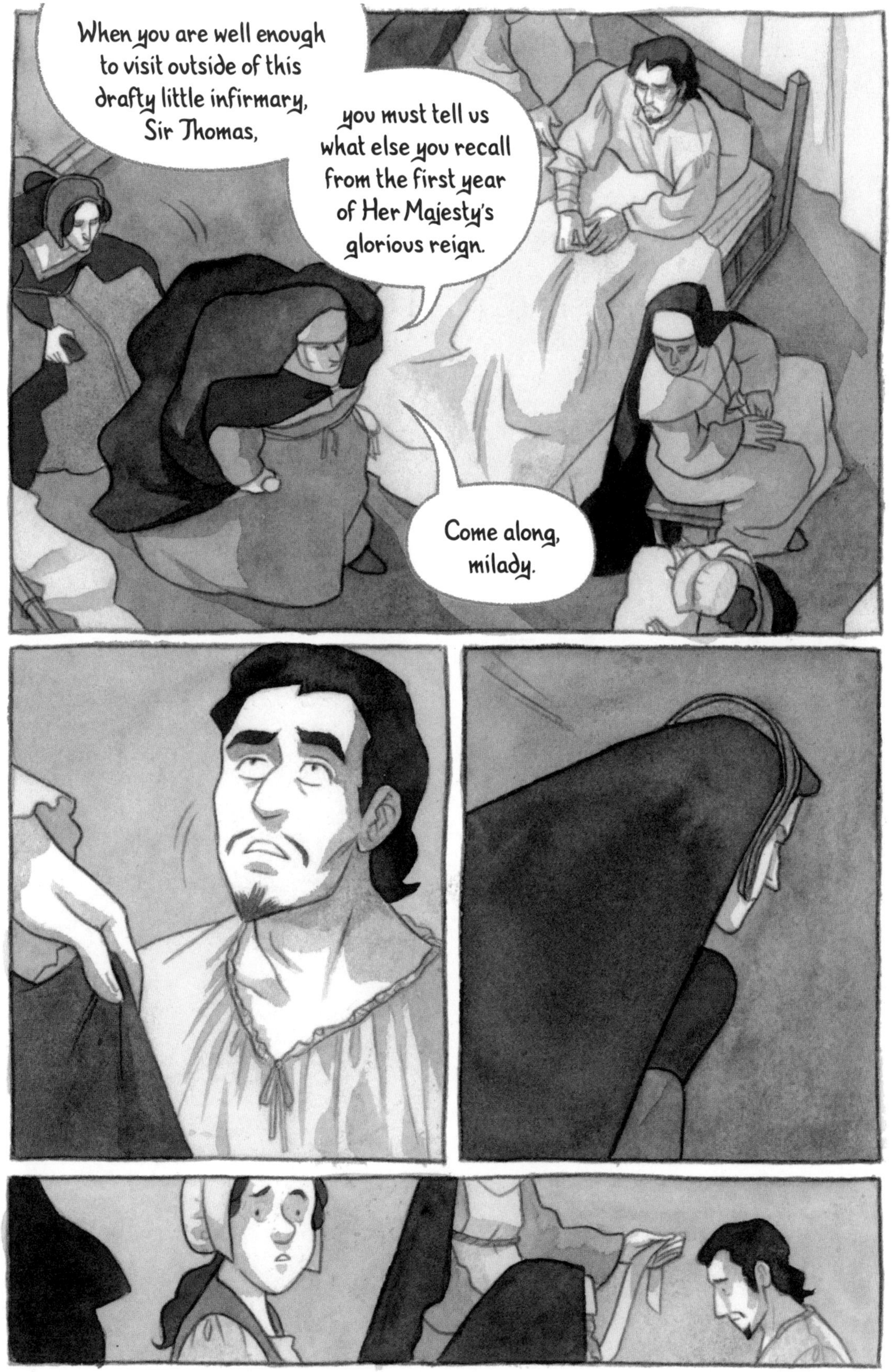
When you are well enough to visit outside of this drafty little infirmary, Sir Thomas,
you must tell us what else you recall from the first year of Her Majesty's glorious reign.
Come along, milady.

Why had Eleanor passed him by so coldly? She didn't call for me, so I had no chance to ask her. I tried to visit Francis on my own, but every time I had a moment to spare, somebody else was already sitting by his side.

Most of the convent found excuses to come and examine the new patient.

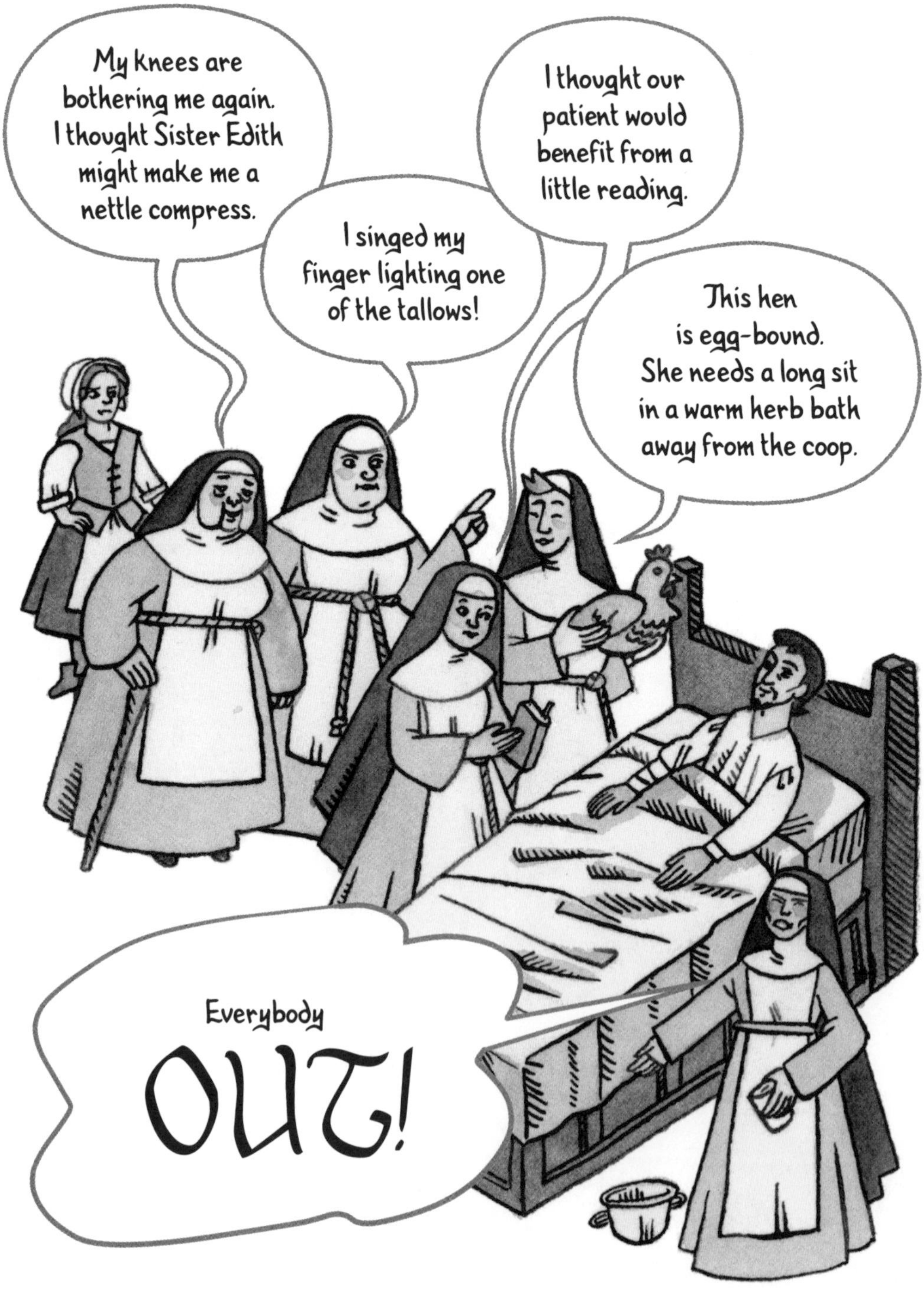
My knees are bothering me again. I thought Sister Edith might make me a nettle compress.
I singed my finger lighting one of the tallows!
I thought our patient would benefit from a little reading.
This hen is egg-bound. She needs a long sit in a warm herb bath away from the coop.
Everybody OUT!

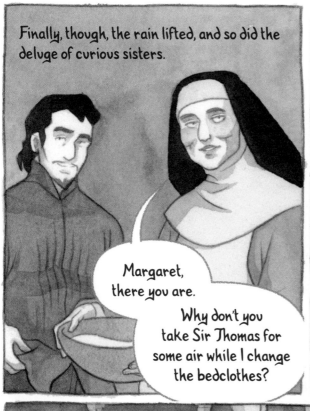

Finally, though, the rain lifted, and so did the deluge of curious sisters.

Margaret, there you are.

Why don't you take Sir Thomas for some air while I change the bedclothes?

I haven't had the chance until now to thank you, Mistress Margaret. I owe you my life.

You should light a candle in Saint Elysia's chapel. She's the one who saved you.

I will.

Did you really come here to rescue Eleanor?

Hmh.

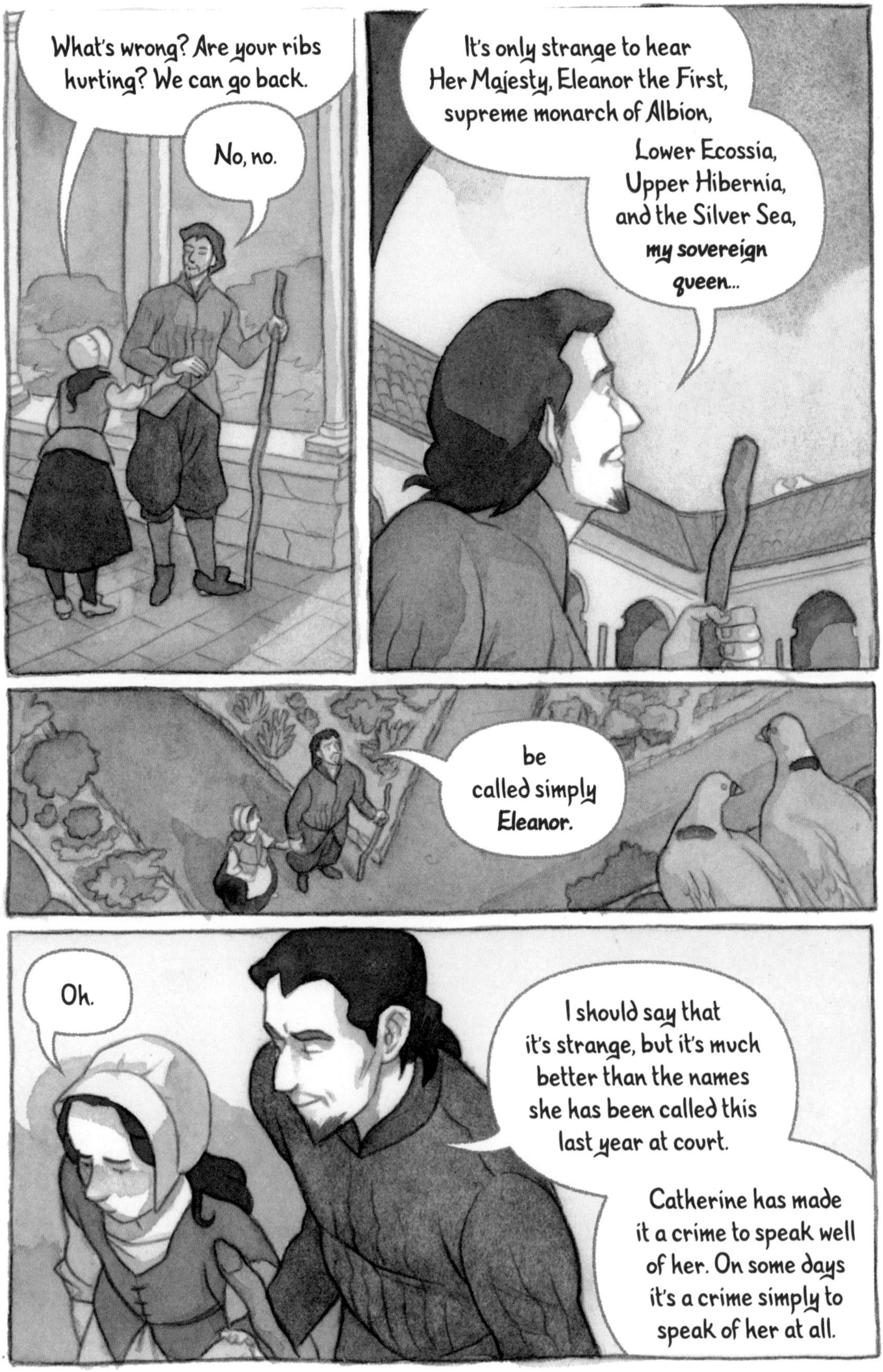

What's wrong? Are your ribs hurting? We can go back.
No, no.
It's only strange to hear Her Majesty, Eleanor the First, supreme monarch of Albion,
Lower Ecossia, Upper Hibernia, and the Silver Sea, my sovereign queen...
be called simply Eleanor.
Oh.
I should say that it's strange, but it's much better than the names she has been called this last year at court.
Catherine has made it a crime to speak well of her. On some days it's a crime simply to speak of her at all.

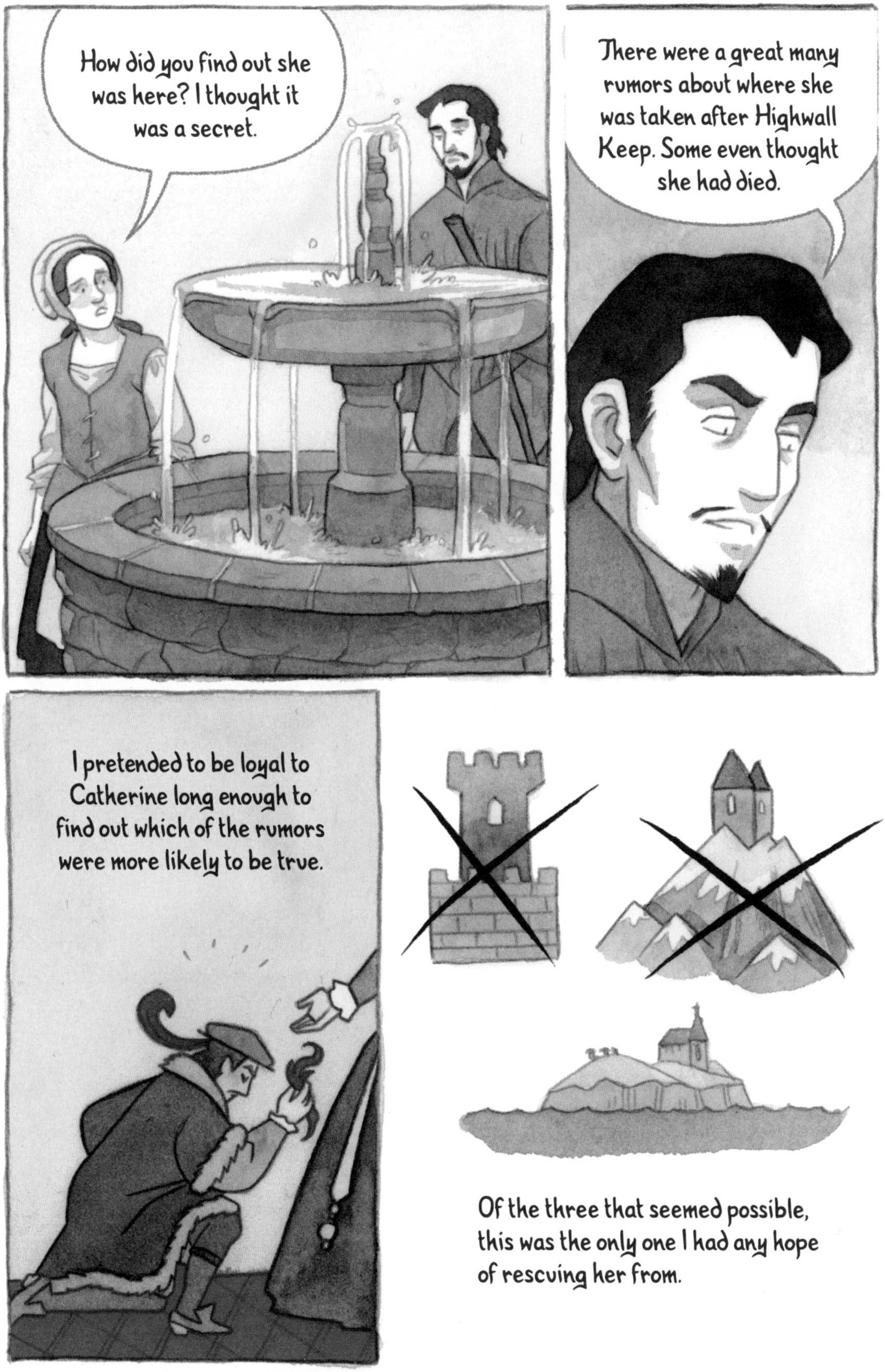

How did you find out she was here? I thought it was a secret.
There were a great many rumors about where she was taken after Highwall Keep. Some even thought she had died.
I pretended to be loyal to Catherine long enough to find out which of the rumors were more likely to be true.
Of the three that seemed possible, this was the only one I had any hope of rescuing her from.

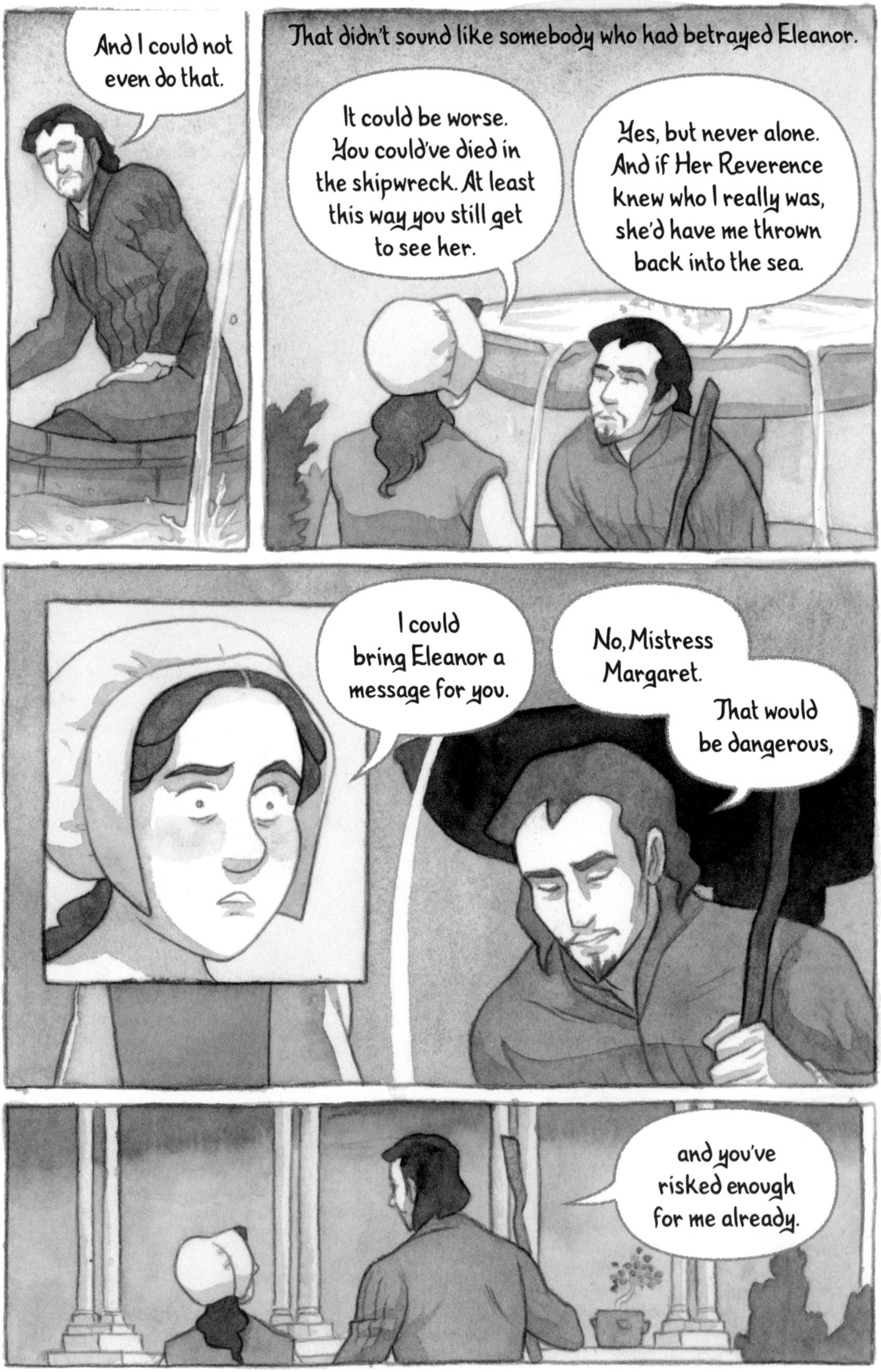
And I could not even do that.
That didn't sound like somebody who had betrayed Eleanor.
It could be worse. You could've died in the shipwreck. At least this way you still get to see her.
Yes, but never alone. And if Her Reverence knew who I really was, she'd have me thrown back into the sea.
I could bring Eleanor a message for you.
No, Mistress Margaret.
That would be dangerous,
and you've risked enough for me already.

I will talk to Eleanor, and if she has a message for you... I'll bring it.

You can't disagree with whatever she decides, can you?

...

-sigh-
No, I cannot.

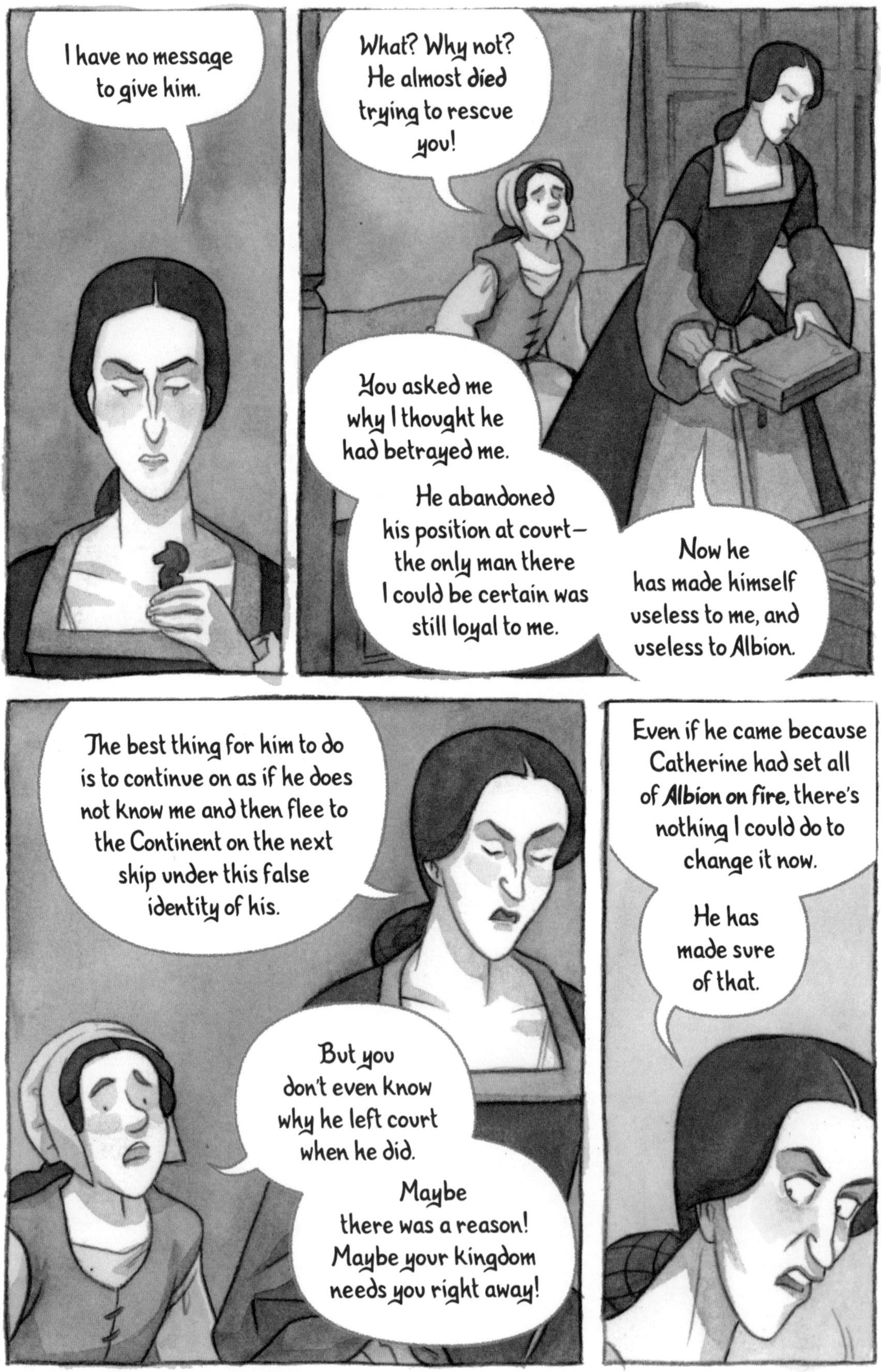
I have no message to give him.
What? Why not? He almost died trying to rescue you!
You asked me why I thought he had betrayed me.
He abandoned his position at court— the only man there I could be certain was still loyal to me.
Now he has made himself useless to me, and useless to Albion.
The best thing for him to do is to continue on as if he does not know me and then flee to the Continent on the next ship under this false identity of his.
But you don't even know why he left court when he did.
Maybe there was a reason! Maybe your kingdom needs you right away!
Even if he came because Catherine had set all of *Albion on fire*, there's nothing I could do to change it now.
He has made sure of that.

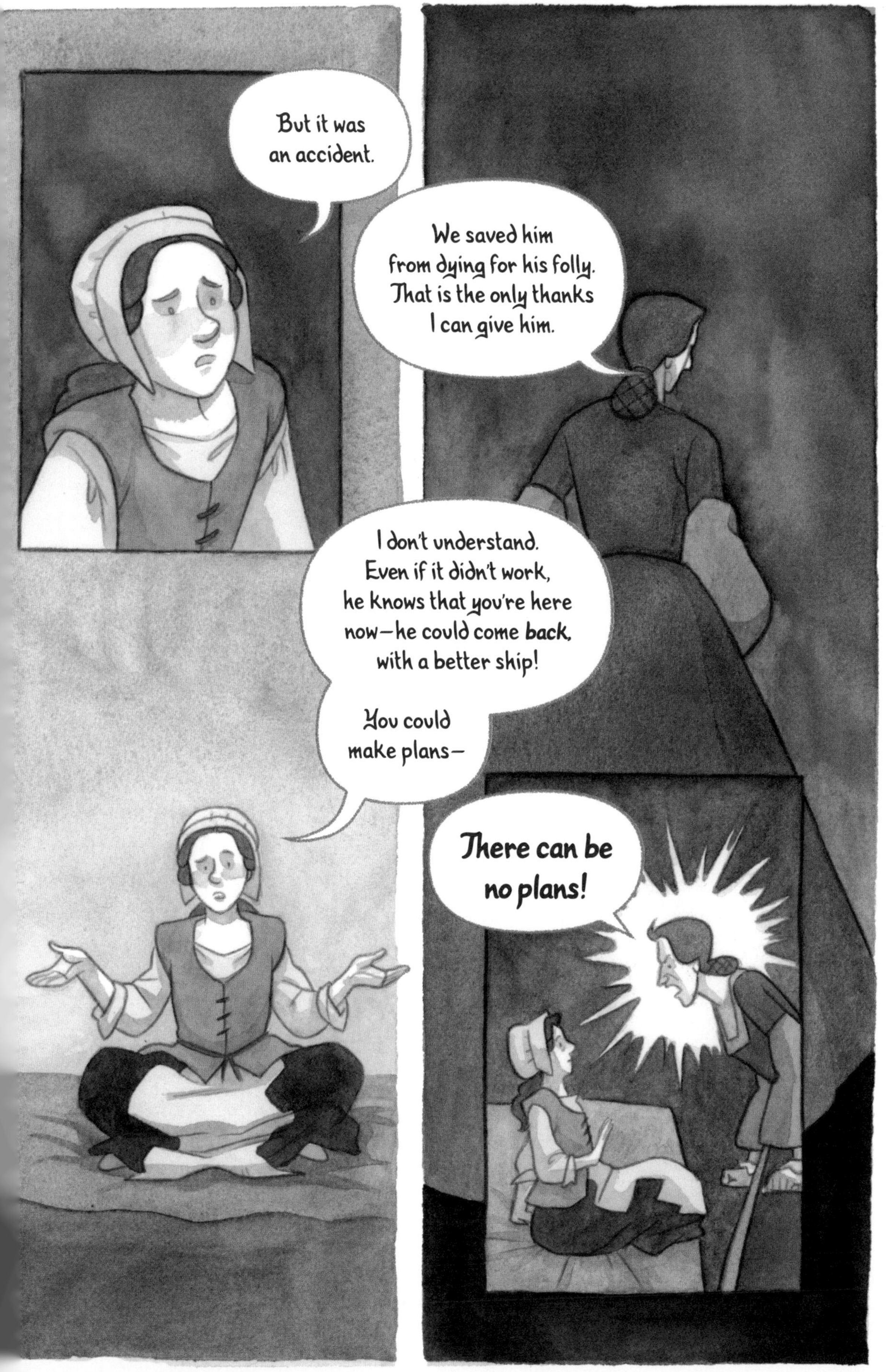
But it was an accident.
We saved him from dying for his folly. That is the only thanks I can give him.
I don't understand. Even if it didn't work, he knows that you're here now—he could come *back*, with a better ship!
You could make plans—
There can be no plans!

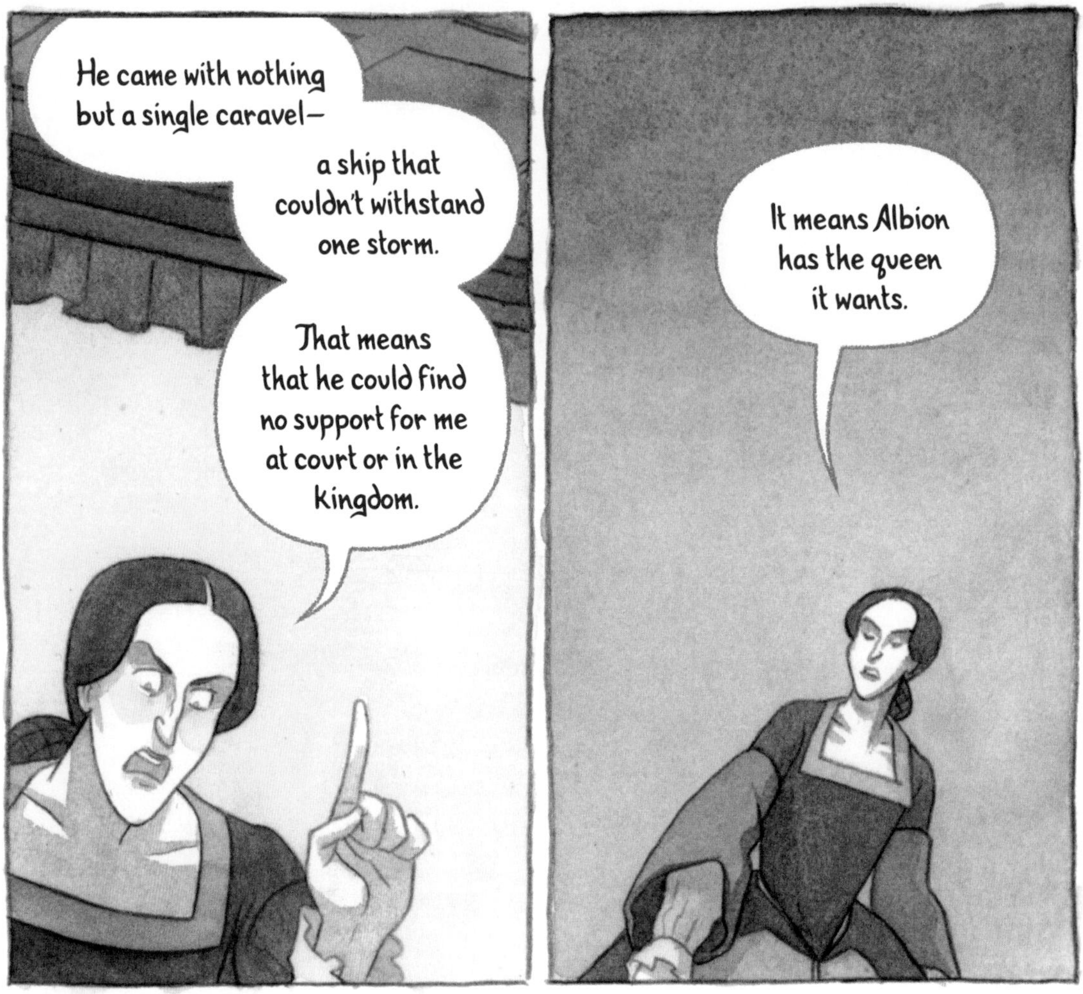
He came with nothing but a single caravel—
a ship that couldn't withstand one storm.
That means that he could find no support for me at court or in the kingdom.
It means Albion has the queen it wants.

I wasn't so sure that was true.

Francis was kind and quiet and brave, and he had risked his life to help Eleanor—despite how awful and strange she could be sometimes. If he still wanted her to be queen, surely other people in Albion felt the same way.

Mother Mary Clemence was the opposite of Francis in every way. She had been happy to hear that Catherine had executed or imprisoned so many of her own subjects, as if it were something to be proud of.

What if I had never met Eleanor at all and simply had to pick between a queen chosen by Francis, or a queen chosen by Mother Mary Clemence?

That was an easy question to answer.

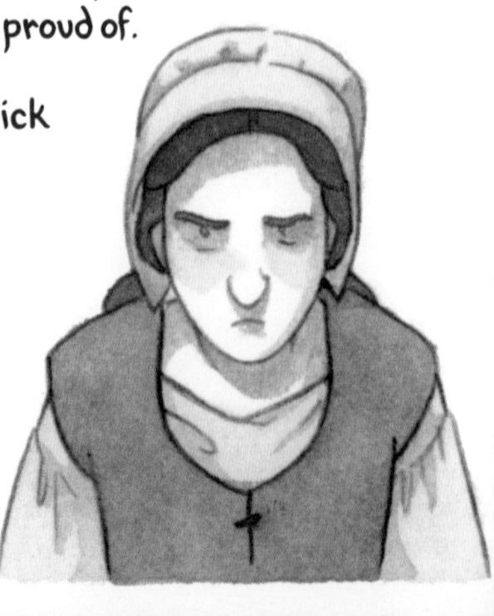

But if Eleanor refused to talk to Francis—the one person who might be able to convince her that there was still hope—then there would be no choosing at all. Not for any of us, and not for Albion.

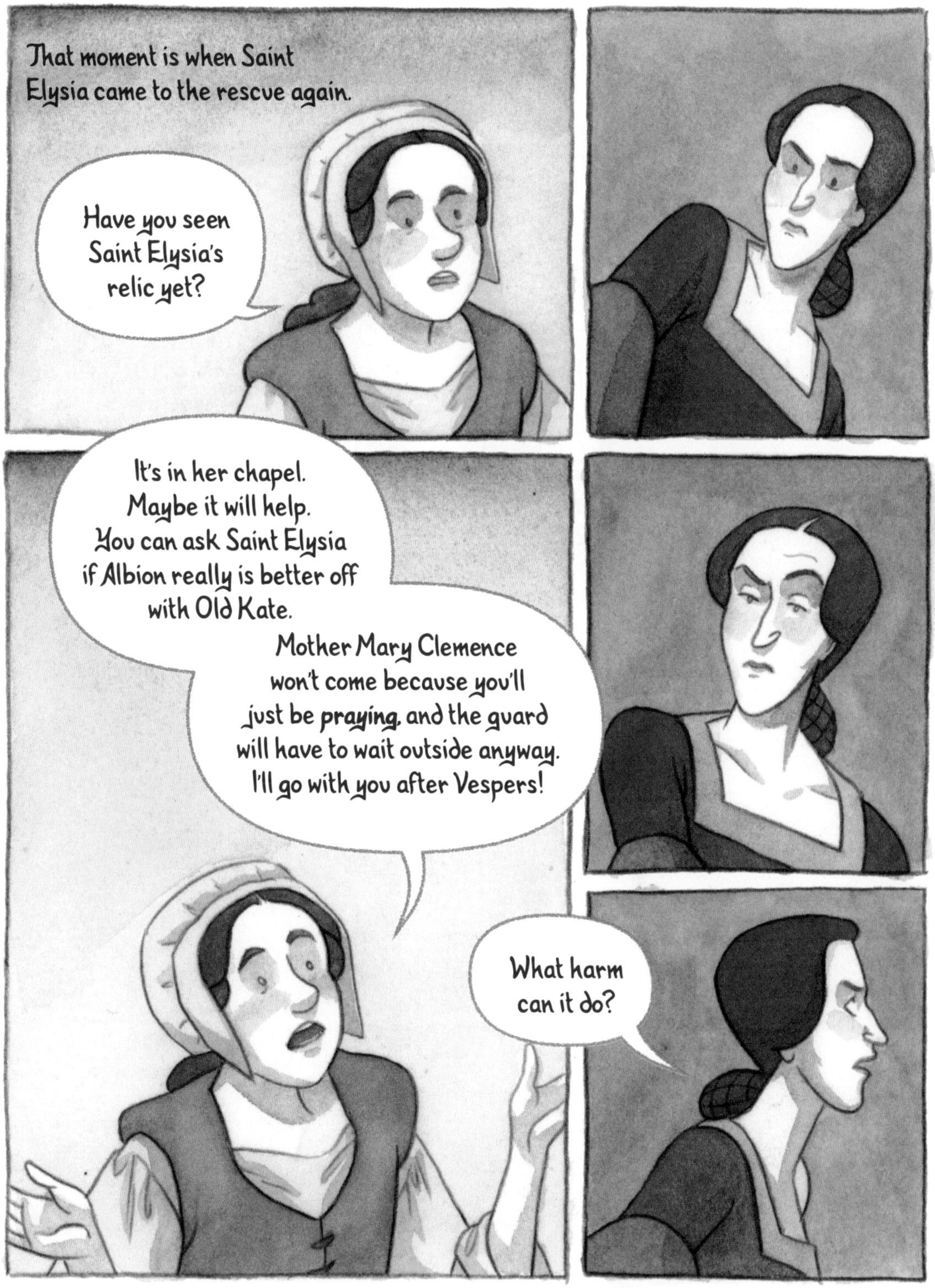
That moment is when Saint Elysia came to the rescue again.
Have you seen Saint Elysia's relic yet?
It's in her chapel. Maybe it will help. You can ask Saint Elysia if Albion really is better off with Old Kate.
Mother Mary Clemence won't come because you'll just be *praying*, and the guard will have to wait outside anyway. I'll go with you after Vespers!
What harm can it do?

There are many, many saints, of course. Saint Elysia isn't the only one.

Saints are mostly people who once walked around and ate breakfast and put their shoes on one at a time, just like you or me. They did something amazing enough that instead of just going to heaven after they die, they become messengers to heaven!

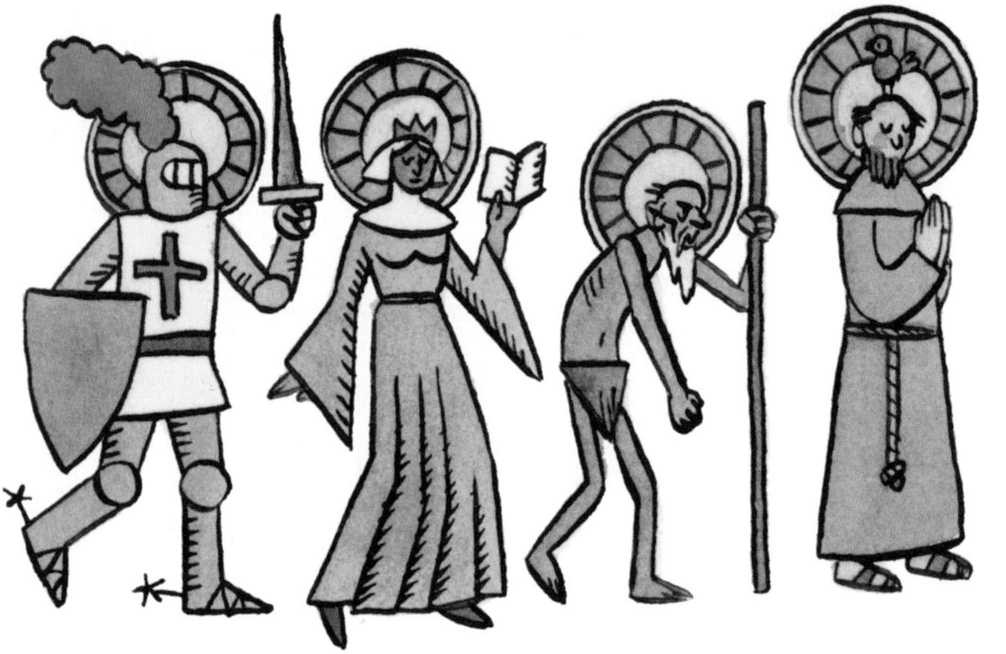

Not everybody gets to be a saint through miracles and good deeds, like Saint Elysia. Some saints died while bravely defending their faith.

Those saints are called **martyrs.**

Martyrs have died in all kinds of awful ways. If something terrible happens to you, it's probably not as bad as being eaten by lions, like Saint Leonisius was.

And if you are being eaten by lions, you know that Saint Leonisius understands.

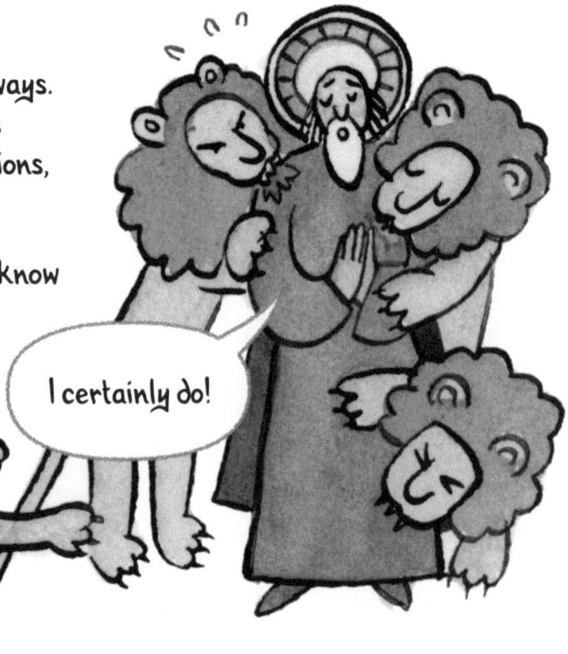
I certainly do!

After someone becomes a saint, she sits in heaven and listens to the prayers of living people, and tries to help them. You can choose to pray to a saint who had a problem like yours when they were alive. Or you can pray to a saint who performed the kinds of miracles you're hoping will happen to you—like curing a sickness or surviving a storm at sea.

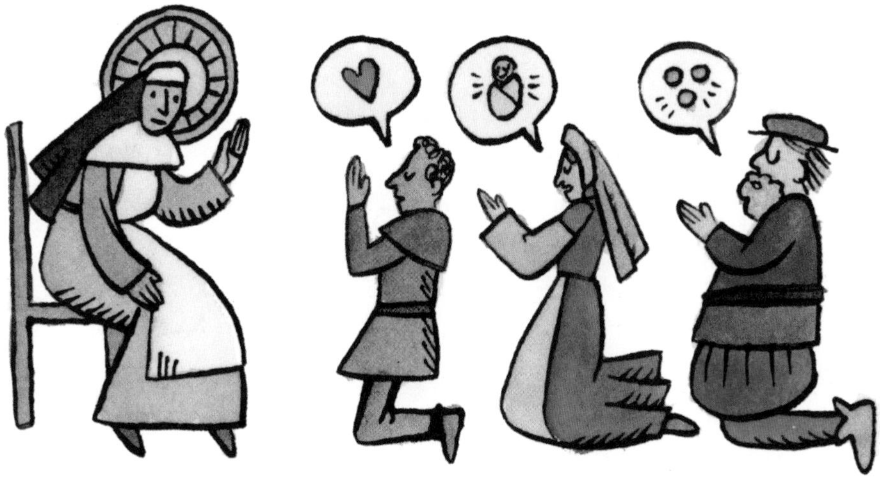

Praying to a saint, or doing something else to honor them, is called **venerating**. You can also pray to a saint in a place that was important to them. Some people think that makes it more likely that a saint will hear you.

Something else that can help you get even closer to a saint is a **relic**. Holy relics are things that used to belong to saints, or important objects that they touched—sometimes they're even *parts* of saints!

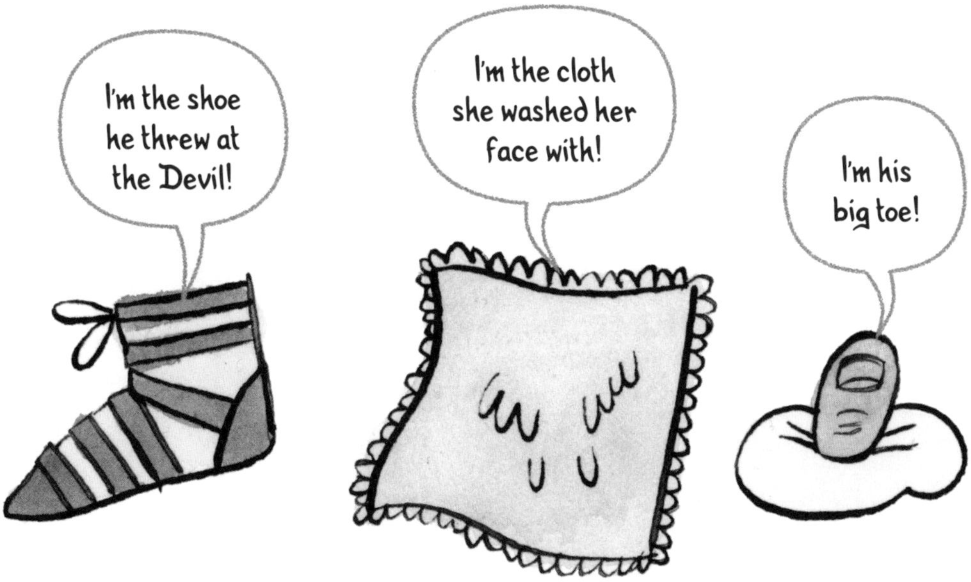
I'm the shoe he threw at the Devil!
I'm the cloth she washed her face with!
I'm his big toe!

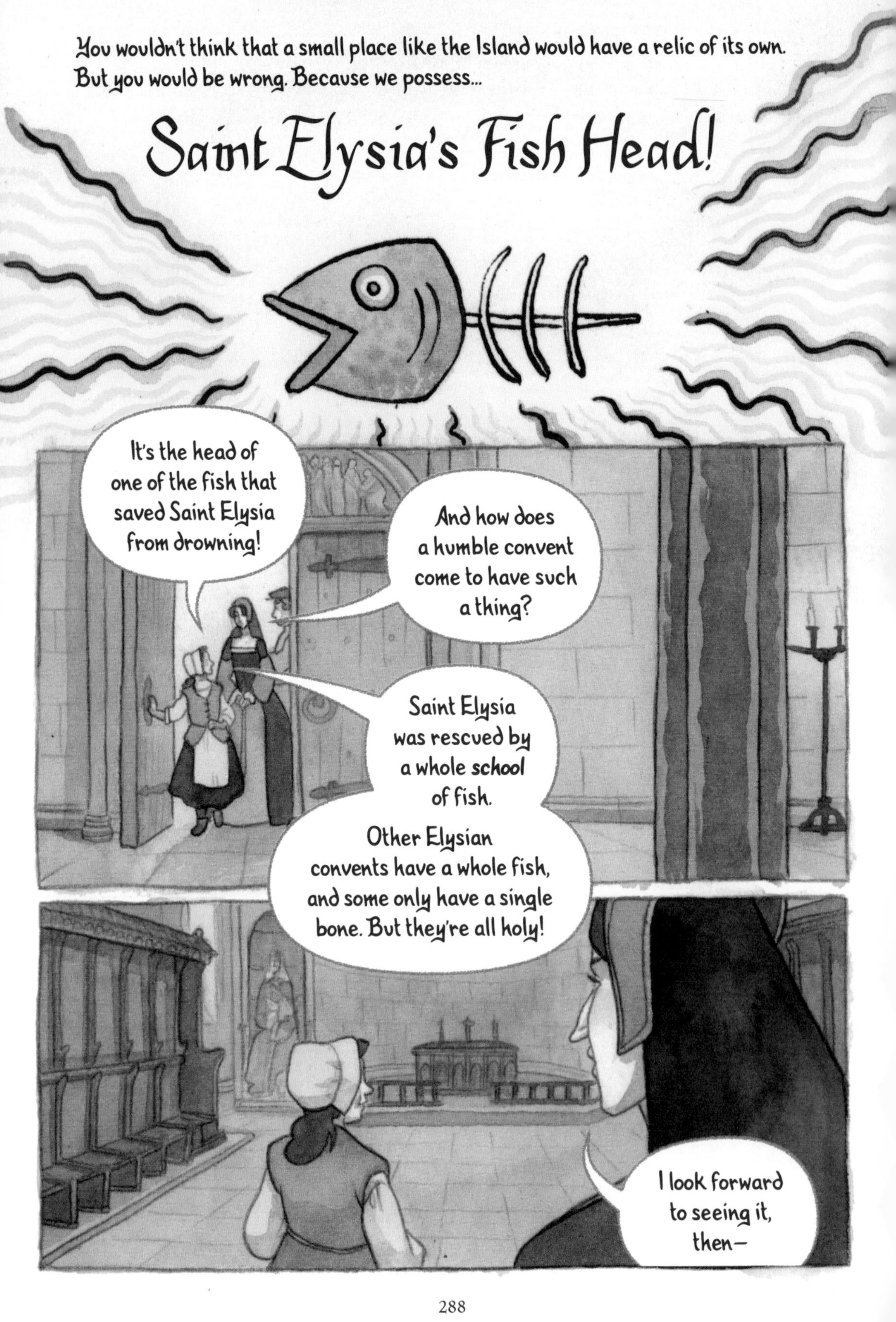
You wouldn't think that a small place like the Island would have a relic of its own. But you would be wrong. Because we possess...
Saint Elysia's Fish Head!
It's the head of one of the fish that saved Saint Elysia from drowning!
And how does a humble convent come to have such a thing?
Saint Elysia was rescued by a whole school of fish.
Other Elysian convents have a whole fish, and some only have a single bone. But they're all holy!
I look forward to seeing it, then—

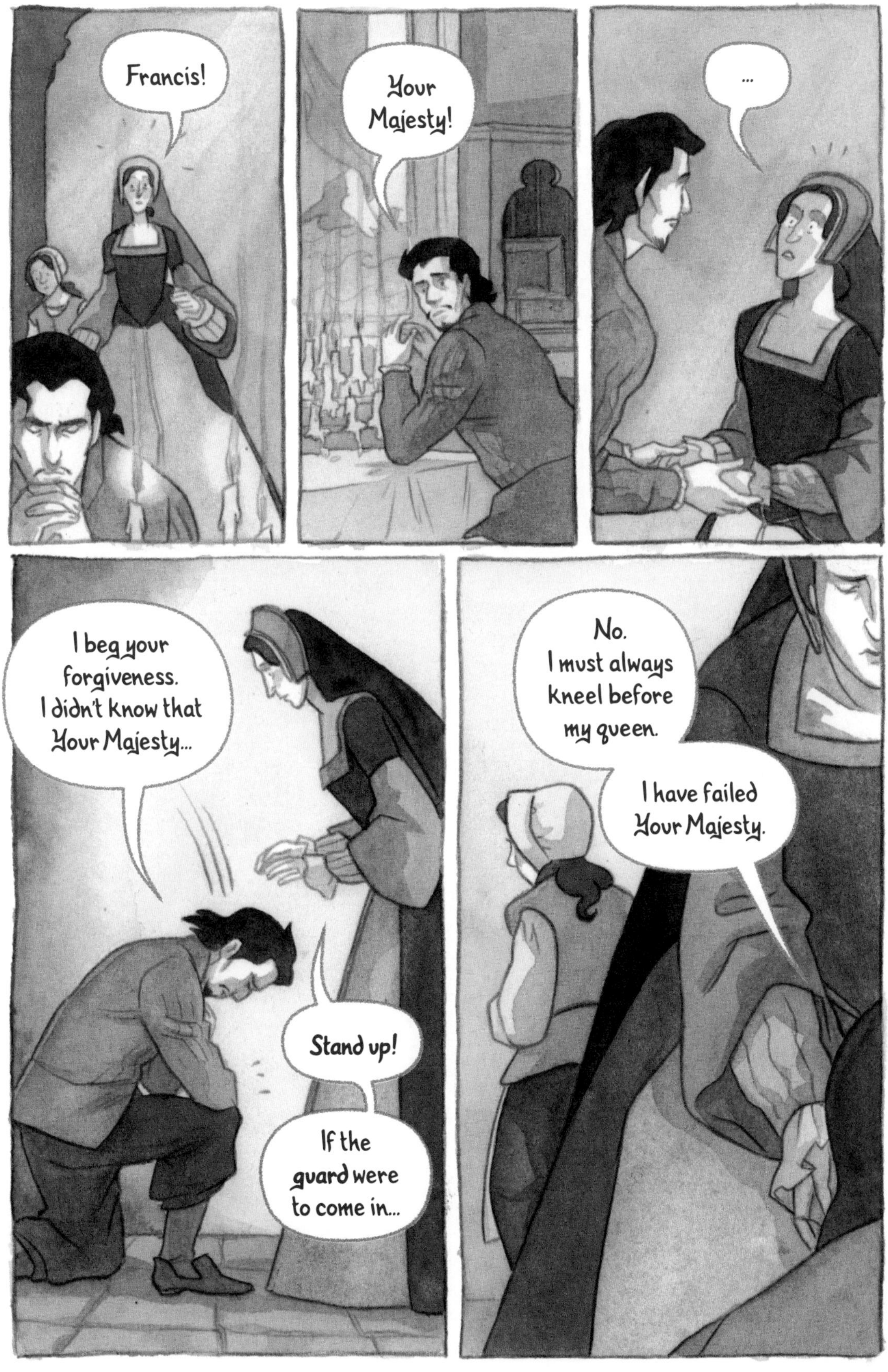
Francis!
Your Majesty!
...
I beg your forgiveness. I didn't know that Your Majesty...
Stand up!
If the guard were to come in...
No. I must always kneel before my queen.
I have failed Your Majesty.

...Nonsense.

I went to sit in the choir,

to make sure that the guard
didn't come in and find them.

But I didn't have to worry.
Harold Carpenter was fast asleep outside.

It was hours yet until the sisters would come
in for their next prayers. The church smelled
of beeswax and dust and smoke and old wood.

It seemed as though even the Sorrowful Son
was fast asleep in his mother's arms.

Had I ever slept in my mother's arms?

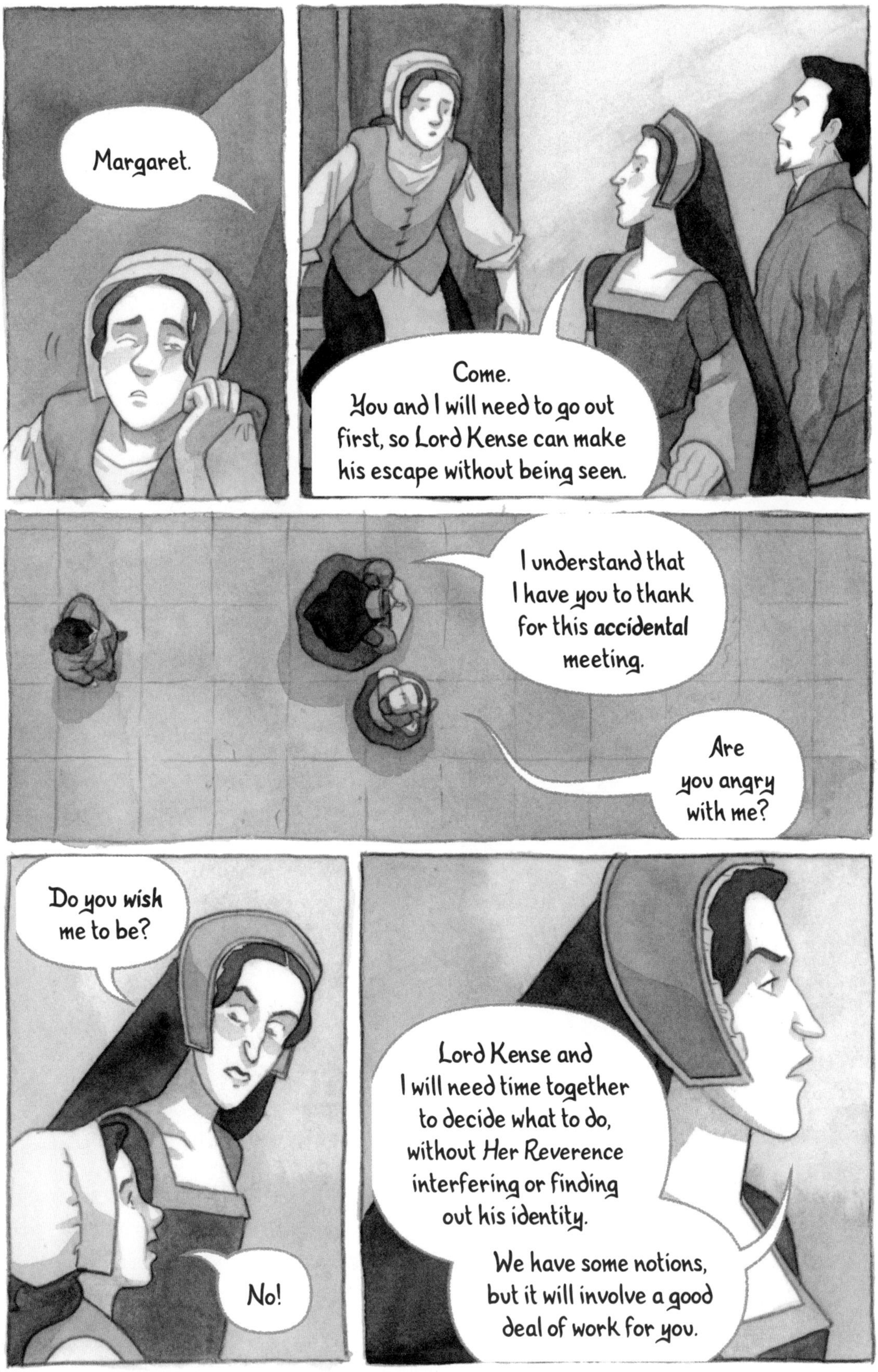
Margaret.
Come.
You and I will need to go out first, so Lord Kense can make his escape without being seen.
I understand that I have you to thank for this accidental meeting.
Are you angry with me?
Do you wish me to be?
No!
Lord Kense and I will need time together to decide what to do, without Her Reverence interfering or finding out his identity.
We have some notions, but it will involve a good deal of work for you.

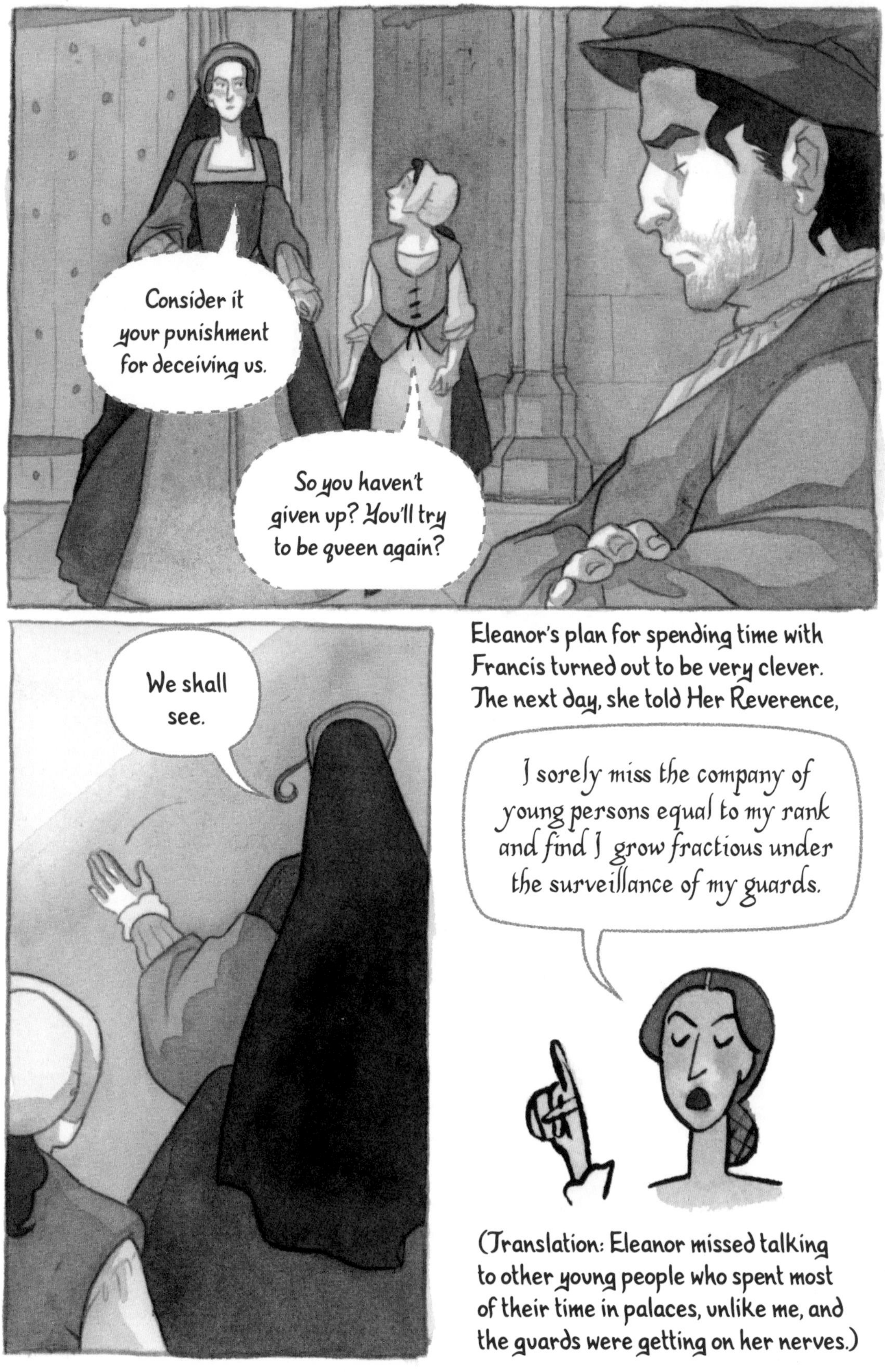
Consider it your punishment for deceiving us.
So you haven't given up? You'll try to be queen again?
We shall see.
Eleanor's plan for spending time with Francis turned out to be very clever. The next day, she told Her Reverence,
I sorely miss the company of young persons equal to my rank and find I grow fractious under the surveillance of my guards.
(Translation: Eleanor missed talking to other young people who spent most of their time in palaces, unlike me, and the guards were getting on her nerves.)

And then:

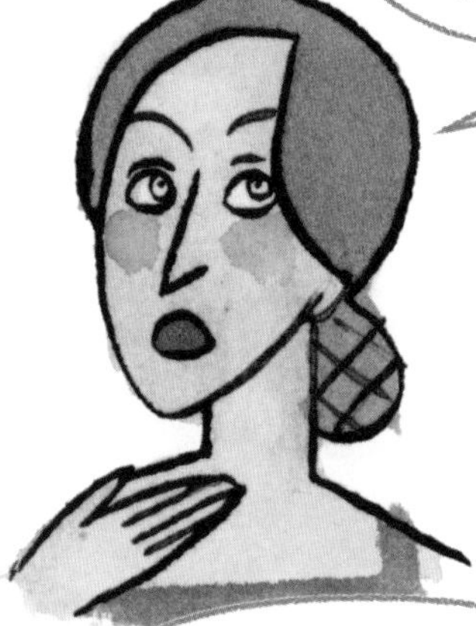

Sir Thomas is a man of discretion and valor, and you can have no objection to his loyalties.
He shall inform me of all the changes Her Royal Highness has wrought on Albion, and I cannot but take moral instruction from his accounts.

(Translation: "Sir Thomas" was very proper, and since he was supposed to be loyal to Queen Catherine, he would spend all his time convincing Eleanor that Kate made a better queen after all.)

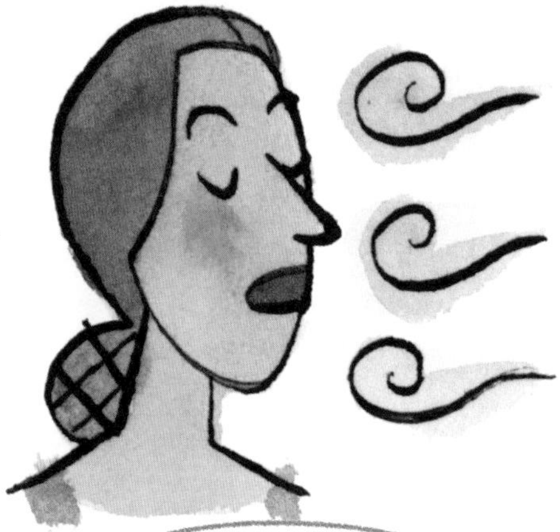

We shall avail ourselves of the curative sea air, so as to remain robust in our confinement.

(Translation: They'd walk around in the cold and wet for exercise, which Mary Clemence and her sore foot would absolutely hate.)

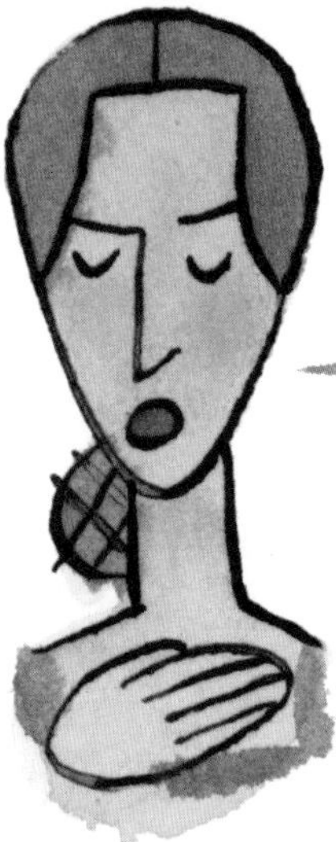

I shall require a chaperone, of course.
The maid, Margaret, has fulfilled the role of lady's companion sufficient to judge propriety, and her unfailing honesty cannot be questioned.

(Translation: I would walk around with them to make sure they got into no mischief, and I could be trusted to give Mother Mary Clemence a truthful report of what they did.)

In other words,

I would have to lie.

The Library on the Island doesn't have very many exciting books.

There are mostly books of prayers, books **about** prayers, and books that teach you languages (so you can pray in them). Only a few of them have good stories. There is exactly one book about love—the kind that you fall into, anyway.

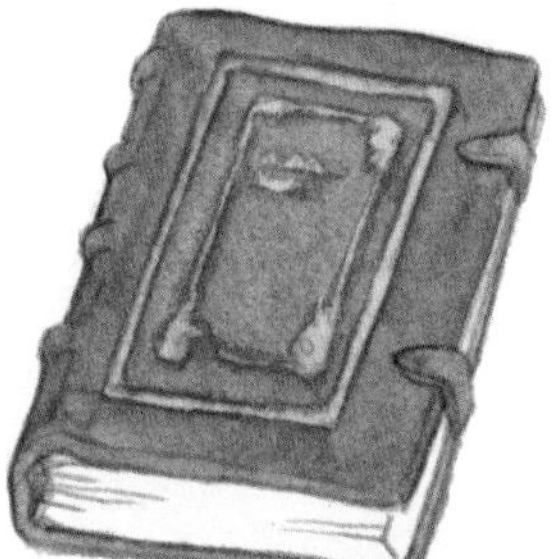

The book is about a knight and a noble maiden.

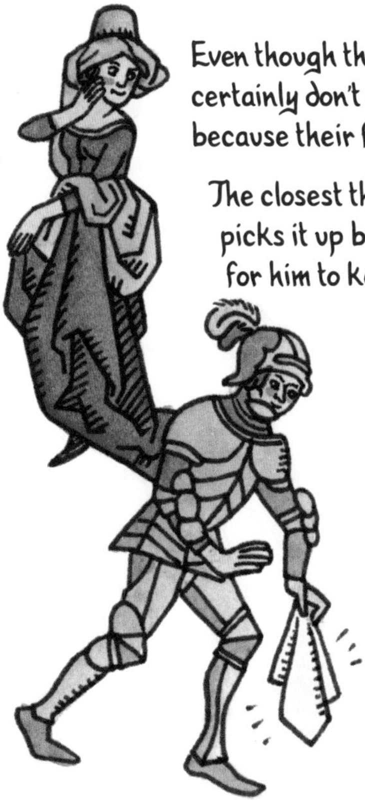

Even though they're in love, they never ever touch, and they certainly don't **kiss**. They hardly even get to speak to each other, because their families have promised to marry them to other people.

The closest they get is when the maiden drops her kerchief, and he picks it up but doesn't give it back to her. He **knows** that she meant for him to keep it, even though she never said.

(Personally, I would be angry if somebody kept **my** kerchief without asking permission, because the embroidery on it took a very long time.)

The maiden becomes very sick, and is about to die, because she's so sad that she can never marry the knight. The only cure is for her to smell a holy rose that grows on top of a mountain far away.

The knight rides through a winter storm and defeats a **whole army** and walks over a bridge of fire that burns his feet, all to get the rose.

He finally returns and brings the rose to her in time. She breathes the rose and is cured, but then he dies at her feet because of all his wounds!

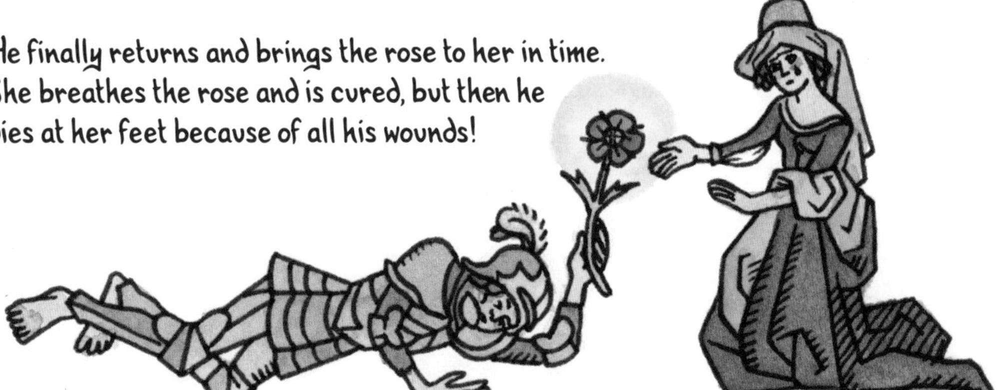

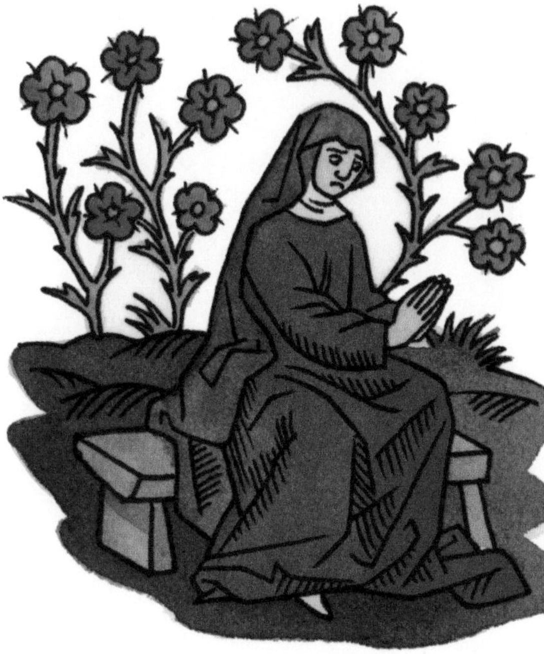

After that, the maiden becomes a nun. (That's the way a lot of stories about maidens end.)

She spends the rest of her life praying for the knight's soul to go to heaven.

I always thought the story was silly.

If that was love, then I was glad that I lived in a convent, where you didn't have to worry about it.

If the girl had just gone straight to the convent at the very beginning, maybe the knight would have lived a long life.

Sister Sybil told me that the book isn't really about the **marrying** kind of love.

It's about loving God so much that you'd give up everything you have, or do terrible and frightening things, or even die, like the saints, if God told you it was the right thing to do.

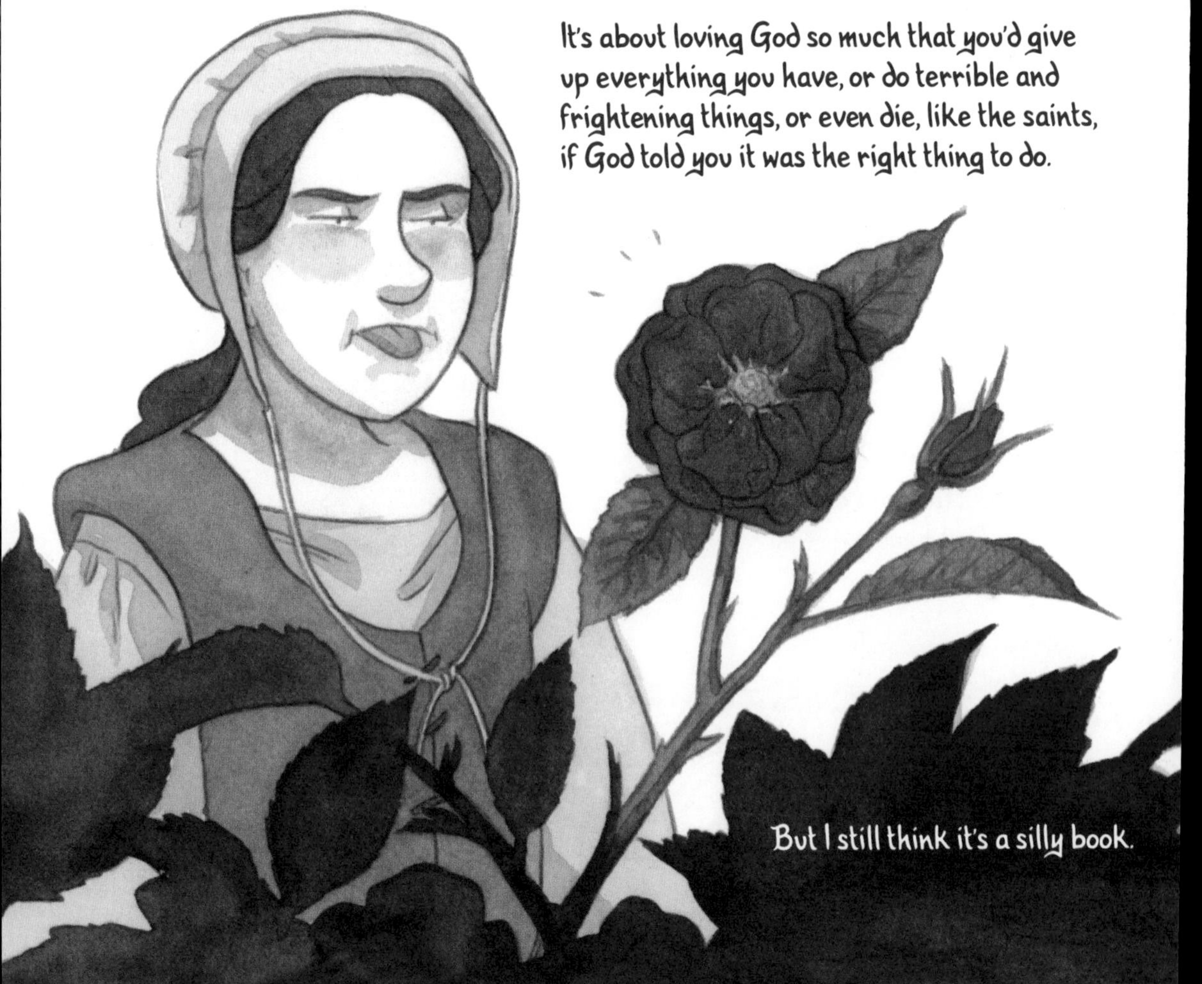
But I still think it's a silly book.

I spent a good part of the winter months walking six feet ahead of, or behind, Eleanor and Francis. Sometimes the weather was too bad for walking and Mother Mary Clemence was in bed with her gouty foot up. Then we sat in the Warming Chamber together while Eleanor played songs on her lute for us, or Francis and Eleanor played chess while I embroidered.

When the weather was good, we would go down to the waves and walk. Twice we went skating on the pond. Francis was very good at it. Eleanor wasn't. He didn't say so.

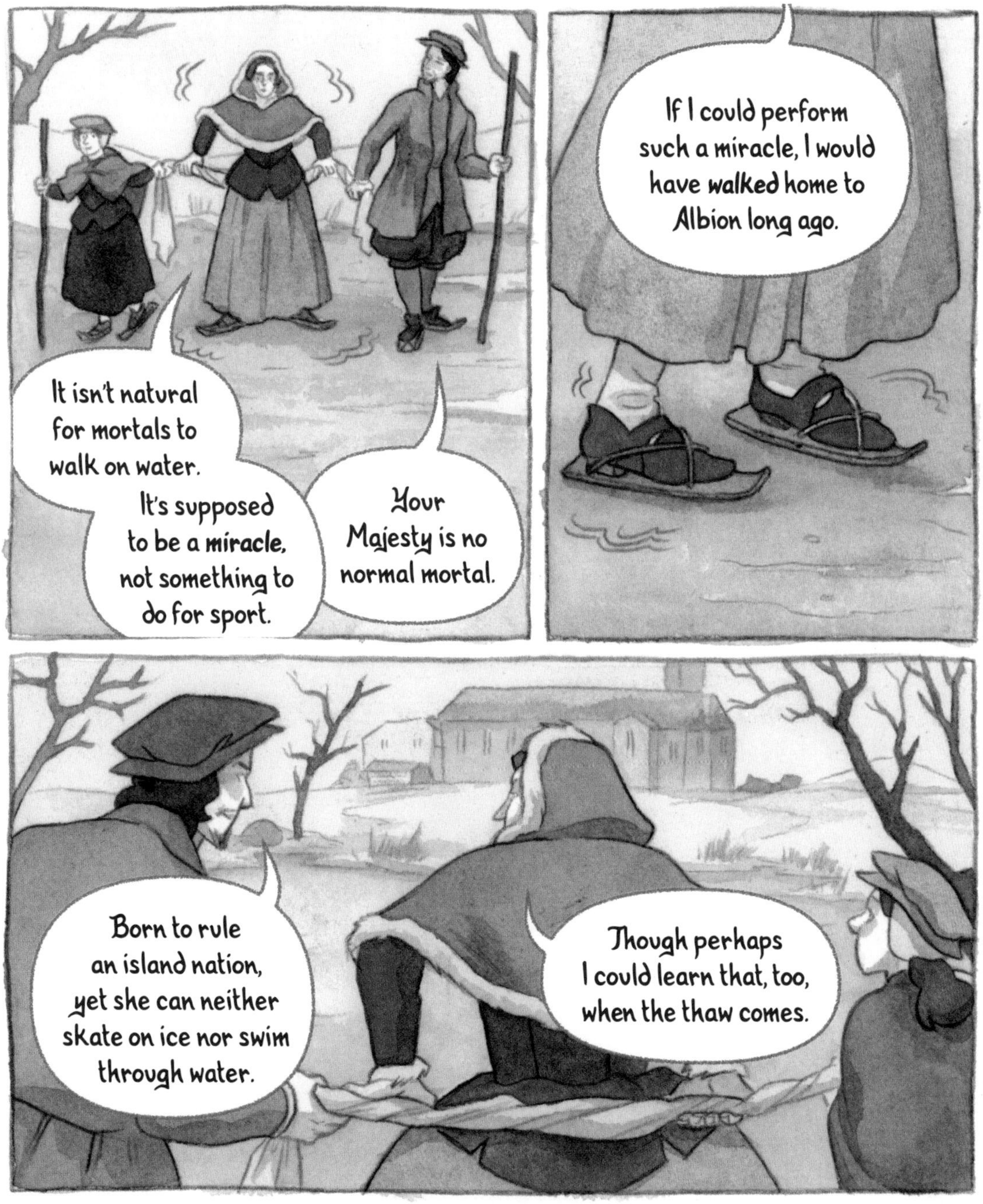

It isn't natural for mortals to walk on water.
It's supposed to be a miracle, not something to do for sport.
Your Majesty is no normal mortal.
If I could perform such a miracle, I would have walked home to Albion long ago.
Born to rule an island nation, yet she can neither skate on ice nor swim through water.
Though perhaps I could learn that, too, when the thaw comes.

But at least twice a week they would have one of their **secret conversations.**
That's when I had to stand a ways away and make sure nobody was coming near who might overhear them.

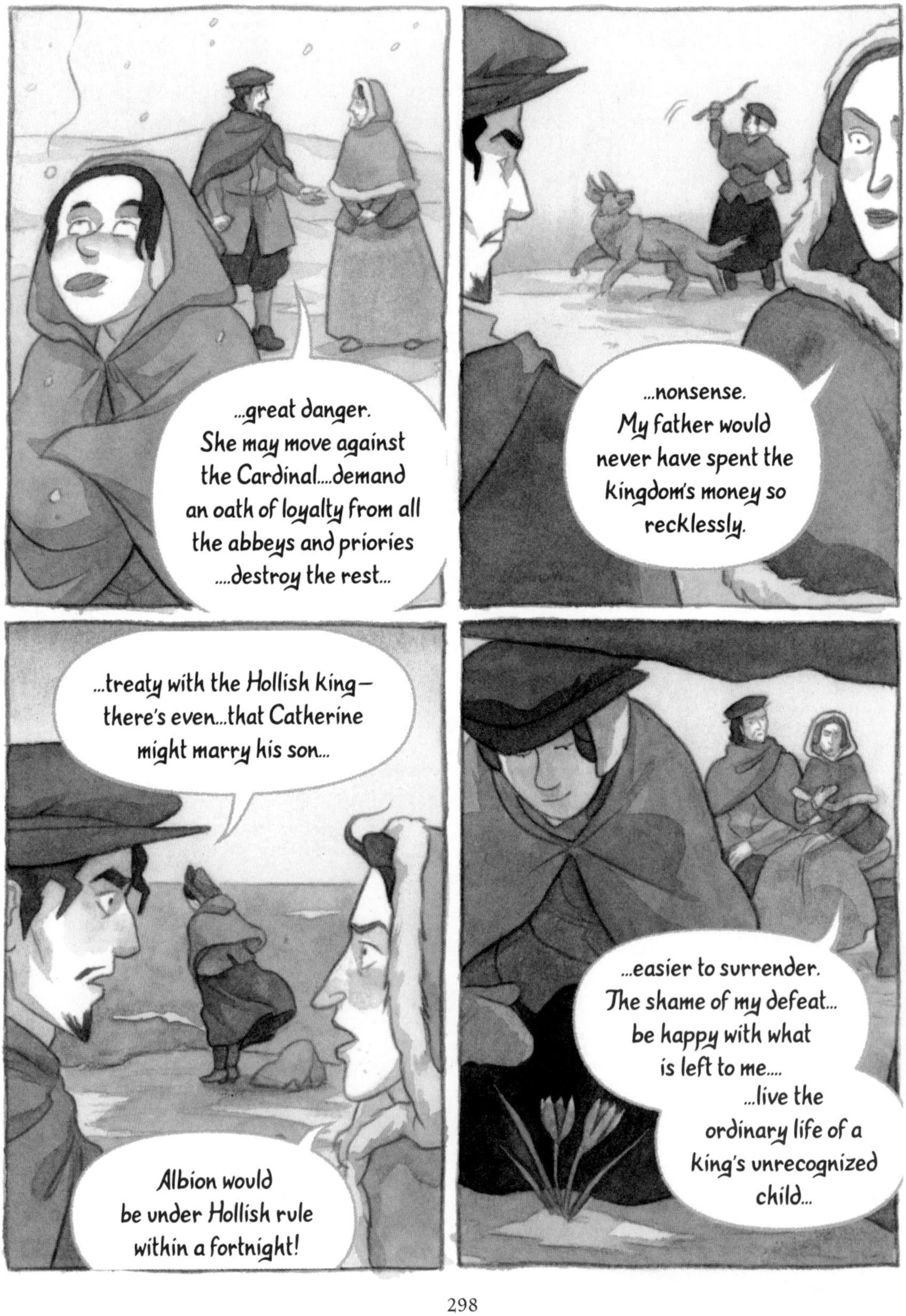

...great danger. She may move against the Cardinal....demand an oath of loyalty from all the abbeys and priories ....destroy the rest...
...nonsense. My father would never have spent the kingdom's money so recklessly.
...treaty with the Hollish king— there's even...that Catherine might marry his son...
Albion would be under Hollish rule within a fortnight!
...easier to surrender. The shame of my defeat... be happy with what is left to me.... ...live the ordinary life of a king's unrecognized child...

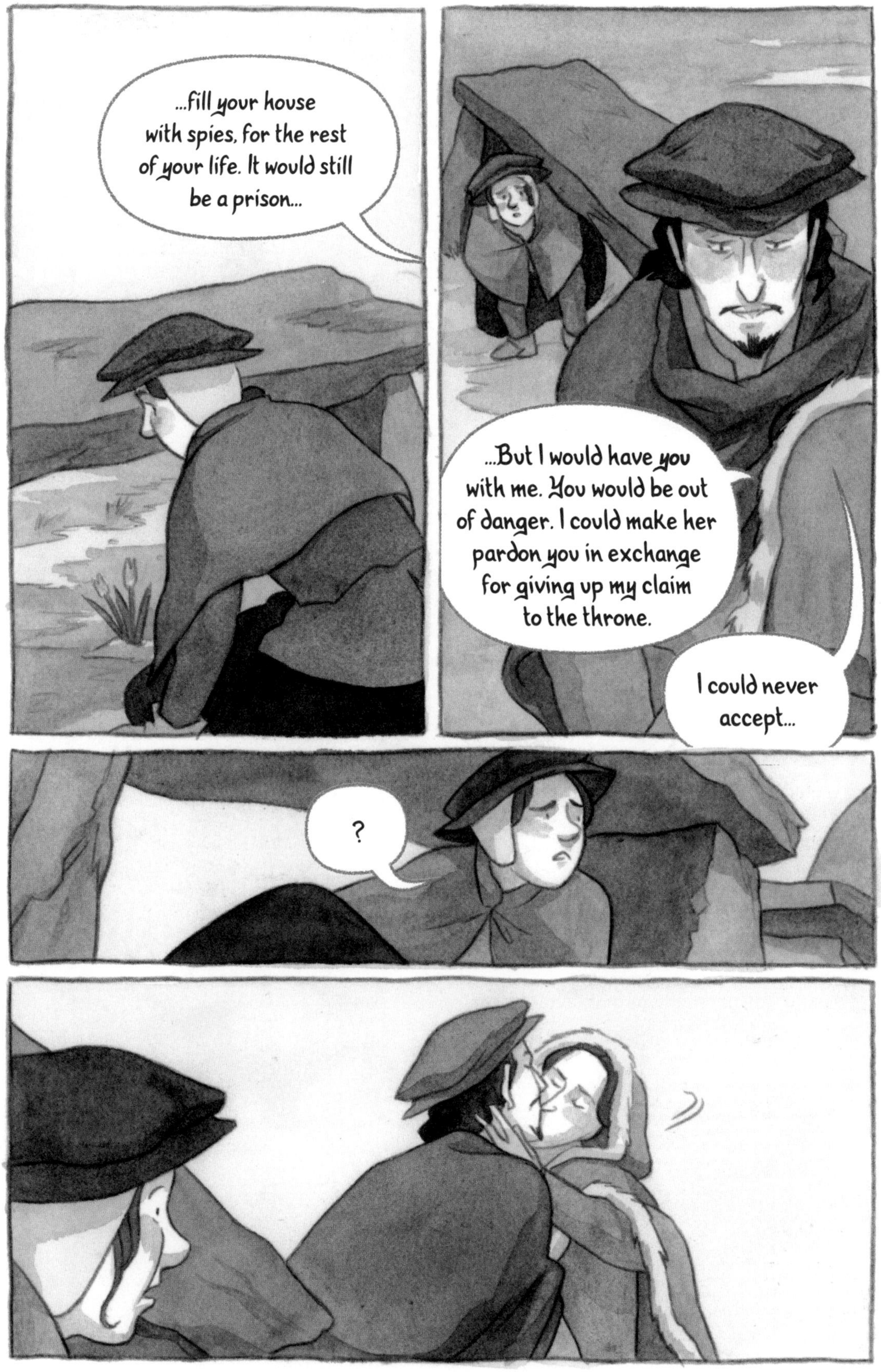
...fill your house with spies, for the rest of your life. It would still be a prison...
...But I would have you with me. You would be out of danger. I could make her pardon you in exchange for giving up my claim to the throne.
I could never accept...
?

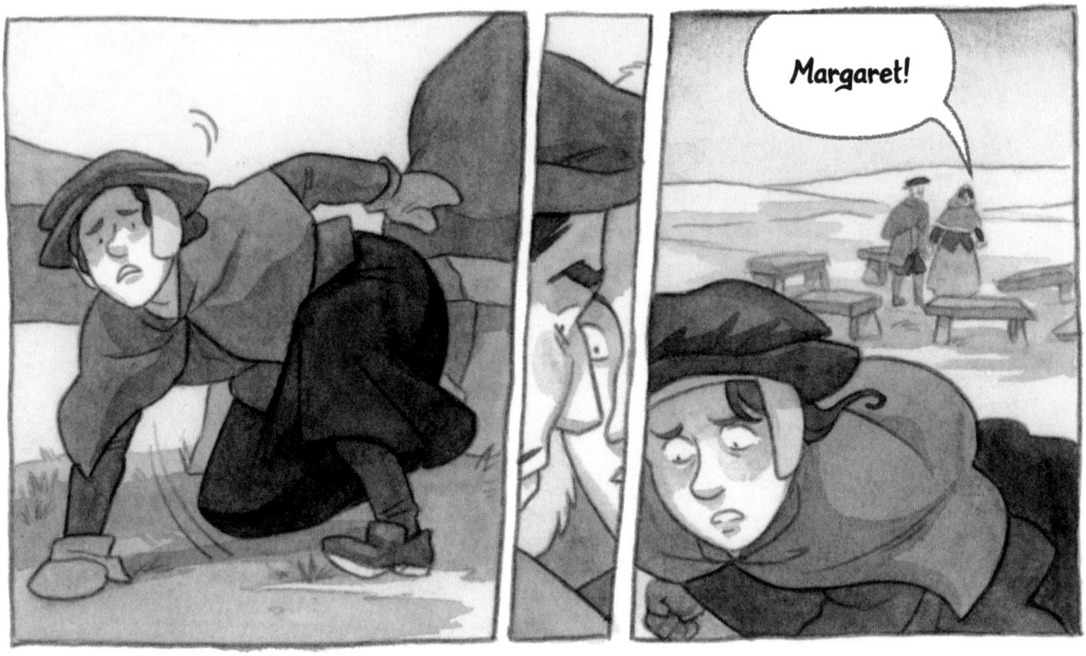
Margaret!

I had never seen a man and a woman kiss. In fact, the only kissing I'd seen at all was Father Ambrose kissing us in church as part of the benediction, but that was *holy*.

I thought Francis was loyal to Eleanor as his queen. How could he *kiss* her? And how could *she* say that she would give up the throne? I thought he had risked his life to give her the chance to be queen again!

Had Francis lied to me? Had he come here like the knight bringing his rose? Had they kissed in Saint Elysia's chapel while I looked out for them?

Kissing was certainly and absolutely not allowed there. Saint Elysia would be *furious*!

And what would happen if Mother Mary Clemence caught them?

Terrible things, and I would be punished right along with them!

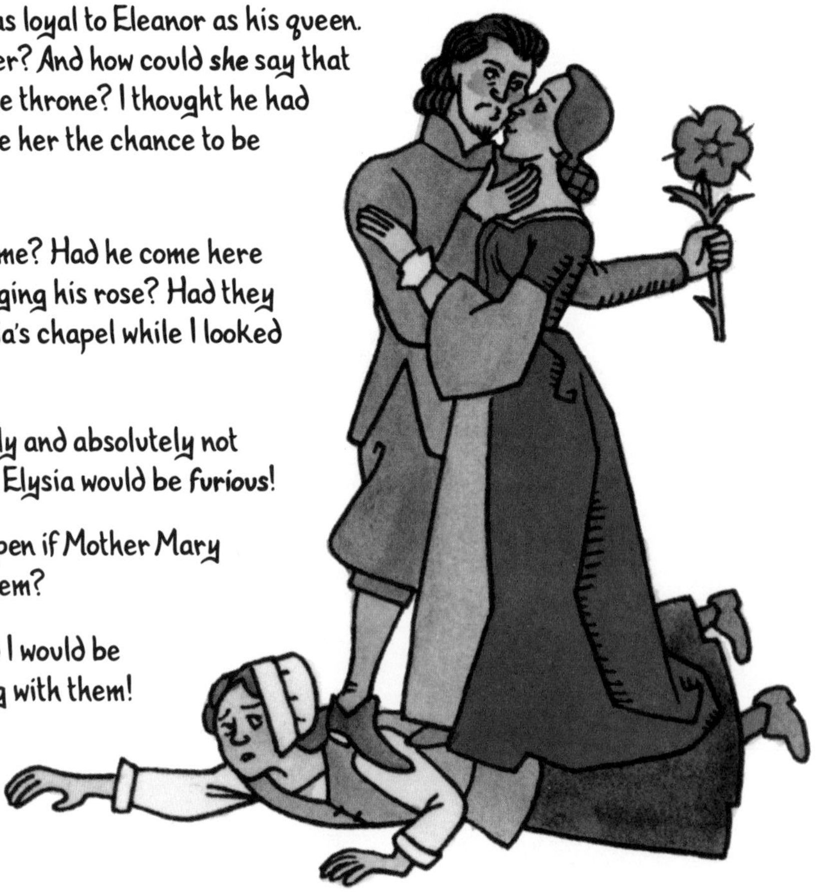

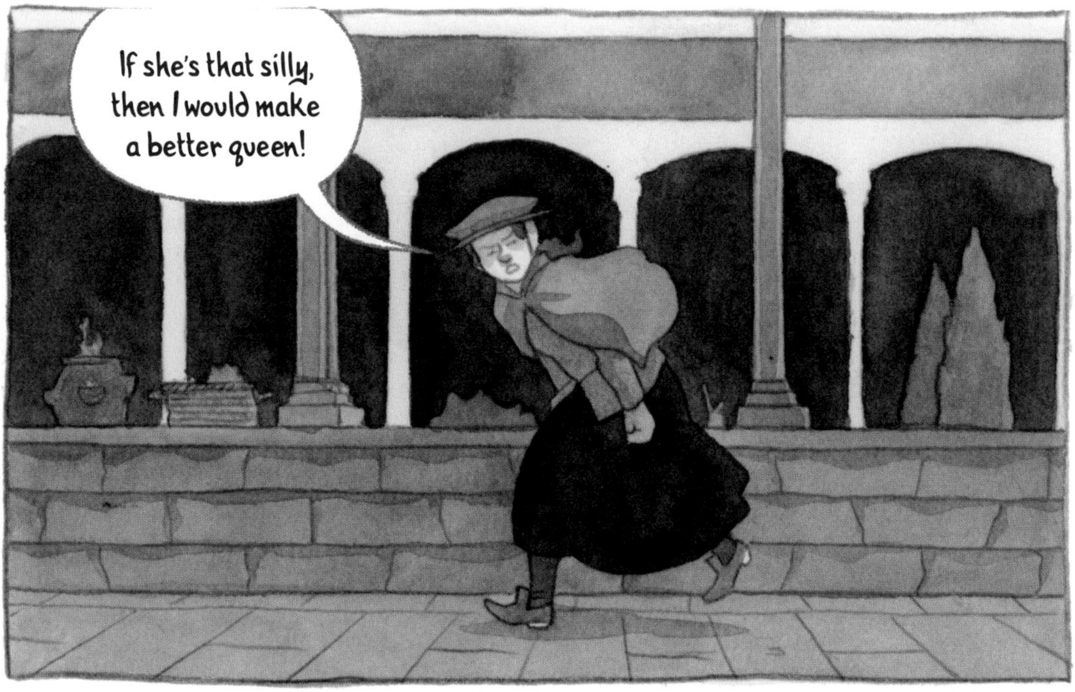
If she's that silly, then I would make a better queen!

And I could be queen. I could tell Mother Mary Clemence everything they'd done and who Francis really was, and have them both sent away (though I would make sure they weren't executed), and I would be taken back to Albion as a hero. Then I would slip away and find my mother, who would be so happy to see me and would have proof that she and King Edmund had been married, so I was the crown princess!

Then I would reveal my true identity to the whole kingdom, and all the people of Albion would realize how good a queen I would be. They'd get rid of Old Kate right away. I would let William out of prison, and I would pardon all the sisters at the convent for their crimes. Eventually I would pardon Francis and Eleanor, but only after they apologized in front of the whole kingdom. If they didn't, they could live on the Island forever and clean out the barn every day until they forgot all about *kissing*!

All Hail Queen Margaret!

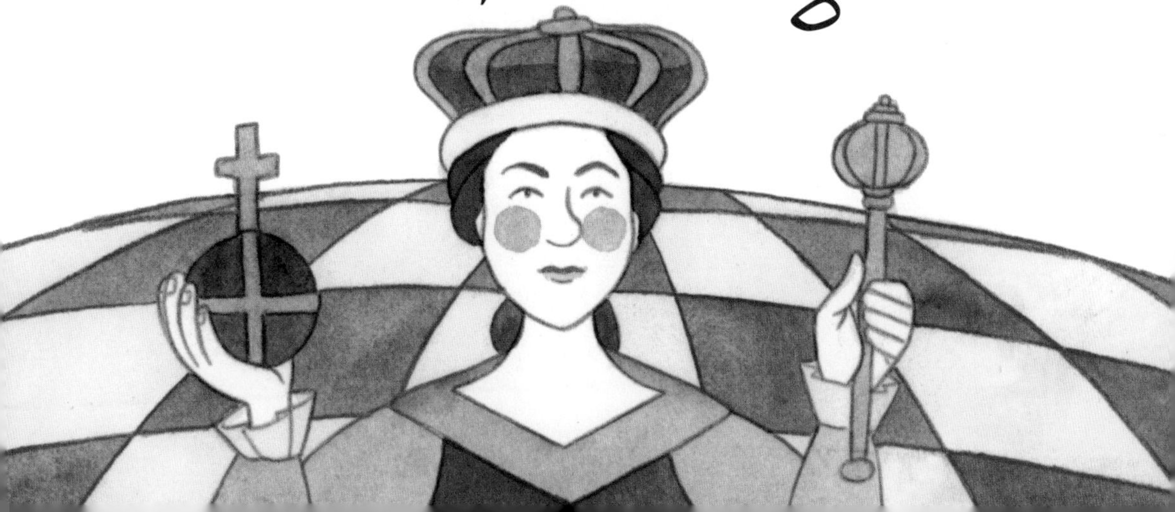

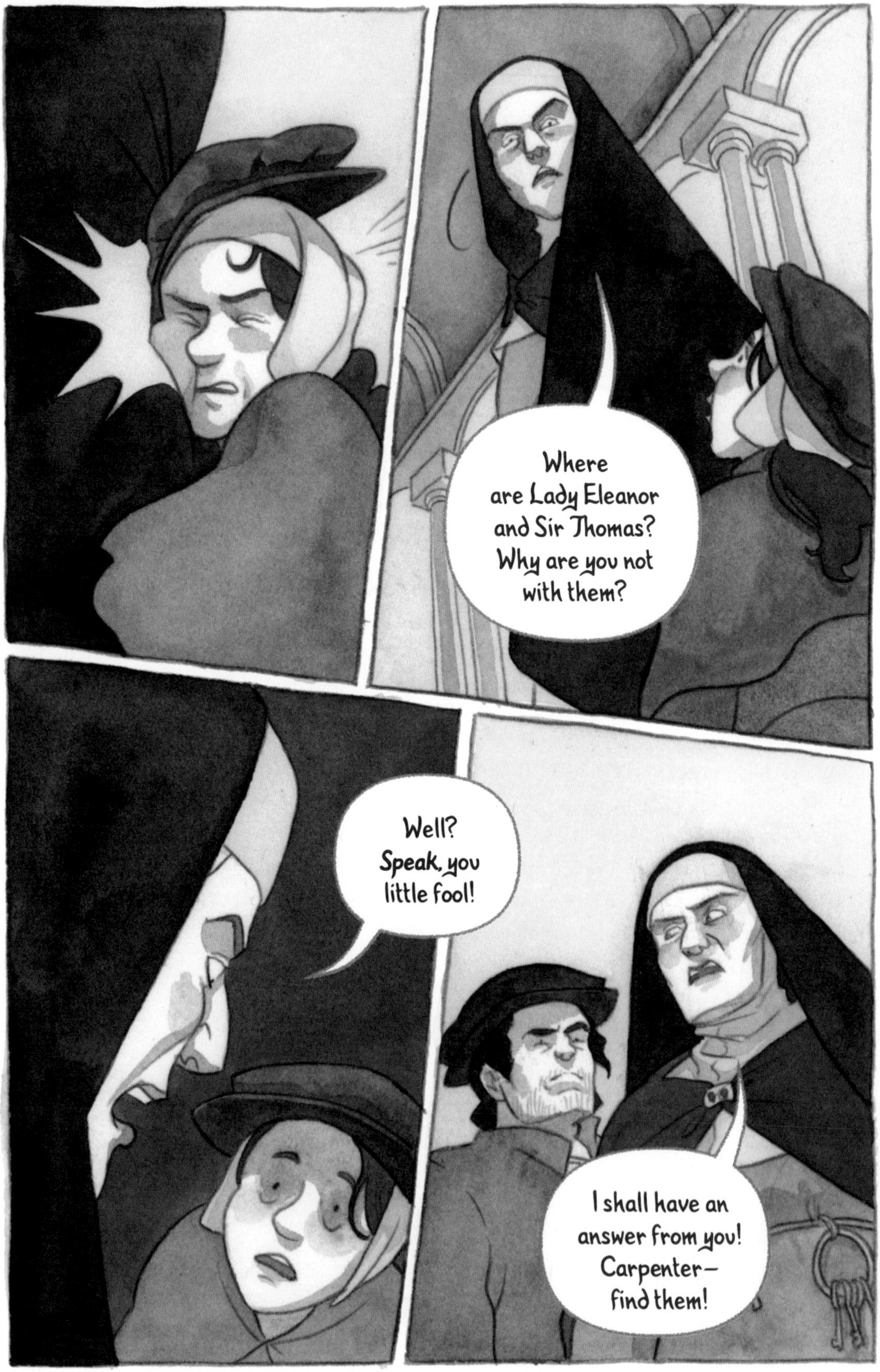
Where are Lady Eleanor and Sir Thomas? Why are you not with them?
Well? Speak, you little fool!
I shall have an answer from you! Carpenter— find them!

She dragged me by the ear all the way to Sister Agnes's chamber and pushed me down into the high-backed chair.

This is a blessed candle, called a *Liar's Taper*. It was made with beeswax taken from a honeycomb in the town of the Sorrowful Son's birth, and its wick was blessed by the Holy Father himself.

Its flame has a very particular property. Do you know what that means?

That it's unusual.

Yes. The flame of this candle is unusual because it only burns the flesh of liars.

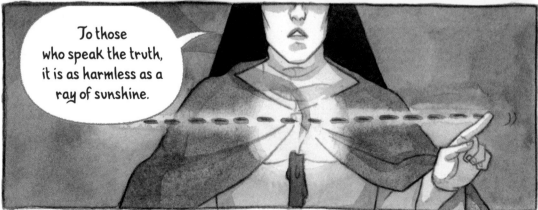

To those who speak the truth, it is as harmless as a ray of sunshine.

303

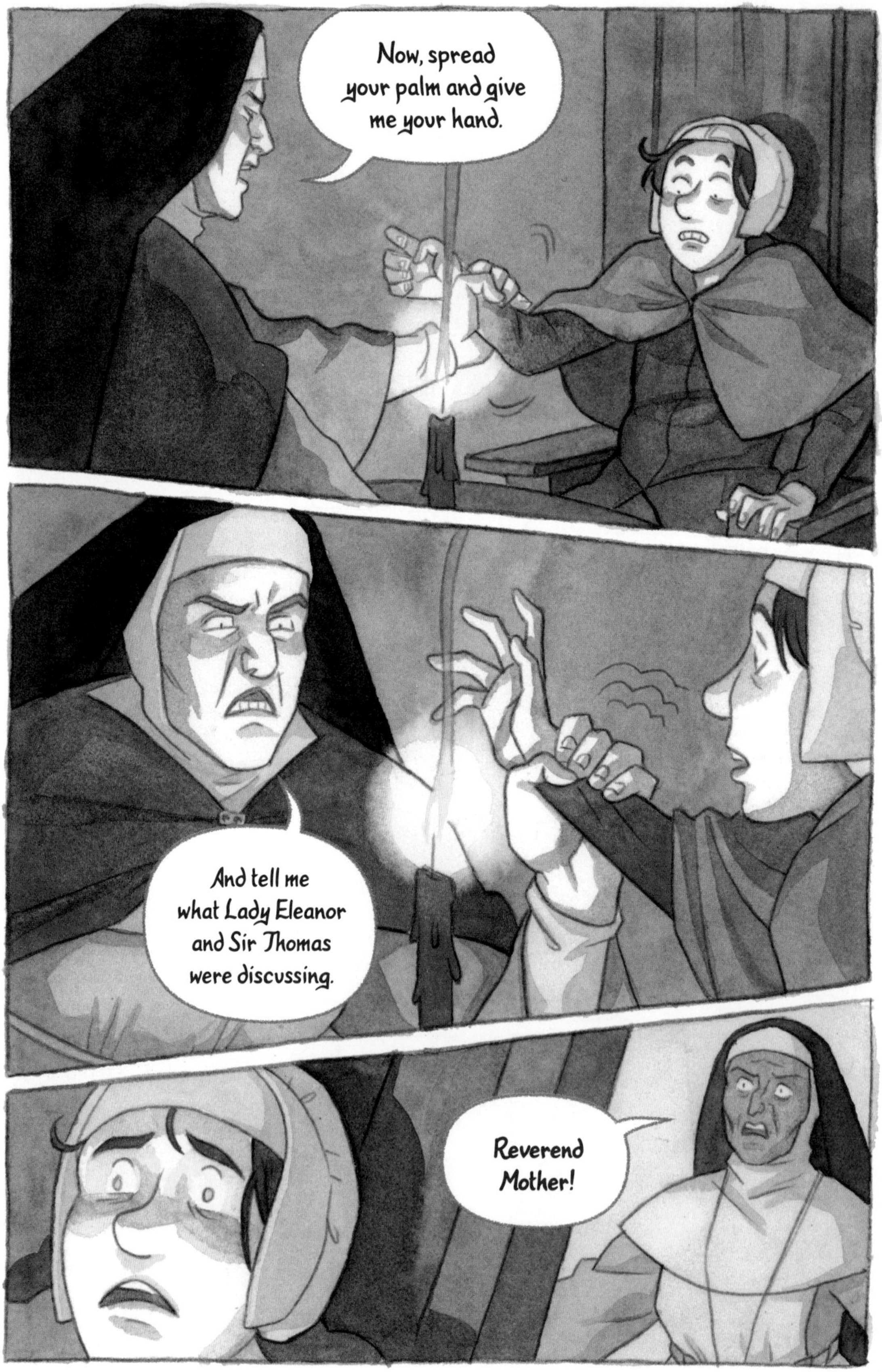
Now, spread your palm and give me your hand.
And tell me what Lady Eleanor and Sir Thomas were discussing.
Reverend Mother!

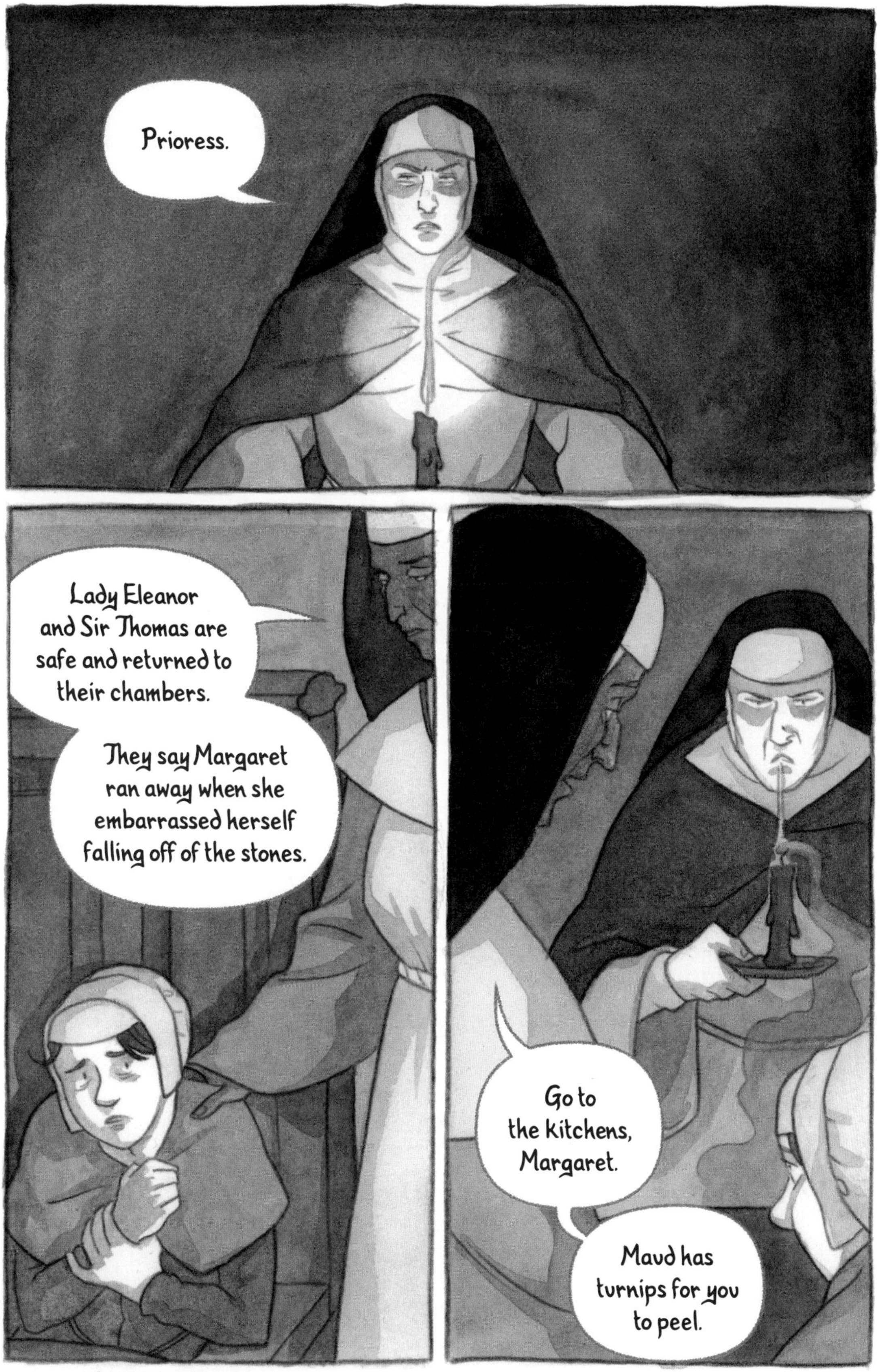
Prioress.
Lady Eleanor and Sir Thomas are safe and returned to their chambers.
They say Margaret ran away when she embarrassed herself falling off of the stones.
Go to the kitchens, Margaret.
Maud has turnips for you to peel.

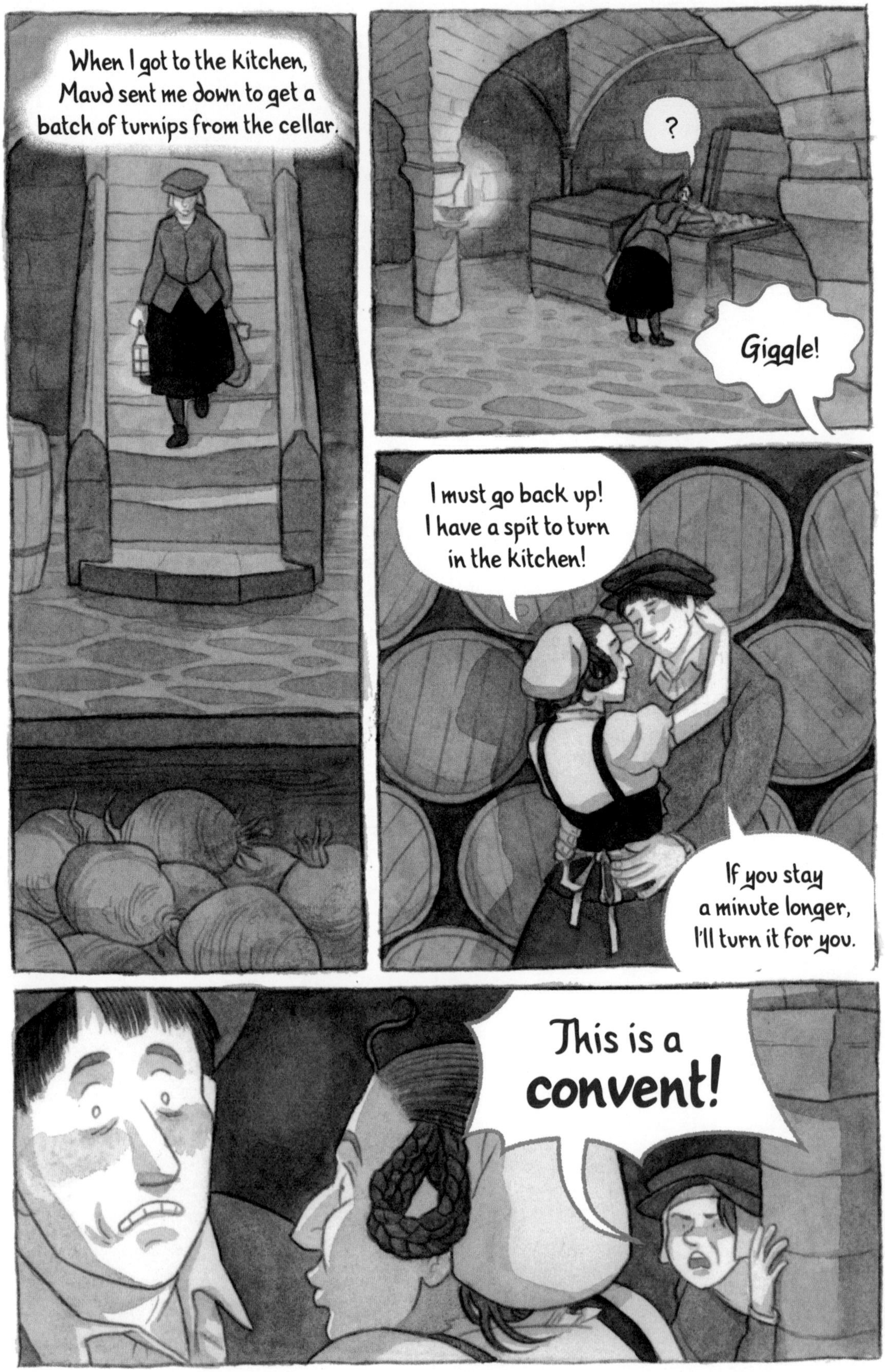
When I got to the kitchen, Maud sent me down to get a batch of turnips from the cellar.
?
Giggle!
I must go back up! I have a spit to turn in the kitchen!
If you stay a minute longer, I'll turn it for you.
This is a convent!

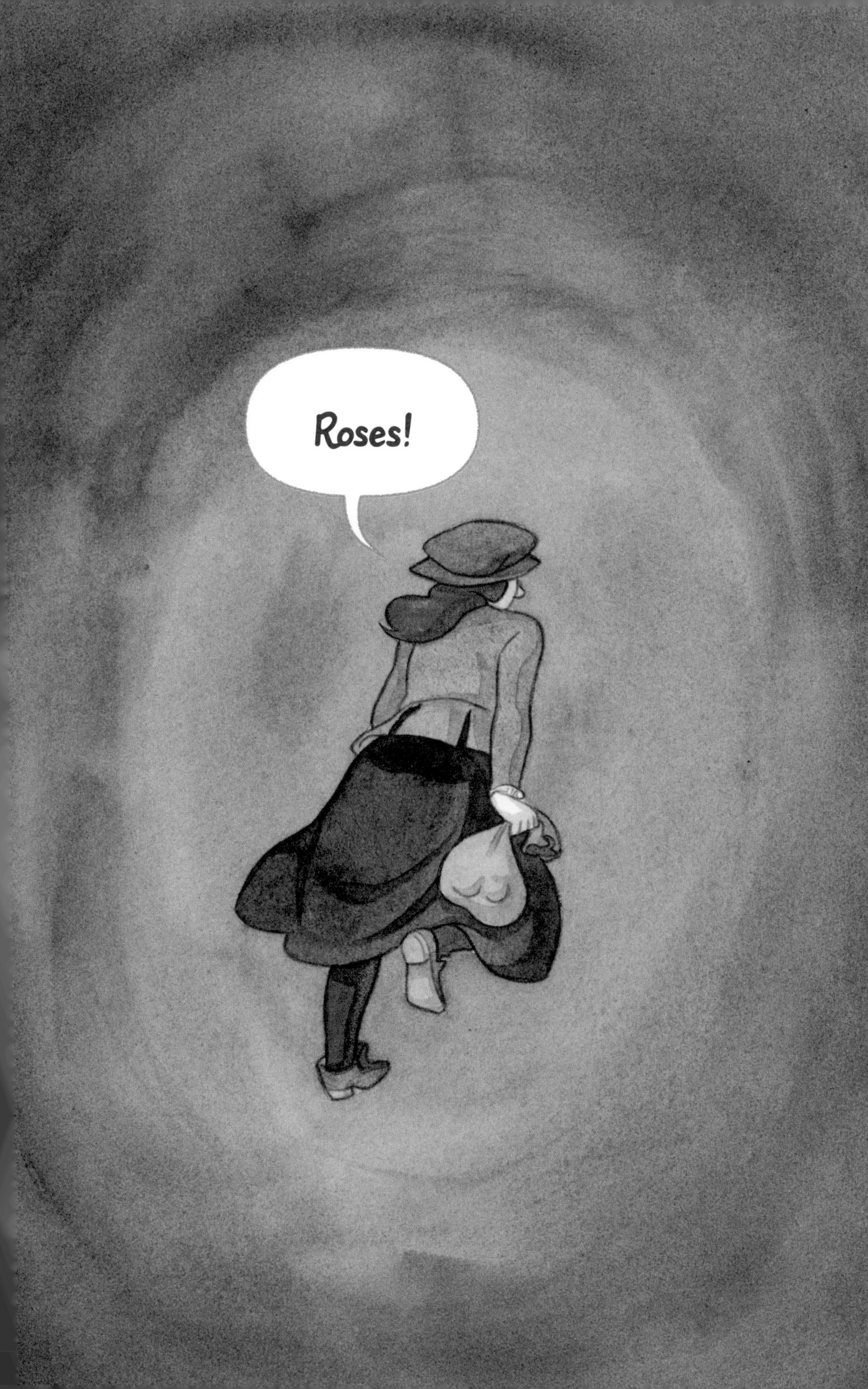
Roses!

The next day, Eleanor sent word for me to meet her in Saint Elysia's chapel.

Francis was not there. Peter Yarrow was her guard and looked at me very nervously as I went into the church. No doubt he was worried that I might tell Maud about his meeting Jess in the cellar.

At least it meant that he wasn't likely to bother us.

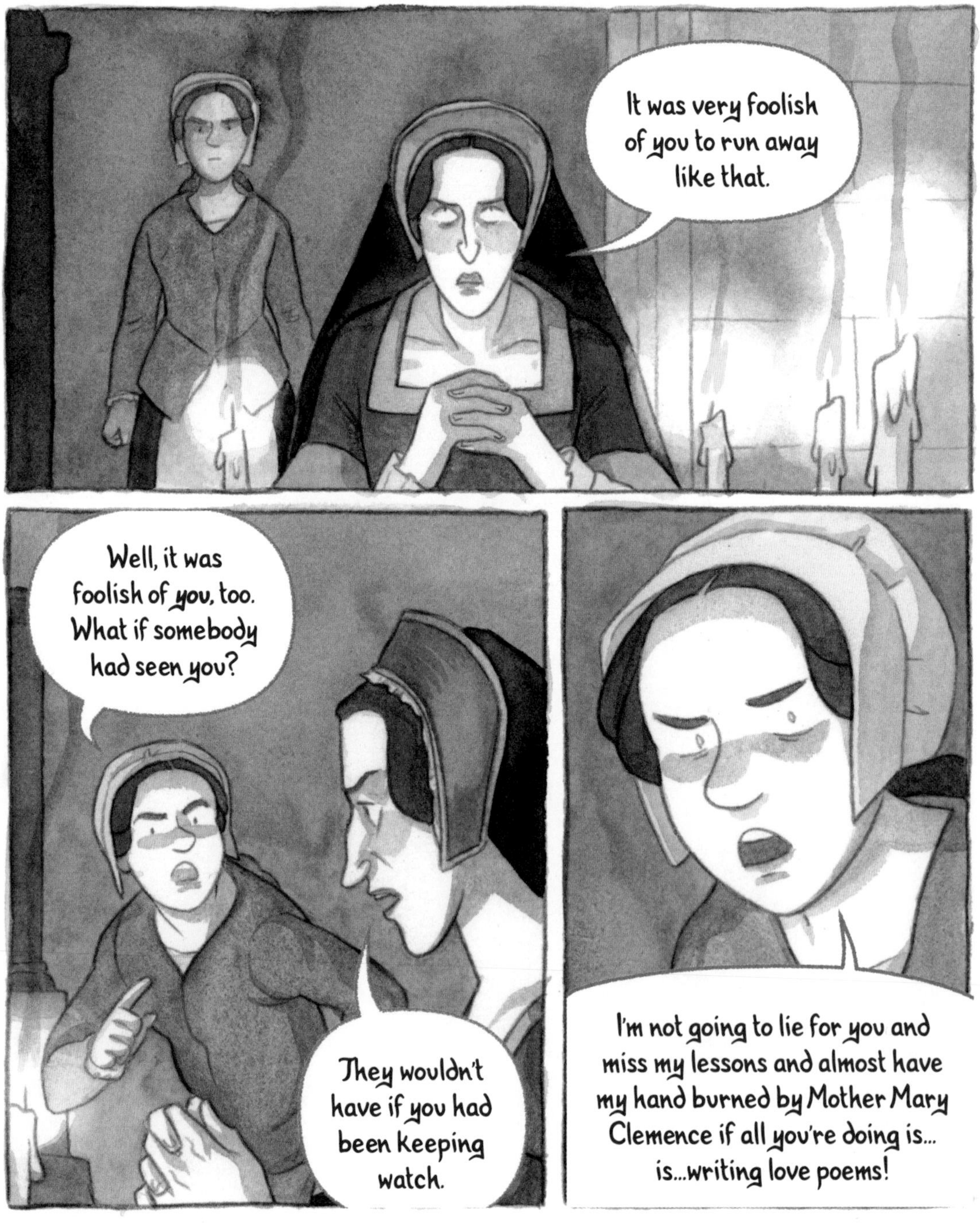

It was very foolish of you to run away like that.
Well, it was foolish of *you*, too. What if somebody had seen you?
They wouldn't have if you had been keeping watch.
I'm not going to lie for you and miss my lessons and almost have my hand burned by Mother Mary Clemence if all you're doing is... is...writing love poems!

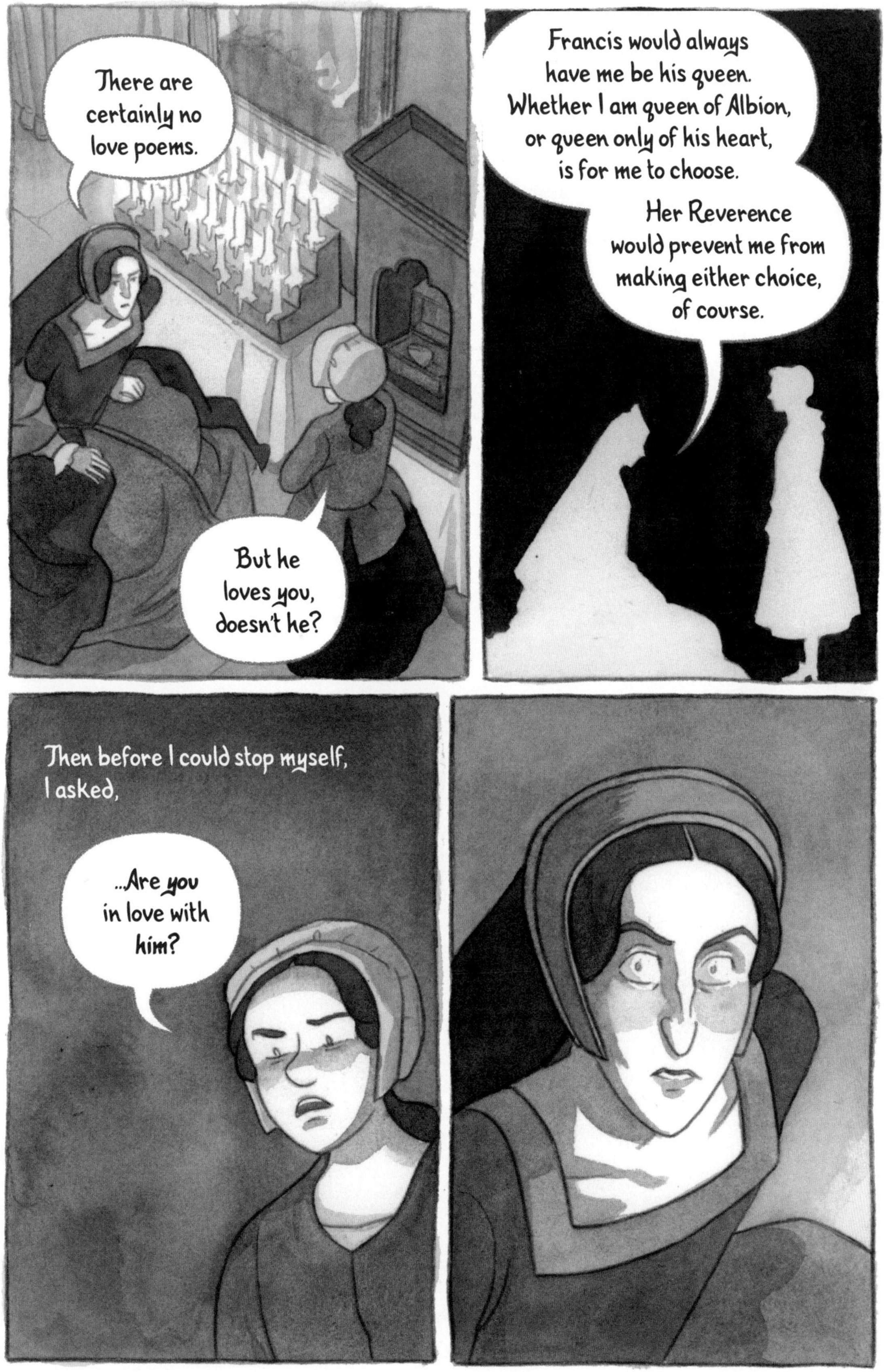
There are certainly no love poems.
But he loves you, doesn't he?
Francis would always have me be his queen. Whether I am queen of Albion, or queen only of his heart, is for me to choose.
Her Reverence would prevent me from making either choice, of course.
Then before I could stop myself, I asked,
...Are you in love with him?

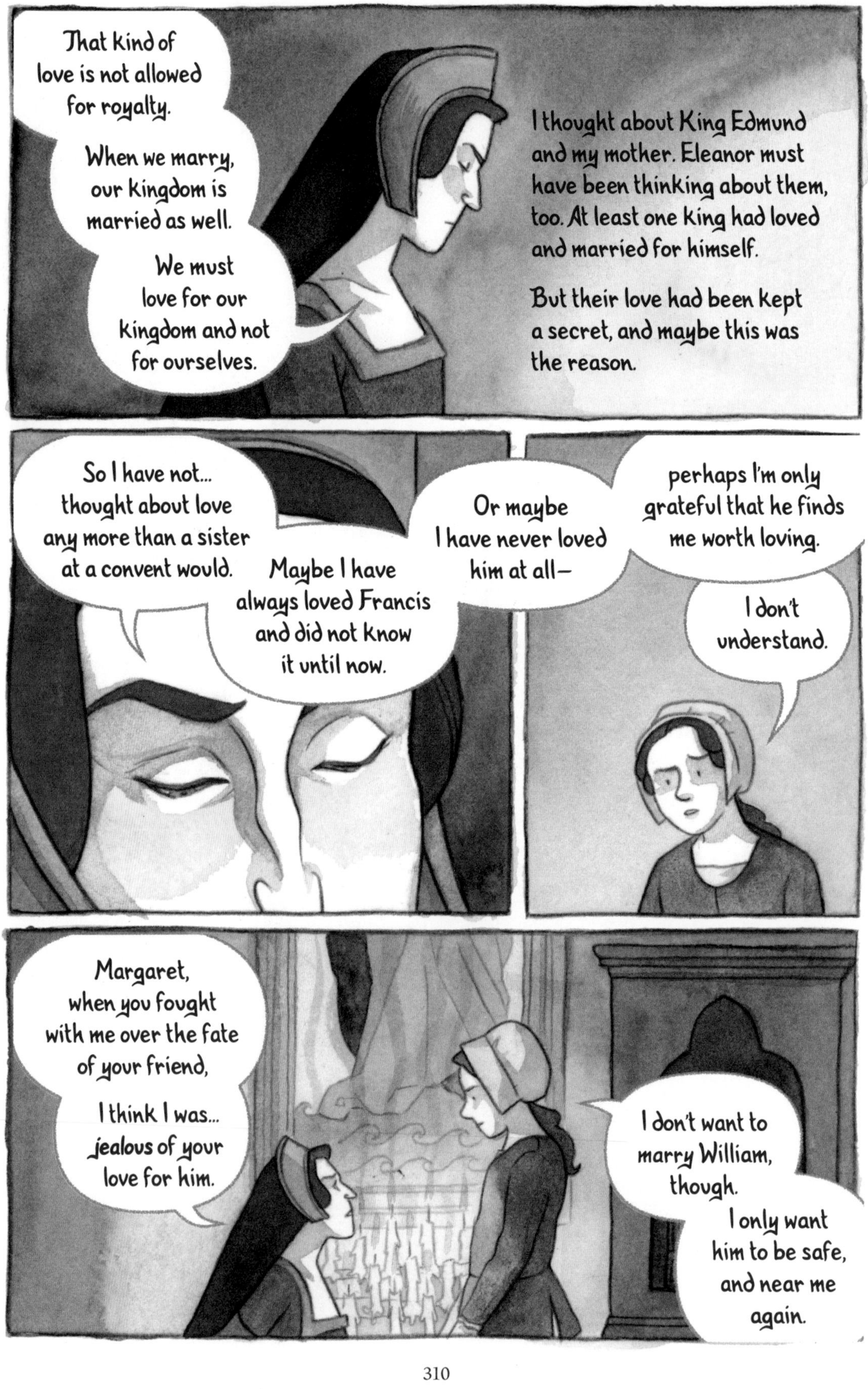
That kind of love is not allowed for royalty.
When we marry, our kingdom is married as well.
We must love for our kingdom and not for ourselves.
I thought about King Edmund and my mother. Eleanor must have been thinking about them, too. At least one king had loved and married for himself.
But their love had been kept a secret, and maybe this was the reason.
So I have not... thought about love any more than a sister at a convent would.
Maybe I have always loved Francis and did not know it until now.
Or maybe I have never loved him at all—
perhaps I'm only grateful that he finds me worth loving.
I don't understand.
Margaret, when you fought with me over the fate of your friend,
I think I was... jealous of your love for him.
I don't want to marry William, though.
I only want him to be safe, and near me again.

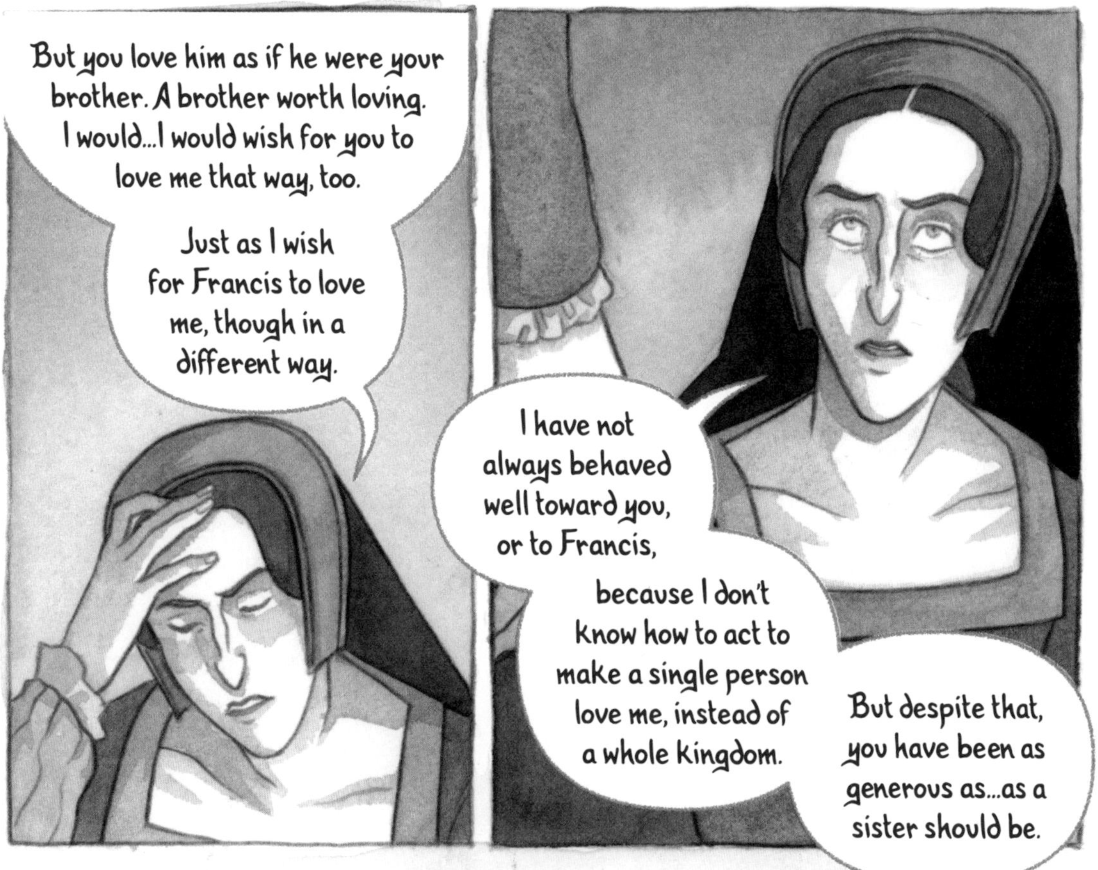
But you love him as if he were your brother. A brother worth loving. I would...I would wish for you to love me that way, too.
Just as I wish for Francis to love me, though in a different way.
I have not always behaved well toward you, or to Francis,
because I don't know how to act to make a single person love me, instead of a whole kingdom.
But despite that, you have been as generous as...as a sister should be.

Everything around me suddenly felt very sharp and alive. Eleanor was going to tell me herself that we were sisters—actual sisters—and that she wanted me to come with her when she left the Island, whether through royal pardon or escape.

Before that moment, every time I thought about leaving the Island, it was just a silly fantasy. Before I knew that I was King Edmund's daughter, I hadn't really thought of it at all, even when William talked about showing me Castle Cameron someday. It would have felt the same if he had talked about showing me a castle at the bottom of the sea.

At that moment, though, my heart started to beat faster, and I held my breath, and for some reason I thought,

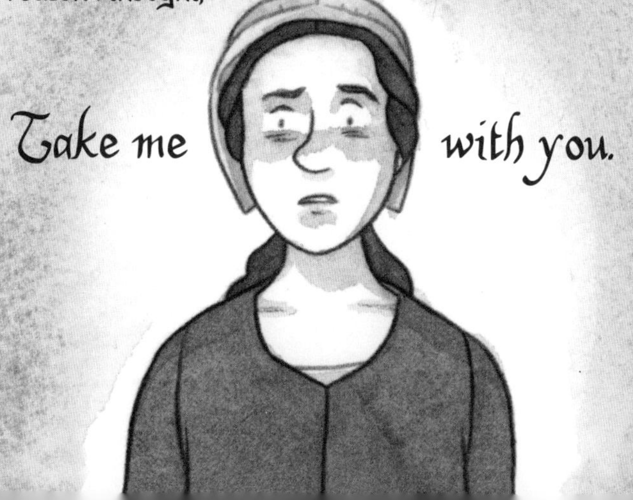
Take me with you.

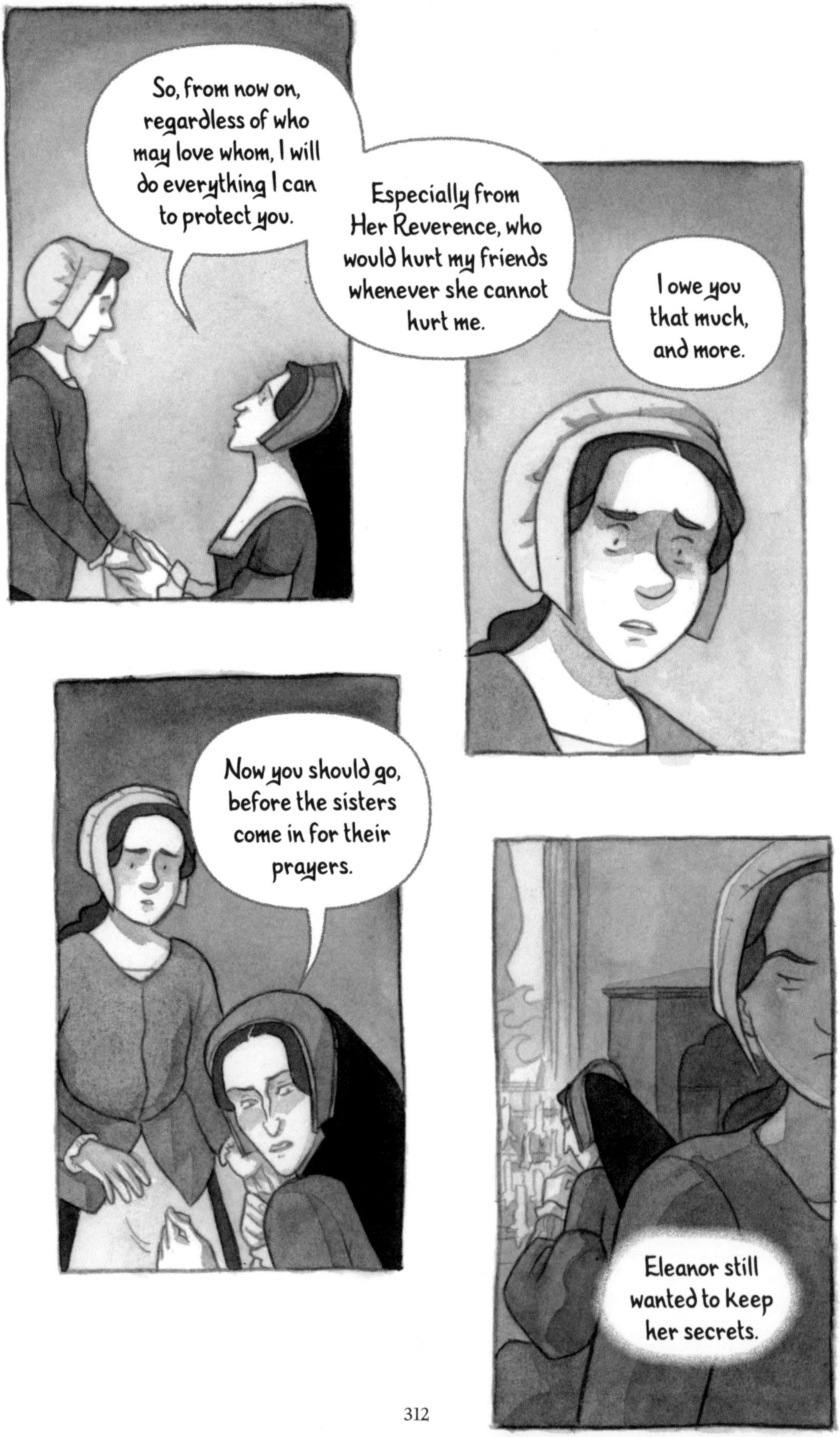
So, from now on, regardless of who may love whom, I will do everything I can to protect you.
Especially from Her Reverence, who would hurt my friends whenever she cannot hurt me.
I owe you that much, and more.
Now you should go, before the sisters come in for their prayers.
Eleanor still wanted to keep her secrets.

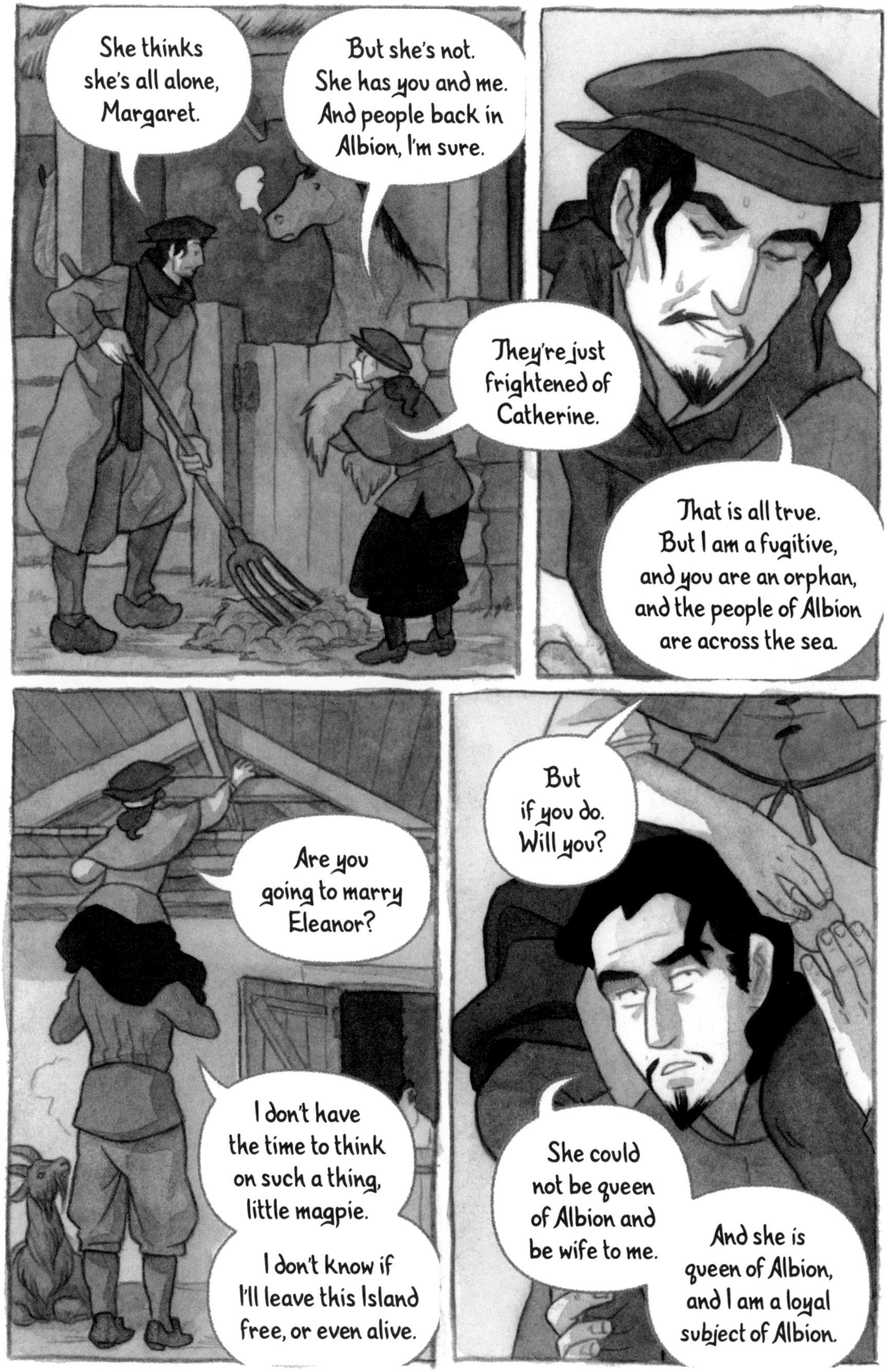

She thinks she's all alone, Margaret.
But she's not. She has you and me. And people back in Albion, I'm sure.
They're just frightened of Catherine.
That is all true. But I am a fugitive, and you are an orphan, and the people of Albion are across the sea.
Are you going to marry Eleanor?
I don't have the time to think on such a thing, little magpie.
I don't know if I'll leave this Island free, or even alive.
But if you do. Will you?
She could not be queen of Albion and be wife to me.
And she is queen of Albion, and I am a loyal subject of Albion.

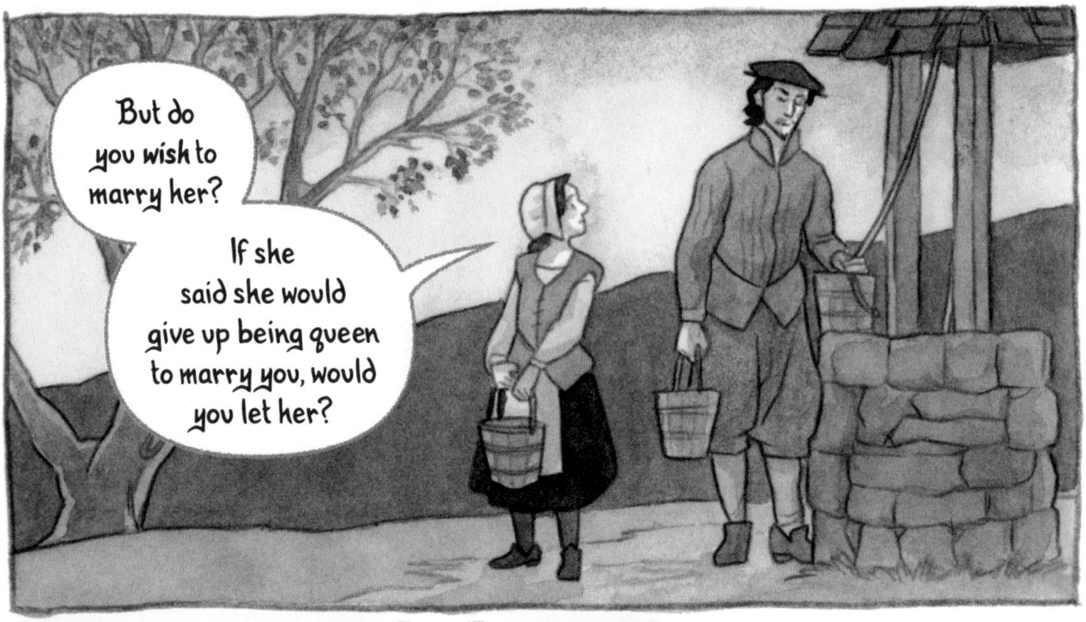
But do you wish to marry her?
If she said she would give up being queen to marry you, would you let her?

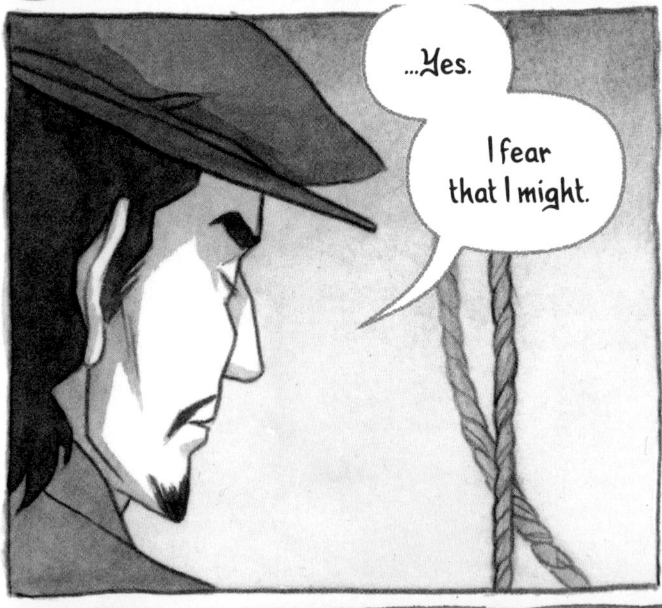
...Yes.
I fear that I might.

I wasn't sure why Francis was frightened. The knight wasn't frightened by all the terrible things he faced to bring the rose to his maiden.

Francis had already risked his life to find Eleanor.

What could possibly scare him now?

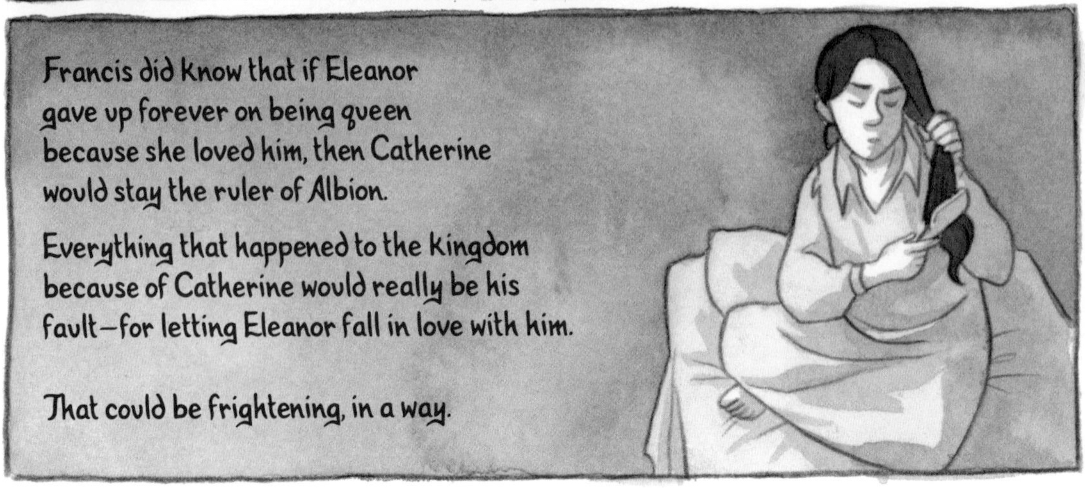
Francis did know that if Eleanor gave up forever on being queen because she loved him, then Catherine would stay the ruler of Albion.
Everything that happened to the kingdom because of Catherine would really be his fault—for letting Eleanor fall in love with him.
That could be frightening, in a way.

Of course, I knew something that Francis didn't. Eleanor and I were sisters. Eleanor thought she was keeping our sisterhood a secret from me. After all, I might try to steal her kingdom, too—or side with Catherine against her.

Like Sister Agnes said, children can be dangerous. As long as I, and everyone else, thought I was just an ordinary orphan, I could never get in the way of Eleanor's plans.

But what if Eleanor told me who I really was, and trusted that I wouldn't betray her? What if she brought me back to Albion with her? King Edmund had married my mother after both Queen Joan and Queen Isabel had died. As long as Sister Agnes had her letter, nobody could argue that I was born out of wedlock.

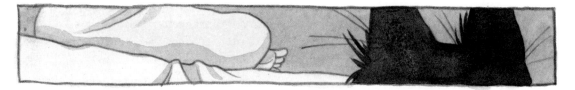

That wasn't true of Eleanor—or of Catherine, either. I was the one daughter of Edmund that all of Albion could agree on! Once everyone knew about me, Catherine would have to admit defeat. Eleanor would get to marry Francis. Both would give up their right to the throne. And I would become the true queen of Albion.

Eleanor could teach me everything I needed to know about ruling a kingdom. It would be just like playing chess together—only, we would be on the same side of the board!

But it seemed as though Eleanor didn't just want to save Albion from Catherine. She wanted to save it by being the *queen.*

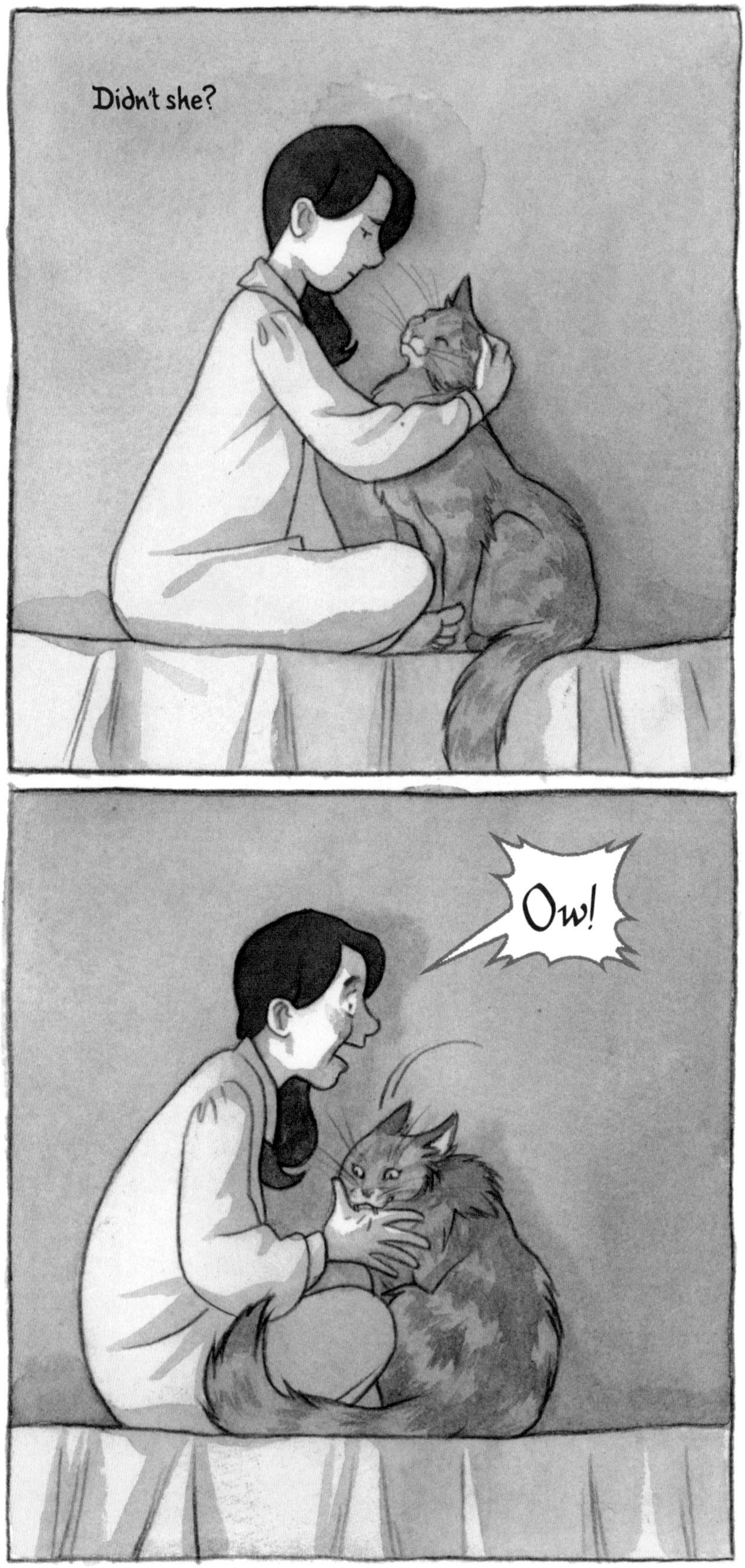
Didn't she?
Ow!

Eleanor had taught me that a queen is the most valuable piece on the chessboard.

You can sacrifice almost any other piece without feeling too badly—there will always be plenty of pawns, and at least one other knight, rook, or bishop.

Although a queen is very powerful, any piece can capture her if she's careless. And you only have one queen. You can lose very quickly if she is captured too soon in the game.

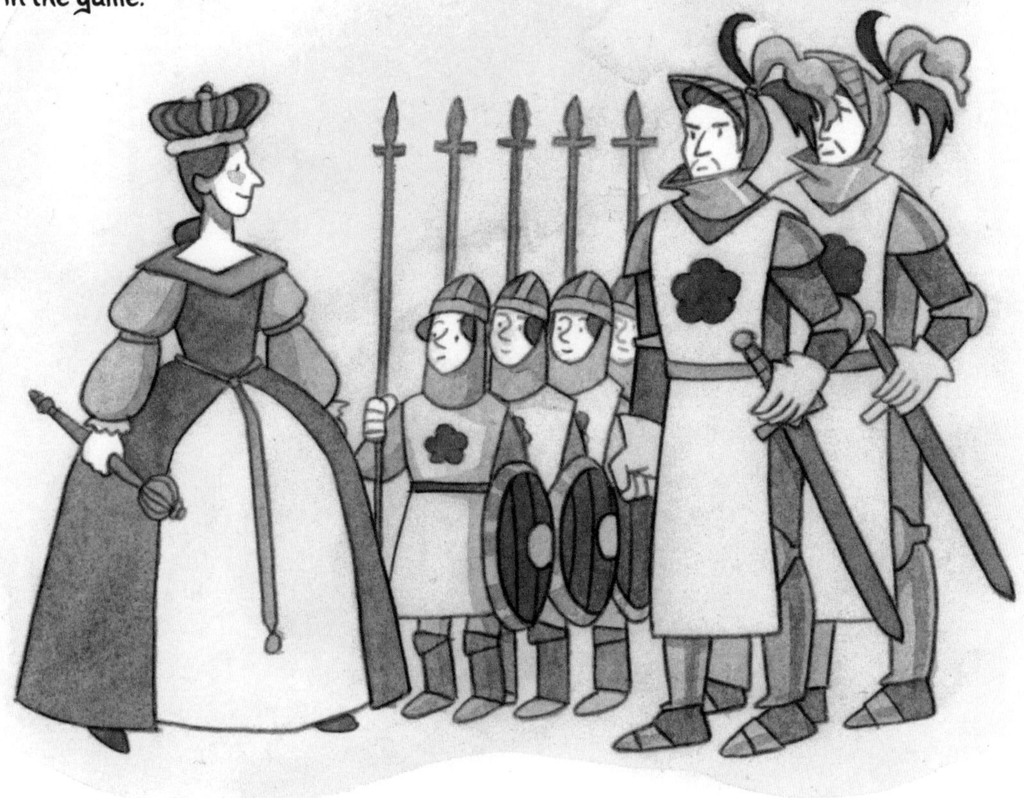

I lost half a dozen chess games to Eleanor or Francis because I was so worried about keeping my queen safe that I hardly used her at all. The other side won—not by being responsible, but by being reckless!

But there is a special move in chess.

If a pawn can creep safely all the way to the other end of the board without getting caught—

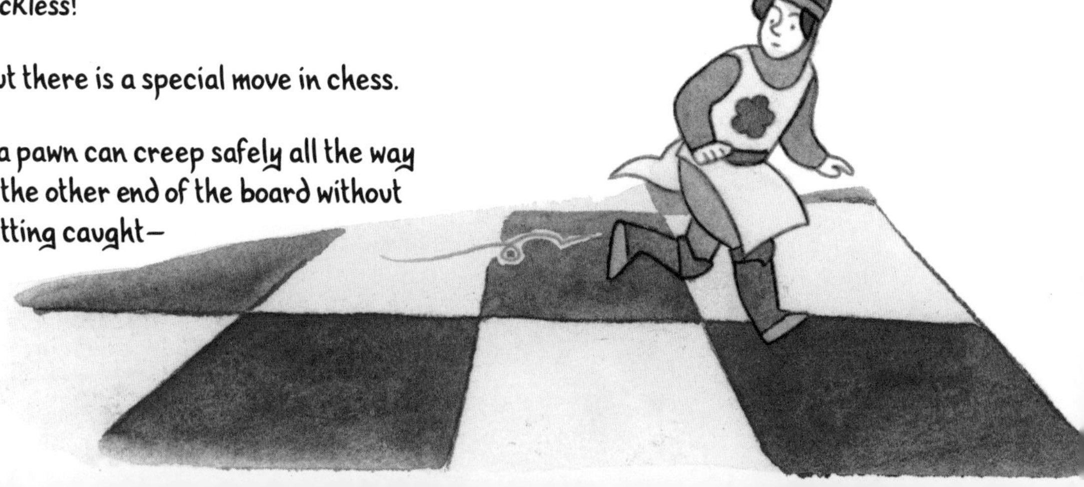

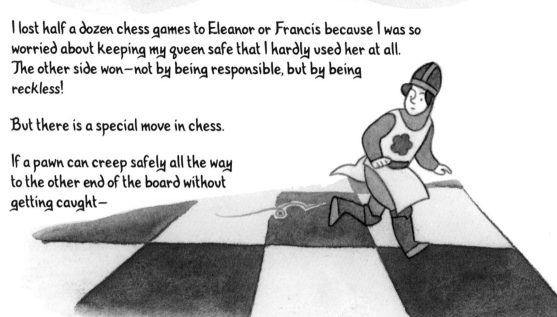

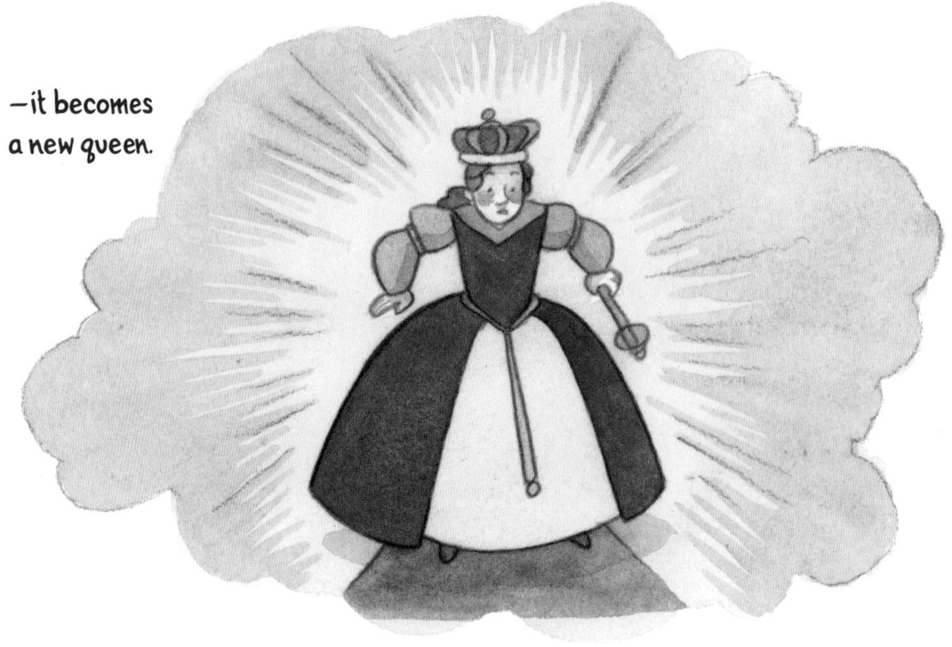
—it becomes
a new queen.

It is much easier to win when you have two queens
and your opponent only has one.

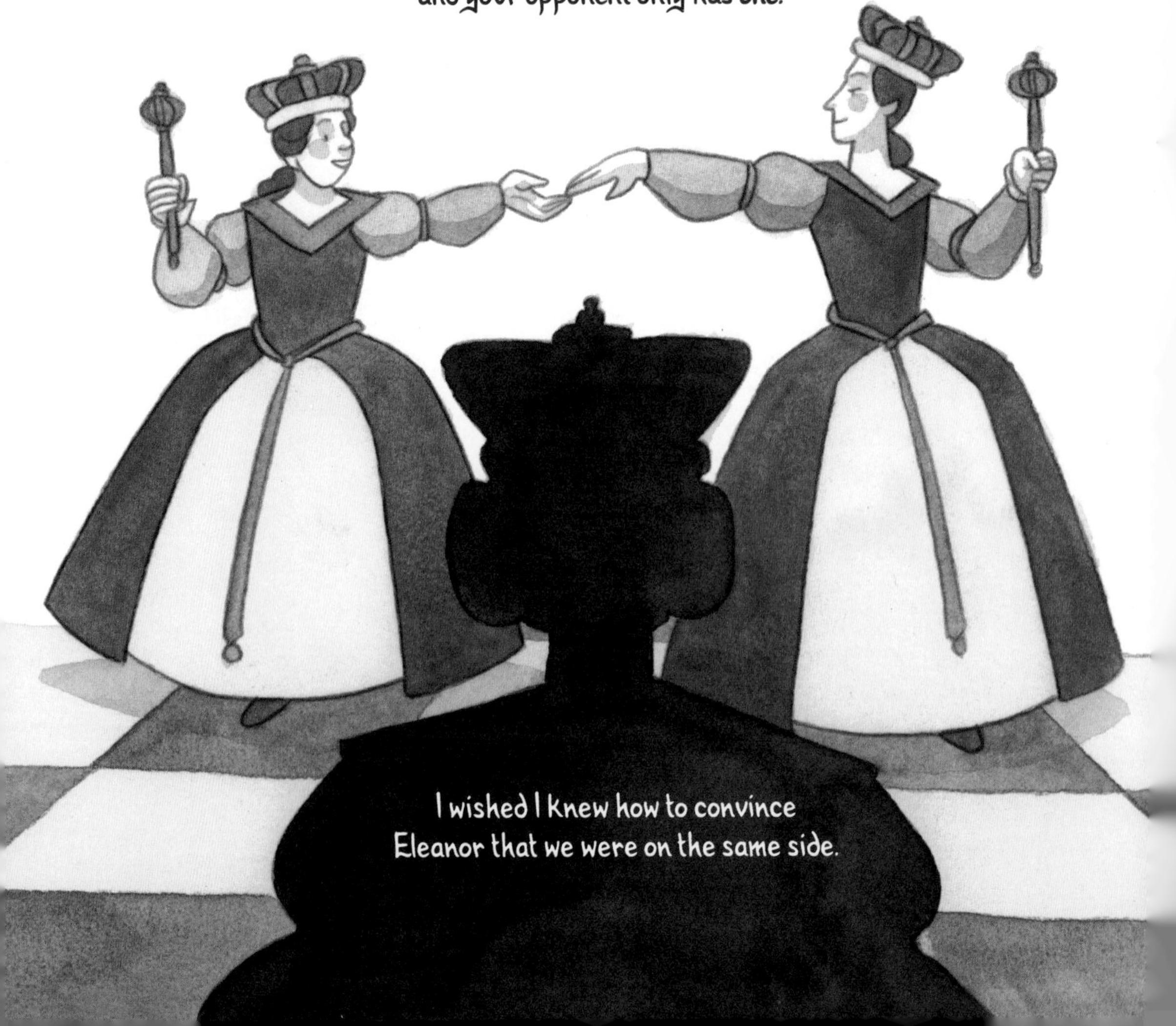
I wished I knew how to convince
Eleanor that we were on the same side.

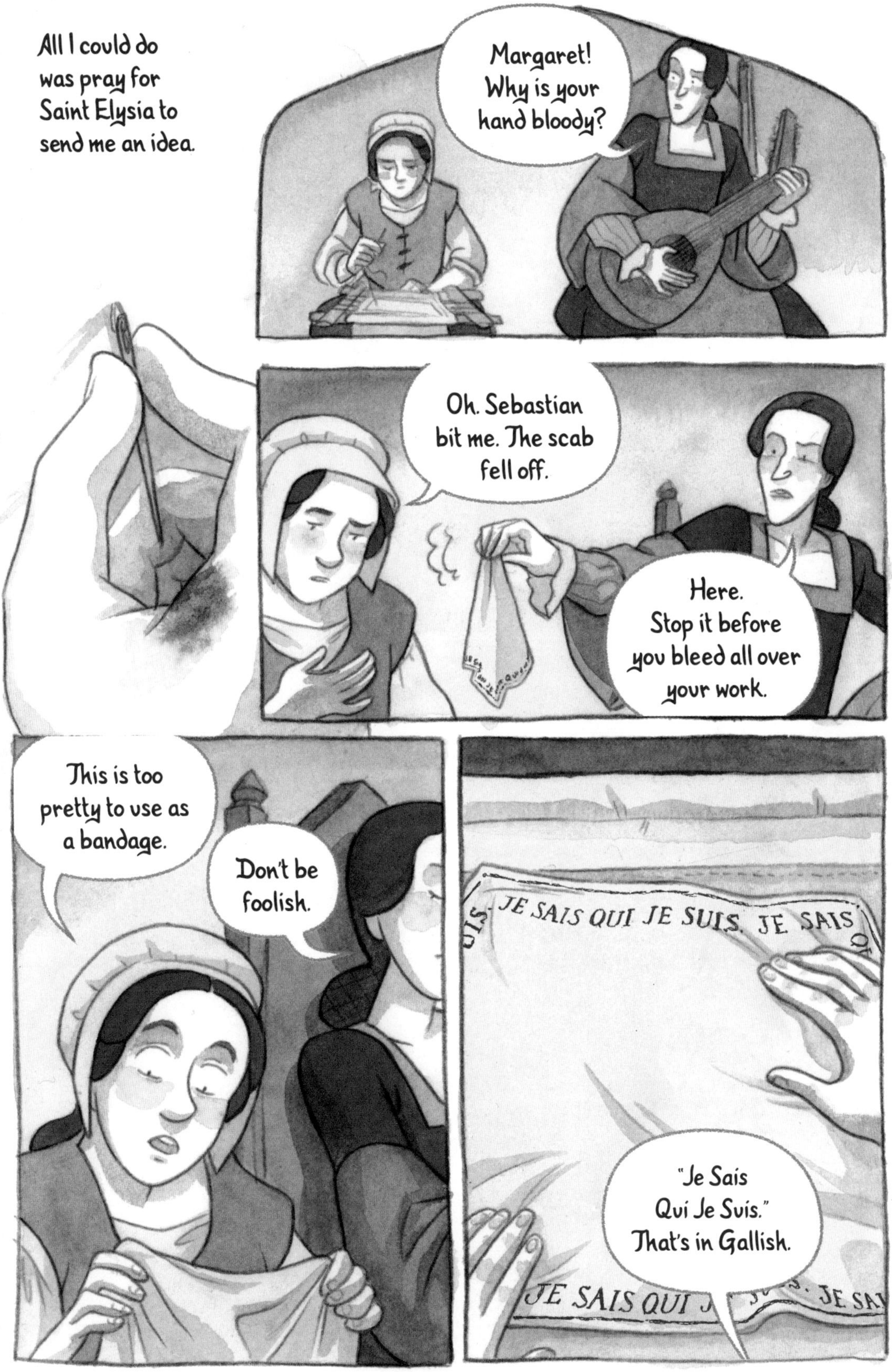
All I could do was pray for Saint Elysia to send me an idea.
Margaret! Why is your hand bloody?
Oh. Sebastian bit me. The scab fell off.
Here. Stop it before you bleed all over your work.
This is too pretty to use as a bandage.
Don't be foolish.
JE SAIS QUI JE SUIS. JE SAIS
"Je Sais Qui Je Suis." That's in Gallish.
JE SAIS QUI

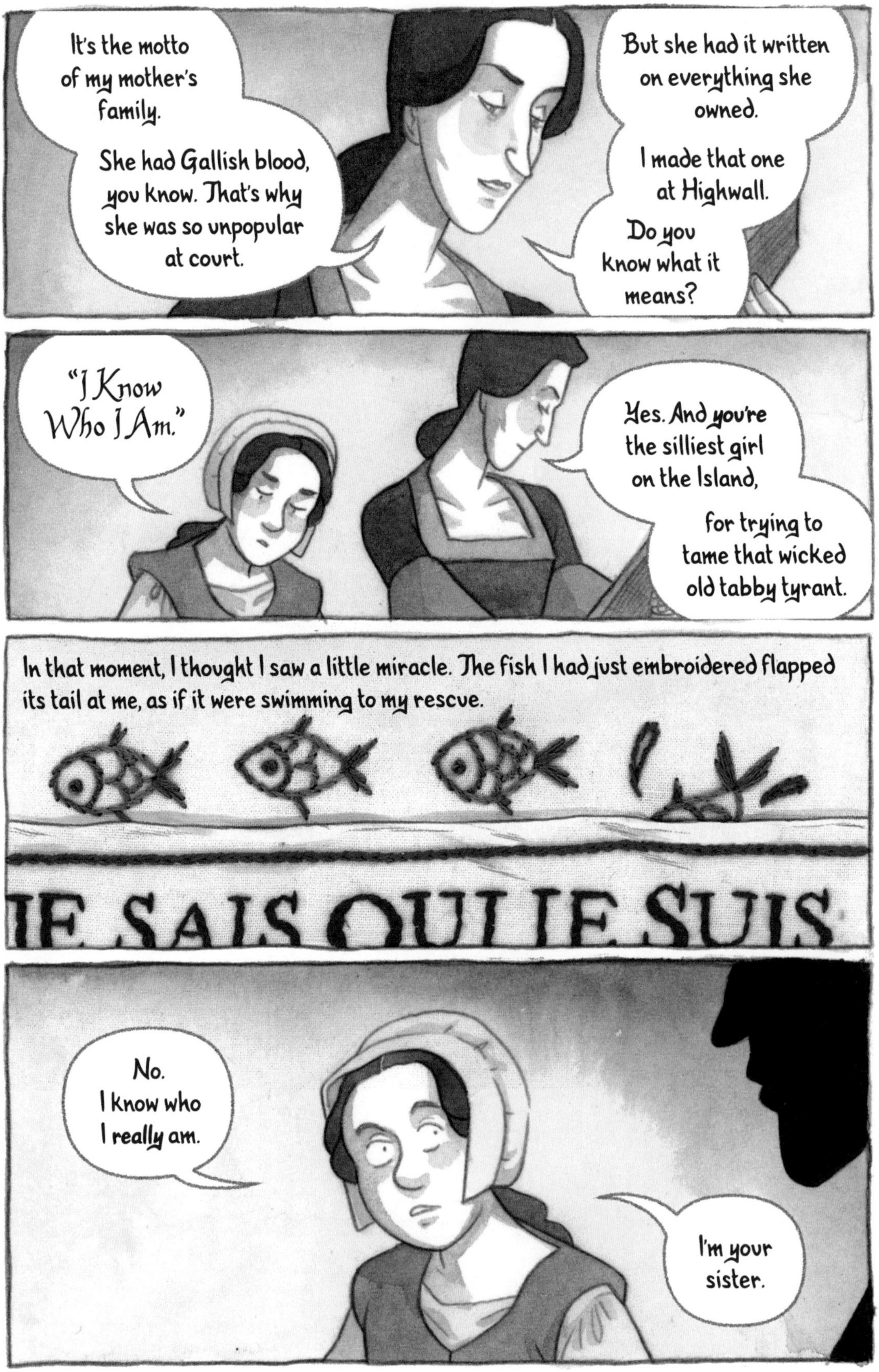
It's the motto of my mother's family.
She had Gallish blood, you know. That's why she was so unpopular at court.
But she had it written on everything she owned.
I made that one at Highwall.
Do you know what it means?
"I Know Who I Am."
Yes. And you're the silliest girl on the Island,
for trying to tame that wicked old tabby tyrant.
In that moment, I thought I saw a little miracle. The fish I had just embroidered flapped its tail at me, as if it were swimming to my rescue.
JE SAIS OU JE SUIS
No. I know who I really am.
I'm your sister.

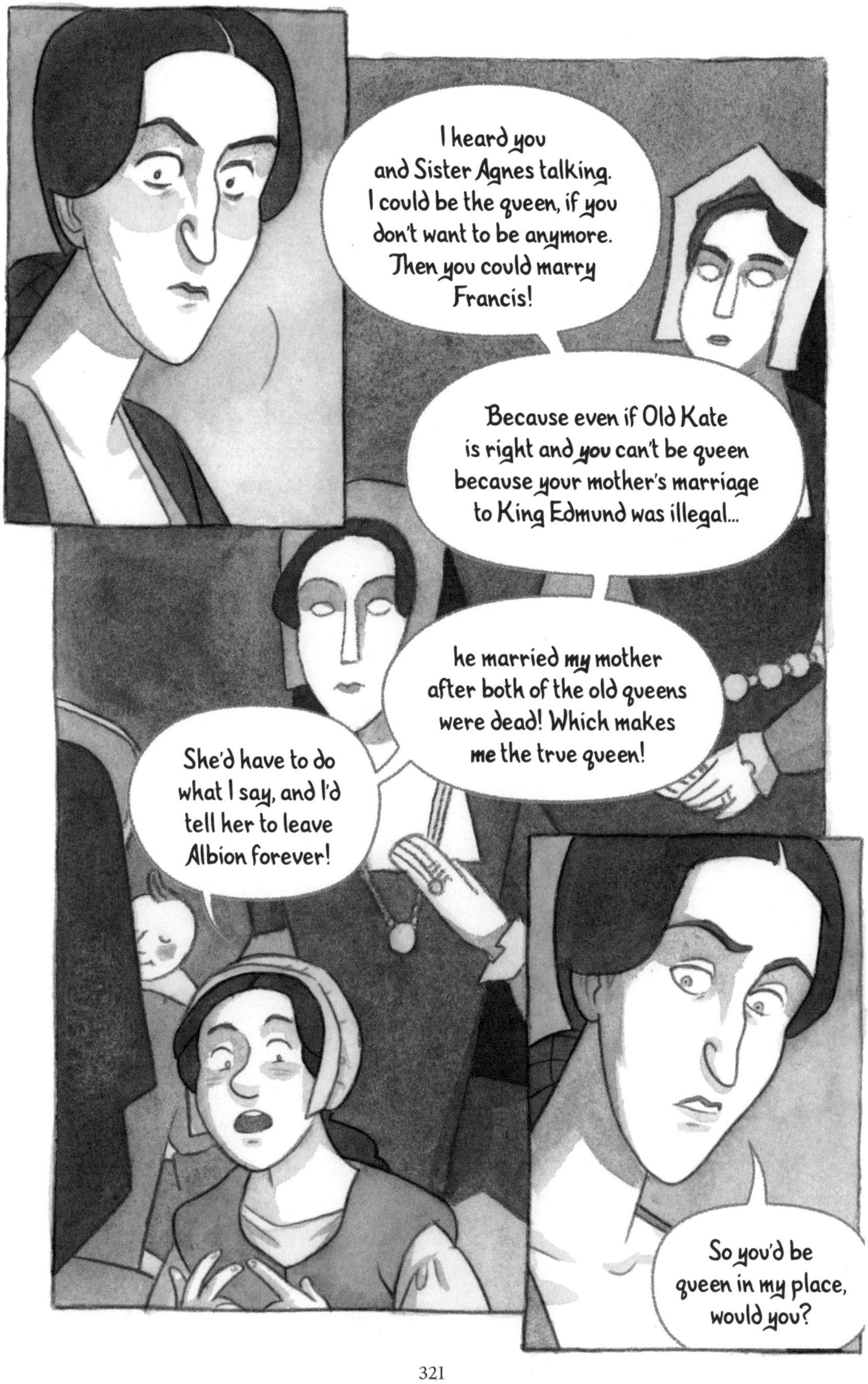
I heard you and Sister Agnes talking. I could be the queen, if you don't want to be anymore. Then you could marry Francis!
Because even if Old Kate is right and you can't be queen because your mother's marriage to King Edmund was illegal...
he married my mother after both of the old queens were dead! Which makes me the true queen!
She'd have to do what I say, and I'd tell her to leave Albion forever!
So you'd be queen in my place, would you?

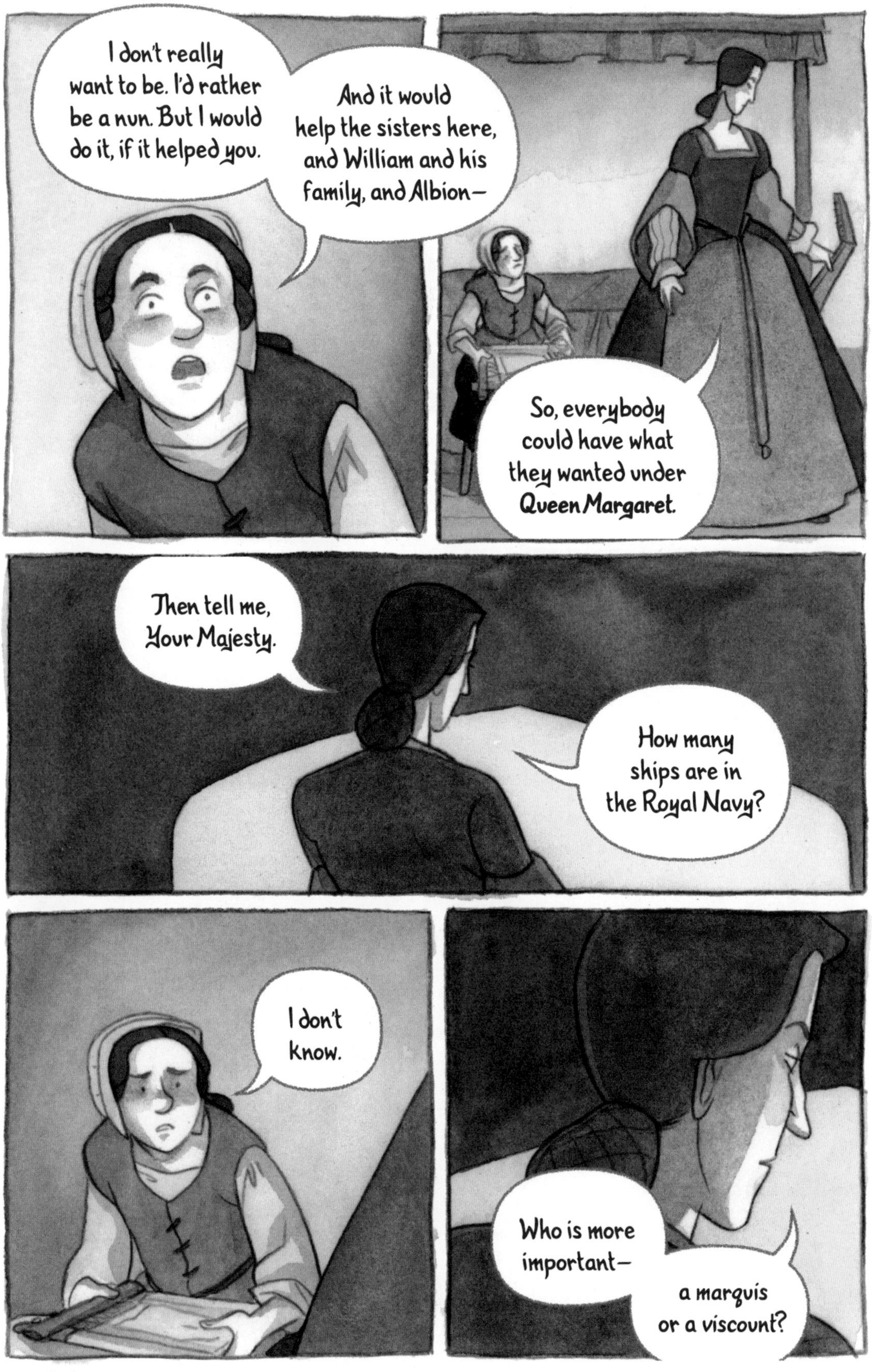
I don't really want to be. I'd rather be a nun. But I would do it, if it helped you.
And it would help the sisters here, and William and his family, and Albion—
So, everybody could have what they wanted under Queen Margaret.
Then tell me, Your Majesty.
How many ships are in the Royal Navy?
I don't know.
Who is more important—
a marquis or a viscount?

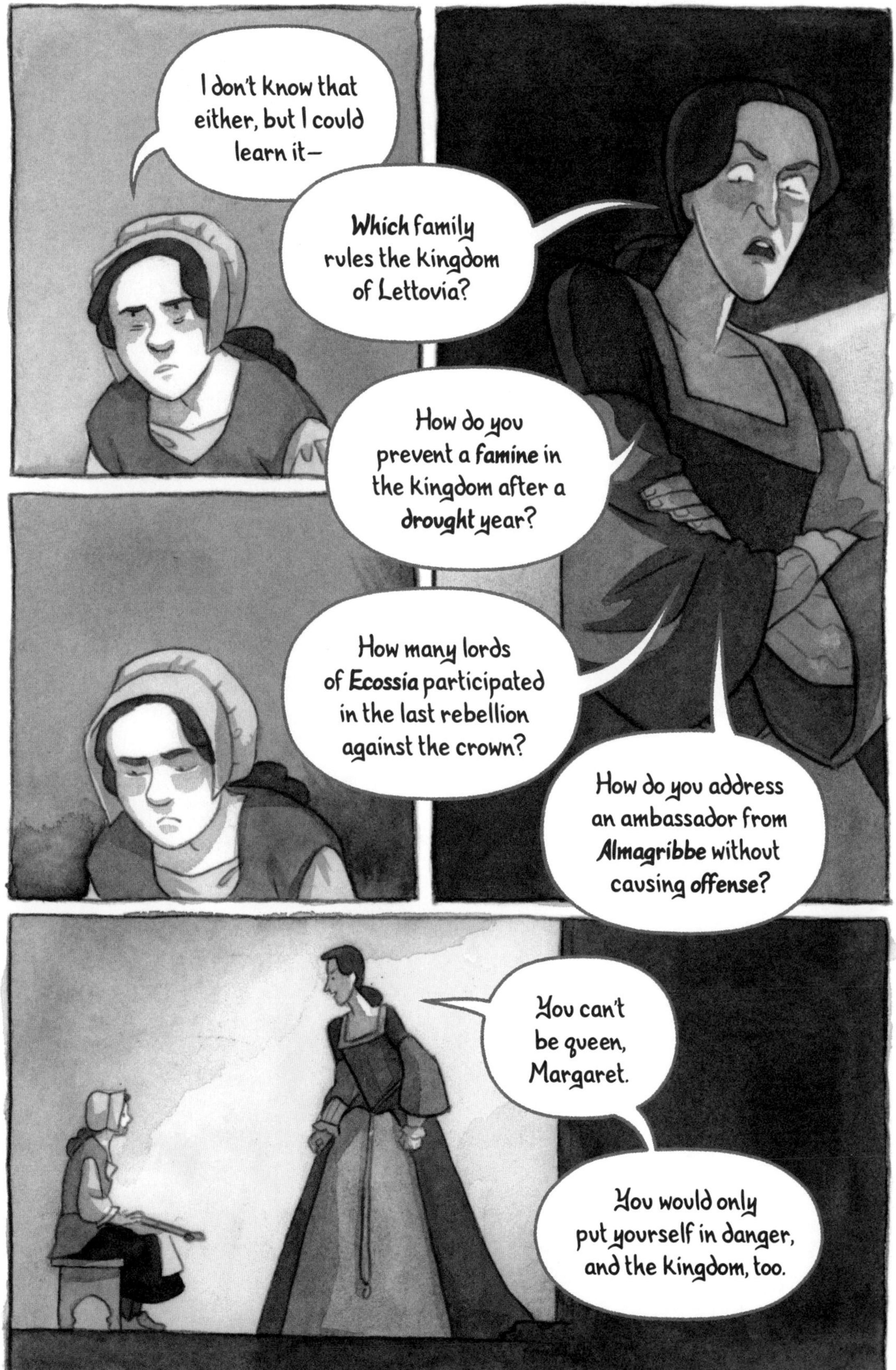
I don't know that either, but I could learn it—
Which family rules the kingdom of Lettovia?
How do you prevent a **famine** in the kingdom after a **drought year**?
How many lords of **Ecossia** participated in the last rebellion against the crown?
How do you address an ambassador from **Almagribbe** without causing **offense**?
You can't be queen, Margaret.
You would only put yourself in danger, and the kingdom, too.

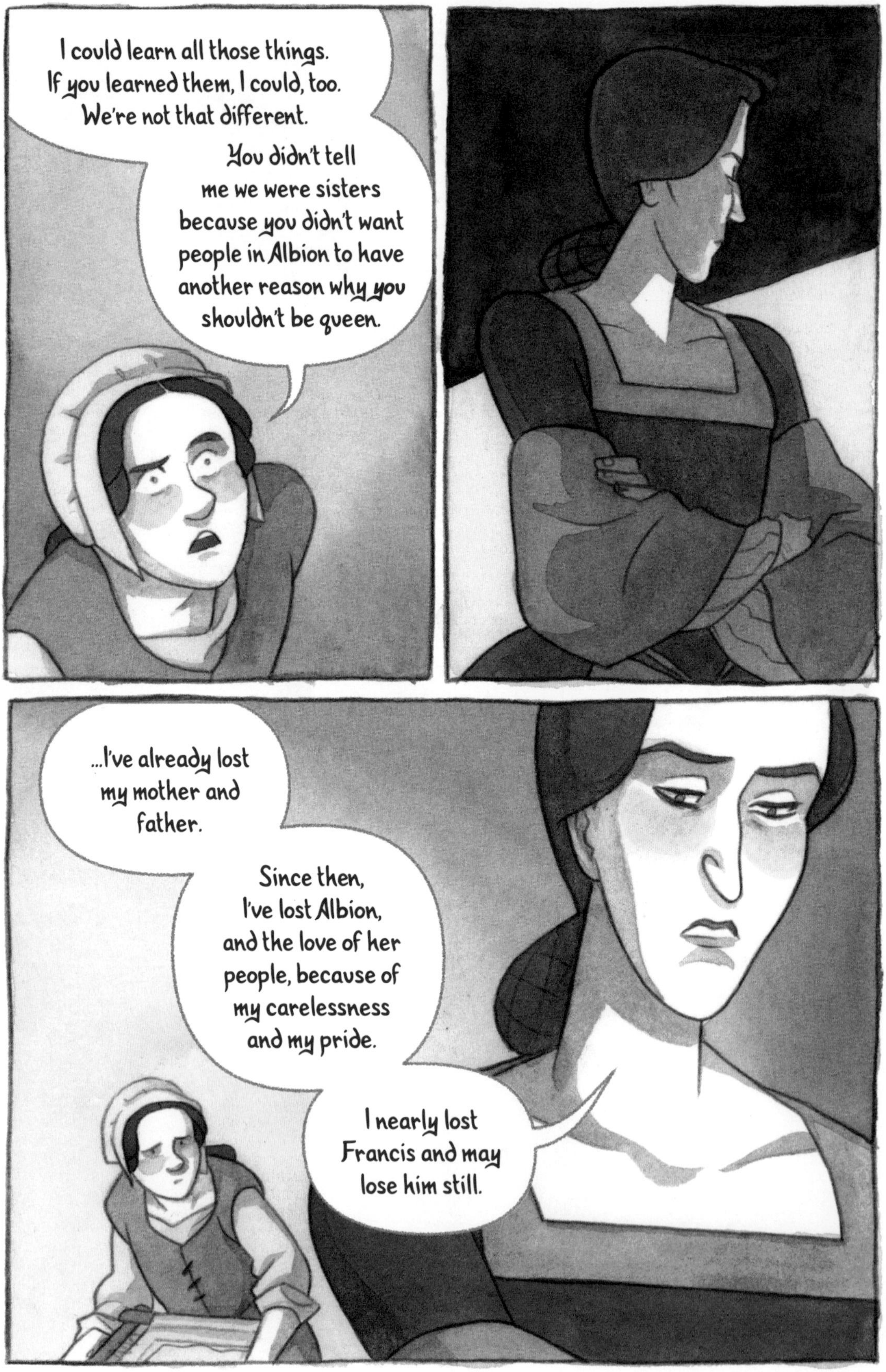
I could learn all those things. If you learned them, I could, too. We're not that different.
You didn't tell me we were sisters because you didn't want people in Albion to have another reason why you shouldn't be queen.
...I've already lost my mother and father.
Since then, I've lost Albion, and the love of her people, because of my carelessness and my pride.
I nearly lost Francis and may lose him still.

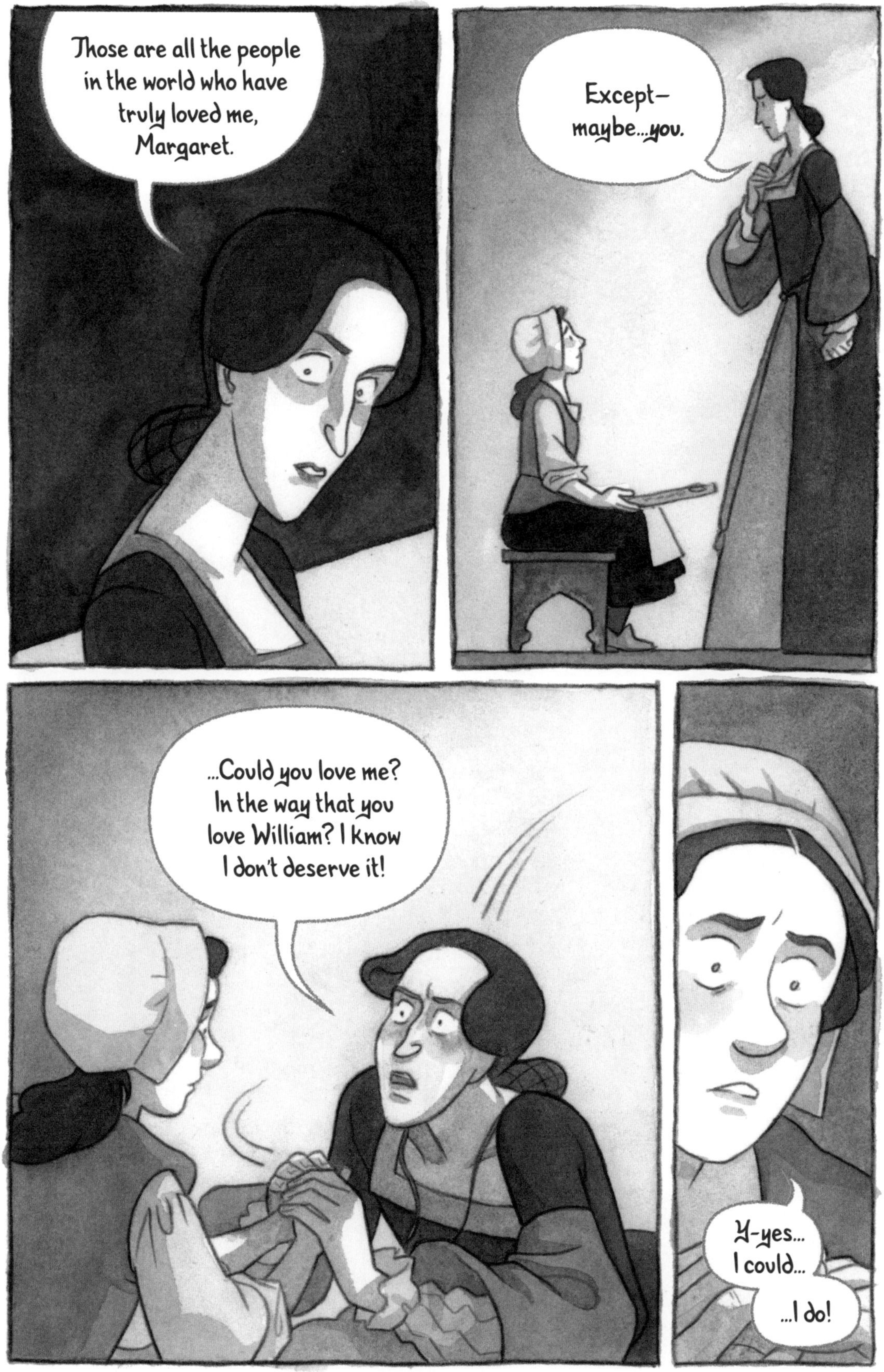
Those are all the people in the world who have truly loved me, Margaret.
Except— maybe...you.
...Could you love me? In the way that you love William? I know I don't deserve it!
Y-yes... I could...
...I do!

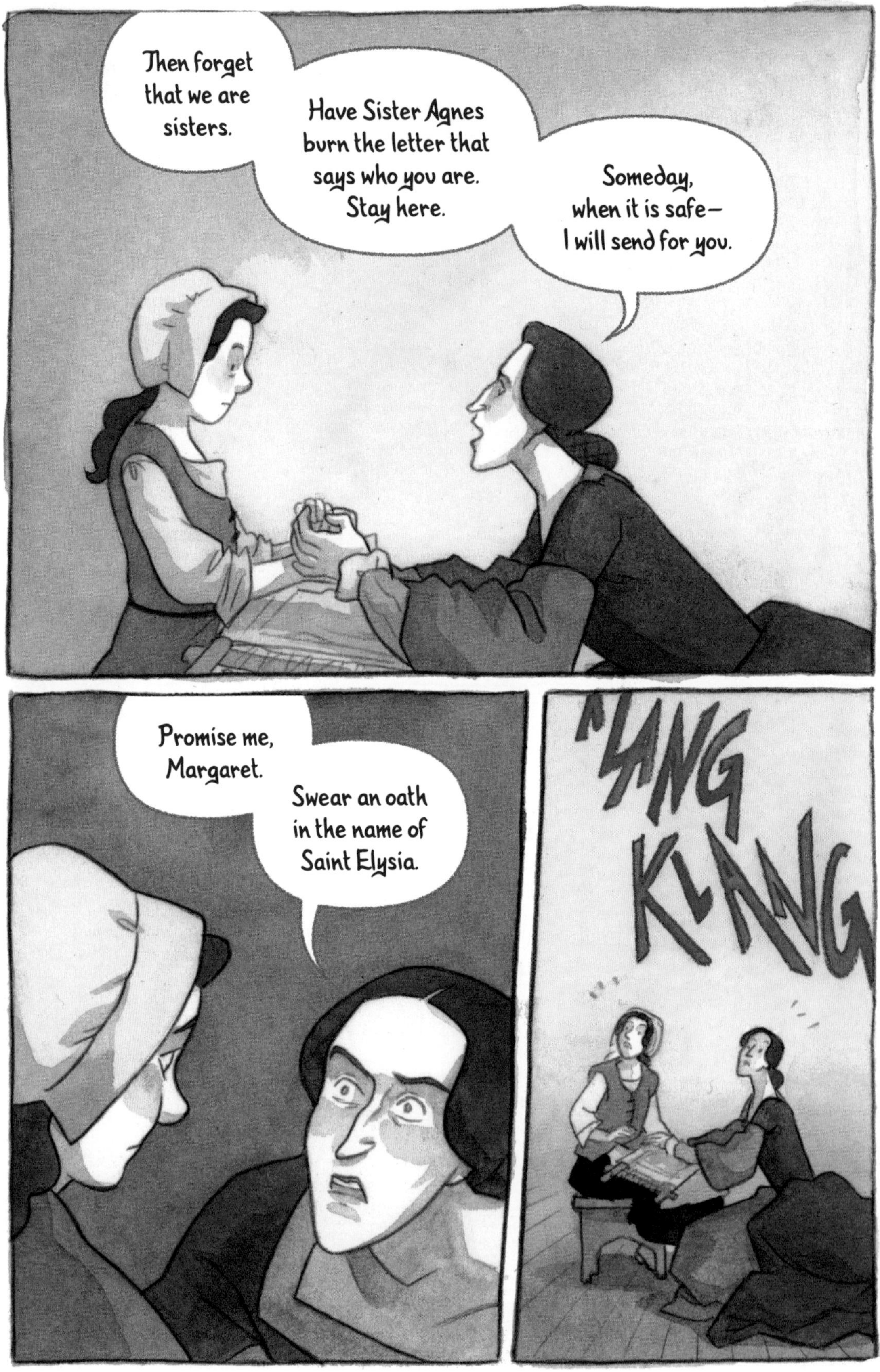
Then forget that we are sisters.
Have Sister Agnes burn the letter that says who you are. Stay here.
Someday, when it is safe— I will send for you.
Promise me, Margaret.
Swear an oath in the name of Saint Elysia.
KLANG KLANG

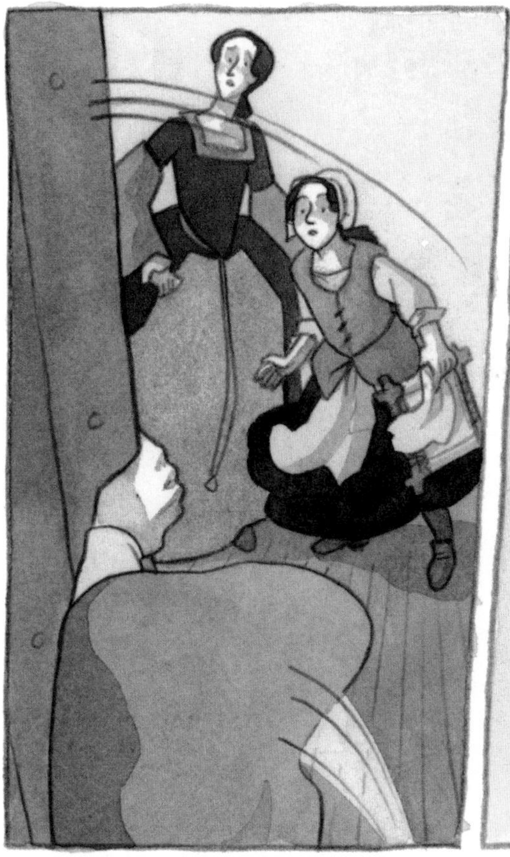

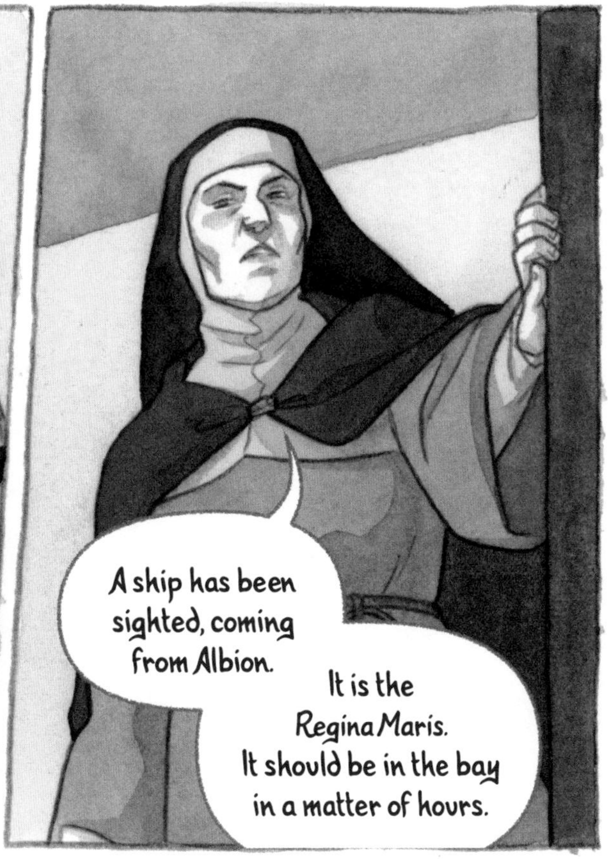

A ship has been sighted, coming from Albion.
It is the *Regina Maris*. It should be in the bay in a matter of hours.

The *Regina Maris* was almost six weeks early.

It normally didn't come until after the Paschal Feast.

The forty days leading up to the week of the feast are very quiet and spare.

Nobody, not even the servants, is allowed to eat any rich foods, or play any games, or sing anything but holy songs.

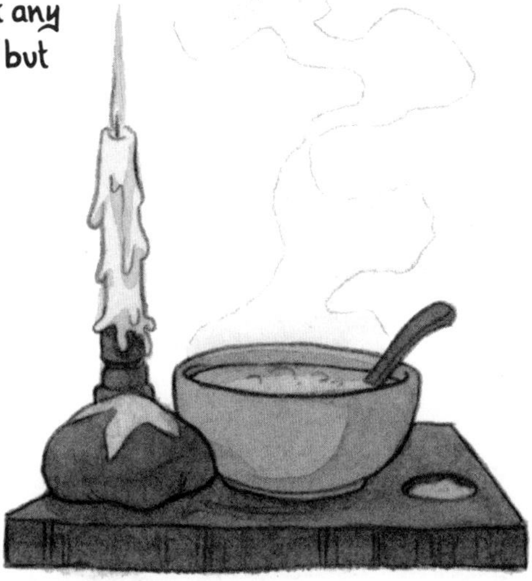

On some days the adults are supposed to fast—that means only eating one small meal for the whole day.

I used to wish I could join in the fasting.

It made me feel like a baby, and William, too, to eat my porridge while everybody else was so grown up and holy.

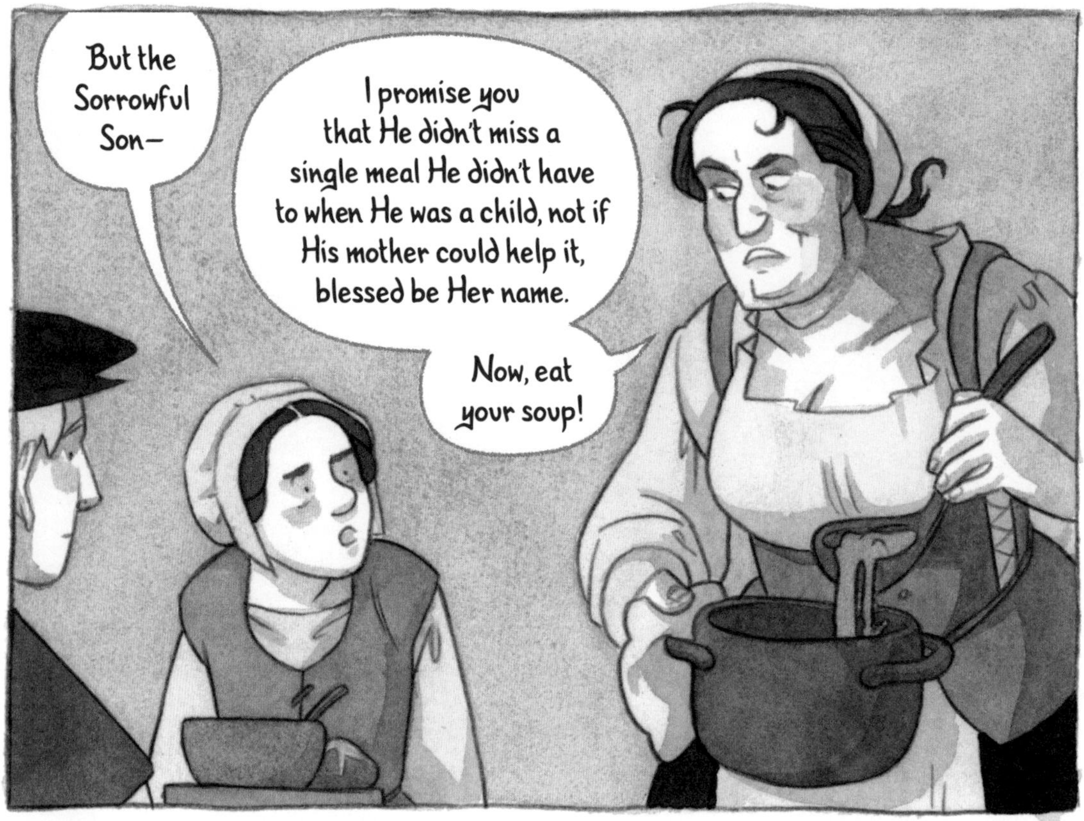
But the Sorrowful Son—
I promise you that He didn't miss a single meal He didn't have to when He was a child, not if His mother could help it, blessed be Her name.
Now, eat your soup!

After that flavorless month, the Paschal Feast arrives, and all the best food appears on the supper table again. Since the *Regina Maris* comes shortly afterward with half a year's worth of fresh supplies, Sister Wynefreed and Maud can empty the cellars without concern.

But the ship coming early meant that there was a lot of work to do, very quickly.

Suddenly the whole Island was busy. Jess and Bess hurried to ready a room in the Guest House for Captain Marley and to start the meal we'd feed to the sailors.

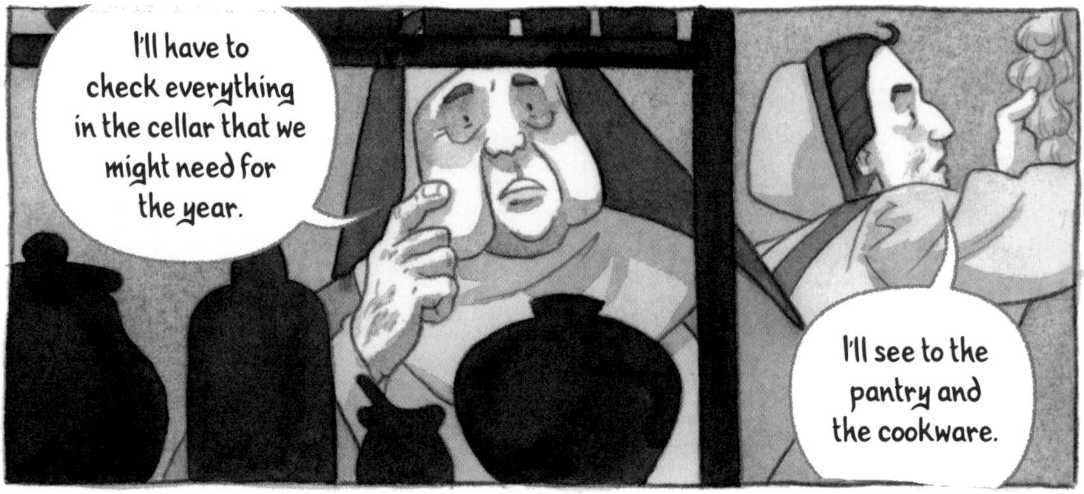
I'll have to check everything in the cellar that we might need for the year.
I'll see to the pantry and the cookware.

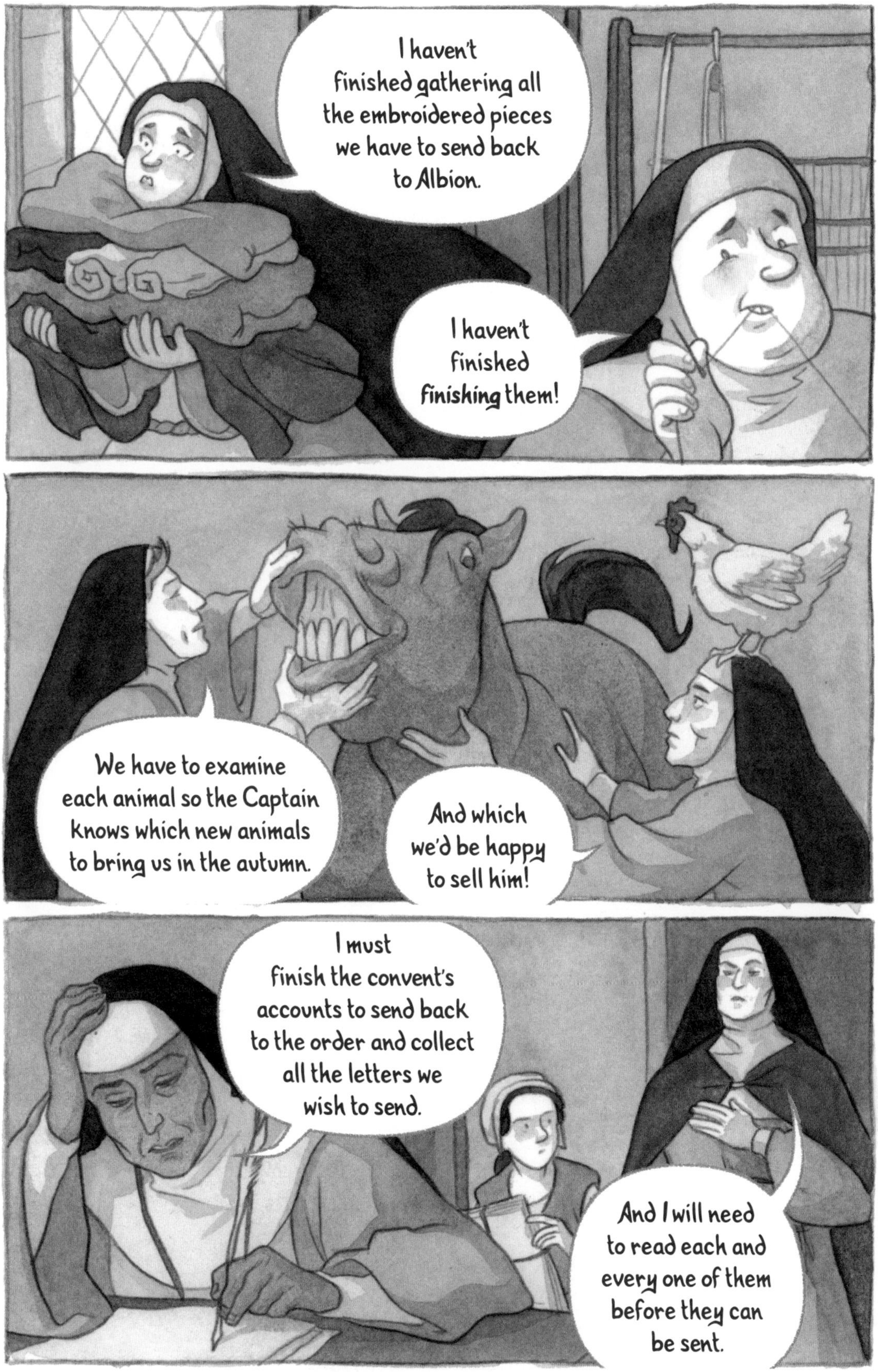
I haven't finished gathering all the embroidered pieces we have to send back to Albion.
I haven't finished finishing them!
We have to examine each animal so the Captain knows which new animals to bring us in the autumn.
And which we'd be happy to sell him!
I must finish the convent's accounts to send back to the order and collect all the letters we wish to send.
And I will need to read each and every one of them before they can be sent.

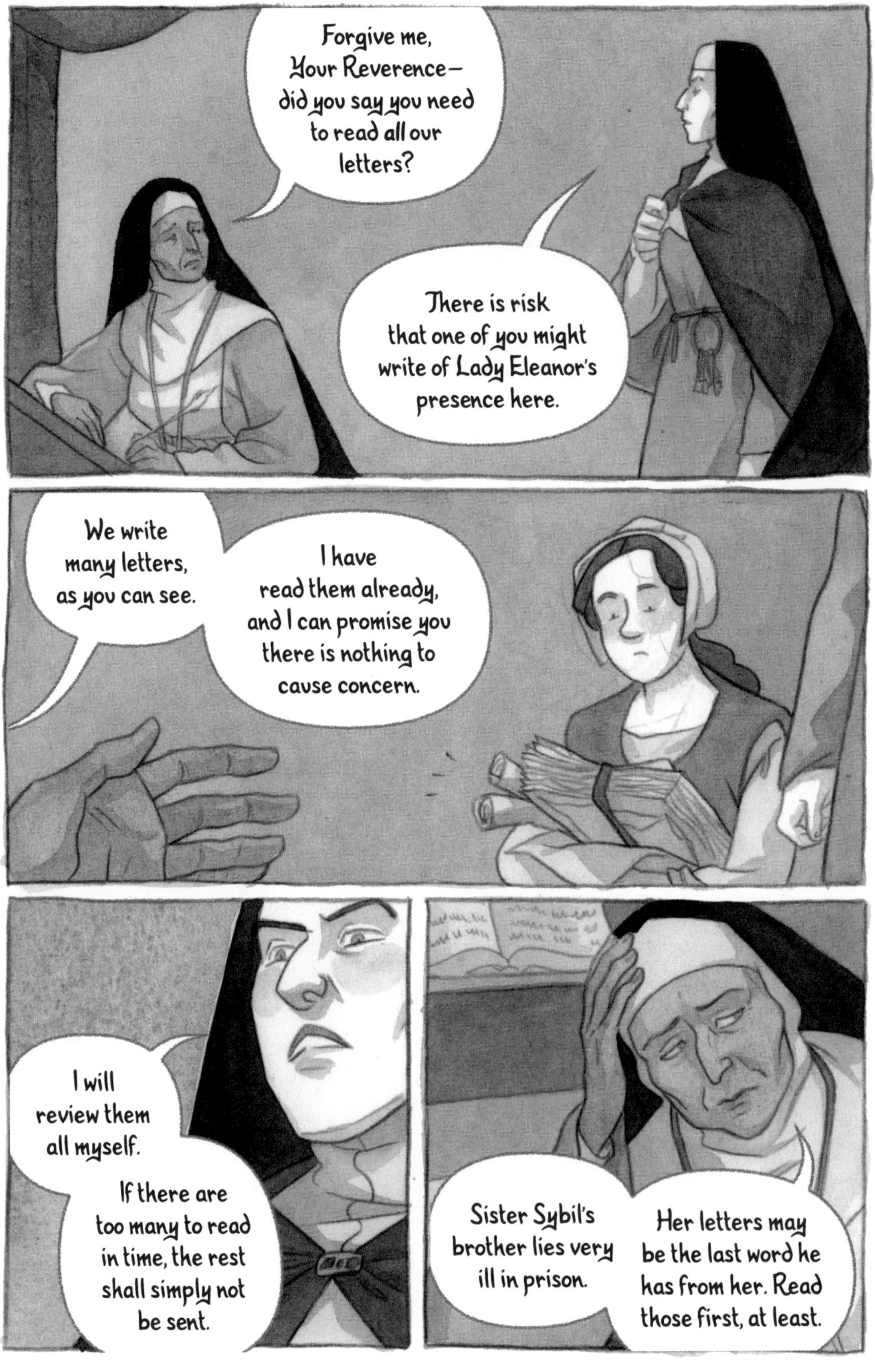
Forgive me, Your Reverence—did you say you need to read all our letters?
There is risk that one of you might write of Lady Eleanor's presence here.
We write many letters, as you can see.
I have read them already, and I can promise you there is nothing to cause concern.
I will review them all myself.
If there are too many to read in time, the rest shall simply not be sent.
Sister Sybil's brother lies very ill in prison.
Her letters may be the last word he has from her. Read those first, at least.

Soon the *Regina Maris* had reached the bay, and it was time for everybody to go down the Stairway to the dock to meet the longboat. I was sent to fetch Francis, and soon I realized the worst thing of all about the ship's early arrival.

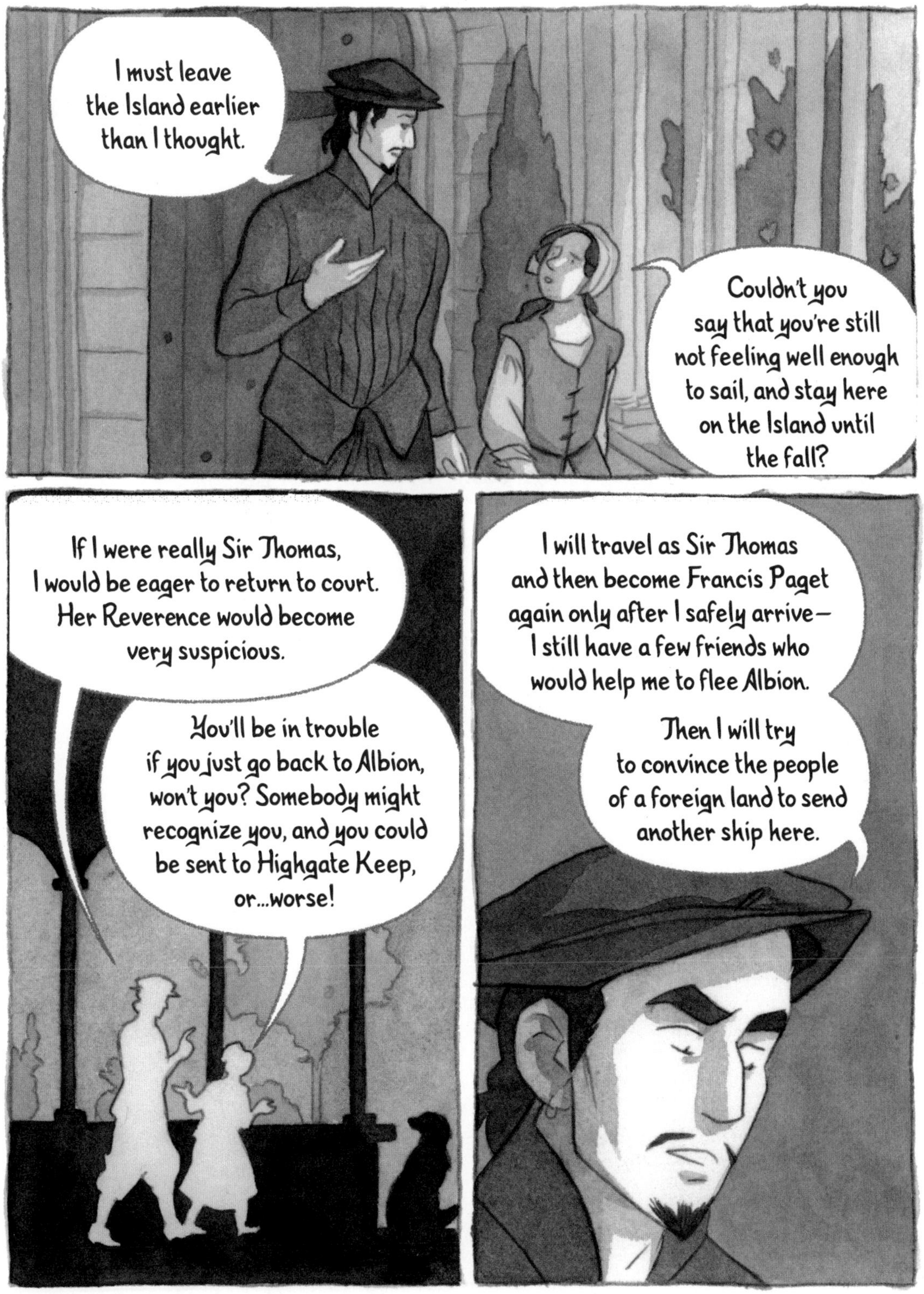

I must leave the Island earlier than I thought.
Couldn't you say that you're still not feeling well enough to sail, and stay here on the Island until the fall?
If I were really Sir Thomas, I would be eager to return to court. Her Reverence would become very suspicious.
You'll be in trouble if you just go back to Albion, won't you? Somebody might recognize you, and you could be sent to Highgate Keep, or...worse!
I will travel as Sir Thomas and then become Francis Paget again only after I safely arrive— I still have a few friends who would help me to flee Albion.
Then I will try to convince the people of a foreign land to send another ship here.

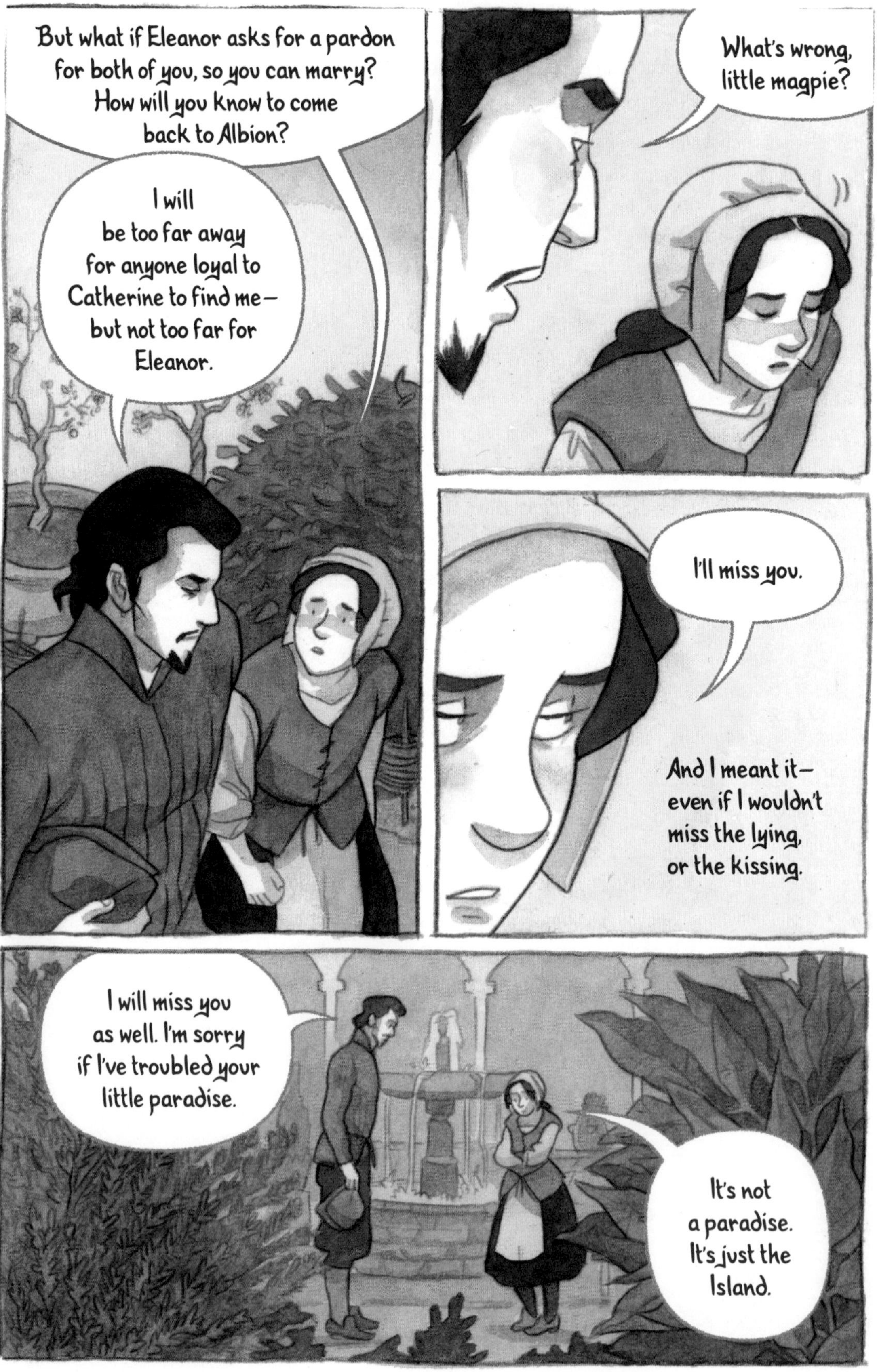
But what if Eleanor asks for a pardon for both of you, so you can marry? How will you know to come back to Albion?
I will be too far away for anyone loyal to Catherine to find me— but not too far for Eleanor.
What's wrong, little magpie?
I'll miss you.
And I meant it— even if I wouldn't miss the lying, or the kissing.
I will miss you as well. I'm sorry if I've troubled your little paradise.
It's not a paradise. It's just the Island.

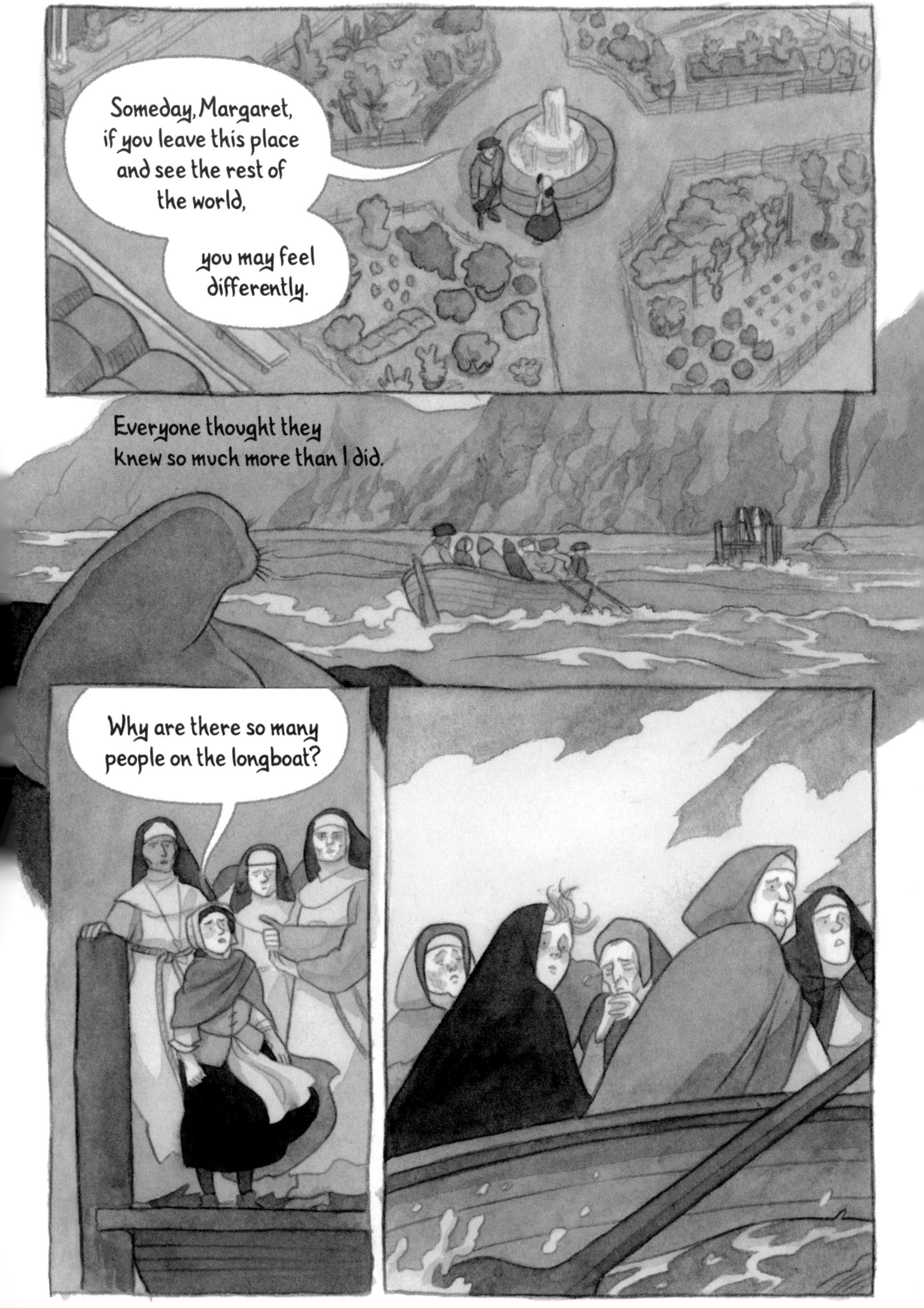
Someday, Margaret, if you leave this place and see the rest of the world,
you may feel differently.
Everyone thought they knew so much more than I did.
Why are there so many people on the longboat?

The *Regina Maris* had never brought more than two new people at a time. It's hard enough to feed just one extra person for half a year without any warning. Six new women and no extra supplies meant that—

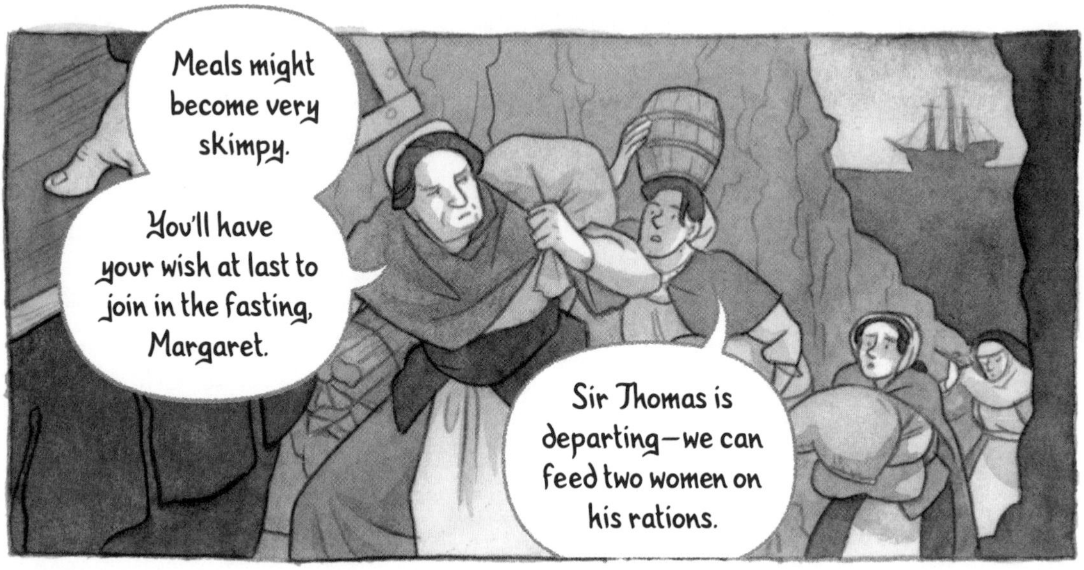
Meals might become very skimpy.
You'll have your wish at last to join in the fasting, Margaret.
Sir Thomas is departing—we can feed two women on his rations.

Who were all these new women? Prisoners, of course.

Some were like Lady Cameron and the sisters—noblewomen whose families weren't loyal enough to the crown. Queen Catherine had found all sorts of new enemies, it seemed. But some of them were already nuns.

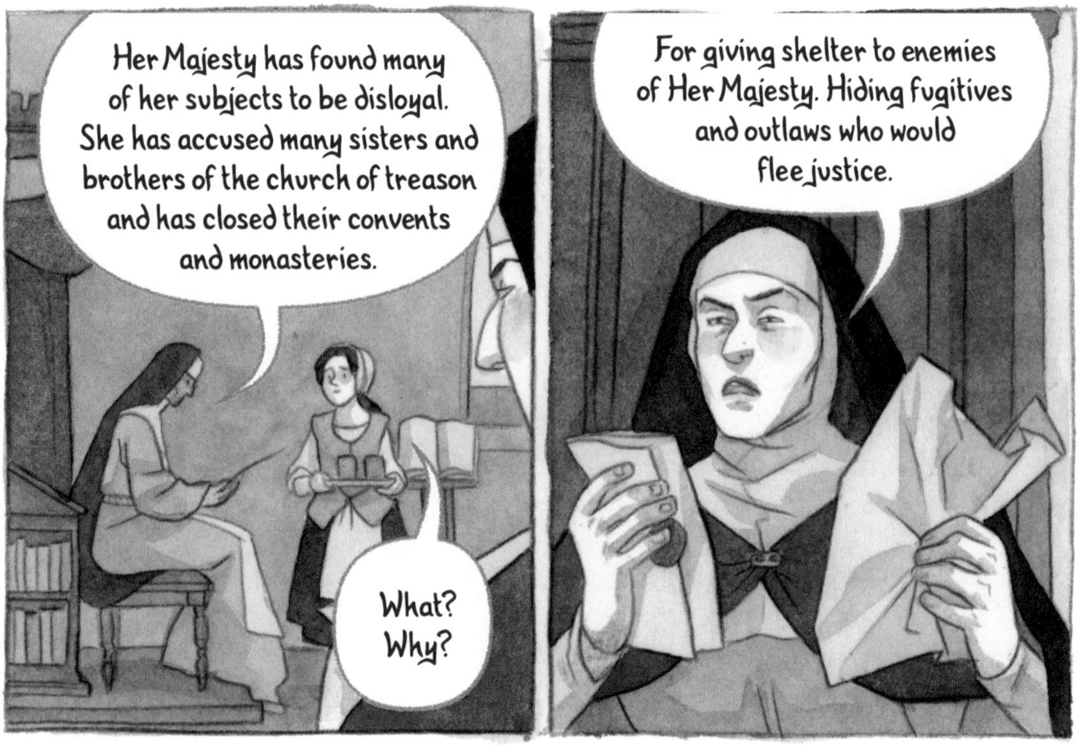
Her Majesty has found many of her subjects to be disloyal. She has accused many sisters and brothers of the church of treason and has closed their convents and monasteries.
What? Why?
For giving shelter to enemies of Her Majesty. Hiding fugitives and outlaws who would flee justice.

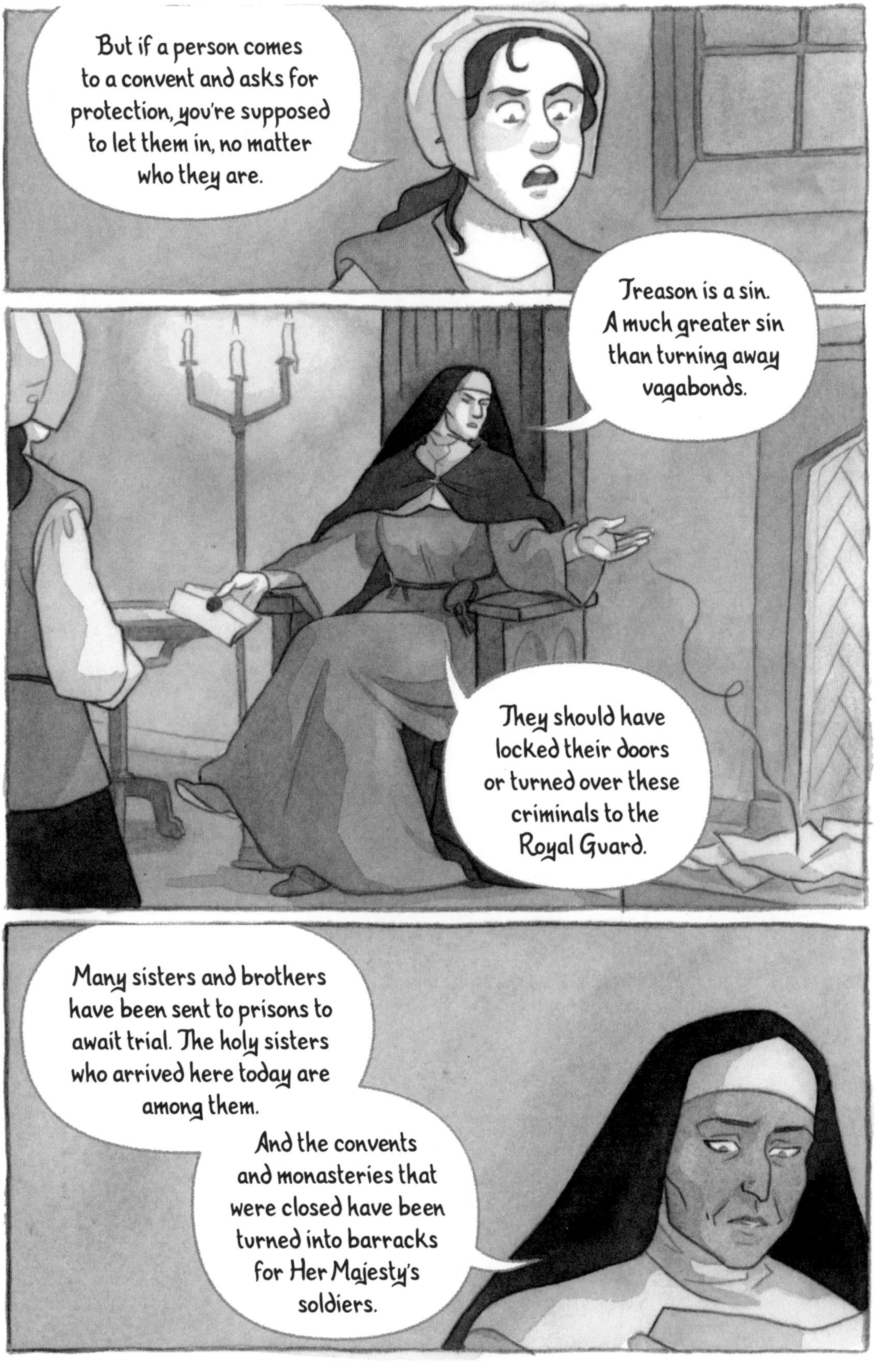
But if a person comes to a convent and asks for protection, you're supposed to let them in, no matter who they are.
Treason is a sin. A much greater sin than turning away vagabonds.
They should have locked their doors or turned over these criminals to the Royal Guard.
Many sisters and brothers have been sent to prisons to await trial. The holy sisters who arrived here today are among them.
And the convents and monasteries that were closed have been turned into barracks for Her Majesty's soldiers.

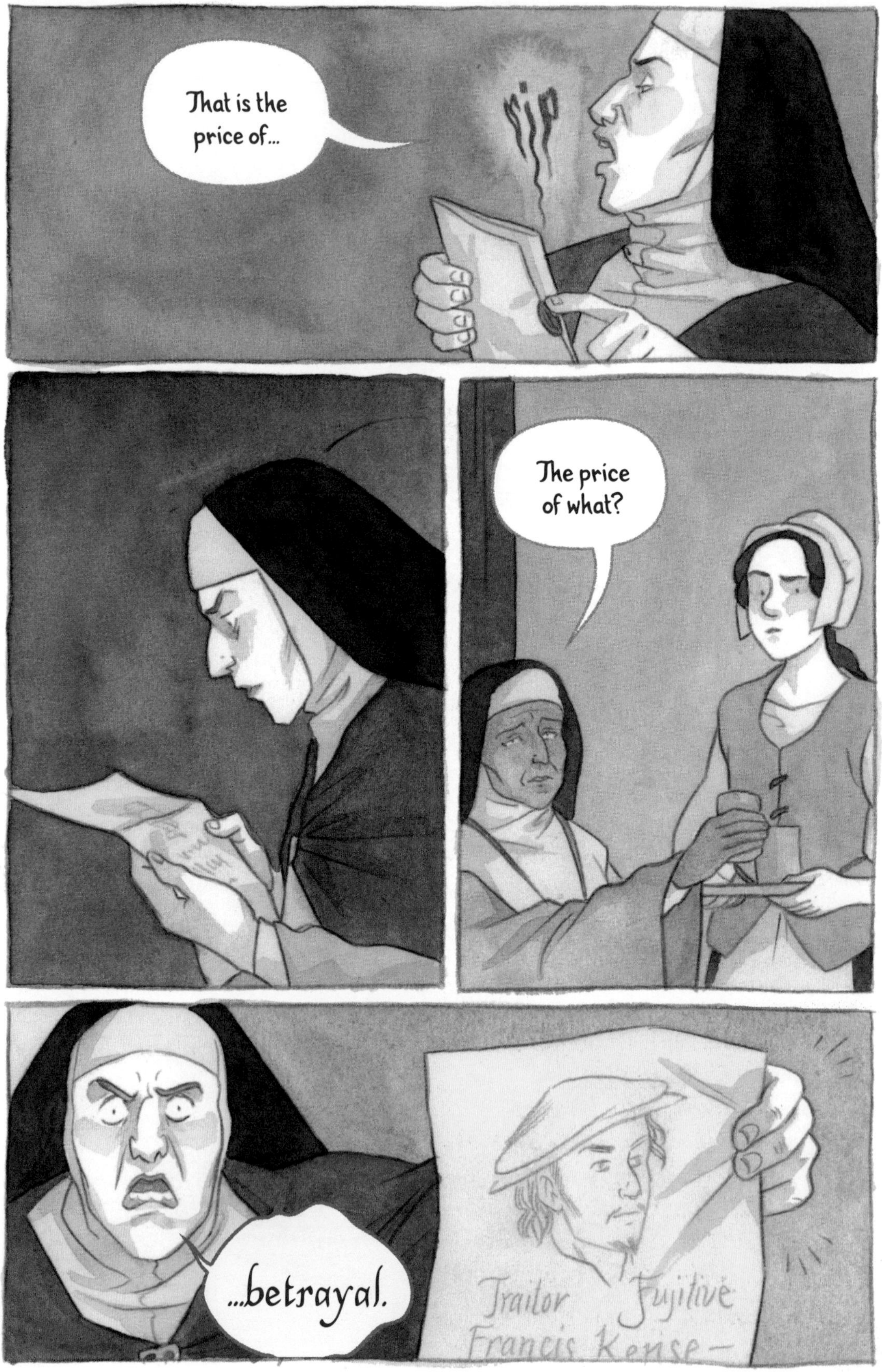
That is the price of...
rip
The price of what?
...betrayal.
Traitor Fugitive
Francis Kense—

I've already told you about martyrs.

Saints who sacrificed their lives for a holy cause. And I've already told you that Saint Elysia wasn't a martyr. But that's because nobody ever even saw her die!

One misty day she went out in a fishing boat—a coracle, like ours—to visit the fishermen who made their living on the waves.

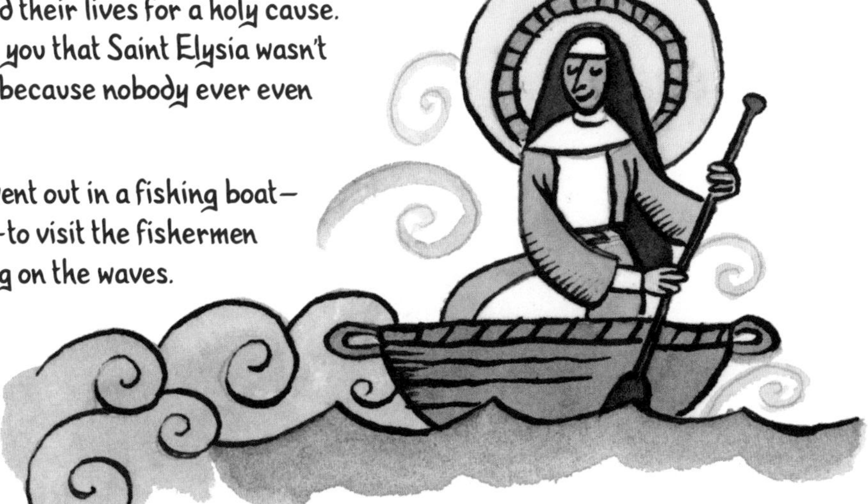

After she had spoken with the last fisherman, she began to row away. But she didn't row back to shore, as he expected she would. Instead she started to row out to sea. When he asked where she was going, she answered,

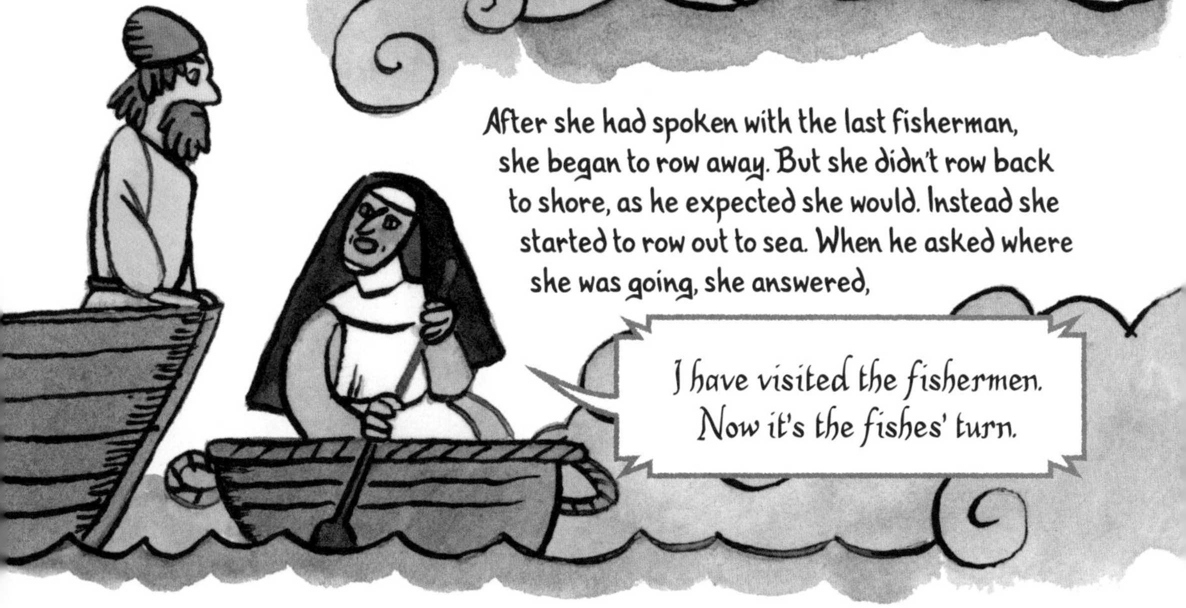
I have visited the fishermen. Now it's the fishes' turn.

There are some versions of the story where she turned into a fish and swam away, but even I think that's a little ridiculous.

There's another version where Saint Elysia rowed away into the mist and was never seen again, at least not by anybody who already knew her.

Sometimes people say they've been rescued from drowning, or warned off of sailing onto rocks, or saved from being captured by pirates, by an Elysian sister in a coracle who rowed away before they could thank her.

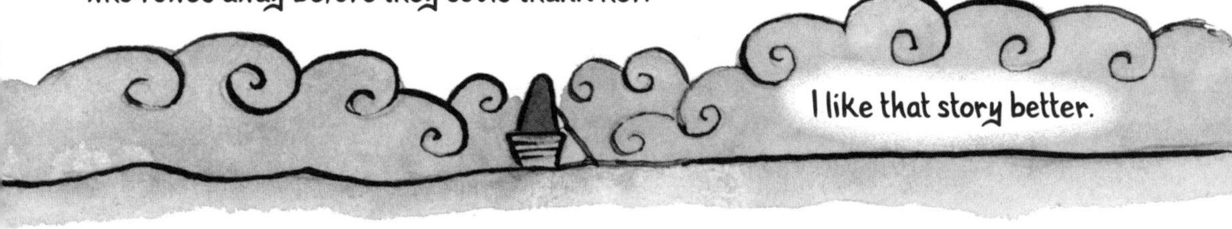
I like that story better.

Traitor

Fujitive

The letter that Mother Mary Clemence had received not only
had a picture of Francis drawn on it but also a description of him
and a list of all the crimes he had committed—or that Queen Catherine
said he had committed. Theft, spying, conspiracy, treason!

Francis had hoped that nobody in Albion would notice he was gone
until after he had already found and rescued Eleanor and they had
escaped to the Continent. But the shipwreck meant that he'd been
trapped here for too long. Everybody in court had had time to realize
that he had disappeared for good, and to discover that he'd stolen
money from the Royal Treasury—enough to buy a ship and to hire
soldiers to help him rescue Eleanor.

The letter said that Francis might be anywhere—in Gallia, or Ecossia,
or even just hiding in Albion in disguise. It said that Francis knew
enough from his time pretending to be loyal to Queen Catherine that
he might have guessed that Eleanor was on the Island. He might try
to come here. If he did, Mother Mary Clemence should have her men
take him prisoner immediately, so he could be taken back to Albion
on the first ship.

Nobody knew that he was already here.
Except for us.

Now we were guilty of treason, too.

Mother Mary Clemence couldn't be quite sure yet who "we" were, though. Eleanor obviously knew that "Sir Thomas" was really Francis. And Francis, of course, knew who he was.

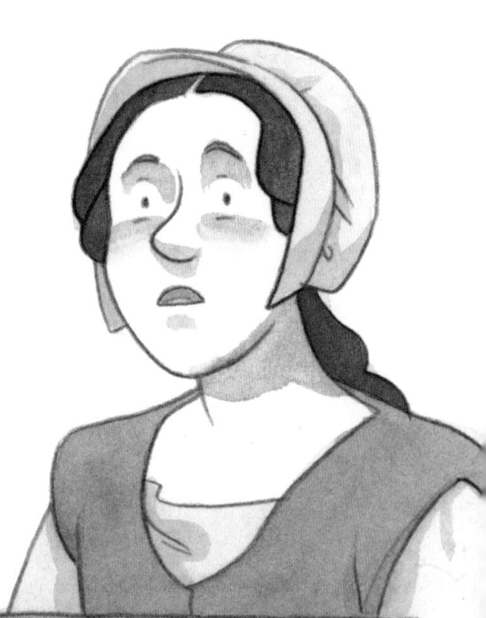

If I had just stood there and pretended to be surprised, Mother Mary Clemence might not have guessed that I knew, too.

She might've kept thinking I was just a silly little girl who played Cherry Pit and daydreamed while Eleanor and Francis whispered plots to each other just a few feet away. At the very least she would've had to go get her awful Liar's Taper.

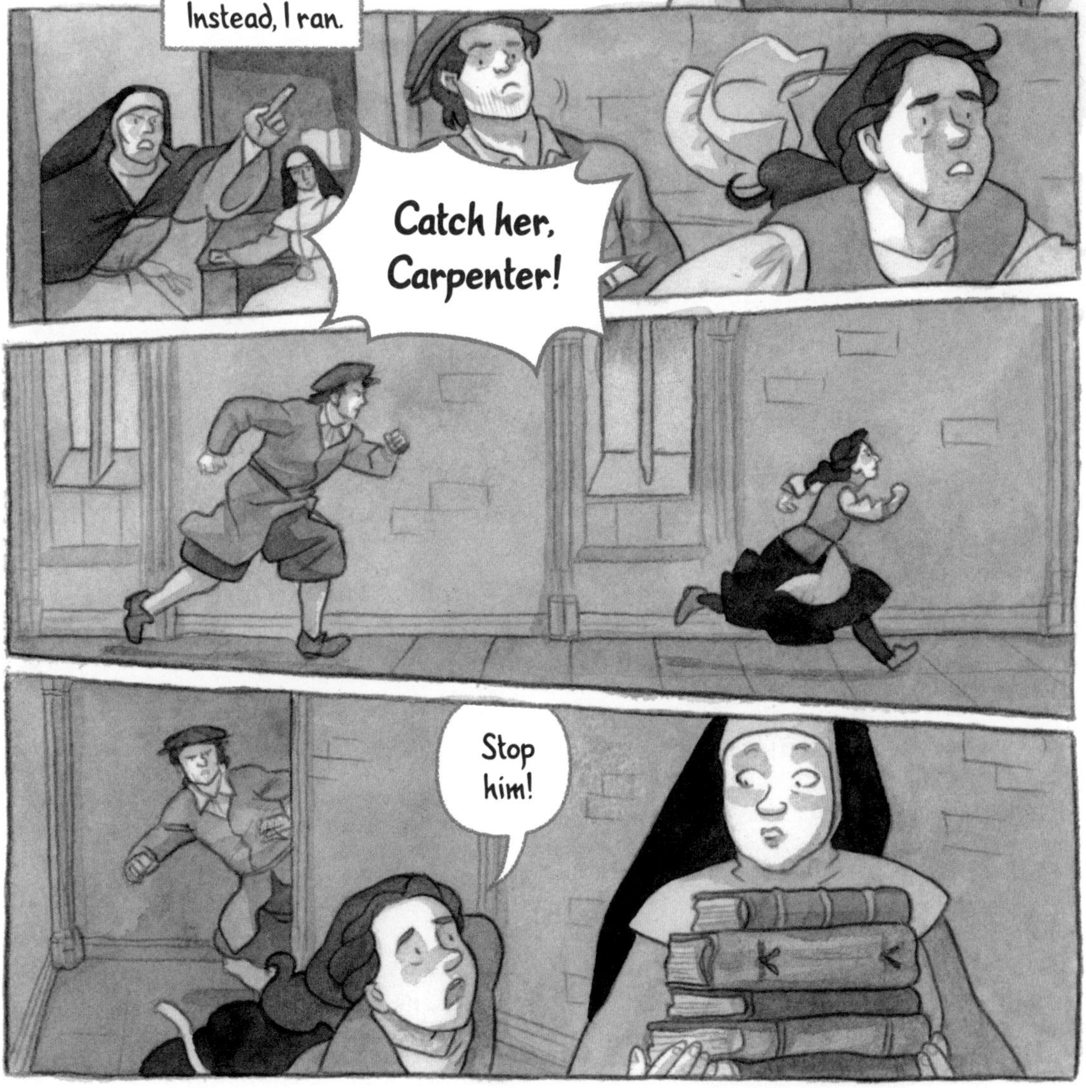

Instead, I ran.
Catch her, Carpenter!
Stop him!

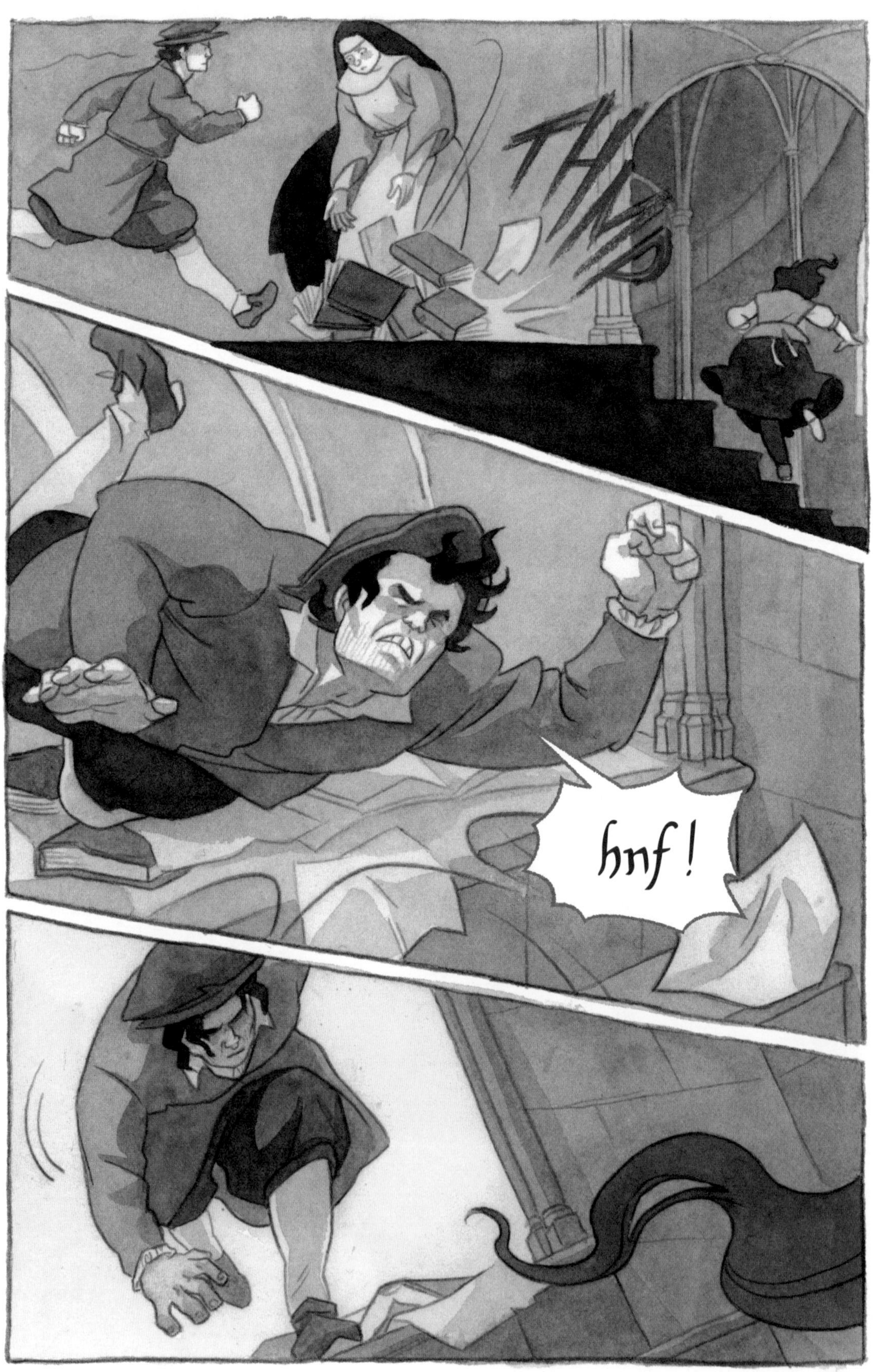
THMP
hnf!

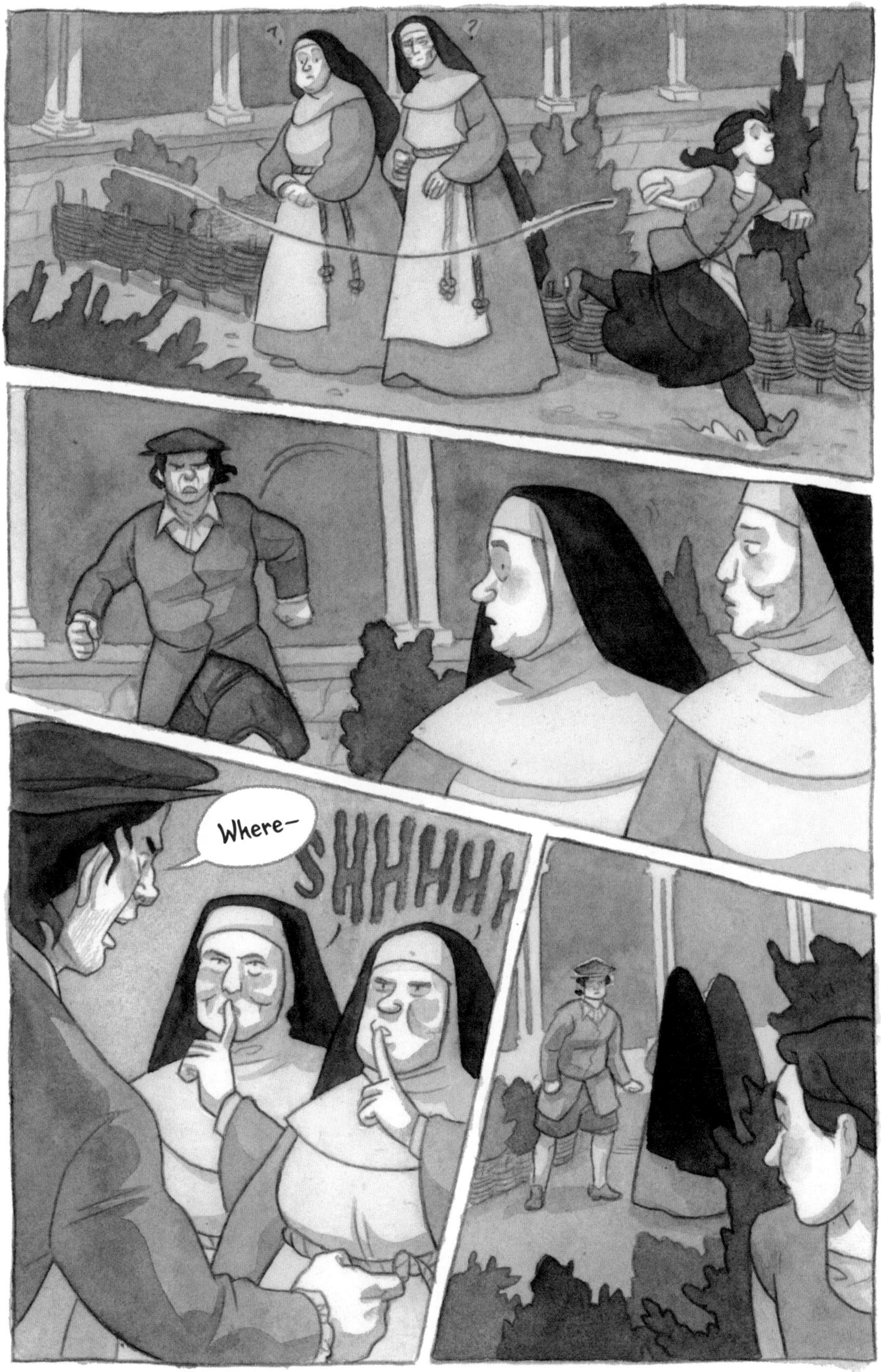
?
?
Where–
SHHHHH

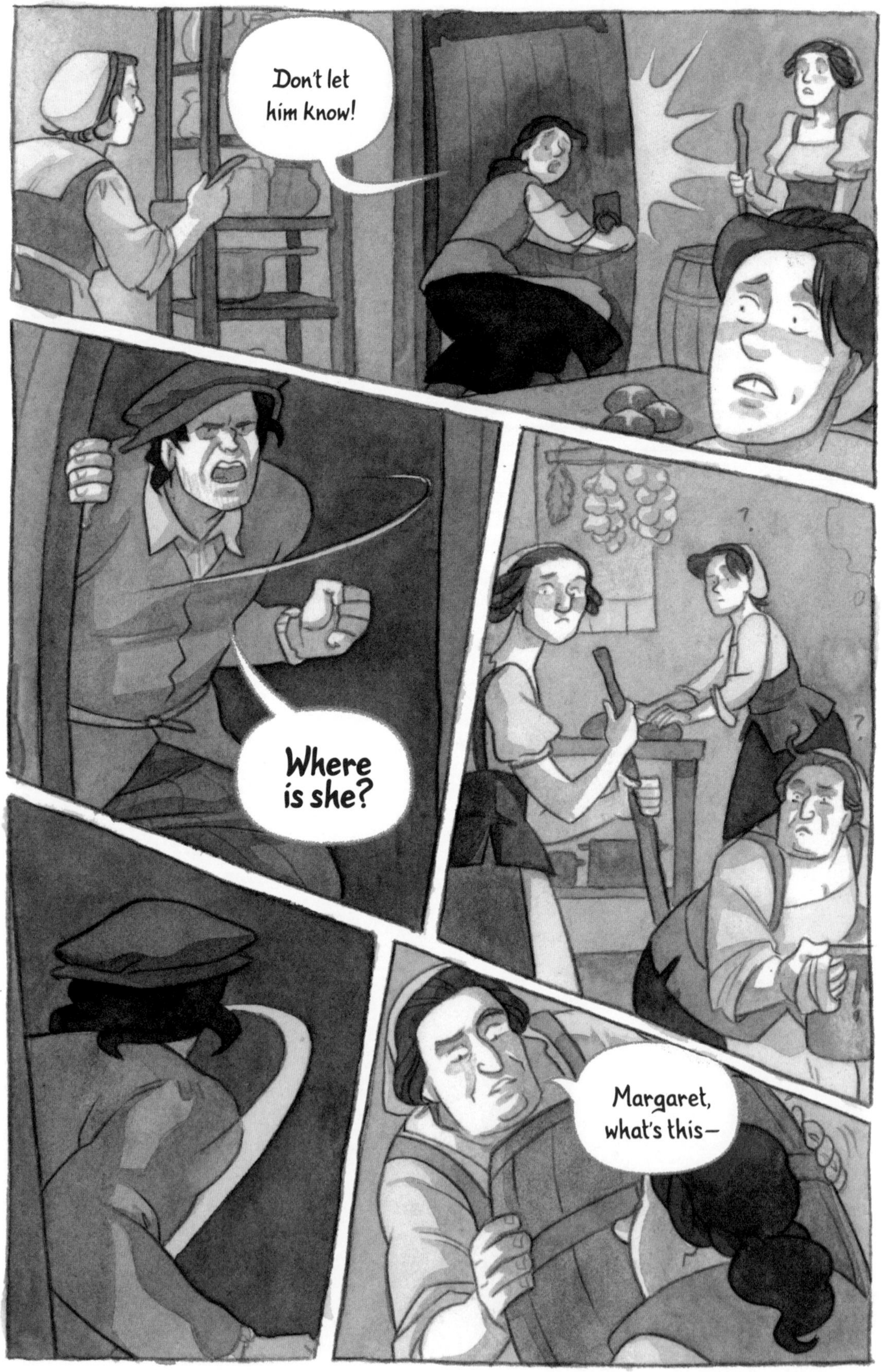
Don't let him know!
Where is she?
Margaret, what's this—

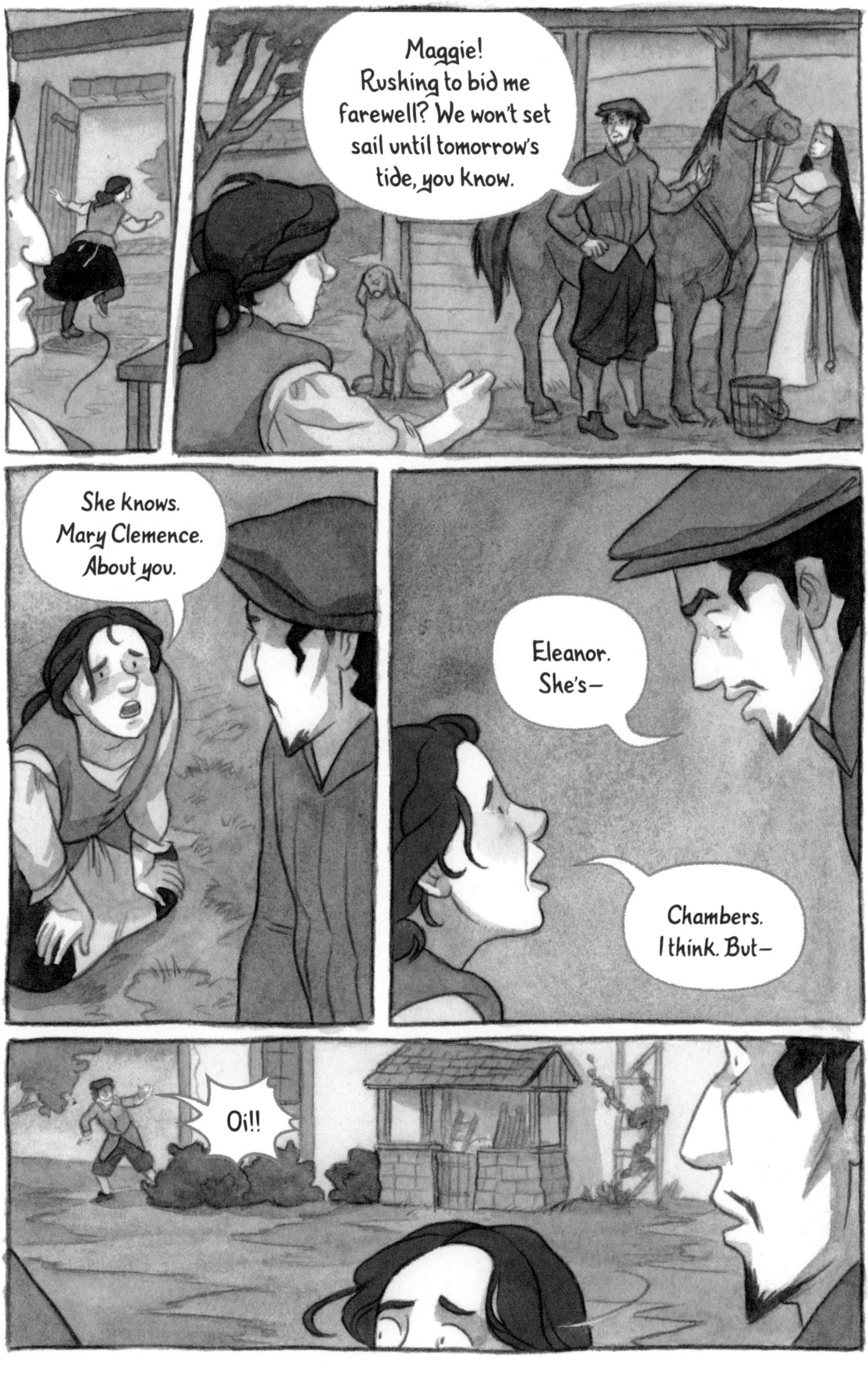
Maggie! Rushing to bid me farewell? We won't set sail until tomorrow's tide, you know.
She knows. Mary Clemence. About you.
Eleanor. She's—
Chambers. I think. But—
Oi!!

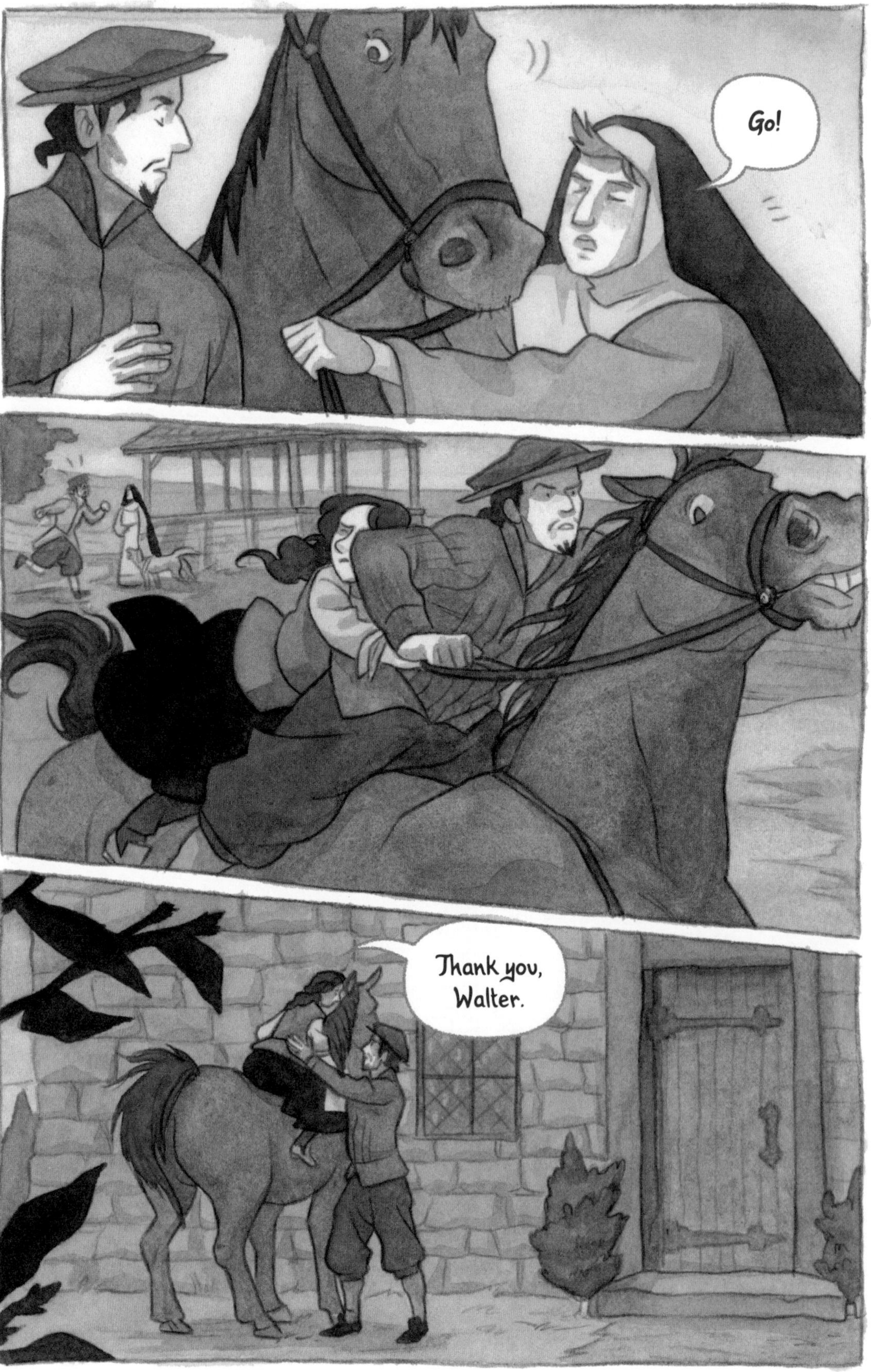
Go!
Thank you, Walter.

We ran up the stairs and into the Guest House. I'm not sure where I thought we'd go after we found Eleanor. I'm not sure Francis knew, either.

The only thing that mattered was reaching Eleanor before Mother Mary Clemence did.

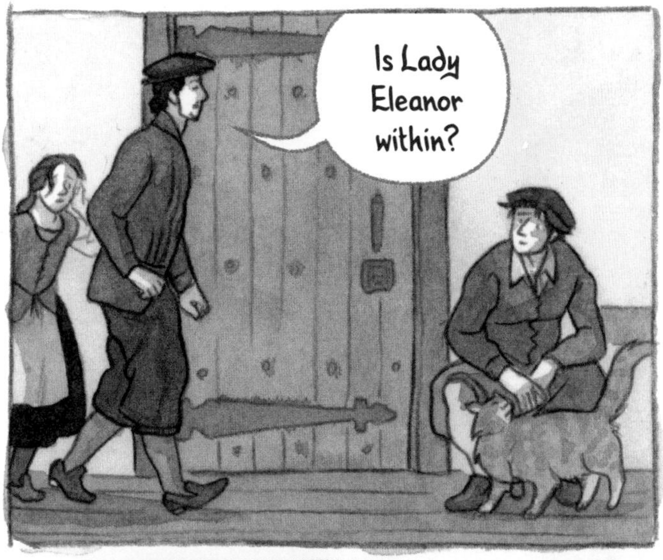
Is Lady Eleanor within?

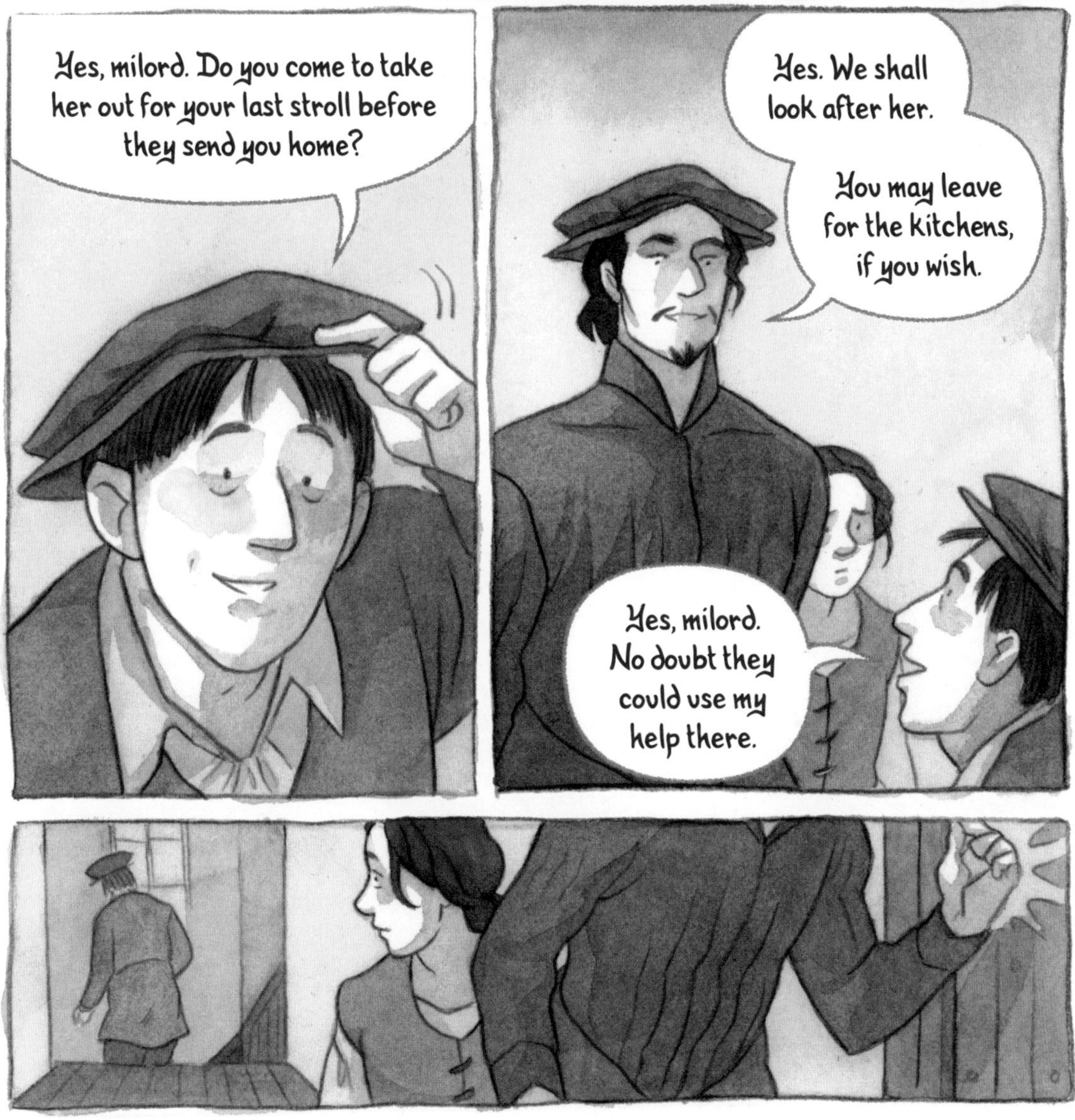
Yes, milord. Do you come to take her out for your last stroll before they send you home?
Yes. We shall look after her.
You may leave for the kitchens, if you wish.
Yes, milord. No doubt they could use my help there.

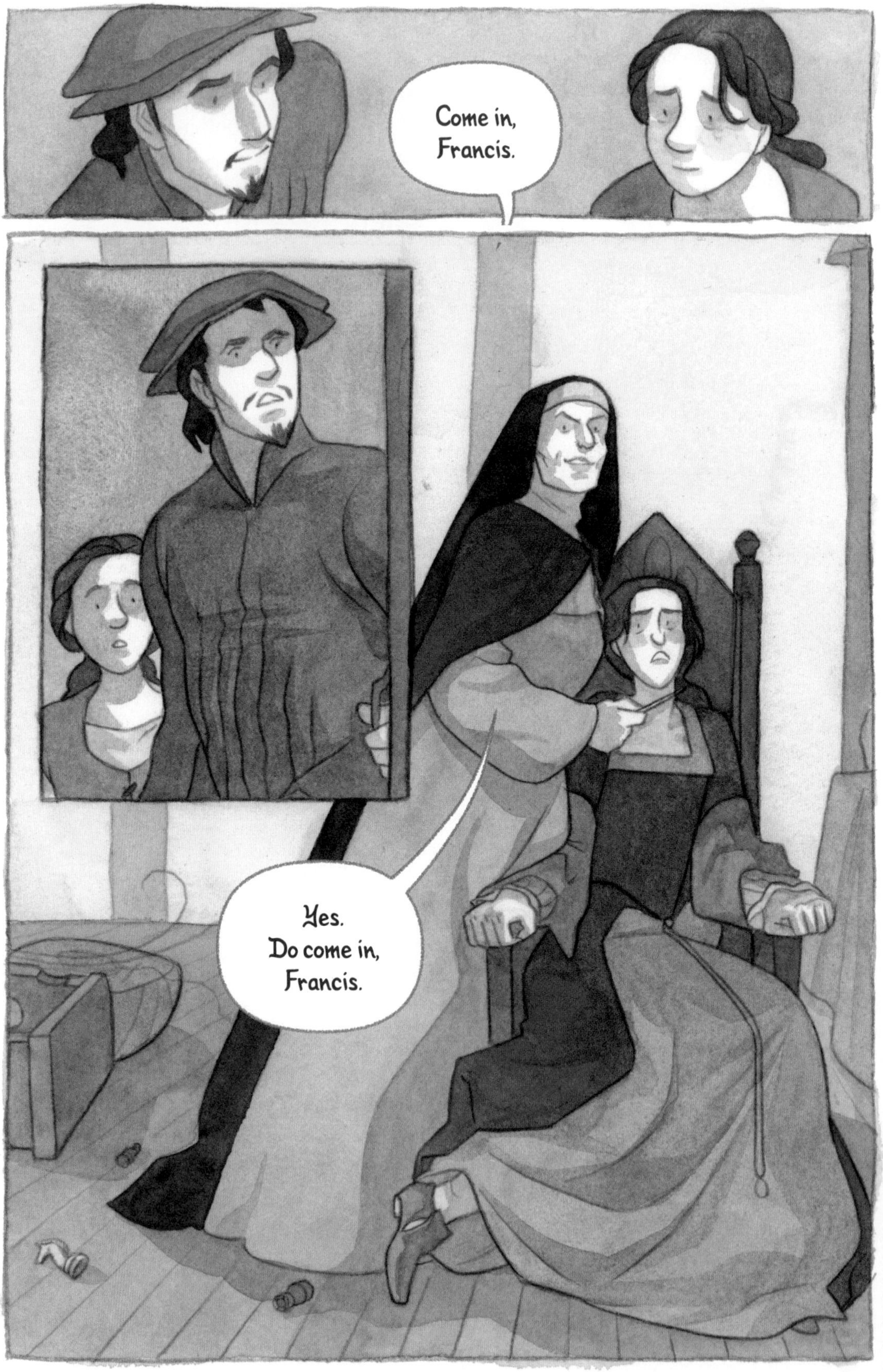
Come in, Francis.
Yes. Do come in, Francis.

Mother Mary Clemence locked us all into separate rooms.

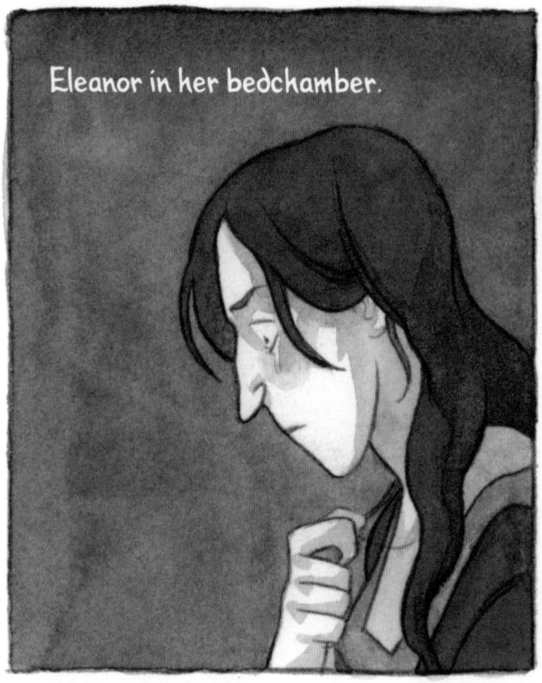
Eleanor in her bedchamber.

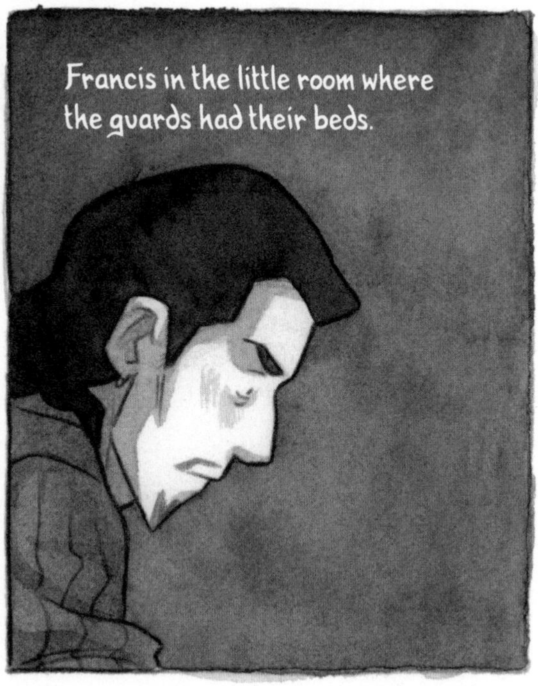
Francis in the little room where the guards had their beds.

My cell in the dorter and the spare chambers in the Guest House were occupied by the women who had arrived on the *Regina Maris*, so I was taken back to Sister Agnes's cell.

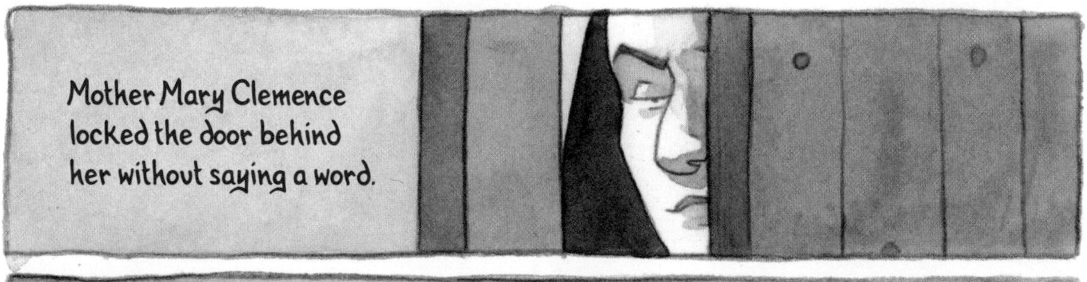
Mother Mary Clemence locked the door behind her without saying a word.

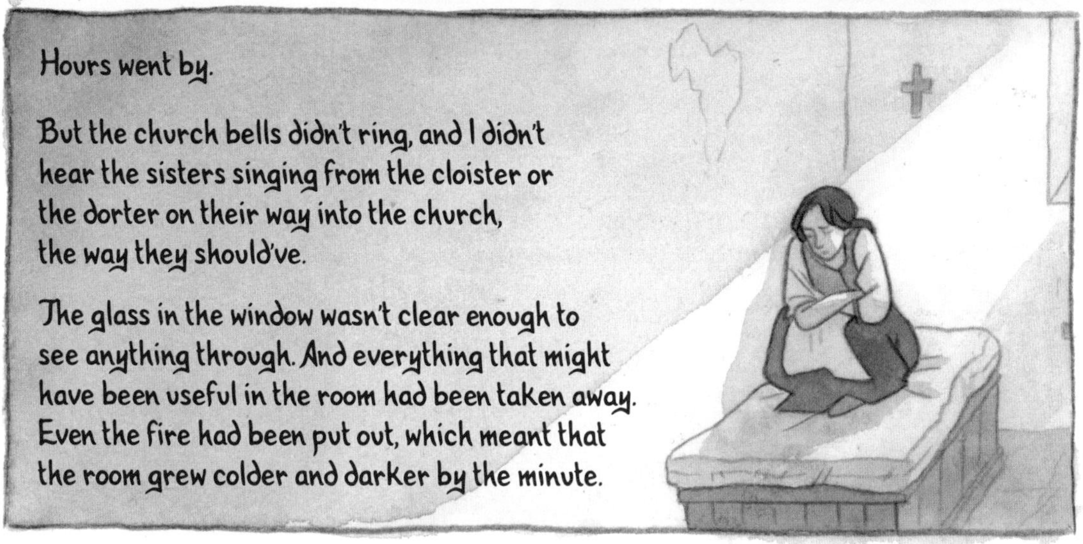
Hours went by.
But the church bells didn't ring, and I didn't hear the sisters singing from the cloister or the dorter on their way into the church, the way they should've.
The glass in the window wasn't clear enough to see anything through. And everything that might have been useful in the room had been taken away. Even the fire had been put out, which meant that the room grew colder and darker by the minute.

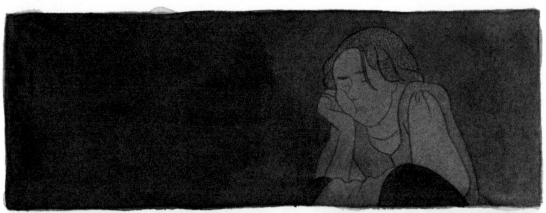

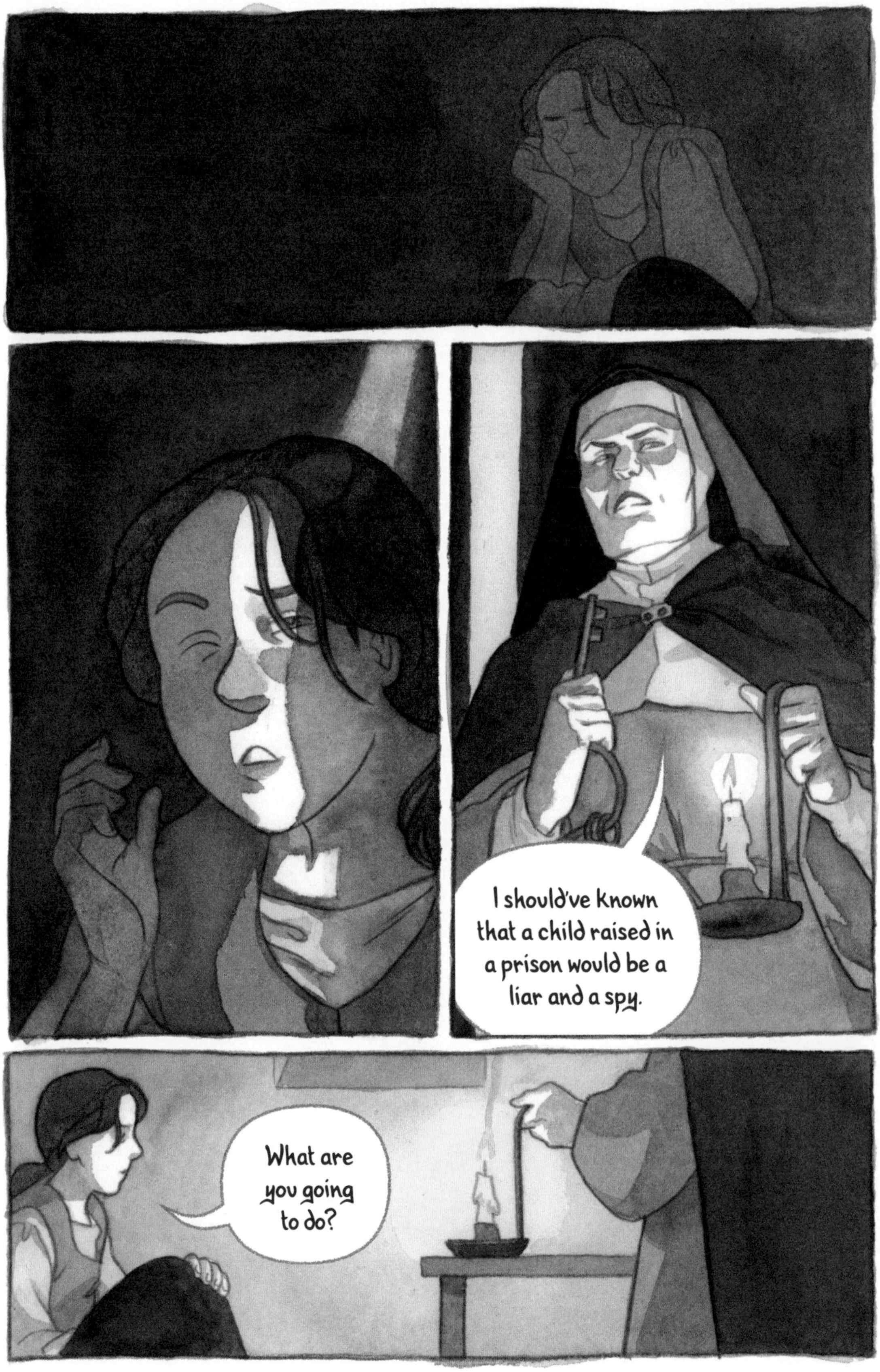
I should've known that a child raised in a prison would be a liar and a spy.
What are you going to do?

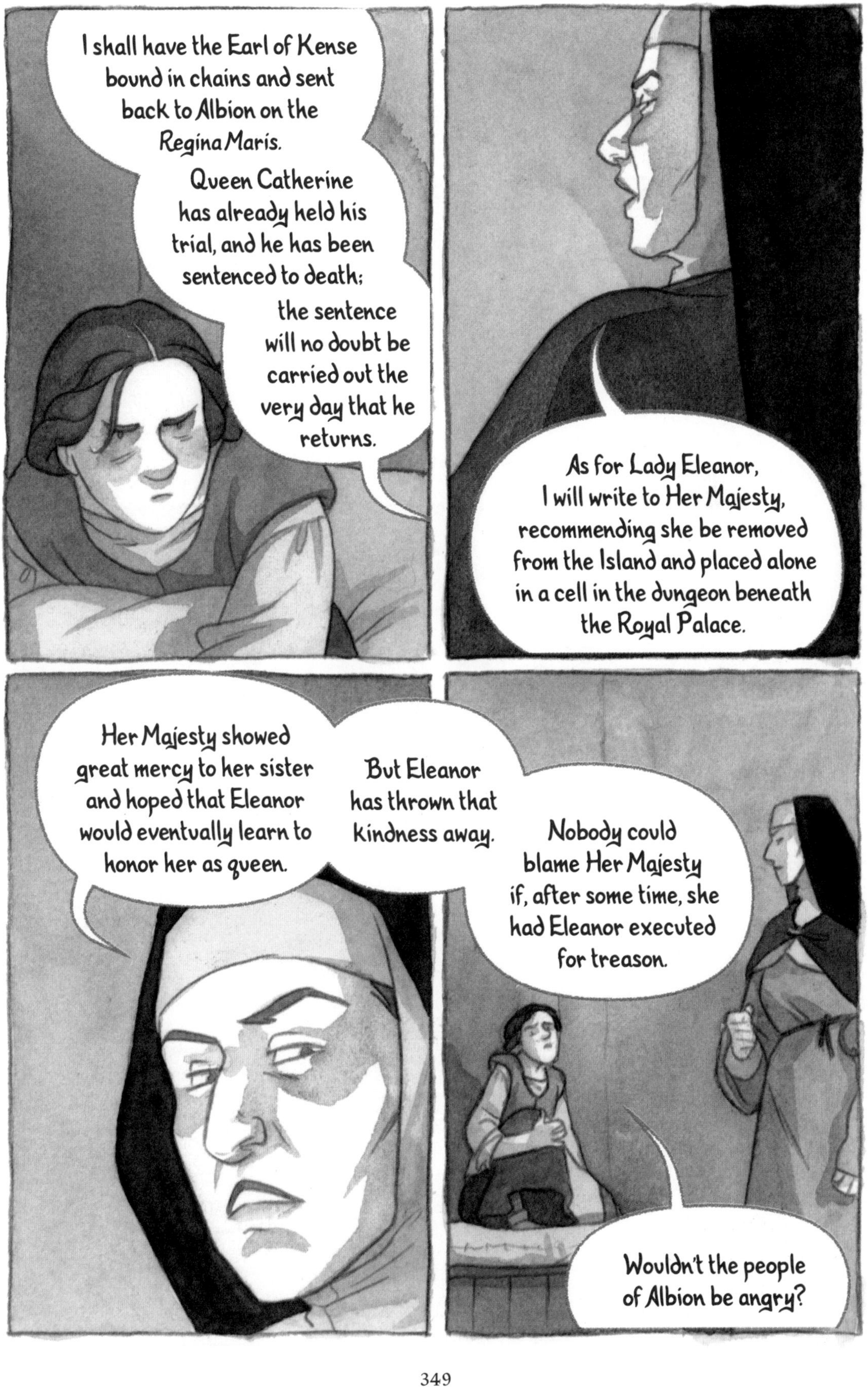
I shall have the Earl of Kense bound in chains and sent back to Albion on the *Regina Maris.*
Queen Catherine has already held his trial, and he has been sentenced to death;
the sentence will no doubt be carried out the very day that he returns.
As for Lady Eleanor, I will write to Her Majesty, recommending she be removed from the Island and placed alone in a cell in the dungeon beneath the Royal Palace.
Her Majesty showed great mercy to her sister and hoped that Eleanor would eventually learn to honor her as queen.
But Eleanor has thrown that kindness away.
Nobody could blame Her Majesty if, after some time, she had Eleanor executed for treason.
Wouldn't the people of Albion be angry?

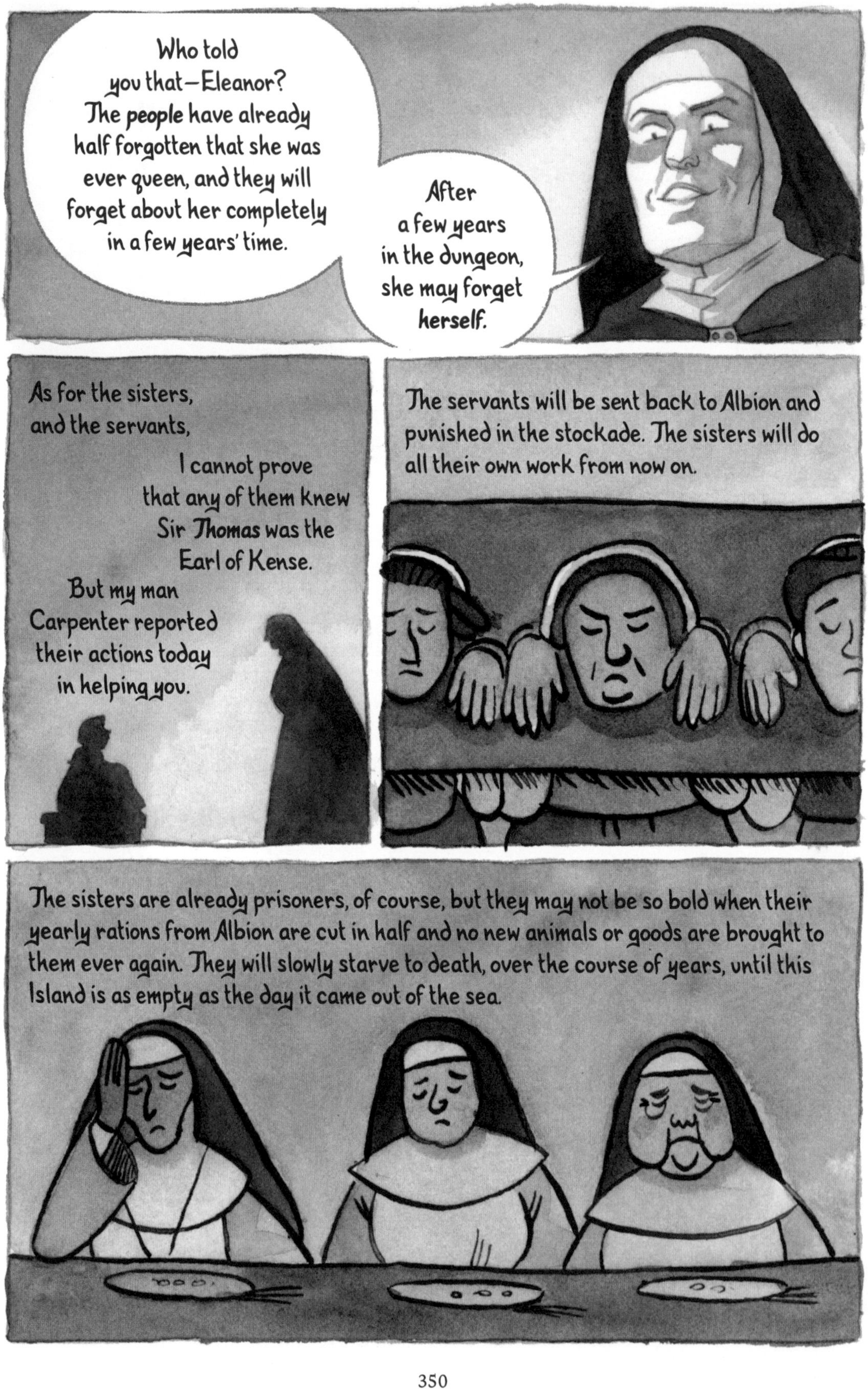
Who told you that—Eleanor? The people have already half forgotten that she was ever queen, and they will forget about her completely in a few years' time.
After a few years in the dungeon, she may forget herself.
As for the sisters, and the servants,
I cannot prove that any of them knew Sir Thomas was the Earl of Kense.
But my man Carpenter reported their actions today in helping you.
The servants will be sent back to Albion and punished in the stockade. The sisters will do all their own work from now on.
The sisters are already prisoners, of course, but they may not be so bold when their yearly rations from Albion are cut in half and no new animals or goods are brought to them ever again. They will slowly starve to death, over the course of years, until this Island is as empty as the day it came out of the sea.

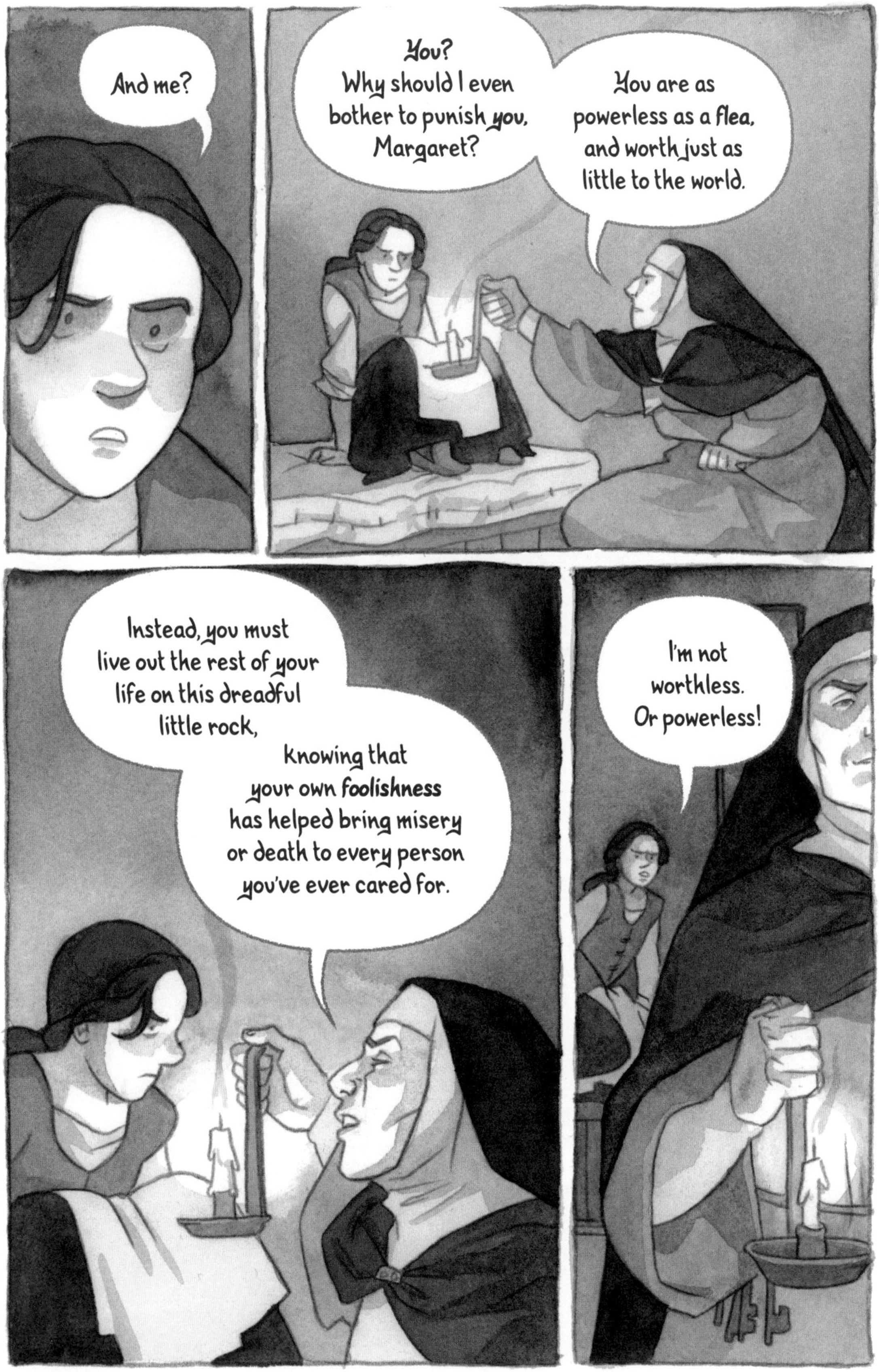
And me?
You? Why should I even bother to punish you, Margaret?
You are as powerless as a flea, and worth just as little to the world.
Instead, you must live out the rest of your life on this dreadful little rock,
knowing that your own foolishness has helped bring misery or death to every person you've ever cared for.
I'm not worthless. Or powerless!

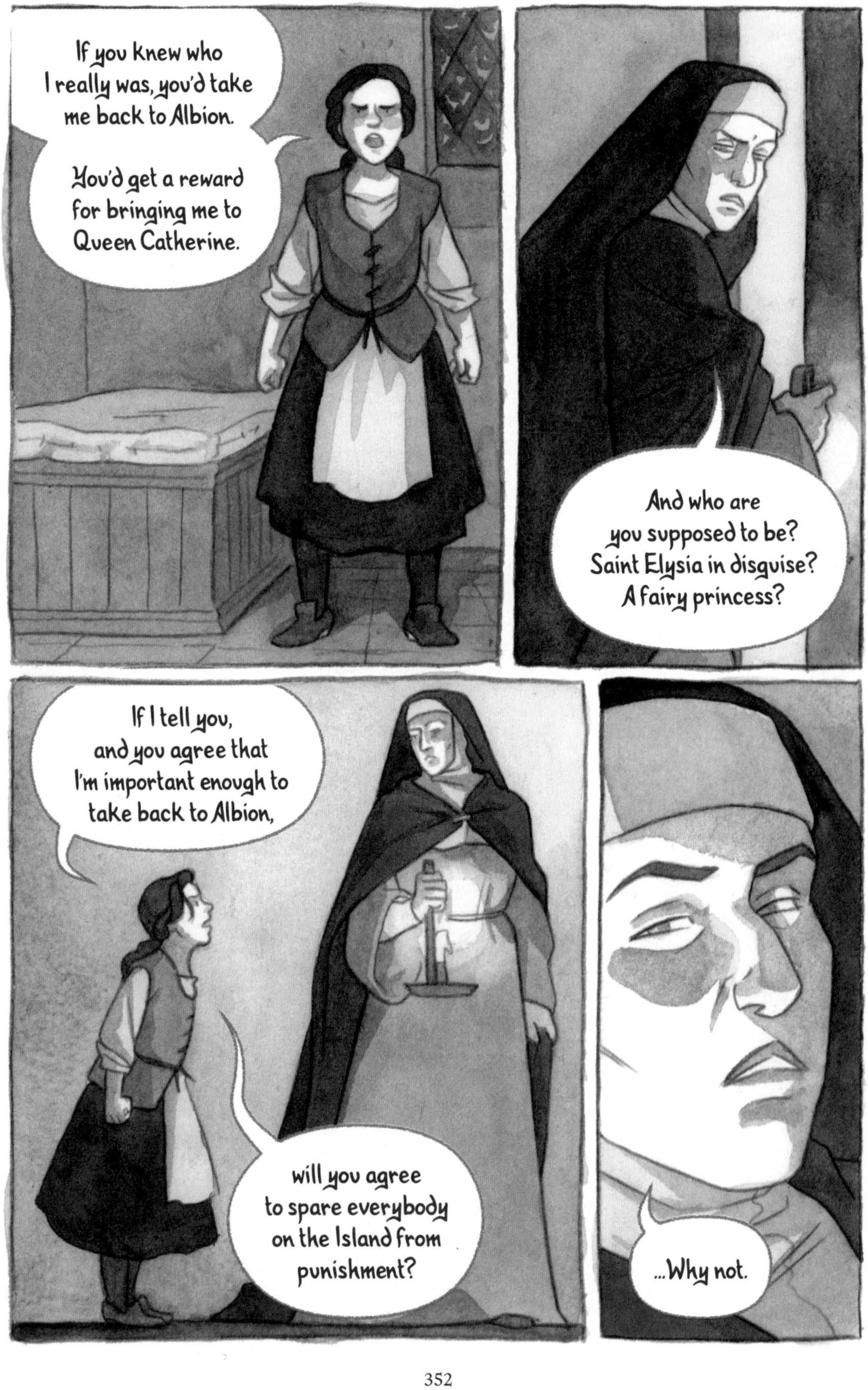
If you knew who I really was, you'd take me back to Albion.
You'd get a reward for bringing me to Queen Catherine.
And who are you supposed to be? Saint Elysia in disguise? A fairy princess?
If I tell you, and you agree that I'm important enough to take back to Albion,
will you agree to spare everybody on the Island from punishment?
...Why not.

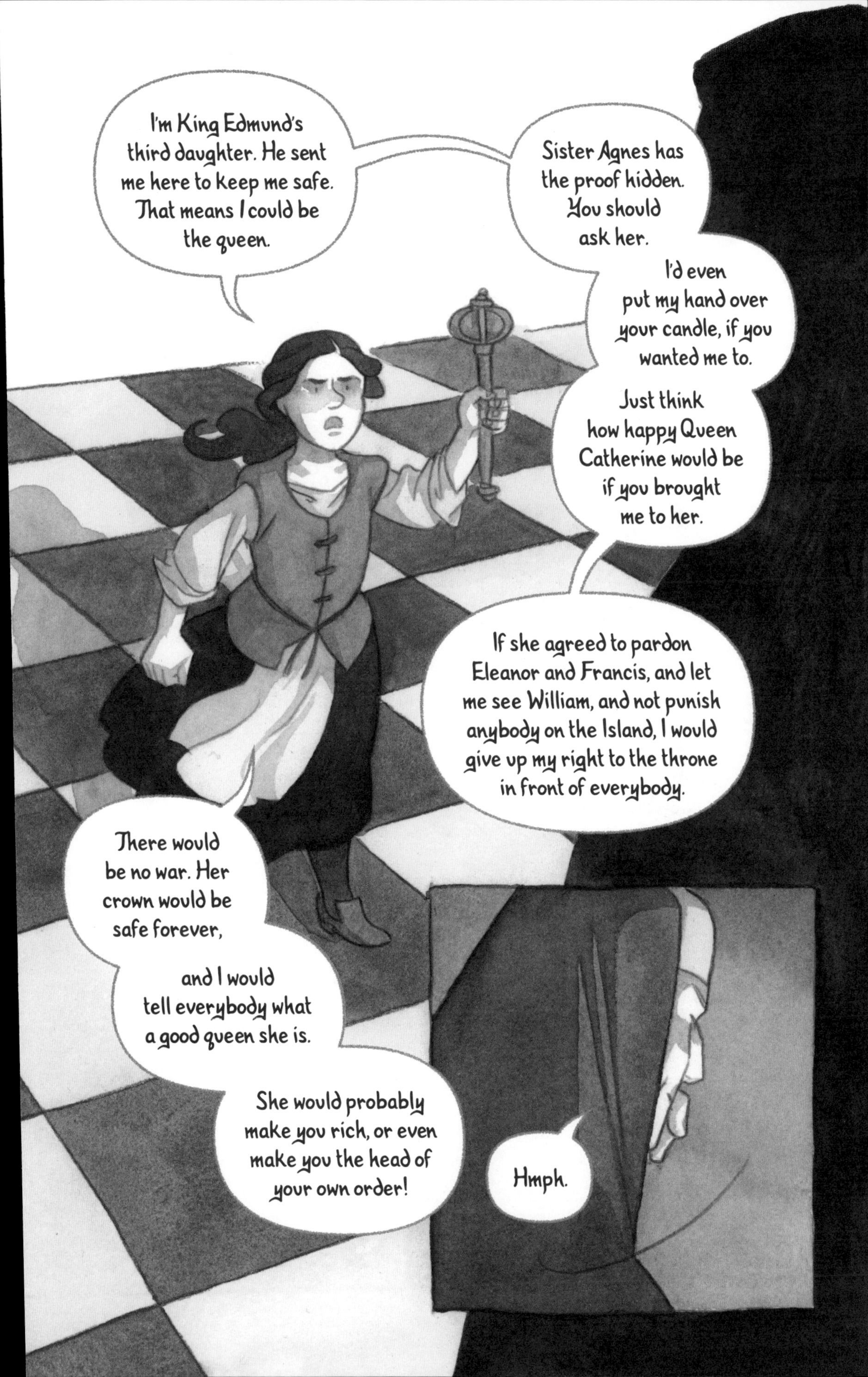
I'm King Edmund's third daughter. He sent me here to keep me safe. That means I could be the queen.
Sister Agnes has the proof hidden. You should ask her.
I'd even put my hand over your candle, if you wanted me to.
Just think how happy Queen Catherine would be if you brought me to her.
If she agreed to pardon Eleanor and Francis, and let me see William, and not punish anybody on the Island, I would give up my right to the throne in front of everybody.
There would be no war. Her crown would be safe forever,
and I would tell everybody what a good queen she is.
She would probably make you rich, or even make you the head of your own order!
Hmph.

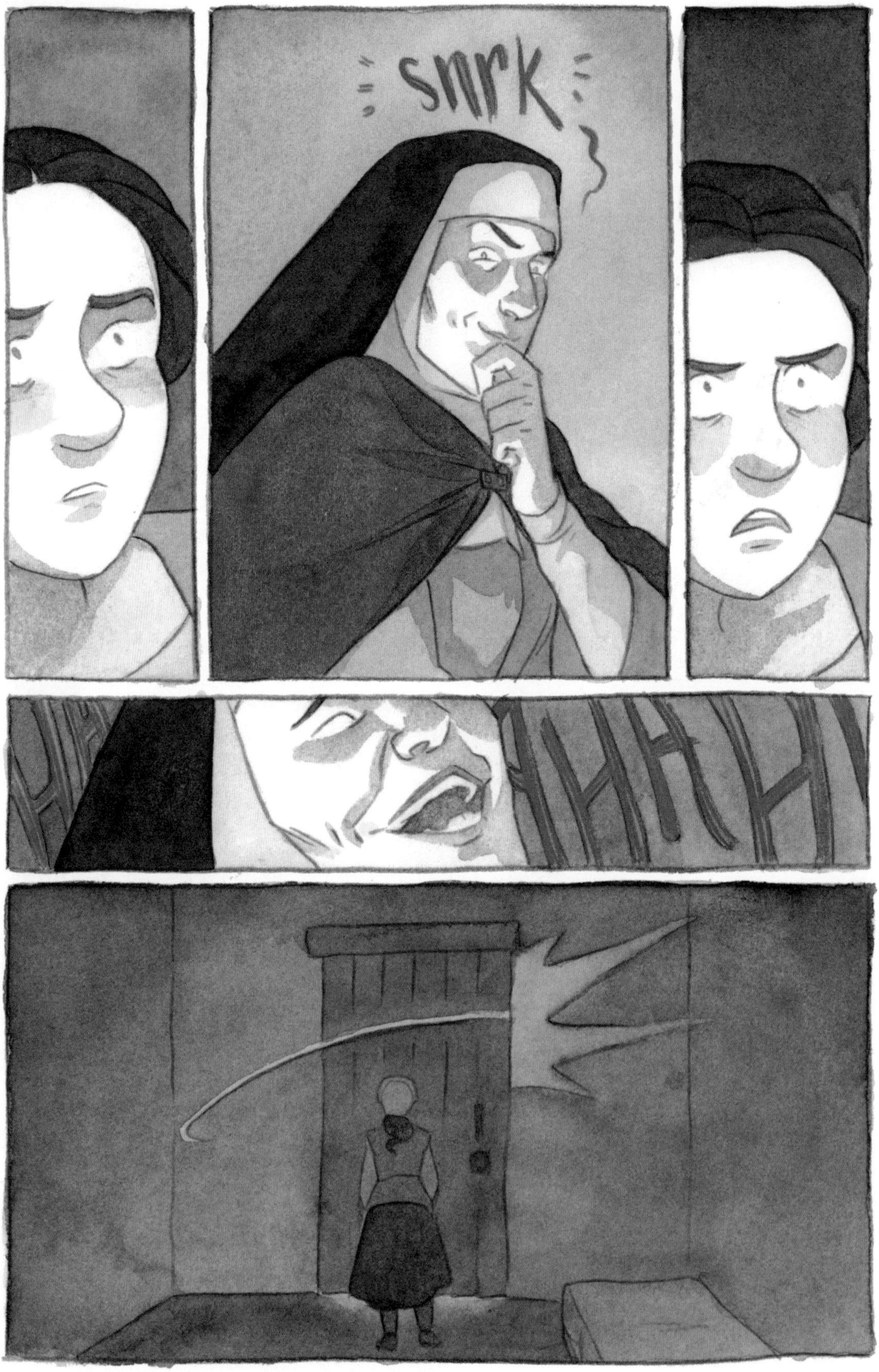
SNRK
HAHAHAHA

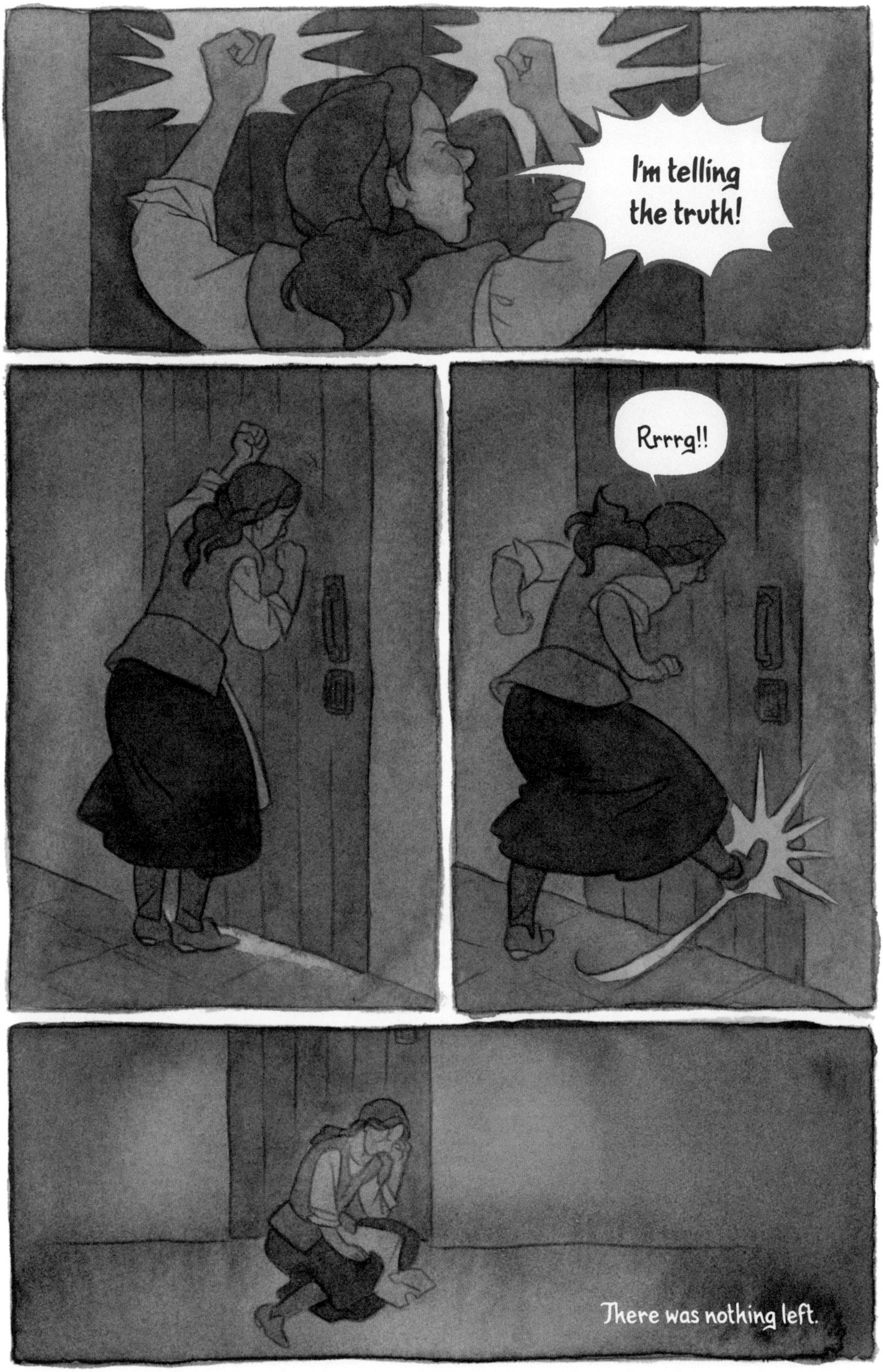
I'm telling the truth!
Rrrrg!!
There was nothing left.

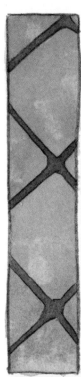

Margaret?

KLUNK

Saint Elysia...?

It's safe to speak. The guards are at Lady Eleanor's and Lord Paget's doors, and Her Reverence is busy questioning His Lordship.

356

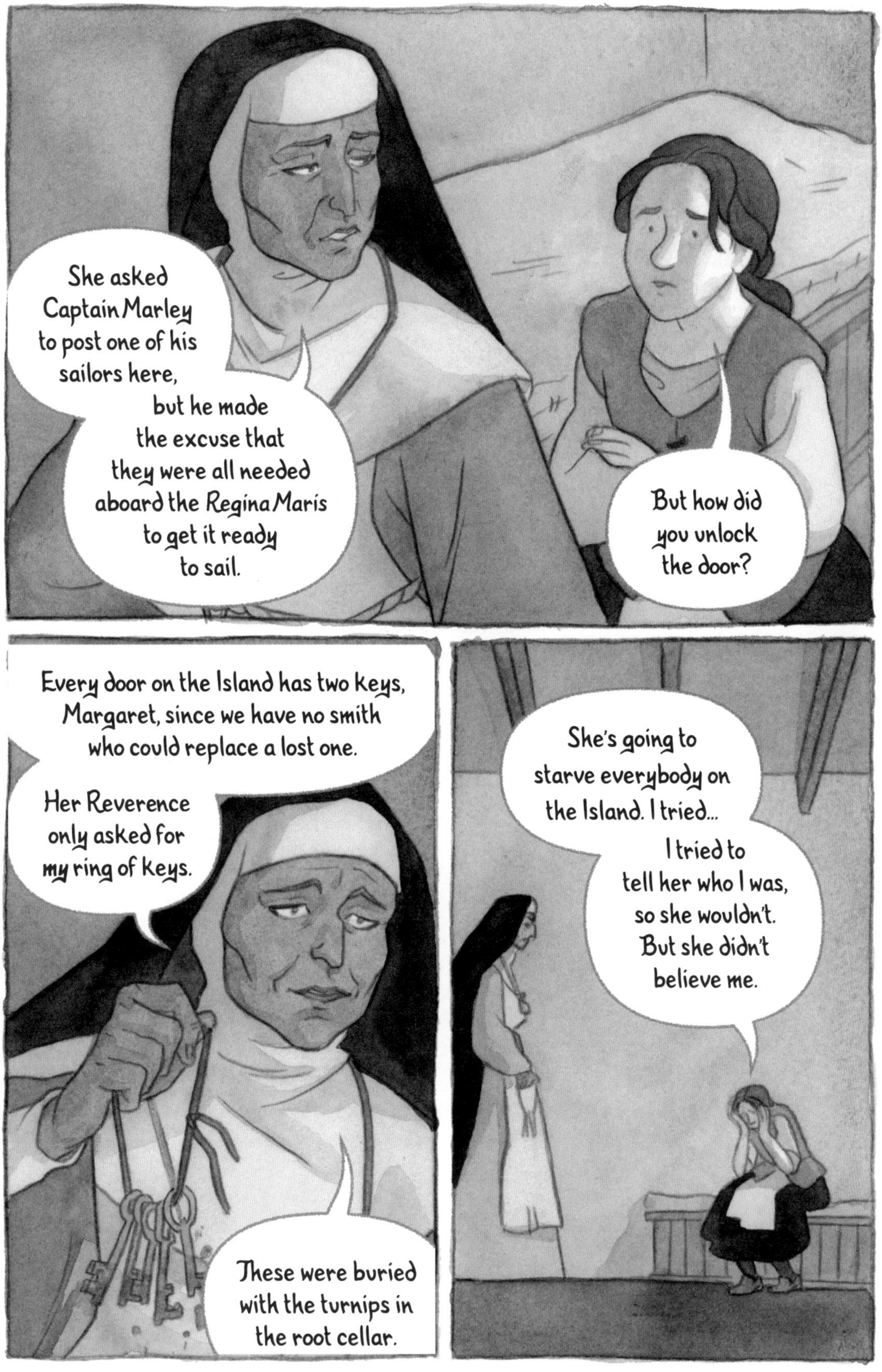
She asked Captain Marley to post one of his sailors here, but he made the excuse that they were all needed aboard the *Regina Maris* to get it ready to sail.
But how did you unlock the door?
Every door on the Island has two keys, Margaret, since we have no smith who could replace a lost one.
Her Reverence only asked for *my* ring of keys.
These were buried with the turnips in the root cellar.
She's going to starve everybody on the Island. I tried...
I tried to tell her who I was, so she wouldn't. But she didn't believe me.

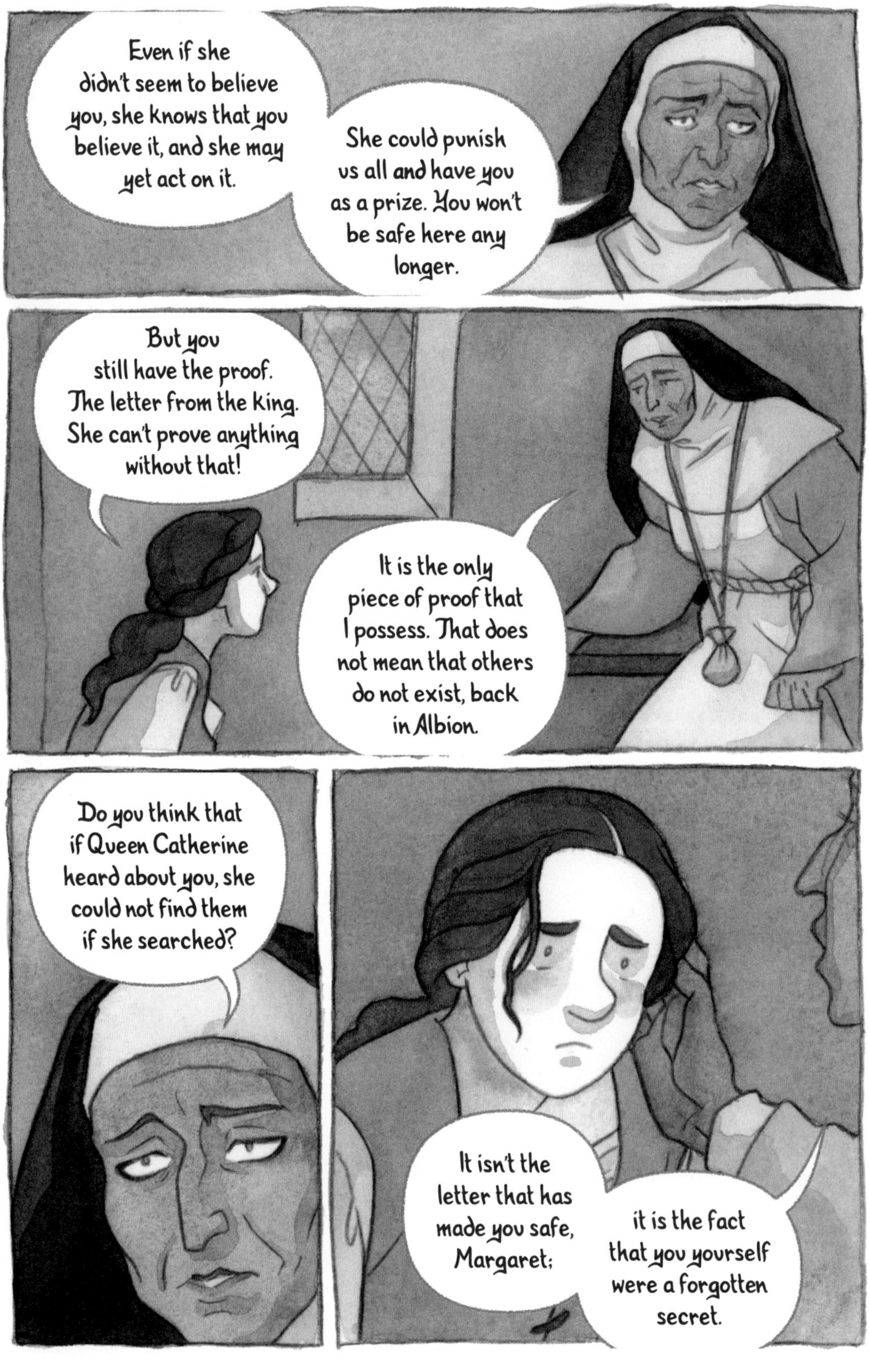

Even if she didn't seem to believe you, she knows that you believe it, and she may yet act on it.
She could punish us all and have you as a prize. You won't be safe here any longer.
But you still have the proof. The letter from the king. She can't prove anything without that!
It is the only piece of proof that I possess. That does not mean that others do not exist, back in Albion.
Do you think that if Queen Catherine heard about you, she could not find them if she searched?
It isn't the letter that has made you safe, Margaret;
it is the fact that you yourself were a forgotten secret.

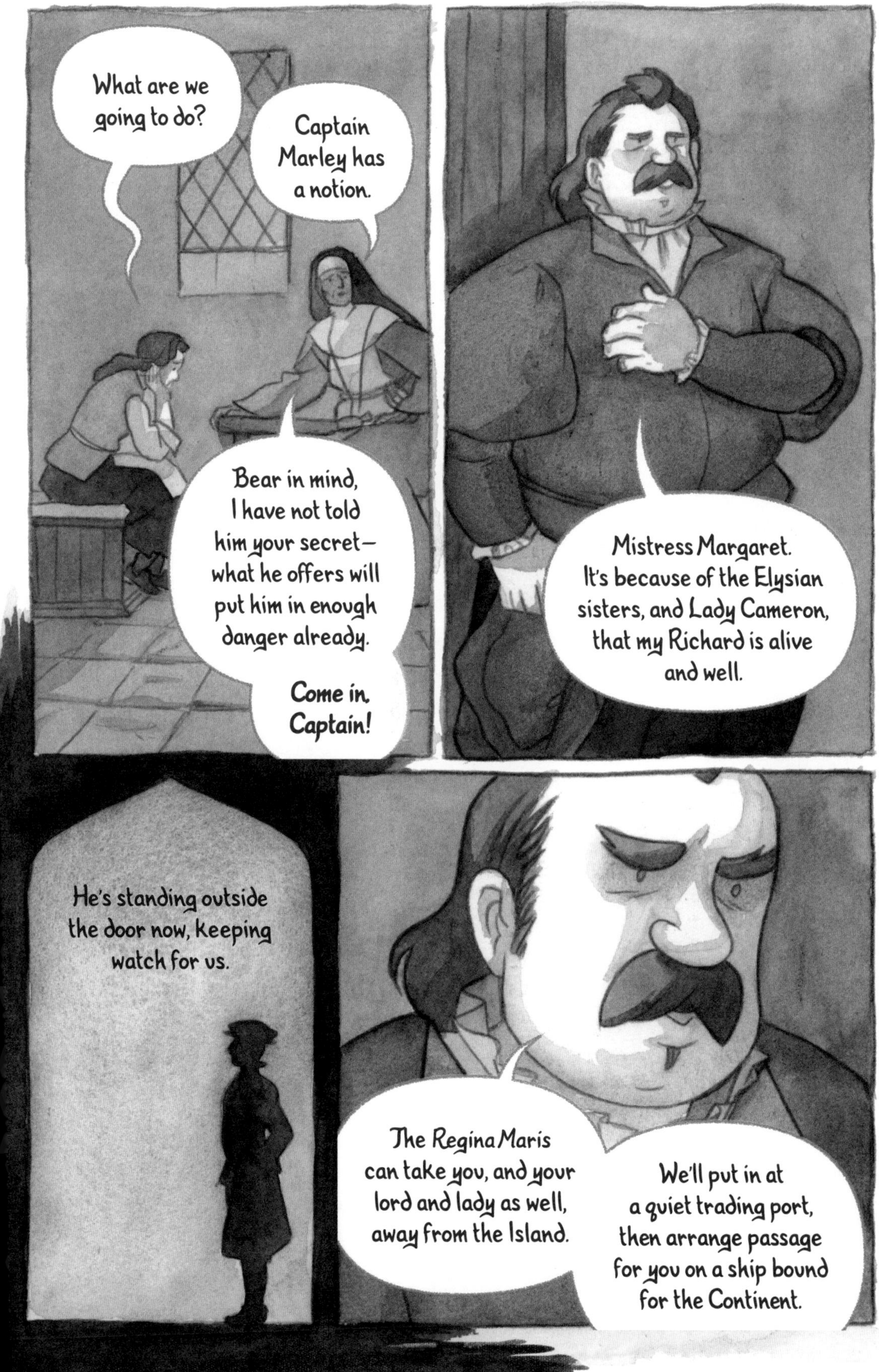
What are we going to do?
Captain Marley has a notion.
Bear in mind, I have not told him your secret—what he offers will put him in enough danger already.
Come in, Captain!
Mistress Margaret. It's because of the Elysian sisters, and Lady Cameron, that my Richard is alive and well.
He's standing outside the door now, keeping watch for us.
The *Regina Maris* can take you, and your lord and lady as well, away from the Island.
We'll put in at a quiet trading port, then arrange passage for you on a ship bound for the Continent.

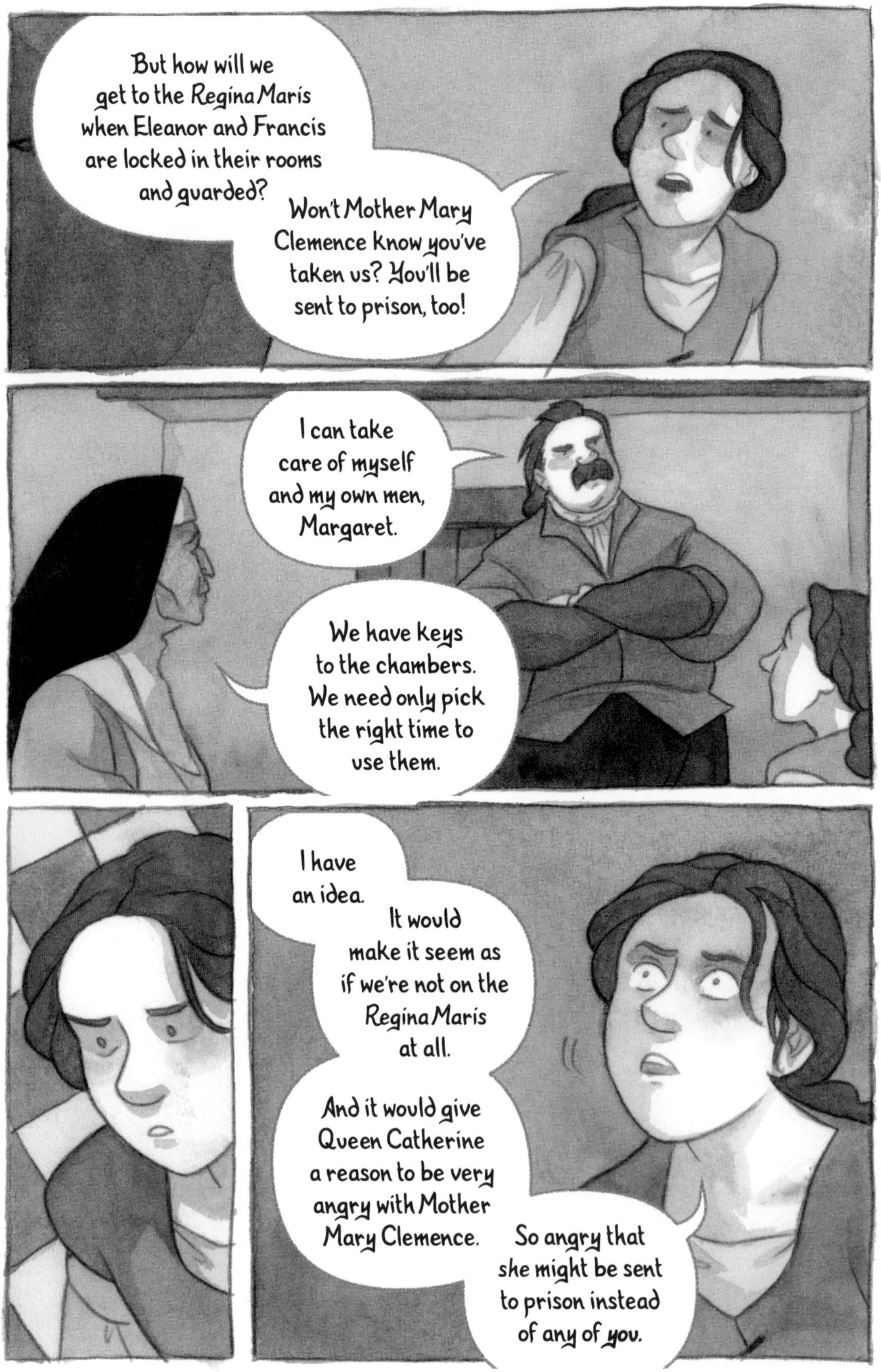
But how will we get to the *Regina Maris* when Eleanor and Francis are locked in their rooms and guarded?
Won't Mother Mary Clemence know you've taken us? You'll be sent to prison, too!
I can take care of myself and my own men, Margaret.
We have keys to the chambers. We need only pick the right time to use them.
I have an idea.
It would make it seem as if we're not on the *Regina Maris* at all.
And it would give Queen Catherine a reason to be very angry with Mother Mary Clemence.
So angry that she might be sent to prison instead of any of *you*.

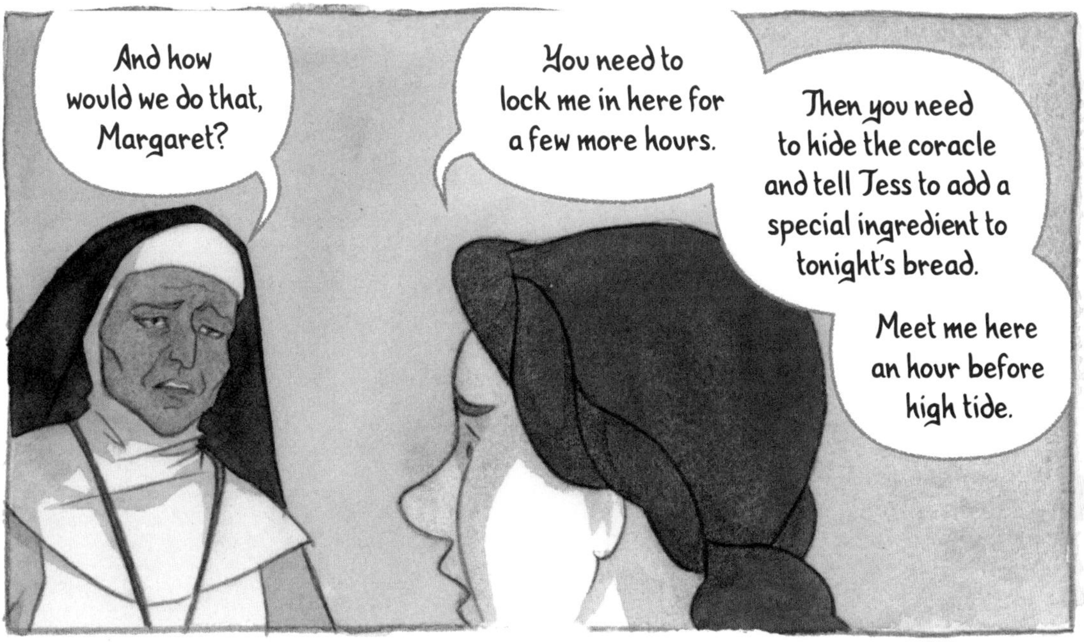
And how would we do that, Margaret?
You need to lock me in here for a few more hours.
Then you need to hide the coracle and tell Jess to add a special ingredient to tonight's bread.
Meet me here an hour before high tide.

I didn't like my own plan very much.

It was better than the one Sister Agnes and Captain Marley had, where everybody we left behind would suffer even more for saving Eleanor, Francis, and me. I spent the next few hours praying to Saint Elysia and Our Lady and the Sorrowful Son and God and everybody in between. I asked the Old People of the Island for their help, because we would need it, and I asked the Queen of the Sea to look out for us, too.

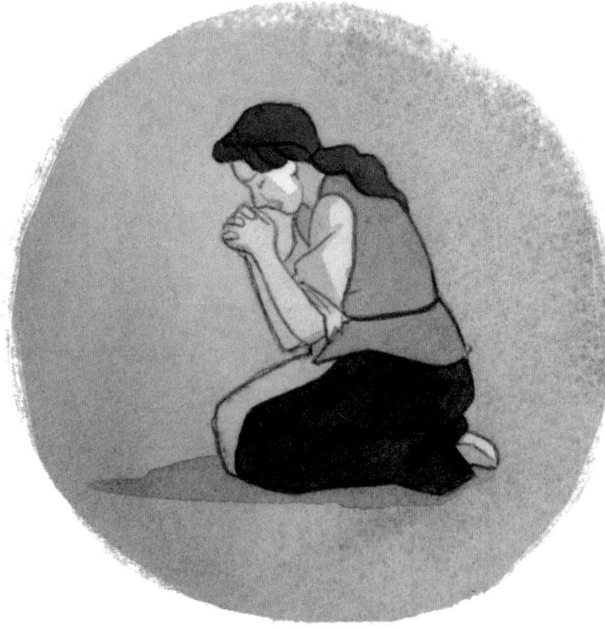

Please let this work.

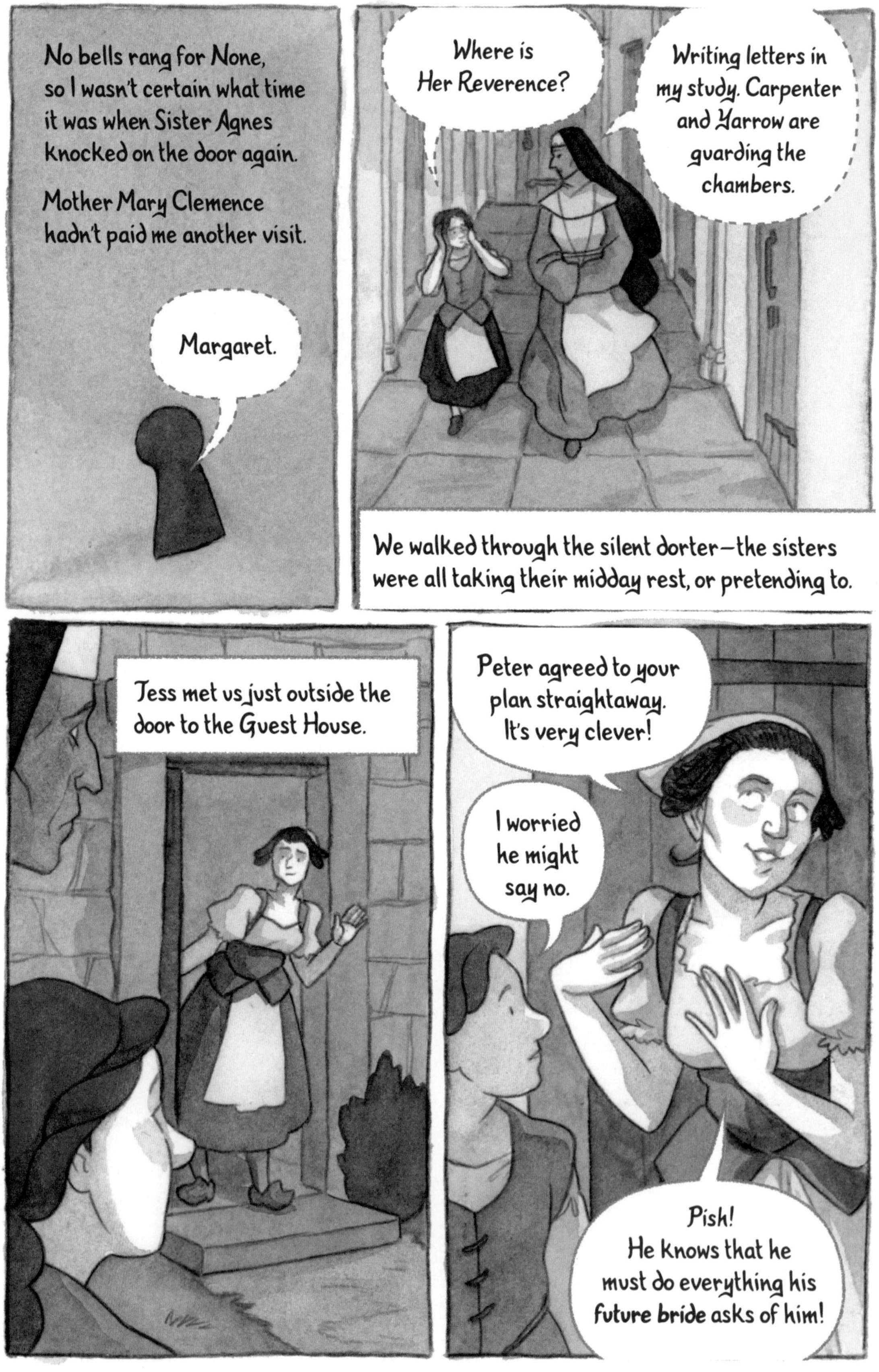
No bells rang for None, so I wasn't certain what time it was when Sister Agnes knocked on the door again.
Mother Mary Clemence hadn't paid me another visit.
Margaret.
Where is Her Reverence?
Writing letters in my study. Carpenter and Yarrow are guarding the chambers.
We walked through the silent dorter—the sisters were all taking their midday rest, or pretending to.
Jess met us just outside the door to the Guest House.
Peter agreed to your plan straightaway. It's very clever!
I worried he might say no.
Pish! He knows that he must do everything his future bride asks of him!

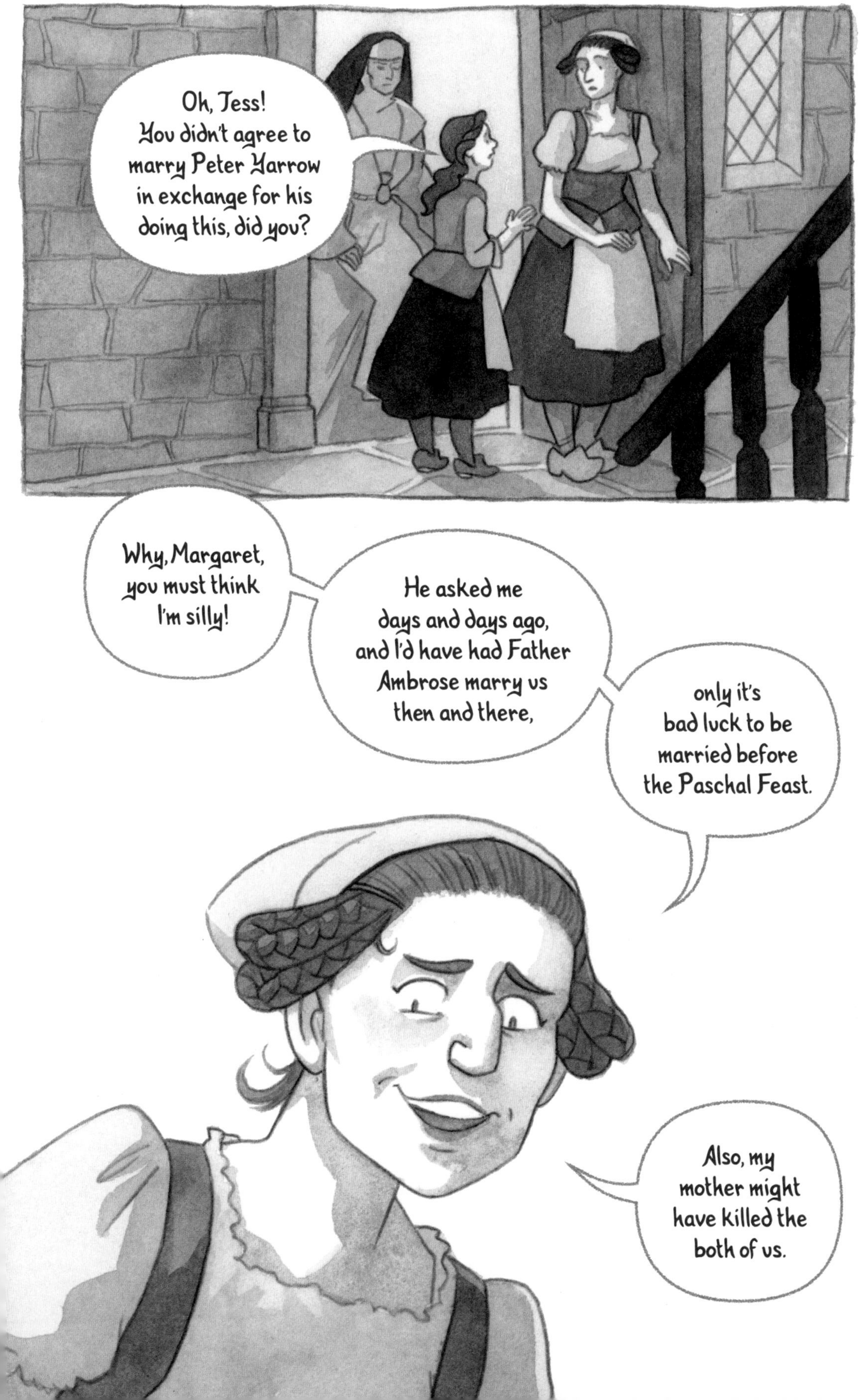
Oh, Jess! You didn't agree to marry Peter Yarrow in exchange for his doing this, did you?
Why, Margaret, you must think I'm silly!
He asked me days and days ago, and I'd have had Father Ambrose marry us then and there,
only it's bad luck to be married before the Paschal Feast.
Also, my mother might have killed the both of us.

Here is what we did.

Sister Agnes gave Jess the keys to the chambers in the Guest House where Francis and Eleanor were each being kept.

Then Jess baked those keys straight into Peter Yarrow's bread and delivered it on his supper plate.

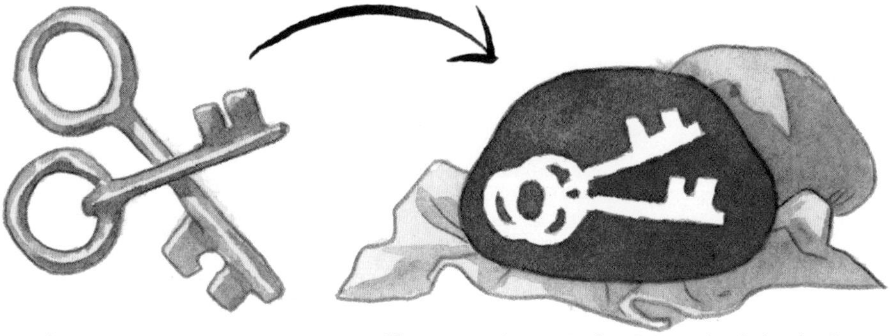

Peter Yarrow was sitting in front of Francis's door at the far end of the hall, and Harold Carpenter was guarding Eleanor's chamber at the other end, near the stairway and the necessarium.

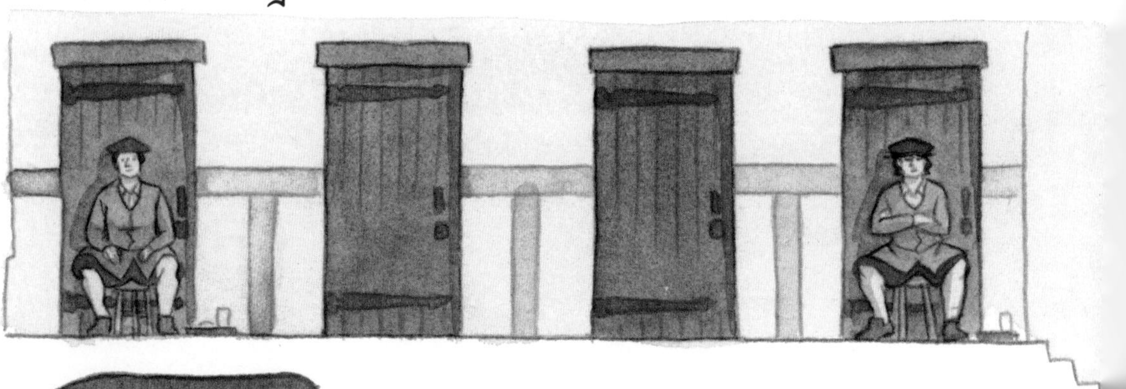

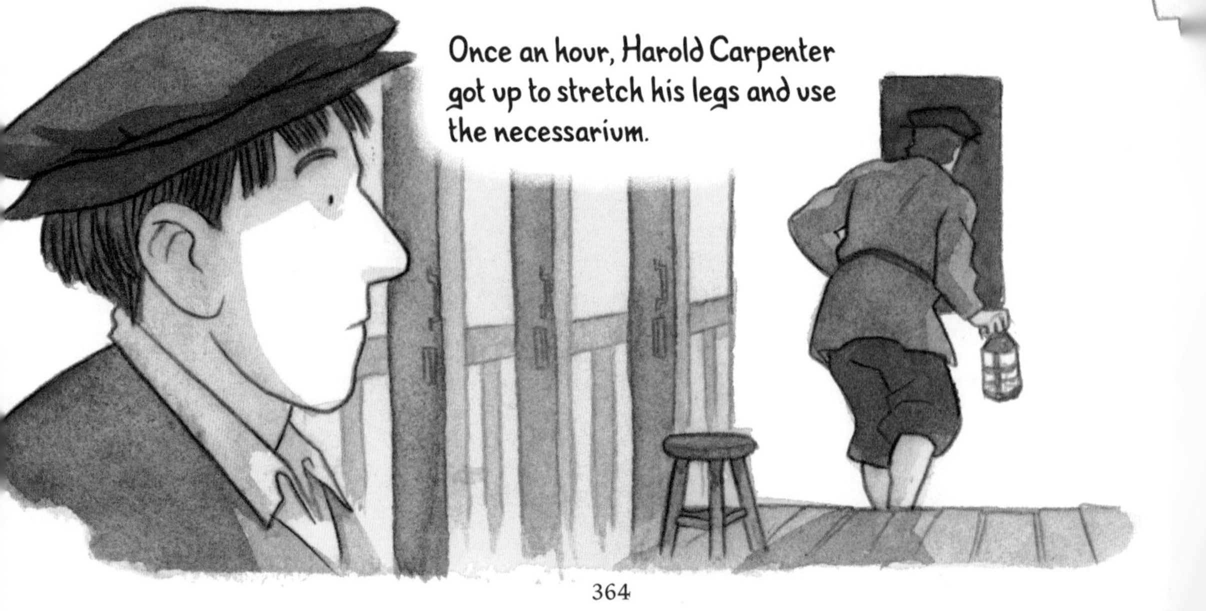
Once an hour, Harold Carpenter got up to stretch his legs and use the necessarium.

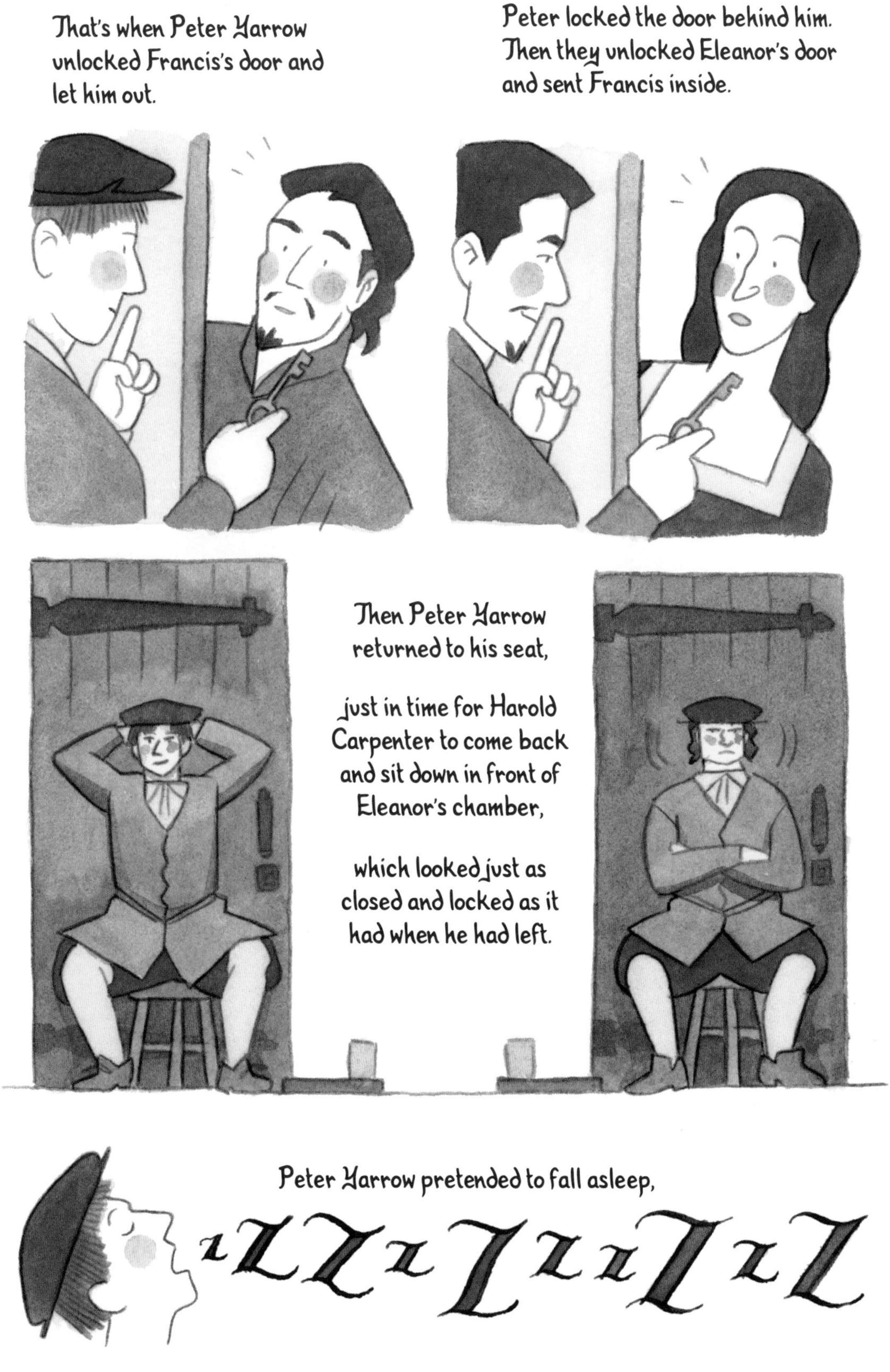
That's when Peter Yarrow unlocked Francis's door and let him out.
Peter locked the door behind him. Then they unlocked Eleanor's door and sent Francis inside.
Then Peter Yarrow returned to his seat,
just in time for Harold Carpenter to come back and sit down in front of Eleanor's chamber,
which looked just as closed and locked as it had when he had left.
Peter Yarrow pretended to fall asleep,
zZZzZzzZzZ

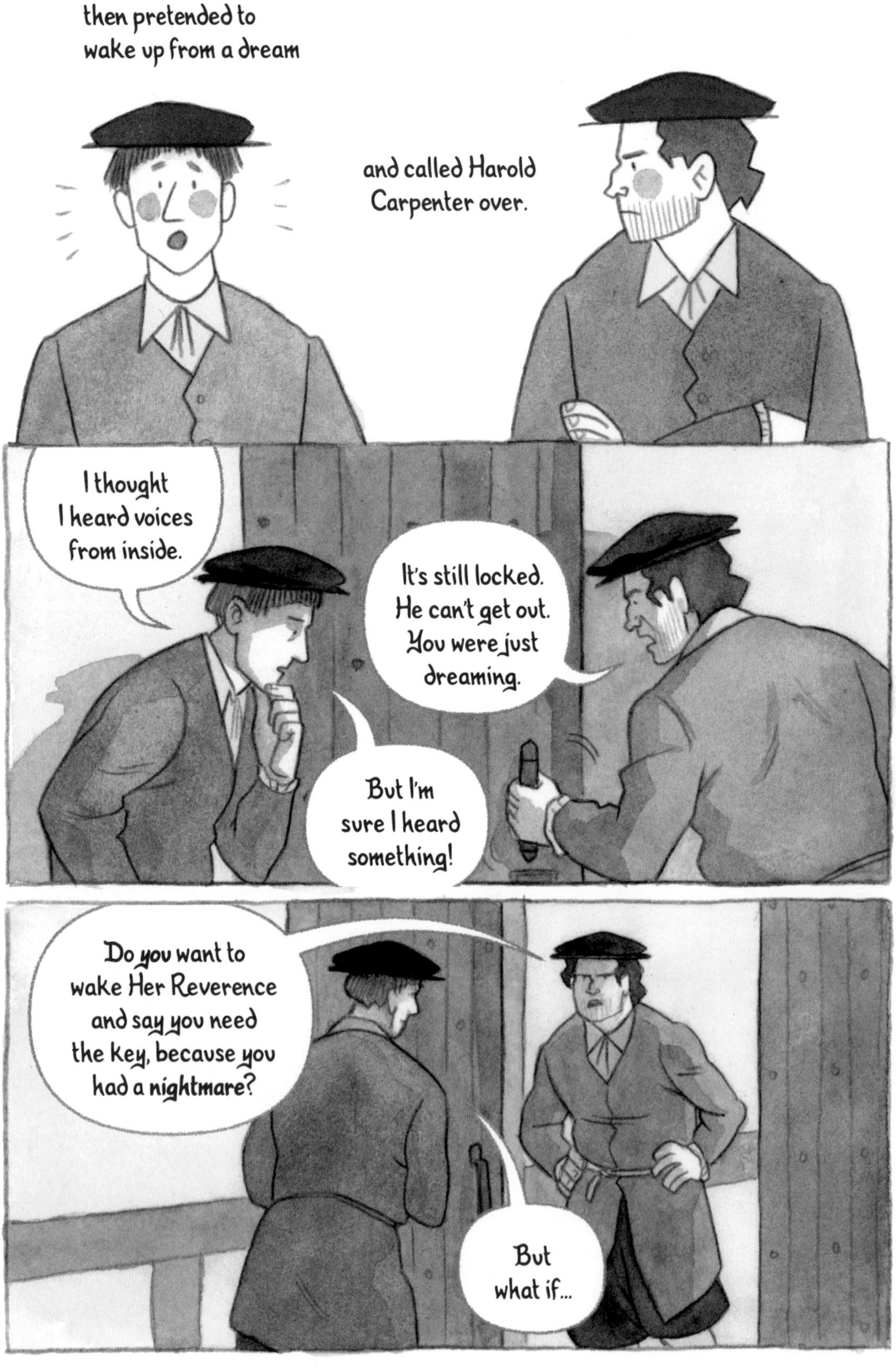
then pretended to wake up from a dream
and called Harold Carpenter over.
I thought I heard voices from inside.
It's still locked. He can't get out. You were just dreaming.
But I'm sure I heard something!
Do you want to wake Her Reverence and say you need the key, because you had a nightmare?
But what if...

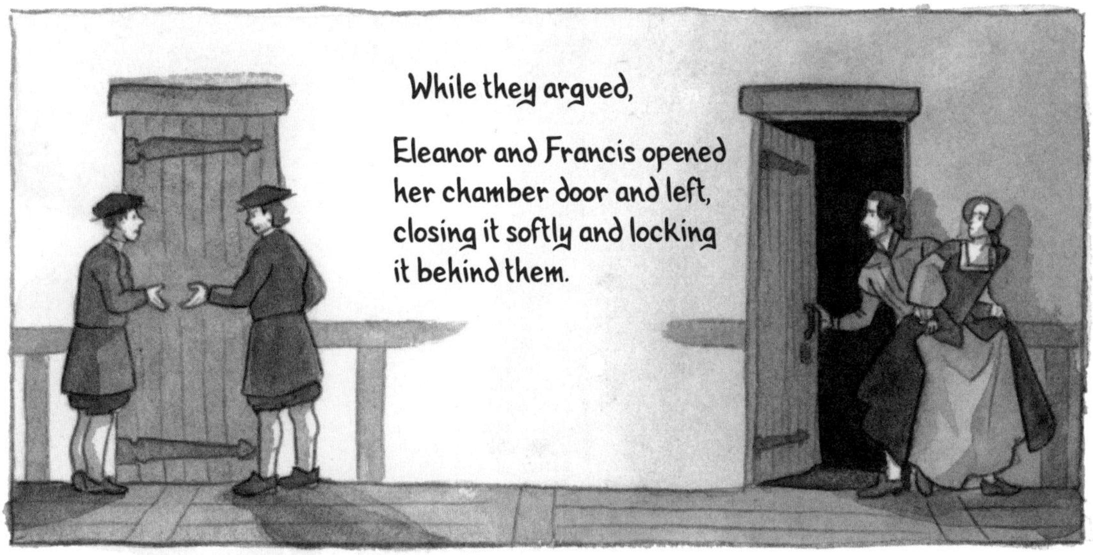
While they argued,
Eleanor and Francis opened her chamber door and left, closing it softly and locking it behind them.

It would seem as if they truly had vanished—either by fairy magic or a holy miracle. After all, the keys were in a ring around Her Reverence's own belt buckle. And it would seem that there was never a time when both Francis and Eleanor could have been let out of their chambers and escaped down the staircase without being seen.

Next, we had to leave the convent.

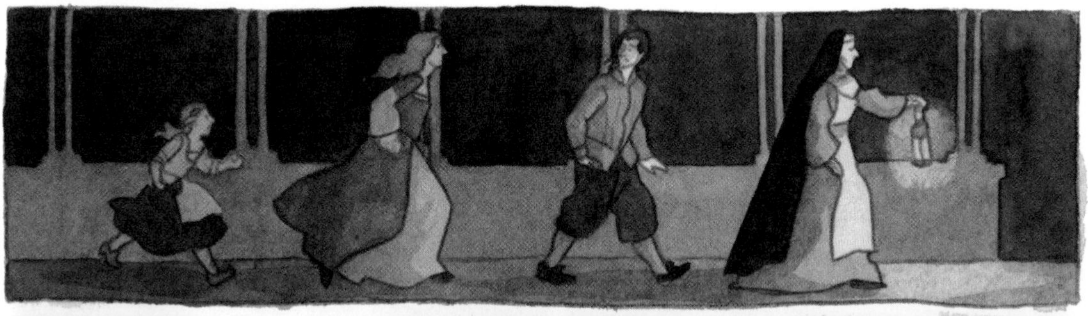

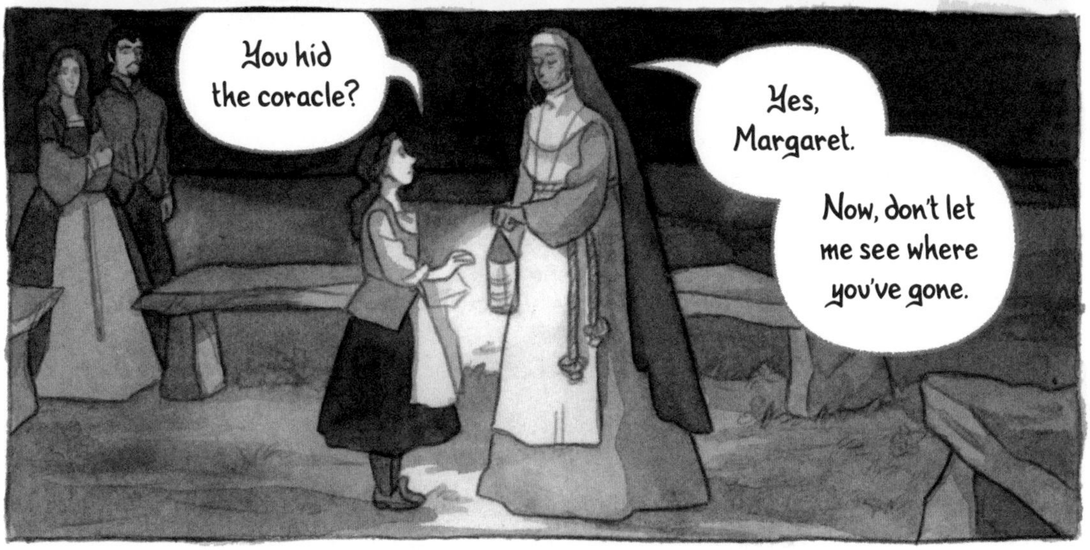
You hid the coracle?
Yes, Margaret.
Now, don't let me see where you've gone.

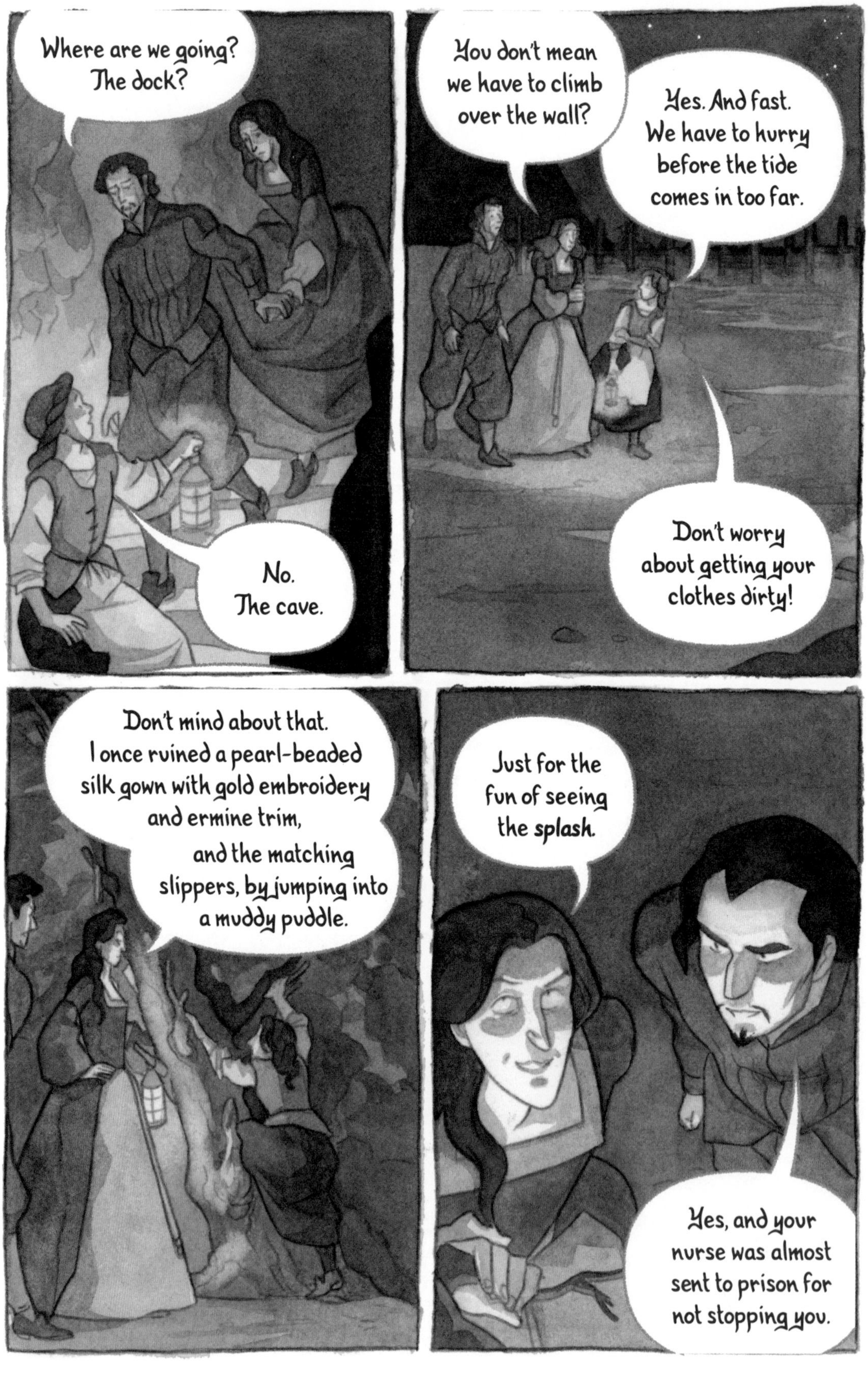
Where are we going? The dock?
No. The cave.
You don't mean we have to climb over the wall?
Yes. And fast. We have to hurry before the tide comes in too far.
Don't worry about getting your clothes dirty!
Don't mind about that. I once ruined a pearl-beaded silk gown with gold embroidery and ermine trim,
and the matching slippers, by jumping into a muddy puddle.
Just for the fun of seeing the *splash*.
Yes, and your nurse was almost sent to prison for not stopping you.

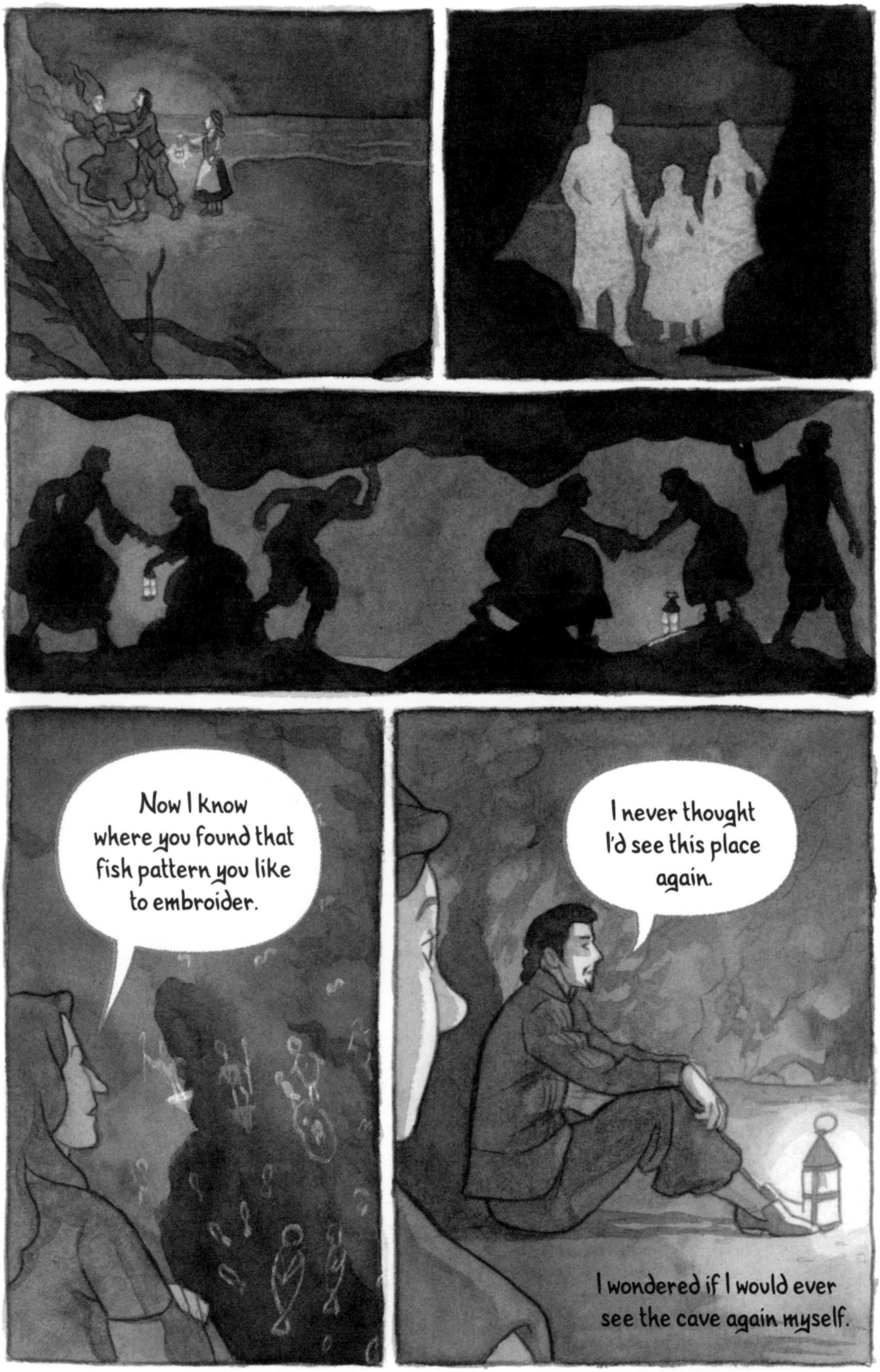
Now I know where you found that fish pattern you like to embroider.
I never thought I'd see this place again.
I wondered if I would ever see the cave again myself.

Or any of the places on the Island. I had loved the thought of seeing some of the rest of the world. I hadn't thought about whether I would still want to see the rest of the world if it meant never coming home again.

The three of us sat in the cave together for the whole day that came. The sunlight that came through the spaces between the rocks above was thin and gray. When the tide came in and filled the tunnel, the sound of the waves and the echoes they made in the cave made it too loud to talk.

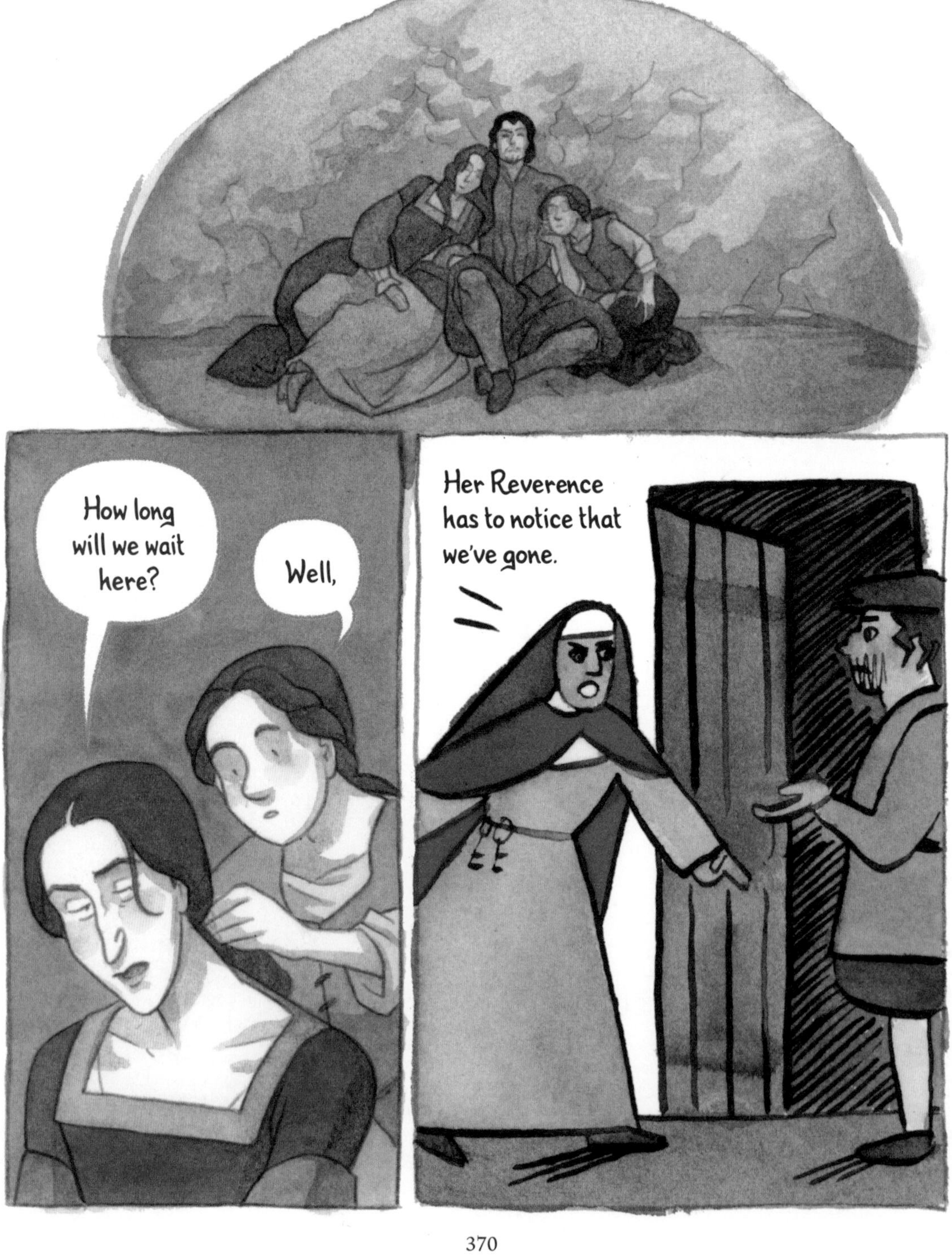
How long will we wait here?
Well,
Her Reverence has to notice that we've gone.

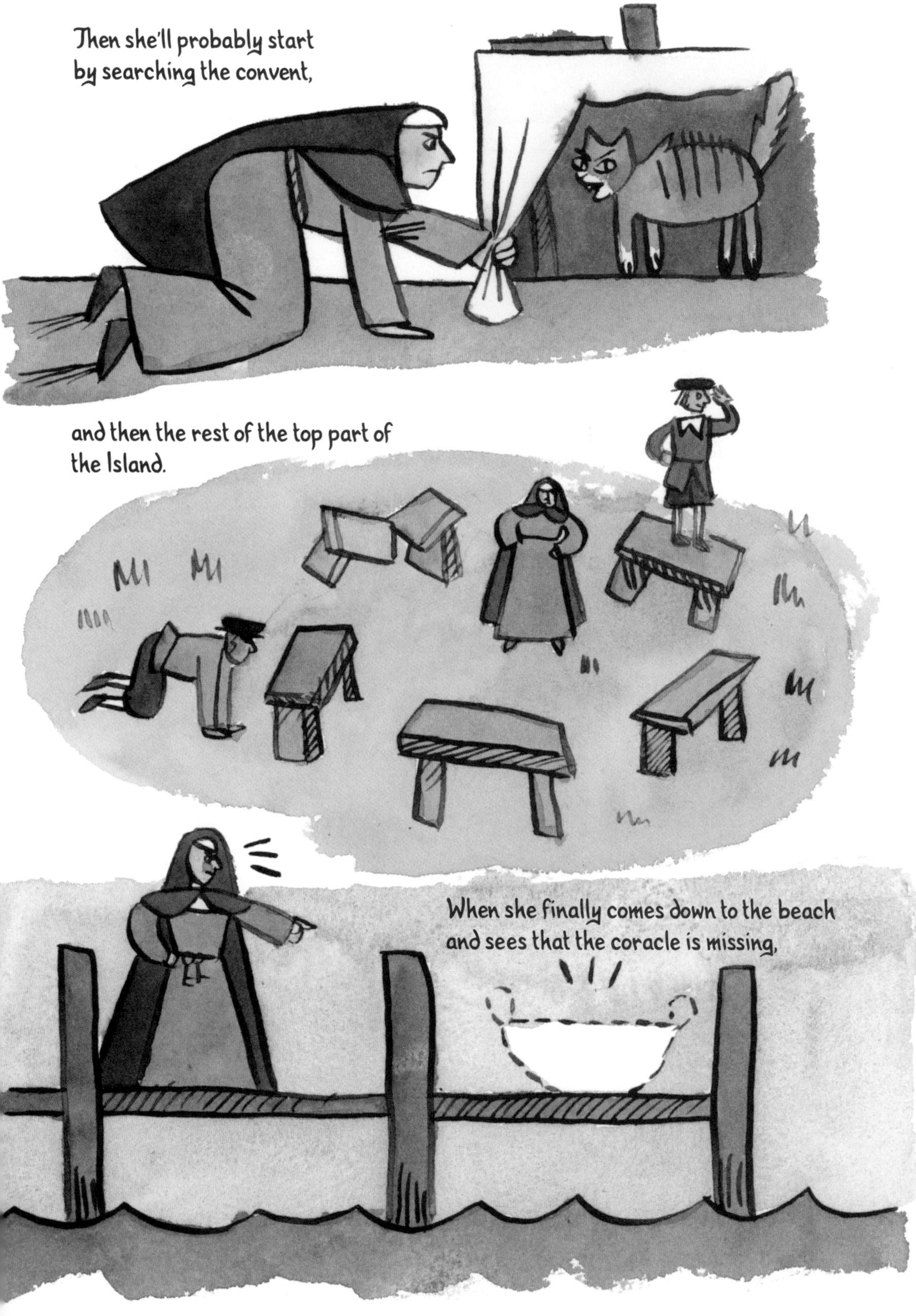
Then she'll probably start by searching the convent,
and then the rest of the top part of the Island.
When she finally comes down to the beach and sees that the coracle is missing,

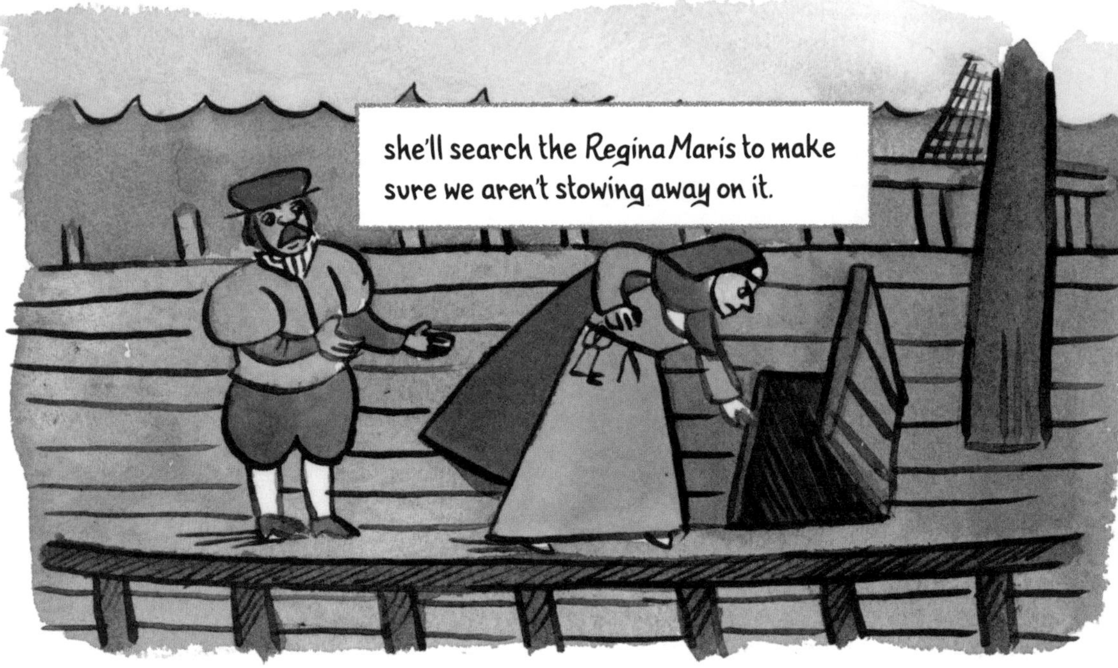
she'll search the Regina Maris to make sure we aren't stowing away on it.

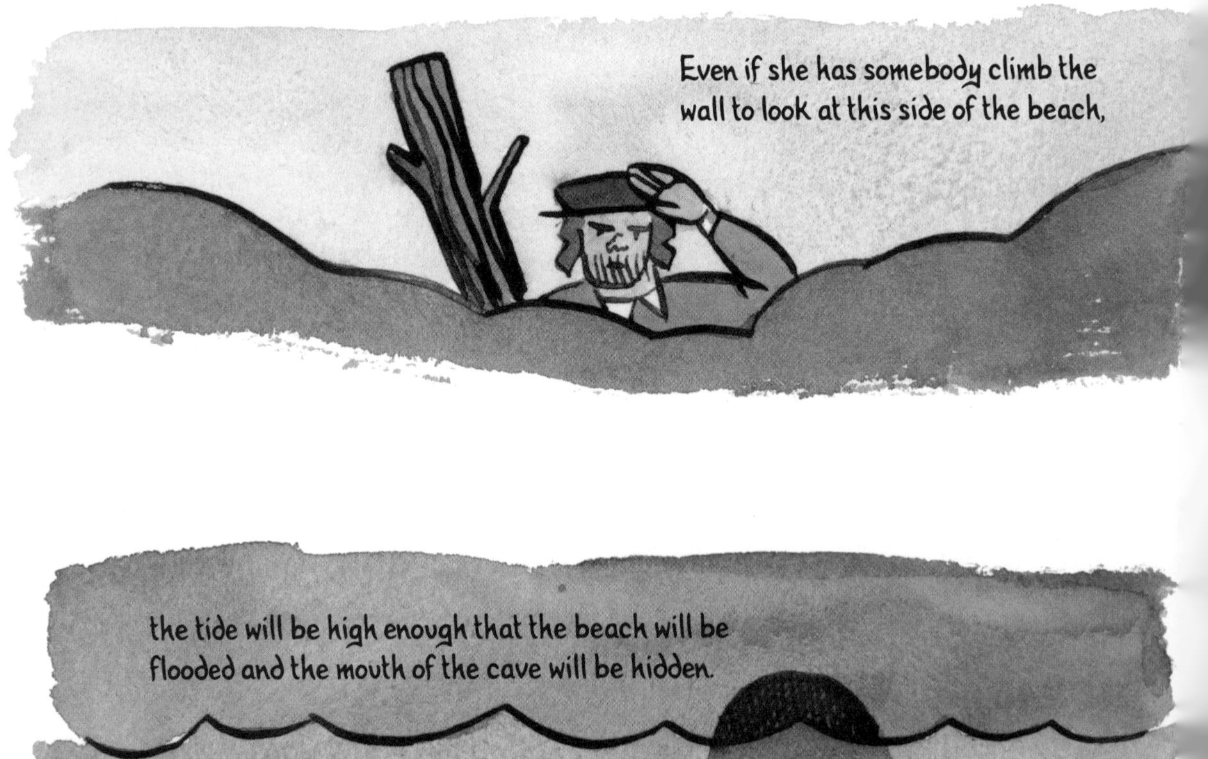
Even if she has somebody climb the wall to look at this side of the beach,

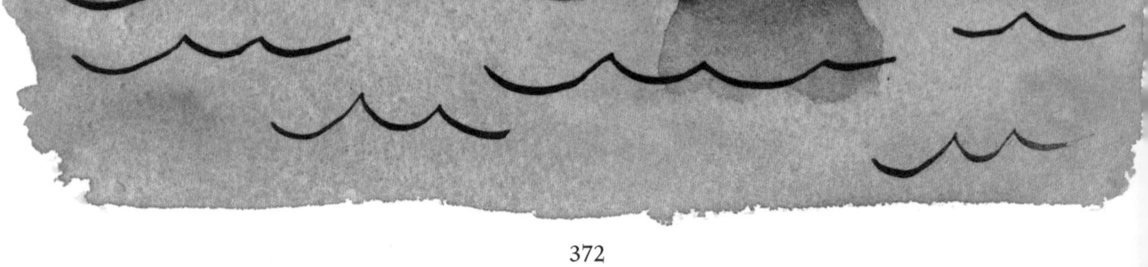
the tide will be high enough that the beach will be flooded and the mouth of the cave will be hidden.

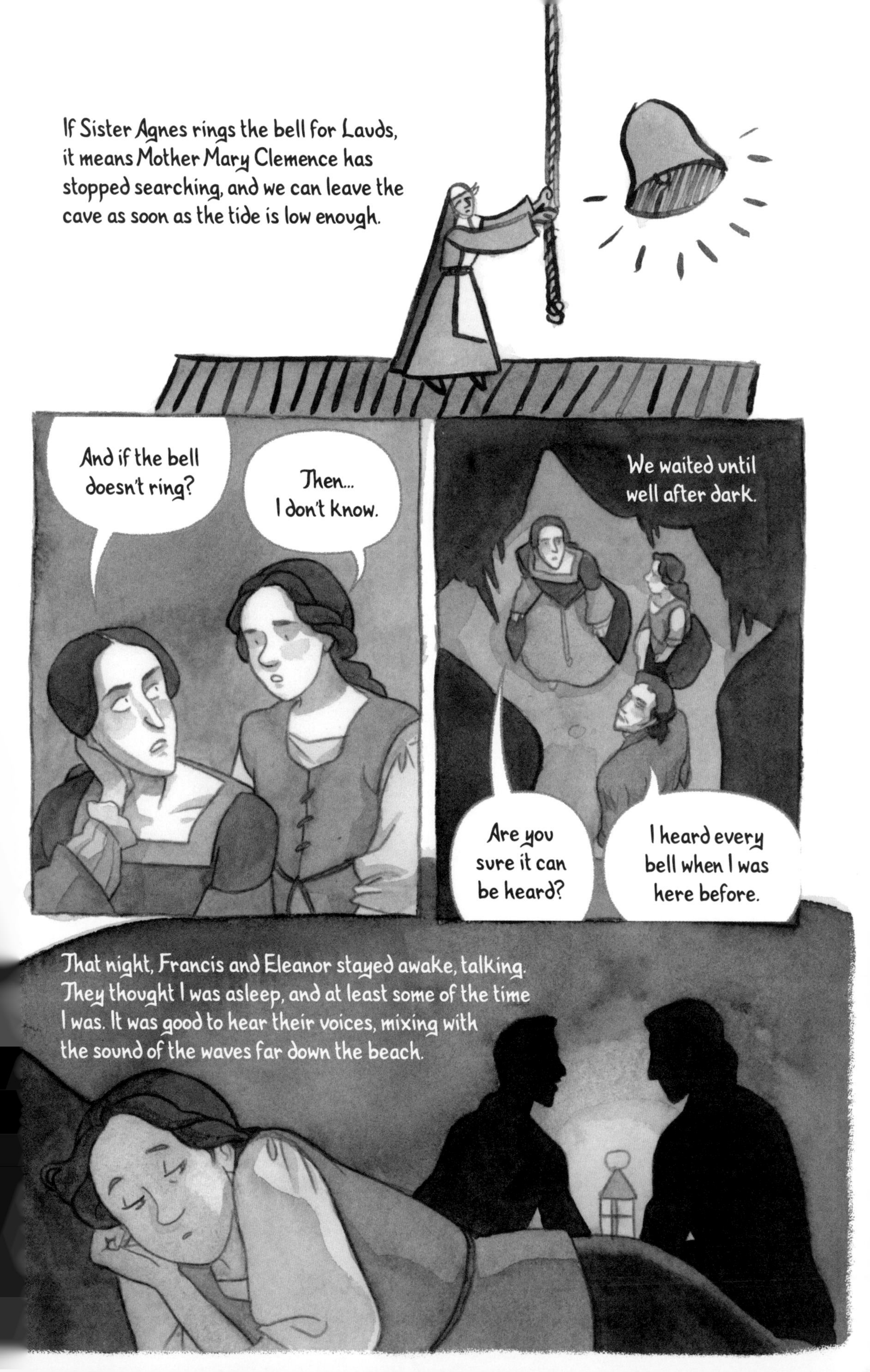
If Sister Agnes rings the bell for Lauds, it means Mother Mary Clemence has stopped searching, and we can leave the cave as soon as the tide is low enough.
And if the bell doesn't ring?
Then... I don't know.
We waited until well after dark.
Are you sure it can be heard?
I heard every bell when I was here before.
That night, Francis and Eleanor stayed awake, talking. They thought I was asleep, and at least some of the time I was. It was good to hear their voices, mixing with the sound of the waves far down the beach.

I imagined that they were my mother and father,
and that I was still a small child, and they were
speaking softly to each other as I slept...

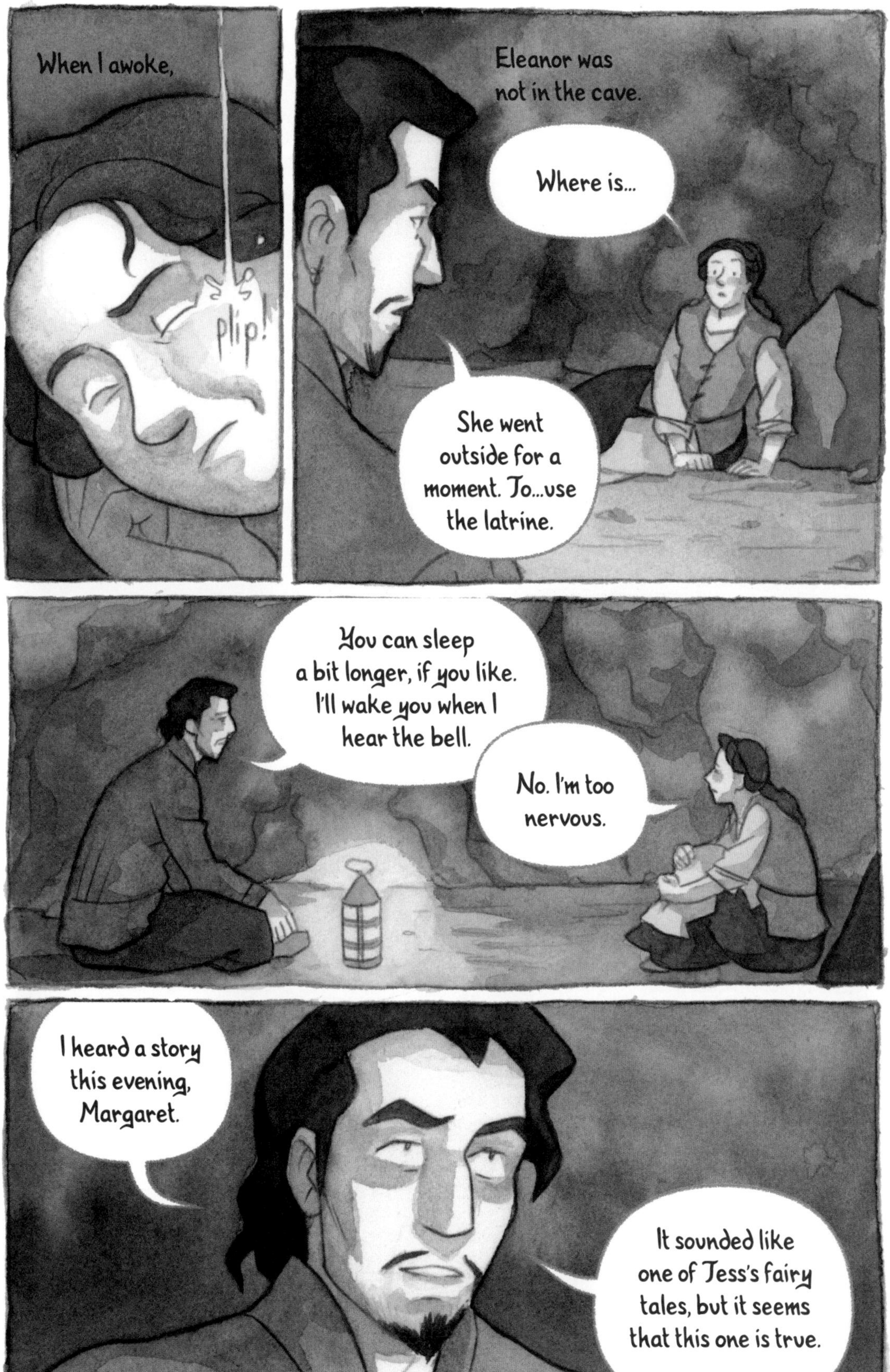
When I awoke,
plip!
Eleanor was not in the cave.
Where is...
She went outside for a moment. To...use the latrine.
You can sleep a bit longer, if you like. I'll wake you when I hear the bell.
No. I'm too nervous.
I heard a story this evening, Margaret.
It sounded like one of Jess's fairy tales, but it seems that this one is true.

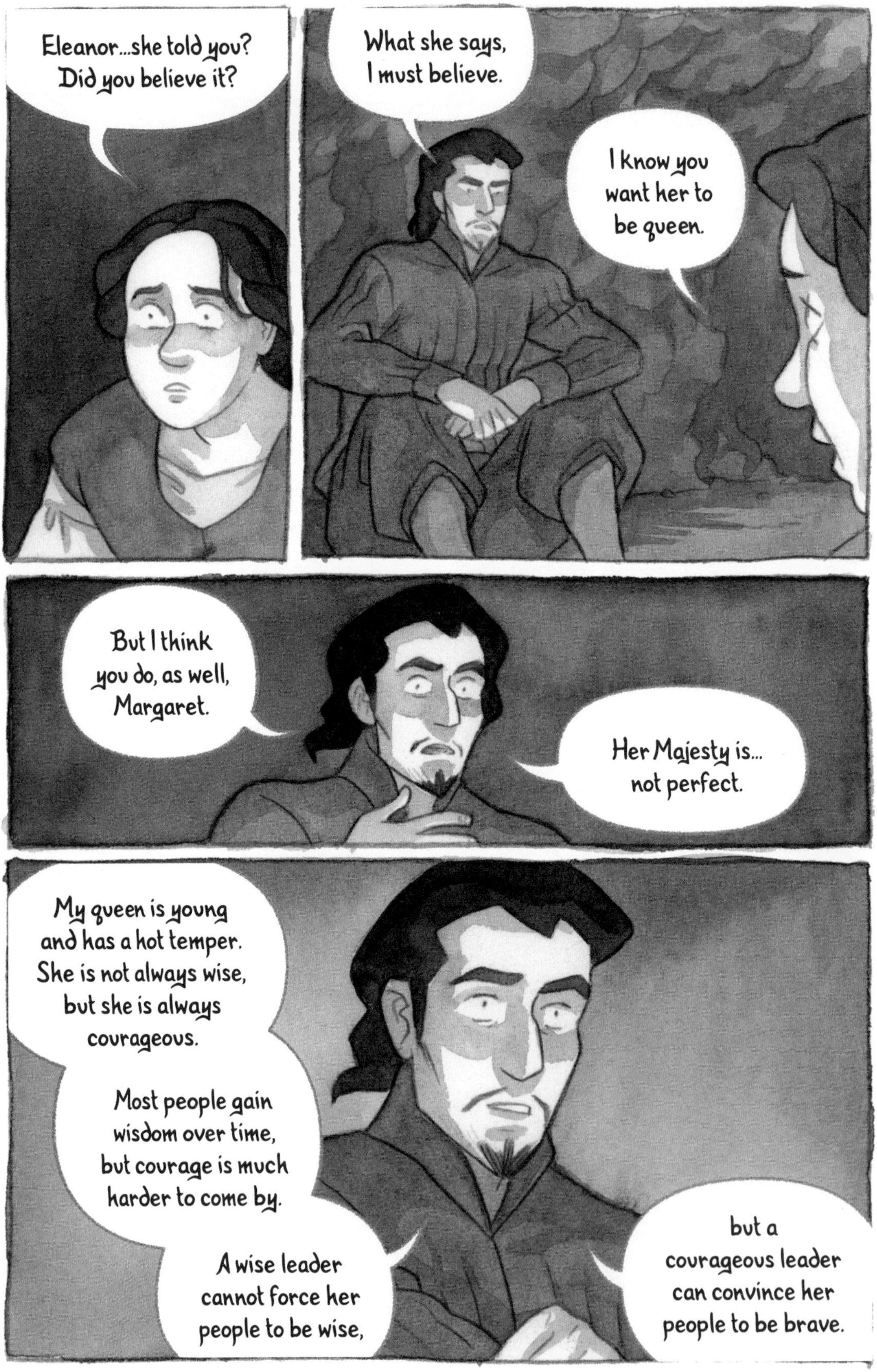

Eleanor...she told you? Did you believe it?
What she says, I must believe.
I know you want her to be queen.
But I think you do, as well, Margaret.
Her Majesty is... not perfect.
My queen is young and has a hot temper. She is not always wise, but she is always courageous.
Most people gain wisdom over time, but courage is much harder to come by.
A wise leader cannot force her people to be wise,
but a courageous leader can convince her people to be brave.

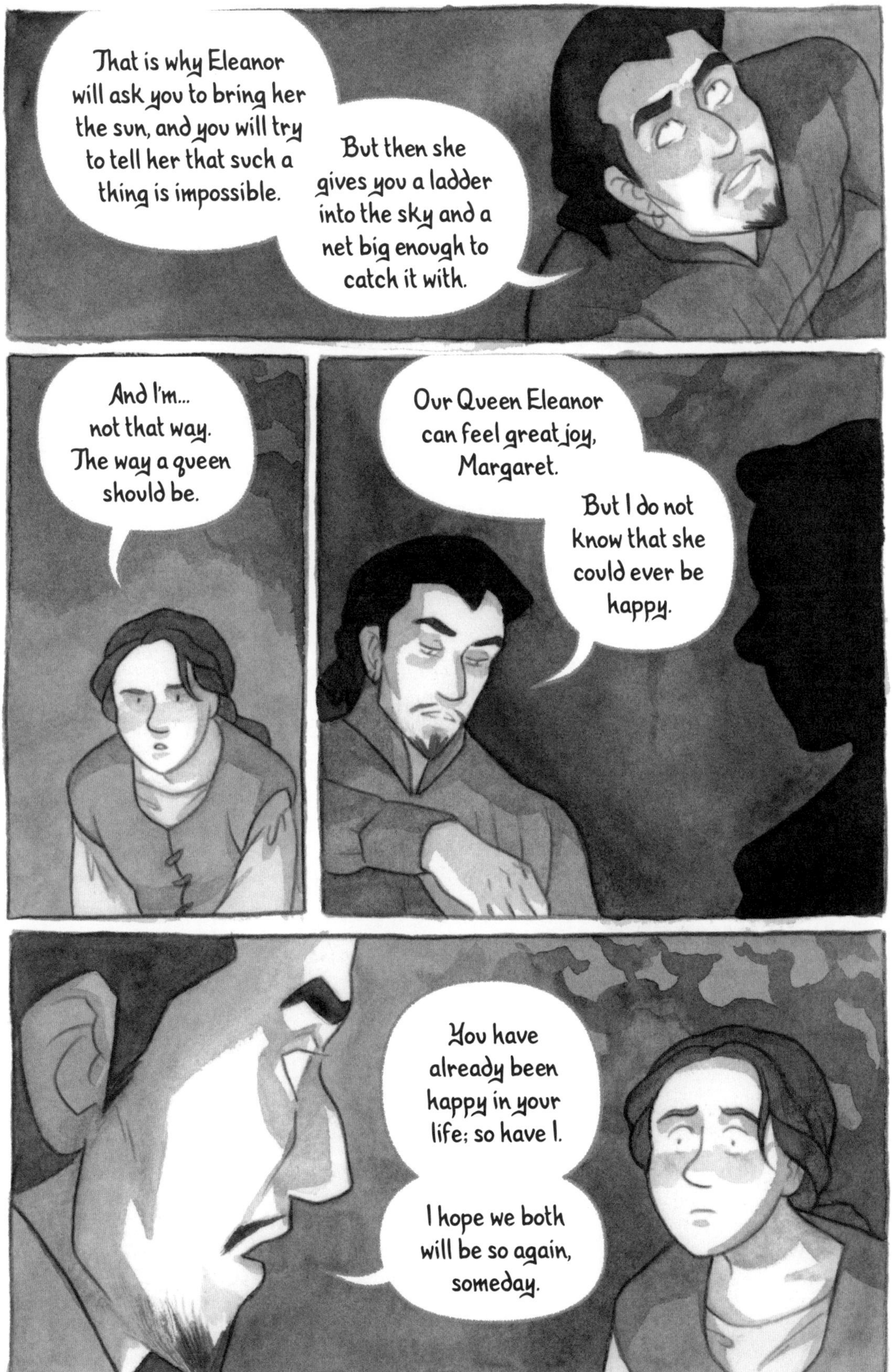
That is why Eleanor will ask you to bring her the sun, and you will try to tell her that such a thing is impossible.
But then she gives you a ladder into the sky and a net big enough to catch it with.
And I'm... not that way. The way a queen should be.
Our Queen Eleanor can feel great joy, Margaret.
But I do not know that she could ever be happy.
You have already been happy in your life; so have I.
I hope we both will be so again, someday.

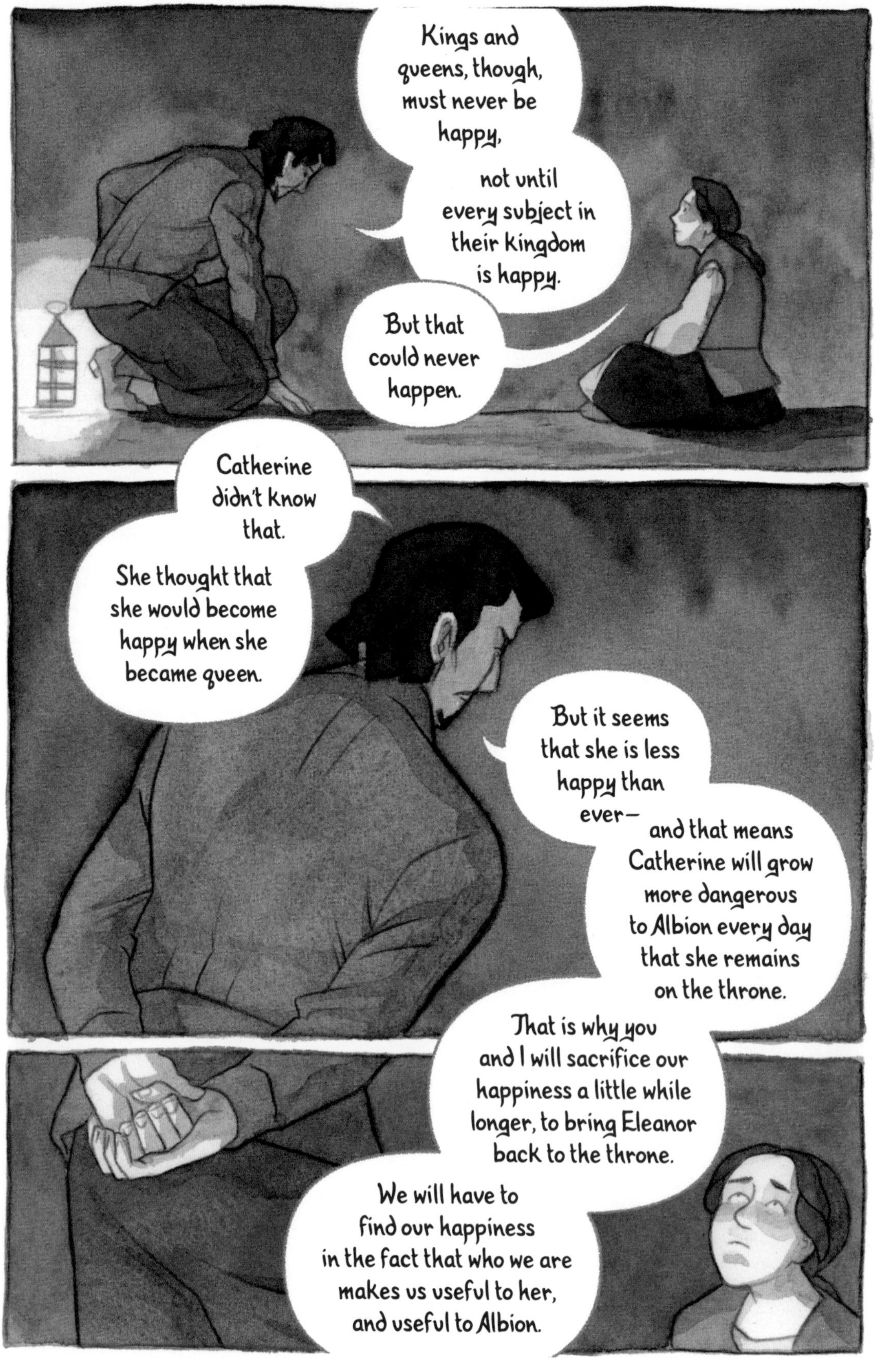

Kings and queens, though, must never be happy,
not until every subject in their kingdom is happy.
But that could never happen.
Catherine didn't know that.
She thought that she would become happy when she became queen.
But it seems that she is less happy than ever—
and that means Catherine will grow more dangerous to Albion every day that she remains on the throne.
That is why you and I will sacrifice our happiness a little while longer, to bring Eleanor back to the throne.
We will have to find our happiness in the fact that who we are makes us useful to her, and useful to Albion.

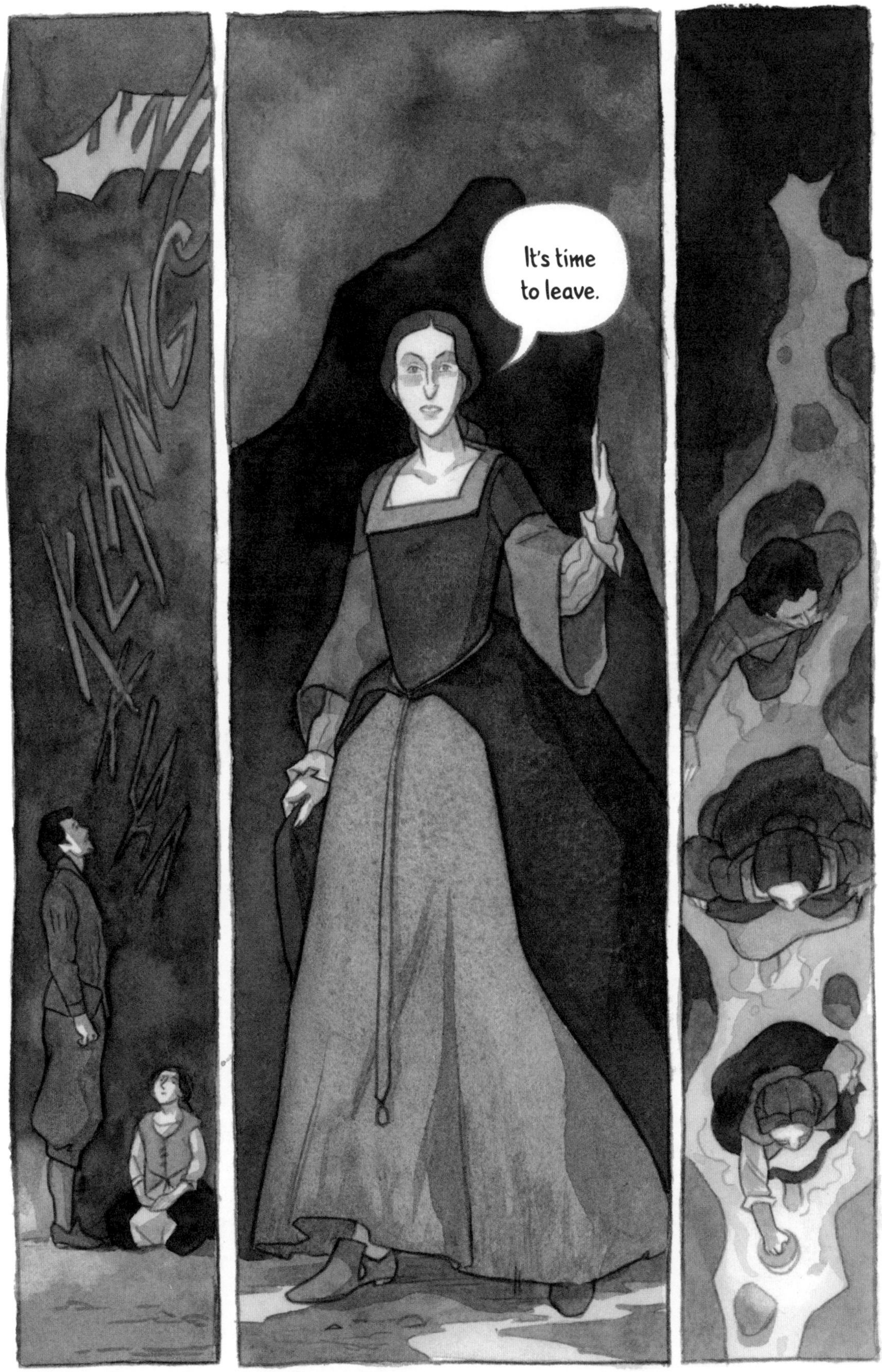
KLANG!
KLANG!
It's time to leave.

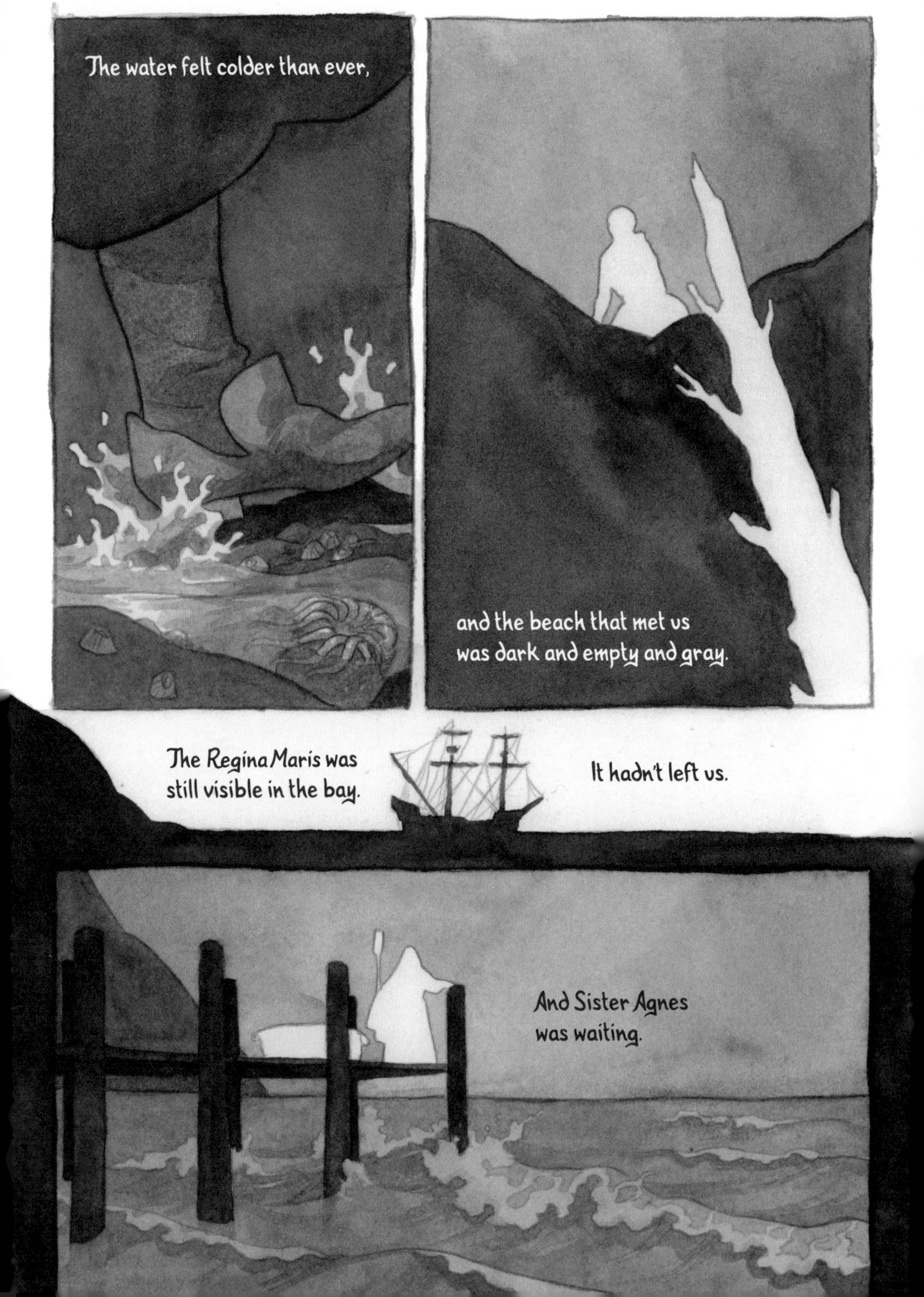
The water felt colder than ever,
and the beach that met us was dark and empty and gray.
The *Regina Maris* was still visible in the bay.
It hadn't left us.
And Sister Agnes was waiting.

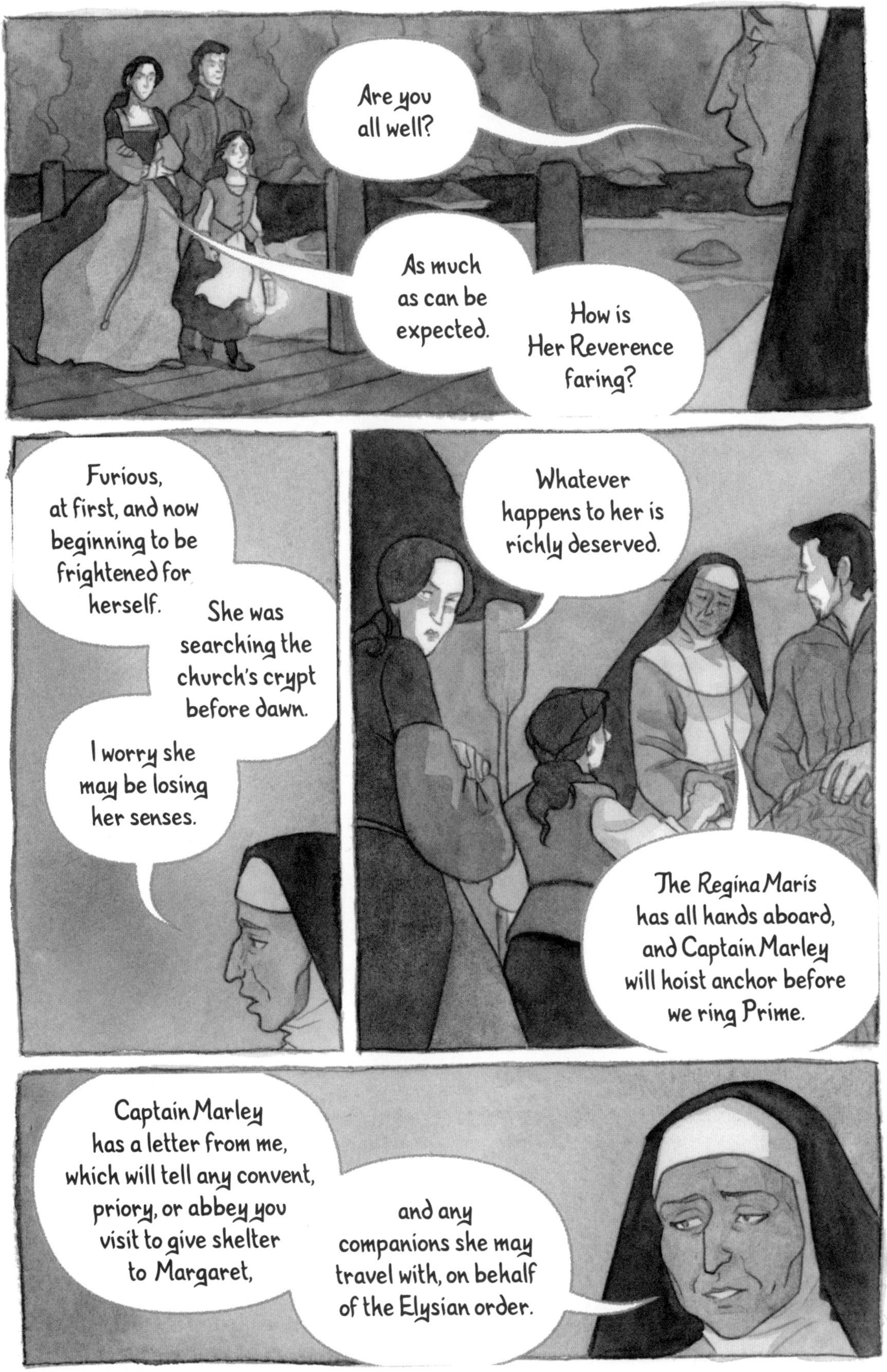
Are you all well?
As much as can be expected.
How is Her Reverence faring?
Furious, at first, and now beginning to be frightened for herself.
She was searching the church's crypt before dawn.
I worry she may be losing her senses.
Whatever happens to her is richly deserved.
The *Regina Maris* has all hands aboard, and Captain Marley will hoist anchor before we ring Prime.
Captain Marley has a letter from me, which will tell any convent, priory, or abbey you visit to give shelter to Margaret,
and any companions she may travel with, on behalf of the Elysian order.

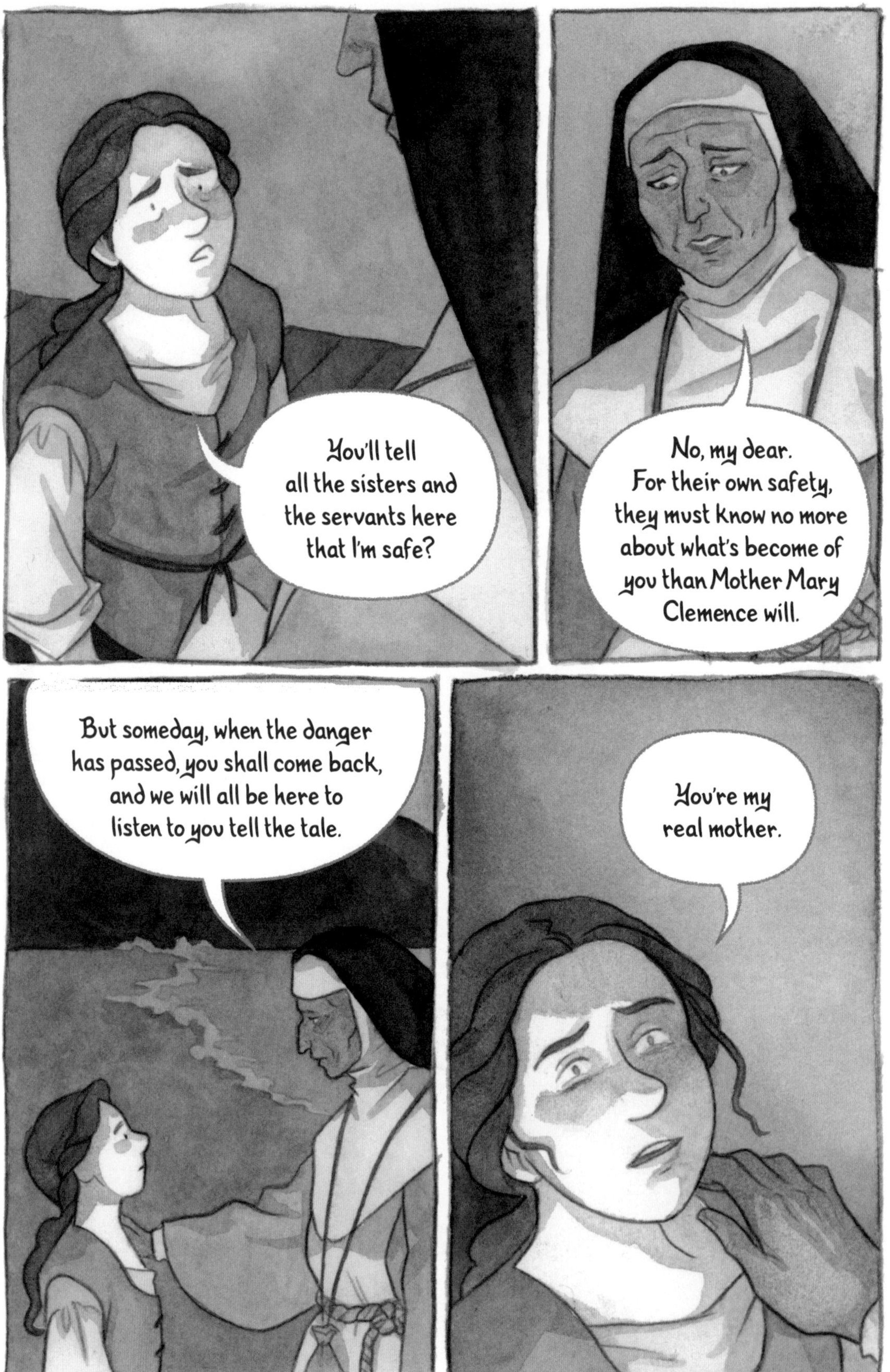
You'll tell all the sisters and the servants here that I'm safe?
No, my dear. For their own safety, they must know no more about what's become of you than Mother Mary Clemence will.
But someday, when the danger has passed, you shall come back, and we will all be here to listen to you tell the tale.
You're my real mother.

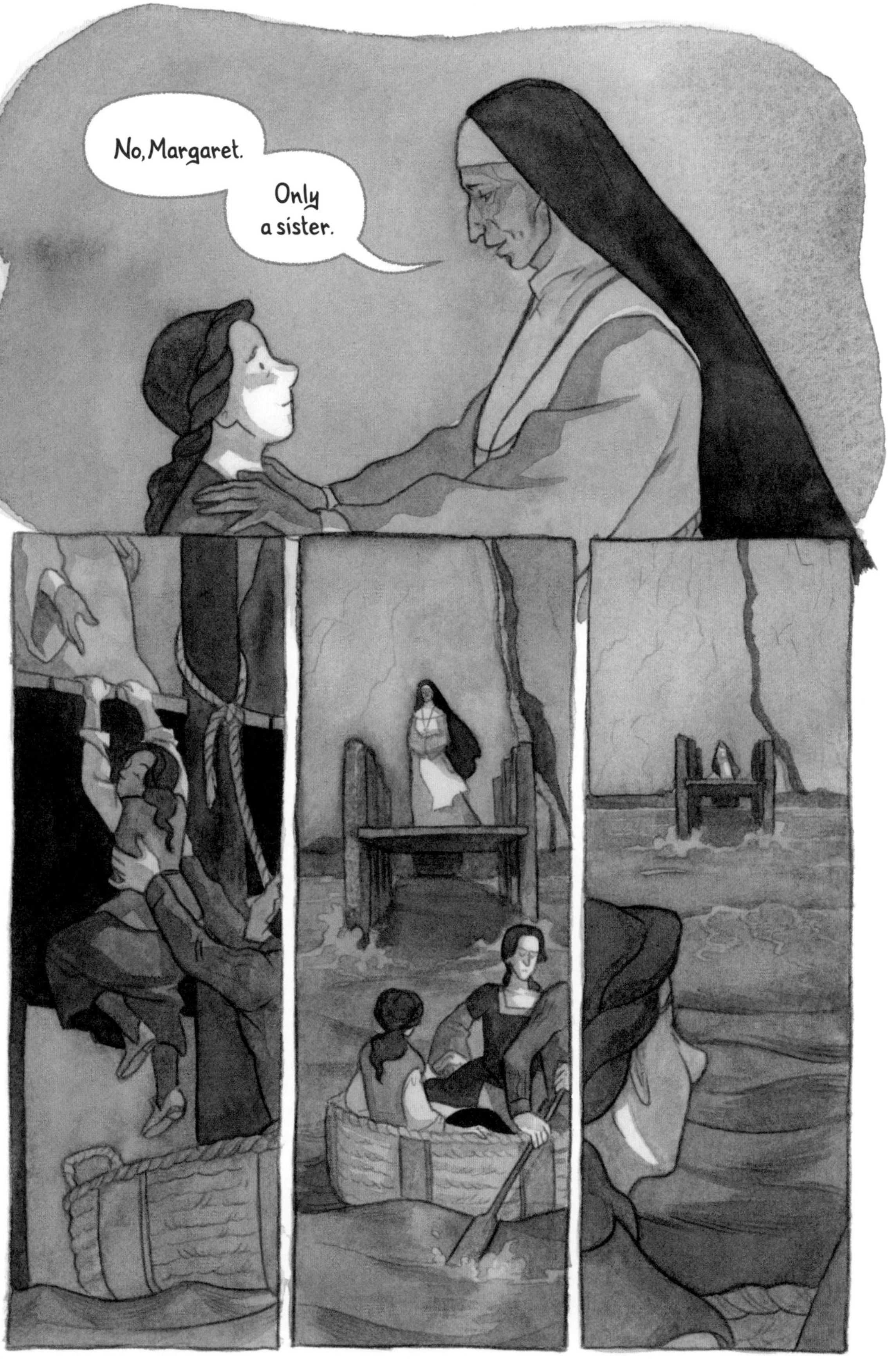
No, Margaret.
Only a sister.

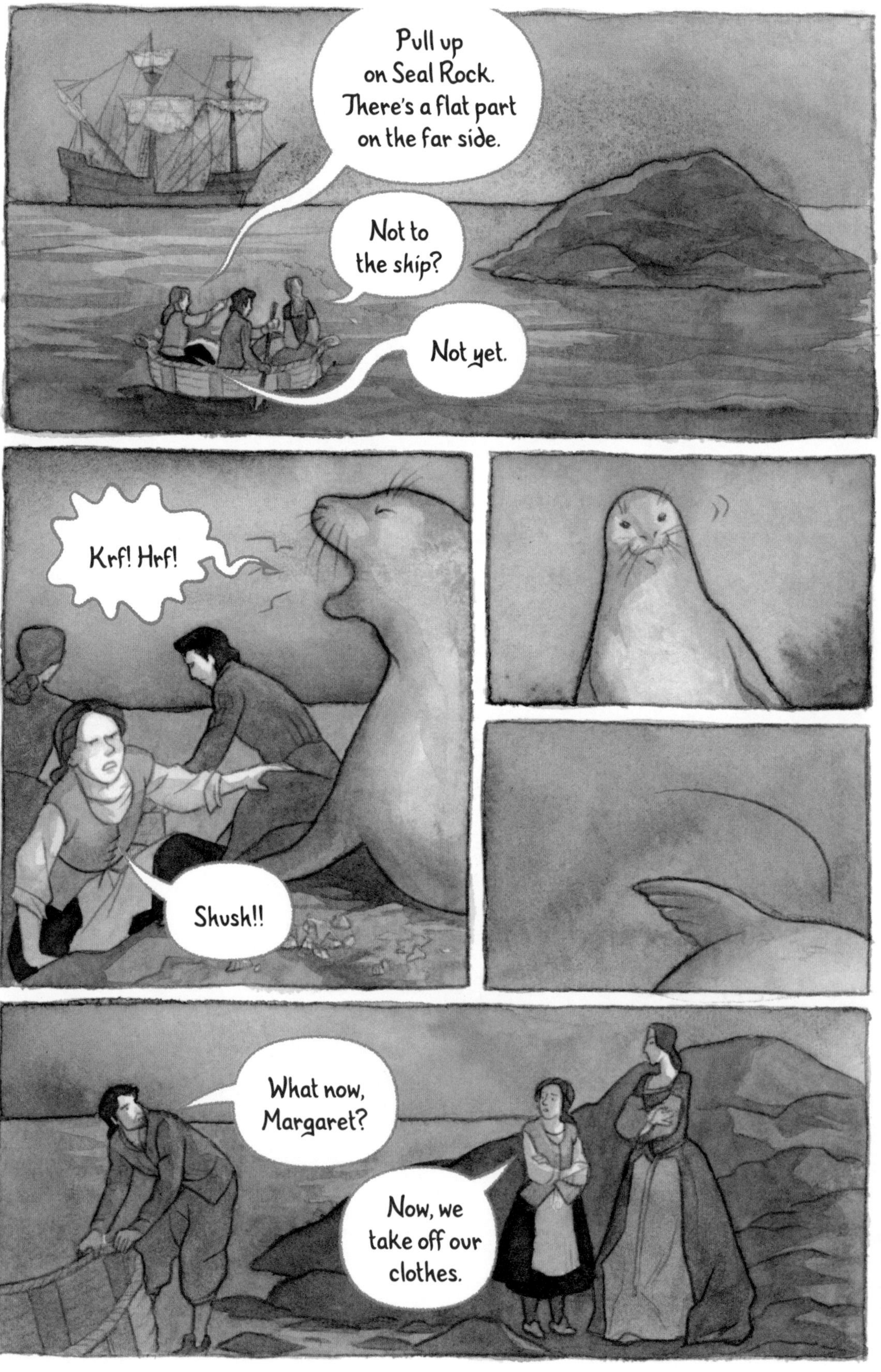
Pull up on Seal Rock. There's a flat part on the far side.
Not to the ship?
Not yet.
Krf! Hrf!
Shush!!
What now, Margaret?
Now, we take off our clothes.

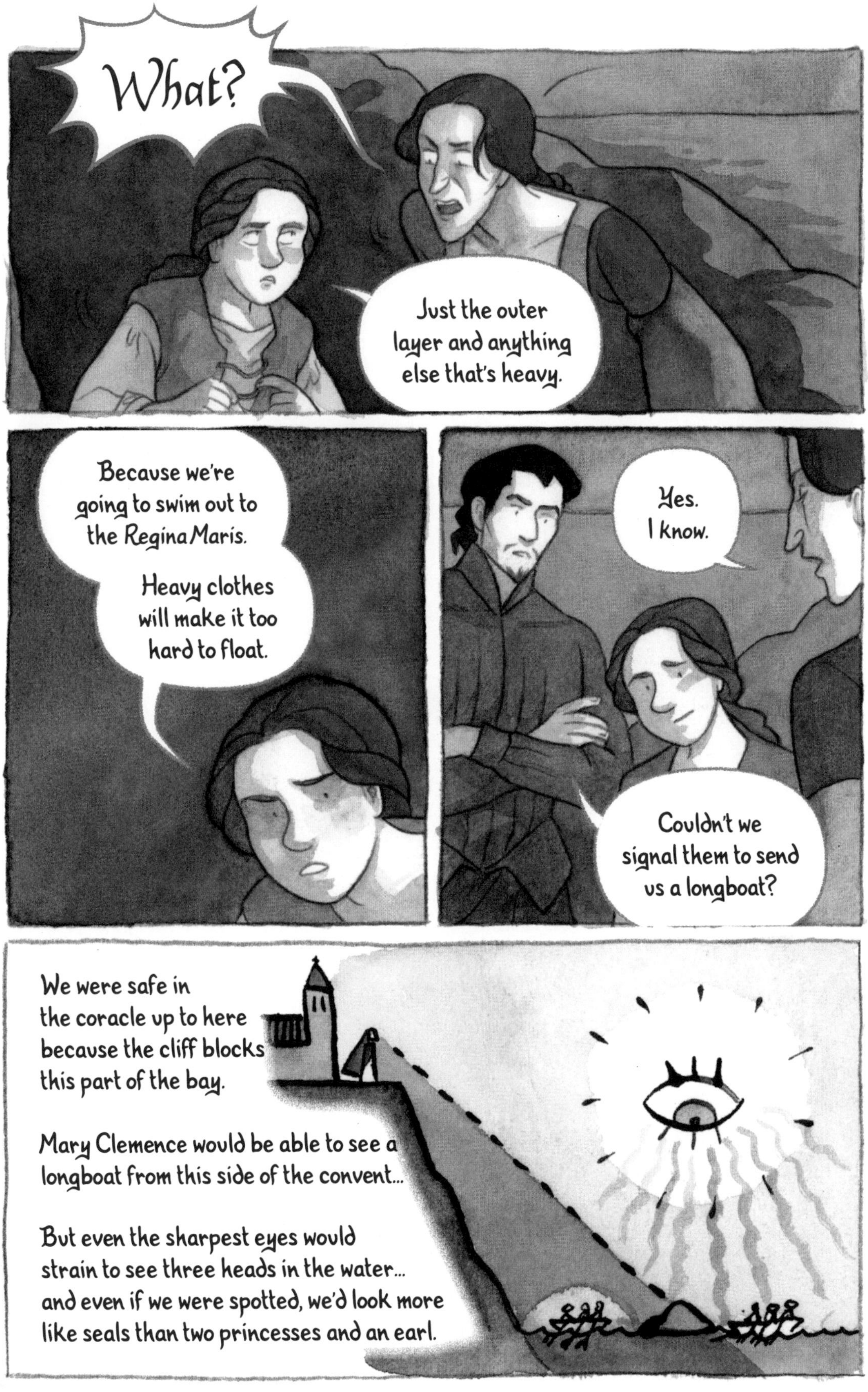
What?
Just the outer layer and anything else that's heavy.
Because we're going to swim out to the Regina Maris.
Heavy clothes will make it too hard to float.
Yes. I know.
Couldn't we signal them to send us a longboat?
We were safe in the coracle up to here because the cliff blocks this part of the bay.
Mary Clemence would be able to see a longboat from this side of the convent...
But even the sharpest eyes would strain to see three heads in the water... and even if we were spotted, we'd look more like seals than two princesses and an earl.

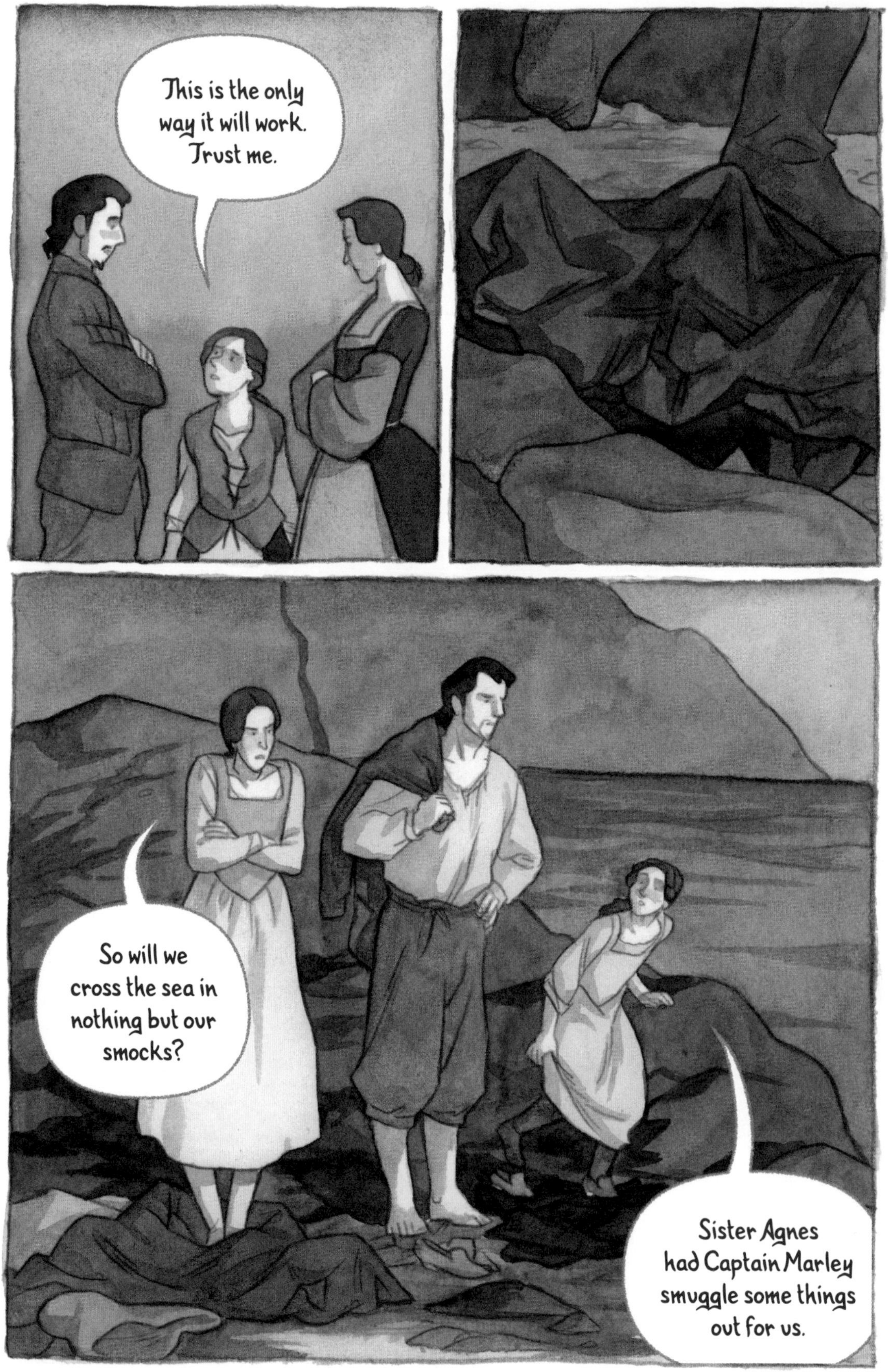
This is the only way it will work. Trust me.
So will we cross the sea in nothing but our smocks?
Sister Agnes had Captain Marley smuggle some things out for us.

I set aside one piece of clothing from each of us.

Then we tied up rocks in the rest.

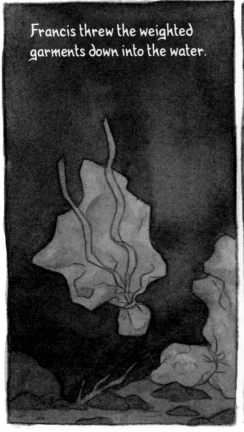

Francis threw the weighted garments down into the water.

What will you do with the rest, Margaret?

We'll throw them into the water, too.

But throw them to the side, so they'll wash up on the beach.

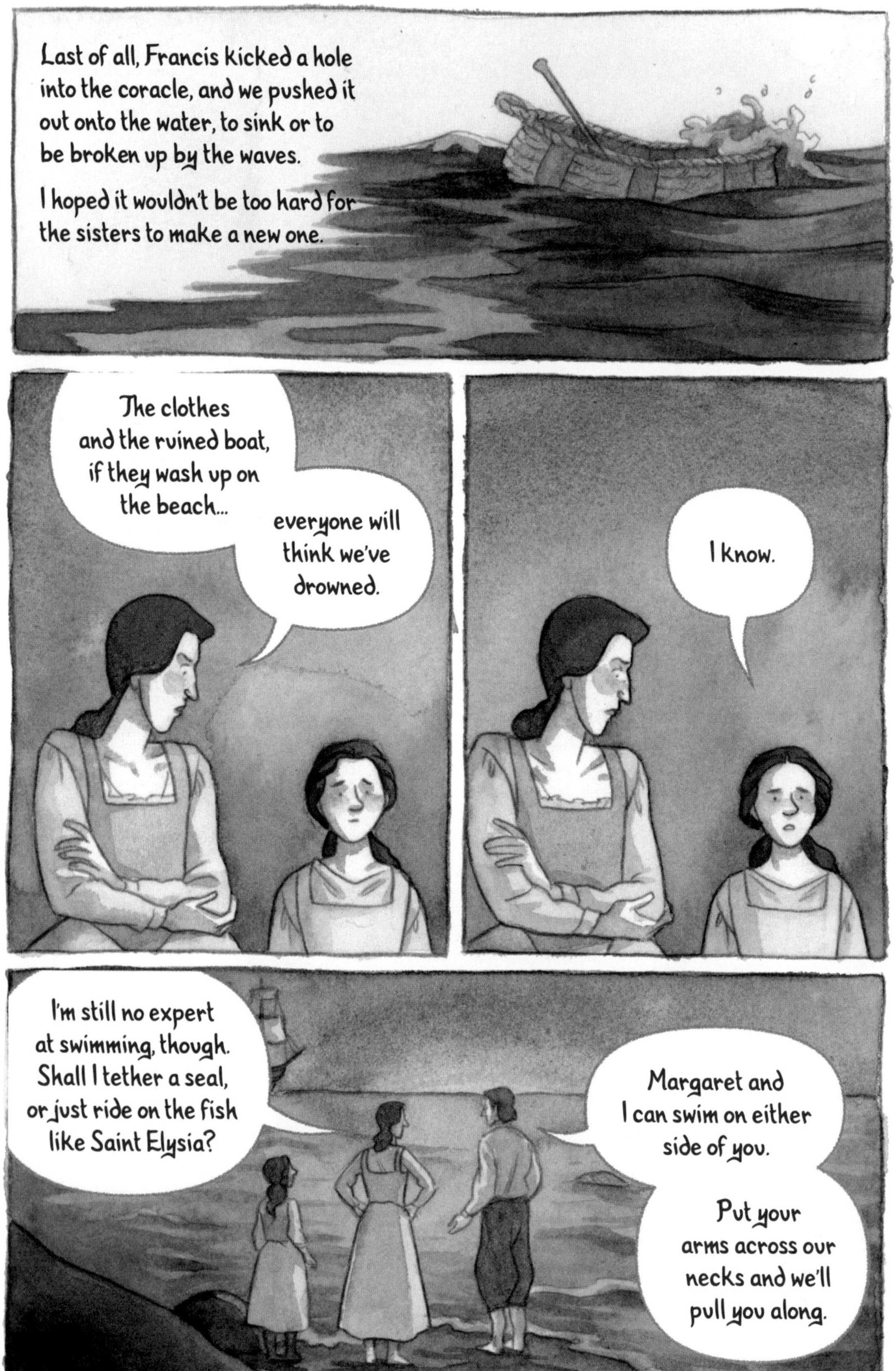
Last of all, Francis kicked a hole into the coracle, and we pushed it out onto the water, to sink or to be broken up by the waves.
I hoped it wouldn't be too hard for the sisters to make a new one.
The clothes and the ruined boat, if they wash up on the beach...
everyone will think we've drowned.
I know.
I'm still no expert at swimming, though. Shall I tether a seal, or just ride on the fish like Saint Elysia?
Margaret and I can swim on either side of you.
Put your arms across our necks and we'll pull you along.

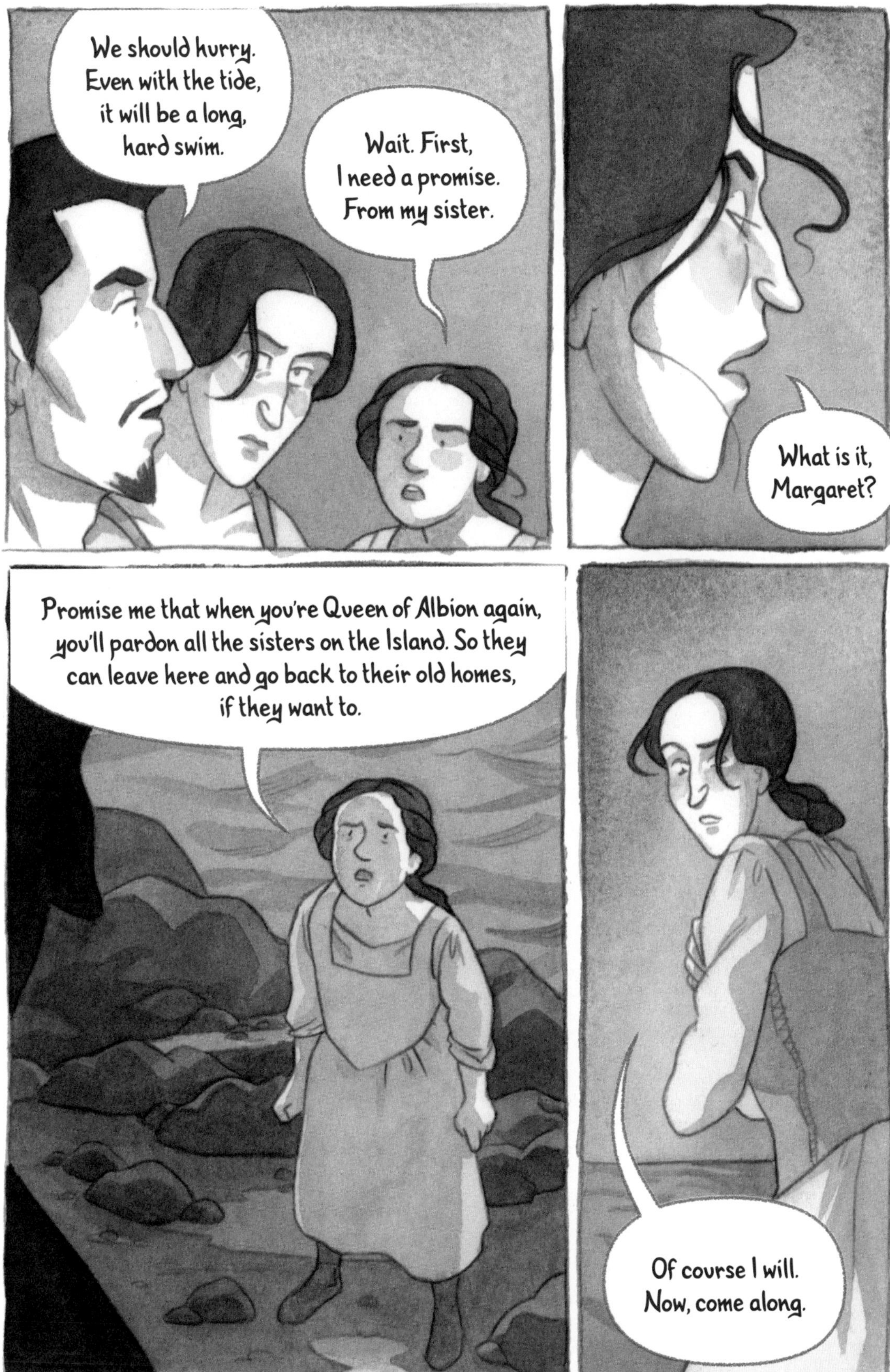
We should hurry. Even with the tide, it will be a long, hard swim.
Wait. First, I need a promise. From my sister.
What is it, Margaret?
Promise me that when you're Queen of Albion again, you'll pardon all the sisters on the Island. So they can leave here and go back to their old homes, if they want to.
Of course I will. Now, come along.

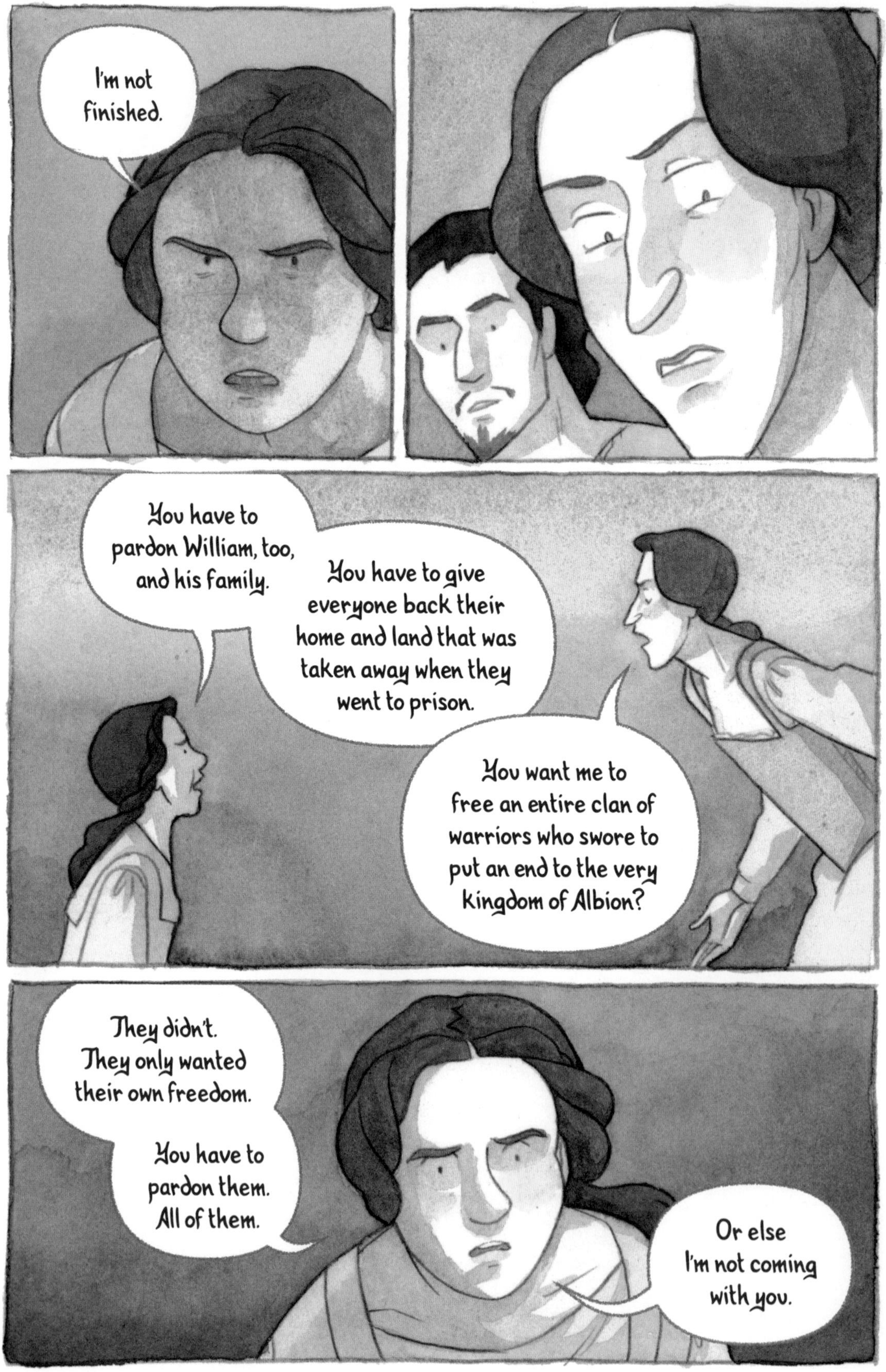
I'm not finished.
You have to pardon William, too, and his family.
You have to give everyone back their home and land that was taken away when they went to prison.
You want me to free an entire clan of warriors who swore to put an end to the very kingdom of Albion?
They didn't. They only wanted their own freedom.
You have to pardon them. All of them.
Or else I'm not coming with you.

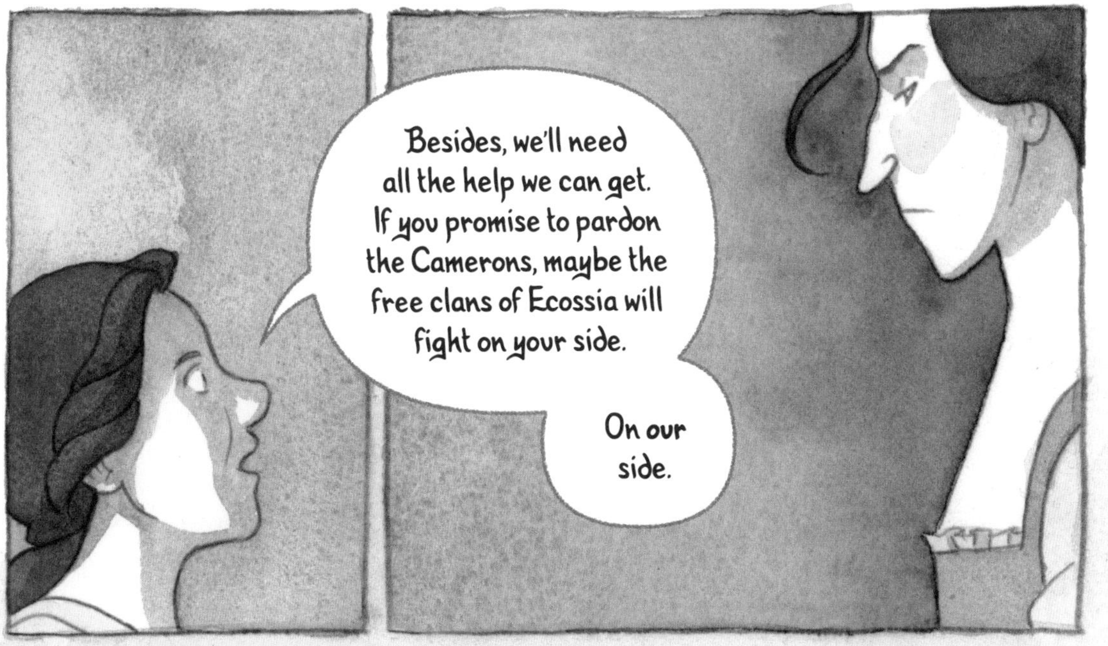
Besides, we'll need all the help we can get. If you promise to pardon the Camerons, maybe the free clans of Ecossia will fight on your side.
On our side.

For a long moment, I thought that I might have made a terrible mistake. That I would stand on that rock and watch Francis and Eleanor swim into the waves and drown, or reach the ship and sail away forever.

And what would become of me? I'd have to borrow a seal's skin and become a selkie and live among the waves. I would swim until the day I finally found the Queen of the Sea in her pale skin and Saint Elysia in her coracle. Together we would set out across the Silver Sea, for the peace and safety of whatever lay on the other side.

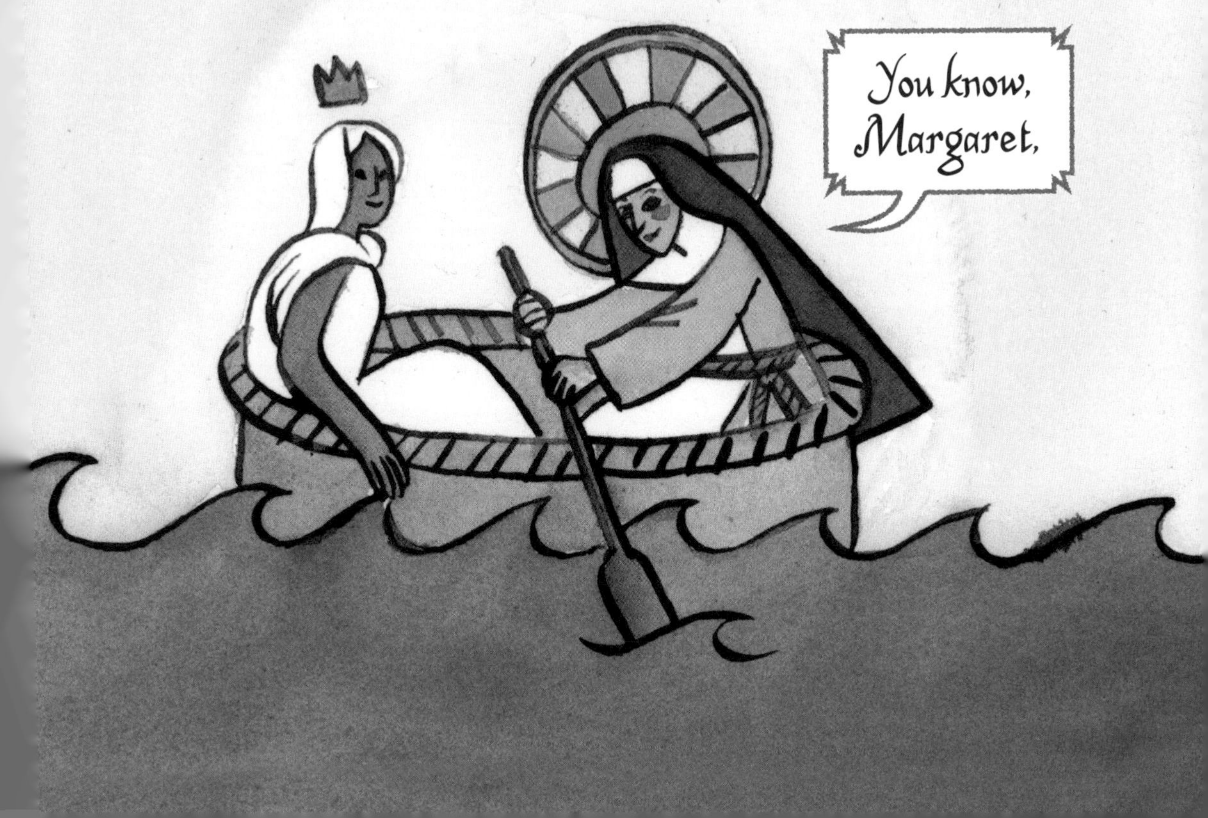
You know, Margaret,

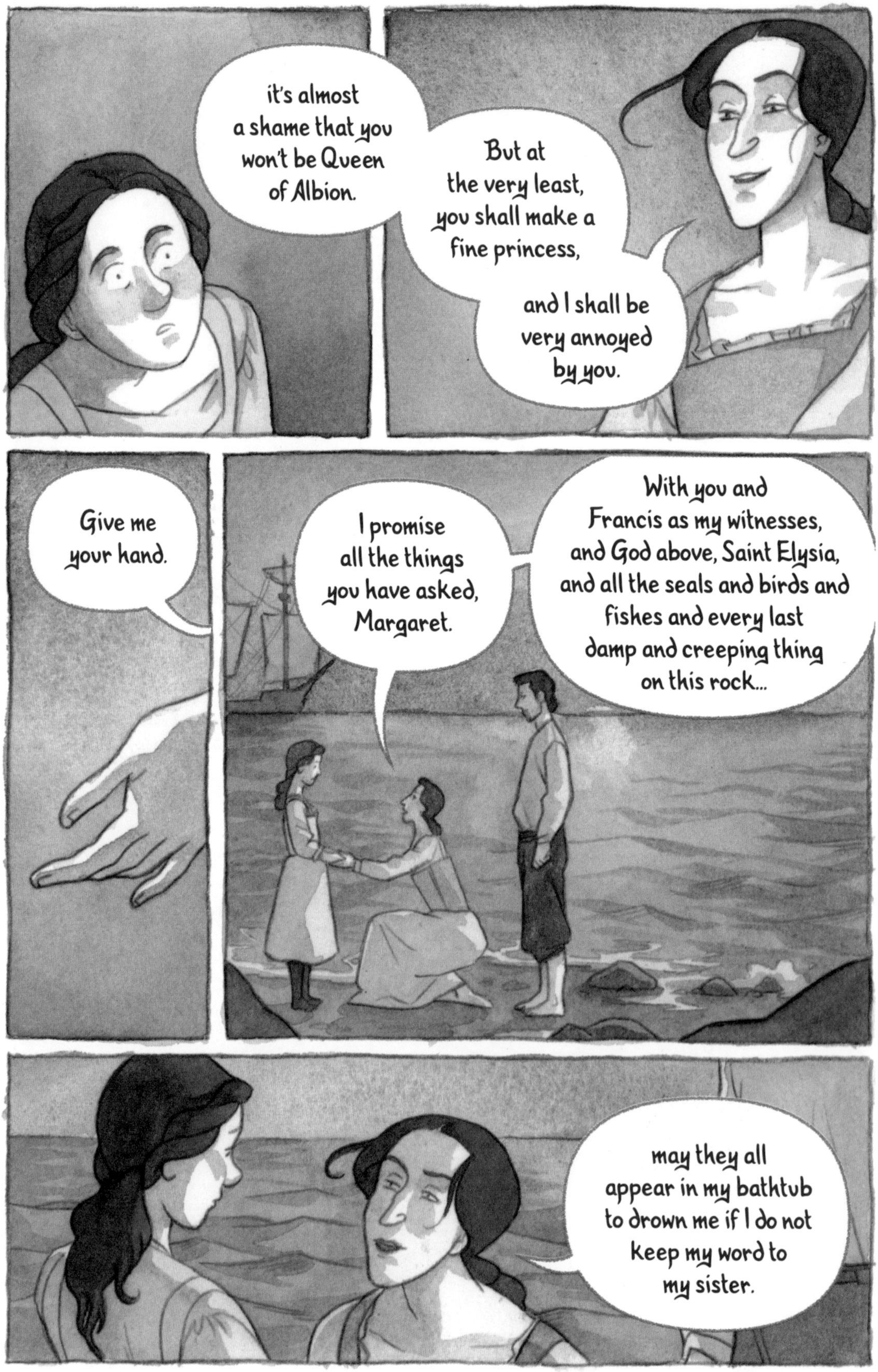
it's almost a shame that you won't be Queen of Albion.
But at the very least, you shall make a fine princess,
and I shall be very annoyed by you.
Give me your hand.
I promise all the things you have asked, Margaret.
With you and Francis as my witnesses, and God above, Saint Elysia, and all the seals and birds and fishes and every last damp and creeping thing on this rock...
may they all appear in my bathtub to drown me if I do not keep my word to my sister.

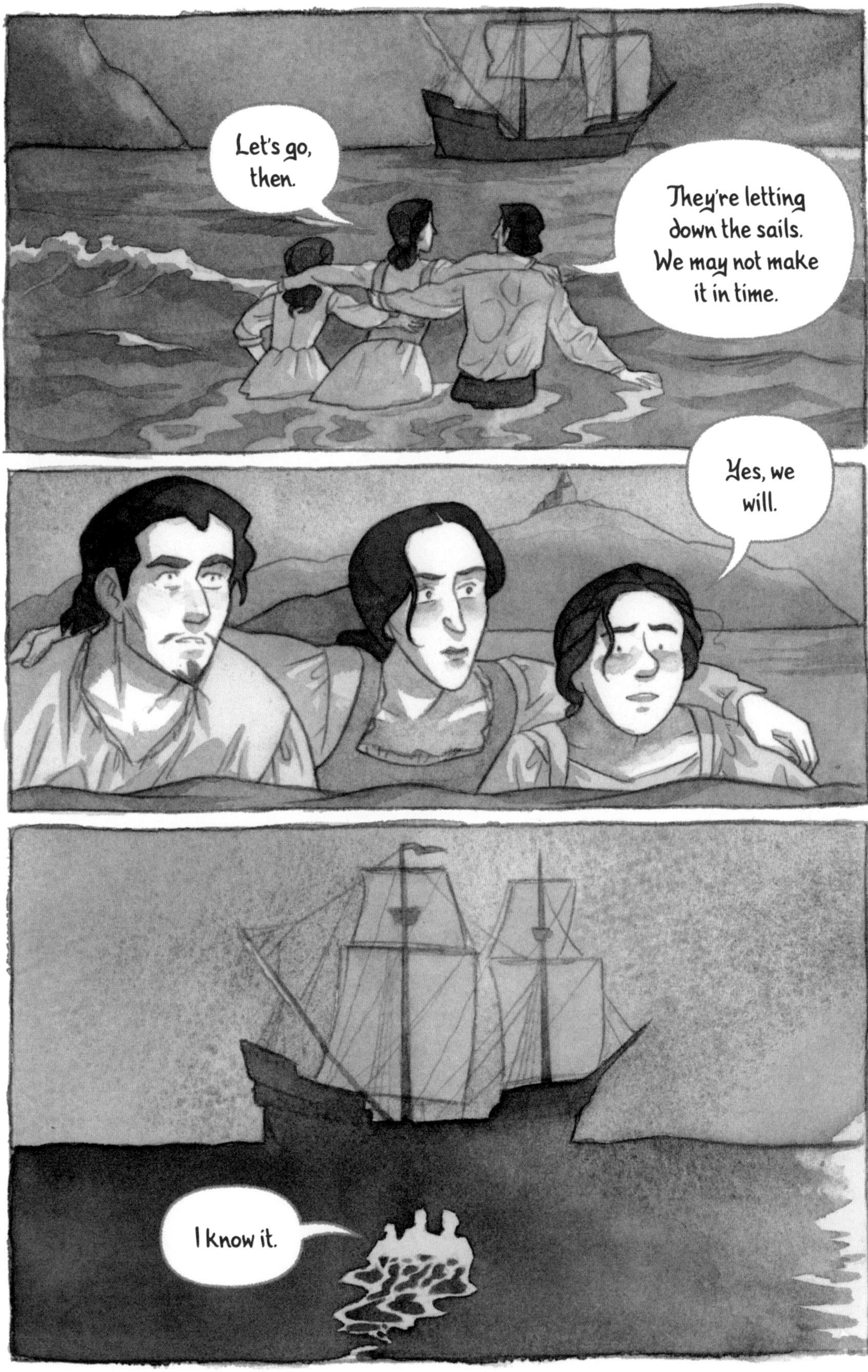
Let's go, then.
They're letting down the sails. We may not make it in time.
Yes, we will.
I know it.

Of course, there is much more that I could
tell you about what happened next to the true
Queen of Albion and her companions.

But for now—

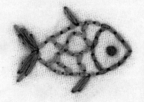

it is enough.

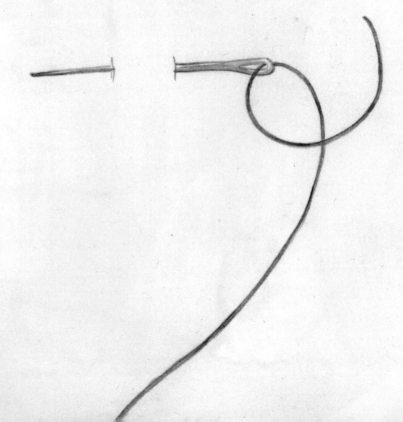

Author's Note

This is not a history book. I love history so much that I know I could never do it justice. Instead, I cherry-picked a few events from the real history of the British Isles in the sixteenth century, during the reigns of King Henry VIII and his daughters, Queen Mary I and Queen Elizabeth I. I also retained many details of daily life during this time. Everything else is either different from its original inspiration or a work of imagination.

The character who bears the closest resemblance to a historical person is Eleanor. Her personality is modeled after Elizabeth I — one of the most famous monarchs of all time. Elizabeth didn't grow up expecting to become a queen. Her younger half brother, Edward, inherited the throne. When he died at fifteen, the kingdom almost fell apart.

After months of chaos, Elizabeth's older half sister, Mary, seized the crown. Mary's plans for England weren't very popular, and when a rebellion broke out, she suspected her little sister. She had Elizabeth captured and ordered her to be taken by boat to the Tower of London, a prison along the River Thames where royal troublemakers were usually sent to be forgotten . . . or executed.

Before they could transport her, Elizabeth sat down to write a desperate letter to Mary, insisting she was innocent and begging for mercy. There was little chance that the letter would change Mary's mind, but Elizabeth knew that if she wrote slowly enough, the tide would rise and the boat would be unable to pass under London Bridge until the next day.

Elizabeth was just twenty years old when she wrote what is now known as the Tide Letter. It was the first of many tides she would outlast. Reading her words made me curious about the story, not of the glorious and confident monarch to come, but of the proud, frightened girl deploying all of her wits to buy just one more day of possibility.

Acknowledgments

With gratitude to Barry Goldblatt, Tricia Ready, Susan Van Metre, D. C. Hopkins for heroic lettering assistance, Erika Moen for bringing Margaret's embroidery to life, Lucy Bellwood, my Helioscope studio mates, M. S. Patterson, Bill Mudron, Sara Ryan, Kate Beaton, Kate Milford, Elizabeth Winslea, the watchful hearts of ST, Comics Camp, my mental health caregivers, my kids at Start Making A Reader Today, the Sapphire Hotel, SPN, Multnomah County Library, and most especially my wonderful parents and my incredible wife, Katie.

For Margaret's adventures beyond the Silver Sea, look for

Prince of the City

coming soon

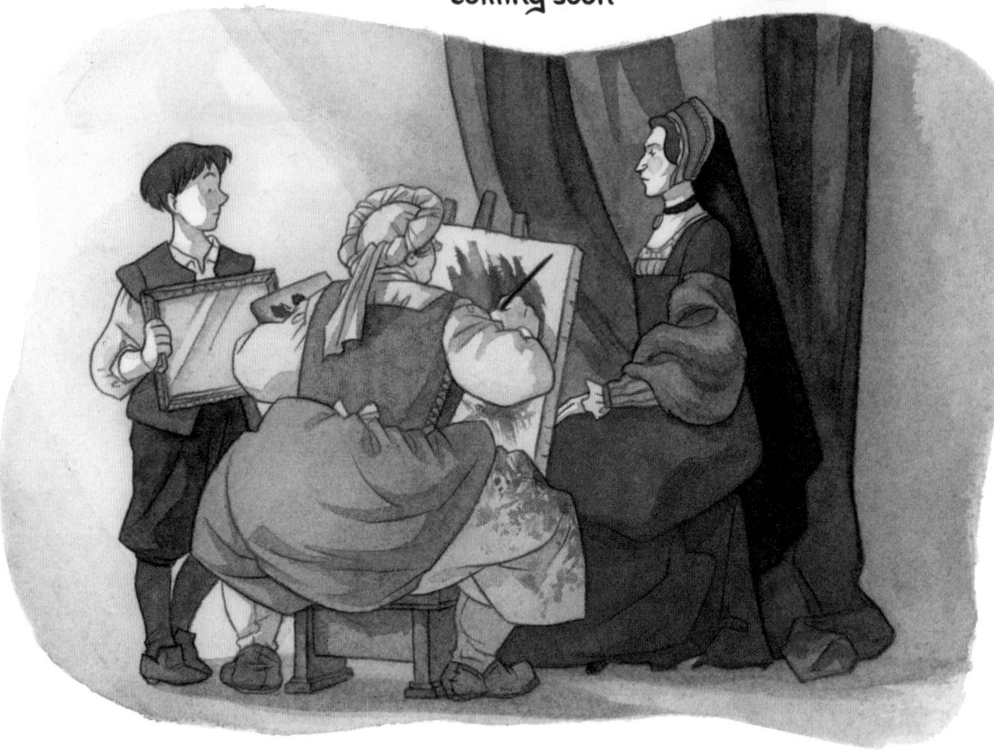

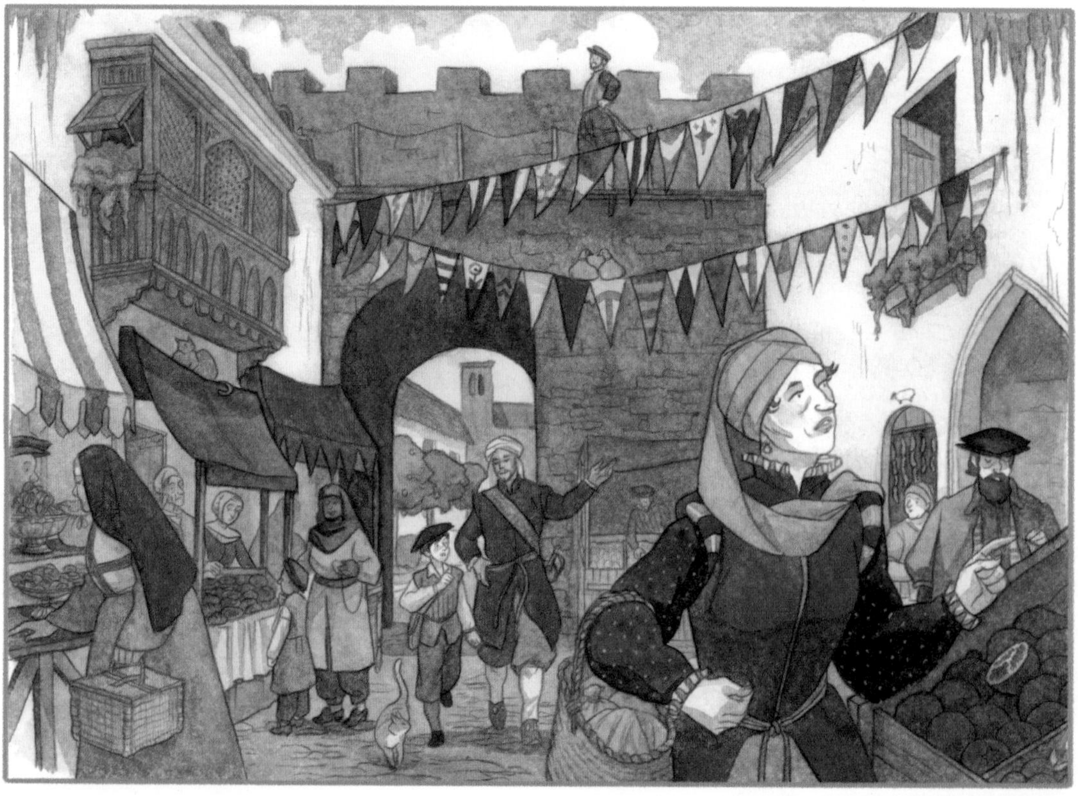